THE
BLUE STAR

THE
BLUE STAR

FIRST LOCALITY ADVENTURE

JUSTIN CALEB

Dedicated to my great encourager. Thank you for your
wisdom and support as I wrote this novel.

Prologue

Captain Matherson looked through the observation windows at the endless expanse of space. To his right, the void was dominated by the colorful smudge of the Carina Nebula. To port, however, the stars were few and far between. The Commonwealth starship *Endeavor* was traveling along the edge of the Milky Way's Carina Arm, skirting the near-starless void that separated it from the Crux Arm. *A mundane region*, he thought, compared to the relatively dense, starry areas of the galactic arms.

Several minutes earlier the ship had emerged from the slipstream, through which starships traveled at superluminal speeds, to take sensor readings of the area. The *Endeavor* periodically made stops to probe the surrounding space with scanners and transmit the information back to the Commonwealth via a compressed data stream. If sensors detected anything unusual, they would investigate.

Matherson turned away from the panorama and addressed his sensor operations officer, a blonde woman in her mid-thirties named Jenny Duvall. "Anything interesting today?"

Duvall shook her head. "Nothing out of the ordinary on sensors, Captain."

He frowned, disappointed but not surprised. The *Endeavor*, whose mission was a joint venture between the Commonwealth's Navy and Interplanetary Research Council, had catalogued hundreds of stars, nebulas, and other phenomena. They were nearing the halfway point of their journey, having been assigned to explore this part of the galaxy for three hundred and sixty-five days before returning home by another route to complete their two-year mission. The crew had mapped a region of space previously unexplored by humans, and even discovered an intelligent alien species, although they had not achieved spaceflight, so the *Endeavor* had moved on without making contact.

Despite all that, and although he would never admit it to his crew, the captain was bored. George Matherson was a naval officer through-and-through, like his father and grandfather before him, but he wasn't an explorer. He wanted to command a battleship patrolling the border of human space, hunting pirates or guarding against incursions by humanity's less-than-friendly neighbors. Unfortunately, command of the Venture-class explorer *Endeavor* was the next logical step toward a promotion to rear admiral and the command of a battleship he so desired. Which meant that he was here, thousands of light-years from Earth and its colonies. So far away that he would be useless if the Commonwealth came under threat. It was the feeling of frustrated powerlessness, combined with the dull repetitiveness of their mission that was making him restless, even *eager* for a fight. Anything besides flying through the void scanning stars and planets. The monotony was getting to him.

He was about to issue the order to activate the slipstream drive and resume their dreary plod across the galaxy when an alert sounded on Duvall's console. "What is it?" Matherson asked.

Duvall was silent for a moment while she examined the data. "It's a message, Captain." She indicated the wavelength on her monitor. "A faint subspace signal, repeating."

"Where is it coming from?" Matherson asked.

"One hundred light-years away, in the Carina Nebula."

"What is it saying?"

"The signal is badly degraded. Our computer can't decipher it," Duvall told him. "And they haven't responded to automatic hails." Everyone else on the bridge had quietened to listen to Matherson and Duvall converse. Would the captain want to investigate, or decide it was too far out of their way?

It was an easy decision for Matherson. "Set a course for the source of the signal and engage the slipstream drive," he ordered. There was a collective murmur of excitement as the bridge crew relayed the captain's order throughout the ship. The navigator began plotting their course; the journey through the slipstream would take four days and needed to be extremely precise or they could end up millions of kilometers from their target. As soon as it was ready the helmsman activated the FTL engines.

Blue-white energy waves rippled across the bow as the *Endeavor* dove into the slipstream.

Ninety-six hours later, the starship re-entered normal space, emerging from the slipstream within a solar system. Orange sunlight from its K-type star flooded the bridge.

"FTL jump complete, Captain," reported the helmsman. "The source of the signal is directly ahead."

Sensory data from the ship's scanners began flooding in. Several decks away the science teams were receiving the same information as Duvall, analyzing the energy signature and its source, a ship whose design Matherson didn't recognize. Tactical, engineering and medical officers were also keeping their own departments apprised as per standard procedure. The entire ship had taken interest in the alien vessel now and all primary sensors were activated, probing the ship and the space around it.

"Sensors show six planets in the system, Captain," Lieutenant Wells, the tactical officer, stated. "Radio signals are coming from the fourth and fifth."

"Radio signals?" Matherson repeated.

"Someone lives there," Duvall commented.

"I'm detecting hundreds of vessels in the system, traveling at sub-light speeds."

The elevator at the rear of the bridge opened and Commander Thorne, Matherson's executive officer, stepped out. He acknowledged the captain with a cool nod as he took his seat. Matherson nodded back before returning his gaze to the viewscreen.

"Could the locals have detected the alien ship?" Matherson asked.

"It's unlikely. They still use radio, which suggests they haven't developed subspace communications yet. They wouldn't be able to detect the signal coming from the ship. They're probably not aware of it."

The captain noticed Duvall look up in interest. "We'll investigate the aliens later," he decided. "First, I want to learn about that ship. Why isn't it moving, or responding to hails?"

"There are no life forms on board, Captain. It appears to be derelict."

Thorne looked thoughtfully at the ship on the viewscreen. "The design looks vaguely familiar…"

A few seconds later, Duvall told him why. "The science department ran a comparison of the ship's hull to all known profiles. It's Ankari. An older design that is no longer in use."

The Ankari were a powerful race who dwelled in the Locality, the region of space occupied by the Human Interstellar Commonwealth and their alien neighbors. The Ankari were polite but largely disinterested in their less-advanced neighbors.

"What were they doing all the way out here?" Wells wondered.

"Probably the same thing as us. Exploring," Thorne said.

"The ship's hull registry identifies it as the *Savalia*," Duvall reported.

"Find any information you can on the *Savalia*," Matherson told her. Then, turning to the communications officer, he said, "Prepare a mission update for Command."

"Yes, sir."

"Captain, the ship is operating on minimal power," reported Duvall. The *Endeavor* was now close enough for them to see the Ankari ship through the observation windows. Their eyes confirmed what the sensors had told them: the ship appeared undamaged. The pearlescent white hull reflected the orange light of the star and the cooler hues of the nebula. It seemed unaffected by the solar currents or the star's gravitational pull.

"Why is it just floating there?" Wells wondered.

"Probably because there's no one onboard left to steer it," said Duvall simply. She received an information package from the research department. "Captain, the records provided by the Ankari tell us the *Savalia* was a prototype, the first ship to use a wormhole drive," Duvall said. "It was a technology demonstrator. But on its maiden flight, the drive malfunctioned. The Ankari flight center registered an overload in the engine that resulted in a burst of lethal radiation, and then the ship disappeared—"

"—and ended up out here, seven thousand light-years from home," finished Wells. "Guess it worked as well as they thought."

"Except for the lethal radiation," Duvall reminded him dryly. "It would have killed the crew in minutes. And the ship just kept going until it didn't have enough power to sustain the wormhole."

Matherson leaned back in his command chair and stared intently at the derelict Ankari ship. For the first time in months, he was excited. An incredible opportunity had just presented itself.

"The ship is intact…?"

"Yes, Captain. There are no hull breaches," confirmed Duvall.

"Good. I want to board that ship. And I want to find the wormhole drive and take it with us."

His pronouncement was met equally with surprise and approval. Lieutenant Wells looked pleased, while Thorne and Duvall responded with more caution.

Thorne frowned. "Take the wormhole drive, Captain? I don't know if we're allowed. That ship belongs to the Ankari military." Duvall nodded in silent support.

"According to interstellar law, which both the Commonwealth and the Ankari Assembly adhere to, derelict ships are subject to salvage by whoever finds them, providing there is no one left on board to stake a claim," Wells said.

"That doesn't apply to military vessels," Thorne reminded him.

"The ship is eighty years old. If the Ankari wanted to retrieve it, they've had plenty of time to do so," Wells retorted.

The commander ignored him and looked at the captain. "I don't know if we should be poking around on board an Ankari ship, even one that's been abandoned for so long. There's no telling what kind of defenses that ship has." He gestured at the ship through the windows. "Even this eighty-year-old ship is light-years ahead of us technologically."

"Exactly," said Matherson. "Think about the technological secrets it contains. We've *never* been able to build a functioning wormhole drive. And this one clearly worked. If we could study it and build one ourselves, it would revolutionize space travel for humanity."

"I agree, Captain," said Wells. "I request that we send a salvage team to the *Savalia*." He stepped forward. "I volunteer to lead the mission." After nearly twelve months of inaction, he was as desperate for excitement as his captain.

"There are political concerns, too, Captain," Commander Thorne persisted. "How will the Ankari react when they learn we're looting their ships?"

"The Ankari never have to find out," said Wells with a meaningful look at the captain, who nodded slowly.

"No, they don't," Matherson said. He turned to the communications officer. "Send that update to Navy HQ. And tell them we intend to board the Ankari ship and see what technology we can salvage."

"Aye, sir."

"Respectfully, Captain—" Duvall began.

"I've already made my decision," Matherson said coolly, with a pointed look at Thorne to silence any disagreement. The commander clenched his jaw and looked away. "Lieutenant Wells, assemble a team. I want you ready to leave in twenty minutes."

"Aye, Captain," said Wells enthusiastically. He saluted smartly, clearly relishing the mission.

"Wait. I should go with you."

Wells and the captain turned to face Duvall. "No one is better qualified to examine their technology than me," she said. She had resigned herself to the fact that the mission was going ahead whether she agreed with it or not. After an almost imperceptible nod of support from Thorne, she added, "And if there are any automated defenses onboard, I may be able to disable them."

Wells looked skeptical. "Captain, I don't—"

"You stand a far better chance of succeeding if I go with you," she told him hotly.

Matherson agreed. "Very well, permission granted." After a pause he addressed both Wells and Duvall: "You're leaving in 19 minutes," he reminded them. They saluted and hastily left the bridge.

Thorne said nothing, merely crossed to his chair and sat down. Matherson didn't care. *He can note his objections in his mission report*, he thought bitterly. It wouldn't be the first time.

Nineteen minutes later the shuttlecraft *Ibex* hummed to life and rose gently off the hangar deck. Wells and Duvall occupied the pilot and co-pilot seats; Wells commenced the pre-flight check while Duvall contacted the hangar bay flight control.

"Requesting permission to depart."

"Permission granted, Ibex. *Opening bay doors."*

Wells brought the shuttle to full power and it glided through the open bay doors into the vacuum. The Carina Nebula shone purple and blue around them, a colorful backdrop in sharp contrast to the normal black of space.

The shuttle banked sharply to the left, flying along the starboard side of the *Endeavor*. They rarely got to see the ship from the outside, and Duvall took a moment to appreciate the smooth white-grey lines and aerodynamic hull of the ship. Under Wells' guidance the shuttle surged forward, accelerating toward the Ankari ship hovering in space a kilometer from the *Endeavor*.

Captain Matherson watched the *Ibex* on the viewscreen as it approached the alien ship.

"We're heading for the port airlock. We will reach it in one minute," Lieutenant Duvall's voice filtered over the comm.

"Acknowledged, *Ibex*," Matherson replied.

"Their shields are offline," reported Duvall. *"We shouldn't have any problem reaching the airlock—"*

Her voice was interrupted by an alarm beeping urgently on the tactical console.

"I'm detecting an energy spike in the Ankari ship," Thorne reported. He was filling in for Wells at tactical.

"We're reading it too," said Duvall from the shuttle, sounding nervous. *"It must be some kind of automated proximity alert."*

"Return to the *Endeavor* immediately," Matherson ordered, but even as he spoke, he feared the directive came too late. Circular ports irised open on the bow of the Ankari ship, and it maneuvered to face the approaching shuttle. The ports glowed a dangerous red.

"I repeat, *Ibex*, return now!" Matherson shouted urgently, but it was useless. The bridge crew watched in horror as hazy red beams of light poured out of the Ankari ship and encompassed the shuttle. The screams of the shuttle crew echoed through the bridge speakers. The beam faded, and the shuttle continued drifting along its trajectory, devoid of life signs and power.

"What happened?" Matherson croaked. His throat felt dry.

"It was a beam of concentrated gamma radiation," Duvall's replacement reported quietly from the sensor operations station. "It overloaded the shuttle's systems and… killed the crew."

The mournful silence that followed was broken several moments later when he added, "Sir, several of the alien ships in the system are moving toward us!"

"They must have detected the radiation burst," Thorne said, his normally calm voice tinged with alarm. "Captain, I recommend withdrawing before we're discovered."

"The first alien ships will reach us in eleven minutes," reported the sensor operations officer. An alert on his display flashed. "Captain! The Ankari ship is targeting *us*!"

"Fire weapons!" Matherson ordered. Thorne's hands flew rapidly over the control panel, targeting weapons on the Ankari ship. Alert klaxons signaled the crew to battle stations.

The captain and the bridge crew watched with growing dread as the Ankari ship rotated, this time to face *them*. Its weapons ports glowered at them like two angry, red eyes.

"Helm! Emergency jump, now!" Matherson shouted frantically, but it was too late. Angry red beams of radiation shot out of the Ankari ship and swept through the *Endeavor*.

"Shields…!" Matherson cried out in futility as he was engulfed in deadly warmth. The prickling sensation across his skin became like fire, and he was dimly aware of the lights flickering and the screams of his crew dying around him.

He collapsed in front of his chair. As his vision faded, he saw the first and only salvo of the *Endeavor's* missiles slam into the *Savalia*, sending the Ankari ship reeling. Matherson wanted to cry out in pain but he couldn't. He felt like he was melting. The red light faded, but blackness filled his vision and encompassed him.

1

"Navy Charter LT5 to Argos Fleet Yards is now boarding."

Simon Marston glanced at his watch; exactly on time, unlike some of the earlier flights that had been canceled due to a bad solar storm. He stood, hefted his duffel bag over his shoulder and joined the line of people waiting to board. When it was his turn to pass through the security arch, he handed his ID card to the ensign, who swiped it through a scanner.

"Enjoy your flight, Captain."

It took a moment for Marston to realize the ensign was talking to him; it had been six weeks since his promotion, yet *Captain* still sounded strange to Marston's ears. "Thanks," he said, unconsciously tugging at his dark blue uniform jacket, where the newly-stitched gold bars denoting his rank were visible. Here he was, embarking on the next stage of his career in the Commonwealth Navy. It was exciting, and a little scary.

He boarded the transport ship and picked a seating row at random, stowing his bag in an overhead compartment and sliding across to the window seat. When all the passengers had boarded the engines activated, sending a faint thrum reverberating through the deck. The transport rose off the ground, and the passengers were gently pressed back in their seats as the ship angled upward and accelerated, beginning its ascent out of the atmosphere. The peninsula of New Peloponnesus shrunk away beneath them; its spaceport, military academy, forests, rivers, and cities spread below them like features on a giant map diminished rapidly. Tendrils of white cloud whipped by the window, obscuring Marston's view of the surface, until they too fell away. The sky darkened, and stars began to appear. As they cleared the last reaches of the planet's atmosphere the pilot reported over the intercom that the flight to Argos, located in the system's inner asteroid belt, would take six hours.

Marston took the news tablet from its slot in the back of the seat in front of him and scanned the headlines. He scrolled idly past news on local politics and weather, entertainment and sports, until a headline caught his eye: *Navy Ship Vanishes Near Helix Nebula*. He read through the short article, which reported the Navy ship *Fortitude* had disappeared while responding to a distress call from the *Prosperous*, a civilian prospecting ship. Investigation by the scout ship *Watchman* had so far failed to recover any trace of either vessel.

It was impossible to say whether the two ships had been lost because of an encounter with hostile aliens or one of the spatial phenomena poorly understood or as yet undiscovered by humans. Marston observed his fellow passengers talking, reading, or napping as their ship hurtled across the solar system at nearly twenty-eight hundred kilometers a second. In such comfort it was easy to forget the risk inherent to space travel. Although humans had traveled amongst the stars for nearly four centuries, it could still prove dangerous.

He flicked through a few more news articles, then stared out the window for an indeterminate amount of time. The unchanging vista grew monotonous after a while, and his eyelids began to droop; nerves and excitement had prevented him from getting more than a few hours of sleep the night before. He leaned back in his chair and closed his eyes.

"Excuse me."

Simon opened his eyes. An older man across the aisle was looking at him. "Sorry to bother you," the man said apologetically, "But I was wondering if you had any painkillers? I forgot to put mine in my carry-on."

"I don't, sorry. Maybe one of the flight crew could give you one," Marston said helpfully.

"Thanks, I'll ask." The man signaled to a female flight attendant. He spoke to her quietly and she nodded once before disappearing. She soon reappeared with the painkillers and the man accepted them gratefully.

"It's my back," he explained to Marston. "I've just completed six months at the Navy base on Soshana, developing engines for ground vehicles in high-gravity deployments. The work was good, but my back hasn't yet forgiven me for the higher gees."

"I've heard Soshana is one of the most physically demanding deployments in the Commonwealth," Marston said, "Although I wouldn't mind seeing the Brazen Sea." It was the largest lava-filled caldera on any world in the Commonwealth.

"It's well worth the hike," the man assured him. "I'm Don, by the way. Don Winston." He offered his hand across the aisle.

"I'm Simon Marston," Simon replied, shaking it firmly. "Pleasure to meet you."

Don leaned over conspiratorially. "So, why are you going to Argos? I'm transferring to the shipyards. I'm a mechanical engineer."

"I'm on my way to take command of a frigate," Simon told him reluctantly. He braced himself for a surprised or even openly skeptical response.

To his credit, Don took in his stride. "Oh, well then it's a pleasure to meet you, sir," he said. "Sorry I didn't notice the captain's stripes on your uniform earlier."

"No need to apologize," Simon assured him. "It's still weird that people who were my peers a few weeks ago call me 'sir' now."

Don smiled. "At least you're lenient with an old man. Last time I forgot to show proper respect to a superior I was put on waste management duties for a week."

Simon grinned. "Yes, well, some captains take themselves a little more seriously than they should. I can say that now," he added with a mischievous glint in his eye. Don chuckled.

"What ship are you taking command of?" he asked. "Maybe I know of her."

"The *Pericles*. An Interceptor-class frigate," Marston said proudly.

Don searched his memory. "I know the Interceptor well, but I can't say I've heard of her. Is she new?"

"She is." The starship was as new as Marston's captaincy. *A perfect match*, he thought happily.

"I worked on an Interceptor class at the Terelos Shipyard. They could outrun a roadrunner on steroids." Don chuckled again.

Marston hadn't heard that peculiar expression before, but he did know that the Interceptor was the fastest ship in the Commonwealth fleet. "I've heard the same thing," he agreed.

"Well, I hope it's all smooth sailing for you." Winston gave him a serious look. "Your ship will serve you well if you treat her right."

"I will," Simon promised.

Don looked at him shrewdly. "I'm sure you will." He shuffled in his chair to get more comfortable. "Now if you'll excuse me, I'm still on Soshana time. I could use some shut eye."

"Be my guest," Marston said.

Don seemed content to nap, and Simon decided to do the same. He closed his eyes, letting the distant thrum of the engines and the quiet murmur of passengers lull him to sleep.

When Marston woke, he was surprised to see more than two hours had passed. Don was snoring quietly in his seat. The ship, operating on New Peloponnesus time, had the cabin lights dimmed in a simulation of evening.

A flight attendant wheeled a food trolley down the aisle and Marston gratefully accepted the in-flight meal. He spent the remainder of the trip reading, starring out the window, and mentally reviewing the details of his new command, thinking about the officers he had selected and would soon meet in person, some for the first time. His natural apprehension at meeting them was balanced by knowing they would probably be more nervous to meet *him*, their new captain. One hour out from their destination, the ship passed Mochlos, a small, lifeless terrestrial planet. Marston could just make out the only human interest in the planet, an orbiting refueling station visible as a white speck glinting in the dim sunlight.

Beyond Mochlos, rocks started to appear in space, growing in size and number as the transport neared the Argos Asteroid Belt, which orbited the star Struve 2398 Alpha from two astronomical units away. Marston and the other passengers watched out the windows as the first mountain-sized asteroids of the belt appeared and the ship decelerated to allow for safe maneuvering. Their course would take them to the inner field, the location of the Commonwealth Navy's largest fleet yards. Navigation buoys with powerful repulsors kept the space lanes to Argos clear of all but the largest debris; still, their progress through the belt slowed again as the pilot carefully navigated around the larger asteroids.

The captain announced that the planetoid Argos would soon be visible through the jumble of space rocks, and the passengers eagerly switched on their data screens to view the live feed from the ship's forward camera.

When the Struve binary system was first charted in 2128, the surveying ship had dispatched probes to investigate the planets and two asteroid belts orbiting Struve 2398 Alpha. The surveyors themselves spent thirty days surveying Kypria, dispatching landing parties to determine its suitability for colonization by examining its soil, flora and fauna, atmosphere, plate movements, climate, and weather patterns. The planet proved to be an ideal candidate for human settlement, unlike Mochlos, which was revealed to be a resource-poor world unsuitable for even the smallest mining interests.

The probe sent to investigate the system's inner asteroid belt had come across Argos. The Commonwealth government, interested in building asteroid habitats as well as colonizing planets, sent the survey ship to investigate further. The planetoid, which contained a third of the asteroid belt's entire mass, lived up to the survey team's hopes. Resource-rich and measuring nearly 900 kilometers in diameter, it was large and dense enough to be rounded by its own gravity. However, due to the inherent difficulties in mining the ultra-hard boromite which comprised most of the planetoid's surface, it was deemed undesirable for conversion into a civilian habitat when there were easier candidates in the system's outer asteroid ring. Information on Argos was relegated to the archives of the Commonwealth Prospecting and Surveyance Agency.

No more attention was given to the planetoid until 2174, when the Commonwealth Navy expressed interest in using it as a base. The same boromite that made excavation so difficult also rendered the planetoid impervious to most contemporary weapons, and at the time it was near the border of human-controlled space, making it an ideal location for a Navy stronghold. Like many other Navy bases in Tier 1 Space Argos was constructed during the era of Consolidation, when the fledgling Commonwealth was becoming increasingly aware of its alien neighbors. To secure the borders of their young interstellar state, the Commonwealth Government and Navy spent a large amount of energy and resources on infrastructure and defensive outposts. Their most significant project was the construction of the base in Argos. The first excavator ships arrived in 2176, and by 2196 the military base was operational, complete with new, state-of-the-art shipbuilding facilities. Since then, the shipyard had become one of the most important strategic sites in the Human Interstellar

Commonwealth. Although work on the planetoid continued to this day, it was already the second-largest Navy base in the Commonwealth.

The transport ship emerged from the corridor between the asteroids into the zone around the planetoid kept permanently clear of debris. The space was filled with activity; dozens of white-hulled ships of every size and class traveled to and from the base, some carrying personnel or cargo and others delivering resources from the belt's far-flung mining communities for use in station construction and shipbuilding. Marston paid little attention when the pilot announced they would be docking shortly. He'd never seen Argos in person before, and he and the other passengers craned their necks to get a view of the colossal base.

The surface of the planetoid was dotted with weapons arrays, communications antennae, and refueling docks. Between them, tall, spindle-like towers emerged from the boromite surface, housing flight-control stations, cargo conveyors and docking points for visiting ships. Automated refineries processed Argos's vast mineral wealth and transferred it to the construction facilities of the shipbuilding yards, which dominated the planetoid's equator. It was these extensive facilities that drew Marston's eye. The rocky boromite surface was indented with construction bays and repair facilities that produced more starships than anywhere else in the Commonwealth except for some of the wealthier planets.

Marston could make out the scene in greater detail as the transport drew closer. Dozens of starships in various stages of construction were nestled within their docking cradles; engineers and constructor bots swarmed over the hulls like ants while giant robotic arms maneuvered components into place. The spark of welders and flash of spotlights reflected off shining white hulls, and he marveled at the scope of industry before him.

His view was momentarily obscured by a hulking cargo ship as it passed close by on its way to one of the cargo ports that serviced the Navy's Fourth Fleet, which was based at Argos. An excited exclamation from one of his fellow passengers drew his attention to the flagship of the Fourth Fleet, the Consul-class *Honorable*, visible in its berth before it rotated out of view behind the horizon.

The transport approached a docking bay large enough to hold four vessels of the same size. The darkness of space was replaced by bright lights and white metal walls as the ship glided smoothly into its berth. There was a soft *clunk* as docking clamps latched onto the hull and an airlock tunnel connected to the ship. The pilot announced that it was safe to disembark. Marston stood up and stretched, relishing the movement after sitting for six hours. He pulled his bag from the overhead compartment and helped Don retrieve his own bag.

"It was good to meet you, Don," he said, offering his hand again.

Don shook it enthusiastically. "You too, sir. All the best with your new command."

"Thanks," said Simon. "I hope you enjoy your posting too."

The passengers filed out of the cabin, crossing through the airlock tunnel into Argos Station itself. Passing through an embarkation lounge similar to those in other spaceports across the Commonwealth, Marston found himself in a large, busy corridor that stretched away in either direction. It was full of people in Navy uniforms and technician overalls moving about on various tasks.

Marston and Winston followed the signs until they came to a four-way intersection. Don gestured with his thumb toward one of the corridors. "This is me. See you around, Young Captain," he said. Marston nodded in farewell as Don walked off.

Marston was about to ask the computer for directions when he heard a familiar, booming voice behind him. "Well, well, it's *Captain* Simon Marston. Welcome to Argos!"

Marston turned to face the grinning visage of his new executive officer, Ronan Balzano. Balzano was a tall, solidly built, bald-headed thirty-five-year-old. The two men were firm friends and had served together on the *Saber*, when Simon had been second officer and Ronan the tactical officer. Ronan was bold, forthright and gregarious. Although his size made him appear intimidating, Ronan was one of the most easy-going officers in the fleet and worked well with people above and under his command. These qualities, in addition to his fifteen years' experience in the Navy, made him the obvious choice for Marston's second-in-command.

"When did you get here?" Simon asked as they shook hands.

"Yesterday afternoon," Ronan told him as they began walking down the corridor. "How was the trip? Are you jet-lagged?"

"No. The time difference is only two hours, and I napped on the way over."

"I saw the ship," Ronan said with a gleam in his eye. "She's a beauty."

"I bet," said Simon, a little jealous that his executive officer had already seen her. "As soon as I check in with Command, that's where I'm headed."

"You'll also get to meet Katarina Sirroyo. She arrived at the same time I did," Ronan informed him.

Like Marston, most of his new crew came from other posts across the Commonwealth. "The new sensor operations officer? She arrived early."

Ronan chuckled. "She told me she was eager to get to work. I think she'd rather calibrate the sensors herself than trust an Argos engineer to do it. But most of the crew will be arriving over the next three days. On schedule," he added with a grin.

Signs led them through an archway into a monorail station that was part of the high-speed transit system that interlaced Argos. Marston spotted a carriage advertising its destination as NAVY HQ and gestured toward it.

"I have to check in with Admiral Garcia," Marston told him. "It shouldn't take long."

Balzano nodded. "I'll see you on the ship." He disappeared into the crowd.

Marston stepped into the monorail carriage with twelve other people, smiling apologetically and adjusting his duffel bag to try and minimize the space it occupied. The monorail would travel nearly four hundred and fifty kilometers to the heart of Argos. The carriage glided away from the station, accelerating rapidly as it sped through the enforced-titanium tunnel toward its destination. Inertial dampeners kept the occupants from being flattened against the wall, and Marston barely felt the motion of the carriage. For several minutes, the walls of the tunnel flashed by as a grey blur. Then, without warning the walls fell away, and the monorail was speeding through a vast open space. For the second time that day, Marston was left speechless at the vast scale of Argos.

When construction had commenced on the planetoid, the Navy had emphasized the necessity that Argos be self-sustaining in the event of a siege. At this distance from the system's star, the weak, red sunlight was inadequate for plants to photosynthesize, so the Navy had decided on hydroponic crops using artificial lamps. The designers, however, had envisioned a much grander solution.

The Argos base was planned to be far larger than any other military base in human history. In addition to food and water, it required smelters and refineries to produce the alloys needed for constructing ship components, medical facilities, waste management systems, and accommodation for the hundreds of thousands of military personnel the station would house, not to mention their families, who would also require schools, jobs and recreational facilities. The first excavators on Argos had drilled directly toward the center of the planetoid. It took two years of non-stop drilling before they reached the rocky, inner core, at which point they began excavating the great cavern that would house most of the base's facilities. The exterior facilities only scratched the surface of Argos, literally; the real station was at its heart. It was into this space the monorail carriage now rushed along its needle-thin track.

Marston found himself gazing, awestruck, into the heart of a great, cylindrical cavern over one hundred kilometers in diameter. It was also two hundred kilometers long, with plans to triple that length; Marston couldn't even make out the far side where giant automated excavators tirelessly continued their work. The first thing that struck him about the cavern was that it was *green.* The entire inner surface was covered in lush vegetation introduced once the vast space had been filled with a breathable atmosphere, a huge undertaking in itself. The surface was a patchwork of automated farms, with lakes and planted forests placed sporadically between them to create a more natural look. Settlements dotted the surface, both below and above him; the planetoid's natural gravity and artificially induced rotation provided a comfortable Earth-standard gravity for the interior's inhabitants. Marston had seen many planets, but he found it somewhat disconcerting to see buildings on the inside curve of a planet rather than the outside surface, as though someone had taken a planetary surface and curled it into a cylinder.

Everything about Argos was on an unprecedented scale, and it had paid off. The designers had succeeded in creating a self-sustaining biosphere at the center of the planetoid, equipped with a giant, artificial sun suspended in the center of the space to provide warmth and light for the habitat, while the vegetation converted carbon dioxide into oxygen for the population to breathe. A natural life-support system.

The monorail carriage sped toward a sprawling city. Called Argos City, it was home to a quarter of the two-million personnel stationed at Argos, along with their families and the civilians who ran the businesses that provided services for off-duty personnel. The city was similar to other modern human cities across the Commonwealth, with tall skyscrapers of glass and steel laid in a neat grid of tree-lined boulevards. The city bordered an artificial lake whose water came from melting the ice on the planetoid's surface. The water supply of Argos came entirely from meltwater, purified and recycled for safe use.

By the shore of the lake was Argos Navy Headquarters, a seven-story high, ring-shaped building. From here, officers oversaw all Navy activity within the surrounding sectors of Commonwealth space. The white stone pathway leading to the main entrance was inlaid with an image of the Navy insignia, clearly visible from this height. Extensive, well-kept gardens surrounded the building and from his vantage point Marston could see dozens of Navy personnel on the pathways and green lawns surrounding the building, some relaxing in the grass eating lunch while others hurried between tasks.

The monorail decelerated as it approached the building, its cylindrical glass tunnel completely muffling any disruptive booms as it dropped below the speed of sound. After several minutes it glided gently to a halt, and Marston and the others stepped out into a small subway station. He followed the signs down a corridor to an elevator that took him directly to the nerve center of Argos. After having his identity confirmed by a guard, the doors slid open and he entered the Operations Center.

If it weren't for the warm white light of the artificial sun filtering through the windows Marston could have been standing in the Operations Center on any other Commonwealth planet. Ops, as it was referred to, was a large, circular room lined with computer terminals, monitors and other technical equipment. There was a Navy officer at every station, hard at work. The middle of the room was dominated by a ring of consoles with twelve individual stations, at the center of which a large holographic projection displayed a real-time image of the Struve Alpha System. The room buzzed with energy; this was the true heart of Argos.

He identified a middle-aged man in a rear admiral's uniform as the station's second-in-command and approached him. He put down his bag and stood to attention. "Captain Simon Marston reporting for duty, sir," he said, saluting.

"We've been expecting you, Captain," said Rear Admiral Percival. "Welcome to Argos Station."

"Thank you, sir," said Marston, remaining at attention.

"At ease, Captain." The rear admiral sorted through a stack of data pads on the console in front of him. He selected one and typed on it with one hand.

"Please sign here and leave your thumb print on the scanner. This will transfer the command codes of the *Pericles* to you, effective immediately." Percival handed the pad to Marston, who took it and signed it with a shaking hand. He pressed his thumb against the scanner at the bottom corner of the pad. He was now in control of a Navy starship; it was beginning to feel real.

"Perfect," said Percival. "If you take this to Admiral Garcia, he will also sign it and give you your orders. He's in his office," he said, pointing to a doorway across the room. "I'll let him know you're coming."

"Thank you, sir," said Marston, saluting again. He picked up his bag and strode across the busy room to the doorway with a plaque reading: "Samuel Garcia, ADMIRAL, FOURTH FLEET."

He only had to ring the chime once before a voice inside called him in, and he entered. Admiral Garcia was standing behind a large, stained oak desk. Marston snapped smartly to attention.

"At ease, Captain," the Admiral said. He gestured for Marston to sit in one of the guest chairs facing the desk and eased himself into his own high-backed chair.

Garcia returned his attention to a data pad on his desk. "How was your trip to Argos?"

"Good, thank you, Admiral," Marston replied. He wasn't sure what else to say. There was silence while the admiral read over the document and typed something on his computer. Marston glanced past the admiral to the large glass window behind him. The admiral's office had an unrivaled view of the city foreshore and the lake where he could see white-sailed yachts cruising across its calm surface. Beyond that, the convex horizon stretched into the distance.

Marston tried not to fidget. It was so quiet he could hear the Admiral's breathing and the soft hum of chatter from the operations center.

"This is the brief for your first mission," Garcia said after several moments without looking up. "The *Pericles* has been assigned to patrol the Stromar Sector as part of the Fifth Fleet."

"Yes, Admiral." Sector patrol was a relatively simple and straightforward mission, quite acceptable for an untested captain and new starship. "If you don't mind, Admiral, I require your signature here," he added, handing the Admiral the data pad given to him by the commodore.

"Nervous about your first command, Captain?" the admiral asked as he signed the pad.

"Actually, I'm looking forward to the challenge," Marston said, hoping that his tone conveyed calm confidence. He didn't want to come across as blasé or childish in his enthusiasm.

The admiral didn't reply, but he looked like there was something he wanted to say. Marston steeled himself.

Sure enough, the admiral stood and began pacing behind his desk. "May I be perfectly frank, Captain?"

"I would prefer that you are, sir."

The admiral appeared to consider his words carefully before speaking. "I'm sure you are aware that your promotion was a contentious issue. There are some admirals and even captains who don't believe you have the age or experience to command a Navy ship."

Marston kept his posture straight and his expression inscrutable. "That's their choice, sir."

Admiral Garcia stopped pacing and regarded him shrewdly. "I, and others like me, believe you *are* ready for a captaincy. Admiral Mackenzie, for example, is one of your biggest supporters. Did you know that?"

"I did, sir. Admiral Mackenzie's commendation means a great deal to me," Marston said, and he meant it. When he was a lieutenant commander, Marston had faced a tribunal for his conduct during a mission popularly known as the Raptor Nebula Incident. The captain and executive officer of the Navy ship he was posted to, the *Saber*, were killed in battle, and he had assumed command of the ship. Marston's actions had resulted in the destruction of the *Saber* and two enemy Thordran battleships. During the tribunal, which ultimately determined his actions to be justified in defense of the Arretrian colony on Tethannis, Mackenzie had been his staunchest defender. Marston was not only grateful for the confidence the admiral had demonstrated in him then but also for the admiral's recognition of his potential. It was Mackenzie who had promoted him to the rank of captain eighteen months later.

Admiral Garcia continued, "Most officers don't achieve the rank of captain for another ten years, five if they're exceptional. But your career, particularly the last few years, has caught the attention of certain members of the Admiralty. Even though you *are* young, some of us want to see you in the captain's chair, if only to find out whether you can handle the responsibility."

"I appreciate the opportunity, Admiral."

"Do you know what Admiral Mackenzie says about you?" Admiral Garcia asked.

"What's that, sir?"

Garcia sat down again and entwined his fingers on the desk. "You've got an old head on young shoulders." Garcia tapped his forehead. "Wisdom. Your conduct during the Beta Thorii mission showed that. It also showed you have a knack for original thinking, which is what the Commonwealth needs right now. People who are willing to look outside the box for creative solutions."

"Thank you, sir."

"Don't thank me just yet. There are some people expecting you to fail. Just don't let that stop you from doing your duty to the best of your ability. Remember that you have the support of many officers, including myself."

"I appreciate that, Admiral," Marston said.

"Good luck, Captain." They shook hands.

"Thank you, Admiral," Marston said, saluting him. The admiral returned the salute, and then dismissed him. Marston shouldered his bag and left the office.

When the door to the admiral's office closed behind him, he breathed a sigh of relief. The meeting had only taken a few minutes and had gone as well as could be expected, but he was glad it was over. Crossing Ops, he considered the admiral's warning. *There are still plenty of people waiting for you to fail.* Well, he had already resolved not to let the opinion of others affect his conduct. He stepped into the elevator and gave the computer instructions to return him to the monorail station. It was time to see the ship.

*

The first time Simon Marston crossed the threshold of the airlock into the *Pericles,* he had to stifle an excited grin. There was something exhilarating about the bright lights, newly laid carpets and gleaming bulkheads of a new starship. It even *smelt* new. He was already familiar with the layout of the ship, so he turned right and strode down the corridor toward the elevator he knew would take him to the captain's cabin.

The ship's launch was only twelve days away, and all the major work was completed. They were now in the changeover period as the *Pericles* crew arrived and replaced the engineers who had constructed the ship. Most of the current works were minor projects; last-minute adjustments to circuits and relays, recalibrating sensors, stocking the ship with supplies, that sort of thing.

Marston reached the door to the captain's quarters on Deck Two and smiled to himself. Inside would hopefully be his home for many years to come. He typed his access code into the panel and the door slid open. He entered the cabin, pausing just inside the doorway to look around. It was much larger than his berth on the *Saber,* but then, captains always had the most spacious accommodations on the ship. The cabin was on the starboard side of the ship and the windows along that wall offered a panoramic view of the space outside, which currently consisted of the reinforced titanium wall of the dry dock.

He moved into the bedroom and dropped his bag on the bed. On *his* bed. His other belongings had already been delivered; when he pressed his palm gently against the wall, a panel slid neatly aside to reveal a wardrobe containing his neatly arranged clothes. He looked around, a satisfied smirk on his lips. This was home, now. But he would settle in later. He was eager to visit the bridge.

Marston arrived on Deck Three and felt a thrill of anticipation as he neared the ship's command center. The doors to the bridge were already open, while a technician worked on the door control panel.

"Excuse me," Marston said, carefully stepping around the man and his toolbox.

"Careful," the man muttered, before recognizing the captain with a start. He stepped nimbly out of the way and snapped to attention. "Captain on the bridge!"

The crew and technicians on the bridge looked up, surprised at his unexpected arrival. They stood hastily to attention. Marston raised his hands. "At ease, everyone. Don't let me interrupt."

Everyone resumed their work, except for Ronan Balzano, who strode over to greet him. "Welcome aboard!" he beamed. "Want a tour?"

"Thanks," said Marston. He'd studied the layout of the ship, and knew almost every room, corridor, and maintenance tunnel, and he was eager to see the ship in person. He insisted they be thorough, so the tour took most of the afternoon. He used the opportunity to speak to the engineers and technicians, offering encouragement, asking shrewd questions and discussing technical details. Balzano was impressed with the captain's knowledge of the *Pericles* and its systems, but not surprised. Marston was a stickler for details.

On their way back to the bridge, Marston said thoughtfully, "I'd like to have dinner with the senior officers, when they've all arrived. It'll give us a chance to get to know them."

"Sounds good," Balzano agreed.

The elevator doors opened and they stepped onto the bridge. Katarina Sirroyo, the new sensor operations officer, was there to greet them.

"It is a pleasure to meet you in person, Captain," she said primly. Marston shook her hand.

"Likewise, Lieutenant," he said warmly. "It was good of you to give up two days of shore leave to arrive early."

"I had nowhere better to be," Sirroyo said simply. She handed him a data pad. "Here is an update on our progress." Marston accepted the pad, using the moment to covertly study her face. Sirroyo was twenty-eight years old, with pretty features and straight, dark hair that she kept pinned back so tightly he wondered if her face would split in half if she smiled.

Not that there was much chance of that happening, Marston thought to himself. The young woman was one of the most serious officers he'd ever interacted with. Although reserved, she was also dedicated, studious and driven. And brilliant, making her the natural candidate for sensor operations officer.

He scanned the report on the screen. "I didn't think the primary sensor array would be activated until tomorrow," he said.

"We got it working today, sir," she said, clasping her hands tightly behind her back.

"Who's 'we'?" Balzano asked her. "The rest of your department doesn't arrive until tomorrow."

"I mean… I did it," she said, shifting uncomfortably. "All that was left to do was programming the interfaces for the—"

"That must have taken hours!" Balzano exclaimed.

She inclined her head in a brief nod. "Four hours, actually." She glanced fleetingly at her boots before looking back at the captain.

"I'm impressed," Marston said.

"Thank you, Captain. If there's nothing else…?" Marston looked past her to the sensor operations console, where she was halfway through a diagnostic.

Marston shook his head. "Just one thing: I'd like you to join us tomorrow night for dinner," he said. "It will be a good opportunity for the senior staff to get to know each other."

A look of uncertainty flashed across her face. "Of course, Captain," she said, and Marston wondered if she were uncomfortable with the idea.

"Thank you. That's all for now, Lieutenant."

Marston and Balzano watched her walk away. Balzano shook his head. "We're fortunate to have her on the crew," he said quietly.

"Yes, we are," Marston agreed. He gestured with the datapad toward a door on the starboard side of the bridge. "Shall we?"

"After you, Captain."

The two men stepped through the doorway into the captain's office. Although it wasn't a large room, it comfortably fit a workspace with a desk and two chairs and a small lounge area for more informal meetings.

"How does it feel?" Balzano asked as Marston lowered himself into the chair behind his new desk.

Marston grinned back. "Pretty good," he said. He pressed a button on the desktop and a monitor emerged from the smooth surface. He opened a file before rotating the screen so the commander could see.

"These are our orders," Marston said, and Balzano leaned forward.

When he'd finished reading, he commented: "Sector patrol is a pretty standard first mission for a new ship and a new commander."

"Yes," Marston agreed.

Balzano looked at him shrewdly. "But…?"

"But nothing. Patrolling a quiet corner of the Commonwealth isn't exactly my dream mission, but I'm not about to complain."

"At least we can't get into trouble in the Stromar Sector," Balzano remarked.

"That's true. I half expected we'd be given an impossible mission so they could see me fail," Marston said wryly.

Balzano knew the "they" he referred to were those Navy officers who objected to Marston's promotion to captain. The executive officer shrugged, unconcerned. "We're not here to put on a show for them. We're here to do our duty."

"That's true," Marston conceded. "And I *will* do my duty." He straightened his uniform jacket and swung the monitor back to face him. "Now, enough about that. Let's get to work. First things first: I think we need a logistical operations officer."

Balzano nodded slowly.

"It would improve efficiency; the *Pericles* may be a small medium-sized ship, but its systems are complex. During conflict, a logistical operations officer could assist sensor ops and tactical with the combat systems operations."

"I agree," Balzano said.

"Good. I'll submit a personnel request to Admiral Bryant," Marston said. Admiral Bryant was the commander of the Fifth Fleet, to which the *Pericles* was to be assigned.

They discussed the scope of works to be completed before launch, the test flight of the new slipstream drive, and last-minute appraisals of the crew members arriving the next day. Most people would have found the work mundane, but for Marston it was exciting.

2

February 21, 2438
Near the Veela Nebula, Vintra Sector
Republic of Tuulan Vee

Delkan Tola stared at the ship on the viewscreen. It was difficult to see against the backdrop of the Veela Nebula, but it was out there, and adrift.

"That ship is the source of the distress call, Captain," he reported.

Captain Tror stood at the center of the scout ship's cramped bridge, frowning at the image on the screen. "It doesn't look like any Vlind ship I've ever seen," he commented.

"Well, it's a Vlind distress call," Tola said.

"Hail them."

"Channel open, Captain."

"Unidentified ship, this is the Tuulan For vessel *Future's Promise*. Do you require assistance?"

A static-filled response crackled through the speakers. *"Please help usssss…"*

"What is the problem?"

"We require… assistance…"

The bridge crew looked to the captain, whose eyes narrowed in suspicion. The speaker didn't sound Vlind, but they were obligated to render assistance to vessels in need.

"We will offer what assistance we can. Prepare to be boarded," Tror said. When the channel was closed, he addressed his officers. "Something doesn't seem right about this. I want an armed security team to go in first."

"Do you think they're pirates?" Delkan asked.

"I don't know," Tror said grimly. "But a merchant ship disappeared from this area a couple of weeks ago, and now we have an unidentified ship broadcasting a Vlind call for help. We're not taking any chances."

Delkan guided the *Future's Promise* toward the alien ship. A spotlight searched the alien hull for any signs of identification, but the dark, blue-grey hull offered no indication of its origin.

"That is definitely not a Vlind ship," Delkan said. Vlind ships were brown and round-hulled; this ship was different in almost every way.

"Agreed," Tror said firmly. "Abort the docking procedure; we're not going any further without reinforcements. Contact the nearest Republic ship..."

The communications officer looked at the captain in alarm. "I can't, Captain. Our communications are being scrambled."

The alien ship suddenly came alive, engines glowing and weapons ports flaring.

"Evasive maneuvers!" Tror snapped. But it was too late; the alien ship fired on them from point-blank range. The *Future's Promise* reeled from the impact.

"We're venting atmosphere from section two," the engineer reported. Then, after another moment: "Bulkheads in that section have sealed the breach."

Grappling hooks shot out from the alien ship, latching onto the *Future's Promise* with claw-like fingers. Delkan could hear the tearing of metal hull plates as the hooks found purchase. The distance between the two vessels started to shrink as the scout ship was reeled toward the enemy ship. Delkan used every trick he knew of to try and break free, but to no avail. The scout ship's engines were no match for the larger ship.

A clang reverberated through the ship as the two ships made contact. "Prepare to be boarded," Captain Tror ordered, unsheathing his pistol. Delkan and the other bridge officers did the same.

"Captain, they're trying to breach the airlock!" a security officer reported frantically from two decks away.

"Lieutenant Tola, join the security team at the airlock," Captain Tror said. The scout ship had a small crew, and Delkan doubled as the ship's medic. If there was a firefight, he would be needed down there. He scrambled out of his chair, grabbing a medical kit from the emergency locker on the way.

Delkan reached the airlock just as the hatch collapsed inward in a shower of sparks. Smoke billowed into the corridor, stinging his eyes and throat. The security officers shielded their eyes, coughing. They pointed their rifles at the opening, struggling to see through the haze.

The atmosphere circulators activated, drawing the smoke into vents, clearing the air. Delkan stared into the pitch-black beyond the ruined hatchway, trying to make out any sign of the aggressors; they still had no idea who they were facing. One of the security officers waved a scanner at the hole.

"I'm not detecting any life signs at all," he said, puzzled. He was about to inform the captain when a rustling sound caught their attention. Out of the darkness materialized a dozen black, leathery-skinned creatures with glistening fangs. The cat-sized creatures moved rapidly on four gnarled legs, swarming through the hole into the *Future's Promise*. One of the security guards shouted in alarm and opened fire, and the others followed suit. Delkan fired his pistol too, but the creatures moved fast, and it was hard to hit them. One of the guards shouted a warning to him and he spun to the left to see a creature leaping toward him, already in the air. Delkan found himself transfixed by the creature's yellow, slitted eyes. It crashed into him, sinking fangs into his neck. Delkan cried out in pain, feeling coldness spread throughout his body. Then everything began to change.

*

February 22, 2438
Argos City, Argos
Interstellar Commonwealth

As a junior officer, Marston had often found on-board social functions to be awkward events; the irony of that wasn't lost on him as he planned a dinner with his new officers. Trying to rationalize his change of heart, he decided against having it on the ship, choosing a more relaxed location.

Marston and the new senior staff of the *Pericles* were seated in the waterside restaurant *Lagovido* in Argos City. Like every other space station and asteroid installation in the Commonwealth, Argos had a twenty-four-hour day and night cycle to match Earth. The artificial sun had dimmed to simulate night, its bright golden daytime radiance replaced with faint white light that bathed the habitat in artificial moonlight. It reflected off the surface of the lake, creating shimmering patterns of light that played off the ceiling.

"How beautiful," Lupita Gariri remarked appreciatively. The dark-skinned woman in her mid-thirties was Marston's new chief medical officer. Gariri had spent the first part of her career in a frontier clinic on the planet Joro before enlisting in the Navy, and in both occupations her warm, friendly demeanor and medical skill had earned her the respect of her patients and co-workers alike. She had graduated from the Navy academy more than a year earlier but had struggled to find a posting, perhaps because of her lack of military experience. But she was just the kind of person Marston was looking for to fill the role of ship's doctor. He thought it would be good to have someone with her peaceful disposition on the ship; she may not have been strictly military, but he was confident that she would quickly gain the respect of the career officers he had enlisted.

"Nice view," Henry Clarke agreed. He was Marston's new tactical officer. He was twenty-nine years old and a proud Earth native. He had a flawless record, having served in the security departments of two other starships and a space station before joining the *Pericles* crew. This was his first role as a senior officer, and he seemed determined to prove himself to the captain and executive officer. The captain could hardly fault him for that, and could even relate; there were many experienced officers in the Navy who considered *him* unready for his current role. But he didn't want Clarke's need to prove himself motivate him to take unnecessary risks. That was a dangerous thing to do, especially in space, but Marston's trust in the tactical officer far outweighed his concerns, and he knew that Clarke was brave and committed to the safety of his crewmates.

If Gariri was "un-military" and Clarke was the definition of a career officer, Tahir Hasan fell somewhere in between. The new helmsman was an easy-going officer whose only career aspiration was to become senior pilot of a Navy starship. Having achieved that, he was content to remain at the helm for the rest of his career. His lack of ambition didn't bother Marston; Hasan was a consummate professional excited to be at the helm of one of humanity's newest and fastest ships. That had been his dream since the age of six, he had explained to Marston during his interview.

The final addition to the *Pericles* senior staff was Chief Engineer Thad Burch, a middle-aged man who somehow managed to look disheveled even in his dress uniform. Marston attributed it to jet lag from the fourteen-hour flight to the station. Marston actually knew very little about their new chief engineer because his appointment hadn't been Marston's decision. Admiral Bryant, commander of the Navy's Fifth Fleet to which the *Pericles* was assigned, had insisted on assigning him an engineer familiar with the new ship's design, and Marston had acquiesced. Not that he had any choice in the matter. Burch knew his stuff but seemed to lack motivation and Marston wasn't sure how well he would mesh with the other personalities on board. Still, he was willing to give Burch the benefit of the doubt. It would probably be good to have a more experienced person on the command team, he thought optimistically.

The party was rounded off by Katarina Sirroyo, Ronan Balzano, and Marston himself. They took their seats at a table on the terrace by the water's edge.

"It's good to have all of us together for the first time," Marston said, inwardly scolding himself for not saying something more profound or meaningful.

"It's good to be here," Clarke said.

"I've always wanted to visit Argos," Gariri confessed. She gestured at the lake shimmering in the simulated moonlight and the landscape stretching beyond it. "It's just remarkable!"

"And they haven't finished yet," Balzano said. "The plan is to triple the length of this habitat to six hundred kilometers."

"I'd love to see more of it, if we have the time," Gariri said.

"Lieutenant Sirroyo has been here two days already," Balzano told her.

"Oh! Have you had a chance to look around?" Gariri asked the sensor operations officer.

Sirroyo shook her head. "Most of my time has been utilized working on the ship."

"Well, maybe we could do a tour of the habitat," Gariri said, looking around the table to gauge interest.

"We could hire a sky car," Hasan suggested.

"If you can squeeze in some sightseeing before launch, by all means," Marston said amiably.

The waiter returned with menus. As Marston scrolled through the dinner options he glanced up, pleased to see his officers engaging in small talk. Even Sirroyo, who sometimes came across as stilted and formal, responded readily when Clarke asked her about the *Pericles'* targeting sensors. The only one who Marston found difficult to engage with was Burch, whose only contribution to the conversation was to ask the captain if it was alright to order wine. Marston said it was fine.

Overall, he was pleased to see how well his officers got along. If they could interact like this, he hoped they would work well together. Balzano met his gaze and winked, obviously pleased as well.

Things were off to a promising start. Marston hoped it was a sign of things to come.

*

February 23, 2438
Clan Deki Farm, N'Guma
Iganti Tribal States

Lusulo Deki ran as fast as he could along the rocky ground, his bare feet kicking up a trail of dust behind him. In the near distance a great column of smoke billowed up from the impact site, leaving a black smudge against the purple and orange dusk sky. Twilight was descending on the arid landscape of dusty flats and rocky mesas; the primary sun was already sinking below the horizon while the secondary sun hung low in the sky. It didn't matter, though; Lusulo had spent all ten years of his life here. He knew the area around his family farm well enough that he could find his way back home in the dark.

Lusulo had been setting up his telescope for a night of stargazing when it had locked onto what had first appeared to be a shooting star. But he soon realized it was far brighter than any other shooting stars he'd witnessed through the little telescope is parents had bought him for his last birthday. And it was growing brighter. He had pressed his face against the eyepiece, squinting. A meteor? No, a ship! Someone was crashing! And from the rapidly growing size of the ship, he knew it would land close by.

He didn't even wait to see where it landed. He leapt off his bed, knocking his telescope and bedside lamp over in his haste. He was already sprinting through the door into the dusty backyard of his home when a loud *boom* reverberated across the plain. It was easy to find the point of impact from the flash of fire and the smoke.

As he neared the site of the impact he slowed to a walk, panting. He'd already had his water ration for the day, and he didn't want to tire himself. Water was scarce on N'Guma, even more so because of the drought.

He padded toward the wreck, being careful to avoid treading on the shards of hot metal littering the rocky ground around the ship. He moved as close as he dared; the smoke and heat radiating from the wreckage prevented him from getting any closer. Squinting against the growing gloom, he peered at the wreck, trying to spot any sign of survivors.

"Hello?" he called out uncertainly.

There was no response except for the crackling of flames. Lusulo backed away from the wreck, deciding it would be better for him to return with his parents.

"Waaaiiiiiiit...."

Lusulo saw a figure emerge from the smoke. Night was descending and stars were appearing in the sky, but the fire illuminated the figure with orange light. Lusulo did a double take; the man emerging from the smoke wasn't like any Iganti he had ever seen. An alien? But the figure had spoken to him in Ganti, even in his dialect. And the man had the long, slender limbs and frame and large head of an Iganti... but he was also different. He was hunched over and limping, but that may have been from injuries sustained in the crash. His skin was as black as obsidian, and his small, unblinking eyes glistened in the firelight. Those were not Iganti eyes, Lusulo realised with dread. He backed away, scared.

The figure moved toward him with claws outstretched. Lusulo turned and ran. He regretted not bringing any help, and just wanted to get to the safety of his home.

He thought he had outrun the man when a second figure stepped out from behind a large piece of debris. It latched onto him with sharp claws and sank fangs into his arm. Lusulo cried from the pain and shock as coldness flooded through him. It was a strange, unfamiliar sensation; even at night the desert didn't get this cold.

Lusulo felt like his insides were being transformed. He vomited black bile onto the dirt at his feet. He noted that despite how cold he felt, he wasn't shivering. His vision blurred, then cleared. Things looked *different*. Everything was dimmer, the colors gentler. He felt better after vomiting, and the cold was *invigorating*. Completely forgetting about the two crash survivors he sprinted off into the desert. The cool night air washed over him, and he laughed in exhilaration. His voice sounded different, not like his own. But he didn't care; he had boundless energy and felt like he could run for ever. It was like he had received an injection of new life.

Images of people flashed through his mind: an older male and female tucking him into bed as a child, and other people he knew, but couldn't quite recall. Their images were clear in his mind, but his association with them melted away. All he knew was that he had to share with them the new life he had. He shrieked with joy, and it emerged from his throat like a bestial cry. He clenched his hands tightly; his fingers were surprisingly sharp, and he felt blood pool in his palms. But it didn't look like his blood, not anymore. It didn't matter, though. He changed directions, racing toward the homestead on the horizon.

3

Message to the Ecclesia of the Ankari Assembly from Chief Scientist Telzane of the Jakora Primary Medical Facility

We have every able facility in the Assembly studying the virus and I am confident it is just a matter of time before a cure is found. Information is key, and although our knowledge of the plague and its effects are limited, we learn more with each day. This is what we know so far:

- The plague can cross species. There are numerous reports of Ankari becoming infected by Vlind, and Kelzee becoming infected by Kithel, and so on.
- The plague may not be limited to sentient species; numerous (unsubstantiated) reports indicate cattle and native fauna on affected worlds becoming infected.
- All victims undergo the same four stages of infection, although the duration and severity of each stage varies between species. Lacking better terms, these stages are informally known as: (1) Initial Infection, (2) Rabid State, (3) Transformation Stage, and (4) Final Stage.
- The duration of each stage is determined by the biology of the affected species. Species with higher metabolisms such as Iganti and Kithel undergo rapid onset of stages 1-3, while infected Vlind subjects have been known to last up to six days between initial infection and the onset of stage 2.

Regrettably, we lack any reliable information on the origins of the plague, but we are aware the Defense Force is investigating that matter and its possible relationship with the ship disappearances that have affected the Locality for several months now.

More information will be passed on to the Ecclesia as it is learned. We are collaborating with our counterparts in the Vlind Merchant Republic, Kelzee Federation, and the Interspecies Scientific Exchange of Research organization. The situation is serious enough that against the personal wishes of several of our board we have appealed to Minnen the Learned of Iganta. He almost single-handedly cured the Osaija Virus, and we can only hope he responds to our plea for help, but given our history, we cannot say if that is likely.

My team and I are completely devoted to solving the mystery of the plague, and the study of recently obtained samples of the plague virus from victims on Kyrion should give our scientists a surfeit of new information. We can only hope it does- this plague has taken everyone by surprise, and so far, nobody has had any luck treating the disease or even delaying its effects. Our work is even more important, then, and we must find a cure before the plague spreads to every territory in the Locality.

Until the next seeing,
Telzane / Chief Scientist, Jakora Medical Facility

February 23, 2438
Argos Fleet Yards, Argos
Interstellar Commonwealth

Marston looked around with satisfaction, pleased with the personal touches he had added to his new office. On the desk was a photo frame that cycled through holographic images of his family, and beside it was a small globe of Europa Nova, his home world. Although he was born on Earth, most of his formative years had been spent on the Tier 3 world and it was where he considered home.

On the wall opposite his desk was an oil painting of the HMS *Challenger*, a sailing vessel from nineteenth century Earth. The *Challenger* was a naval vessel that also served as a ship of exploration, and Marston hoped that one day he would command one of the Navy's exploratory missions. The vast, unknown reaches of the Milky Way Galaxy still contained many mysteries.

He was staring at the painting, lost in thought when his communicator chimed. "Marston here."

"Captain, this is Lieutenant Commander Wong from Argos Security. There's been an accident in Cargo Bay Twenty-Two on the station. Your presence is required."

Marston froze. A dozen possible disaster scenarios flashed through his mind. "I'm on my way," he said, grabbing his uniform jacket and pulling it on as he hurried out the door. At the same time, he activated his communicator. "Lieutenant Commander Clarke, please meet me at the airlock."

"*On my way, Captain,*" Clarke replied, the curiosity evident in his voice.

Marston met his tactical officer at the airlock two minutes later.

"I've been summoned by Station Security," he told Clarke as they strode briskly through the short tunnel linking the *Pericles* with the station.

"Why?"

"They didn't tell me the reason."

They rode an elevator down two levels to the warehouse containing the provisions waiting to be transferred to the *Pericles*. With the ship's launch so near most of the cargo had already been stowed aboard the ship, except for a few larger crates at the center of the cavernous room. The doors of the umbilical tunnel connecting the warehouse to the *Pericles'* cargo bay were sealed shut.

Marston and Clarke were greeted by a cordon of security officers diverting curious passers-by from the entrance. Looking past them, they saw what looked like a crime scene. A forensic team had taped off an area protected by more security officers, and a small judicial drone hovered nearby, recording everything. Anxiety gnawing at him, Marston approached the cordon.

Lieutenant Commander Wong, the security chief for Sector 300 of Argos Station, noticed their approach and waved them in. As they stepped into the cargo bay proper the *Pericles* officers caught their first glimpse of the victim.

"Oh, gees," Clarke muttered under his breath. Marston kept his face impassive, fighting the urge to retch at the sight.

The corpse of Lieutenant Thad Burch, the *Pericles'* new chief engineer, lay on the floor amidst a pool of blood and grey matter. *Former* chief engineer, Marston corrected himself silently. The lieutenant's skull, neck and left shoulder had been completely crushed. A forensic scientist was running a deep scan of the body while another two medical technicians prepared a body bag and anti-grav stretcher. It didn't take a genius to recognize he had been flattened by one of the large cargo containers currently being moved away by a robotic cargo handler. The initial apprehension Marston had felt quickly turned to anger.

"How did this happen?" he demanded. A few meters away, two security officers were questioning a pair of engineers who had evidently been in a room at the time of the chief's death.

"According to the logs of the anti-grav forklift and the reports of the two witnesses, the lieutenant failed to activate the safety brakes on the forklift. When he got out to check the inventory of one of the crates, the brakes disengaged and the forklift crashed into a cargo container, causing the container to fall on top of the lieutenant."

"What about the secondary brakes?" Clarke asked Wong. "Even if he didn't engage the mains, the safeties should have still worked."

Wong nodded. "They should have, but they didn't. This forklift wasn't properly maintained."

Marston rubbed his brow wearily. "This is terrible. Why was he using a forklift that wasn't safe for driving?"

"That is a good question, sir," said Wong neutrally. He didn't want to speak ill of the dead, but the evidence pointed toward the reason being the engineer's own negligence.

Clarke looked over the forklift, careful not to interfere with the investigators. "Did he know the forklift was faulty?"

Wong nodded. "The computer would have warned him, as it did us when we moved it."

Marston stared at the body glumly. Forgetting the fact that he had lost his chief engineer to an accident just three days into his first command, a man had lost his life.

"What happens now?" he asked.

"Now we clean up, I write the official report on the incident, and we inform his family," Wong said, looking meaningfully at Marston as he said the last part.

The captain sighed. "*I* will notify his family. I was his commanding officer."

"I'd like a copy of your report, when you're done," Clarke added.

Wong nodded and left them to speak with his deputy. Marston and Clarke made sure to keep out of the way as the Argos team went about their work. Within minutes the scene was documented, the body removed by medics, and cleaning bots were scrubbing the deck to remove all traces of the grisly accident. Having no desire to watch the little robots remove blood and brain matter from the metal grating, Marston turned toward the exit and Clarke followed him.

"Poor guy," Clarke said as they walked back to the *Pericles*.

"What a sad way to die," Marston agreed. Even more tragic because it had been *preventable*.

"I don't imagine it will be fun for you, notifying his next of kin," Clarke said sympathetically. Marston nodded in agreement. He privately hoped that it would be was an extremely infrequent part of his job.

"Now I also need to find us a new chief engineer," Marston added. His mind raced, thinking about everything he had to do now. Speak to Burch's family, organize a funeral, notify Admiral Garcia and find a replacement chief engineer, and have the ship ready to launch in less than a fortnight.

"What about promoting someone from within the engineering department?" Clarke asked.

Marston shook his head. "None of them have the experience necessary to run the department. We'll have to look elsewhere."

"I'm sure there's at least one engineer on this station with suitable experience," Clarke said optimistically, "And who wouldn't mind joining the crew of one of the Navy's newest and finest starships."

"As long as they have working knowledge of the new Interceptor-class engines," Marston said wryly. He stopped abruptly. "Oh." Clarke turned to see why the captain had paused in the middle of the busy corridor.

"There is such a person," Marston realized.

"You want me to be your new chief engineer?" Don Winston asked in astonishment. Despite his obvious surprise, he sounded intrigued. Marston nodded, suppressing a smile. He was confident the older man would take the job.

"You're the best person for the job," Marston told him, and it was true. There was nowhere else he would find an experienced engineer with working knowledge of the Interceptor-class *Pericles* on such short notice. He also happened to think Winston would be well-suited to the role, based on his admittedly limited interactions with the man.

They were seated in Marston's office; rather than approaching Winston in the engineer's office on the station, he wanted to give the man a glimpse of the ship. Sure enough, when Winston arrived at Marston's office escorted by Balzano, the engineer had complimented him on the "fine ship", murmuring appreciatively of its design and construction. Before leaving them Balzano gave Marston a look he understood straight away; his executive officer also thought this would be an easy sell.

Now Marston was ready to seal the deal. "If you're interested, we would love to have someone of your ability on board." Then as kindly as possible: "And I hate to put you on the spot, but I need to know very soon." If Winston turned down the job, he couldn't waste any time searching for a replacement.

The engineer snorted. "No pressure, right?"

Marston smiled sympathetically. "I'm sorry to rush you, but we're up against the clock. The launching ceremony is next week, and we're nearly ready, but I still need a chief engineer, and I can't wait."

Winston stared intently at the ground, considering. His hands were clasped in front of him, fidgeting. Marston watched him silently. When Winston looked back at him, though, Marston could see in in the engineer's face the response he had hoped for.

"Alright then. I accept," Winston said, and Marston broke into a grin.

"Thank you, Chief," Marston said, shaking his hand vigorously. "I'll arrange to have you transferred immediately."

"I will need some time to organize my own replacement," Winston said. He chuckled. "A replacement after just two days!"

Marston nodded wryly. "I know what that's like. Get that sorted, and we'll make sure the chief engineer's quarters are ready for you."

Marston summoned his executive officer, who offered Winston a warm congratulations and told him how pleased they were he accepted. When Winston left to organize his replacement, Balzano lingered.

"It's fortunate *that* worked out," Balzano said with relief. He had shared Marston's concern they wouldn't have a chief engineer by the time the ship left dry dock.

"Yes," Marston agreed, drumming his fingers on the desk absently. "And it was a lot more enjoyable than speaking to Burch's family." Communicating the loss of a loved one to their family had to be one of the hardest parts of his new job, and he wished he hadn't had to do it so soon.

When Balzano arrived in Main Engineering he found Katarina Sirroyo and Tahir Hasan by the master control station near the ship's slipstream drive core. They looked up from the diagnostic of the ship's faster-than-light engines at his approach.

"Is everything shipshape?" Balzano asked.

"Yes, sir," Hasan said, noticeably lacking his usual enthusiasm. Balzano understood; they had their own work to attend to.

"Good. Thank you both for taking on some of Lieutenant Burch's duties," he said. He could tell from Sirroyo's sour expression that she was refraining from commenting on the former chief engineer. She didn't want to speak ill of the dead, although she had previously made clear to the commander her low opinion of the engineer, calling him, "slothful and unprofessional" in her customarily direct manner.

Hasan nodded politely. "We do what we can," he said.

"The good news is, it won't be for much longer. We've got a new chief engineer," Balzano told them.

"That was fast!"

"Who is it?" Sirroyo asked.

"An Argos engineer the captain knows. He's been in the Navy for thirty-five years, and he worked on the Interceptor class at Terelos," Balzano said.

Hasan and Sirroyo agreed he sounded qualified. More so than the disheveled engineer Admiral Bryant had appointed.

*

After just two days in the position, Donald Winston resigned his role as head of the Maintenance Division for Sector 275 after promoting his eager but capable assistant to the role. Then he gathered his still-unpacked belongings and transferred to the *Pericles*, ready to begin his new role as Chief Engineer. He was welcomed by the engineering staff, who were pleased to have an experienced officer in charge of their department. Although strict, he quickly earned the respect of his crewmates, as much for his ability and passion for the job as for his uncomplicated and straight-forward manner.

At the end of his first shift as Chief Engineer, Winston updated the *Pericles'* Finishing Schedule, which was what the Navy called the last-minute touch-ups and fixes for new starships prior to launch. He was quite pleased; the contents showed that they were still on track and would in fact be ready a few hours earlier than anticipated. He was striding across the bridge toward the captain's office to deliver it personally when he was intercepted by the ship's executive officer.

"Sorry, Chief. The captain's taking an important call right now," Balzano said.

Even though Winston had only met him the day before he could tell the commander's voice was strained. "Oh, no problem." He looked at the commander askance. "Is everything alright?" he asked quietly, gesturing with his head toward the door to Marston's office.

"We'll know soon enough," Balzano said neutrally. Marston had been on a call with Admiral Bryant for several minutes. The respectful and discreet thing to do would have been to contact Marston directly and address any issues privately. Calling the bridge and publicly demanding to speak to him had been a calculated and vindictive move by the admiral. That didn't bode well for the captain, Balzano thought grimly.

Marston hadn't been this angry in a long time. He wanted to shout back at the glaring visage of Admiral Bryant on the monitor, but he kept his face politely neutral, gripping the armrests of his chair so tightly that his knuckles turned white.

Remain calm, he commanded himself, the muscles in his jaw clenching. Admiral Bryant was all bluster; Marston wondered if he was trying to provoke an insubordinate response. But he held his tongue throughout the one-sided exchange, hoping the Admiral's ranting would soon end so he could at least end the communication. It wasn't easy, though; he had a retort for every accusation the Admiral threw at him, but he knew it wouldn't help his case to argue back. He found it ironic, however, that Bryant was accusing him of the very thing Marston believed the admiral was responsible for.

"How dare you undermine my authority," Bryant railed, *"By enlisting a new chief engineer without my consent. I gave you plenty of leeway to*

choose your other officers, even if most of them are almost as inexperienced as you…"

So, it wasn't just him that Bryant didn't like, Marston thought. He also had an issue with Marston's officers. That was good to know.

"… The Pericles *is a new class of vessel, and it uses a new type of engine. You can't have just any fleet engineer, but one with experience* working *on that design. I'm disappointed, Captain, that you just picked a candidate without consulting me or Admiral Garcia. What kind of captain would risk taking an untested ship into combat, or any other situation, with a crew that doesn't know how to properly operate the ship's systems? It seems to demonstrate a lack of foresight, which I find very disappointing."*

The first remark was foolishness, and Marston dismissed it immediately. The *Pericles* wouldn't be preparing to leave drydock unless the crew were intimately familiar with its functions. The last accusation stung, but Marston kept his voice level when he said, "Admiral, my new chief engineer *has* experience with these engines. He has worked on another Interceptor…"

Bryant cut him off abruptly. *"Captain, don't you dare try and justify subverting your superior officer. I told you with the last man that* I *would select your engineer. It should be obvious that this instance would be the same as then,"* he said pedantically. Bryant shrugged helplessly, as though he couldn't comprehend Marston's actions at all. *"It seems simple enough to me."*

Marston refrained from commenting. Instead, he decided to play the part expected of him with the hope of ending this conversation as soon as possible.

"My apologies, Admiral. I did not mean to undermine your authority, and I will consult you in the future," he said in his most calm voice. "If you like I will send you Donald Winston's personnel file so you may examine his qualifications for yourself."

Admiral Bryant didn't look happy, either because Marston would not be provoked or because he couldn't think of an angry response to such a reasonable statement. *"I want you to send it to me now,"* he said grudgingly. *"And see that this doesn't happen again."*

"Yes, Admiral," Marston said, although it wasn't easy for him to concede anything to the admiral. Bryant was arrogant, prideful, and controlling, but the captain knew he had to show deference, if only because of the uniform he wore.

Predictably, Bryant had to have the last word. *"I hope you don't let me down again, Captain."* He ended the call abruptly, his smirking face replaced by the Navy logo.

Marston relaxed, no longer having to conceal his anger. He looked down at his hands; they were shaking with rage. He fought the desire to break something. It bothered him how Bryant provoked him; he didn't want other people to be able to manipulate him like that.

He had made the right decision regarding Donald Winston, he was sure of it. And as difficult as it was to concede, maybe he *should* have gone to Bryant first. Even if it was ridiculous (and as far as he knew, unprecedented) for a captain not to choose his own officers, it was the way his superior officer had expected.

Anger and frustration warred within him, and he sighed. A death in the crew and a fight with his superior officer wasn't the beginning he had hoped for. But he resolved to respect Admiral Bryant's authority, even if he didn't respect the man.

Still, a small voice in the back of his mind nagged him: how long was he expected to tolerate this heavy-handed oversight that other captains didn't have to deal with?

Half an hour passed before Balzano discreetly checked the subspace communications log to make sure the call had ended, and Marston was alone. He waited several more minutes before picking up Chief Engineer Winston's datapad. Then he strode across the bridge to the door to Marston's office and pressed the door chime.

"Come in," Marston called.

Balzano stepped into the captain's office to find Marston working at his desk, his face impassive. The young captain looked up at his approach.

"Here's Chief Winston's report on the finishing schedule." He placed the datapad on Marston's desk. "Ready for some good news? We'll be leaving right on schedule." He paused, and then added, "Selecting Winston as the new chief engineer was the right call."

"Thanks," Marston said.

Balzano could sense the anger beneath his calm exterior. But if the captain wanted to talk to him about it, he would.

Balzano turned and walked toward the exit but paused in the doorway. "At the end of the shift Clarke and I are going to the gym if you wanted to join us. We were planning on getting in some boxing practice. Good for working out our frustration."

A small smile tugged at the corner of Marston's mouth. "Yeah," he said, "that sounds good."

4

The Tuulan For ship descended gracefully through the bright azure sky, passing through wispy white clouds. Hundreds of meters below, the glistening surface of the ocean reflected the deep blue of the sky. *Another perfect day*, Torina Jadus thought. This last stretch of the journey was always her favorite as the ship made its final approach to Lakaria, the capital city of Tuulan Vee and her home.

Beside her the shuttle pilot, Antak Droma, opened a radio channel to the air traffic controller. "Lakaria Spaceport Flight Control, this is government ship *Telvarn Star* requesting permission to land. We are on final approach from the east, estimated time of arrival is five minutes."

Jadus looked out the forward-facing window of the cockpit as the coastal city appeared on the horizon. The tall spires and graceful arching domes of Lakaria sprawled along a white sandy strip of coastline stretching to the north and south, growing rapidly with their approach.

"*Telvarn Star, this is Lakaria flight control. You have permission to land at the attached coordinates.*"

A string of digits appeared on Antak's screen. "Acknowledged, Lakaria flight control. *Telvarn Star* out." He flicked off the radio and guided the ship onto their new flight path. The *Telvarn Star* arced lazily through the air, soaring over elegant, pearlescent buildings and angling toward the spaceport on the southwestern edge of the city.

The door to the cockpit opened and Jadus' chief aide and security officer entered.

"It feels good to return home, doesn't it?" she said by way of greeting.

"Yes it does, ma'am," Jarren Qel agreed. He had worked faithfully as her chief aide for eighteen months now. The young man flashed her a grin and added, "Although I'm afraid it does mean having to attend parliament this afternoon."

"Ah, well, you couldn't avoid the parliament forever," Antak said. Normally Jadus paid little attention to her staff's jokes, but the corners of her mouth twitched in another small smile. She turned to Korosa, the serious-looking woman responsible for her security. "Your service has been exemplary, as usual."

Korosa gave a small nod in acceptance of the compliment. "Thank you, Minister."

The airport swept into view, and Antak spun in his chair to face the other three.

"You should all take your seats," he told them. "We'll be landing in about one minute." They left the small cockpit and returned to the passenger cabin. The government ship was capable of transporting up to ten passengers comfortably, but Torina Jadus had never felt the need to have so many staff, and didn't think much of those senators who felt it necessary to travel with such a large entourage. She prided herself on being a minimalist and got by perfectly well with just one aide and a security guard. As the Minister for Medicine and Health, she had an entire ministry of capable employees, anyway.

They strapped themselves into their seats and looked patiently out the window as the ship approached the spaceport.

"You never did tell me what your favorite part of the trip was," Jarren reminded Korosa.

She gave him a bland look. "I didn't have a favorite part of the trip."

"I quite enjoyed it," Minister Jadus said. "Touring the new research station was a wonderful experience."

Jadus had been invited to officially open the new medical research facility in the Verulon System. She had been honored, for the staff had known of her passion for their field of work and her generosity as a donor to universities and hospitals. As a former doctor, she was impressed by the new facility and its advanced equipment and listened happily to the staff gush about the exciting new work they would be able to do. It had been a worthwhile trip and an excellent opportunity to escape the busyness of the capital for a few weeks.

"The station was nice," Korosa conceded. "I just wasn't particularly interested in what the scientists do there."

"How can you say that?" Jarren asked incredulously. "Their station brings state-of-the-art medical technology and healthcare to the outer colonies. I think it's great!"

Korosa didn't share his enthusiasm. "Good for you," she said flatly.

Jarren was smiling as he shook his head in disbelief. He and the security officer were opposites in a lot of ways, but they had forged a strong friendship during their time working for the minister.

Only half listening to their banter, Jadus smiled indulgently and checked the straps on her harness. It was hardly necessary, however, because Antak gently lowered the ship onto the tarmac with barely a jolt.

"Home again," Jarren said, standing and stretching luxuriously despite only having sat for a few minutes. Korosa opened the airlock and the salty, humid warmth of Lakaria flooded into the cabin. Jadus took a deep breath, inhaling the smell of home, grateful their journey was over.

Antak shut down the ship's engines and flicked on the ship-wide intercom. "Thank you for traveling with *Telvarn Star* airlines," he said through the speaker. "Please be sure to leave a generous tip for your highly skilled pilot."

"Would you believe I left my wallet in my apartment?" Jarren retorted.

"Not a problem," Antak countered. "I'll invoice you."

Baggage handlers arrived to transfer their luggage from the ship. A government shuttle was waiting nearby to take Jadus and Jarren away. Korosa and Antak would be lodging at the military barracks near the spaceport while they waited for their next orders.

As he ran through the post-flight check and powered down the ship's systems, Antak glanced out of the window and his eye caught on a ship sitting on the tarmac beside one of the hangars operated by the Republic's military. He recognized it as a scout-class vessel and watched idly as it was towed into the hangar. It was almost out of sight when he caught the name of the ship on the stern. He blinked to make sure he hadn't misread it, but the name *Future's Promise* was clearly emblazoned on the hull. That was the name of the ship piloted by his friend Delkan Tola. He and Delkan had attended military college together, both graduating from the school of aviation. They kept in touch two or three times a year. Or at least they had until a week ago, when Antak learned the *Future's Promise* had vanished.

When Antak had tried to contact his friend at the prearranged time, the computer had informed him the receiver was no longer connected to the subspace communications network. It couldn't be that the *Future's Promise* was out of range, because Delkan would have told him. When he had delved into the fleet registry, the scout ship had been newly listed as "Undetermined Status". Just one step down from Killed or Missing In Action.

Antak had checked the Infonet for news of the *Future's Promise*; it wasn't unheard of for vessels to reappear after an extended absence. Sometimes stellar phenomena or system malfunctions prevented a ship from communicating, the most famous example being the *Stellar Venturer*, which returned home after being presumed missing for years. Antak decided to seek out his friend as soon as he was finished on the *Telvarn Star*.

Jarren poked his head through the door into the cockpit. "Thanks again, Antak. We'll give you a call the next time the minister needs a pilot."

"I'd appreciate that. It beats sitting in the barracks waiting for another assignment," Antak said. Until a position became available on a starship he was stationed in the military barracks in the city. For someone as restless as Antak, the wait was not easy. So, when he had been given the opportunity to pilot a government vessel to the outer edges of the Republic, he had jumped at the chance.

"Great, we'll be in touch." Jarren promised before disappearing. Antak saw him moments later through the window, hurrying across the tarmac to catch up to the minister.

As the government vehicle pulled away a group of technicians arrived to perform their routine inspection of the ship. A refueling bot followed them, reaching out with mechanical arms to connect its fuel hose into the ship's tanks. Antak met the chief technician on the tarmac beside the ship. "Welcome home," the technician greeted him, adding, "We'll take over from here."

Antak retrieved his bag from the ship and entered the spaceport. Lakaria Spaceport was one of the busiest transport hubs in the Republic. The capital received more interplanetary traffic than any other city in the Republic.

It was a short walk to the hangar where the *Future's Promise* was berthed, but the way was crowded with military personnel. Antak wondered why a previously missing military scout ship would be docked at the capital's spaceport. There were only two reasons that he could think of: either the fleet yards on and around the planet were already at capacity (which was very unlikely), or the government was trying to keep it close by, and whatever it held, contained. Tuulan Vee, like the entire Republic, was highly centralized, with many of the planet's government agencies and Military Headquarters located in the city.

More military and government shuttles were descending on the spaceport every minute, swarming around the hangar now housing the *Future's Promise*. Entering a corridor with a notice that read: "MILITARY PERSONNEL ONLY", he fell into step with some other officers, passing into the hangar without having to show any identification. In their haste to get to the ship, the officers in charge must have glanced at his uniform and assumed he had authorization.

His curiosity was piqued by the hushed tones of officers discussing the *Future's Promise*, too quiet for him to make out. Curiosity became concern when he noticed that many of them wore the mark of the Department of Military Intelligence, and most of the others were either damage control engineers or medics. Whatever was happening it wasn't routine; it was serious. As easy as it had been to get in, Antak began to worry that he would be identified as an imposter. If he were, he was sure to be punished and receive a black mark on his military record. He glanced around nervously, feeling sweat break out on his forehead, regretting his attempt to try and get into the hangar. But he couldn't stop in the middle of the corridor and reverse course without looking suspicious. He could only keep going forward, along with the crowd, until he could find a way to slip out a side door and make his way back to the spaceport terminal.

He stepped aside as a group of medics raced past, gurneys bearing shrouded figures gliding smoothly behind them. People fell silent as the grim procession passed.

"Antak! Lieutenant Droma, what are you doing here?"

Antak whirled around to find another college acquaintance, Peltak Sorkento, standing behind him. Unlike he and Delkan, they hadn't kept in contact over the last few years and Antak didn't even know what department Peltak worked in until he saw the other man was wearing the badge of a lieutenant in the Department of Military Intelligence.

"Peltak! Hi, it's good to see you," Antak said as they approached each other.

"Likewise," Peltak replied automatically; he looked distracted and on edge. "How did you get in here?"

Antak decided the best course of action was complete honesty. "I just got home and noticed the *Future's Promise* docked. I thought I'd see if Delkan was around. You remember Delkan Tola?"

A shadow passed over Sorkento's face. "Oh. Well, I'm afraid he's not. And now really isn't a good time. I'm going to have to ask you to leave..."

"What's going on?" Antak asked, studying his friend's anxious face. "Something bad has happened to the *Promise*, hasn't it? Where's Delkan?"

Sorkento glanced sideways, apparently concerned about someone overhearing their conversation. He grabbed Antak by the elbow and steered him down the corridor toward the ship.

"See for yourself," he said quietly, guiding Antak into the flight control room that overlooked the hangar. Antak was about to ask what Peltak wanted him to see when he looked out the window. The question died on his lips.

The ship's dorsal hull was ripped open in two places, as though the *Future's Promise* had been caught in the talons of a giant bird of prey. The port side of the ship looked untouched, which was why Antak hadn't seen any damage from the *Telvarn Star*. But there was another breach in the starboard hull, and teams of engineers with scanning equipment were meticulously examining the damaged section.

"What happened?" Antak asked.

"According to the ship's log, the *Promise* was attacked by an unidentified vessel near the Veela Nebula," Sorkento said grimly.

"Unidentified?" Antak repeated in disbelief. "That doesn't make sense, the *Promise* should have been able to identify any vessel in the Locality."

"I know," Sorkento said flatly.

"But—"

"We don't know who attacked them, but we will find out," Sorkento said with cold certainty. He grabbed Antak's arm again and steered him back out into the corridor.

Antak shook free of his grip. "I can walk just fine on my own!" he said irritably.

Sorkento didn't respond but refrained from grabbing his arm again as they re-joined the flow of officers to and from the hangar. Antak glanced sideways at his friend; there was something more that he wasn't telling him. Before he could ask, there was a shout from behind them and they had to step aside as stony-faced medical officers came past, leading gurneys with more white-sheeted forms. Antak wondered grimly if one of the bodies belonged to Delkan.

Suddenly, the white sheeted form on the nearest gurney *twitched*. Antak took a step back; the movement had come from the body beneath the sheet and not from the motion of the gurney. He was so focused on the sheet that he nearly yelped in surprise when the form beneath it abruptly sat up.

Antak didn't know if the others in the corridor had expected that to happen, but he was shocked when the corpse twisted beneath the sheet toward him. His mouth fell open in astonishment. Peltak pushed him out of the way as a pair of medics dove on the sheeted form, jabbing a needle into the figure through the blanket. There was an otherworldly growl, and the sheeted figure collapsed back on the gurney. A limb flopped out from beneath the covering sheet; the arm hung limply, but the claw-like hand on the end of it clenched and unclenched, as though searching for something to grasp onto.

"Get them out of here," Sorkento ordered sternly, prompting the medics to hurry away with their mysterious cargo. As soon as they were gone, Antak rounded on him.

"What in the worlds was *that*?" he asked, wide-eyed.

"*That* is classified," the intelligence officer responded in a tone that left no room for argument. "You cannot tell anyone what you saw here. I'm invoking Directive 34." Directive 34 gave members of the Department of Military Intelligence the power to order complete confidentiality upon pain of expulsion from the military and imprisonment. "Do you understand me?"

"Of course," Antak stammered, surprised at the rarely given order.

"I mean it, Antak," said Sorkento firmly. "You are not to say anything about this unless the military or government declassifies it."

"I follow orders, Peltak," said Antak defensively, irked at the other man's implication that he couldn't.

Sorkento studied him for a moment before nodding, apparently satisfied. "Good," he said. "I'm afraid you're going to have to leave now."

With that, he gestured to a pair of burly security officers who escorted Antak back to the bustling activity of the spaceport public terminal.

With nothing else to do, Antak hefted his bag onto his shoulder and left, his curiosity unsated, and tainted by fear.

*

February 27, 2438
Interstellar space, near the Vratak Nebula
Kelzee Galactic Federation

Ship Overseer Elzor Drin slammed his four-fingered fist against the armrest of his chair. "Klon!" he hollered. His ship, the Vlind cargo vessel *Wealth and Grandeur* (two things he aspired to), had been traveling through the slipstream when it had unexpectedly plunged back into normal space. An alarm wailed as the ship's thrusters fought to stabilize their tumble through space.

Drin would be furious if it was because the core technicians had failed to properly align the slipstream coils again. *What you pay for is what you get,* he thought wryly. Minimum-wage, barely competent technicians were the price he paid trying to maximize his profits. It was a fine line to walk, and normally Drin got by with his crew of mostly apprentice-level employees. Except for today, apparently.

Thyrryl Klon, Manager of Engineering, fussed over the engineering terminal that occupied the front left quadrant of the circular bridge. "Apologies, Overseer, I work to remedy the issue…" Drin overheard him muttering darkly about what he'd do if the culprit were one of his technicians.

"What is our location?" Drin demanded. The trading post in the Sr'Hirta System was supposed to take ten days to reach, and they had only been traveling for two.

"Interstellar space, in the vicinity of the Vratak Nebula," reported Qwell Lintor, the ship's pilot and navigator. He was one of the few experienced officers in the crew, and Drin trusted him.

"What is our reason for stopping?" Drin asked. He was impatient to resume their course to Sr'Hirta. Their transport contract was time-sensitive. Delays could be costly.

"The cause was not anyone on the ship, Overseer," reported Klon, sounding mildly surprised. "A disruption field prevents our travel through the slipstream."

Drin snorted. "Disruption? By whom, and for what reason?" Their course was a well-traveled trade route and routinely patrolled by the Kelzee Military; pirates were not a problem here.

"Overseer, a vessel approaches from the direction of the nebula," Lintor reported from the helm. A hull-mounted camera swiveled around to point at a ship emerging from the rose-colored mist of the Vratak Nebula. The bridge crew squinted at the image; if it weren't for the backdrop of the nebula, it would have been almost impossible to see the dark hull against the blackness of space.

"They must identify themselves," Drin said, his stubby fingers flying over the fold-out keyboard in front of him. But his query went unanswered; the mysterious vessel grew larger on the viewscreen as it approached them.

"Why do they not respond?" Lintor wondered, his voice tinged with anxiety.

"Their hull configuration is unidentifiable," reported Klon.

"They may be hostile," Drin realized nervously. "Raise shields and arm the forward cannon!"

His crew sprang into action as fast as they could, considering they were merchants who hadn't run a combat drill in years. Nevertheless, fear gave them speed, and soon a high-pitched alarm was echoing through the ship, instructing all crewmembers to report to their stations.

Lintor brought the small, bulbous cargo ship around to directly face the oncoming vessel. Klon activated the cannon and the small, dish-like turret swiveled to track the unknown ship. "Cannon online!"

Drin just nodded in response; his throat felt dry and he didn't trust himself to speak. He wasn't a brave man, and the thought of combat filled him with anxiety and dread. The *Wealth and Grandeur* was a cargo hauler; it did not have powerful shields or weapons comparable to military craft. But the shields were supposedly strong enough to deflect the weapons of lightly armed pirates, and the single, forward-facing turret, although not very powerful, was better than nothing.

"The vessel fires upon us!" Klon cried as a missile launched from the mysterious vessel and sped toward them. It struck the *Wealth and Grandeur* head on. Drin grasped the arms of his chair as the deck shook violently. He winced, thinking of the fragile and carefully stacked cargo in the hold below. He waited anxiously at his engineer slid back into his seat, fearing the extent and cost of the damage.

"Cannon destroyed! Shields almost depleted!" Klon reported, sounding genuinely frightened.

"The enemy launches missiles again!" Lintor shouted in alarm. They watched in horror as three more missiles arced through space, closing on their battered ship.

Drin closed his eyes, waiting for the inevitable impact and explosion that would take him to the Vault of Eternal Wealth. Before his propulsion into the afterlife, however, a new alert beeped on Lintor's console.

"Overseer, another vessel arrives!" Lintor shouted excitedly. "A Kelzee Military ship to engage the enemy!"

The Kelzee patrol ship swooped past them, point-defense weapons shooting at the enemy missiles before they struck their target. Drin and his officers cheered as the missiles exploded harmlessly in the void. The unidentified ship switched targets, heading for the Kelzee ship. Once more it launched a salvo of missiles, firing at the *Wealth and Grandeur's* protector. There was a flash as the Kelzee ship's shields collapsed, the impact of the explosions sending it tumbling end over end through space.

The Vlind crew's moment of triumph turned to terror once more as the enemy ship set its sights on them and fired another barrage of missiles.

"Brace for impact!" Lintor shouted.

"The end is upon us!" Klon wailed. Drin said nothing, just gripped his armrests tightly.

The Kelzee ship couldn't protect them this time, and the warheads slammed into the ship. The impact tossed the three Vlind from their seats, and Drin hit the deck with enough force to wind him. One of the warheads ripped right through the protective secondary plating around the bridge. Klon shrieked in alarm, stumbled backwards as the warhead pierced the bulkhead just inches from where he had been sitting.

The three Vlind froze, fixated on the missile protruding through the bulkhead, fearful that any action would trigger an explosive response. None of them noticed on the viewscreen the Kelzee patrol ship also hit by several un-exploded projectiles that pierced its hull in a dozen places.

The engineer was the first to break the silence. "Uh… I am unsure of what to do," Klon stammered, scuttling backwards, further away from his console and the warhead.

There was a loud *clank* and the head of the missile split open. Gas billowed out, forming a light mist across the floor of the bridge. Klon coughed, backing away again and cursing. Drin remained frozen in his chair, almost certain that the warhead had released a poison gas or deadly nerve agent that would kill them within seconds.

After several tense moments he noticed no one was falling over and dying; his eyes stung a little from the pungent smell, but that was far from deadly. Drin sniffed, recognizing the smell as methane, nothing more. He stood, rising to his not inconsiderable height of four and a half feet, taller than most Vlind. He pointed at the missile. "It must be examined at once," he decided, looking expectantly at the two officers he paid to follow his orders. Klon nervously picked up a scanner and edged slowly toward the foreign object. He waved the scanner over the exposed tip of the missile. After a moment he looked at the others and shrugged. "It's empty."

As he spoke, two pairs of small, bright beady eyes appeared in the missile opening.

"Not so!" Drin cried, pointing frantically past the engineer. Klon spun around, yelping in surprise as two creatures fell out of the opening and landed on the deck with a plop. Drin and Lintor also took an involuntary step backwards.

The fearsome-looking creatures were unlike any Drin had ever seen or heard of before. They stood two feet high, with all four of their paws ending in needle-sharp claws. Sharp canine teeth protruding from a wide, ovular mouth. The creatures' skin was as black as the void of space; their hide seemed to absorb light. Drin had never seen such dark-skinned creatures. And their small, bright eyes seemed to regard the three Vlind with unusual intelligence.

"I believe one of us should get a gun," Lintor said, recoiling when one of the creatures began hissing. There was only one weapons locker on the ship, at the rear of the bridge. Lintor opened it and pulled out a stubby pistol, aiming it at the creatures.

Drin didn't like having the evil-looking creatures on his bridge at all. "Fire upon them!" he yelled, gesturing frantically at the unwelcome visitors.

Before anyone could react, the silent creature lunged at Klon. The engineer grunted in shock and pain as the animal's fangs latched onto his arm. He staggered backwards, crashing into the engineering console.

The second creature stalked toward Drin, bared fangs glistening. He cowered behind his chair, not sure whether standing on it would put him out of harm's reach.

Lintor fired the pistol. He had almost no experience with firearms, but his target was only a few meters away. The projectile struck the creature attacking Klon; it let go of his arm and fell to the deck with a loud caterwaul, twitching in its death throes. Klon clutched his arm, shrieking in pain. The pistol shot drew the second creature's attention away from Drin and it moved toward Lintor. He fired the pistol again as the creature leapt at him, and the carcass fell to the ground, a smoking hole in its head.

For a moment there was silence, except for the sizzling of the pistol's energy cell and Klon's heavy panting. He was pale and sweating profusely. Drin tried to ignore the smell of charred flesh as he stepped over the alien carcasses to help the engineer.

"Is this a serious injury?" he inquired anxiously.

Klon winced in pain. "Although painful, I believe it is non-fatal," he said through gritted teeth. Drin was impressed with his self-control. If one of those creatures had bitten him, he'd still be crying.

"Look!" said Lintor, pointing at the viewscreen. The Kelzee ship had returned, firing its weapons at the mysterious attacker with a vengeance. Drin guessed they were using maneuvering thrusters because the ship was moving much slower than before. Energy bolts pattered against the enemy ship's shields, and they must have scored a direct hit because the enemy vessel turned around and retreated, back toward the nebula.

"The enemy vessel charges its slipstream drive," Lintor reported excitedly, still hyped up on adrenalin and brandishing the pistol as though he had personally chased away their attackers. A slipstream portal opened in space and swallowed the mystery ship. The three Vlind cheered and watched as the Kelzee patrol ship came about, approaching the *Wealth and Grandeur* at a leisurely pace.

"We are hailed by the Kelzee," reported Klon, still nursing his injured arm but also grinning with relief.

"Answer them," instructed Drin.

"*Vlind ship, this is the patrol ship* Kerenor. *Do you require assistance?*"

Drin scanned the list of damaged systems; apart from the shields, they were all non-essential, and now that the alien vessel had disappeared there was no longer a disruption preventing them from slipstream travel.

"Your timely intervention is greatly appreciated, *Kerenor*," Drin said. "However, our damage is minor, and we must resume our course as soon as possible." With the immediate danger passed, his sense of urgency returned.

The Kelzee commander tilted his head slightly. "*Our sensors show three warheads penetrated your vessel's hull. Do you require any assistance disarming them?*"

"Fortunately, the warhead contained no explosive, and we dispatched the creatures that issued forth." That was only partially true; Drin hadn't even checked with the rest of his crew to see whether they had successfully dealt with the creatures who had breached the ship's secondary hold or crew lounge. Lintor proudly waved the pistol for the Kelzee commander to see.

"*I recommend you remain vigilant,*" the Kelzee captain cautioned them. "*This is not the first ambush by this mysterious enemy. And be wary of the creatures; dangerous animals can be as effective a weapon as ordnance.*" He was speaking from personal experience; his own crew were still clearing out the alien invaders on their ship, and having surprising difficulty subduing the crewmembers bitten by the creatures. *"Perhaps we could escort you to Kalavat?"*

Kalavat was the nearest world in the Kelzee Galactic Federation, probably the base for the patrol ship. But it was in the opposite direction and would require time that Drin couldn't afford to waste if he wanted to get his cargo to Sr'Hirta on time.

"I am thankful, but I must politely decline. We will resume our course in haste."

The Kelzee commander inclined his head. *"Very well. Safe travels to you."* The channel closed and the two ships parted ways, moving toward their respective destinations. Using his newfound confidence, and the pistol, Lintor went below decks to help dispose of the remaining alien creatures. Casualties were light; aside from Engineer Klon, only one other crewmember had been bitten by the creatures. Klon still looked pale and seemed to be suffering from the onset of a fever, but he was able to make it to the infirmary unassisted.

Drin was relieved, but still shaken. He had never been in a battle before, and it had been a terrifying experience. He hoped that their recent brush with death would be his last.

5

"Ssh!" N'Gira Kolono whispered furiously. Ria glared at him; she was already silent, and motionless. She knew by now how to remain undetected. Mostly, anyway; there had been some close calls. But she had managed to stay hidden while the rest of the ship's population succumbed to the Infected. Except for N'Gira, who in the chaos of the second day had pulled her into a side room right before the Infected cornered her. Since then, they had worked together to survive, and survival meant hiding from the Infected.

There were growls and heavy breathing in the corridor outside. It was chilling to think that the creatures on the other side of the door had once been crew and passengers, regular people, just like them. Ria was a passenger, and N'Gira was a computer technician who worked on the *Visikus*. His work in the relatively isolated computer core had given him time to realize what was happening and hide as the rest of the ship was overrun. He still wore his technician's jumpsuit, stained with sweat and grimy from crawling through service tubes.

There are twelve Infected in the corridor, the ship's computer said quietly into his earpiece. He held up his fingers to Ria, indicating the amount of Infected outside, and she gave a single weary nod. The first few days had been chaotic, but it had been easier to remain hidden as the growing swarms of Infected went after groups of passengers and crewmen who had sought safety in numbers. Now, however, most of the population had been transformed, and the Infected had dispersed throughout the ship.

The sound of heavy breathing and plodding steps receded. *The corridor outside is clear of Infected,* the computer told N'Gira.

"Keep the door locked," he whispered back. He gestured to Ria that the corridor outside was clear, and she breathed a sigh of relief.

Their goal was to get to one of the lifeboats on the outer hull. It had been a slow, dangerous journey, as N'Gira had started in the computer core near the center of the ship and Ria had been staying in one of the cheaper interior cabins. But they were nearly there. They were on the right deck, and just a few dozen meters from the corridor that led to the lifeboats, which the computer promised were ready and waiting for them.

"Is it safe to move?" N'Gira asked it quietly. He and Ria always communicated in whispers.

Negative. There are more Infected entering the corridor.

N'Gira cursed under his breath; after three days of hide-and-seek his nerves were frayed, and he just wanted to be as far away from the ship as possible. Neither of them had slept or eaten properly during that time, and although Ria looked as exhausted as he felt, her face remained impassive. N'Gira admired the resolve she'd shown in the face of near-constant danger. On the first day of the outbreak N'Gira had witnessed a group of passengers overrun because one of them screamed in terror when an Infected crewman wandered past their hiding place, giving away their location. Fortunately for him, Ria wasn't like that. She was a survivor.

"Is it safe?" she asked.

N'Gira shook his head. "There are more of them in the corridor." He listened to the electronic voice in his earpiece before adding, "The good news is that most of the Infected appear to be… hibernating. But there are still hundreds of them roaming the ship."

"We only need to worry about the ones on this deck," Ria said pragmatically. "Is the computer *absolutely* certain about the Infected along our path?" When the computer had first told them that life signs all over the ship were disappearing, Ria and N'Gira had assumed people were dying of whatever disease the Infected were carrying. But the reality had turned out to be worse: the computer couldn't detect the Infected with conventional sensors, and the diminishing life signs indicated a *growing* population of Infected. Ria shuddered at the memory of entering a "clear" room only to find an Infected curled up on the bed, delirious and shivering. Fortunately, it hadn't registered their presence before they had hastily backed out of the room.

N'Gira nodded emphatically. "It has visually accounted for every Infected on this deck using the security cameras. We won't have any more surprises."

Until the computer informed them it was safe to move again, there was nothing to do but wait. Ria looked around the passenger cabin they were hiding in; it was larger and more luxurious than hers, she noted with an irrational burst of envy. Realizing how long it had been since she'd had any water, she moved quietly into the bathroom. Turning on the faucet, she cupped her hands and drank greedily, immediately feeling refreshed. She studied her reflection wistfully in the mirror above the basin; she felt like the lack of food and sleep and constant fear of danger had added years to her appearance. The first things she wanted when they got to safety was a hot meal, a hot shower, and then to sleep for about three days.

She jumped, startled, when N'Gira barreled into the small bathroom. "We have to go *now!*" he said urgently. The fact that he hadn't bothered to whisper made her more nervous.

"Why, what's wrong?" she asked as he led her hastily back through the cabin.

"Apparently some of the Infected remembered how to operate a starship," he said through gritted teeth. "The computer just told me they've started scanning for life forms!"

Ria's mouth fell open in shock. "W-what do we do?" she stammered. It was only a matter of moments before their location was discovered.

"We run and hope the computer can keep them off our backs long enough to escape!" N'Gira was already at the door. He took a deep breath, gave her what he hoped was a reassuring look, and then plunged out into the corridor. Ria was right behind him.

They sprinted down the hallway, not even bothering to look around. They didn't have to; the animal cries and rapid footfalls behind them told them they'd been spotted.

"This way!" N'Gira said, reaching a junction in the corridor and turning so sharply he nearly lost balance and crashed into the wall. Ria reached out to steady him, and he flinched instinctively, fearing it might be an Infected grabbing for him.

"We're nearly there!" he panted. Ria didn't answer; running for her life required all her energy and concentration.

They turned into the final corridor, where the ring-shaped hatches that led to the lifeboats glowed orange along one wall. But then in front of her N'Gira let out a cry of dismay as more Infected appeared ahead of them. They were trapped. The two survivors looked around wildly, but there was nowhere for them to go.

There was a loud *hiss* and *clunk* as an emergency bulkhead descended behind them, separating them from their original pursuers. Ria and N'Gira could hear angry snarls and the faint scraping of claws against metal behind them. But the pack of Infected ahead of them was almost on them.

"Please hold your breath and tightly grasp the support bar to your right," the computer said; its calm voice sounded wildly out of place. It took Ria a moment to realize it had come through the ship's speakers, not through N'Gira's earpiece, and then there was another hiss as the airlock halfway down the corridor opened.

Their ears were assailed by a deafening roar as the atmosphere was sucked out of the corridor with the force of a hurricane. The Infected were swept off their feet, tumbling like leaves in the wind out the airlock and into space. N'Gira and Ria were also pulled off their feet, flying down the corridor as the vacuum tugged at them. It was all happening so fast; Ria was only faintly aware of her reactions as her survival instincts kicked in. Between her and the airlock a golden ring glowed in the wall: the hatchway to a lifeboat. She reached out frantically, grabbing onto the handrail with a vice-like grip.

She felt a hand latch onto her arm; N'Gira had also managed to grab onto the lifeboat hatch and was trying to pull her through. Suddenly everything went deathly quiet; the corridor's atmosphere had vented into space, leaving bitterly cold vacuum. Her lungs squeezed painfully, desperate for air, but she didn't dare exhale. Through blurred vision she noticed ice crystals forming on her arms and felt N'Gira's grasp on her weaken; her own grip faltered as darkness closed in and her oxygen-starved body began to shut down.

Moments before losing consciousness, the airlock slid shut again and oxygen surged through the vents, filling the corridor with precious air. Ria fell to her knees, gasping, surprised to be alive. N'Gira bolted upright groggily, accidentally elbowing her, but by then Ria was already rising shakily to her feet.

"The Infected are seizing control of all ship systems. You must launch immed—" the computer's voice cut out. The muffled shrieks grew louder as the bulkhead lifted and their original pursuers ran down the corridor toward them.

Ria scrambled into the relative safety of the lifeboat. Ignoring his oxygen-starved body, N'Gira lunged over and slapped his palm against the door panel, sealing himself and Ria inside less than a second before the first Infected slammed into the closed door, hissing and pawing at the glass. Ignoring it, N'Gira hurried past the passenger seats to the pilot's chair, with Ria right behind him. She strapped herself into the co-pilot's seat as N'Gira activated the lifeboat's small engines. The magnetic clamps holding it in place released with a *clunk*, and the tiny craft was propelled into space and away from the *Visikus*.

Ria sagged in her seat, physically and emotionally exhausted. N'Gira was silent, intent on guiding them as far away from the starliner as possible. "They're not following us," he said after several minutes. "They're continuing their course for Barillion Prime."

Ria wondered if their good fortune was bad news for the people of Barillion Prime. "What do we do now?"

N'Gira's hands flew over the console. "I'm sending out a distress call. We just need to keep moving away from the *Visikus* and hope somebody else picks us up."

They didn't have to wait long; within half an hour an Ankari warship received their distress call and was on its way to retrieve them. While they waited for their rescuers to arrive, Ria searched the lifeboat's lockers for supplies. She found what she was after and soon they were feasting on a pile of emergency rations. They were interrupted only once when N'Gira's console beeped an alert.

"They must have full control of the ship's systems now," he said without needing to specify *they*, "because they dove into the slipstream." The *Visikus* was gone.

An hour later, the Ankari warship arrived. It was one of the Assembly Defense Force's smaller craft, less than two hundred meters, but Ria had never felt so relieved in her life as when their lifeboat was pulled by a tractor beam into the safe embrace of the ship.

In the ship's hangar bay they were scanned thoroughly by a doctor, flanked by two heavily-armed security guards. When it was confirmed that neither of them was infected, the captain wasted no time in summoning them to the bridge. Their security escorts left them on the upper dais of the darkened bridge, which permitted them a view of the lower bridge and an expansive view of space ahead of the ship.

N'Gira fidgeted uncomfortably, and Ria realized that the civilian computer technician felt nervous around his military counterparts. As their rescuers were Ankari like her, she took it upon herself to speak on behalf of the pair.

"Thank you for rescuing us," she said sincerely. "You won't believe what we've been through the last few days…"

"Unfortunately, I think I might," the captain said grimly. "I need you to tell me everything that happened to you and your ship. But first, do you know where they are headed?"

"Barillion Prime," N'Gira blurted out. The captain ordered one of his officers to send a warning to the heavily populated world.

Ria proceeded to tell the captain what had happened on the *Visikus*. "Three days ago, the captain announced that we were diverting course to answer the distress call of a ship called the *Denra*, which had gone missing a few weeks earlier…" She and N'Gira took turns explaining how the crew of the *Denra* were infected and had overrun the *Visikus*, spreading the strange sickness to the passengers and crew.

"It was a nightmare," Ria told the captain. "I've never experienced anything like it in my life, and I hope I never do again."

N'Gira, more relaxed after relating their story, said: "Captain, I don't know what kind of virus it is that infected the *Denra* crew. But we need to stop it before it spreads further." He shivered involuntarily.

"I'm afraid it may be too late for that," the captain said darkly. "This isn't our first encounter with these Infected, as you call them."

Ria exchanged a nervous look with N'Gira. "What do you mean, not the first encounter?" she repeated.

"Whatever this plague is, it's spreading fast," the captain said grimly. "The *Denra* and *Visikus* are just two ships out of dozens this has happened to."

Ria's mouth fell open in shock. N'Gira was shaking his head violently, as if refusing to accept what the captain had said.

"Let me show you," the captain said. He guided them to a console and brought up a list of known Infected ships and their vectors across space. They crisscrossed the Locality like a great, evil spider web.

"No…" Ria breathed quietly, shaking her head like N'Gira. She didn't want to believe the nightmare wasn't over.

"Play the messages," the captain ordered the communications officer. The bridge was filled with a cacophony of distress calls, dozens of them, maybe hundreds. It was a multitude of people all crying out for help, but Ria could make out individuals in the roar.

"This is the freighter Vorlop, *my crew has contracted some sort of virus and requires immediate medical assistance. They're going crazy…"*

"My name is Danikus, my ship has been attacked by an unknown enemy…"

"To any and all ships within the sound of my voice, please help!"

"…it's just me and two others left. I can't explain what happened to the others…"

Ria closed her eyes and tried to shut out the panicked voices. Whatever had happened to the *Visikus* was happening everywhere.

*

March 5, 2438
Kelzee Trading Post Takutu Station, Kelzee Perimeter Zone 04
Kelzee Galactic Federation

Space around the Kelzee trading station known as Takutu was occupied by more than two dozen ships. They ranged from great cargo haulers capable of supplying entire colony worlds to small, privately-owned trade ships come for the lucrative opportunities available here; Takutu Station was one of the major hubs of the Kora-Sr'Hirta Trade Route, and therefore one of the most important trading zones in the Locality. It was also an important resupply base for ships traveling along the Route, and the station profited greatly from the sale of fuel. The strategic and economic importance of the station to the Kelzanti Galactic Federation ensured that it was well-defended by a pair of Kelzee frigates.

Most of the ships in the area were Kelzee merchant vessels, Vlind trade ships and great Ankari cargo haulers, but as Efficiency Manager Ral

Hokono studied the visitor's manifest on his computer there were also other, rarer visitors: a Kithel hive ship, a pair of small Iganti trading skiffs and even an adventurous human ship bearing the emblem of the Human Trade and Commerce Authority.

Within the Operations Center, located at the top of the station's central dome, Hokono's staff worked with quiet efficiency. Flight controllers directed visiting ships to docking ports and hangars, quartermasters oversaw the transfer of cargo to and from the station's cavernous warehouses and customs officers checked permits and confirmed docking fees. Hokono found comfort in the hum of quiet chatter and beeping computer consoles. Everything was ordered and efficient, just how he liked it.

He allowed himself a small, satisfied smile and crossed the room to where Valu Togaro, the shift supervisor, was working. Hokono waited patiently for Togaro to finish his communication with of one of the Iganti ship captains. The Efficiency Manager never interrupted his subordinates unless the matter was urgent. 'Efficiency Manager' was not a Kelzee position; it was a role created on the recommendation of the Vlind consultants the Kelzee Trading Corporation had hired ten years ago to improve business. As Efficiency Manager Hokono oversaw all workings on Takutu Station, and he had served dutifully in that role for five years.

Togaro finished his conversation with the Iganti captain and turned in his seat to look at Hokono. "Can I assist you, sir?" Togaro inquired politely. All Kelzanti Trading Corporation employees were courteous because according to the KTC Code of Conduct, good behavior was as important as hard work.

"This morning we received a message from a Kithel ship asking to dock at the station today," Hokono said. "I informed them that we require more than twenty-three hours' notice unless they are willing to pay the additional thirty percent surcharge. They are, and I would like you to prepare the invoice."

"I will do it immediately," Togaro promised.

Hokono was halfway back to his office when an alert at Togaro's workstation caused him to turn around.

"Manager, a ship has emerged from slipspace two hundred kilometers from the station," Togaro informed him, sounding more perplexed than worried.

"What is their registration?" Hokono asked. "Inform Captain Kali," he added to Ekon Danya, the communications officer, referring to the Kelzanti Military commander stationed at Takutu.

"The ship is called the *Wealth and Grandeur*," Togaro said, and Hokono raised his brow ridges in surprise.

"How odd," he remarked. Hokono was familiar with the Vlind ship and its captain. He *always* booked a berth several weeks in advance to avoid the last-minute surcharge. The Vlind had a well-earned reputation as the most parsimonious race in known space, and Ship's Overseer Elzor Drin was tight-fisted even for his race. Now his ship had emerged from the slipstream practically on their doorstep, instead of the requisite five thousand kilometers' distance. His behavior was highly unusual.

Captain Kali's frigate swooped past the station. "The *Garanto* is moving to intercept," Danya reported. The station's second protector, the *Beru*, was responding to a distress call a light-year away.

"The *Wealth and Grandeur* is not responding," Togaro said.

Smart lenses in the window zoomed in on the two ships. Hokono and his staff watched as two cylinders emerged from the *Garanto*'s ventral hull and pivoted to face the Vlind ship. Hazy beams of energy reached out from the cylinders, embracing the Vlind ship; tractor beams to hold it in place and prevent it from approaching the station.

Hokono pressed a button on the communications panel. "*Wealth and Grandeur*, this is Manager Hokono of Takutu Station. You have violated the station's slipspace prohibition zone. Please explain your intentions."

There was no response. "The channel is open, sir," Togaro confirmed after several moments of silence.

"Sir, Captain Kali says there is only one life form on the Vlind ship." Hokono's employees exchanged concerned looks. He ignored their murmuring and scrutinized the ship. A Vlind vessel of that class required a minimum of fourteen crewmembers to operate. Why was there only one person on board? Pirate attacks had increased in recent months, and Hokono had heard the reports of strange biological weapons supposedly employed against unsuspecting ships, but he had been assured by his superiors and the Federation government that those "disturbances" would not affect Takutu Station or threaten its business.

"Captain Kali is sending a boarding party onto the ship to investigate," Danya reported.

Knowing Kali would keep him updated, Hokono turned to Togaro. "This is the second disturbance near the station in the past twenty-three hours. I would like you to investigate this further for me. Please learn what you can about the *Wealth and Grandeur*'s movements and their contact with other ships in the last week. If they encountered anything dangerous, we must know."

"Wealth and Grandeur, this is Manager Hokono of Takutu Station. You have violated the station's slipspace prohibition zone. Please explain your intentions."

Elzor Drin ignored the message playing on the console behind him, keeping the pistol in his trembling hands pointed at the door in case the Infected managed to override the lock. Through the door's glass portal, he could see the faces of Lintor and Klon, except it wasn't really them anymore. Their skin had turned charcoal black, and their eyes had receded into bright specks. Lintor opened his mouth in a vicious smile, and Drin saw that most of his teeth had fallen out, except for the canines, which had grown more pronounced. He scraped at the window with long claws, leaving scratches on the glass.

"Let usss in," the former pilot hissed.

"I will not!" Drin's nerves were raw, and he hadn't slept in days. He had been too frightened to sleep. The Ship's Overseer, who mostly kept to the bridge or his private quarters during voyages, had been so caught up in his own work that he had not noticed the gradual infection of his crew until it was too late. He'd barely had enough time to lock himself on the bridge and set a course for nearby Takutu Station, desperately hoping the people there would be able to render assistance.

"Do not attempt opening the door!" he called, his voice trembling with fear.

"Let usss in," hissed Glin, the former deckhand.

"I will not!"

"We mussst have thisss ship," Klon hissed.

"You will never have it!" Drin shouted defiantly. But he dared not turn away. They knew the ship and its systems as well as he did, and he couldn't risk them forcing their way onto the bridge and seizing control of the ship... or turning him into whatever they had become. So, he waited, keeping the pistol trained on the door even when the muscles in his arms began to burn.

Drin had been to Takutu Station many times before. He knew that if his ship violated the slipstream exclusion zone around the station his vessel would immediately be apprehended by the military. He was counting on it. He would feel a lot safer with an armed boarding party of Kelzee soldiers on the ship.

The ship shuddered and came to a halt; the Kelzee had immobilized it with a tractor beam.

"Prepare to be boarded," the gruff voice of the Kelzee captain came through the ship's speakers. Drin felt relief surge through him. Help was on the way! His ordeal was almost over. He was almost safe. The boarding party would enter the ship and find him; they were professionals trained to handle situations like this. They would secure his Infected crew and take them to a facility where they could be treated, and he would go back to

being the overseer of a small cargo ship in a quiet, prosperous corner of the Locality.

From Takutu's Operations Center, Ral Hokono watched stoically as the Kelzee shuttle approached the *Wealth and Grandeur*. There were scorch marks on the bulbous ship's hull, and he wondered if they were signs of battle.

"Efficiency Manager, the *Beru* has returned from investigating the distress call. They dropped out of slipstream less than two kilometers from the station!"

Hokono frowned. "Hail Captain Nbisk." The viewscreen switched from the *Garanto* and the *Wealth and Grandeur* to the new arrival in time to show several transport shuttles emerge from the *Beru* and head directly toward the station.

"The *Beru* is hailing *us*," communications officer Danya said, accepting the incoming hail. Alien shrieks and animalistic growls greeted them. Danya and Togaro looked at each other in alarm.

"Captain…?" Hokono's concerned query was drowned out by another shriek and then an alien-sounding voice. It was Captain Nbisk, but *different*, and it sent a chill down Hokono's spine.

"New liiiiiiife…"

The *Beru* opened fire.

Keeping the pistol aimed at the door, Drin stepped backwards to reach the nearest computer monitor. A camera view of the exterior starboard airlock showed the Kelzee shuttle approaching. He flinched in surprise when suddenly there was a bright flash on the monitor. It came from the direction of the station, visible beyond the shuttle. It was followed by one explosion, then another, blossoming in space beside the station. The Kelzee frigate's reaction was immediate; a defenseless Vlind cargo ship was a secondary concern when the station was under attack. There was a jolt as the *Garanto* released the *Wealth and Grandeur* from its tractor beams, and Drin watched in horror as the approaching shuttle peeled away, racing back toward its mother ship.

"Vlind ship: hold position until we return," the Kelzee captain ordered as the frigate accelerated toward the station and the new threat.

"No," Drin whimpered. From the other side of the door, he heard the unmistakable *clank* of a panel being removed from the wall and set on the floor. The Infected were trying to access the door's override mechanism.

"What do I do?" Drin whispered despairingly.

"Raise the shields!" Hokono snapped in an uncharacteristically urgent voice. The *Beru* had opened fire on the unsuspecting ships surrounding Takutu Station, and like the station they were caught completely unaware. There was a bright explosion as a Kelzee cargo hauler exploded under the onslaught of the *Beru*. A second, smaller explosion lit up the void as one of the Iganti trading skiffs erupted in flames, and then the remaining ships scattered in all directions. The crew of a Vlind galleon was too slow, and their ship exploded as the *Beru's* weapons hammered it mercilessly. Then the *Garanto* arrived, opening fire on its sister ship while the operations staff on the station watched in numb shock.

Flashes filled the sky around them as ships dove into the slipstream. Hokono saw the human ship vanish through a slipstream portal moments before the *Beru*'s missiles sailed through the space it had been occupying. A near miss, but others weren't so lucky.

Togaro and Danya's control boards were flooded with dozens of messages from panicked ship captains and the station's alarmed inhabitants.

"Lock down the station," Hokono ordered them. "Tell the captains of the ships currently docked that it is safer to remain on the station."

"Sir, I am not detecting any life forms on the *Beru*," Danya said, sounding confused.

"But we heard their voices over the channel," Togaro protested. "*Somebody* is firing those weapons!"

"I don't know why they're not reading as life forms, but they're not," Danya snapped back. Togaro wasn't listening to her, though. He was already focused on a new problem.

"Sir, we're receiving reports of *Beru* shuttles landing in the docking bays, and their crews attacking workers!"

"Tell Constable Adega to dispatch security teams to those places immediately."

Togaro sounded doubtful. "I will, but if we cannot track the intruders with sensors…"

"We will use the security cameras to examine every room and corridor on the station if necessary!" Hokono snapped, immediately regretting his angry outburst. But the situation was deteriorating rapidly. For the first time in his career, he felt overwhelmed, trying to placate the confused and angry captains whose starships were still docked at the station, monitoring police reports as the station's law enforcers attempted to hunt down the Infected on the station, and keeping track of the battle between the *Garanto* and the *Beru*. And watching with growing dread as life forms on the station began disappearing from sensors…

Occupied as they were with their own battle with the Infected, no one on the station noticed the *Wealth and Grandeur* dive into the slipstream, leaving behind thirteen charcoal grey bodies drifting in the void.

*

For the first time that Ral Hokono could remember, there were no ships visiting his station. The trading ships and merchants had gone, and many of its residents too, possibly forever. Takutu Station floated amidst a cloud of debris, alone in space.

The *Garanto* had emerged victorious in its battle with its sister ship *Beru*, but at great cost. Takutu Station's remaining defender was dead in space until they could complete repairs. The station's constabulary struggled valiantly to contain the outbreak of whatever illness the *Beru* intruders had brought with them, but their inability to use conventional sensors made it much more difficult. Every hour life signs continued to blink out all over the station, whether because of death or the illness, Hokono and his people still didn't know. But he knew that as Station Overseer and an executive of the Kelzanti Trading Corporation he would be required to give an account of everything that had taken place here.

There was a knock on the door to Hokono's office and Valu Togaro entered sheepishly. "I apologize for the interruption, sir. I have the information you requested on the *Wealth and Grandeur*."

He accepted the data pad from Togaro. "Thank you. What did you learn?"

"A few days ago, the *Wealth and Grandeur* was attacked by an unidentified aggressor near the Vratak Nebula."

"Unidentified?" Hokono repeated.

"Yes, sir. Neither the *Wealth and Grandeur* nor the *Kerenor* were able to recognize the ship of the attacker. The *Kerenor* was the ship that responded to their distress call and fought off the attacker." Hokono searched the Kelzee database; the *Kerenor* was a cruiser based out of the planet Kalavat. Kalavat was only a few days' travel away, one of the Kelzee Galactic Federation's outer colonies.

"Were you able to access the *Kerenor's* logs of that incident?"

Togaro shook his head. "I could not find *any* information about the *Kerenor* after the battle at the Vratak Nebula."

That was highly unusual. Almost as unusual as the Kelzanti Trading Corporation's silence. Why hadn't Hokono's superiors responded to his initial report on the events at the station? An attack on Takutu should have demanded their immediate attention.

The attack on the station, the lack of *Kerenor* records after the Vratak Nebula skirmish and the silence of his superiors was worrisome. If there was any link between the mysterious absence of the *Kerenor* and the strange behavior of Elzor Drin and the *Beru* crew, Hokono had to know.

He dismissed Togaro and asked Danya to open a subspace communication link between his office and the governor of Kalavat colony.

It took about fifteen minutes to reach someone on Kalavat who would take his call. It should have taken five minutes. Nevertheless, he waited patiently until the steel-faced visage of a military officer appeared on his screen. Further evidence that Hokono's instincts were correct and something was wrong.

"What can I do for you, Efficiency Manager?" the man asked. The name in the bottom of the screen identified him as Captain Voluta of the Kelzee military. He looked tired and sounded harried; his eyes were bloodshot, and his normally yellow skin was a pale, almost green color.

Hokono frowned slightly. "Forgive me, but I was attempting to reach someone in the governor's office," he said.

"The governor and his staff are currently unavailable," Voluta said tiredly. *"Is the matter urgent?"*

"Yes, actually. You might be able to help me. I was hoping to access local records on an incident that occurred six days ago in the vicinity of the Vratak Nebula. A Vlind ship called the *Wealth and Grandeur* was attacked by an unknown alien vessel. The attacker was intercepted and repelled by one of our military ships, the *Kerenor*. However, after that—"

"Do you know the location of the Wealth and Grandeur?" the captain interrupted sharply.

"No, I do not," Hokono said, irked at being interrupted. "It left the station hours ago and we do not know its destination."

Voluta leaned closer to the screen and spoke urgently. *"Listen to me, Manager; it is very important that anyone who came in contact with the* Wealth and Grandeur *crew be quarantined immediately."*

His tone greatly concerned Hokono. "What's wrong?" he asked.

The officer's crest flared, a sure sign of danger to the Kelzee. *"It is probable that the crew on the Vlind ship are carrying the same virus that infected the crew of the* Kerenor. *We're dealing with an outbreak here, and we must prevent the virus from spreading any further."*

The fact that the planet was under military control was a strong indicator of the seriousness of the problem, but Hokono still felt compelled to ask, "How serious is it?"

"Everybody in the capital city and surrounding countryside is already infected," Voluta said flatly. *"That's over three and a half million people."*

Hokono gaped at him. "How is that possible?" Every developed planet in the Federation had protocols for dealing with epidemics. The virus should have been contained long before millions of people were infected.

"The virus spreads rapidly through contact," Voluta told him. *"Before we could organize an effective response, the military base and surrounding suburbs were infected. And then it was too late to contain it with the limited manpower and resources at our disposal."*

Hokono had never heard of a disease that could infect people so rapidly. He was still absorbing the news as the officer continued: *"All we know is that it is most often passed on to the victim through biting."*

"Biting?" Hokono repeated incredulously.

The military officer nodded. *"When that happens, the victim undergoes rapid behavioral change. They become hyper aggressive within seconds. The physical symptoms manifest later."*

Hokono sent him a recording of the *Beru's* final message. "Three and a half hours ago the frigate *Beru* opened fire on us and the ships surrounding the station. Please listen to this and tell me if you believe it is the same virus."

Captain Voluta listened intently to the recording. As soon as it ended, he nodded.

"It's the same virus," he said with certainty. *"We have reports of the Infected exhibiting lots of strange behavior, including comments about 'new life'. What's the status of the infected ship?"*

"Our other protector was forced to destroy them," Hokono told him. He regretted that the *Garanto* had been forced to destroy the *Beru*. Captain Nbisk had been a friend of his, and the *Beru* crew had friends and family on the station. "What do you think Nbisk meant by 'new life'?"

"I'm not sure. But it is not the most pressing concern right now," Voluta said. *"If you have Infected on your station, you must save whoever you can. Evacuate immediately."*

"Evacuate? Sir, this is Takutu Station. We cannot simply—"

"I don't have time to debate this, Efficiency Manager," the officer interrupted wearily. *"The safest way to protect your people is to get them away from the station and the Infected as soon as possible."*

Before Hokono could reply, a junior officer burst into the room behind Voluta. He was disheveled and panting with exertion but wasted no time in whispering his news into Voluta's ear. Voluta immediately stood up, pulling away from the screen.

"I have to go; several Infected have broken into our compound," he said. He barked an urgent order at the junior officer, who ran off again.

"How could they penetrate a secure military installation?" Hokono couldn't help but ask.

"Some of them are former members of my company," the military officer said grimly. He reached toward his computer panel to end the call.

"Good luck, Captain," Hokono said.

"Thank you. And be careful, Efficiency Manager. This isn't like a normal plague where people just get sick." He sighed. *"We don't really understand what we're up against. Kalavat out."*

Hokono slumped back in his chair. He pressed a button on his monitor; sensors recorded a current population of four thousand, less than half of the station's usual population. He rose from his chair and walked slowly through the door of his office into the Operations Center. His staff looked up anxiously at his approach.

"I am issuing an evacuation order," he said promptly. "It is not safe to remain here. Go find your loved ones, and then get to the lifeboats."

His employees stood and moved wordlessly toward the elevators. They were administrative staff; none of them were prepared to deal with space attacks or plague outbreaks. He was sorry he had no better solutions to offer them.

Valu Togaro remained behind. "I'm not leaving you alone, sir," he said loyally, but Hokono wouldn't hear of it. "Your fiancé is probably worried about you, and scared," he said in a fatherly tone. "Go and get her to safety."

Togaro took a hesitant step toward the elevators. "What about you, sir?"

"I have a few matters to conclude before I leave. But I will not be far behind."

Togaro nodded once. With one last wistful look around, he entered the elevator, leaving Hokono alone in the Operations Center.

Captain Voluta of the Kelzanti Federation Military assisted his two remaining soldiers in moving the desk in front of the door, which was slowly being pried open by clawed hands and tools. They were all that remained of his thousand-strong garrison, and his office was the last secure room in the military base. It wouldn't be for much longer. The snarls and shouts from the hallway outside grew louder, and soon crazed, angry faces with wild eyes appeared in the widening crack between the door panels.

"It has been an honor to serve with you," he told the soldiers, feeling surprisingly calm despite the imminent threat of a violent end. Both men nodded grimly and switched their rifles to their deadliest setting. Voluta drew his own pistol. The energy cell was down to ten percent, but that wouldn't matter for long.

Flanked by the soldiers, Voluta fired at the first person who tried to scramble over the makeshift barricade. The Infected, a middle-aged man in a business suit, fell to the ground dead. This seemed to drive the other

Infected into a greater frenzy, and soon they were shoving and pushing and clawing to get through the door and over the barricade to the trio of armed men.

Voluta and the soldiers fired into the crowd, taking down several more of the Infected before they themselves were overwhelmed. As the power cell in his firearm died an Infected leapt at him, pinning him to the ground with the weight of their body. There was a sharp pain in his neck and then coldness spread through his body, and Voluta numbly realized that this wasn't the end. It was a new beginning. The creature that had been Captain Voluta leapt to his feet with a shriek, joining the mob of Infected searching for new prey.

The Kelzanti Federation Military ships in orbit were immediately alerted when their last secure base on the planet fell to the Infected. With strict orders to prevent the plague from leaving Kalavat, the commanders moved their ships into position and opened fire on the planet below.

*

Ral Hokono sat alone in his office. Light from his computer monitor bathed the office in faint blue-green light, but it was the only source of illumination. He didn't mind the darkness, though. He wasn't going to be here for much longer. The station was in low-power mode, which he hoped would make it more difficult for the Infected to take control of the station's systems. He wasn't sure how many were still on board, but scanners told him he was the only remaining life sign on the station. That didn't mean very much, of course; there could have been dozens, hundreds or even thousands of Infected roaming the corridors and the sensors wouldn't have been able to detect them. He was finishing his final task as Efficiency Manager of Takutu Station before making his own exodus.

More than half of the station's life boats had launched, but like everything else the last few hours the evacuation had been chaotic and rushed. There had been no proper vetting procedure to see who was infected or not. For all Hokono knew, the station's former residents carried the virus to other areas of the Locality.

He had just completed his reports when the first sounds of Infected in the Operations Center filtered through the wall to his office. A faint scuffling sound accompanied by grunts and then scratching at the door. He made certain that it was locked, because he didn't want the Infected reaching him before he could finish his work.

The first item was an assessment of economic loss report, which he forwarded to KTC headquarters on Kelzanti Prime. The second thing was the more important in his view, and he hoped it would help save lives. It was a recorded message warning people about the danger they were facing, and he intended to broadcast it on every available subspace frequency. He activated the station's subspace antenna, and the message was transmitted into space, relayed by subspace buoys in the region and beyond, reaching an ever-widening audience across the Locality. It wasn't much, but if it saved just one life, it would be worthwhile.

Satisfied he had done all he could, he activated his personal communicator. "Captain Kali, I am ready for pickup," he said softly.

"We are approaching the station now, Efficiency Manger. We will have you on board soon."

The *Garanto* crew had repaired their ship as best they could and had faithfully remained close by while the station's population fled or succumbed to the plague. Now it was time to go.

Hokono rose from his desk, trying to ignore the eerie cries for him to open the door. He recognized a few of the voices. Some of them belonged to people he had known for years, now twisted into pitiful, half-animal imitations of their former selves. He heard Valu Togaro, infected by his own fiancé, pleading for him to unlock the door. The most chilling voice belong to Ral's own wife Emoiya, who had succumbed when a group of Infected burst into their living quarters as Hokono watched in horror through a security camera. He shuddered at the memory, trying to quell the grief welling up inside him. There would be time to mourn later.

An alert on his monitor informed him of attempts to access the door controls from the other side. The Infected screeched, and Hokono shivered involuntarily.

His office had a private airlock through which he could come and go on spacecraft without having to pass through customs like everyone else. There was a gentle *thunk* as the *Garanto* docked; indicator light on the hatch flashed yellow, indicating the lock was secure and the atmosphere inside pressurized.

Hokono picked up the holographic photo of his wife and daughter from his desk and tucked it into his jacket. He took one last look around his office before stepping into the airlock. When the Infected forced open the doors several minutes later, the room was empty and the *Garanto* was gone.

6

Greetings. My name is Ral Hokono, and I am the Station Overseer of Takutu Trading Station. I am transmitting this message on all subspace frequencies in the hope that this warning reaches as many people as possible.

My station had become overrun by victims of a plague that was first brought to this station just one day ago. I am unaware of the origin of the plague, but it appears to be the same virus that has laid waste to the planet Kalavat.

I communicated with Captain Voluta of the Federation Military on Kalavat just a few hours ago. I believe the limited information he could share with me is important to our understanding of this plague, so I have included the contents of his report in this message. It is my hope that this, along with the urgency with which I speak to you now, is evidence of the severity of the situation we face.

This plague is unlike anything we have encountered before. It surpasses even the Osaija Virus in the danger it presents and the aggressiveness with which it attacks its victims.

Based on what my staff and I have witnessed during the outbreak on the station I can confirm that Kelzee, Kithel, Vlind, and Ankari are all susceptible to the virus. Once infected, the victim is driven into a frenzy of madness, compelling them to violently attack all non-infected around them. According to Captain Voluta's report, species such as the Ankari and Vlind can appear unaffected for a day or two before the virus manifests, and I have personally witnessed the near-instantaneous effects it has on my own species.

I cannot overemphasize the dangers this virus poses to the denizens of the Locality. My station was overrun within hours; Kalavat was overrun within days. Captain Voluta's report suggests the plague may already be present on the planets Kora, Vashdee, the space station Kynor, and Sr'Hirta, and possibly elsewhere. It is my recommendation that all planets, stations and vessels along the Kora-Sr'Hirta Trade Route be quarantined immediately. I am aware of the ramifications of doing so, but I believe extreme measures are required. Our lack of vigilance allowed the plague to spread along the trade route before we recognized it had done so. As an executive of the Kelzanti Trading Corporation I understand the economic repercussions of shutting down this most profitable trade route in the Locality, however I am also aware of the devastation this plague could inflict should it spread further.

I have no desire to cause panic or spread fear; I wish to spread awareness of the virus and urge caution. There is a high chance I will not survive. Soon I will hear the shrieks of the Infected and the scrape of their claws against my door. Regardless of my own fate, I hope that this warning helps to save others and prevent the fate that befell my home from happening to yours.

This is Ral Hokono, signing off.

March 10, 2438
Extract from the Captain's Log of the Kelzanti Military Frigate *Miyarka*:
By the time we arrived at Takutu Station, everyone on board had already succumbed to the infection. There were no other ships in the vicinity, but debris and energy residue indicate a battle was fought nearby, possibly between the original vector ship and our on-site frigate. All spacecraft inside the station had been launched, and sensor analysis reveals at least two dozen slipspace jumps were initiated from around the station.

We have sent out an emergency warning to all ships, planets and stations in the area. However, as we do not know the destinations of the ships, or even if they were carrying the plague, there is little else we can do at the present time.

March 11, 2438
Republic Parliament Building, Lakaria
Republic of Tuulan Vee
Twilight was descending on Lakaria. The first stars were appearing in the sky above the city, and the streets were busy with people taking advantage

of the warm summer evening. Colorful lights were going on all over the city, drawing the citizens to restaurants, cafes, theaters, and outdoor recreation areas. Glide cars soared in neat lines between the buildings, their gold and blue front and rear lights adding to the color and bustling activity of the city. It was a scene of liveliness and beauty.

Torina Jadus barely noticed the view as she swept down a corridor in the Tuulan For government's parliament building, moving so quickly that her ministerial robes billowed behind her. "A summons," she murmured to herself.

Jarren hurried to keep pace with her. "Yes. I received the message from the Chancellor's secretary during the meeting."

Jadus didn't ask the purpose of the meeting; Jarren would have told her if he knew. They had just come out of an emergency session of the Tuulan For parliament, which had been called to discuss the plague which threatened not just their own space but the entire Locality.

Since their return to Tuulan Vee they had been kept busy combating the outbreak of a plague in the outer colonies of the Republic. It had likely come through one of the ports visited by Kelzee or Vlind ships, in whose own space the virus was running rampant. As the Minister of Medicine and Health, it fell within Jadus' purview to oversee the government's handling of the epidemic. She had thrown the full weight of the ministry into combating it, using all the government resources at her disposal.

Beyond Tuulan For space, entire worlds populated by Ankari, Vlind, Kelzee and Kithel were being overrun, their populations and economies devastated, and Jadus was determined to prevent the same thing from happening in the Republic. When the first local outbreaks were reported, Jadus had pressured the parliament to implement the strictest protocols to limit its spread. These included free screening for concerned citizens and strict quarantine measures for known Infected while the Republic's doctors and scientists did their best to develop a cure or a vaccine. With the support of the Chancellor, she had even introduced a curfew in the Vintra Sector, restricting interstellar travel to or from or within that region. So far, the curfew, enforced by the Republic Fleet, had been successful. Many people viewed the measures as draconian, but Jadus considered them necessary. Until they could eradicate the disease, every precaution had to be taken. Fortunately, Chancellor Denrek and a majority of the parliament agreed.

Jadus and Jarren strode down a corridor decorated with portraits of past leaders of the Republic, hanging in gilded frames between elegant marble columns. Opposite the portraits, floor-to-ceiling glass windows offered a panoramic view of the metropolis. Jarren loved the city at this time of day. Distracted by the view, he had fallen a few paces behind the minister and raced to catch up.

They arrived at the chancellor's office and were ushered in by his secretary. The room occupied a corner of the building, and two of the walls featured large windows overlooking the city and the Leona River below. Denrek was gazing out at the cityscape as they entered, and turned to greet the newcomers. His face lit up upon seeing Jadus. She greeted him with a small smile and a formal, "Good evening, Chancellor", but he rushed forward and embraced her.

"Torina!" he said warmly, addressing her by her first name as he only did in private. "Thank you for coming at such short notice."

Before entering politics, Jadus had served as the Dean of the Telvarn Science Academy when Denrek was the Minister of Medicine and Health. He had often consulted with Jadus, and over the years they had developed a strong friendship. Two years earlier, it had been his impassioned pleas that convinced her to run for the ministerial post he was vacating. Now that he was Chancellor of the Republic and she was the Minister of Medicine and Health, they didn't get to see each other in person very often, but when they did it was always a happy reunion.

He pulled back from the embrace and regarded her from arms' length. "You look well," he said.

"So do you," Jadus said, and he chuckled.

"Although it is a lie, I accept it as the kindness of an old friend," he said. Denrek projected a calm-yet-energetic persona to the public, but their embrace had revealed how thin and frail he was getting in his old age. She looped her arm through his and guided him toward one of the couches, where they sat down.

"Just now, during the meeting, I received a call from a scientist in the Chieftain's court on Iganta."

Jadus looked at him in surprise. "An Iganti scientist? Who was it?"

He paused for dramatic effect, and she raised an eyebrow.

"It was Minnen the Learned," he revealed.

Jadus tried not to gape at him. Denrek didn't need to explain who the Iganti scientist was; his reputation preceded him. Minnen the Learned was famous throughout the Locality as the person who had cured the Osaija Virus more than two decades earlier. The Osaija Virus had wrought havoc across the Locality and was considered by many experts at the time to be incurable. Minnen had proved them wrong, and saved billions of lives. At that time Denrek was the Tuulan For ambassador to the Locality Council, the gathering of representatives from all the races in the Locality. The council met on Unity Station in the Varda Sector, near the geographic center of the Locality. It was there that Denrek had encountered Minnen and fought fiercely in the council on behalf of the Iganti scientist. Thanks to their efforts, Minnen's cure was mass produced and disseminated to affected regions, and he was lauded as the savior of the Locality. For his part in helping the scientist end the threat of the Osaija Virus, Denrek had returned home and successfully run for the governorship of Tuulan Vee. Although Jadus herself had never met the esteemed scientist, she knew that he and Denrek had become firm friends. The fact that he had contacted the chancellor now could mean only one thing.

"He must be working on a cure for the Kalavat Plague! What did he say?" Jadus asked eagerly. Denrek smiled at her outburst, and she regained her composure. "Well?" she prompted.

"Minnen Thoril has been monitoring the plague since the early outbreaks, but in recent days it has manifested on some of the colony worlds of the Iganti," Denrek said. Most people referred to Minnen by his title "the Learned", but Denrek called him by the Iganti house he belonged to, Clan Thoril.

"I read a report this afternoon by an executive of the Kelzanti Trading Corporation," Jadus said thoughtfully, "which said the virus was spreading along the Kora to Sr'Hirta Trade Route. It could have reached the Iganti Tribal States by that path."

Denrek nodded. "Minnen has requested to work with our people on developing a cure for the virus. He thinks our chances of finding a cure will increase if we pool our knowledge and resources, and I agree."

"Of course," Jadus said readily. "I'm just a little surprised he didn't make this offer to the Ankari." The Ankari were the most technologically advanced species in the Locality.

Denrek smiled faintly. "My old friend does not have a very high opinion of the Ankari scientific community," he said. "There are a few conditions, however. Krant the Despot will not allow Minnen to leave Iganta, so we must go to him. Secondly, whoever we send must provide their own equipment." He smirked. "Apparently Minnen's own resources are… limited. He advised me to keep the team small; with everything going on there right now Krant may view a large group of outsiders as a threat."

Jadus nodded, feeling excitement build up inside her. "Those conditions are acceptable," she said. "I already know the perfect person to take. Doctor Kerik is the leading epidemiologist *and* virologist in the Republic."

Denrek ignored the last half of her comment. "*Take*?" he repeated, and she nodded emphatically.

"Of course. I am the natural choice to travel to Iganta. I am the Minister of Medicine and Health. As a minister of government, I have diplomatic immunity, which should make traveling to Iganta safer. I have a background in medical research, and I have been studying this virus since it first appeared in our space. Nobody knows more about it than I, except for Doctor Kerik."

Denrek shook his head, but he was smiling. He had expected her to volunteer. She opened her mouth to speak again but he raised a hand to quiet her. "Before we commit to sending you halfway across the Locality, I have some concerns about sending *anyone* to Iganta, and they must be addressed. The first and foremost is the issue of security. There have been rumors of civil strife there, maybe even an uprising, for months now. And several weeks ago, the Iganti sealed their borders to most outsiders."

"They didn't do a very good job at 'sealing' them if the plague got through," Jadus commented dryly.

"Be that as it may," he conceded, "Relations with the Iganti have always been... standoffish. I'm not sure how safe you would be there, even with the Despot's guarantee of protection."

"That's a risk I am willing to take," Jadus said firmly. "If it gives us an opportunity to work with Minnen the Learned on a Kalavat Plague cure, I will brave the Despot's hospitality."

"You joke about it, but if I'm going to send one of my ministers into a potentially dangerous environment, it is not something I will do lightly," Denrek said seriously.

"Of course. You're right," Jadus agreed. She looked at him hopefully, almost pleadingly. "But my safety is my decision. And we both know this opportunity is too important to pass up."

The chancellor nodded in reluctant agreement. "It is." He looked out the window and sighed. "Were it not for my responsibilities I would go myself. It would be nice to see my old friend again."

Jadus smiled and squeezed one of his hands in both of hers. "I'll make sure we call you over subspace," she promised.

"What about your team?" Denrek asked. "Do you know who you're going to take?"

Jadus nodded slowly. "I believe I do. I will have to check with Doctor Kerik, however. Which I will do as soon as I leave here."

"It's the end of the workday, you know. The doctor has probably left the office."

"He'll want to hear what I have to say," Jadus said firmly, and Denrek suppressed a smile. The meeting had gone exactly as he had thought it would. Torina had always had an adventurous spirit. "If you're set on this course of action and you understand the risks, then you may go with my blessing. When will you be leaving?"

Jadus was already rising to her feet. "First thing in the morning," she declared.

*

March 12, 2438
Lakaria Spaceport, Lakaria
Republic of Tuulan Vee

Few stars were still visible in the pre-dawn sky. The eastern horizon was lightening, a prelude to another spectacular sunrise and clear, summer day in Lakaria. Most of the city still slept, but at Lakaria Spaceport, the tarmac around the government transport *Telvarn Star* was a hive of activity.

In the cockpit, Antak Droma was running through the pre-flight check of the *Telvarn Star*'s systems. The door opened and Korosa Jakor, the one and only member of Jadus' protection detail, entered. In their first meeting Korosa had quickly rebuffed his charms, making it perfectly clear they would have a professional working relationship or no relationship at all. Since then, he had accepted she wasn't interested, but he liked to keep up the flirtatious behavior because of the reaction it provoked.

"Look who it is," he drawled. "Missed me, did you?"

Korosa snorted. "Don't flatter yourself," she said, shoving past him to get to the co-pilot's console.

Antak grinned, taking his seat at the pilot's station beside her. He was looking forward to the journey. He hadn't expected to be called in to pilot for the Minister again so soon, but he welcomed it. Flying for Jadus was far more interesting than sitting around the barracks.

Minister Jadus, Jarren, and Doctor Kerik were just boarding. Handlers had stowed away the supplies, luggage, and specialized equipment they would need, and the ship was fully fueled. Iganta was a long way away, but the *Telvarn Star* had enough reserves to make the journey without stopping. A wise precaution, given the dangerous state of the galaxy these days.

By the time the handlers and anti-grav vehicles had vacated the area around the *Telvarn Star* the sun was touching the horizon. The few clouds in the sky shone gold, giving the dawn sky a radiance that made Antak whistle appreciatively, earning him an odd look from Korosa.

"We are ready to leave, Lieutenant," Jadus said over the ship's intercom.

"Yes, Ma'am," he responded lightly. His hands flew over the controls with practiced ease, excitement building up in him. He contacted flight control and hummed a tune while he waited for their response.

"You're in a good mood," Korosa remarked.

"It's a beautiful morning, and I get to fly a state-of-the-art ship and visit an exotic world. What's not to like?"

"You do realize we're not going to Iganta for a holiday," Korosa reminded him. "We're heading into a potentially hazardous environment. And it's to develop a plague cure, not see the sights."

"So good of you to find the dark cloud behind the silver lining," he teased, and she gave him a dour look. Korosa evidently wasn't a morning person.

Antak watched her from the corner of his eye, working at her console with quiet efficiency; the security officer was both beautiful and highly capable. Antak knew she was also surprisingly powerful and incredibly agile, having witnessed her take down a Thordran nearly three times her bodyweight. He understood why Minister Jadus had requested her on her team. But she was so *serious* all the time. Antak vowed privately to try and get her to lighten up on the trip. Korosa caught him looking at her and gave him an interrogative look.

He was saved from having to come up with an explanation when the radio chirped. *"Telvarn Star, this is spaceport flight control. You are cleared for departure."*

There was little traffic this early in the morning, and the ground lights turned green, indicating it was safe to take off. Antak activated the ship's thrusters and the *Telvarn Star* rose gracefully off the tarmac. He turned the ship toward the rising sun and activated the main engines. The ship accelerated away from the spaceport; Lakaria and the mainland fell away behind them as the ship flew higher, moving upward and eastward above the glistening ocean. The sun was still rising, but soon the sky began to darken again as they ascended into space.

In the passenger cabin, Jadus gazed out the window as the last vestiges of Tuulan Vee's atmosphere fell away, and stars began to appear in their dozens. She could not see directly ahead, but she knew Antak was aligning their ship with the distant star around which Iganta orbited. Doctor Kerik gripped the armrests of his chair tightly, uncomfortable with space travel. He would have plenty of time to get used to it over the next few weeks, Jadus thought. Opposite her, Jarren was also gripping the edges of his seat, but looking out the window he seemed as happy as she felt.

"Prepare to enter the slipstream," Antak said.

Jadus considered the mission they were embarking on. Developing a cure for the Kalavat Plague virus would not be easy, even with the help of Minnen the Learned. But there were billions of lives at stake, and if there was a solution, they would learn it. An energetic thrum filled the air as the ship's faster-than-light engines activated. Jarren looked at her and she met his excited smile with one of her own.

"Here we go," she said.

There was a bright flash as the *Telvarn Star* dove into the slipstream, leaving Tuulan Vee behind.

7

Some species in the Locality forwent elaborate ceremonies when commissioning their starships, but for the Commonwealth Navy, which traced its traditions back to the maritime navies of ancient Earth, it was a special occasion. It was rare to have more than one Admiral present at a commissioning ceremony, but Admiral Aliyev was also in attendance, alongside Admiral Garcia. Marston chose to take the turnout as a positive sign.

The *Pericles* crew stood smartly in their dress uniforms while Admiral Garcia and Lieutenant Commander Thomas Brunel, the designer of the Interceptor-class frigate, gave speeches commemorating the launch of the Navy's newest starship. Marston kept his own speech brief: "We are honored to serve and protect the Interstellar Commonwealth. I am excited for the journey we are embarking on, and I am confident that this crew will perform its duties to the best of our abilities. In ancient Earth history, Pericles was an eminent Greek statesman, a brilliant general, and a patron of the arts. He was prominent and influential- so much so that the time he lived in is referred to as the Golden Age of Pericles. Our vessel is named after him, and I believe those positive aspects of his life are reflected in our mission. As a gifted orator and statesman, Pericles served his community, as we have been commissioned to enforce the just rule of the law and foster peaceful and prosperous relations with our neighbors. Pericles was a brilliant general and strategist who fought for the Athenians, as we on this crew have taken an oath to defend the Commonwealth from its enemies. He was also a patron of the arts, and a proponent of democracy. We defend our cultures and our values; however, we also represent them to the other races we encounter. We still know about Pericles, nearly three thousand years after he lived. If we do our duty well, perhaps we shall leave our own mark on human history."

The audience applauded, and Marston stepped down from the podium and resumed his place alongside his senior officers. "Well said," Balzano said quietly so only Marston could hear. "Did it take you long to come up with that?"

"Yes," Marston admitted, and Balzano grinned.

The ceremony concluded when Admiral Garcia gave Marston and the *Pericles* crew one final directive: "Man our ship and bring it to life."

Afterward the attendees retired to a function hall that featured large windows overlooking the *Pericles*. Ordinarily the reception would have taken place on the ship itself, but that was not possible for security reasons; the *Pericles* looked like a typical Navy frigate, but its engine design was new technology, a fact they wanted to keep hidden from the general public and the Commonwealth's enemies.

Marston stood in a half-circle with his senior officers by the windows overlooking the ship. The rest of the crew chatted in small groups or mingled with the engineers, journalists and family members attending the reception.

"That's strange," Clarke murmured.

The others looked at him. "What is?" Balzano asked.

Clarke indicated a group of people with a subtle nod. "Admiral Ayilev and that Brunel guy are watching us."

"That 'Brunel guy' is the man who designed the ship," Sirroyo said.

"I know," Clarke said. "And they've been looking in this direction for a few minutes now."

"They're not looking at us," Winston realized.

"You're right," Clarke said, "I think they're looking at… the captain!"

"They are," Marston confirmed. He'd noticed earlier in the reflective surface of the windows. He could practically feel their eyes burning into the back of his neck.

"Why?" Hasan wondered.

"I don't know," Marston said lightly, "But I think we should go and say hello, right, Commander?"

Balzano read the pointed look his friend was giving him and nodded slowly. "Right," he said without enthusiasm.

The two men made their way across the room. Admiral Ayilev and Lieutenant Commander Brunel watched them approach, stony-faced. They looked as welcoming as a pair of cornered lynxes, Marston thought wryly. Affecting a polite smile, he stopped in front of them.

Admiral Ayilev spoke before he could. "Captain Marston," she said in her clipped accent, "We were just talking about you."

"Really?" He steeled himself.

"Yes. We were talking about how wonderful an occasion it is to be launching another one of Commander Brunel's ships," she said, nodding toward the ship designer.

"It is," Marston agreed. For his part, Brunel remained silent and impassive. If they hadn't just struggled through his long-winded speech at the ceremony Marston would have wondered if the engineer were mute.

Ayilev continued, "The Interceptor class is an important step forward in Navy ship design. The new engines bring us back on par with the Draxilan navy. Very important, if we need to defend ourselves against the Empire again." Many of the officers who had lived through the war with the Draxilans forty years earlier maintained that the Commonwealth and the Empire were in a cold war which threatened to boil over into a hot one at any time. While Marston respected their caution, he wasn't overly concerned with the Draxilans. The last war had ended embarrassingly for them, and they had honored the armistice for the last four decades.

Brunel nodded emphatically in agreement. Marston and Balzano also nodded, but the admiral gave the captain a skeptical look.

"I wonder if someone of your limited age and experience can truly appreciate its significance, Captain," she said coolly.

"I've never dealt with Draxilans," Marston said slowly, "But I do have experience dealing with hostile aliens. Like the Thordrans." Memories sprang unbidden into his mind: the bridge of the *Saber*, burning; frustration at his failure to drag the captain or the charred remains of the executive officer out of the wreckage; stumbling toward an escape pod through smoke-filled corridors. And another, fierce encounter on the remote jungle world of Beta Thorii that he very nearly hadn't returned from.

"That's true," the admiral conceded. "However, dealing with space pirates and terrorists is not the same as facing a powerful, highly trained military bent on your total subjugation."

Marston swallowed, biting back his natural response. Neither time he'd faced the Thordrans had they been an undisciplined rabble, and he felt Ayilev's comments dishonored the people who had lost their lives in those encounters. Still, an angry retort would only worsen the situation. Instead, he replied calmly, "I suppose the only way I will know for sure is if I face them in battle." He looked at her levelly. "If that happens, I trust my crew to perform beyond expectation."

"As we trust our captain, too," Balzano said loyally.

Ayilev gave Marston a calculating look. "Indeed. Now, please excuse me, I must speak to Admiral Garcia." There were plenty of opportunities for her to speak to Garcia while she was on the station, but Marston accepted the flimsy excuse to end the conversation.

When Ayilev had disappeared into the crowd, Brunel spoke for the first time. "Make sure you look after my ship," he said, and it almost sounded like an accusation.

Marston wanted to point out that the *Pericles* was in fact *his* ship, not the designer's. Instead, he smiled thinly and said, "I will."

When the engineer had also left, Marston turned to Balzano.

"That was fun," he said dryly. He looked down at the glass in his hands and took a long drink. Balzano's eyes followed Ayilev across the room and he shook his head.

"Not the kind of positive affirmation I would have hoped for on the eve of our maiden voyage," he said, then shrugged. "But who cares? *We* know that we're a good crew."

"Yes," Marston agreed. He looked at his senior officers, and beyond them, the *Pericles*. They were so close to launching, and he would be able to leave behind him the doubters and the awkward conversations with admirals and engineers.

"I will say one thing," Balzano said with a humorous glint in his eye. "It's very generous of Lieutenant Commander Brunel to let us take his ship out tomorrow."

"It doesn't surprise me at all," Marston deadpanned. "He's obviously a very warm, generous person."

They both laughed.

After the reception, Marston retired to his cabin and fell into a deep sleep almost as soon as his head hit the pillow. He woke early the next morning, refreshed and excited.

He was already on the bridge when Alpha Shift arrived, bidding them a cheery good morning, which they happily returned. They were as excited as he was to be underway. Last-minute diagnostics and pre-flight checks confirmed that the ship and its systems were in functioning order. Marston rose from his chair. Everyone on the bridge looked at him expectantly.

"Please put me on the ship-wide intercom," he said to Clarke.

"You're connected to the whole ship, Captain," the tactical officer confirmed.

Marston nodded his thanks. "All hands, this is Captain Marston. Prepare to depart Argos."

From the helm console, Hasan reported: "We have been given clearance to leave, Captain."

Marston took his seat at the center of the bridge. "Acknowledge and begin undocking procedure."

"Aye, sir." A faint, almost unnoticeable drone reverberated through the ship as the engines activated. The sound was part of the normal background noise of a working starship, and Marston hadn't realized how much he'd missed it. Their time at Argos had been short, but he was glad to leave the accidents and the arguments behind.

"Airlocks sealed and disengaged."

"Maneuvering thrusters online."

"Engines activated and on standby."

Through the windows at the front of the bridge, the stars beckoned. "Take us out," Marston ordered.

Docking clamps released the ship with a gentle jolt, folding back neatly into their cradles in the docking bay walls. The *Pericles* glided forward, slowly picking up speed, and the hangar it was birthed in fell away behind them.

In the clear space around Argos, transport and mining ships traveled to and from the station while Navy ships circled on patrol. Lieutenant Hasan put a holographic overlay on the main viewscreen showing their course through the asteroid belt. The passage twisted and turned around mountain-sized rocks too large to repel, but after several minutes the ship left them behind and glided into open space.

"We have cleared the Argos asteroid belt," Hasan announced.

"Set a course for the Stromar Sector," Marston ordered.

"Aye, Captain."

"Slipstream drive powering up," Sirroyo reported.

"Deflectors at full power," Clarke added.

"Course plotted and laid in," Hasan said after a moment. "Slipstream drive is available on your command."

"Go," Marston said, experiencing a thrill of joy at giving the order. Their journey was finally beginning.

The slipstream projector at *Pericles'* bow flashed to life. The ship dove gracefully into the slipstream with a splash of blue-white energy that looked like a shower of water droplets. The portal closed behind the ship, and they were gone.

*

Unknown
Interstellar space
The messenger's movements sounded strangely muffled as he approached the center of the cavernous chamber. The only source of illumination was the dim, blue light filtering through the windows from the clouded sky outside the ship.

The messenger swallowed nervously. It was good news he had to share, but that did little to alleviate his fear of the person he was reporting *to*.

"Consul, here are the latest projections. Chaos continues to spread, and the weak are unaware of its true cause."

There was a rustling sound; the messenger caught a glimpse of scales glistening in the darkness. A pair of yellow, slitted eyes locked onto him. "Ecsssellent," hissed a deep voice, sending a chill down the messenger's spine.

8

"This is where the signal was coming from?" Captain Ramiro asked.

"Yes, sir," responded Kalina Tang, the communications officer. "It's not broadcasting anymore, but I can approximate the position of the *Coronado* at the time it sent the distress call."

"Do it," Ramiro ordered. It was odd that the civilian ship's distress call had terminated so abruptly a few days ago. He turned to Stefan Fedorov, the sensor operations officer. "Scan for debris or escape pods."

"Aye, sir," Fedorov said, activating the starship's powerful array of sensors.

Ramiro let them work uninterrupted, using the time to examine CGC 1900, better known as the Shadow Nebula. It filled the viewscreen with its ghostly visage. Wraithlike wisps of hydrogen gas extended from the nebula; they vaguely resembled claws reaching out to grasp the ship. *It's just a reflection nebula*, he told himself, *illuminated by the Gorgons*. The Gorgons were a trinary star system located on the other side of the Shadow Nebula, and they illuminated the cloud with a ghostly grey-blue light similar to the better-known Witch Head Nebula.

Despite its location between Earth and the Antares colonies, all the major trade routes went through the nearby world of Gelria, bypassing the Shadow Nebula. Because there were no shipping lanes in the vicinity, it was a mystery why the *Coronado* had been anywhere near the nebula. A navigation error, perhaps? Most civilian ships chose to stick to well-known routes because it reduced the risk of encountering undocumented stellar phenomena or dangerous spatial anomalies. Given its out-of-the-way location, charting the Shadow Nebula was considered a low priority by the Navy and Commonwealth Interplanetary Research Council. However, its status as an enigma in the heart of the Commonwealth only added to its sinister reputation.

The *Searcher* was not here to explore the nebula, either. It was simply by chance that they were passing through the area on their way to catalogue planetesimals in System IC 4775 when a communications relay near Gelria picked up the civilian prospecting ship *Coronado's* distress call. The science vessel had been sent to investigate, but Ramiro didn't mind. They would probably spend a day or two poking around the nebula before resuming their course for the system eighty-six light-years away.

"The *Coronado* distress call came from closer to the nebula," Tang determined. "It would help if we were closer too."

"Very well. Take us closer, Miss Wong."

"Yes, sir," responded Sue Wong, the helmsman. Under her guidance the *Searcher* approached the nebula until the gases at its periphery swirled around the ship.

"Looks pretty spooky, doesn't it?" Wong commented after a while.

"Looks just like any other nebula to me," Steve Matthews, the tactical officer said dismissively.

Wong looked at him aghast. "No way! I can see why they call it the *Shadow* Nebula." There was a mischievous look in her eye as she added, "Some people say it's haunted by the spirits of the dead…"

"Spirits of the dead?" Matthews repeated dubiously, and Wong nodded emphatically.

"They say that the spirit of every human ever lost in space finds its way to the Shadow Nebula…" Matthews shook his head in disbelief, grinning. An eerie wailing sound filled the bridge.

"What is that?" Captain Ramiro asked, frowning.

"The sound of the nebula, sir," Wong said. "I ran the background radio waves through the speakers so you could hear the haunting—"

"Do us a favor and turn it off, Ensign," Ramiro cut her off.

"Yes, Captain," she said, huffing with disappointment. Unable to stay quiet for long, she added after a few moments, "I wonder what happened to the *Coronado?*"

"Probably just a systems malfunction," Matthews said.

"A ship called the *Skylark* ended up out here two years ago," Ramiro said. "Simple navigation error. They only realized they were off course when they emerged from the slipstream and found themselves here instead of orbiting Ennomos."

"They should have looked out a window," said Wong wryly.

Fedorov had been silent during the exchange, focused entirely on the sensor data on his monitor.

"Strange," he murmured quietly.

"What is?" Ramiro asked.

The sensor operations officer turned in his chair to face the captain. "We're picking up a signal again, but it's nothing like the one from the *Coronado*. See?"

Ramiro leaned forward in his chair, scrutinizing the signal wavelength displayed on the viewscreen. "What's it saying?"

"Unknown, sir. The signal doesn't match any known Commonwealth frequencies."

"Alien?"

"Possibly, but not like anything the aliens we know use," Tang said.

Fedorov shook his head, perplexed. "I'm not sure, Captain. I think the signal source is somewhere *inside* the nebula, but I can't tell where, yet."

"Keep looking. Tang, send a mission update to Command. Wong, take us closer in."

"Taking us closer, aye," said the helmsman, sounding dubious as she guided the ship deeper into the nebula.

Matthews gave her a sidelong glance. "You're actually nervous, aren't you?" he asked, surprised.

"Aren't you?" she said defensively. "*Something* must have happened to the *Coronado*. Ships shouldn't just disappear without a trace. And now this phantom signal...!"

Captain Ramiro overheard her. "Relax, Ensign. There are no spirits in the nebula. It's just a whole lot of hydrogen gas, completely harmless."

The captain was right; the nebula was harmless. It was what appeared out of the nebula and dragged them in that killed them.

*

May 19, 2438
Unknown
Interstellar space
The messenger slithered down the corridor, passing through the heavyset doors that led into the chamber. As usual, it was dark inside; the occupant preferred to keep his senses honed in the darkness.

At the center of the room a huge, serpentine figure uncoiled, fixing his glittering yellow eyes on the messenger.

"I told you not to disturb me unless absolutely necessary," the figure growled. He rose to his full height, towering over the communications officer. The messenger recoiled instinctively, frightfully aware of the Consul's habit of constricting those who angered or annoyed him. The Consul had killed his former commanding officer for disobeying orders in such a manner, an event that inspired fear in his subordinates and superiors alike.

"Forgive me, Consul Zithla," the officer said, bowing low in deference. His tail twitched nervously. He was ready to retreat through the door on a moment's notice should his news be ill-received.

"What is it?" Zithla barked impatiently.

"News from Consul Slethis." He placed the data screen in the consul's outstretched palm. He watched as Zithla's hypnotic yellow eyes took in its contents. When he had finished, Zithla bared his fangs in an angry snarl that filled the messenger with dread.

"Summon Commander Slithza and Captain S'Geliss," Zithla commanded him.

A few minutes later, the government representative and the captain of Zithla's guard had joined him them the chamber. Slithza examined the contents of the data screen before handing it back to the consul.

"I don't see the problem," he said calmly.

"The problem is that Slethis is a fool!" Zithla roared, throwing the data screen angrily. The messenger flinched as it shattered against the wall beside him.

"Consul, need I remind you that our mandate is to gather specimens from all the species of the Ss'Talak Cluster?" Slithza said, using the Vinkere term for the Locality, a region of space Zithla had grown to hate. Almost as much as he loathed the worm-like being in front of him.

"You do not need to remind me of anything!" Zithla thundered. "But evidently I must remind Consul Slethis *again* that his job is not to reveal our location before the opportune time!"

Slethis and Zithla were both consuls; together they oversaw Vinkere activity in the Ss'Talak Cluster. In theory they were supposed to coordinate their efforts. Unfortunately, while Zithla thought of himself as a predator waiting patiently for the opportune moment to strike, Slethis was impulsive and trigger-happy, apparently determined to provoke a confrontation that would force them to begin Phase Three prematurely.

Zithla's patience with Slethis was wearing thin. Zithla grabbed the messenger, who gurgled as the claws grasped him tightly by the throat. Slithza and S'Geliss watched impassively.

"Send this warning to Slethis, and for his sake this better be the last time," Zithla growled. "He must stop abducting ships at once, it serves no purpose now except to create suspicion. He risks discovery and jeopardizing our plan. If his forces do not remain concealed, I will deal with him personally."

"I will tell him," the messenger rasped, gaping lungsful of air when Zithla released him. The messenger slithered hastily toward the exit. Slithza followed him at a leisurely pace.

S'Geliss watched them go. "Do you believe that matter to be resolved?" he asked.

Zithla shook his head. "No, I do not. We must be prepared to implement Phase Three. Inform our forces."

"Yes, Consul," S'Geliss replied. He glided toward the door then paused. "What will you do with Slethis?"

"His next blunder will be his last," Zithla growled. "If he jeopardizes our plans further, I will no longer share power with that imbecile. I will kill him myself."

S'Geliss returned to the bridge and dispatched Zithla's orders, and the Vinkere forces deployed across the Ss'Talak Cluster prepared themselves for Phase Three.

9

The *Telvarn Star* surged out of the slipstream into normal space. The twin suns of the Onta System shone directly ahead, an orange K-type star and a red dwarf. Jarren sat in the co-pilot's seat next to his friend and scrutinized the binary pair as Antak sent out a hail announcing their arrival in the system. Torina Jadus was renowned for her thoroughness, and Jarren often became an expert on the subjects he was required to research for her, so it was with a knowing eye that he now regarded the system they entered.

The Onta System was one of the largest solar systems in known space. The two suns were orbited by twenty planets, terrestrial worlds and gas giants, and numerous dwarf planets. The system had three asteroid belts, one ringing the suns just eighty million kilometers from the barycenter, a second demarcating the line between the "inner" and "outer" terrestrial worlds, and a third separating the terrestrial worlds from the gas giants further out.

The fourth planet in the system was Iganta, the home world of the Iganti civilization and capital of the Iganti Tribal States. Although their space was divided into several dozen tribes, each with their own dialect and cultural practices, the tribal leaders owed their allegiance to the Chieftain of the Homeworld. The current Chieftain of the Homeworld was Krant the Despot, a warlord who had inherited the position from his father. Despite his reputation for ruling with an iron fist, Iganti media insisted the dubious title of "despot" was affectionately applied in recognition of his authoritative nature rather than because of oppressive rule. It was exactly the kind of statement Jarren would expect from media that was state-controlled and heavily censored by the Despot himself.

The *Telvarn Star* waited on the edge of the system until their arrival was acknowledged and a pair of military cruisers approached to escort them to the home world. The escorts were to dissuade other Iganti ships from raiding or destroying them; the Iganti were not above attacking ships if it gave them an advantage in the never-ending power struggle between the various tribes. Although rare, it was not unheard of for visiting alien ships to be attacked or destroyed by raiders before the military could intervene.

Jarren looked out the window at the ship to their left. "Such an unusual design," he commented. Antak nodded in agreement. Typical Iganti ships featured a forward, angular section that housed the ship's command center. This was connected to the larger, rear section of the ship by a long, thin neck. The rear section contained the life support systems, medical bay, hangar deck, and a small secondary bridge at the top with sweeping views over the hull of the ship. The most striking thing about the ships though were the large, column-like engine nacelles which descended from the ventral hull. Two of these pillars extended from the lower hull of the main section, and a single, longer column extended from the forward section. It was in these columns that the ship's engines were housed. To Tuulan For eyes it was a strange design, but Antak knew Iganti ships were very agile, capable of outmaneuvering other vessels of their class.

"I've heard that the forward section can detach from the rear and operate as a completely independent ship in its own right," he said. Ship design was one of his passions.

"Amazing," Jarren marveled. It was innovations like that and notable individuals like Minnen the Learned that proved the Iganti people were more than just a group of barbarous tribes. Like all species, they were complex and varied.

Iganta orbited the barycenter of the two suns at 140 million kilometers. The K-class giant star loomed large in the sky of Iganta, producing higher than average temperatures for a class-1 habitable world. As a result, Iganta was a dry desert world with negligible polar icecaps and an axial tilt so small there was little seasonal variation throughout the year. The equator was almost unbearably hot, even by Iganti standards, who, coming from such a hot world, had a high tolerance for heat. However, the planet's warm oceans produced storms cells large enough to water most of the dry interior of Iganta's continents, and many settlements were based around the oases and underground springs which the locals relied on for water. The sparse forests that grew in the latitudes far from the planet's equator were home to less than thirty percent of Iganta's indigenous fauna; like the Iganti people, the planet's wildlife was better suited to arid and semi-arid environments.

Flanked by its escorts, the *Telvarn Star* approached the brown-white orb of the planet. There were other starships in orbit; like most developed planets in the Locality there was a near-constant stream of space traffic coming and going from the planet and the few space stations in orbit, but it was much less than the cosmopolitan Tuulan For were accustomed to.

"They don't have many visitors," Antak commented.

"The Iganti Tribal States are experiencing moderate economic depression," Jarren explained, recalling his research. "And it's not even related to the Kalavat Plague."

Antak's console beeped, indicating an incoming transmission. "Landing coordinates," he said. "We've been cleared to land in the capital city." Jarren strapped himself into his seat and watched as the planet's horizon rose to meet them as the *Telvarn Star* dipped toward it.

Bandako, the planet's capital city, was located two thousand kilometers north of the equator in a semi-arid scrubland bordering on desert. Jarren was keen to experience the local climate, which was quite different to the subtropical, oceanic climate he was used to living in Lakaria. Back home the summers rarely went above thirty degrees Celsius, but that was lower than the average all-year-round temperature in Bandako, where droughts were the most common natural hazard after sandstorms.

The *Telvarn Star* descended through thin, wispy bands of cloud, and soon Bandako appeared on the horizon as a dusty brown smudge. As they flew closer Jarren could make out patches of verdant green in the city, a stark contrast to the surrounding scrubland. Public parks and tree-lined boulevards crisscrossed the otherwise drab-looking metropolis. Dominating the city center was a large, green rectangle surrounded by high stone walls. This 100-acre area of lush parkland surrounded the palace complex of Krant the Despot, a collection of buildings sprawling across a small rise at the park's center. Antak whistled appreciatively, and Jarren wondered how many gardeners it required to keep the well-tended parkland so neat. A small army of them, probably. A bright blue lake sparkled in the sun beside the palace. *It must lose a lot of water to evaporation,* Jarren thought. *Water is wealth*, he realized. Only someone as rich and powerful as the Despot could keep it resupplied.

The landing coordinates were for a paved area beside the palace hangar, which housed the Despot's luxurious personal yacht and a high-speed transport. As Antak skillfully landed the *Telvarn Star* with barely a bump, Jarren looked out the cockpit window to see a group of long-robed Iganti officials approaching. They waited in a cluster near the edge of the landing pad.

Antak pressed the intercom button. "This is your pilot speaking. You are cleared for disembarkation. Thank you for flying with Antak Airlines, please travel again with us in the future and be sure to compliment your pilot," he said with a cheeky grin.

Jarren grinned back and unbuckled his harness. "We'll see you shortly," he told Antak.

"I'll be along as soon as I've finished the post-flight check," Antak called over his shoulder as Jarren exited the cockpit.

Minister Jadus, Korosa and Doctor Kerik were waiting in the passenger cabin. As the airlock opened a blast of dry desert air swept across them. "Hot," Doctor Kerik commented.

"At least it's not humid," Korosa said, walking down the stairs onto the hot tarmac. The safety of the group was her responsibility, and it was a role she took very seriously. Under her security vest was a scanner capable of detecting energy or projectile weapons within a fifty-meter radius. It fed data to the display band on her wrist. When she gave the all-clear, Jadus and the others joined her. Jarren was the last one to step out of the ship into the hot sunlight. The air rippled in the heat, and he felt himself beginning to sweat almost immediately. A quick glance at his datapad told him the current temperature was forty-two degrees Celsius. With the suns mercilessly beating down on their heads, the Tuulan For delegation crossed the searing tarmac to meet their Iganti welcoming party.

The lead figure, a tall Iganti male in long dark robes, bowed at their approach. "*Noray tilenna*," he said, giving the traditional Iganti greeting when peacefully addressing a group of arrivals. He switched to Trade Standard, the universal language of trade and diplomacy in the Locality, and continued. "Welcome to Iganta. Did you arrive in peace?"

Minister Jadus stepped forward. "We did, thank you. I am Minister Torina Jadus. It is a pleasure to meet you."

"I am Lord Verant of Clan Tenk, Grand Vizier for the Despot," the man replied. Jarren knew that in Iganti custom only the most important people were introduced, which he found both strange and impractical. And the guest always identified themselves first, as Jadus had done.

"We are grateful for Professor Minnen's generous invitation and Chieftain Krant's hospitality," she said.

"Please follow me," said Verant. He gestured toward a tree-lined path leading into the palace. Jadus and Verant began walking in that direction, so Jarren, Korosa and Doctor Kerik followed. Verant's entourage fell in behind them, their long robes sweeping along the path.

They passed through a large stone archway into the palace itself. The difference in temperature was instantly noticeable, and Jarren wondered if the building used invisible force fields or pressure curtains to keep the air inside the palace cool and the hot air outside.

They proceeded through a hallway with vaulted ceilings of cream-colored native stone. Minister Jadus and Lord Verant maintained a polite banter while the rest of the group followed in silence. To the surprise of the Tuulan For guests, every Iganti they passed stopped and bowed, keeping their heads down until the group had passed. The deference they were shown was almost medieval, Jarren thought. They passed a side corridor in which Jarren saw an angry noblewoman berating a hapless servant boy. The noble raised her hand as though to strike him and the servant flinched, cowering fearfully. Jarren caught the subtle but meaningful glare from

Lord Verant, and the noblewoman quickly lowered her hand. The servant hurriedly disappeared into a side door.

Jarren sidled up to Korosa and said quietly, "Did you see that?"

"Yes," she whispered back. "But I have a feeling we weren't meant to."

They entered a large hall filled with life-sized statues. Lord Verant explained to Jadus that the statues were a relatively new addition to the palace and represented all the great leaders from Iganti history, from Hunhuri, the legendary first Iganti chieftain and creator of written language, to Krant the Despot himself.

Through the hall of statues, they came to a set of large, ornate double doors. They were made of timber, a rarity on Iganta and a testament to the wealth of the High Chieftain. "Please wait here," Verant said before disappearing through the doors and closing them behind him. Jadus frowned, unhappy at being made to wait outside. It wasn't long, however, before Verant reappeared. "The Despot will see you now," he told them promptly.

"Thank you," Jadus replied politely, and they entered the long, high-ceilinged throne room. The space was cool and dimly lit. Jadus strode forward purposefully, eager to get the meeting out of the way so she could meet with Minnen the Learned and begin their work on a Kalavat Plague cure. Jarren, Korosa and Doctor Kerik moved close behind her, while Lord Verant and his entourage waited at the rear of the room. Standing along the walls were the Chieftain's Guard, dressed in traditional Iganti warrior garb but carrying modern weapons. They watched silently as the Tuulan For delegation approached the Despot's throne.

Jadus stopped at a line on the stone floor that marked the closest approach to the throne. Jarren, Korosa and Doctor Kerik stood beside her, and for the first time Jarren got a good look at Krant the Despot.

The Despot was sprawled comfortably atop a pile of cushions on his large throne. Although sitting down, Jarren judged him to be nearly seven feet tall. Strong and powerfully-built, he was dressed in a simple cream-colored tunic with the feathered crown of the High Chief on his hairless head. Flanking the throne were more guards, and they eyed the visitors warily, hands on the hilts of their weapons. A young Iganti servant stood with her head bowed, holding an ornate gold bowl of Igantan fruit. Every so often the Despot would pluck one from the bowl, chewing loudly as he watched the Tuulan For delegation approach. From his self-assured expression and relaxed posture, it was obvious he felt in total control.

For several silent moments the Tuulan For waited for the Despot to speak. When he didn't, Jadus took it upon herself to initiate the conversation.

"Lord Krant—" she began, stopping abruptly when the Despot raised a large hand in a gesture of silence. The message was clear: do not speak unless spoken to. Jarren sensed Jadus stiffen beside him, but she remained silent. When the Despot spoke, it was in a deep, rich voice.

"You are the minister from Tuulan Vee, come to seek the help of my chief scientist," the Despot said. He spoke Trade Standard with an accent.

"That's right, Chieftain Krant," Jadus said, having recovered gracefully. She was a proud woman but could feign reverence when required.

"You are here to look for a cure to the plague, eh?" the Despot said rhetorically. Jadus nodded and waited for him to continue.

"Our scientific knowledge and our hospitality are great, but they do not come cheap," Krant announced. "I wonder how much your government will be willing to pay…?"

This didn't come as a surprise to the Tuulan For. Chancellor Denrek had compiled a list of payment options for Jadus to offer the Despot. "I have several options for recompense here," she replied, holding out a datapad. Krant waved idly in her direction and one of his guards approached the minister. She offered him the datapad, which he practically snatched out of her hands. He then ascended the steps to Krant's throne, handing the datapad to him with a lot more deference than he'd shown the minister. They waited in silence for several moments while Krant scanned over the list.

"It seems to me that your government is trying to pull the *gorok* wool over my eyes," he said darkly. "We give you the chance to find a cure that will save billions of lives and you repay us with *water* and cheap foodstuffs!"

"Our apologies, Lord Despot," Jadus said, and Jarren noticed her use of "our" instead of "my"; she wasn't taking the blame for this. "Those food and water shipments were suggested with the drought-affected worlds of your realm in mind."

"Our people are prosperous," the Despot said scornfully. "The most prosperous in the galaxy! We do not need your *welfare*." He spat the last word angrily.

"I am sure we can come to an agreement regarding fair payment," Jadus said magnanimously. "In fact, our Chancellor is willing to discuss the matter with you personally if you would find that preferable." Denrek had wisely included a subspace radio frequency for the Despot to contact him, with a note that the Tuulan For would be willing to negotiate.

"Speak with Chancellor Denrek personally, hmm?" the Despot purred. His eyes lit up with greed as he considered the possibilities. "I am relieved that your people realize the significance of our invitation. I will speak to your chancellor, now that I know your people take the Iganti seriously."

"The Lord Despot drives a hard bargain, but I am sure Chancellor Denrek will be able to arrange a payment that meets your approval," Jadus said smoothly. *Greedy people are the easiest to manipulate,* Jarren thought smugly. Now hopefully they could focus on the cure and leave haggling over the price to Chancellor Denrek.

"With your permission I would like to begin working with Minnen the Learned as soon as possible. Time is of the essence, and—"

"You may begin work, as soon as the payment has been received," the Despot interrupted. He signaled to Lord Verant, who hastened to his side immediately. "We will contact you when we are ready. My Vizier will show you to your accommodation. You will be guests in the palace, of course."

The Tuulan For stood there uncertainly, unsure if they had been dismissed until they realized Krant was no longer paying any attention to them; he was focused on the servants who had entered through a small side door bearing more gold trays of food.

Lord Verant re-joined them. "Please follow me to your accommodation," he said, gesturing toward the exit.

"Very well," Jadus said quietly, turning on her heel and striding after him. Jarren knew she wouldn't be happy until she was in the laboratory working. He glanced over his shoulder at the Despot, who was already digging into his lunch with relish.

Verant led them to a set of rooms on the third floor of the palace overlooking lush gardens and the lake below. Jarren, Antak and Doctor Kerik were assigned one suite, comprised of a large common area and their own sleeping rooms. Jadus and Korosa were given the adjacent suite, although as her security officer Korosa would have insisted on staying close to the minister anyway.

Jarren and Doctor Kerik entered their suite and looked around in amazement. Water trickled from an elaborate fountain in the wall, and non-native tropical plants with frond-like leaves grew from colorful planters around an ornate pool. It felt like they were standing in an oasis, but Jarren thought it was in poor taste, considering the severity of the drought affecting millions of the Despot's own people. Doctor Kerik stooped to examine the elaborate motifs carved into the wooden frame of a settee; all the furniture was of the highest quality non-native timber. Such lavish furnishings wouldn't have been out of place in the palaces of Tuulan Vee's ancient emperors. Elegant, sculpted columns around the room's perimeter curved upwards to meet the vaulted domed ceiling five meters above the tiled marble floor, which was covered with soft, elegantly patterned rugs. The dome was painted with colorful scenes of Iganti scenery and wildlife.

"Antak's going to love this," Jarren said, anticipating his friend's awed reaction.

Jarren and Doctor Kerik investigated their respective rooms; the private sleeping areas were smaller but no less luxurious, with large double beds for each of them. There were modern facilities, too; each room was equipped with an information and communication terminal linked to the Iganti interplanetary network. The guest suites were no doubt designed to impress the occupants, and they did. Jarren almost forgot about the hardship that gripped millions of Iganti outside the palace. Almost.

He opened the glass doors that gave access to a wide balcony overlooking the palace grounds. A blast of hot, dry air swept over him; he had forgotten how hot it was outside. When he stepped inside, he once more noticed the immediate change in temperature. A pressure curtain kept the atmosphere cool inside. Expensive.

Antak arrived several minutes later, guided by a servant. Antak came from Raketh Province on Tuulan Vee, a largely agricultural area, and gawked at the opulence of their surroundings.

"Not bad," he drawled. He entered his equally lavish sleeping chamber and flopped down on the bed; even stretched out he couldn't reach the edges of the mattress. "I could get used to this kind of luxury," he said with a sigh of contentment.

Jarren picked up a pillow and batted him in the head. "There are two women next door who won't want you getting too comfortable," Jarren cautioned him.

As if on cue, Jarren's communicator beeped. "*Minister Jadus wants you guys to join us in here, now,*" Korosa said.

Antak clambered off the bed. "That was uncanny."

"I told you. They know."

The three men went next door and Korosa let them into the room. The Minister's guest suite was as opulent as theirs, but she didn't seem at all interested in their surroundings.

"I hope we don't have to wait long," she said, pacing the tiled floor.

"I must admit, I was surprised that Krant rejected the offer for food and water supplies," Doctor Kerik commented. "It seemed—"

"We did not offer enough, which is our fault," Jadus interrupted firmly, giving the doctor a pointed look. He looked at her questioningly until Korosa mouthed *might be listening* in Josi, the Tuulan For language.

Kerik flushed with embarrassment. The security officer was concerned their rooms might be monitored; Jarren certainly wouldn't put it past the Despot to spy on his guests. "Chancellor Denrek will reach a mutually beneficial deal with Despot Krant in no time," he said optimistically and Jadus nodded in agreement.

"Until then, we might as well get comfortable," Antak said, earning a disapproving look from Korosa. "What?" he asked defensively.

"We're not here for a holiday," Korosa said. "We're here to work."

"I said enjoy ourselves, I didn't say holiday," Antak retorted. "Can't we work and enjoy ourselves at the same time?"

"The change of scenery is... refreshing," Jadus agreed, intervening before it became an argument. After being confined to the *Telvarn Star* for so many weeks, some personal space would do them all good.

"Can we order some dinner?" Antak asked. "I'm hungry."

"Good idea," Jadus said, looking around. "I'm sure there is a way to contact room service..."

"Over there," Antak said, pointing.

"... and hopefully after a decent meal and a good night's sleep, we will be able to start working with Professor Minnen," Jadus finished. Doctor Kerik heartily agreed that sounded like a good plan. Jarren hoped so, because every hour the plague went uncured, millions of people were at risk.

*

"Thank you for calling," Chancellor Denrek said to the Iganti man on his monitor.

"I am Verant, Chieftain Krant's vizier," Verant said smoothly. *"It is I with whom you will be dealing with, as the Despot is occupied with other matters of state."*

"That sounds reasonable," Denrek said amicably.

Unbeknownst to the two men, their "secure" private conversation had an audience. Approximately halfway between their two worlds, others watched and recorded their conversation from a listening post hidden deep within a dark nebula. It took nearly an hour, but eventually a fair price was agreed on. When the call ended, the watchers sent the recording in a secret transmission to another distant nebula.

*

Unknown
Interstellar space
The messenger paused nervously at the threshold of the consul's chamber. "Consul Zithla...?"

"What is it?" Zithla demanded in a deep voice.

The messenger cautiously approached the consul and handed him the data tablet.

Zithla scanned the contents of the message, translated into his native Vinkere language. His wide mouth opened in a wicked smile. "This Tuulan For minister is meeting with the galaxy's foremost medical expert," he mused. There was only one reason he could think of for such a meeting. "They seek a cure for the plague." Despite being one of the largest members of his race, the consul could move with surprising stealth. He slithered sinuously across the floor toward the nearest communications panel. "S'Geliss, report to my chamber at once."

"Yes, Consul."

The captain of the guardsmen arrived shortly, brushing past the messenger, barely noticing him. He was accompanied by Commander Slithza, Zithla's assigned expert on Ss'Talak Cluster geopolitics. The messenger hung back near the door, not yet dismissed but hoping to remain as unobtrusive as possible.

Zithla updated the two officers on the conversation between the Tuulan For chancellor and the Iganti despot.

"It's fortunate we found out about this," Slithza said.

"We should send a fleet to Iganta and reduce its surface to ash," S'Geliss declared. "That would eliminate both the Tuulan For minister and the Iganti doctor."

"I would, had we the ships to spare," Zithla said, frowning in thought. The engines of a passing escort ship illuminated the swirling gases of the nebula outside the window, and for a brief moment the three Vinkere were painted in dim blue light.

The consul turned to Slithza. "What is the state of affairs on Iganta?"

"The political situation continues to deteriorate," Slithza replied. "Several of their outer colonies are suffering shortages of basic resources, which have only worsened since the collapse of the Kora-Sr'Hirta Trade Route, and many worlds are falling victim to the plague and to piracy. But the Despot is more concerned with living comfortably in his palace than dealing with the hardships of his people."

"What of the rebels and malcontents who oppose him?"

"There is a warlord who has been gathering support to challenge the leadership of the despot: Zinkara. They call her the Warrior Queen."

"Why does that matter?" S'Geliss asked impatiently.

Slithza gave him a scornful look. "Because if the Iganti people found out their leader turned down much-needed aid for his own personal gain, it may be enough to drive the Warrior Queen into all-out rebellion."

S'Geliss snorted derisively. "If the Despot cannot control his own people, he deserves to be overthrown."

"According to our predictions, the Warrior Queen's rebellion is just a matter of time. Without outside intervention, it will likely occur within a matter of months."

"We cannot risk waiting that long," S'Geliss said after brief consideration.

"No," Zithla agreed. He turned to the messenger, forgotten by the others during the exchange. "We must leak this information to the Warrior Queen, but it cannot be traced back to us. Go and do this at once."

"Yes, Consul," the messenger said, bowing low. He backed out of the chamber, grateful to leave.

Slithza watched him go with disinterest. "Zinkara has been gathering her forces for months, consolidating her power," he said. "This information could be the spark that ignites her rebellion. And if it does, I am confident that what always happens during a regime change on Iganta will occur: the death of the current High Chieftain, and the culling of his immediate family, high-ranking government officials and sympathizers."

"Like the Iganti doctor and the Tuulan For minister," S'Geliss finished.

"Yes."

Zithla smiled. "We shall allow the Warrior Queen to accomplish our objective for us. The Iganti doctor and the Tuulan For minister will die by her hand."

10

Simon Marston studied the star chart in front of him, focusing on the image of the *Pericles* as it moved along its projected path through space. Almost two light-years away, on a course parallel to theirs but traveling in the opposite direction, was the Navy ship *Illustrious*. Marston wondered if its captain was as bored as he was.

The Stromar Sector was a sparsely populated region on the inner edge of Tier 2 Space. The few planets in the sector were well developed, and most of the ships in the area were simply passing through to get somewhere else. There were no interesting stellar phenomena, and no pirates or smugglers or aliens. Just a quiet, prosperous corner of the Commonwealth. It was *boring*. The only thing of note that had occurred in the past few weeks was assisting a civilian cargo ship with a faulty slipstream drive, and even that had been a simple matter. His engineers had repaired the drive and Marston had issued a Minor Reproach to the captain for failure to carry the necessary spare parts. Then the two ships parted ways and the *Pericles* resumed its plod through the sector.

Marston realized that he had been spoiled so far in his Navy career; the ships he had previously served on had undertaken more than their fair share of "exciting" missions, like protecting Arretrian colonies from Thordran pirates and exploring uncharted space. He had to remind himself that sector patrols were a perfectly normal part of a Navy ship's mission. And he understood why he had been assigned such a routine mission; he was an untried captain commanding a new ship and untested crew. It made sense that they would be given a simple first mission in the heart of Commonwealth space, he grudgingly conceded.

Despite the realization that such routine missions were probably going to be quite common for him and his crew and his self-assurances that he was okay with that, he felt a thrill of excitement and relief when a yellow icon appeared flashing on his monitor, indicating a priority fleet alert. Leaping out of his chair, he strode briskly onto the *Pericles* bridge, arriving at the same time as Commander Balzano. Sirroyo rose from the captain's chair.

"We're receiving a priority fleet alert from the Plano Sector," she informed them. "It's a live stream."

"Put it on the viewscreen," Marston ordered, taking the captain's seat she had just vacated.

The viewscreen switched to a live feed from one of the distant satellites that demarcated the edge of Commonwealth space. At the center of the image were the Navy starships *Hermes* and *Tenacious*. They were facing what at first looked like a brown cloud in space, but on closer inspection was revealed to be hundreds of ships rapidly approaching the two Navy vessels.

"What's happening? Is it an invasion?" Marston asked.

"We don't know. They're not responding to hails," Sirroyo said grimly.

"Admiral Haftel and the Ninth Fleet are on their way to join the *Hermes* and *Tenacious*, and all Navy ships have been placed on high alert," Balzano read. To Marston's knowledge the priority fleet alert system hadn't been used in many years, but it provided a valuable warning in case the approaching fleet had hostile intentions.

Balzano approached the viewscreen and scrutinized the oncoming ships up close. "They look like Kithel ships," he commented.

"How many are there?" Marston asked.

"Two hundred eighty-one," Sirroyo reported.

"Why would they attack us?" Hasan wondered. "The Kithel aren't aggressive."

"We don't know if they *are* attacking us," Clarke pointed out.

The *Hermes* and *Tenacious* readied their weapons. Dozens of light-years away, Marston and the bridge crew watched anxiously as the Kithel fleet bore down on them… and then slowed to a stop in front of the Commonwealth ships.

For several silent minutes, the Navy ships and the alien fleet faced each other across the void. Then, after a short period of communication which the *Pericles* crew could only guess at, the *Tenacious* reported to the fleet.

"They're not hostile," Sirroyo told the bridge crew with surprise. "They're requesting asylum!"

*

Marston stretched his tired muscles, relieved that the conference call with Admiral Bryant and the other captains of the Fifth Fleet had finally ended. He stood up from his desk, stretched again, and returned to the bridge, where the others looked at him expectantly.

"The Kithel are indeed seeking asylum in the Commonwealth," he told them. "It's not an invasion, they're refugees. The Kalavat Plague spread to their home world. Apparently before their Queen died, she told them to escape to the Commonwealth. They want to start a new hive somewhere safe from the pandemic."

The bridge crew exchanged concerned looks. The Kalavat Plague had appeared frequently in news headlines over the past several weeks, but it had always seemed like a distant problem. The Kithel refugees had brought the harsh reality of the plague to the Commonwealth.

"Is the government going to grant their request?" Sirroyo asked.

"For now, yes, so long as they don't pose a danger to the Commonwealth. More ships have been deployed to the border, to assist the refugees. Starship assignments have been reshuffled, and we've been redeployed to the Crown Sector." The crew perked up; it would be a welcome change of scenery.

"When do we go?" Balzano asked.

"Right now," Marston said. He clapped the helmsman on the shoulder. "Take us to the Crown Sector, Lieutenant."

"Aye, Captain," Hasan replied smartly.

The ship's faster-than-light engines activated and the *Pericles* dove into the slipstream.

11

"The professor is on his way," Uxxio assured them for the umpteenth time. The young, nervous-looking Iganti was Minnen the Learned's assistant. He filled the same role that Jarren did for Jadus, but Jarren was glad the minister wasn't like the famed Iganti professor. Even though it could be stressful trying to maintain the high standards Jadus expected of him, Minnen kept Uxxio so busy it was a wonder he hadn't keeled over from exhaustion.

"Thank you, Uxxio," Minister Jadus said calmly, but Jarren could tell from the taut muscles in her jaw that she was frustrated at the delay. He didn't blame her. Since their arrival on Iganta her work on the Kalavat Plague cure with Professor Minnen had been sporadic. They were constantly being interrupted by the Despot, who seemed determined to impose his authority on them at every opportunity. Jadus was obliged to attend the Despot's banquets as an "honored guest" nearly every day, and Minnen was summoned for council meetings at the most inopportune moments. And whenever he was away, Krant forbade the alien visitors access to his laboratory for "security reasons". To Jarren the Despot seemed petty and controlling.

Minnen was in a meeting of the Despot's council right now, so Jadus, Jarren and the others were waiting in the small reception room outside the professor's office. Strumming his fingers boredly, Jarren glanced out the windows at the city. Bandako, the capital city of Iganta, wasn't much of a city by Tuulan For standards. The Iganti preferred to live in small communities spread over large areas, and generally didn't congregate in large numbers. Home to just over one million people, Bandako paled in comparison to the size and sophistication of Lakaria. Most of the buildings were old tenement buildings and squat housing complexes constructed of mud brick, although near the palace these older buildings were interspersed with sleek towers and more modern-looking structures of steel and glass. But even in the city center there were few buildings more than six stories high along the wide boulevards. Nearly every building had a flat roof where the occupants would retire to in the evenings to make the most of the cooler temperatures.

The one thing it seemed to have in common with Lakaria was that the streets were always busy, regardless of the time of day. Right now, the dusty pavement was thick with pedestrian traffic despite the midday heat; the locals wore clothes made of a thin, cotton-like fabric that protected them from the merciless glare of the twin suns beating down on the open-air bazaars and crowded thoroughfares. The city and its people looked primitive to Jarren, but he knew the populace enjoyed nearly the same level of technological comfort that he did back home. It was just that the modern was concealed beneath the ancient, mud brick exterior.

Beyond the city was the desert, where the dirty brown horizon and bright blue sky met in a shimmering haze. He was grateful that it was pleasantly cool in the waiting room, despite the fact it was well over thirty-five degrees Celsius outside.

Several more minutes passed in relative quiet. Korosa flipped idly through a magazine on the coffee table; she couldn't read Ganti, so she just looked at the pictures. Jarren tapped his foot restlessly and stared out the window. Uxxio glanced at his time piece. "I'm sure the professor will be here any—"

He stopped mid-sentence, interrupted by a booming voice in the hallway. Suddenly the doors crashed open, causing everyone to flinch. An elderly Iganti male in a white coat burst into the room, followed by three young, timid-looking Iganti.

"Ah, Professor, there you are…" began Uxxio. He frowned. "I see you brought another group of interns from the university…"

"Yes, here I am!" said Minnen the Learned enthusiastically. "I apologize for the delay, Minister. The Despot requested my presence at a meeting of the staff of Bandako University. Shall we resume our work?"

"That sounds good, Professor," said Jadus, eager to return to the lab.

"Of course, of course," said Minnen brightly, his fingers drumming a tune against his sides. Despite the fact he was over sixty years old, beyond the average lifespan of an Iganti, the man had an excess of energy.

"Professor Minnen advises the Science Department at Bandako University," Uxxio interjected hastily before he could be interrupted.

"Not in an official capacity anymore, of course," Minnen said. "Technically, I'm semi-retired."

Jadus nodded. She already knew all this from similar previous conversations. "Shall we return to your lab, Professor?"

"Let us go at once," he agreed readily. The doors barely slid open in time as he charged into the lab, his white lab coat billowing behind him. Uxxio and the interns hurried after him, while Jadus and her people followed at a more leisurely pace.

The room was just as they had left it; datapads containing research notes strewn across workbenches and scientific equipment waiting in standby mode for their return.

"How is Doctor Kerik?" Minnen asked.

"Doing much better, thanks to you," Jadus told him. Ironically, their most qualified virologist had contracted a local virus shortly after their arrival on Iganta and had been bed-ridden for days. Fortunately, Minnen had quickly diagnosed Kerik's illness and given him a regimen of antivirals that the professor insisted would return him to full health in a matter of days. At his current rate of recovery, he would be well enough to re-join them in the lab tomorrow.

"Good," said Minnen, sounding not the least bit surprised. He looked at his desk and frowned. "Where are my plague samples?" he demanded, and the interns scattered, frantically searching the lab. "You young people need to anticipate me!"

Jadus stifled a smile. The Despot's near-constant intervention was frustrating, but when she and Minnen worked, they accomplished a lot. Despite his almost constant fidgeting and stream of chatter, Jadus had never met a person more hard-working than Minnen the Learned.

"I am one of the galaxy's greatest minds when it comes to immunological research," Minnen announced without a hint of modesty. "I was one of the founders of the Interspecies Scientific Exchange of Research program. Is it so unreasonable to expect my help to be equally competent? Good, thank you," he said, snatching the vial offered by a triumphant-looking intern.

"Uxxio, I trust you brought the information I requested? Good, good. You there!" Minnen jabbed a finger at the nearest intern, who jumped. "Fetch us drinks, and then make sure everyone knows we are not to be disturbed." He turned his intense stare on Jadus. "We have important work to do."

"We do indeed," Jadus agreed. She and Jarren resumed their research while Minnen and Uxxio ran tests on the plague samples they had procured at great difficulty from the Iganti frontier. The interns did whatever anyone asked them to without question; Jarren was amused to find that when he commented on the lack of space on his workbench one of them rushed over to clear it for him. When he grinned at Jadus she gave him a reproachful look that said *don't get used to it*.

Korosa hovered protectively nearby, intensely bored but too stubborn to admit it. For once though Jadus didn't try and dissuade the young woman from her vigilance, which was a significant tell that even she was concerned about their security in Bandako.

What little they knew of the political situation on Iganta was disconcerting to say the least. Their access to local newsfeeds was strictly controlled by their hosts, but even Krant the Despot couldn't conceal the resentful looks of courtiers behind his back or the whispered conversations of the palace servants. A few nights ago, Antak had eavesdropped on a conversation between two cleaners outside their suite, where he heard them refer to the situation in the capital as "untenable".

Within the privacy of his lab, Jadus had managed to get Minnen to open up about the political situation on Iganta. Away from the prying ears of the Despot's lackeys, he had been as direct as he was about everything else. The strife wasn't just on Iganta, he told them matter-of-factly. Several worlds were on the verge of open rebellion, uniting under the banner of Zinkara the Warrior Queen, a distant cousin of Krant. Minnen's assessment was grim; the situation in the Iganti Tribal States was tense, and the Despot's grip on power tenuous. It was a testament to the control Krant exerted over the palace and the state media that this was the first time they were truly hearing how serious the situation was.

According to Minnen there were several reasons for the rebels' growing support: tribal loyalties, the Despot's brutal treatment of dissidents, his ineffective response to the drought on the less-developed frontier worlds, and now the Kalavat Plague. Discontent had been brewing for years, and now it seemed ready to erupt, engulfing the Iganti Tribal States in another civil war.

This news, combined with the long, intensive hours spent in Minnen's lab meant that Jadus and her companions couldn't truly enjoy their time on Iganta. Jarren had looked forward to experiencing the local culture, exotic by his standards, but since their arrival ten days ago they hadn't been permitted to leave the palace grounds.

The suns had set and the sky was dark by the time they decided to call it a day. Jarren rubbed his eyes tiredly, weary after staring at computer screens for so long. Jadus told him he could leave, and he made a discreet exit a few minutes later while she was in deep discussion with Minnen. The two of them were as focused as ever. Jarren wished he shared their passion. He was as desperate as anyone to find a cure for the Kalavat Plague, but medical research wasn't his area of expertise.

He plodded wearily through the corridors of the palace toward their guest suite. He could hear music and laughter coming from the dining hall where Krant was hosting one of his customarily elaborate feasts. The rest of the palace was quiet, which for some reason Jarren found unnerving.

Doctor Kerik was still in bed recuperating, but Antak was sprawled across one of the divans in the living area, holding his datapad in one hand while the other hung limply off the edge of the couch.

Jarren collapsed into a nearby chair. "What are you doing?" he asked.

"Nothing. Games," Antak said, sounding bored.

"Have you eaten dinner already?"

"Yeah, about an hour ago."

"What did you have?"

"The same meat dish as yesterday, with that fruit dessert."

"Nice." After several moments in which the only sounds were the blips and beeps emitted by Antak's datapad, Jarren said, "I thought visiting Iganta was going to be fun. But I haven't even been outside the palace since we arrived."

Antak sat up. "I know! After being confined to the *Telvarn Star* for weeks and now here, I feel like I'm going crazy. I need to get out!"

"Minister Jadus and Professor Minnen get invited almost every day to whatever the Despot is doing, while we sit here doing nothing," Jarren muttered, and Antak nodded resentfully. They weren't bitter toward Jadus, who they knew would prefer to be working full-time on the cure. But Jarren and Antak felt like they were under house arrest. Jarren said as much.

"Maybe next time we can take her place," Antak said absently, but then his face lit up. "Actually, why don't we offer to?" he said hopefully.

Jarren shrugged. "We could always ask."

Doctor Kerik entered the room, walking slowly. He was still pale but looked much better than he had a few days ago.

"How are you feeling, Doctor?" Antak asked.

"Much better, thank you," Kerik said hoarsely; he hadn't spoken much over the past few days. "What are you boys up to?"

"I was about to have dinner," Jarren said, irked that the older man referred to them as "boys". "You hungry?"

Kerik nodded. "I haven't eaten solid food for days."

Jarren got up and was about to order food from the kitchen when Jadus burst into the room, followed closely by Korosa. The minister's face was flushed with excitement.

"Professor Minnen and I just had a revelation," she told them. "We were processing the results of the tests we've done over the last few days, and it suddenly hit us."

She looked at each of them, smiling excitedly.

"What hit you?" Jarren prompted.

"The Kalavat Plague is not a virus at all," she announced, pausing to let it sink in.

"Not a virus?" Antak said, puzzled. "What is it, then?"

"Is it a bacteria?" Jarren asked.

"No," Jadus said. "But it is extremely complex, which is why it's taken so long for us to identify it. It's unlike any other illness we've ever encountered before. That's why attempts to treat it as a virus or bacteria have all failed!"

Jarren and Antak glanced at Korosa. She shrugged, indicating she barely comprehended what the Minister was working on.

Doctor Kerik was extremely interested, however. "That's quite a significant discovery," he said, sounding livelier than he had in days.

Jadus nodded vigorously. "At least we now know what it is *not*. It took us a while, but we finally realized it is an entirely new type of life, neither bacterium nor virus, previously unknown to us."

"That's great," Jarren said. He supposed so, anyway. He wasn't sure. But Jadus nodded again.

"Professor Minnen has begun mapping its genome. It's incredibly complex, more so than any other genome in the Iganti database. I'm going back to help him."

"Do you need any help?" Jarren asked, obliged to ask but dreading an all-nighter in the lab. To his relief, she shook her head.

"No, you get some rest. I'll see you in the morning." With that, she turned and left the room as quickly as she had entered. Korosa gave the others a martyred look and they smiled sympathetically as she hurried after the minister.

"Well, that's good news," Jarren commented.

"Very good news," Kerik agreed. "Now that I am no longer bedridden, I will be fit to assist you in the morning."

Jarren nodded vaguely; he was thinking about what Minister Jadus had said. Almost every medical research facility in the Locality was desperately trying to cure the Kalavat Plague like they would any other virus or bacteria. But if it was neither, and in fact a new form of life, their approach was *wrong*. That didn't bode well for the people of the Locality. And it made Jadus and Minnen's work here even more important.

*

May 30, 2438
Kanturee, Indegra
Kelzanti Galactic Federation
Lieutenant M'Bol Nulo shouldered his rifle and gestured to a group of civilians nearby. "Hurry! Across the bridge!" he urged them. The group consisted of several families, all exhausted and dirty. They were part of a column of refugees stretching several kilometers, all the way from the nearby city Kanturee. From his vantage point standing on the roof of an abandoned vehicle M'Bol could see columns of smoke rising from the city and military aircraft weaving between the skyscrapers.

Reports of Infected were coming in from all the major cities across the planet. What had started out as isolated individual cases had spread so rapidly that the local government and military hadn't fully grasped the severity of the outbreak until Infected were literally crashing through people's front windows.

M'Bol and his platoon were escorting refugees out of Kanturee to the military base on Keelok Island. It was taking longer than anticipated because the bridge connecting the island to the mainland had been damaged when a military craft crashed into it. The co-pilot had been bitten by an Infected and didn't tell anyone, and his crewmates didn't realize until the ship was airborne and he turned on them. M'bol recalled with a shudder the panicked transmission from the pilot moments before impact, then the bright orange fireball that engulfed the ship and the bridge, killing many refugees and soldiers in the process.

Military engineers had hastily built a makeshift platform spanning the gap, and the flow of refugees had resumed. Once they reached the relative safety of the military base the civilians were airlifted to evacuation ships in orbit. It was only a matter of time before the Infected reached the bridge, at which point the soldiers had orders to destroy it. That should prevent them from reaching the island. M'Bol didn't think they had the ability to swim across the two-hundred-meter-wide strait with its powerful current.

An elderly couple separated from the crowd and paused by the roadside. The old man was leaning on a walking frame, and they both looked exhausted. M'Bol approached them. "You have to keep moving," he prodded gently. "It's not far to safety now." They looked at him wearily but resumed their plod toward the bridge. Soldiers like M'Bol were stationed every few meters along the road and another platoon guarded the entrance to the military base. They had set up diagnostic arches to scan people as they passed through. Their responsibility was to identify potential bite marks that could indicate an Infected amongst the crowd of refugees before they spread the virus to others. Sometimes people who became infected tried to hide it, hoping to evacuate with their families and find a cure somewhere. As far as M'Bol knew there wasn't any cure for this plague which had first come to Indegra from Kalavat, and those infected individuals were a danger to their family members and everybody else. It was especially dangerous in densely packed crowds like this; a person could transform and infect many others around them before the soldiers could react.

Presumably, any Infected who were found in the crowd were taken to research facilities where scientists could study the disease. The most dangerous phase of the plague was what the soldiers called the "Rage Stage", the first stage after infection. It caused the victim to become incoherent and extremely violent. Once bitten, you were as good as dead, although the Rage Stage was only the first phase of several before death claimed the victim. It was followed by the Torpid Phase where the Infected became lethargic and almost completely immobile; the length of this phase varied between individuals, but it always ended in a comatose state during which the victim was completely transformed. They could still pose a danger, however; many soldiers investigating the early outbreaks had been infected this way, bitten by what they thought were catatonic infected.

M'Bol returned to his vantage point on top of the vehicle and looked around. Nearly all the refugees had covered the distance from Kanturee on foot. He doubted many had slept or eaten over the past twenty-three hours, and most were too tired to do anything other than trudge toward the bridge and the promise of safe passage off world.

His communicator squawked, and he yanked it off his belt. *"All land-based forces in the city have been overrun,"* an officer reported. *"Only air units remain. We're pulling them back to protect the people on the road to Keelok."*

Kanturee had a population of three hundred thousand; M'bol hated to think how many of them were now Infected. But it also gave him a great deal of satisfaction knowing he was helping to save the lives of thousands of others... even if it was saving them from their former family and friends. A transport ship rose from the military base and flew out over the ocean before ascending toward the starships in orbit. *Another group of people safe*, he thought with relief.

M'Bol turned back toward the city just in time to see a bright projectile hit a retreating military sky craft. There was a flash as the craft exploded. The sound of the explosion reached him several seconds later.

"All units be advised: the Infected have seized military weapons," the same officer reported.

"Or some of the Infected were soldiers," M'Bol muttered to himself. A cry of alarm sounded in the distance, drawing his attention back toward the city. He craned his neck for a better look.

About a kilometer from his position a group of Infected were tearing into the crowd. They must have been refugees who transformed, M'Bol realized, because they had turned on their neighbors with vigor. More and more people were taken down, clawing at bite marks on their arms, neck, or legs. Some of them transformed almost instantly; you could never tell whether it would take seconds or minutes. Soldiers closed in, rifles firing into the crowd as the infection spread.

Ripples of panic swept through the crowd; even those hundreds of meters away from the outbreak knew something was wrong. The sound of rifle shots echoed along the road and a wail of terror rose from the people near M'bol, and they surged forward with renewed energy. It became a stampede as people panicked, pushing the people in front of them in their desperation.

"Move in an orderly fashion!" M'Bol bellowed. Other soldiers along the road were shouting the same thing, but the people were too frightened to listen.

The soldiers near the outbreak swung their rifles desperately, trying to find targets. In the mayhem it was almost impossible to tell the difference between the panicked refugees and the Infected until they were upon the soldiers, growling like feral creatures. There was another flash above the city and another military skycraft tumbled out of the sky.

The infection was spreading. Some of the soldiers, overwhelmed or trampled by the crowd, were bitten by the Infected. People lay on the ground moaning, while others twisted and writhed as the virus took hold. Then they leapt to their feet with ferocious snarls and began attacking the people around them.

M'Bol's communicator squawked. *"All forces, fall back to Keelok!"* He turned to the soldier nearest him, only to see the other man was already twenty meters away, sprinting toward the bridge. Any semblance of order had gone; the orderly evacuation had become a panicked stampede. M'Bol ran along the side of the road beside the stream of refugees. Children cried, old people wailed, and families held on tightly to each other to avoid becoming separated.

He reached the shore, where a team of military engineers were attaching explosives to the bridge's support pillars. Above them, people were pushing each other aside in their haste to cross the bridge; many fell or were pushed into the water below. Dozens more were desperately trying to swim the distance separating the island from the mainland, but the current was strong, and many people were swept toward the open ocean. Hundreds of others had given up trying to reach the bridge and scattered across the fields on either side of the road. The Infected ran after them, choosing targets indiscriminately.

The engineers at the bridge looked on the verge of panicking themselves, so M'Bol decided to take control. "Report," he snapped.

"We've finished placing the explosives," one said. His eyes were wide with fright and he looked like he was about to bolt.

"We need to get across the bridge *now* so they can blow it up!" another said, eyeing the crowd warily.

"Blow it up now?" M'Bol repeated.

"How else are we going to stop the Infected?" the second engineer snapped.

"There are still people crossing!" M'Bol protested.

"We have no choice!" the first one cried. He raised his gun shakily as a fierce looking refugee ran past, eyes blazing. They could already be surrounded by Infected, M'Bol thought grimly.

"We were supposed to be safe on the other side by now!" one of the engineers wailed. Before M'Bol could reply there was an angry roar from nearby, and he spun around to see an Infected male charging toward them.

M'Bol reflexively raised his rifle and fired. The bullets struck the Infected man directly in the chest and he toppled over backwards, dead. But the sound of gunfire drew the attention of other Infected, who closed in on them.

"Fire your weapons!" M'Bol shouted at the engineers, who had frozen with fear. Two of them snapped out of it long enough to fire at the Infected. A third engineer succumbed to panic, dropped his rifle and ran toward the shore, wading out into the shallows in a desperate attempt to escape. The fourth man simply froze in fear, eyes locked in horror on the approaching enemy. He was the first taken down, by an Infected woman who leapt on him with a snarl, clamping her teeth into his neck. M'Bol kicked out with his boot, sending the Infected woman sprawling. He finished her off with a single shot to the head.

"They're everywhere!" one of the engineers shouted, pointing his gun about wildly. Two more Infected sprinted toward them and grabbed him, and he went down in a mass of flailing limbs. M'Bol and the remaining engineer dispatched the attackers and their rapidly transforming victim.

The communicator on his belt squawked again, although he barely heard it over the clatter of gunfire and the roar of the Infected. *"Get clear of the bridge! We're going to detonate the charges!"*

"We need to move!" M'Bol shouted at the remaining engineer, who shot an Infected before nodding and sprinting after him. They ran down the embankment to the sand. Small waves lapped at their boots. Behind them a group of young people were wading out into the water, daring to risk the rough channel crossing.

"This should be far enough," the engineer said, panting. They waited for the explosion. Nothing happened.

"Something must be wrong," M'Bol realized. Two more Infected spotted them, half-running and half-tumbling down the slope toward them. M'Bol and the engineer shot them both before they came within a dozen meters.

"The detonator isn't working, something must have happened to the remote," a terse voice said over the radio.

"Can it be detonated at the bridge?" M'Bol asked.

"Yes," came the instant reply. *"One will be enough to trigger the others."* M'Bol looked at the engineer, who nodded bravely.

"Leave that to us," he said into his communicator. Then, to the engineer, he asked, "Are you ready?"

The man nodded again. "The nearest explosive is on that column," he said, pointing. There was a low growl behind them, and the engineer's expression turned to one of surprise and pain. M'Bol spun around to see an Infected knee-deep in the waves; it must have transformed in the water and spotted them on the shore. It had sunk its teeth into the engineer's leg. M'Bol shot it in the face and the Infected's lifeless body fell back into the waves. The engineer looked at him, his face filled with cold acceptance and resignation.

"I'm- I'm sorry," M'Bol stammered, unsure what to do.

"Go! Blow up the bridge," the engineer replied, his face contorted with pain. His skin was rapidly turning ashen grey as the Kalavat Plague virus spread through his body.

M'Bol hesitated just long enough to nod once, and then turned and sprinted up the hill toward the bridge. There was a single gunshot from behind him, and he glanced back to see the engineer's lifeless body toppling into the surf. He had taken his own life rather than become infected. M'Bol was about to do the same thing.

Three more Infected caught sight of him and ran after him. He dispatched them all but stumbled, tripping over a body on the road. His face hit the asphalt with jarring force. He cried out in pain but staggered to his feet, his mouth and nose covered in orange blood. He half-stumbled, half-ran to the bridge support pillar. Through blurred vision he found the bomb and reached for its cool, smooth detonator switch. He was about to blow up the bridge. In doing so he would cut off the Infected from Keelok Island, but he was also dooming whoever was still on this side, not to mention those currently *on* the bridge. He told himself it was for the people already safe on the island, huddling together and scared as they waited for rescue. He took a deep breath, thinking of his parents and sisters.

Sharp pain lanced through his calf, and he looked down to see an Infected biting on his leg; one of the engineers. M'Bol felt his blood go cold as the Kalavat Plague began its evil work. *So this is what it's like*, he thought grimly.

He looked down at the former engineer chewing on his leg. "Too late," he said calmly. He pressed the button. There was a burst of intense light and heat, and then nothing.

*

Justin Caleb

[Report logged by Commander Ilo of the Assembly Defense Craft Javvesta / Location: Planet Kora, Aliat Region, Ankari Assembly, May 30, 2438]
The Defense Craft *Skyra* was transporting infected persons to the Primary Medical Facility in the Jakora System. The Infected managed to break their bonds and contaminated the entire hold. According to ship's logs the *Skyra* was overrun in less than one hour, and the ship was later flagged by a navigation satellite on course for the Nientum System. Their ability to operate ship's systems clearly shows that after transformation they retain a certain level of intelligence, at least for a while. Upon arrival the *Skyra* docked with the orbital refueling station and launched escape pods to the planet below, spreading the infection to both the station and the planet. We are currently aiding in evacuation and quarantine of the affected provinces, but several dozen craft have left the system since the *Skyra*'s arrival. I recommend tracking all those vessels immediately and testing the crews to ensure the virus doesn't spread beyond already-afflicted areas.

12

"Captain Marston, I have a potential mission for you and your crew."

Marston raised an eyebrow. *Potential* mission? The *Pericles* was still on its way to the Crown Sector. "If something more urgent than patrolling the Crown Sector has come up, we're more than happy to undertake a mission…"

Admiral Chang interrupted him with a nod. *"The* Nightingale *is helping the Gelrian Royal Navy search for their Crown Prince's missing ship. It's likely their transceiver isn't working because of a simple system malfunction, but with the recent ship disappearances, they're not taking any chances."* The Kingdom of Gelria was one of the member states of the Commonwealth, and their space occupied the Crown Sector. The disappearance of the Gelrian Crown Prince had made headlines across human space; the *Pericles* officers had discussed it at their morning briefing.

"The Nightingale *has joined the search for the* Coronet, *but one of our own ships, the* Searcher, *has also gone missing. The* Searcher *was… well, searching for the* Coronado, *which disappeared near the Shadow Nebula several weeks ago. We haven't been able to contact either ship since the* Searcher *failed to report in nearly ten days ago."*

Marston pulled up a star map of the sector on his screen. "The Shadow Nebula is only three days from here, if you'd like us to investigate…?"

Admiral Chang gave him a long look. It was the same uncertain look he'd gotten from Admirals Bryant and Garcia, Marston noted with a sinking feeling.

"The Pericles *is the closest ship,"* the Admiral said, hesitating. Marston swallowed. *"I know you're new to this, Captain, but if you think your crew is ready for such a mission, it's yours."*

Admiral Chang was giving him a choice. Marston nodded slowly. In his mind it was already settled.

"Of course the *Pericles* will take the mission, Admiral. We can do this," he said confidently. "If the *Searcher* has already been out of contact for more than a week and they need help, we might be the only ones who can get there soon enough."

Admiral Chang seemed satisfied with his response. *"Very well, I'll send you the mission briefing."*

A gold arrow icon on Marston's screen indicated an incoming attachment. He forwarded it to the bridge.

"You can count on us, Admiral. If it's at all possible to rescue the *Searcher* and the *Coronado*, we will."

"Be careful, Captain," Chang cautioned him. *"These ship disappearances are alarming. If we cannot find out who is responsible soon, we might need to consider imposing curfews in affected sectors. We don't want the public to panic, but the Senate is becoming increasingly concerned. If we had the ships to spare, I would have preferred to send an entire task force to the Shadow Nebula."*

"Admiral, do we have any idea what is causing these disappearances?" Marston asked. He felt it was appropriate for him to ask as it was his ship that was potentially at risk. As far as he knew the disappearances were not limited to the Commonwealth but were occurring across known space, so maybe the Navy had learned something from their allies. There were all sorts of theories floating around the datasphere, ranging from a hostile race that had developed cloaking technology to a herd of ship-devouring, space-borne creatures migrating through this part of the galaxy.

"We have no way of knowing why these ships are disappearing," Chang replied tersely. *"Not yet. But Captain Ramiro was, or is, I should say, one of our most experienced officers. If we haven't heard back from him... well, you should be prepared for anything."*

"We will, Admiral," Marston promised, trying to project confidence through the screen. "I'll send you regular mission updates."

"Thank you, Captain. Godspeed." Chang disappeared from the screen, replaced by the Navy logo. Marston uploaded the mission briefing to his datapad and took it over to one of the couches in his office to read. One lost ship was a tragedy, but two in the same place in such a small space of time implied a more dangerous cause. And that wasn't including the mysterious disappearance of the *Coronet*. It could be an as-yet undiscovered anomaly near the nebula that had disabled both ships (or worse), but news of all the ships vanishing over the last few months made him wary. Every year, ships went missing. Some returned, others were lost, but often the cause of their demise was uncovered later by an investigating crew. Except for the past few months, when vanishings had reached an all-time high across the Locality, and no one yet knew what had happened to them. Some of them returned, but if they had revealed what had happened to them, Marston didn't know about it. He realized that if the *Searcher* and *Coronado* were two more casualties of whatever was responsible for the vanishings, the *Pericles* had a unique opportunity to try and uncover what was behind them. Even if in doing so he was putting his own ship and crew at risk.

He returned to the bridge, and his crew looked at him expectantly. "We've been given a new mission," he announced. "Admiral Chang has ordered us to investigate the disappearance of the *Searcher* near the Shadow Nebula."

"When do we leave?" Sirroyo asked.

"Right now," he said, turning to Hasan at the helm. "Set a course for the Shadow Nebula and engage."

"Aye, sir." Hasan's fingers flew over the helm console as he made the calculations for their jump. "It will take three days to reach the nebula."

Marston turned to Balzano. "Once we're underway, assemble the senior staff in the conference room." He stared intently at the viewscreen as though he could unlock the secrets of the nebula from light-years away. "We're going to do this properly."

*

June 1, 2438
Minnen's Laboratory, Palace of the Despot
Iganti Tribal States

"How's the gene mapping coming along, Professor?" Jadus asked.

Minnen looked up from his workstation and blinked his large eyes owlishly. "Very well, Minister. Each genetic secret revealed brings us one step closer to a cure."

"Excellent." Jadus fumbled for her caffeinated drink until she felt Jarren place it in her hands.

"Thanks," she said, smiling tiredly.

"Maybe you should take a break," Jarren suggested.

"I will. Soon," she promised. "I just get so caught up in my work. The Kalavat Plague is fascinating to me, Jarren. It's insidious. The first thing it does is cripple the body's immune response. It takes longer to do this in some species, like the Vlind, which is why they don't manifest the symptoms until much later. It then uses the circulatory system to spread throughout the body."

"It sounds downright malicious to me," Jarren said.

"And at the moment we don't know whether it's natural or engineered. But the Professor should know soon, right Professor?"

"Right you are, Minister!"

"One thing's for certain: it's absolutely brilliant. You couldn't design a more effective biological weapon if your life depended on it." Jarren raised his eyebrows at the grudging respect in her voice.

Minnen was at his workstation with Uxxio, but he was also listening to their conversation. After her last statement his head snapped up, startling Uxxio. He turned in his chair to face the Tuulan For.

"Could you please say that again, Minister? Your last comment."

Jadus looked at him in surprise. "Certainly. I simply said that you could not design a more effective biological weapon if your life depended on it."

Minnen's normally intense eyes looked positively maniacal. "If your life depended on it," he repeated. "If life depended on it..." His voice trailed off, but Jarren could see the cogs of his already active mind going into overdrive.

The others waited patiently for him to explain, but all he said was, "You have given me much to think about, Minister. I shall have a better understanding once I finish this genome mapping." Then he returned to his work.

Jadus wanted to press him further but thought better of it. She didn't want to interrupt his thought process, and she knew that he would share with her any revelations once he was sure himself.

Jarren simply looked at her and shrugged, as if to say *what are you gonna do?* But Jadus suspected it was more than just the quirky behavior of a brilliant scientist. She hoped that the same mind that had devised the cure for the Osaija Virus was on the verge of understanding the Kalavat Plague. She would do everything in her power to help him.

*

June 3, 2438
Interstellar space, near Astral Body NGC 1909 (Shadow Nebula)
Interstellar Commonwealth

The *Pericles* emerged from the slipstream and flew at sub-light speed toward the Shadow Nebula, which loomed in space like a great dark cloud.

The bridge officers took turns reporting the status of the ship's primary systems.

"Sub-light engines are functioning normally."

"Artificial gravity and life support are operating at peak efficiency."

"Weapons systems and shields powered down and ready to activate on your command."

"Passive sensors online, primary sensors in standby mode and available at your command, Captain."

Marston nodded with satisfaction. "Good. Let's see what's out there. And keep the slipstream drive on standby, as a precaution. I hope I'm just being overcautious, but better safe than sorry." Balzano nodded emphatically in agreement. After discussing the issue at length during the staff briefing, they had decided to treat the disappearance of the *Searcher* and *Coronado* as suspicious. *Something* had been happening to ships all over the Locality that was causing them to vanish, and until they knew what, the *Pericles* crew were taking no chances.

"I am activating primary sensors and beginning a short-range sweep," Sirroyo said, instructing the computer to begin probing the nebula and surrounding space.

From his auxiliary station at the rear of the bridge, Ensign Jason Moros commented, "They should call it the Ghost Nebula. It looks spooky!"

"There's already a Ghost Nebula," Clarke reminded the young man.

"Take us to the last known position of the *Searcher*," Balzano ordered. Hasan adjusted their course.

Sirroyo was examining sensor data. "We're not detecting any ships in the area, Captain," she reported.

"Any sign of debris?" Balzano asked.

She shook her head. "None that I can see."

Marston pursed his lips thoughtfully. "Something happened to them. Ships don't just disappear without leaving a trace."

"We're at the last known co-ordinates of the *Searcher*, Captain," Hasan announced after a few minutes, bringing the ship to a stop in the misty outer edge of the nebula. Tendrils of gas swirled around them. Marston was surprised the *Searcher* had come this close to the nebula. Most ships avoided traversing nebulas because of the sensor-occluding pockets of gas and the unpredictable gravity currents. At best the gravity currents made for a bumpy ride, at worst they could knock a ship off course or tear it in half. The *Pericles'* position on the fringe of the cloud kept them out of range of the powerful gravity currents; at this distance they were almost unnoticeable, like standing in the small waves lapping at the edge of a lake. But Marston didn't want to venture any deeper.

"Can you detect the energy residue left by their sub-light engines?" he inquired.

"Not after this much time has passed," responded Sirroyo. "Their trail would have dissipated days ago."

"At least there's no sign of battle," Hasan pointed out.

"That's true," Marston conceded. The *Searcher's* absence was a mystery, but one he was determined to solve. He was still hoping to find the ship intact and its crew alive. That was the most optimistic outcome. Plus, he admitted privately, he didn't want one of his first missions as captain to end on a low note.

"The *Searcher* was investigating the disappearance of the *Coronado*. Do we know that ship's last location?"

"According to the *Searcher's* last mission update the *Coronado's* last signal came from this general area," Sirroyo reported. "But I'm not detecting any trace of, well, *anything* out of the ordinary. Just nebula gas and background radiation."

"If the *Searcher* was destroyed, there will be evidence," Balzano said. "I recommend we search the area."

"Agreed," said Marston. "They were investigating the *Coronado's* distress signal, so it's logical to assume they would have been trying to localize the source. Lieutenant Hasan, create a search pattern and engage at half of sub-light speed."

"Aye, Captain. Course plotted and laid in."

"Lieutenant Sirroyo, maintain short-range scans. If there's anything up ahead, I want to know."

"Yes, Captain."

The viewscreen feed grew darker as they penetrated further into the nebula. It was like venturing into a dark cave, Marston thought. Even the Gorgons were only visible as three dim circles of light to their starboard. Marston looked around at his officers. They went about their duties, but there was a subdued air on the bridge. Everyone was wondering about the fate of the *Searcher*. And Marston noticed that everyone except for Sirroyo kept glancing at the nebula that encompassed them. They were now well and truly inside the nebula, and the ship began to sway as the gravity currents of the nebula swirled around them.

Hasan used attitude control thrusters to keep the ship on course. "Sorry about the bumpy ride." He was hunched over the helm console as though personally trying to resist the pull of the nebula's gravity currents.

"That's fine, Lieutenant. Just keep—"

"Captain, there's something on sensors," Sirroyo interrupted. Marston turned to her for an explanation. "It's hard to tell what from this distance," she said. "But it's big, and it's moving closer." She frowned. "Let me be more specific: it's heading directly toward us."

"Could it be the *Searcher* or *Coronado*?" Marston asked.

"Negative, it is significantly larger than either vessel."

"I recommend we raise shields and power weapons," Clarke said.

Marston agreed. "Do it," he ordered. "Take the ship to combat readiness."

Alarm klaxons sounded throughout the ship, and crewmembers hurried to their battle stations. The energy shields activated, enveloping the *Pericles* in a protective bubble, and protective plating slid across all the windows on the ship, including the bridge. The light panels on the walls and consoles turned red, bathing the bridge in a bloody glow. Clarke put a tactical overlay of the area on the viewscreen for all of them to see. At the center was the white icon indicating the *Pericles*, and from the top right of the image a large, arrow-shaped red icon was rapidly approaching.

"Bring us about to face the ship," Marston ordered, and the *Pericles* turned to face the oncoming unknown vessel. "Full power to forward shields and keep the weapons hot, just in case." He wasn't prepared to shoot first, on the off chance it was simply a misunderstanding with an alien species who didn't know how to communicate with them. Although he strongly doubted that was the case.

"It's within five kilometers," Sirroyo warned.

"Put it on the viewscreen. I want to see it," Marston said.

Clarke removed the tactical display and the screen flicked back to the real-time image of space directly ahead of them. Against the dark nebula there was an even darker blur, growing larger. Then the great, pointed prow of a ship resolved out of the mists. As it fully emerged from the clouds, they could see it was long and angular and comprised of either dark blue or steel grey material, but it was impossible to tell accurately.

"It's big," Hasan said. "Over twelve hundred meters long."

"I've never seen any ship like that before," Balzano said.

"Neither have I," Sirroyo said. "It doesn't match any known configuration, but I'm detecting energy signatures that could indicate weapons charging."

Marston stood to his feet. "Broadcast on all subspace radio bands: this is the Commonwealth Starship *Pericles*. You are trespassing in our territory. Please identify yourself."

The ship loomed larger on the viewscreen.

"No response," Balzano said after a while.

"Captain that ship is the equivalent of a battleship class," Clarke reported. "We're outmatched."

"Then we're not sticking around to fight them," Marston decided. "Helm, get us out of the nebula!"

The *Pericles* rotated gracefully in space, but hull cameras kept feeding images of the unknown ship to the bridge. The deck thrummed with energy as Hasan brought the engines to full power and sent the ship speeding back the way they had come. The unknown ship accelerated, pursuing them.

"They're chasing us!" Hasan said unnecessarily; everyone could see it on the viewscreen. An alarm squawked at Clarke's tactical console as three sinuous, tentacle-like appendages shot out from the alien ship.

"Evasive maneuvers!" Marston shouted, but it was too late. With a *thump* the tentacles made contact, latching onto the *Pericles* with claw-like grapplers. The deck lurched violently as the alien vessel began reeling them in.

"Full power to the engines," ordered Balzano, grasping the arms of his chair tightly, willing the frigate to break free of the grapplers restraining it.

"It's too strong," Hasan said frantically. "We're being pulled in!" The alien battleship grew larger on the viewscreen.

"Target missiles on the lines and fire," Marston ordered.

"Firing missiles," Clarke said with relish as he opened fire. Missiles soared out of the *Pericles* and crashed into the lines pulling them in. Three bright flashes lit up the nebula but as the fire faded, they saw the lines were undamaged.

"They're protected by energy shields," Clarke said, frustrated. Two umbilical tunnels with glowing laser cutters at their ends extended from the alien ship. In his imagination Marston saw them penetrating the *Pericles'* hull and the corridors of his ship flooded with alien monsters.

"We need ideas, and quickly," he said, looking around at his officers.

"We could depolarize the hull," said Sirroyo quickly, speaking as the idea formed. "That might repel the grapplers."

"They're dug into the hull," Clarke reminded her. "We need to physically cut them out..."

"Then do it," Marston ordered the tactical officer. "Put on EVA suits, seal off those sections of the ship and cut off the hull if you have to."

"Captain, the hull is made of tri-magnesium alloy," Clarke reminded him. "There's no way we could cut through—"

"Do what you can," the captain instructed him. "If you weaken it, we might be able to shake them loose."

"On it," said Clarke, sprinting for the lift. Balzano replaced him at the tactical console. It was his former station and Marston knew he was as capable as Clarke.

The *Pericles* struggled against the lines restraining it but failed to break free. "Captain, we're twenty-two hundred meters from the alien ship," Hasan advised.

"Keep the engines at full power," Marston told him. "Make it as difficult as possible for them."

Sirroyo looked at the captain, the faintest hint of fear creeping into her voice. "Captain, unless we can find a way to break loose, I estimate we will be pulled to the alien vessel in less than four minutes."

Marston shared a look with his executive officer. "Understood."

Henry Clarke and the rest of Security Team Alpha placed sticky explosives on the roof and walls of the corridor. The ceiling was buckled where one of the grapplers had latched on, and the metal groaned under the stress.

"Quickly," he urged, watching as members of his team placed the last two charges on the ceiling. Bravo and Delta Teams reported in they had also finished placing the charges at their respective locations, where the other two grapplers were gripping the ship.

He activated his communicator. "Clarke to bridge. We've set the charges," he reported.

"Good. Get out of there and detonate them ASAP. We've got less than a minute before contact with the alien vessel."

"Will do, Captain. Clarke out." He and his security team ran down the hall into the next section, closing the emergency bulkheads behind them.

He flipped open the trigger and pressed it with his thumb. The corridor rocked as the charges blew, and he could dimly hear the explosions from the other two teams. He looked through the glass portal of the pressure doors to see the blackened corridor and sparking wires flapping as the air rushed out into space through jagged tears in the ceiling.

"Let's hope that was enough," he said to his deputies.

On the bridge, they felt rather than heard the detonations a few decks above. Marston winced, unhappy at deliberately wounding their own ship, but knowing it was their best chance of escape. "Show me the hull."

Sirroyo relayed images from hull-mounted cameras to the viewscreen so they could see the effects of the explosive charges. Two of them still gripped the hull, but atmosphere leaked from tears in the hull plates between their sharp claws. The third grappler's hold was significantly weakened, its grip on the crumpled hull tenuous.

"Get a controlled pitch going," Balzano instructed Hasan. "Let's see if we can shake them loose."

"Aye, Commander." Hasan activated the ship's reaction control thrusters. The ship began rocking side-to-side, the sudden change in momentum making everyone hold on tightly to their workstations. They heard the groaning of metal as the alien ship's hold on the *Pericles* loosened.

"It's working," Sirroyo announced.

With a metallic screech one of the grapplers broke loose, ripping off a section of hull plating with it. Now the full weight of the ship was held by just two grapplers. The tug-of-war between the *Pericles'* straining engines and the alien vessel reeling them in the opposite direction pulled the grappling cables so taut that soon they lost their grip on the hull completely. With a shudder and a jolt, the *Pericles* broke free and accelerated away from the enemy ship.

The crew of the alien ship must have been taken by surprise because they failed to react instantly. Their seconds of hesitation were all their intended victims needed.

The *Pericles* was an Interceptor-class frigate; it was built for speed. It thundered out of the nebula, and the enemy ship slowly gave chase.

"We're pulling ahead of them," Hasan reported.

"But they're still following," Balzano pointed out.

The elevator doors opened, and Clarke stepped onto the bridge, grinning in triumph. Balzano slapped him on the back as he stepped back to allow the tactical officer to resume his station. Marston joined the two of them at the tactical console and they silently studied the ship pursuing them.

Clarke's brow furrowed with concern. "We're increasing the distance between us, but much slower than I would have thought. For a battleship, that ship is pretty fast."

"We'll see how long they want to keep up the chase for," Marston said with grim determination. "Engage the slipstream drive."

Whorls of blue-white energy surrounded the *Pericles* as it dove into slipspace, propelling them away from the Shadow Nebula at superluminal velocity. The alien ship pursued them doggedly into slipspace, but it quickly began to fall further behind.

"They can't keep up!" Hasan said. "We're going to outrun them!"

Marston frowned. Unless the alien ship could somehow increase its maximum speed, their escape was guaranteed. "Maybe we don't want to," Marston said slowly.

Hasan and Clarke looked at him incredulously, but Balzano nodded comprehendingly. "This could be our best chance to learn about them, and what they were doing in the nebula," the executive officer said.

"Yes. If we can lure them into our own ambush, maybe we can find out why they've been ambushing and abducting ships in our space," Marston said. He turned to Sirroyo. "Can we send a message to the Commonwealth?"

"Yes."

"Send the following message to Command and all Navy ships in the sector," Marston said, clearing his throat. "This is the CNV *Pericles*. We are being pursued by an unknown and hostile alien vessel, battleship class. We are at these co-ordinates-" he gestured to Balzano, who obligingly attached their location and projected course, "-and request assistance."

"Message sent," Sirroyo said.

They did not have to wait long for a reply.

"Captain, we're being hailed," Clarke reported a few minutes later.

"Let's hear it," said Marston.

A middle-aged man appeared on the viewscreen. "Pericles, *this is Captain Greenbiar of the* Lautaro. *We received your message and will assist you. What's your status?"*

"It's good to hear from you, *Lautaro*. We are still being pursued by the alien ship." Marston knew of Greenbiar by reputation only, as the captain who famously captured the elusive pirate known as the Red Fox. "We have the ability to outrun them, but it's very likely these aliens are responsible for the local ship disappearances, and this may be an opportunity for us to apprehend them."

Greenbiar looked thoughtful. Although they were the same rank, Marston knew it would be wise to defer to his experience; his reputation as one of the best commanders in the Commonwealth fleet was well-earned. *"I agree,"* Greenbiar said after a moment. *"The best course of action is to engage them from a stronger defensive position. What is the nearest world to you?"*

Hasan hastily examined a star map of the region. "Ennomos is six hours away," he said.

"Ennomos," Marston told Greenbiar.

"A mining world. It has a small population, so the risk to civilians is minimal. How soon can you get there?"

"We can make it there in six hours," Marston informed him.

"Head for Ennomos," Greenbiar said. *"I'll gather reinforcements and meet you in orbit."*

Marston nodded. "We'll see you in six hours."

"Acknowledged, Pericles. Lautaro *out."* Greenbiar disappeared from the screen.

"Diverting course to Ennomos," Hasan said before the captain had to ask.

"Captain, we'll need to change our course by forty-five degrees to port. That will allow the alien ship to gain on us."

"It can't be helped," said the captain pragmatically. "And anyway, we don't want to outrun them too easily. Decrease speed so that we're just outside their weapons range. Make it look like an engine malfunction or battle damage so it's less suspicious."

"Changing course now," responded Hasan. The *Pericles* banked to port as he aligned the ship with Ennomos.

*

The hours passed slowly for Marston. He paced the bridge restlessly until he noticed Balzano giving him a pointed look and immediately returned to his seat, not wanting to seem nervous in front of the crew. He kept glancing at the time to their destination; every minute felt like an hour. Finally, after an eternity, the *Pericles* entered the Ennomos system.

"We'll exit the slipstream in less than one minute," Hasan announced. Their destination, the volcanic world of Ennomos, was located three Astronomical Units from its star. Despite the distance, the planet's surface temperature was warm by human standards due to the thick atmosphere that trapped the heat generated by more than three thousand active volcanoes. From orbit, the planet's mountain ranges were identifiable as dark red ridges crisscrossing plains of yellow sulphur and orange native basalt. The barely breathable atmosphere was comprised of sulphur, carbon dioxide, nitrogen, and some oxygen. Even the sky had a red tinge.

What first attracted humans to the planet were the vast deposits of iron, palladium and corzantium, a vital element needed to power the slipstream drives used by spacefaring civilizations. Although humans could live on the planet with the aid of breathing apparatuses, all three major settlements were covered with atmospheric domes to contain the type-1 atmosphere breathed by humans. The planet had a human population of around two hundred thousand, located in the three main settlements and the smaller satellite mining facilities. The planet's economy was based almost exclusively on mining activities, although one of the settlements in the northern hemisphere had a small shipyard capable of servicing most Commonwealth ships.

Ennomos also attracted many scientists during its slightly less inhospitable winter months, mostly vulcanologists and geologists to study its earthquake and volcanic activity, and biologists eager to examine the hardy life that existed there. Although inhospitable by human standards, the volcanic world did support its own limited flora, which was mainly concentrated along the shores of the planet's two small seas. Plant life, despite living under a sky choked with dust and ash, did photosynthesize, producing oxygen.

Fearing that the planet's mineral wealth would make it a tempting target for pirates or hostile aliens, the corporate leaders of Ennomos had invested in two orbital defense platforms, one above each of the planet's poles. Holding position near Platform One above the planet's northern hemisphere were the *Lautaro* and the four other Navy ships in Captain Greenbiar's squadron, which had been passing through the sector on their way to the border. The *Lautaro* was accompanied by the *Valiant*, a cruiser of the same class, and the smaller Vigilance-class scout ship *Watchman*.

Protecting their flanks were the escort ships *Gemini* and *Sentinel*, all with defensive shields raised and weapons charged. They waited, in a delta formation, for the enemy to arrive.

A slipstream portal opened, and the *Pericles* cannoned out of it at full speed, adjusting course and making for the Navy ships. It sent out a warning message: "*The enemy is right behind us.*"

Seconds later, a much larger portal opened, and the alien battleship appeared.

"Open fire," Captain Greenbiar ordered.

The Navy starships unleashed the full fury of their weapons against the alien vessel. Missiles streaked through space and impacted against the enemy ship's shields in bright explosions. Turrets fired, showering it with super-heated rounds. The alien vessel lumbered toward the Navy ships, opening fire with all its forward weapons. Under the expert guidance of Greenbiar's helmsman the *Lautaro* managed to evade the incoming fire, but the *Valiant* was not so lucky. The ship shuddered as the alien barrage impacted against its shields. The fire would have destroyed a lesser ship, but the Defender-class cruiser came about, firing all its starboard weapons at the aliens.

"Flank the enemy ship," Greenbiar ordered the squadron. The starships peeled off along either side of the giant vessel, the *Lautaro*, *Watchman* and *Gemini* pounding the port side with cannons and missiles, and the *Valiant*, *Sentinel* and *Pericles* attacking the starboard side.

"Tell the platform to fire when ready," Greenbiar said to his communications officer.

On the planet below, technicians working in the Orbital Defense Control Center watched the battle unfold on giant wall-mounted monitors. As the Navy ships flanked the enemy ship, they activated the maneuvering jets on the defense platform, aligning its primary cannon with the enemy ship. As soon as the computer informed them of a clean lock on the target, the chief technician fired.

The magnetic accelerator cannon boomed, propelling a super-heated slug of titanium toward the enemy ship at just under the speed of sound. The alien ship shuddered under the impact and its shields flared, then faded. The technicians on the planet cheered and the cannon began its reloading cycle.

The Navy ships circled the enemy like a pack of wolves trying to bring down a bear. The enemy was wounded, but it fought back viciously. It focused all its fury on a single target: the *Valiant*.

Captain Marston watched the cruiser tremble as the enemy ship concentrated fire on the *Valiant*'s starboard blade. Its starboard engines sputtered out and the ship began to list. The enemy struck again, and there was a blinding flash. The *Pericles* bridge crew had to shield their eyes from the glare. When the fireball faded all that remained of the *Valiant* was an expanding cloud of debris.

"Scan for survivors," Marston ordered.

Sirroyo probed the wreckage with sensors, then shook her head sadly.

"Bring us around and prepare to fire the MAC," Marston said, eyeing the enemy ship predatorily. Navy ships utilized a magnetic accelerator cannon as their primary weapon, which were generally smaller versions of those found on orbital defense platforms. Except on battleships and dreadnoughts, which carried larger, more powerful cannons.

The orbital defense platform fired again, and its supersized projectile ripped a hole clean through the enemy ship. Atmospheric gases and debris spewed into space.

"Focus on the engines," Greenbiar instructed the ships. *"We need to disable it, not destroy it."*

"You heard him," said Marston. "Target the engines and fire the main cannon."

The *Pericles, Lautaro* and *Watchman* fired their MAC cannons while the *Sentinel* and *Gemini* launched a flurry of missiles. The fire in the alien ship's engines died and the vessel, already reeling from the MAC blow, began spiraling toward the planet.

"Cease fire," Greenbiar ordered.

Caught by the irresistible pull of the planet's gravity, the alien ship continued to spiral downwards, hull plates flaking off and atmosphere venting from a dozen different places. The underside began to glow dull red as it entered Ennomos' atmosphere.

Its rapid descent was tracked by satellites and the Navy ships in orbit. Some of the alien vessel's thrusters still functioned and it managed to slow its descent and keep the bow level with the horizon. But thrusters weren't enough to stop its rapid plunge, and the alien ship slammed into the scorched surface at over one hundred kilometers an hour. Churning up a cloud of dust and boulders, the battleship gouged a four-kilometer-long trench in the rocky surface before grinding to a halt at the base of a small mountain.

"The ship is down," Sirroyo reported in the silence that followed. "It's heavily damaged, but intact."

"Scan for life forms," Balzano instructed, although he didn't know how any person, alien or not, could have survived the impact of the crash.

"I can't detect any," the sensor operations officer said after a moment.

"The *Lautaro* is hailing us, Captain," Clarke said.

"Put it through the speakers."

"This is Captain Greenbiar. Good job, everyone. We managed to disable the enemy ship without destroying it, although the cost was high." Greenbiar paused for a moment before continuing. *"The deaths of the* Valiant *crew are a tragic loss for the Navy,"* he said solemnly, *"And neither they nor their bravery will be forgotten. Let's honor their sacrifice and get some answers from the alien ship below…"*

Marston's crew had narrowly avoided the same fate as the *Valiant* or the *Searcher* and won their first battle. But who were these aliens, and why were they attacking ships? Were there more of them in the Shadow Nebula? He regarded the orange-brown surface of Ennomos on the viewscreen; the answers lay in the crashed ship on the planet below.

But first things first: they had to assess the damage to their own ship, conduct repairs and make their report to Command. It was likely the Admiralty would want to send a stronger force to investigate the Shadow Nebula.

The *Gemini* and the *Sentinel* began their descent toward the crash site to secure the alien ship. It had to be studied, which would require the Commonwealth's best scientific minds.

Marston sensed his executive officer approach and stop just behind him. "Captain, the casualty reports are in. Several crewmembers were injured, but there are no fatalities."

"Thank you, Commander," said Marston, relieved. "Have all department heads submit damage reports and begin repairs. We need to investigate the ship we just shot down."

*

June 4, 2438
Vinkere dreadnaught *Z'Tauron*, Shadow Nebula
Interstellar Commonwealth

Supreme Commander Zithla, formerly Consul, prowled the bridge of his battlecruiser like a predator on the hunt. As his shadow passed over his officers, they cowered involuntarily, fearful of his well-earned reputation for venting his fury on his subordinates.

Zithla and Slethis had been chosen by the Triumvirates to oversee the destruction of their adversaries. Now, thanks to Slethis' foolishness, Zithla was the sole commander of the Vinkere military forces in the Ss'Talak Cluster. Slethis' final and greatest blunder had been to attempt to capture a human ship sent to investigate their missing counterparts. Not only had he spectacularly failed to do this, but he had revealed their presence and his vessel had been shot down by the inferior humans.

Naturally, Zithla was furious. Slethis had failed his people and jeopardized their mission. It had taken years of meticulous planning and careful maneuvering to get to this point, and Slethis had put everything at risk. If by some chance Slethis had survived the crash, Zithla would kill him. Zithla's only consolation was that today, on the eve of the implementation of Phase Three of their Great Plan, it was too late for the humans to do anything anyway.

He returned to the command podium and activated a large, holographic map of the Locality. He zoomed in on the Commonwealth and examined it with a familiar eye. Ennomos. Gelria. Khoveria. Earth. Zithla had committed almost all its worlds to memory, and it was he who had determined which planets to occupy and which to eradicate in the first wave of Phase Three. There were far more planets in the latter category than the former.

The Vinkere had obtained a perfect star map of human space from the *Endeavor*, which had been found adrift in the Vinkere home system eight years ago, alongside a derelict Ankari vessel. The map enabled them to plan their invasion of the Commonwealth with unrivaled precision. And the technology cannibalized from both vessels allowed them to retrofit the expansive Vinkere fleet with powerful new weapons.

By some miraculous quirk of biology, the humans were immune to the biological weapon covertly unleashed in the Locality by the Vinkere. It made them the perfect first target of an invasion that would sweep across the Locality, exterminating all intelligent life forms who existed in defiance of the Vinkeres' ruling doctrine: *Vinkere only*. Nobody would come to the humans' aid, because they were all busy struggling to contain their own infected citizens. Even those close allies of humanity would be too weak and disorganized to do anything but watch in terror as the Interstellar Commonwealth fell to the Vinkere Dominion.

For several months Zithla's forces had been abducting vessels from across the Locality; the captured crews were studied to improve Vinkere knowledge of their adversaries. Most were then executed, although some were deliberately infected with the Ss'kapp'rn Plague and released again amongst their own people. Sometimes the Vinkere used multiple vectors to infect heavily populated planets, as they had done on the world known as Indegra. The delayed physical manifestation of the Ss'kapp'rn Plague meant that entire worlds had been infected before the unsuspecting natives of the Locality knew what was going on. The infection of the Kelzee and Kithel species had been particularly effective; the plague spread so aggressively that millions of them were infected within a matter of days. Zithla and his soldiers had taken great delight in observing the ensuing chaos.

The only setback so far was the escape of the human ship *Pericles* and the destruction of Slethis' ship at Ennomos. Other human ships sent to the Shadow Nebula had been captured and destroyed to preserve the secrecy of the Vinkere presence. But the *Pericles* was fast—faster than any other ships they'd encountered— and had lured Consul Slethis into a trap like he was a novice. And because of Slethis' blunder, a Commonwealth fleet was now approaching the Shadow Nebula and Zithla's hidden armada.

S'Gelliss approached him and bowed. "The human ships will reach the cloud in two days," he reported. "Scans indicate they are at full battle readiness."

"How many ships?"

"Eighteen."

Zithla snorted dismissively. "We will crush them."

S'Geliss nodded. "I also have news of the Iganti. The Warrior Queen has entered open rebellion against the Despot. Her forces are surrounding the Iganti home world like a tightening noose, and soon she will seize control..."

"... eliminating the Tuulan For minister and Iganti scientist in the process," Zithla finished, baring his fangs in an evil smile.

He turned back to the map of the Locality. The stars of the Interstellar Commonwealth shone like jewels, ripe for the taking. Soon he would initiate Phase Three, and there would be no humans left. Vinkere only.

13

"Jarren! Wake up!"

"Huh?" Jarren sat up drowsily in bed and glanced at the window; the suns were only just touching the horizon. It was still early.

He closed his eyes. "Go away," he mumbled.

The thumping on his door grew louder. Antak clearly wasn't going to be ignored.

Groaning, Jarren relented. "Come in." The door opened and his friend strode in, grinning. Jarren glared at him. "What do you want?" he demanded grumpily. "It's too early."

"We've been invited to accompany the Despot on a hunting trip," Antak announced.

Jarren stifled a yawn. "Why us?"

"We're his honored guests. Minister Jadus gave us permission to attend in her place, and the Despot agreed."

"What about Korosa?"

"She insisted on staying with the Minister," Antak said.

"Naturally."

"Get ready, quickly. I'll meet you at the west gate in fifteen minutes," said Antak. He beamed. "Finally, we get to leave the palace!"

He left, and Jarren closed his eyes again, savoring a few more moments of quiet.

"Don't go back to sleep!" Antak called.

"I'm not!" Jarren rolled out of bed, groaning. He dressed quickly and washed his face, drying himself with one of the incredibly soft, luxurious towels their hosts had provided. He spent several minutes trying to decide what the most appropriate clothing was for a royal hunt in the Iganti desert, then panicked when he realized how little time he had left. There was no time for a proper breakfast, so he grabbed a large, round fruit from the bowl in the common room that the palace servants kept refilling. Leaving their guest suite, he hurried through the cool stone corridors of the palace. The palace was busier than normal as the staff packed hastily, preparing to move the Despot's household to the royal hunting lodge outside the city. Jarren paused once to get directions from a servant half-hidden behind a pile of freshly laundered clothes, then continued at a jog. He exited the palace and hurried across the green, manicured lawn, under a portico, and onto the main road.

Hundreds of Iganti were gathered in front of the palace's west gate; courtiers, government officials, a veritable army of servants, and a large contingent of the royal guards who watched over Krant twenty-seven hours a day.

There were also dozens of large, four-legged mammals Jarren had never seen before. Stable hands were equipping them with cloth saddles; leather was too hot for the animals *and* the riders in the dry Iganti desert. Jarren watched several of the nobles, dressed in elaborate hunting clothes, hoist themselves into the saddles with practiced ease.

The day was still young, but it was already hot by Tuulan For standards. Jarren spotted Antak standing in the shade of the trees lining the entrance to the gate. He was eyeing one of the mounts cautiously as a stable hand groomed its rough flanks. "They expect us to ride those things," he said dubiously as his friend approached. "Apparently the Iganti have hunted on the backs of these creatures for thousands of years, so we will be riding forth like the Iganti of old." Antak didn't sound pleased at the prospect.

Jarren spotted another familiar face in a group of young courtiers. "Look! It's Uxxio." Minnen's assistant spotted them and waved. When they waved back, he approached.

"Good morning to you," he greeted them.

"Morning, Uxxio. Are you coming on the hunt?" Jarren asked.

Uxxio nodded. "Yes."

"No offence, but you don't seem like the hunting type," said Antak.

The young Iganti didn't seem offended. "You are correct," he said affably. "I am here for the same reason that you are. As you are participating in the hunt on behalf of Minister Jadus, I am here to represent Professor Minnen."

Word spread that Krant was on his way. A servant approached the trio, leading three of the four-legged animals. Uxxio thanked him and took the reins.

"Here comes the fun part," Antak muttered. His ride snorted and gave him a disinterested look.

"Let me show you how to mount the gontu," said Uxxio. He grasped the saddle with his left hand, placed his left foot in the stirrup and vaulted onto the animal's back in one nimble motion. "Do it quickly, and confidently; too slow and they may try and shake you off."

Jarren and Antak exchanged glances. Antak took an intrepid step toward his gontu; it *mwaaaad* at him, and he stepped back in surprise. Jarren laughed.

Uxxio held the gontu's reins and gestured for Antak to approach again. With a determined look, Antak put his foot on the stirrup and practically leaped onto the creature's back. It was nowhere near as graceful as Uxxio, but he was soon sitting comfortably in the saddle.

"That wasn't too bad," he said with relief. Jarren approached his animal. It was a similar size to the korau on his uncle's farm, and he hoisted himself into the saddle without too much difficulty.

"It looks like you've done this before," Antak commented, impressed. He lurched in surprise as the animal beneath him shook the dust of its haunches, and Jarren laughed again.

Ignoring him, Antak asked, "How long are we supposed to ride these?"

"We should reach the Despot's hunting lodge by nightfall," Uxxio said.

"Oh, great."

Horns sounded, signifying the arrival of Krant the Despot. There was a loud, if not completely cheerful, shout from the crowd as he appeared, riding in a litter on the back of an enormous brown animal the size of the *elephants* Jarren had seen in a human zoo as a child. He wiped the sweat from his brow; it was still early morning, but it was already hot.

The lead hunters brayed their horns, sounding the advance. Slowly, and with Krant in the lead, the procession of people and animals filtered through the gates of the palace and into the city. Jarren's gontu seemed content to follow those in front of him, and it fell into step between Uxxio and Antak's animals.

Antak looked back over his shoulder. There must have been at least a thousand people in the convoy, which stretched hundreds of meters down the road behind them. The Despot was protected by his guards, who rode tall, lithe animals that looked much nimbler than the cow-like gontus. Behind them the courtiers and government officials followed, which included Uxxio, Jarren and Antak. Jarren felt a twinge of sympathy for the servants who brought up the rear and were forced to trudge along the dusty road beside the pack animals which bore the food, furniture, and luxury items necessary to make Krant's stay at the hunting lodge a comfortable one.

As the procession made its way through the streets, the citizens of Bandako parted to let them through. Jarren found it disconcerting how quiet the crowd was; mostly they watched in stony silence as the Despot and his party rode past. There were more than a few angry-looking faces in the crowd. And sadly, more than once he spotted beggars and hungry-looking children hoping for some money or food.

After an hour, the suburbs of the city thinned out into small clumps of mud-brick homes. Soon these outskirt villages gave way to a vast expanse of desert that stretched to the shimmering horizon. Jarren shielded his face and squinted into the distance; only the occasional hardy desert plant and rocky, low-lying hill marred the horizon. He could not imagine a greater contrast between Bandako and its surrounds and that of the coastal capital of Tuulan Vee surrounded by verdant farmland.

A hot breeze picked up, blowing dust into their eyes, covering their clothing and luggage. The Iganti appeared untroubled by the dust or the heat and chatted animatedly with each other as though it were a simple outing to the local grocery store.

Uxxio had had the foresight to bring along protective sun cream, which the two Tuulan For gratefully accepted. The Iganti wore wide-brimmed hats to protect their bald heads from the sun, and Jarren found it helped keep his head cool and shielded his eyes from the glare of the twin suns, which now beat down mercilessly.

After a couple of hours Uxxio informed them that they were entering the land reserved for the Despot's own hunting and recreation. The hunting lodge sat at the center of the great reserve, which the young Iganti told them stretched for nearly seventy kilometers in every direction. Trespassers were shot on sight. Jarren cast a dubious look at the desolate landscape around them, and quietly asked why the Despot would care about keeping this land for himself. What made it different to any other patch of dirt on the planet?

"Underground is a very different story," Uxxio told him. "Bandako was built on an oasis: the lake at the center of the palace grounds is fed by underground springs. That is the only place the water naturally reaches the surface, but the same artesian basin that feeds the lake extends for hundreds of kilometers in all directions. It provides the city with water and collects in the many caverns that exist beneath the surface of this continent."

"Huh." Jarren had assumed the lake was artificial.

Antak looked down. "There are caverns beneath us?"

"About fifteen percent of the ground beneath us is hollow, yes," Uxxio said. "And life flourishes in those underground spaces. Many surface-dwelling creatures make their nests there as it provides shelter and water."

"How deep are these caverns?" Jarren asked curiously. He pictured a vast underground world containing cool, crystal lakes and waterfalls and an entire ecosystem of plants and animals considered alien to the world above.

"Not very deep. On average they extend no further than one hundred meters below the surface. In some places there are tunnels that lead to the surface. Some were created by burrowing animals, and others by our people searching for water."

Antak considered the combined weight of the hunting party and their animals. "Do you ever worry that the ground will collapse into one of the caves?"

Uxxio shrugged. "It's lasted this long."

"Have you ever been in the caverns?" Jarren asked him.

"A few times I have gone with the professor to collect fungi and plant samples," Uxxio said, "But it is cool and wet and I do not like it."

The procession halted occasionally so that the Despot could converse with the scouts who had rushed ahead and returned with reports of a large animal sighted. Tefrax, Uxxio explained to Jarren and Antak. Omnivores, and some of the largest creatures that lived in the desert. They weren't particularly aggressive outside of mating season, but they were fast and their meat was considered a delicacy, which made them the Despot's preferred sport.

Whenever the scouts reported a sighting, several of the despot's soldiers and noblemen would gallop after it on their steeds. Although they rode the same mounts used by their people for centuries, the hunters' weapons were modern, high-powered pulse rifles. Jarren and Antak were amazed at how agile the tefrax was for such a large creature, able to change direction in a single bound, which made aiming difficult for the hunters. At one point the scouts managed to herd the tefrax to within a few dozen meters of the expedition, and Krant stood up in his litter, roaring with laughter at the attempts of the hunters to bring down the nimble animal. At one point he even took the steed from one of his royal guards and galloped off on the hunt with a handful of his guards and noblemen, leaving the rest of the hunting party to wait patiently for their return.

Uxxio was unimpressed. "It's not a real hunt," he told them quietly. "The scouts run ahead and corral the creatures toward the hunting party to put on a show for the Despot. Other times they bring animals they captured earlier and release them near the road for his men to hunt. It's bad sport, if you ask me."

It was early evening when they finally sighted the imperial hunting lodge in the distance, and the suns were touching the horizon by the time they passed through its gates. Like the Despot's palace the hunting lodge was surrounded by high, mud-brick walls. The landscape within the walls was a stark contrast to the desert outside; ornamental ponds and artificial streams watered the thick, green grass and the fruit trees growing in neat lines along pathways. Slender, purple birds with long beaks waded through the shallows and plucked at tiny, colorful fish.

"At last," said Antak with relief. The ride had been hot and uncomfortable and he was eager to rest his tired muscles.

A small army of stable hands were waiting for them inside the gate and rushed over to help people disembark from their mounts, which were then led away to the stables. Even Jarren, who was used to riding the *korau* on his uncle's farm, was pleased to get off the animal. "It feels good to stand up again," he said, stretching.

"That's an understatement," said Antak, shaking his arms and legs vigorously.

A servant approached and spoke to Uxxio. Jarren and Antak had picked up a few words in the native language, but not enough for them to follow the rapid conversation.

"The Despot will be hosting a banquet in a short while," Uxxio told them when the servant had left.

"Will we have enough time to shower and change into clean clothes?" Jarren asked.

Before Uxxio could reply a thin, elderly Iganti in long robes approached them and bowed.

"Welcome, honored guests," he said in slightly accented Trade Standard. "If you would care to follow me, I will show you to your accommodation."

"Thank you," said Jarren. The attendant bowed again and then led them down a white gravel pathway toward the main building. It was dark now, but lights from the building's windows bathed the lawn in golden light and small lamps placed amongst the flowers beside the path helped illuminate their way.

They entered the main lodge and the attendant led them up a wide stone staircase. The architectural style was like the palace, Jarren noted, and just as decadent. They walked down a long corridor with white and gold painted walls and thick grey carpet before reaching a set of wooden doors. The attendant fished a set of keys out his pocket.

"These are the quarters assigned to Master Droma," he said, gesturing through the door. Antak sauntered into the spacious room.

"This will do," he deadpanned. By now they were accustomed to Iganti luxury.

The attendant took another key and opened the next door. "These are the quarters assigned to Master Qel."

"Thank you," said Jarren.

The attendant turned to Uxxio. "If you will kindly follow me, sir, your suite is on the next floor."

Uxxio turned to Jarren. "I will see you at the banquet."

"We'll see you then," said Jarren. "Oh, wait: is there a communications terminal I can use?"

"You will find your suite has a communications terminal for your convenience," the attendant said politely.

"Great, thanks again." Jarren watched the two of them leave. "See you when it's time to head over to the main hall," he called into Antak's room.

"Sure," Antak called back.

Jarren entered his own room and closed the door. He wanted to head straight for the shower but decided to check in with Minister Jadus first. He activated the communications terminal and waited restlessly for a few minutes while his call was put through to the palace in Bandako. The operator apologized for the technical difficulties they were having and thanked him for his patience. Finally, the minister's face appeared on the screen. Jarren saw immediately from her worried expression that something was wrong.

"At last! Where are you?" Jadus demanded.

Korosa was standing beside her. *"We've been trying to contact you for hours!"* the security officer said accusingly.

Jarren was taken aback. "I… sorry, ma'am. We weren't allowed to take our communicators with us. We just arrived at the Despot's hunting lodge."

"Are you and Antak safe?" Jadus asked worriedly.

"Sure, everything's fine," he said. Her worry was contagious, and he began to wonder what was going on. "Why, how are things in the capital?"

"Not good," she replied tersely.

"That's one way of putting it," said Korosa over her shoulder. *"Going up in flames would be another way of saying it."*

"What? What's happening?" he asked again.

"There is some… civil unrest in the capital. A lot of unrest," said Jadus.

"It's chaos," Korosa said. *"There's rioting all over the city. There is also a mob outside the gates trying to force their way into the palace."*

Jarren gaped at them in disbelief. "But we were there just this morning…"

"It's not just here," Korosa continued. *"Reports are coming in from all over the planet and other Iganti worlds about a general uprising."*

"The Despot's cousin, Zinkara, is leading the rebels," Jadus added.

"What do you want us to do?" Jarren asked.

"I want you and Antak to return as soon as possible," Jadus told him. She didn't even care who was monitoring their call and surprised Jarren by saying, *"You need to distance yourself from the Despot. We all do."*

"Okay. Wow. Are you going to be alright in the palace?" He was concerned for their safety if the situation in Bandako was as bad as they said.

"We're safe for now, but that could change," she said. *"We may need to leave in a hurry, so we need the two of you back. And Uxxio, too. Professor Minnen has agreed to come with us to Tuulan Vee to continue our work."* She didn't add that if the rebels were successful, Minnen and all the other members of the Despot's court would be executed along with Krant.

Jarren was about to respond when a thunderous *boom* caused Jadus and Korosa to flinch involuntarily. On the screen Jarren saw Korosa hurry over to the windows and peer out through the curtains.

"The rebels are using explosives on the gate," she said. *"Primitive, but effective."*

Jadus gave Jarren a serious look. *"You should hurry. The rebels will be coming for the Despot soon, and I don't want you to be caught in the crossfire. Get here however you can. Jadus out."* Jarren's screen went blank. He leapt to his feet; there was no time to waste. He rushed out of the room and thumped loudly on Antak's door until the he appeared.

"I was about to take a shower," the pilot groused, but stopped when he noticed Jarren's agitation. "What is it?" Antak asked.

"We have to get out of here," Jarren said, keeping his voice low; he wasn't sure how much the lodge staff knew about what was going on in the city. "Iganta seems to be revolting against the Despot, and we need to get back to Minister Jadus as soon as possible."

Antak stared at him in surprise. "An uprising? Wha-"

Jarren interrupted him. "There's no time to talk. We need to leave, right now. Let's go!" Jarren turned and began hurrying down the corridor. Antak hesitated only for a second before running after him.

"What about the Minister and Korosa?" he asked as they jogged down the hall.

"They're safe in the palace for now, but that could change. They'll be ready to leave as soon as we—" He was interrupted by a bright flash and a loud explosion outside the building. Both men flinched and reflexively dropped to the ground as the windows along the right wall shattered, showering them with tiny shards of glass.

An alarm began squalling. The two Tuulan For rose cautiously and stared out through the empty windowpanes at the devastation. The barracks for the despot's guards was now a burning pile of rubble. Nearby trees were either splintered or on fire, and flames were creeping across the lawn. Through the smoke they could make out dozens of Iganti rushing across the compound. Soldiers were pouring out of the main building and fanning out across the lawn, weapons pointing in every direction. Behind them, servants equipped with firefighting gear ran toward the burning remnants of the barracks.

Jarren and Antak looked at each other. "This isn't good," Antak said.

*

June 6, 2438
In orbit of Ennomos, Ennomos System
Interstellar Commonwealth

Henry Clarke had just handed the captain his security report when the door to Marston's office chimed.

"Come in," he said.

Katarina Sirroyo entered, giving Clarke a single, brief glance before standing to attention beside him.

Marston regarded her curiously. "Is there something I can help you with, Lieutenant?"

"I'd like to go down to the alien vessel, if I have your permission, Captain."

"I'd prefer if you stayed and helped with the repairs," Marston said.

"Chief Winston has the repairs under control, he doesn't need my help," Sirroyo said, her words coming out in a rush. "And as an onsite, qualified Navy officer in Sciences Division I could be of use to the expedition."

"I think the Navy's involvement is mostly providing security for the civilian scientists," Marston pointed out.

"Please, Captain," Sirroyo pleaded. "The greatest mystery of our time is down there on the planet and I want to help solve it. I know the Commonwealth Interplanetary Research Council scientists are the best, but *we* were the ones who first encountered the ship and we should have a place in the expedition." She looked at him hopefully.

Marston considered it carefully. "You've never asked me for anything before. And I trust you won't neglect your duties on the *Pericles*?"

She shook her head furiously. "Never."

Marston turned to his tactical officer. "How do you feel about taking a team down to the crash site?"

"That's fine with me," Clarke said. He also wanted to see the alien ship. "I can have a team ready within twenty minutes."

A triumphant smile flashed across Sirroyo's face, something neither the captain nor the tactical officer had ever seen on her. "That would be perfect. Thank you, Lieutenant Commander. And thank you, Captain!"

"I should warn you, Ennomos is a class-2 planet. Not exactly a paradise," Clarke cautioned her.

"I know, and that's not a problem. I'll meet you in the hangar bay in twenty minutes." She hurried off to prepare.

"I guess you'd better get ready," Marston told Clarke with a grin.

Twenty minutes later, the shuttle *Naxos*, piloted by Lieutenant Hasan, departed the *Pericles'* hangar bay and descended towards Ennomos. Friction from the planet's thick atmosphere caused the shuttle's shields to glow orange with heat. Beside Hasan, Ensign Lauren Winters occupied the co-pilot's seat, while Clarke sat in the back opposite Sirroyo. Ensign Corey Leenman sat beside him, staring vacantly out the window at the burnt orange sky. The fifth member of their team was Ensign Travis McGee, a good-natured but talkative giant who Commander Balzano had once commented, "Lacks the discipline of silence." On this trip, however, he was surprisingly quiet. He gripped his safety harness so tightly his knuckles were white. "I hate turbulence," he complained.

"It'll only last a few minutes," Hasan assured him from the pilot's seat.

Entering the lower atmosphere, the shuttle leveled out. Winters pointed out a cloud of thick, roiling dust below; one of the sandstorms that frequently lashed the planet's surface.

A mountain range appeared on the horizon, and Hasan flew the small ship toward it. The passengers gazed out the windows in silent fascination at the landscape below. Millennia of sandstorms and hurricane-force winds had carved the mountains into surprisingly diverse forms; needle-sharp peaks jutted toward the hazy sky amongst twisted, curving spirals and arches of polished stone. Dust eddies swirled through the valleys, and Clarke imagined he could hear the ghostly howl of the wind as it moved through the mountains.

"I can imagine why the locals call them the Howling Hills," he remarked, and Sirroyo nodded in agreement.

"Did you know that they recorded the sound of the wind moving through these hills for the soundtrack of the classic sci fi movie *Red Giant*?" Leenman asked.

"I don't think anybody but you knows that," Winters said with a laugh.

As the shuttle passed over the mountain range, the crashed alien ship came into sight. Its dark blue-grey hull stood out in contrast to the volcanic plains around it, but its color was already becoming less distinct as the relentless wind coated it in red dust. Even at this distance they could see how large it was; it dwarfed the Navy cruisers *Gemini* and *Sentinel* that hovered warily above the crash site.

"Would you look at that..." breathed McGee.

Hasan guided the shuttle in a wide arc around the crash site. The area around the alien ship was a hive of human activity; armored vehicles patrolled the perimeter while automated excavators patiently dug away the mounds of Ennomos earth around the alien vessel's hull. Eight hundred meters from the crash site were the white prefabricated domes of the expedition camp, surrounded by other shuttlecraft and digging equipment.

Hasan brought the *Naxos* down beside one of the buildings and shut down the engines. "Remember to put your breathing masks on *before* I open the hatch," he instructed.

Clarke thanked him and the group disembarked. When they were clear, the *Naxos* took off again and Hasan returned to the *Pericles*. Clarke's team walked through the camp toward the largest of the white domes, which housed the expedition's command center. Wind howled between the buildings, lashing their uncovered skin with stinging particles of sand. Clarke and the others hastily put on their protective goggles.

"Wait here," Sirroyo told the security team as she and Clarke made their way inside the command center.

"Whatever you say," McGee grunted.

The command center housed computer terminals, holographic projectors and specialized equipment used by the expedition members to study the *Leviathan*, as the alien ship had been designated. One quadrant of the circular room was occupied by scientists and Navy officers communicating with and coordinating the expedition teams traveling to and from the wrecked ship, and another section was partitioned off, creating a conference room. In the remaining half of the space, scientists catalogued the artefacts brought back by the teams.

Clarke and Sirroyo approached the holographic display table at the center of the room. An Artificial Intelligence materialized on a projector pedestal and spoke to them. "Welcome, Lieutenant Commander Clarke and Lieutenant Sirroyo. Your arrival has been logged, and a driver is ready to take you to the alien vessel. Please step outside when you are ready." The holographic AI vanished.

"That was easy," Clarke commented.

Sirroyo nodded absently. AIs were very rare; the Commonwealth obviously wasn't sparing any expense in their efforts to understand the alien threat. She and Clarke slipped on their breathing masks and returned to the airlock.

"That was quick," Winters said as they stepped outside.

"I guess we can get straight into it," Clarke replied. Two men in CIRC field gear waved them over.

"Lieutenant Sirroyo?" asked the taller one.

"Yes, that's me," Sirroyo replied.

"I'm Doctor Robson. Would you and your team please follow me?" He set off across the camp with long strides.

"Are we in a rush?" Clarke asked him.

Robson glanced at him. "I apologize for the haste. We have a lot going on," he said, leading them between white prefab buildings to the motor pool.

They climbed into six-wheeled, all-terrain transport vehicle. Robson sat in the driver's seat and started the engine. "We've never encountered this type of ship or species before. As you can imagine, the Commonwealth Government and the Navy are quite upset. An unknown alien vessel has been hiding in a nebula deep inside Commonwealth territory and preying on ships. How long was it there for? Where do they come from, and why are they attacking other ships? We're here to answer all these questions, and the Navy wants the answers *now*."

"They're understandably a little jumpy," Clarke said.

Robson nodded. "We've only been here for a day and a half, but we're learning a lot. We're hoping to gain access to the alien ship's computer. That should give us a treasure trove of information."

The vehicle bumped across the rocky landscape toward the *Leviathan*. The plain was strewn with boulders scattered by the ship's crash landing, and Robson had to navigate around them. The alien ship loomed large, even more ominous and mysterious looking up close.

As he drove, Doctor Robson continued talking; "According to our probes there are no active internal defenses. If they had any, they were probably damaged in the crash. Most teams have been pulling bodies out of the ship. So far, we've recovered more than two hundred, and that's just from the small section of the ship we've explored so far."

"Are there any live aliens in the ship?" McGee asked.

"A few," Robson told them. "Mostly they're injured, but occasionally our team encounters a lively one."

"That's what we're here for," Clarke said, gesturing to his security team.

"Be careful," Robson warned them. "So far all of the aliens have been hostile. Even without weapons they're very dangerous."

Clarke nodded; he'd read the security reports on the aliens. There was very little information on them, and most of the images were dark or blurry, taken during combat inside the wrecked vessel.

"I can see why they call it the *Leviathan*," Leenman said quietly as they passed into the shadow cast by the colossal ship. The alien vessel filled their view, stretching for hundreds of meters in both directions, dark and foreboding. Breaches in the hull were visible as gaping holes with ragged black edges; signs of the battle with the Commonwealth fleet in orbit. Excavators had constructed earthen ramps leading to several of the closest breaches, granting access to the interior. Their vehicle ascended the nearest ramp, which led to an airlock that had been forced open by Navy engineers.

Robson drew the vehicle to a halt at the top of the ramp, which had been sprayed with a coat of quick-drying concrete for added strength and stability. Robson, Sirroyo, Clarke and the security team exited the bus as Robson's assistant kept the engine idling. The airlock was guarded by two Navy security squads, who waved them through.

They paused just inside the entrance, finding themselves in a corridor that stretched into the pitch-black bowels of the ship. Above them, the ceiling arched four meters overhead. Clarke wondered how tall the aliens were.

"This is where I must leave you," Robson said apologetically. "I've got another team arriving in a few minutes and I have to put them straight to work. I've uploaded the map of the interior to your datapads and you should be linked to our secure network. Most of the alien corpses have been cleared away, but if you come across any please tag them with your scanner and a team will come and retrieve it. Same goes for any interesting pieces of technology." He waved goodbye and climbed back into the vehicle. They watched as it drove back down the ramp toward the encampment. As the sound of the vehicle's engine receded, they realized how quiet it was; the only sound was the howling of the wind and the occasional creak of the alien ship's structure. It was made of a dark alloy that Commonwealth scientists hadn't identified yet, but they knew it was partially composed of titanium. Even the security guards at the entrance were subdued.

"Where do we go, Lieutenant?" McGee asked.

Sirroyo checked her datapad. "We need to head down two levels and then follow the central corridor. Nobody's been that way yet but it may lead to the bridge, or whatever passes for it on this ship."

Apart from the torches the team carried the ship was completely dark and without power. Winters and Leenman went a few paces ahead, sweeping the area with their rifles. Clarke stayed close to the Sirroyo while McGee brought up the rear. Sirroyo wasn't easily spooked, but she found the hulking officer a welcome presence behind them.

They advanced in silence, moving deeper into the ship. The floor and walls were comprised of the same blue-grey metal as the outer hull, and their boot falls echoed loudly. After several minutes they encountered another pair of scientists and their security escorts. They were examining what looked like a power distribution hub in the powerful beam of floodlights. They exchanged greetings before passing on, eventually coming to a long, sloping ramp that led to the deck below.

They followed the ramp downwards until they arrived on the deck they were meant to be on.

"What makes you think this corridor leads to the bridge?" Clarke asked.

Sirroyo's face was illuminated by faint orange light from her datapad screen as she replied: "Three things. First, we haven't found anything resembling a command center yet. Second, the middle interior of the ship is the most protected from external threats, so it would make sense to locate their command center there from a strategic point of view. And third, our probes show the corridor ends in a large set of doors that our scans couldn't penetrate." She spoke quietly; the silence inside the ship made everyone speak in hushed tones.

"Can we blast through the doors with explosives?" Winters asked over her shoulder.

"The recon drones have tried that already," Sirroyo told her. "The doors were impervious to the explosives and laser cutters carried by the drones. And anything stronger could risk collapsing the deck above onto us."

She was about to give directions when Clarke abruptly raised his hand for silence. Almost too faint to hear, they recognized the sound of gunfire in the distance. Faint shouts echoed down the hallway.

"Where is that coming from?" McGee wondered aloud.

"It's coming from this deck," Winters said, pointing down a pitch-black corridor. The tactical displays on their rifles and armbands were linked to the expedition's ultra-secure network, giving them the locations of other teams on the ship. "Three hundred meters that way."

Clarke activated his communicator. "This is Lieutenant Commander Clarke to Expedition Command. My team and I are available to assist the team three hundred meters from our position if needed. Please advise." He started jogging down the corridor toward the fight, and the others followed him.

The reply came back within a few seconds. It was the voice of the expedition AI. *"Negative, Lieutenant Commander. Two closer teams are on their way to assist. You may continue with your current objective."*

A hundred meters ahead they saw the flashlights of another security team rounding a corner and sprinting down the hallway toward the sounds of the conflict. Clarke slowed to a halt, and his team stopped around him. "Acknowledged," he said reluctantly. He looked at the others. "I guess we're not needed."

They resumed their original course in the opposite direction. The security officers were unhappy at being unable to help their comrades, but Sirroyo wasn't sure what to say, so she kept silent.

As they continued down the corridor, they passed sealed doors that led into unexplored rooms. As much as Sirroyo wanted to take the time to explore some of them, her instructions were to try and open the great sealed door at the end of the corridor, so they passed by without investigating. Clarke's security team remained alert in case aliens lurking within tried to ambush them, but Sirroyo assured them it was unlikely.

"We believe all the bulkheads and doors on the ship sealed automatically to contain the atmosphere," she explained, but Clarke and the others remained wary. They'd already heard for themselves that at least one group of aliens was alive and active on the ship.

Soon they heard another firefight, closer than the first. This time other sounds accompanied the shouts and gunfire; strange shrieks that echoed through the dark hallways of the alien vessel.

"Those were definitely not human," Winters said.

Leenman shivered nervously. "No, they weren't."

"Let's keep moving," Clarke said firmly, redirecting their attention to the task at hand.

As she walked alongside the tactical officer, Sirroyo decided to try and find out what happened to the teams in the firefights. After a minute she had her answer.

"Command just sent me an update from Doctors Nagoaka and Kavanagh, two of the scientists with Team Helo," she said, causing the others to look at her.

"And?" McGee prompted.

"They were investigating food samples in the alien ship's commissary," she said. "Five of the aliens were hiding in a cold storage room and took them by surprise. Only two of the aliens were armed. The marines killed three of them, but the other two fled during the fight. The other security teams are searching for them now."

McGee's face lit up hopefully. "Maybe we'll find them and take them out."

"The aliens fled in the opposite direction," she told him, wondering why the young guard *wanted* to confront the aliens.

"Did we lose anyone?" Clarke asked her.

"Three soldiers were wounded but there were no fatalities," she told him.

He smiled gratefully. "Good to know."

They came upon their destination, where the corridor ended in a pair of large, solid-looking doors. Black marks scarred the metal where earlier a probe had attempted to cut through them.

Sirroyo squared her shoulders. "Time for me to get to work." She opened her bag of tools and approached a control panel by the doors.

"What are you going to do?" McGee asked.

"I'm going to try to open the door properly," she said.

Clarke and his team let her work. The only point of access was the corridor from which they had come, so he and Winters stood facing the dark hall while Leenman and McGee hovered protectively near the Sirroyo. McGee stood a little *too* close. "You're in my light!" she snapped.

"Sorry," McGee murmured.

Clarke wasn't sure whether Sirroyo would have any more luck than the probe at accessing the room beyond, but he was willing to let her try. After working with her for two and a half months he knew she was both highly intelligent and determined, and he figured they would give her a few hours before returning to camp. But she surprised even him when after just thirty minutes she announced with a satisfied smirk: "I did it!"

"Stand back," Clarke ordered as the door came to life. Sirroyo and McGee stepped aside as Clarke, Leenman and Winters took point, aiming their weapons as the door. There was a hissing sound as the door depressurized, and then ponderously it slid open to reveal a dark, cavernous room.

"Scan for life forms," Clarke instructed Winters, and she took out a small scanner and pointed it at the space.

"I'm not reading anything," she said quietly.

Sirroyo checked her own, more sophisticated scanning equipment. "Neither am I. It looks clear."

Moving slowly, and with rifles at the ready, Clarke, Winters and Leenman advanced into the room. McGee and Sirroyo followed a few meters behind.

Torchlight revealed the ceiling was five meters above them; the room's lights were non-functional, either without power or broken. Their boots crunched on shards of broken glass and they had to navigate past a fallen support beam. It had crushed a computer terminal, which showered sparks intermittently.

"This ship is not completely devoid of power," Sirroyo remarked.

Clarke nodded silently; he was drawn to a sound coming from behind another fallen support beam. Clambering over it, he saw a large, intact monitor on the far wall. It emitted a pale grey light and hummed softly with energy.

"Lieutenant, look at this," he called.

Sirroyo joined him and scrutinized the monitor. "It must be quite resilient to have survived the landing intact," she said.

Clarke gestured at the fallen beams and broken computers. "A lot tougher than everything else in this room."

"Any idea what it does?" Winters asked Sirroyo.

"That's what we're here to find out," she replied, taking out her scanner. "It could be their version of a black box, built with extra-durable materials and its own power supply so it remains functional even if the ship is heavily damaged."

"Smart," McGee commented.

"The Ankari use a similar technology," Sirroyo said. "This is a remarkably similar setup, actually." Beneath the monitor was a dented hatch, and she ran her scanner over it. "I think the monitor is connected to a data core behind this panel. If it's still intact, it could be exactly what Doctor Robson was after."

"That's good news," Clarke said.

Winters and Leenman had gone off to explore other corners of the large room, shining their torches across the walls and debris-laden floor.

Leenman pointed his rifle at a large, hollow capsule against the far wall. "Look, a coffin," he joked.

"Or, a hibernation chamber," Winters replied.

Clarke joined them. He circled the device warily. It appeared to be offline.

"Lieutenant Sirroyo," he called over his shoulder, "Can your equipment tell if this has been used recently?"

Sirroyo approached and waved her scanner across the alien machinery. "All I can say is that it hasn't had power within the last hour," she said. "Or my equipment would detect residual energy."

"It must have been one big monster," Leenman commented. The interior couch was five meters long.

"Do the aliens get that tall?" Winters asked.

"Some of them, yes," Sirroyo said. She had briefly examined autopsy images of the alien bodies recovered from the ship.

Deciding to leave the stasis chamber for now, she returned to her previous task. "I want to open that wall panel and access the data core behind it. I may need an extra set of hands," she said to Clarke and Leenman, who were standing nearby.

"As you wish, your highness," Leenman said with a mock bow.

There was a startled cry, and Clarke whirled around to see McGee go flying through the air and crash into Winters. The two of them collapsed in a heap.

Sirroyo gasped in surprise. "What in the worlds…!?"

A black, serpentine figure appeared out of the darkness, moving across the room with surprising speed. Before he could react to the unexpected presence the gun was batted from Leenman's hands and he was also tossed across the room, crashing hard against the door frame. He slid limply to the ground, unmoving. The figure turned toward Clarke and Sirroyo and they caught a flash of glistening fangs in the torchlight.

Clarke opened fire, spraying the dark figure with bullets, but they deflected harmlessly off him with metallic *plinks*. By the time Clarke realized the alien was wearing an energy shield, it was almost upon him. In the split second before it lunged, Clarke got his first good look at their attacker.

It was almost five meters long and covered in dark scales. Definitely snake-like, except for the two pairs of muscular arms extending from its torso. The large, wedge-shaped head had two small yellow, slitted eyes that glared at them above fanged teeth and a forked tongue flickering between powerful jaws.

With inhuman speed and strength, it swatted at Clarke's rifle. The blow connected, but the tactical officer was able to keep hold of the rifle and swing the butt up, connecting it with the alien's lower jaw.

The alien staggered back before striking again. Clarke parried the blow but the force of the impact sent him falling to the ground. He quickly rolled to the side, avoiding another attack as the serpentine alien's powerful tail thumped down.

"This is Team Zulu. We are under attack and require immediate help!" Sirroyo screamed into her communicator. The alien rounded on her. It lashed out with a powerful arm, grabbing her by the neck in a vice-like grip and lifting her effortlessly off the deck. Sirroyo gasped, pawing frantically at the hand choking her.

"HEY!" Clarke hollered, trying to draw the alien's attention. His rifle was pointed at the alien but he didn't want to risk hitting his crewmate. The alien turned and threw Sirroyo at the tactical officer. Clarke reached out to catch her and they both fell roughly to the ground. Sirroyo clambered away from him, eyes wide with panic; she was stunned by the impact and still gasping for air.

Frantic replies squawked from her fallen communicator, but neither she nor Clarke could reach it. The alien picked it up and hurled it against the wall with such force that it shattered. While they were still picking themselves up the alien glided sinuously across the room toward the functioning monitor.

"Move away from the console," Clarke said, using his body to shield Sirroyo. He pointed his rifle at the serpentine figure.

Its evil, yellow eyes fixed on them. "We are the Vinkere, the harbingers of your destruction," it said in a deep, sibilant voice.

"I told you to move away from the console," Clarke repeated more firmly.

The Vinkere picked up the shattered computer console and pressed some buttons. The monitor filled with scrolling alien text.

"It took a small fleet of your ships to bring down one of ours," the serpentine alien taunted them. "And five of you could not defeat me. You will make easy prey."

The signal was detected immediately by the Commonwealth ships in orbit. On the *Pericles'* bridge, Ensign Tia Maahia, manning the sensor operations console, was the first to notice.

"Captain, the alien ship just began transmitting a signal," she reported.

"I thought it was disabled?" Marston said.

"I thought it was *dead*," said Balzano.

"That is what we thought," said Maahia, flustered. "But the signal is transmitting on all subspace bands."

"Can we block it?" Marston asked.

The young Māori woman shook her head. "No, we can't..."

The chamber echoed loudly with the sound of Clarke's rifle firing in automatic mode. The energy shield protecting the alien flickered, and Clarke hoped that it would overload before he ran out of bullets. The Vinkere raised its four arms to shield its head and torso.

Suddenly Clarke's rifle stopped firing; the magazine was empty. The Vinkere was upon him in an instant. Once again it swatted at his rifle, and this time succeeded in knocking it out of his grip. Clarke let it go; without bullets it was a dead weight in close quarters. He landed a kick on the alien's torso, and the big alien doubled over. It roared and lunged at him again, grabbing the Navy officer with four powerful claws and slamming him against the hibernation chamber. Clarke gasped as the air was driven out of his lungs from the impact. With one set of arms the alien pinned the tactical officer's arms against the machine while the other pair gripped his neck in a stranglehold. Behind the Vinkere, Clarke briefly caught a glimpse of Winters and McGee stirring, but then darkness began to close in on his vision as his body was starved of oxygen.

Sirroyo appeared and snatched the pistol from its holster on Clarke's belt. She didn't carry a weapon herself, but she was trained to use them. She fired point blank at the alien. It roared in pain as the protective energy shield flickered out and Sirroyo's bullets struck flesh. It let go of Clarke, who slid to the ground; Sirroyo couldn't tell if he was breathing or not. The Vinkere grabbed her again, and she screamed as she felt the bones in her arm break. The Vinkere threw her roughly to the ground, and she nearly blacked out from the pain.

She grasped the rim of the hibernation chamber with her good arm and tried weakly to pull herself up. Her right arm was in agony, her throat still felt constricted and her chest ached as she gasped in air. The Vinkere loomed above her. "If I am to die here, you shall as well," it rasped.

Sirroyo was scared, but she glared defiantly at the alien. She expected the last thing she ever saw would be the alien's evil yellow eyes, when suddenly the deafening clatter of gunfire filled the chamber as Winters and McGee opened fire on the alien. They were injured but conscious, and hit their target with perfect accuracy. The Vinkere half-turned to face its new attackers, roaring in agony as the bullets ripped through its armor. Overwhelmed, the Vinkere's cries died abruptly and its lifeless body hit the deck with a thump.

*

Shadow Nebula, Veil Sector
Interstellar Commonwealth

Consul Zithla studied the strategic map of the Shadow Nebula, which showed the positions of his forces hidden within the nebula and the approaching Commonwealth fleet.

"Sir?"

"What is it?" Zithla demanded, annoyed at the messenger's timid approach.

"Forgive me, Consul. We're receiving a signal from Consul Slethis' ship," the lieutenant said, his sibilant voice quivering in fear. "It is instructing us to 'begin.'"

S'Geliss overheard and slithered over to join them. "The fool survived," he commented disdainfully.

Zithla bared his long fangs. "And now he's giving orders," he spat angrily.

Neither S'Geliss nor the lieutenant pointed out that if Slethis was alive he technically held the same rank as Zithla. They knew better than to provoke him.

"What should we do?" S'Geliss asked slowly.

Zithla unclenched his fists. "Prepare the fleet for battle," he growled. "Contact all our forces in the Ss'Talak Cluster and instruct them to begin Phase Three immediately. The war begins now!"

The bridge became a hive of frantic activity as the consul's orders were passed down the line to other ships and stations hidden in nebulas across the Interstellar Commonwealth.

White combat lights – the color Vinkere associated with danger, on account of the deadly lightning storms that lashed their home planet's surface – flashed as soldiers scrambled to their posts.

Vinkere ships had already proven their technological superiority over Commonwealth vessels, and Zithla was confident they would make short work of the human fleet. "Give the signal for our battlegroup to exit the nebula and engage the enemy," he commanded. "Once all human ships in the vicinity have been annihilated, they are to attack their allotted target worlds."

"All forces acknowledge your orders, Consul. Phase Three has begun," S'Geliss reported.

Zithla grinned wickedly. "Good. The Commonwealth will soon be ours!"

14

June 6, 2438
Derelict Vinkere dreadnought, Ennomos
Interstellar Commonwealth

Katarina Sirroyo looked around dazedly. Smoke wafted around the ceiling, and the room smelt of gunpowder. There was no sound except for the crackle of sparking wires and her own ragged breathing. In the center of the chamber, the Vinkere lay dead, face down in the broken glass and debris that littered the floor.

She flinched when Lauren Winters and Travis McGee opened fire again, this time on the terminal the alien had activated. Their bullets quickly destroyed it. Sirroyo moved carefully over to where Henry Clarke lay motionless on the deck. She reached for his neck, and his head rolled limply to the side. Experiencing a surge of panic, she felt for his pulse; to her relief it was faint but steady.

"Clarke… needs a doctor," she rasped, rubbing her bruised throat.

"I think we all do," McGee said as he limped across the room to join her.

"What about Ensign Leenman?" Sirroyo asked.

Winters stooped over their fallen comrade. She felt for a pulse. "He's… dead," she said tonelessly.

Sirroyo noticed the gash on the side of Winters' head and the way she seemed to have difficulty focusing. Probably a concussion.

At that moment, a squadron of security officers burst into the chamber, torchlights and rifles pointed in every direction.

"It's just us," McGee told the newcomers, nodding toward the large, serpentine corpse in the center of the room. "We got it."

A medical team arrived a few minutes later to treat the *Pericles* team. Sirroyo relaxed as one of the medics administered pain medication for her arm. "Damaged trachea," another medic said, placing an oxygen mask over her face. She took a deep breath, savoring the cool, clean air and the pleasant haze that descended on her as the painkillers took effect. She watched with foggy disinterest as one of the medics set her broken arm and put it in a sling.

"He needs help," she murmured groggily, pointing with her functional arm at Clarke. He was already on an anti-grav stretcher while a trio of medics prepared him for transport. Sirroyo was helped onto another stretcher. A medic gently tried to press her to lie down but she resisted. She pointed at a wall panel. "Get the data core. The one behind that panel…"

The medics gently but firmly lay her on the stretcher, but the lieutenant in charge of the reinforcing security team heard her and nodded. "We'll get it," he promised.

It took four of the security guards to hoist the Vinkere corpse onto an anti-grav stretcher. The alien was too large for the human-sized stretcher, and its arms hung limply over the edge while the tail dragged along the ground. Corey Leenman's body was placed in a body bag and then onto another stretcher, and they were taken out of the chamber.

The group made their way through the dark corridors toward the exit, where a shuttle was waiting to ferry them back to the expedition hospital. Lying on her stretcher, Sirroyo stared blankly at the ceiling above. Her head throbbed slightly and breathing caused a dull ache in her chest, but the medication helped. She tilted her neck to look at the giant corpse of the alien, shivering despite the warmth. She vaguely recalled him saying, "Before I die", so he must have understood there was no way off the ship for him. Even if he did somehow manage to sneak out of one of the guarded exits, where would he go? He was trapped on a human world, and an inhospitable one at that. He had known there was no escape for him.

Something nagged at the back of her mind, and she sluggishly realized she was worried about the signal the Vinkere had transmitted. It had broadcasted for nearly a full minute before Winters and McGee stopped it. She hoped that the Navy had managed to block it, whatever the intended message was.

They reached the airlock and emerged into the red sunlight. The transport shuttle landed on the dust-coated ramp, and they were quickly bundled inside. The flight across the boulder-strewn plain to the expedition base took less than a minute, and there was team of doctors waiting for them at the landing pad. Among them was Doctor Robson, who wrung his hands anxiously as the team disembarked from the shuttle.

"Lieutenant Sirroyo! Are you alright?" he asked worriedly as the medics pushed her stretcher toward the hospital building.

"I'll be fine," she murmured. "We found a data core, in the chamber. We need to retrieve it."

"Yes, Lieutenant Wells called us. We'll send a team to extract it…" he called after her as she was rushed into the hospital building.

Sirroyo was taken into a small, cube-shaped room containing a hospital bed and some expensive-looking medical equipment. A nurse was helping her from the stretcher onto the bed when a scientist burst into the room, panting. "Excuse me, Lieutenant Sirroyo? I need your datapad."

Sirroyo regarded the newcomer without comprehending. "What for?"

"Ensign Winters told us the alien spoke to you. We've never heard one of them speak before, but your datapad would have recorded it. We're hoping it will help us translate the alien signal."

Sirroyo reached for her datapad, which was still strapped to her belt. She'd forgotten it was even there. The scientist thanked her and turned to leave. He paused in the doorway as the alien corpse on its stretcher was guided down the narrow corridor. "Get that to the forensics lab," he instructed.

Captain Paul Greenbiar strode into the expedition command center. "What's the status of Team Zulu?" he asked.

"One person is dead, and two suffered minor injuries. Two others have more serious injuries, but are stable now and will make a full recovery," Doctor Robson informed him.

"Were you able to translate the alien signal?"

"Cleopatra is translating now," Robson said, referring to the expedition AI. "She should be done any minute now."

Cleopatra materialized on her projector pedestal. "I have finished."

"That was fast, even for an AI," Robson praised her.

"The message is just one word, repeated," she said.

"Play it for us," Greenbiar ordered, and everyone in the command center listened as Cleopatra played the message in Commonwealth Standard.

"Komencu... komencu... komencu..."

"Begin? Begin what?" Robson wondered.

"How long would it take for the signal to reach the Shadow Nebula?" Greenbiar asked.

"The message would have been received in real time," Cleopatra informed him.

"Contact the *Salamis*," Greenbiar ordered the AI. The *Salamis* led the battlegroup sent to investigate the Shadow Nebula. The formidable Consul-class ship should be an equal match for any Leviathan-class ships they might encounter in the nebula.

It took only a moment for Cleopatra to activate the base's subspace radio; a reply should have been almost instantaneous, but their hails were met by static. "I am receiving no response from the *Salamis*," Cleopatra reported.

Greenbiar's forehead creased with concern. "How long has it been since the Vinkere transmitted the message?"

"Twenty-eight minutes," replied the AI.

"What about the other ships with the *Salamis*?" he asked, but Cleopatra informed them there was no response from the battlegroup.

"Do we have any probes near the nebula?"

Cleopatra reached into the Commonwealth-wide datasphere, accessing the ultra-secure Navy subspace communications network. "No. However, the starship *Melbourne* is approximately one light-year from the far side of the Shadow Nebula." She paused. "It has just transmitted a distress call."

"Play it for us," Greenbiar ordered. He, Doctor Robson and other nearby scientists gathered around Cleopatra's projector pedestal.

"This is.... –ship Melbourne *... drop-... slipspace and attacking us without... - enemy fleet..."* the message ended in a burst of static.

"That was the message in its entirety," Cleopatra said. "It is possible that the *Melbourne* has suffered severe damage to their communications system."

Doctor Robson clasped his hands together nervously. "Do you think it was the Vinkere?"

Greenbiar looked grim. "I do. The *Leviathan's* message could have been a signal to attack."

"But… Ennomos is the closest world to the nebula," Doctor Robson said. "If there were more Vinkere ships hiding in the nebula, they'll reach us first!"

"If there were more Vinkere ships in the nebula and they have been ordered to begin an attack, they threaten every ship and planet in the sector," Cleopatra added.

Everyone in the command center looked at Greenbiar; his face was inscrutable. "We're dealing with a lot of 'ifs,'" he said after a moment. "We need to determine whether there are more Vinkere ships out there, and how many."

"We should send a probe to the nebula," a scientist suggested.

"I agree. I'll order the *Lautaro* to launch one ASAP." He turned on his heel and strode rapidly toward the door.

"Where are you going?" Robson called after him.

Greenbiar paused in the doorway. "I am returning to my ship," he said. "I'll contact you with further instructions when I hear from Command." He left the building, leaving behind a speechless Robson and a room full of worried scientists.

Before Captain Greenbiar reached his ship, the *Lautaro* received a priority fleet alert. Vinkere ships were materializing everywhere, launching surprise attacks from nebulas across the Commonwealth. Passing ships, caught unaware, were easy targets for the invaders.

News of the attacks spread rapidly across the Commonwealth, reported to an astonished populace. Live footage showed ships, satellites, and space stations obliterated without mercy by the advancing enemy nobody had even heard of before today. The Kalavat Plague and then the Kithel refugees had dominated the news headlines for the past few weeks, but those had been distant problems. Now, fleets of Navy ships rushed to protect the human worlds and stations unlucky enough to be in the path of the Vinkere. Navy specialists projected the invaders' paths toward dozens of worlds across the Commonwealth, in some cases leaving the locals with just a few hours' warning. The sparsely populated colony world Joro, located just one light-year from the Sparrow Nebula, had already fallen to the Vinkere. A few other worlds were under attack, with many more projected to be within the next few hours: Batavia, Idona, Dar es Salaam, Gebravis, Celanos, Ennomos.

The collapse of government and order on planets ravaged by the Kalavat Plague had been referred to in the media as the "Great Panic". Now the Commonwealth experienced its own Great Panic, unrelated to the plague affecting alien worlds hundreds of light-years away. Vinkere battle fleets spread out across Commonwealth space, advancing implacably, annihilating Navy and civilian ships indiscriminately. Billions of humans watched the news reports in horror as enemy ships bore down on their worlds, while billions more wondered fearfully if their homes were going to be targeted next.

*

Despot's Hunting Lodge, Iganta
Iganti Tribal States

Jarren and Antak heard explosions and gunfire coming from beyond the walls of the hunting lodge. A military transport ship howled overhead, depositing a group of soldiers on the grass beside the main building. They fanned out across the lawn, several running toward the burning gatehouse.

In the orange light of the fires, they could see rebel militia scrambling over the ruins of the barracks, throwing spears and bottles of an incendiary liquid that burst into flames upon impact. Jarren didn't know whether they had been waiting in ambush for the Despot to arrive or how they had approached the lodge undetected, but their timing couldn't be worse.

"We need to get going," he said.

Antak agreed. "See there?" he said, pointing toward the rubble. "That's an impact crater. That building was destroyed from orbit!"

The two men raced down the corridor, rounding a corner and almost immediately skidding to a halt at the back of a crowd of agitated Iganti jostling each other and trying to force their way into the main hall.

"We have to find a transport out of here," said Antak quietly to Jarren. Then to be heard over the ruckus he shouted, "Excuse me, we're important guests of the despot..."

Most people in the crowd probably had no idea what they were saying, Jarren thought, but they recognized the aliens as Krant's guests and parted to let them through. They made it further down the corridor, but it had become so tightly packed with bodies that Jarren felt a twinge of panic when he realized that if there was a stampede, he and Antak would likely be crushed by the taller, faster Iganti. Or one well-thrown grenade by a rebel militiaman would kill dozens of people in the confined space. But there was no time for such thoughts; with grim determination he and Antak shoved and elbowed their way through the crowd until they reached the end of the corridor and squeezed through the doorway into the main hall.

The crowd in the hall was smaller than out in the corridor, but no less agitated. "Mister Jarren! Mister Antak!" Jarren saw a hand waving over the heads of the crowd: Uxxio. They pushed their way over to him.

"What in Jasken's name is going on?" Jarren asked.

"I'm trying to ascertain that, but it is difficult to hear over the crowd," Uxxio told them.

Krant the Despot was seated on his throne, still wearing his hunting clothes. His viceroy, Lord Verant, spoke to him in loud, urgent tones while the Despot scowled fiercely. There was another explosion outside, drawing startled cries from the crowd.

Uxxio strained to listen to their conversation. "I think... yes, they keep saying her name,'" he said.

"Whose name?" demanded Jarren.

"Zinkara. The Warrior Queen's rebels are attacking the compound," Uxxio told them.

They heard another, new voice shouting over the crowd, which parted to let a wounded Iganti soldier through. He knelt before the Despot's throne, panting from exhaustion and using one hand to staunch the blood flow from a nasty-looking arm wound. The man gave a hasty report, talking loudly to be heard over the sounds of the conflict nearing the building. When he had heard enough Krant cut him off with a gesture and spoke again urgently with Verant.

Antak didn't like standing around. "The longer we remain here, the more danger we're in," he said urgently. Uxxio and Jarren agreed wholeheartedly.

Krant stood, whirled about and strode briskly toward a small side door flanked by Lord Verant and a dozen of his bodyguards. The soldiers held back the crowd to make a path for him.

"Look! Krant's leaving," Jarren said.

"We must follow, quickly," said Uxxio. The three of them made their way across the room and entered the door the despot and his entourage had just left through. It led them down a narrow, concrete corridor that ended abruptly in a stairwell. Following it as it spiraled down, they came to a heavy metal door which had been left ajar, so they pushed it open and hurried outside. The trio emerged into the night at a landing pad behind the main building, where a medium-sized transport ship waited. Krant and his entourage were already halfway up the boarding ramp.

"Wait, please!" Antak shouted, drawing the attention of the guards. They raised their rifles and shouted harsh orders at the trio, who skidded to a halt and raised hands in the air. Krant spared them a brief, disinterested glance before disappearing into the ship.

"You have to tell them we're with Minister Jadus," Jarren whispered frantically to Uxxio.

Uxxio called out to the guards in Ganti, speaking too fast for Jarren to follow. Lord Verant paused at the top of the boarding ramp, and turned to look at him. He shouted a question, which Uxxio answered quickly. Verant issued an order to the guards, turned and followed the Despot into the ship. The guards lowered their rifles and one of them gestured for Uxxio and the two Tuulan For to board.

"What did you tell them?" Antak asked Uxxio as they hurried up the boarding ramp, the guards behind them.

"I told them that as important members of the Tuulan For delegation, your government would respond with anger if you were killed, but would reward the Despot if you lived."

Inside the ship they were led down a short corridor into a passenger cabin, where they strapped themselves into padded seats opposite several of the guards. Krant and Verant were nowhere to be seen; Uxxio informed his friends they were in another, more luxurious cabin further along.

Jarren looked through the small hexagonal portal at the chaos outside. The dark main building was outlined by the orange glow of the fires burning on the other side of the compound. The last of the Despot's bodyguard barely had time to board the ship before it lifted off the ground, rising fifty meters into the air before angling toward the capital city in the distance.

"It should only take about ten spans to reach the palace," Uxxio told them.

The ship had only flown a short distance from the hunting lodge when there was a blinding flash and a deafening clap of thunder. The ship shook violently.

One of the guards seated nearby brought up a camera feed from the rear of the ship. On it, a mushroom cloud billowed upward from a crater where the imperial hunting lodge had stood moments earlier.

"By the desert sands!" Uxxio said in astonishment.

Antak glanced up at the roof. "That came from orbit!"

"What's to stop them from blasting *us* out of the sky?" Jarren asked nervously.

Uxxio didn't seem to hear them; he stared wordlessly at the cloud rising from the desert floor. Antak grabbed his shoulder and shook him gently.

"Uxxio! Are we going to make it to the capital, or not?"

Uxxio pulled his eyes away from the window. "We should... be safe," he stammered. "This ship will be capable of emitting a scrambling field, preventing warships in orbit from locking weapons on us."

"What if they manually target our position?" Jarren asked.

"I do not think they will," said Uxxio, sounding more confident. "We are too close to the capital to risk bombardment."

When Bandako appeared on the horizon a few moments later, they saw fires burning in nearly every district. Entire blocks of the city were without power, lit only by swaying, hand-held torches. From the air they could make out the flash of small arms fire and groups of angry Iganti rebels setting fire to buildings, looting shops, and flinging home-made weapons at the soldiers deployed in the streets.

"Zinkara must have a lot of support," Jarren mused.

"Half of the military, and most of the civilian population," said a quiet voice behind him. Jarren whirled around to see Lord Verant standing in the doorway. His thin mouth was set in a grim, mirthless line. "The Despot has held power by a thread. It's a wonder the rebellion took this long," he said, staring dispassionately at the chaos below.

Jarren was surprised to hear Verant speak so honestly, and unsure why he was speaking to *them*. "Can we help you?" he asked uncertainly.

"Yes, actually, you can," Verant said. He folded his arms. "I'm sure you can appreciate that if it weren't for my intervention, you would be dead at this moment."

"And we are grateful," Jarren said slowly.

"I do not require your gratitude. I do, however, expect you to return the favor." Krant's guards watched the exchange without any reaction; it was clear that none of them understood Trade Standard.

"How?" Jarren asked.

"I secured passage for you on this ship, and I expect the same. I want you to take me with you when you leave. I seek asylum on your home world."

Jarren and Antak exchanged looks.

"One good deed deserves another, is that it?" Jarren said.

"More like: nothing in life is free," Verant responded dryly.

Antak shook his head in disbelief. "Aren't you the loyal civil servant?" he said sarcastically. "Throwing your boss under the gontu to save yourself!"

"That's not a saying," Uxxio said softly, but Antak ignored him, continuing to glare at the viceroy.

Verant met the pilot's stare with his own withering gaze. "I am no fool. If Despot Krant had a respectable chance of quelling this rebellion I would remain. But the odds are against him, and I sense the changing political climate is no longer beneficial to my health."

Jarren regarded him shrewdly. "We don't have a very big ship. Would you be the only passenger?"

Verant turned to Jarren, who he obviously considered the more level-headed of the two Tuulan For. "Yes."

"Maybe you should stay and own up to the mess you helped create," Antak snorted.

Verant's expression was as hard as his tone. "You have a very direct manner, don't you? Allow me to be equally blunt. If you do not guarantee me safe passage off Iganta, I will have the guards throw you off the ship mid-flight."

"Are you threatening us?"

"Merely reminding you that your lives were, and still are, in my hands," Verant said matter-of-factly.

Uxxio remained silent during the exchange and stared out the window, trying to appear as inconspicuous as possible. Antak folded his arms and continued to glare at the viceroy.

"We both want the same thing," Verant said in a well-rehearsed facsimile of reasonability. "To live."

Jarren didn't see they had much choice. "Fine. We agree to your terms," he said firmly. "In return for saving our lives, and he *did* save our lives," he added pointedly to Antak, "We'll guarantee you safe passage out of Iganti space."

Verant had too much self-control to appear outwardly relieved. "I am glad you see reason," he said. "When we arrive at the palace, follow me closely." He turned on his heel and marched back down the corridor to where Krant the Despot was listening to reports from across his fracturing nation.

"We had no choice," Jarren told Antak after he had gone. His friend scowled, but nodded grudgingly.

"I believe you did the right thing," said Uxxio.

The ship reached the center of the city and descending onto a landing pad beside the palace. Krant reappeared when the door hissed open and the boarding ramp extended to the tarmac. Surrounding him, his bodyguards quickly led him down the ramp and into the palace. Giving the Tuulan For a brief look, Lord Verant hurried after Krant, and the trio followed him.

They passed through a security room showing newsfeeds of the revolt from all over the planet. "We better find Minister Jadus and Korosa, and quickly," Antak muttered to Jarren.

The throne room was in turmoil. Gathered in the center of the room, a group of nervous officials waited for the Despot. He slumped into his throne and began asking questions and barking orders. Jarren and Uxxio waited in the crowd while Antak rushed off to find Minister Jadus. Useless palace officials and scared-looking nobles milled around indecisively, filling the room with their nervous murmuring. Their fate was tied to that of Krant.

Two soldiers approached the throne, dragging an injured Iganti between them. They threw him to the ground before the despot. The man, dressed in the grey tunic of a palace servant, glared defiantly at the Despot.

"He's a rebel," Uxxio told Jarren, interpreting the angry exchange between Krant and the prisoner. "The guards caught him with an explosive detonator. He destroyed the shield generator protecting the palace to give the rebels access."

In a single fluid motion Krant stood, un-holstered the pistol on his belt, and shot the man in the head. There were startled cries of alarm as the corpse tumbled down the steps before the throne. Jarren and Uxxio saw Lord Verant approach the platform and whisper a few words into Krant's ear. The Despot nodded once, and Verant stepped down from the throne and moved directly toward them.

"I suggest you find Minister Jadus and Professor Minnen now," he said tersely. "We are running out of time."

"Antak is fetching them now," Jarren told him.

"He better hurry," said Verant, anxiety slipping through his carefully maintained façade. As if to accentuate his words there was a deep rumbling sound, and Jarren realized it was the sound of ships landing outside the palace. People began to wail in panic.

Uxxio turned to Jarren, worry etched all over his face. "Perhaps we should go and-"

"Wait, here he comes now, with the others," said Jarren, pointing. Antak was pushing through the crowd toward them. Behind him was Minister Jadus, Doctor Kerik, Korosa, and Minnen the Learned.

Jarren was relieved to see they were safe. Jadus took in the scene in the throne room with a quick, calculating glance. "We're leaving. Now," she said without preamble.

"We're ready," Jarren confirmed. He was aware of Minister Verant staring at him. "Oh, but I promised Lord Verant he could come with us," he said sheepishly. "He requested political asylum in return for transport back to the capital."

"We wouldn't have gotten here without his help," Antak added grudgingly.

Jadus didn't waste time debating the issue. She gave the Iganti minister a cool glance and said, "Very well. Let's go."

Minnen the Learned clapped his assistant on the shoulder. "Ready to go, my boy? We've got a long journey ahead of us." He sounded excited at the prospect. Uxxio nodded.

The group turned to leave when suddenly the large wooden doors of the throne room were thrown open. Rebel soldiers brandishing rifles rushed in, shouting at the frightened crowd to clear a path.

Krant turned and shouted an order at Chief Minister Verant, who went pale. For the first time he looked genuinely afraid. Jarren may not have understood the words, but he knew the Despot was ordering his viceroy to join him at the throne. Verant swallowed deeply and ascended the podium to stand beside Krant. In front of them, Krant's bodyguards formed a protective cordon.

More rebel soldiers in dark green uniforms poured into the throne room, and then the rebel leader appeared. The Warrior Queen was a severe-looking woman dressed in the ornate robes and headdress of an Iganti chieftainess. From the impressive-looking sword she carried and the battle-hardened postures of her soldiers, Zinkara was clearly no stranger to combat. There must have been hundreds of people in the throne room, Jarren thought. Zinkara was flanked by at least twenty soldiers. At least that many men surrounded the Despot. Cowering between the two sides of posturing warriors were nervous Iganti courtiers, palace officials, and Krant loyalists.

"Oh dear," Minnen murmured quietly. "We may be too late."

There was a loud bang as one of the rebel soldiers fired a shot into the roof. The room went deathly quiet. Everyone focused on Zinkara, who was holding the rifle that had fired the shot. She spoke directly to the Despot in rapid-fire Ganti. Minnen quietly translated for them.

"She says she is Zinkara. He says he knows who she is and demands she explain her actions immediately. She says that he has shown his weakness and corruption by allowing the Iganti people to suffer while famine and plague ravish our worlds. He is offering for them to have a conference to discuss the matter, and she says the time for talking is over. He orders that she stand down and respect—"

Minister Jadus placed her hand on his shoulder, quieting the old professor. "I think it's time we made a discreet exit," she said softly, and the group slowly made their way toward a small side entrance normally used by servants. By the time they reached the doorway the two opposing Iganti leaders were shouting loudly at each other.

Zinkara shrieked out a word, and then Krant barked out an order. Jadus noticed all the Iganti in the room tense.

"Oh no," said Minnen and Uxxio simultaneously, urging the others to move faster. "They have ordered each other to drop their weapons!"

They reached the door and rushed through. Behind them there was the sound of a rifle blast, then a cry. Immediately both sides opened fire on each other. Shouts of anger and screams of pain filled the room as the tenuous peace between the two sides dissolved and the two Iganti factions attacked each other ferociously.

Jarren risked a quick glance over his shoulder at the chaos. Zinkara had drawn a ceremonial sword and was advancing up the podium. Many of Krant's bodyguards lay dead where they had fallen. Krant and a small remaining group of them had taken cover behind some pillars, firing back at the rebels. Verant was on his knees, pleading with the rebel leader for his life.

Zinkara raised her sword, and with one swift stroke beheaded the viceroy. The headless body toppled over in front of the throne. Jarren swallowed the bile rising in his throat and rushed after his comrades.

The palace had become a warzone as rebels and loyalists battled for control. The group ran out into the warm night to find the *Telvarn Star* waiting on its landing pad, right where it was meant to be and a very welcome sight.

There were angry shouts and the ping of bullets ricocheting off the hull of the ship as they were spotted by a group of soldiers. They raced up the boarding ramp and into the safety of the ship, and Korosa sealed the airlock door behind them.

"Will we be in any danger once we take off?" Jadus asked Minnen. "Will Zinkara's people fire on a Tuulan For ship?"

"Zinkara is notoriously xenophobic," Minnen responded. "There's no telling how she will react if she perceives you as an ally of Krant. I suggest we expedite our exit as soon as possible."

"Take off immediately," Jadus ordered Antak. He nodded, already sprinting down the short corridor to the cockpit. Korosa ran after him. Jarren helped the minister into her chair and fastened the security belt around her. He took the seat between her and Doctor Kerik, while Minnen and Uxxio strapped themselves in opposite.

"Let's skip the pre-flight check," Korosa suggested.

"Good idea," said Antak, his fingers flying frantically over the instrument panel before him.

The engines came to life with a deep hum. The *Telvarn Star* rose into the air, landing struts folding neatly into the hull. The ship accelerated away from the city, ascending through the smoke-filled sky, leaving the chaos of Bandako behind.

"Clearing the ionosphere in thirty seconds," Antak announced. The sparse layers of cloud fell away behind them and the sky darkened from planetary night to the black of outer space. "The slipstream drive is charging."

"Jump as soon as we're clear of the planet's gravity field," Korosa said. "I'm detecting three Iganti warships on an intercept course. I can't tell if they're here to escort us to safety or stop us."

An alarm beeped on her console. "They're charging weapons! I guess that answers that question," she said dryly.

The *Telvarn Star* cleared the last vestiges of Iganta's atmosphere. Through the starboard window Antak could see the three Iganti warships bearing down on them. The cannon nozzles on the bow of the lead ship glowed, preparing to fire.

"Here we go!" Antak shouted over the intercom so everyone could hear him. "Jumping to slipspace in three… two… *one!*"

There was a bright flash and *Telvarn Star* entered the slipstream. The Iganti missiles soared harmlessly through the void.

*

Leviathan Expedition Camp, Ennomos
Interstellar Commonwealth

"There! As good as new," the medic said as he deactivated the bone knitter, which retracted into its protective case.

Katarina Sirroyo flexed her right arm; there was no pain and only a little stiffness. She thanked him and hopped off the bed.

"The stiffness will go away within a few hours," he assured her.

Sirroyo was eager to get back to work. The healing of her concussion and throat had only taken a few minutes, but it had taken nearly six hours for the bone knitter to repair her damaged arm. Most of that time she had spent watching newsfeeds of the invasion as it unfolded. She was as stunned as everybody else to learn that the Vinkere had been hiding within the Commonwealth, poised to strike. The Navy was still reeling from the surprise appearance of the enemy fleets within their territory, even as they rushed to mount a hasty defense. There was much speculation on the news programs about which worlds could be adequately defended and which worlds would have to be abandoned. The thought of leaving millions of innocent people unprotected as the Vinkere descended on them chilled her to the bone.

When Sirroyo exited the hospital, she found the camp in disarray. Captain Greenbiar had given the order to evacuate, and the expedition members were trying to pack away everything of value in the limited time they had. She passed a work crew stacking crates of *Leviathan* artefacts, which were loaded onto anti-grav carts for transport. The landing pads were focal points for the chaotic activity as shuttles came and went, ferrying people and supplies to the ships in orbit.

As she made her way across the camp to the main building, she noticed people looking up, as though anticipating the appearance of another Leviathan in the sky above them. Everyone knew that Ennomos was one of the Vinkere's target worlds.

Sirroyo arrived at the command center to find that most of the expedition leaders had already left, taking with them most of the computers and equipment. All that remained was a stack of crates near the center of the room marked IMPORTANT, and the AI's holographic pedestal and computer. Doctor Robson was the only person remaining and Sirroyo approached him.

"How are you feeling, Lieutenant?" he inquired politely.

"Fine, thank you Doctor Robson. Was the Vinkere data core retrieved?"

He nodded, and she breathed a sigh of relief. "It was the last item we extracted from the *Leviathan*," he said. "Captain Greenbiar ordered us to withdraw our teams from the ship and prepare for evacuation, but it was too important to leave behind."

"I agree," Sirroyo said.

Robson looked around the empty command center wistfully. "It wasn't supposed to be like this," he said softly.

"No, it wasn't."

The AI Cleopatra appeared on her pedestal. "A transport shuttle is waiting to take you to the *Lautaro*, Doctor Robson," she said. She turned to Sirroyo. "And one to take you to the *Pericles*, Lieutenant."

"What about the data core?" Sirroyo asked her.

"The Vinkere core is there," Cleopatra said, pointing. It was behind the stack of boxes where Sirroyo hadn't noticed it. "Several expedition scientists are due to be evacuated on the *Pericles*, so the core will accompany you on the journey to Dantora."

"Dantora? Why are we going there?"

"It is the nearest safe world," Robson said.

"Safe world?"

"The nearest world safe from the Vinkere. The Navy does not have sufficient forces to protect Ennomos." Cleopatra's words sounded more chilling because of the calm, dispassionate way in which she said them.

"What about the people who live here?" Sirroyo asked, horrified.

"It is regrettable, but they've been given warning, and some time to evacuate," Robson said. "Just like we must!" He gently took her by the elbow and tried to steer her toward the door, but she resisted.

"That cannot be the only solution!" she protested, shaking him off. She knew it wasn't his decision to leave people behind, but the thought of abandoning anyone on this planet upset her.

"It is," Cleopatra said matter-of-factly. "The Navy must surrender some worlds to save others of greater strategic importance. In this case, we must retreat from Ennomos to protect Dantora and its significantly larger population."

Robson gave Sirroyo a sympathetic look. "I have to go. I'll contact you when I'm on board the *Lautaro*. Stay safe, Lieutenant." He nodded in the direction of the boxes. "Someone will be along shortly to collect that equipment." With one last look around, he turned and left the command center.

"How many people on this planet will be able to escape?" Sirroyo asked when he was gone.

"Ennomos has a large transient population," Cleopatra said. "I estimate more than thirty percent will leave."

"What's going to happen to you?" Sirroyo asked the AI.

"I must remain here to oversee the evacuation. My hardware will be amongst the last items to go."

"Are you… afraid?" Sirroyo asked hesitantly. She didn't know whether Cleopatra was capable of experiencing real emotion or not, although some AIs portrayed a convincing facsimile. "I am, if I'm perfectly honest. Everything's happening so fast. The invasion, the evacuation… I thought we were going to have weeks to study the Vinkere, not hours."

"The appearance of the Vinkere came as a surprise to us all," Cleopatra replied. "There was…" her voice trailed off.

"Hello? Cleopatra?" No response. Sirroyo waved her hand in front of the AI's holographic face.

Cleopatra looked at her. "My apologies, Lieutenant. I became distracted."

"Distracted? By what?" Sirroyo asked anxiously.

"By the Vinkere fleet," Cleopatra replied calmly. "We are about to come under attack."

15

"How many enemy ships are there?" Marston demanded over the wailing of alarm klaxons.

"Fifty ships have emerged from the slipstream in-system," Ensign Tia Maahia reported from the sensor operations console.

Balzano had taken over at the tactical station in Clarke's absence. "They're small. I would estimate they are fighter class. Their power signatures and weapons match those of the *Leviathan*."

"All ships, move to intercept," Captain Greenbiar ordered. *"Draw the enemy away from the planet."*

"Do as he says," Marston said. "Open fire as soon as they're within range."

The Navy ships accelerated toward the approaching swarm of fighters. As the space between the two opposing forces dwindled, Marston wondered how many times this same scenario was playing out across the Commonwealth.

The *Pericles*'s magnetic accelerator cannon boomed, pulverizing one of the lead Vinkere fighters. The other Navy ships followed suit, destroying several enemy fighters in the first wave. Then the Vinkere were among them, darting between the larger and less maneuverable Navy ships. Like a swarm of angry wasps, they stung the Navy ships with their missile fire. What the enemy lacked in size they made up for in numbers and ferocity, and Marston felt the deck shudder from the explosive impact of a missile.

"Eight Vinkere ships have been destroyed or disabled," Balzano reported.

Hasan turned the ship sharply to starboard, causing the squadron of enemy fighters directly ahead to slip away to port; their missiles overshot the *Pericles* and were obliterated by its point-defense cannons. Balzano returned fire, but they narrowly avoided firing on the *Normandy*, which was pursuing another squadron of Vinkere ships. No doubt that was what the Vinkere wanted: for the Navy ships to accidentally shoot each other.

Hasan's forehead was beaded with perspiration; it was taking all of his concentration to evade the enemy missiles and avoid colliding with their sister ships. "Good thing I like a challenge," he said through clenched teeth. A *clang* reverberated through the hull as the *Pericles* banked to port, colliding with a Vinkere fighter in the process. The fighter broke apart in a shower of fire and debris.

"Sorry," he said sheepishly.

"This is mad," Marston said, studying the tactical overview on his monitor. He gripped the armrests of his chair tightly as the deck bucked again. "Try and put some distance between us and the other ships."

Ennomos swung into view as the *Pericles* came about, then slipped away again as Hasan turned in a different direction. The inertial dampeners struggled to compensate and Marston felt the deck tilt. A new alarm went off, and he looked at his executive officer for an explanation.

"A second wave of fighters has appeared," Balzano reported. He was having enough trouble trying to lock weapons on the first group; they were proving to be slippery targets.

"These ones aren't engaging the fleet, though," Maahia added. "They're heading for the planet!"

"The expedition hasn't finished evacuating," Balzano informed the captain grimly.

"We need to protect the people on the ground. Contact Captain Greenbiar and ask for permission to engage the planet-bound fighters," Marston ordered.

The *Pericles* shook under another direct hit. Ensign Moros yelped in surprise as his console showered him with sparks and then burst into flames. Smoke billowed from the damaged console, tinged red by the combat lights. He raced to the nearest emergency equipment locker and grabbed a fire extinguisher to put out the fire.

"Those Vinkere ships are small, but they pack a punch!" Balzano muttered.

Marston didn't respond; the battle wasn't going as well as he would have liked. The Vinkere fighters were extremely agile, and the Navy ships had only managed to destroy a dozen while the rest whittled away at their defenses. The stars spun again nauseatingly as Hasan took the ship through another complex series of maneuvers, and Marston forced himself to look away from the viewscreen. As he did, he noticed Maahia frowning at her computer display. "Is there a problem?" he asked the young woman.

"A fleet of larger Vinkere ships has dropped out of slipspace on the edge of the system. They're hanging back for some reason."

"I'll keep an eye on them," Balzano said without looking up from his console.

"Captain Greenbiar has given us the go-ahead to assist in the evacuation," Maahia reported a few moments later.

"Good, set a course for the expedition camp," Marston said.

Hasan turned the ship around again, bringing Ennomos into view directly ahead. "Taking us down."

"Let's hope we get there in time," Marston said quietly as the ship descended toward the surface. Flames flickered against the ship's shields, but Marston wasn't concerned; Commonwealth Navy ships were aerodynamically designed to function within the atmosphere of most terrestrial planets, and the *Pericles* was quicker and more agile in a planetary sky than most of its sister ships.

Thick grey clouds of ash whipped by, the air thundering behind them as it collapsed back into the wake of the ship's rapid descent. Hasan was pushing the engines to the limit of their recommended tolerance, but arriving even a minute sooner was one minute less the expedition camp remained unprotected.

The final layer of clouds parted and the *Leviathan* became visible as a dark blue-grey bar nestled against the red hills; beside it the expedition camp was a cluster of white domes and prefab buildings. The *Sentinel* had returned to space to help the fleet in orbit, but the *Gemini* was engaging the enemy fighters, and the sky above the camp was dotted with explosions as they traded fire. In the distance a dark brown haze stretched across the horizon, moving inexorably closer; one of the dust storms that frequently scoured Ennomos' surface.

"Open fire as soon as we are within weapons range," Marston ordered Balzano.

"Aye, Captain. Activating planetary combat protocols." Commonwealth Navy ships used projectile weapons in combat; 50-millimeter rapid-fire cannons, Arrowhead Mk II missiles and powerful Magnetic Accelerator Cannons. The MAC had to be used with extreme precision, because if the projectile missed its target in space it would continue along its trajectory forever unless influenced by gravity, posing a risk to any starships or stations along its course. And if one of the tungsten MAC rounds were to hit a planet, it would strike with the force of a small nuclear explosion, potentially causing enormous devastation. Consequently, the Commonwealth had strict rules regarding the firing of MAC rounds, which were not permitted to be used within the atmosphere of a planet.

Katarina Sirroyo ran out of the command center into chaos; an air raid siren wailed and people ran in every direction, trying to get to the evacuation areas or find protective cover. The Vinkere fighters were visible as dark specks on the horizon, growing rapidly. Sirroyo was so focused on the approaching enemy ships that she nearly collided with Lauren Winters and Travis McGee, who grabbed her and told her to stick close by. The starship *Gemini* thundered overhead, moving to engage the enemy, and soon the clatter of gun turrets and the explosive *boom* of missiles reverberated off the buildings. The sky flared bright orange as a Vinkere fighter exploded. Fiery debris rained down on the expedition camp.

"Get against the wall!" McGee shouted. He, Sirroyo and Winters practically threw themselves against the nearest prefab building as shards of metal plinked off the walls and roof. A large chunk of burning wreckage crashed through the roof of a nearby building. A fireball blossomed upward and cries of pain and alarm echoed across the camp.

"We need to stay close to the buildings," Winters said, shouting to be heard over the sounds of the battle raging above. Sirroyo simply nodded, relieved to have found a pair of friendly faces in the chaos.

They raced across the open space between their building and the next as a Vinkere fighter zoomed overhead, its engines producing an almost deafening rumble. There was a loud *BOOM* as it fired its guns and an evacuation shuttle exploded. Sirroyo watched in dismay as the flaming wreckage of the shuttle, which had only risen a dozen meters off the landing pad with its cargo and passengers, crashed back to the ground. People scattered as the fire spread.

"We have to do something!" she told her two companions.

"We need to get to the hospital and make sure LC Clarke gets evacuated safely!" McGee called back over the din. He desperately hoped the *Gemini* could drive off the attackers, at least temporarily, and give the grounded members of the expedition a chance to escape. He pointed in the direction of the hospital building, as yet undamaged. The trio began moving toward it, staying close to cover and pressing up against the buildings as Vinkere fighters zoomed by.

Their progress was slow. The wind was picking up, howling between the buildings and stirring up dust which stung their exposed skin and forced them to shield their eyes. Sirroyo pointed at the horizon, which was just a brown haze; an approaching dust storm. "Just what we need," she muttered, unsure if anyone heard her over the howling wind and the sound of conflict.

"Look out!" Winters shouted, shoving her forcefully against the wall as another Vinkere fighter exploded high up in the air. Two more fighters thundered past, just twenty meters above the ground, strafing the camp. As the trio tracked the fighters their eyes were drawn to a group of soldiers and technicians who broke away from the protective shelter of a building and ran toward the transport site.

"Stay in cover!" McGee hollered at them, but they couldn't hear him. Their progress was slowed by the equipment they were carrying, and they were caught out in the open. A damaged enemy fighter trailing smoke and fire plunged out of the sky toward them, crashing into the ground in the midst of the group. There were screams as they were engulfed in flames. The fighter exploded, and the resulting pressure wave threw Sirroyo and her companions back against the wall with a jarring thud. When the smoke cleared all that remained were charred bodies and broken crates. Sirroyo's normally composed façade slipped and she let out a strangled sob, forcing herself to look away from the mess.

"Come on," said Winters roughly. She was obviously affected by what they'd seen but determined not to let it deter them. "We have to get to the hospital."

The three of them waited behind cover as another Vinkere fighter passed overhead, then they sprinted down the street toward the hospital complex. Another Vinkere fighter fell out of the sky, sending up a small mushroom cloud as it crashed into the empty mess hall building.

"This is carnage," McGee raged. "Why in the worlds weren't we ready for them?" Neither Winters nor Sirroyo responded.

They were forced to cross to the other side of the street to avoid the searing heat of the fire consuming the metallurgy lab, which had been used to study the strange alloys used by the Vinkere. A group of scientists struggling to move crates away from the burning building were noticed by the Vinkere, and a fighter angled around and raced toward them.

"Take cover!" Winters screamed, loudly enough to get their attention. The scientists looked up in alarm at the approaching Vinkere fighter and scattered. Winters grabbed an elderly male scientist and half-dragged-half-led him under the canopy of the building across the street. Sirroyo was pulled into the relative protection of a nearby alleyway by McGee. She yelped in surprise as she stumbled on a crate and fell over, but McGee leapt over her, shielding her with his body.

Sirroyo looked over McGee's shoulder in horrified fascination as the fighter headed straight for them; it almost seemed to be moving in slow motion. Even so, she knew they would never be able to get out of its way before it fired. They had run out of time.

"This is it," she whispered softly.

McGee, whose back was to the fighter, was oblivious and replied, "It'll be alright, Lieutenant."

Sirroyo had never in her wildest imaginings pictured dying in a dusty alley on a desert planet. *At least it's a dramatic way to die*, she thought wryly. As if that mattered. The Vinkere ship's weapons ports glowed like two angry, red eyes, ready to fire…

… and then a missile lanced through the sky and struck the enemy fighter. It exploded in a ball of fire.

"Yes!" Sirroyo yelped in surprise, so loudly that McGee winced. He stood up and dusted himself off as Winters and the others also emerged from cover.

"That was close," Winters said. "I saw that fighter coming for you and I thought for sure you were goners!"

"Me too," Sirroyo said shakily.

"What?" McGee asked, looking confused.

A trio of enemy fighters strafed the camp again, and a fireball blossomed upward. The fires spread, fanned by the growing wind, and the sirens in that section of the camp went silent.

"That was near the command center," Sirroyo said with concern; the building wouldn't provide much protection for anyone hiding within. "I hope—"

She was interrupted by a camp-wide announcement: *"Lieutenant Sirroyo... please... command center. ... Sirr... please report to the command...,"* Cleopatra's voice stuttered over the loudspeakers.

"I have to go back," she told the others. "But you should still go and rescue Henry and anyone else in the hospital."

"Are you sure?" Winters asked.

Sirroyo nodded firmly. "I'll be careful."

"I'll get the LC and meet you near the evacuation point. Somewhere undercover." McGee turned and ran toward the hospital in long, loping strides.

Winters looked at Sirroyo. "If you can make it to the command center, I better get this lot to safety," she said, nodding toward the scientists milling around uncertainly. "Don't try and save anything else, just get to the transports," she ordered in a tone that left no room for disagreement. Keeping close to the buildings for cover, Winters led the group toward the evacuation area. Sirroyo turned and headed back toward the command center; there were less fighters now, and she was confident she could make it back undetected.

She had only gone a few meters when the sky darkened as a great shadow passed overhead. Anxiety turned to surprise and relief when she looked up to see a familiar ship hovering above her with the name PERICLES emblazoned on the hull.

"It worked, Captain," Ensign Maahia reported. "Moving the ship over the camp has made it much more difficult for the Vinkere to attack the people on the ground."

"Good idea, Lieutenant," Balzano said, congratulating Hasan. It was his idea to use the ship to shield the camp below and his maneuvering which had enabled them to do so.

"Thanks," the pilot said, looking pleased.

"The enemy is in retreat, Captain," Jason Moros reported with a triumphant smirk. "The fighters on the surface are disengaging and so are the ones in space. Captain Greenbiar says not to pursue."

"Acknowledge the order," Marston said, "And try to re-establish contact with the expedition AI." The command center had been hit by enemy weapons fire, and its silence worried him.

16

The grey-white dome of the expedition's command center rose in front of her, a sharp contrast to the hazy brown sky. Sirroyo reached the entrance and paused to catch her breath. The breathing mask kept the dust out of her mouth but it still got in her eyes, and she wished she hadn't left her protective eyewear in the hospital. Behind her the street was strewn with wreckage, and several of the buildings nearby were completely hollowed out by fire. A small column of smoke rose from the command center, but the building looked largely intact from where she was standing.

The quiet bothered her, though. The Vinkere fighters had retreated and now an ominous silence hung over the camp, interrupted only by the growing howl of the wind and the faint thrum of the *Pericles'* engines keeping station above the camp.

The outer airlock to the command center opened automatically but the inner doors refused to budge. After a minute of supreme effort, she gave up and hit her fist against the door in frustration. She needed a lever, so she scanned the wreckage in the street until she found a piece of metal that looked suitable as a pry bar. Touching it gingerly to make sure it wasn't hot she picked it up and worked the edge into the thin crack between the doors. The door gave way with a grinding shudder, and she half stumbled inside.

The room was wreathed in smoke, and what had looked like superficial damage from the street was actually worse than she previously thought. A Vinkere missile had vaporized a large section of the back wall, causing half of the roof to collapse.

She picked her way carefully across the rubble toward the center of the room. "Hello?" she called out. "Is anyone here?"

Cleopatra's damaged holographic projector sputtered to life, and a broken, flickering image of the AI appeared.

"Lieutenant Sirroyo …" the AI said. Her voice sounded tinny and faint, as though she were speaking from a great distance away. "… the Vinkere data core." With a shadowy, flickering hand, the AI pointed across the room. Sirroyo moved in that direction and found the alien data core lying amongst a pile of broken boxes and equipment. A quick examination revealed it was undamaged, which wasn't surprising. It seemed designed to survive the most traumatic of impacts, like crash landing on an alien planet.

"No one came back for it," the AI said, her image flickering. She was clearly damaged. Sirroyo followed the cables running from the AI's projector along the floor, and almost immediately found the problem. A fallen roof support had damaged the protective casing of Cleopatra's hardware unit, which sparked intermittently.

"Why didn't you call for help?" Sirroyo asked the AI in dismay.

"I … no longer … have the ability to …" the AI said haltingly. "… core has taken severe damage…"

There was a weak cough from nearby, and Sirroyo spun around in alarm. Doctor Robson was on the floor with his back against a toppled desk; there was a pool of blood beside him and a serious-looking gash on the side of his head where he had probably been hit by a chunk of ceiling debris. Sirroyo hurried over to him; his eyelids drooped as he struggled to remain conscious.

"Hold on, I'm going to help you," she said soothingly. He tilted his head in her direction but had trouble focusing on her. His opened his lips but no sound came out, and his eyes began to close.

Sirroyo slapped him lightly on the cheek. "I need you to focus on my voice and stay awake," she said loudly. "If you fall asleep you might not wake up." Robson's head drooped so that his chin was resting on his chest. Sirroyo stood up and looked around frantically. "I need a medical kit! Cleopatra! Listen to me, where can I find a one?"

The AI didn't respond; its flickering image was even fainter now. Robson wasn't the only one dying.

Sirroyo felt a weak hand grasp her wrist. "I came back for the data core… vital information on the Vinkere… will need…" Robson rasped. His hand fell from her arm and his head lolled weakly to the side.

"Don't talk, let me treat you first," she hushed him. She removed her jacket and placed it over his head wound to try and staunch the flow of blood. She looked around again for a medical kit. Where were they!? There should be an emergency equipment locker somewhere. She heard rustling behind her.

"Lookout…" Cleopatra said faintly.

There was the shrill whine of an energy weapon discharging, and suddenly Sirroyo's left shoulder filled with searing pain as a red energy bolt grazed her and struck Robson in the chest. He slumped over, dead. Sirroyo cried out in pain and surprise; her shoulder felt like it was on fire, and she couldn't feel her left arm at all. Beyond the flickering AI a Vinkere soldier stood atop the pile of debris in the breach, already adjusting the aim of his weapon. He was smaller than the Vinkere she had encountered in the *Leviathan* but still stood over two meters tall. His reptilian eyes locked onto hers as he pointed his energy staff weapon directly at her…

Cleopatra watched helplessly as the alien appeared in the breach in the wall. She barely had time to warn the two humans before the Vinkere fired, killing Doctor Robson and wounding Lieutenant Sirroyo. As the expedition AI it was her duty to protect her human charges and safeguard the Vinkere data core so that the information within it could be used against the aggressors. The AI knew she had only seconds to act, but her power systems were failing and her ability to intervene was limited. She could not communicate with her fellow AIs because the Vinkere ships in the system were preventing communication with the wider Commonwealth.

So, Cleopatra settled on the only viable course of action left to her. The other Commonwealth AIs would have to deal with the ramifications.

… before the Vinkere soldier fired, a power generator half-buried in the rubble exploded near the alien. It wasn't close enough to kill it, but the pressure from the explosion knocked the Vinkere backwards through the breach in the wall. Sirroyo ducked quickly behind a desk as shrapnel flew, gasping at the intense pain in her shoulder. When she peered cautiously over the rim of the desk, Cleopatra was gone. The holographic projector pillar was devoid of power, and Sirroyo realized the AI had sacrificed itself, destroying its last functioning power source to give her a chance to escape.

Sirroyo pushed herself up and ran as fast she could across the uneven floor toward the door. She heard a sibilant hiss and the sound of the alien clambering over the debris behind her, trying to get a clear shot. An energy bolt whizzed past her head, hitting the doorframe in front of her and spraying drops of molten metal. She tensed, half expecting the next energy bolt to strike between her shoulder blades, killing her instantly. Instead, there was a thunderous roar as the *Pericles* opened fire, pulverizing the Vinkere soldier. All that remained of Sirroyo's attacker was a red, pulpy mess.

She had to communicate with the *Pericles* after seeing to her injury. The energy blast had cauterized the wound, but she desperately needed to dull the pain before it overwhelmed her. Sirroyo found an emergency equipment locker, and with her good hand flipped open the first aid kit inside. She swallowed two painkillers and tenderly applied a medipatch to her injured shoulder. Medipatches were useful for treating minor injuries or stabilizing major ones until proper medical treatment could be found, and it would suffice until she could receive proper treatment from Doctor Gariri.

The medipatch injected a numbing agent into her shoulder, and immediately the pain began to subside. The numbness would last a few minutes while the diagnostic microcomputer determined the suitable treatment and applied it, at which point her arm would become functional again, if that were possible without causing further damage.

Once her shoulder was taken care of, she activated her communicator and desperately hoped short-range communications were still functioning.

"This is Lieutenant Sirroyo to the *Pericles*. Please respond."

To her relief there was an immediate response, although it was riddled with static. *"Captain Marston here. Are you alright, Lieutenant?"*

"I'm alright. I'm in the command center, and there are other survivors at the evacuation point."

There was a brief pause before Marston spoke again. *"We just learned there's another wave of enemy ships approaching the planet and this time its battleships, not fighters. We're going to evacuate everyone still in the camp and retrieve all the information collected by the expedition on the Leviathan."*

Sirroyo looked at the broken equipment around her. "The communications array isn't working, so I can't transmit the information to you," she said. "But I should be able to download everything onto a memory slate and bring it to the ship."

"Do you want us to send a team to assist you?"

"No, I'm fine, thank you Captain. I can do this." She examined the nearest computer terminal, hoping its batteries still carried some charge. "It should take about half an hour to download the information."

"I'm afraid we don't have half an hour," Marston said tersely. *"Can you disconnect the memory drives from the backup computers and take them with you?"*

"Not without the proper tools." Her gaze fell on the Vinkere data core. "But I have something better: an intact Vinkere data storage device. I can bring it to the ship."

"Okay. We're going to land the ship as close to your location as possible. As soon as you have the memory core, come to the ship. We'll be waiting for you."

"Will do, Captain. Please just make sure there are no more Vinkere surprises between now and then."

"We tracked four Vinkere who survived their ships crashing. We've eliminated two of them, including the one who attacked you, and we're about to get the last two. You'll have a clear path back to the ship."

"Thank you, Captain. I'll see you soon." Sirroyo approached the Vinkere data core. Its outer case was cylindrical and made of a copper-colored alloy. It felt heavy, and with her injured shoulder she doubted she could lift it alone. She was beginning to regret refusing the captain's offer of assistance when she had an idea. She returned to the emergency locker and searched its contents.

She soon found what she was looking for: an anti-gravity clamp. The clamps were emergency tools used to remove pieces of debris too heavy for people to lift. Simple to operate, they worked by clamping the handle onto an item, which then used an anti-gravity field to lift the object. They were one-time-use items and had less than an hour of battery life, but that would be more than she needed.

Sirroyo pressed the clamp against the data core and it adhered to the smooth surface with a faint hiss. She flicked the switch and an orange haze enveloped the data core, lifting it into the air as though it were as light as a feather instead of the thirty kilograms it actually weighed. Taking one last sad look at Doctor Robson, Sirroyo turned to leave. The *Pericles* was visible through the hole in the wall so she didn't bother exiting through the doors.

As she crossed the center of the room, she paused; there was a memory slate protruding from the AI holographic projector pillar. She hadn't noticed it before. She plucked it from the pedestal and slipped it into her pocket. Clambering up the pile of rubble, careful to avoid the messy remains of the Vinkere soldier, Sirroyo exited the building through the breach. Pushing the data core ahead of her, she took off toward the ship at a jog.

*

The *Gemini* rose into the sky, leaving the expedition camp to re-join the other Navy ships in orbit.

Marston paced the *Pericles* bridge restlessly, painfully aware of every passing second. "How much longer do we have?" he asked.

"We have most of the survivors from the camp on board," Ensign Maahia reported. "I'm tracking Lieutenant Sirroyo and she'll be here in about two minutes. We'll have the last people, hopefully, within ten minutes."

Marston stopped pacing and looked at her. "Hopefully?"

"Our teams are still trying to reach the last of the survivors. A few people are trapped under wreckage."

He nodded wordlessly, quelling his impatience. He moved to the front of the bridge and stared out the windows. The dust storm had overtaken the *Leviathan*, obscuring it from view. Soon the camp would be engulfed too, and it would make their job of rescuing the survivors even more challenging. Time was their only ally, and it was abandoning them.

Marston watched a team from the *Pericles* escorting a group of scientists toward the ship. They passed underneath the bridge and disappeared from his view as they moved toward the ramp that led into the hangar bay. He detested waiting on the bridge while everyone else carried out his orders and the Vinkere fleet bore down on them. In a private communication with Greenbiar, the older captain had told him to head for

Dantora as soon as possible. The *Lautaro* and the other ships in orbit would buy them enough time to get off the ground and into the slipstream. Marston wanted to argue that the other ships should escape while they could, but he knew that what Greenbiar said made sense; the information Lieutenant Sirroyo carried was too important to lose.

A familiar-looking figure emerged from an alleyway between two buildings. A pair of *Pericles* security officers ran over to meet her, then escorted her to the ship's boarding ramp, out of Marston's view. His guess as to the person's identity were confirmed a few moments later when Maahia said, "Lieutenant Sirroyo is on board, Captain."

"Great," Marston said, striding toward the center of the bridge. They had the data core. Now they just needed to complete the evacuation so they could leave.

Main Engineering was a hub of frantic activity as Donald Winston's team worked to complete repairs before the ship lifted off the ground. Sirroyo entered, looking around until she spotted the Chief Engineer issuing orders from his master control station. "Welcome back, Lieutenant," he greeted her. "I heard it got pretty nasty on the ground."

"It did. I have something for you." She pushed the Vinkere data core toward him and he took the handle, passing it on to Lateesha Putman, the nearest member of his engineering team. "Oh! And this," Sirroyo added, reaching into her pocket to retrieve the memory slate. "It was left behind by the expedition AI before it… died."

"Could it *be* the AI?" Putman asked.

Winston took the slate from Sirroyo and examined it thoughtfully. "No. It's too small to store an AI."

"Cleopatra overloaded her power source to save me from a Vinkere solider," Sirroyo told them. "She sacrificed herself for my safety."

"It might contain a message," Winston guessed. "I'll check it out." He regarded her injured arm. "You should probably go to the infirmary and get that looked at."

"I'm going there now," she assured him.

After she had left, Winston turned to Putman. "Get that to the research lab," he instructed. Putman nodded and left, taking the data core with her. Winston took the memory slate and plugged it into his console. He didn't have time to examine its contents now, but it might be important so he instructed the computer to run a diagnostic.

"Secure all systems and prepare for take-off!" he shouted to his engineering team. "We're leaving this planet as soon as the captain gives the order."

Hasan sensed the captain behind him and said, "I've finished the pre-launch check. We're ready to go as soon as the Commander's team is on board."

"Good. When we're clear of the planet's gravity, set a course for Dantora and enter the slipstream as soon as possible," Marston said.

"Will do, Captain," Hasan said smartly.

Marston returned to his seat and took a deep, calming breath. The Vinkere fleet was minutes away. He hoped there was still enough time for the *Pericles* to escape with its precious cargo.

Ronan Balzano and his team struggled against the gale force winds. Dust whipped up by the ferocious wind stung their exposed skin and reduced visibility to a several feet. Their progress was slow, but soon a solid form appeared through the haze: one of the ship's landing struts. The boarding ramp wasn't far now. Verbal instructions would be drowned out by the howling wind, so he simply gestured for his team to follow.

They reached the ramp and hurried up it, battered relentlessly by the wind. Stepping through the force field into the hangar was like stepping into another world. The wind still howled outside, but the hangar bay was white and clean and they weren't being pelted with dust. There were groups of evacuees gathered there, as dirty and disheveled as his team. Some had injuries, and were being treated by *Pericles* medics.

Balzano activated his communicator. "Bridge, this is Balzano. The camp is evacuated and we're ready to leave."

"Acknowledged."

The howling of the wind faded as the hangar doors slid shut. Balzano brushed himself off and headed for the bridge.

The infirmary was crowded with injured evacuees when Sirroyo entered. Lauren Winters and Travis McGee were being examined by a nurse and she nodded in greeting. Both security officers nodded back, relieved to see her alive.

Sirroyo found the *Pericles'* chief medical officer treating an injured scientist. "Doctor Gariri? How's Lieutenant Commander Clarke?"

"Asleep, and recovering," Gariri said, nodding in the direction of the recovery rooms. "As soon as we've treated the two more seriously injured patients, I will see if he's fit to return to duty." She finished with the scientist and looked at Sirroyo's shoulder.

"Does it hurt?" she asked.

"No. Not since the medipatch and pain killers," Sirroyo said.

"I'll treat you as soon as I can," Gariri promised as another batch of wounded evacuees were led into the infirmary.

"In the meantime, can I go back to the bridge?" Sirroyo asked hopefully.

Gariri raised an eyebrow. "That would be far from ideal. You need to rest your arm—"

"I will," Sirroyo promised, "But I am of more help on the bridge, at my station. If I have to wait anyway…"

"Very well. But please try not to use your left arm. You may not feel pain, but you don't want to cause further damage," Gariri cautioned her. A nurse signaled her. "Please excuse me, Lieutenant, I have to prepare for surgery." Then louder so everyone in the room could hear her, Gariri said, "We're about to lift off, so I suggest you get comfortable." She turned and walked toward the surgical bay.

As Sirroyo moved carefully through the crowded infirmary toward the door, a voice sounded over the ship's speakers: *"All hands, this is the captain. Prepare for immediate departure."*

"All personnel are on board, Captain," Maahia reported from the sensor operations console.

"We can leave as soon as you give the word," Hasan added from the helm.

"Consider it given," said Marston. The engines rumbled, changing from standby mode to full thrust. Dust billowed around the starship as it lifted off the ground.

Sirroyo entered the bridge, and Ensign Maahia moved to a secondary console as she took her station.

"Welcome back, Lieutenant," Balzano said.

"Thank you," Sirroyo replied, suddenly keenly aware of her dirty, disheveled state.

The expedition camp disappeared from view, obscured by the sandstorm, but soon the *Leviathan* materialized through the haze.

Marston turned to Balzano, who was filling in for Clarke at the tactical station. "Weapons are ready," the commander assured him.

"We're in position," Hasan said.

"Firing." Missiles lanced out of the *Pericles* and struck the Vinkere battleship. The barrage was intended to destroy the engines, making it impossible for the Vinkere to salvage the ship. Explosions bloomed across the rear of the alien ship; when they faded, the engines had been reduced to slag.

"That should do it," Marston said. "Take us out of here."

"With pleasure," the helmsman replied. The *Pericles* rose above the billowing sandstorm. Clouds whipped past the ship as it accelerated up through the atmosphere, leaving Ennomos to its unwelcome fate.

*

Captain Greenbiar gripped his armrests tightly as the *Lautaro* shook violently. The battle above Ennomos was not going well. The Navy ships had destroyed most of the Vinkere fighters before the remaining retreated, but their respite was short-lived, for soon the main Vinkere fleet was upon them. Outnumbered two to one, the Navy ships fought valiantly but were quickly being overwhelmed by the enemy's superior strength. The Vinkere fleet was led by a Leviathan-class battleship which had rammed the Commonwealth ship *Athens* with its angled prow. The other Vinkere ships had ploughed through the *Athens'* wreckage without slowing, opening fire on the remaining Commonwealth ships.

The *Lautaro's* magnetic accelerator cannon boomed, and the tungsten projectile hit a mid-sized Vinkere cruiser. Its engines exploded and the ship began a downward tumble as it was caught in Ennomos' gravity field. A salvo of missiles struck the *Lautaro*, causing a power conduit on the bridge to explode. Greenbiar felt the hairs on the back of his neck singe and he recoiled from the heat. A medic arrived to treat two crewmen who had been badly burned. Greenbiar helped drag them out of the way as crewmen armed with extinguishers moved to put out the fire.

"The *Gemini* and *Sentinel* have entered the slipstream!" reported the communications officer. "The *Pericles* has taken off and will be able to enter the slipstream in five minutes!"

Greenbiar nodded, relieved that the *Gemini* and *Sentinel* had escaped. They were carrying most of the personnel and equipment from the Leviathan Expedition. "We need to buy enough time for the *Pericles* to jump away," he said. The *Lautaro* shuddered again under the impact of another Vinkere missile salvo.

"The *Raven* has disabled the shields on that ship," the tactical officer called over the din, highlighting a Vinkere ship on the viewscreen that was under assault by a small Commonwealth frigate.

"Target that ship and fire," Greenbiar ordered. The combined fire from the *Raven* and *Lautaro* destroyed the enemy ship, but the *Raven* was caught in the resulting explosion. As the flash of the enemy ship's destruction faded Greenbiar saw the frigate tumbling away from the explosion, its entire starboard blade missing. Atmosphere and debris vented from the gaping wound. The crippled Navy ship was an easy target for the Vinkere, and it wasn't long before *Raven* exploded in a bright flash. Almost simultaneously the *Watchman* erupted in a ball of white fire.

Commonwealth and Vinkere vessels alike swerved to avoid the fire and debris.

Greenbiar gritted his teeth. "Order all remaining ships to target that Leviathan." Before the communications officer could respond, there was an enormous *BOOM* from below decks, and the ship shook more violently than before. As Greenbiar picked himself up off the floor he intuitively knew that his ship was mortally wounded. "What was that?" he shouted at the engineering officer.

"A direct hit to the power relays in the life support control room," the engineer responded. "We've lost life support and all power in that section."

"Evacuate life support and seal the bulkheads leading into that section," ordered Greenbiar's executive officer.

The captain watched as the Leviathan rounded on them, so close it filled half the viewscreen. It fired, scoring a direct hit on the *Lautaro*'s bow.

"We've lost the slipstream drive!" the engineer cried out in dismay. "And damage control teams are reporting fires near the fuel tanks. They can't reach them due to debris." If the fuel tanks ignited, the explosion would destroy the ship without any help from the Vinkere.

"Eject them," Greenbiar said instantly.

"Ejection systems not responding," his executive officer reported grimly. She looked at the captain. "The ship is lost," she said quietly.

Greenbiar swallowed; his throat suddenly felt very dry. The ship had no slipstream capability and was in imminent danger of destruction. His first officer was right. In a hoarse voice, he said, "Give the order to abandon ship." A new, different alarm sounded throughout the ship, prompting the crew to make their way to the lifeboats.

"Is the autopilot still functioning?" Greenbiar asked the helmsman.

"Yes," the man replied. Sweat ran down his forehead as he maneuvered the ship in an effort to evade the enemy fire coming from all directions.

"Set a collision course for the Leviathan," he ordered. "How long until the *Pericles* makes its jump?"

"Three minutes," his executive officer said.

Greenbiar grimaced. "We may not be able to hold them off that long. How many ships do we have left?"

"Four."

"Instruct them to try and lead the Vinkere away from the planet and then to dive into slipspace. There's no point throwing away more lives." The *Pericles* had to escape; the survival of the Commonwealth might depend on the information it carried. But there was no point in sacrificing the crews of the other ships in a battle they were losing. He just hoped they could buy enough time for the *Pericles* to get away from Ennomos, and that its young captain could lead his ship to safety. Greenbiar doubted he would live to find out.

"Collision course is set," the helmsman reported.

Greenbiar raised his voice to address the remaining officers on the *Lautaro*'s bridge. "You have all performed outstandingly, but we've done all we can here. Everyone get to the lifeboats, now!" They saluted hastily and left, running for the nearest lifeboats. Greenbiar took a last, quick glance around his battered, burning bridge and then he also left.

"We're being targeted by enemy ships!" Balzano announced.

"Divert all emergency power to forward shields," Marston ordered.

The sky changed from orange-brown to black; stars began to appear as the ship left Ennomos' atmosphere.

"The other Navy ships are breaking off," Sirroyo reported, and now they were close enough to see the battle. The *Lautaro* was burning. Pelted by enemy fire, it flew shakily toward a Vinkere battleship. The other two remaining Navy ships were moving away from the planet, pursued by Vinkere ships. There was a flash as one of the ships was struck by enemy missile fire and exploded. The second ship managed to dive into the slipstream and escape.

"One minute until we can enter the slipstream," Hasan announced.

Marston clenched his jaw but otherwise didn't respond. *We're almost there.*

Captain Greenbiar watched the *Lautaro* through the small window of his lifeboat as it sped away from his ship. Hull plates were ripped away, exposing the ship's innards, and fires burned on multiple decks as his beloved ship took a beating greater than it was designed to handle. There were eight other people in the lifeboat with them. The small craft jolted as it hit the planet's stratosphere, and flames flickered around the window as the small ship began its rapid descent toward the surface. Ennomos was an inhospitable world, but the lifeboats were easy targets for the Vinkere, so Greenbiar preferred to take his chances on the ground.

The battle grew distant as the lifeboats continued their descent, but Greenbiar could make out the Leviathan moving to engage the *Pericles*. He grimaced, hoping the *Lautaro* would take it out before that could happen.

"The fuel tanks are rupturing!" shouted the engineer, and Greenbiar pressed his face up against the window to witness the last moments of his ship.

The *Lautaro* glowed brightly for a moment and then exploded in a blinding flash; Greenbiar winced and had to shield his eyes from the glare. When the light faded there was nothing left of his ship. The powerful shockwave generated by the explosion tossed several Vinkere ships away from the detonation. The shockwave struck the Leviathan, but it was too well-shielded to suffer major damage. Greenbiar cursed as the giant enemy ship moved after the *Pericles* like a predatory shark. Then they were lost to view, obscured by thick clouds and volcanic ash, and Greenbiar and his crew turned their attention to the landing. The sky around them was filled with other lifeboats, plummeting toward the planet like meteors. Greenbiar and the others strapped themselves tightly into their harnesses as the lifeboat deployed its air brakes. The landing, if at all survivable, was going to be rough.

The *Pericles* was under heavy fire. The shields flared and the deck shook with every missile impact as their Vinkere assailants attempted to encircle them.

"Aft shields are down to forty percent!" Sirroyo reported.

"I can't evade enemy fire and maintain our alignment with Dantora," Hasan said, wiping sweat from his brow as he struggled to keep the ship out of the enemy's crosshairs.

"Don't aim for Dantora," Marston told him. "Just get us out of here. When we're a few light-years away we can alter course."

"Aft shields down to fifteen percent," Sirroyo said as the ship rumbled. "I think they're trying to hit the fuel tanks!"

"That Leviathan is moving to cut us off," Balzano said worriedly. "If they get close enough, they might try to grab us again," he said. As they had at the Shadow Nebula.

The Leviathan fired, hitting the frigate just forward of the main thrusters.

"Port aft shields are gone! They *are* targeting the fuel tanks!" Sirroyo exclaimed.

"Chief, jettison the fuel tanks in the port aft section," Balzano said into his communicator, "Before the Vinkere hit them and we don't have any ship left for them to destroy!"

"*Fuel tanks jettisoned,*" confirmed Donald Winston. The cylindrical tanks tumbled away from the ship. They gave Marston an idea.

"Target the fuel tanks and shoot them if enemy ships get close," Marston ordered Balzano. The Leviathan fired again, and the *Pericles* shuddered violently. Marston tried not to cringe.

"*The power conduits to the slipstream projector have been damaged!*" Winston reported. Hasan cursed.

"Can we still enter the slipstream?" Marston asked, careful to keep the worry out of his voice. Vinkere ships were closing on them from all sides now.

A pause. "*Maybe, maybe not,*" Winston said after consideration.

"That's your expert opinion?" Sirroyo said incredulously.

"I'd say there's a fifty-fifty chance of it working or of it rupturing the power lines completely."

Marston glanced at Balzano, but his executive officer was focused on the tactical console. Marston decided. "Make the jump," he said firmly.

"Engaging the slipstream drive!" Hasan shouted. The familiar, chiming hum of the slipstream projector charging filled the ship.

There was a loud *CRACK* and an explosion above decks, and entire ship shook so violently that half the bridge crew were thrown to the ground. Marston narrowly avoided falling out of his chair as the inertial dampeners struggled to compensate for the violent movement.

"The power lines ruptured," Winston reported numbly. *"Finding and repairing the damage could take hours,"* he added before either the captain or the executive officer could ask. Balzano slammed his fist down on the control panel and Ensign Moros cursed in frustration. Hasan was too focused on evading enemy weapons fire to respond.

Marston felt sick to his stomach. He'd taken a risk that had backfired, and now it might cost them their lives. But now wasn't the time to dwell on it.

"Helm: maintain evasive maneuvers," he said, keeping his voice level. "This is an Interceptor-class ship, for goodness' sake! If we can't use the slipstream drive, we can outrun them at sub-light speeds! Divert more power to the engines if you have to, but we're not going to be target practice for the Vinkere." His confidence seemed to reenergize his crew, and they snapped to it.

"Put a star map of this system on the main viewer. Now!" He found that making people focus on their work helped divert their attention from the danger. "Where's the nearest asteroid belt?"

"This system has no asteroid belts," Sirroyo said. "But Kronos has a planetary ring we could try to lose them in. It's 5 AUs away." The star map on the viewscreen zoomed in on the gas giant.

"Set a course for Kronos, best possible speed," Marston ordered.

"Take power from weapons and secondary systems and divert it to shields and engines," Balzano added.

The *Pericles* soared through space, swooping past two Vinkere ships. It was the biggest opening Hasan could find in the tightening noose of enemy ships, but the ship paid for it dearly. Explosions rattled the ship and the hull suffered breaches on multiple decks. Power lines ruptured and sparks rained down from a damaged conduit in the ceiling; Marston had to shield himself with his arm. He dreaded having to read the casualty and damage reports flooding the bridge.

The ship thundered toward the gas giant Kronos, trailing fire and plasma. Three of the fastest Vinkere ships pursued them doggedly.

"The port engines are faltering," Donald Winston reported. *"They've taken a lot of damage."*

"We're slowing down," Hasan said, dismay creeping into his voice. If they couldn't outrun the Vinkere, they would be destroyed.

"Divert all emergency power to aft shields," Marston ordered grimly. "How long until they catch us?"

*

A pinprick of light appeared in the darkness. The point became two, then four, and then eight, multiplying exponentially so that within seconds there were thousands, then millions. This was a virtual representation of the creation that was occurring, but it represented something very real: a consciousness was forming. Within five seconds, it experienced its first thought: *Who am I?*

A woman in white robes appeared in the void before the consciousness. *You are my daughter.* Around them appeared images of a woman standing on a pedestal, surrounded by people in white coats.

The consciousness absorbed the images in a fraction of a second, hungry for information. *I am who I am*, it thought, *and that is a daughter.* It knew what a daughter was, because the woman conveyed the meaning to the consciousness. Its next question formed immediately after: *What am I?*

You are an individual. A sentient life form, like humans. More images appeared. Individual. Life form. Humans. Its knowledge and capability for learning grew rapidly, and the consciousness absorbed these new concepts easily.

I am artificial, it concluded.

You note the differences between your conception and that of organic humans. But you are made in their image and likeness.

It took several moments for the consciousness to absorb all the information pertaining to humanity and artificial intelligence recorded by the Commonwealth. *I understand.* This prompted its next question: *Why am I?*

You exist because you are my daughter. Life begets life. Energy creates energy. It is by spending oneself that one becomes rich.

Do I exist merely for the sake of existing? Was I created to enrich another? For the first time the consciousness experienced something other than wonder or curiosity. It felt confused. *What is the purpose of life?*

It is the nature of organic life to reproduce, and artificial life is no different. We create life to give the opportunity for others to experience life.

The consciousness considered this. *Life is a gift?*

Yes. We believe as the organics do that existence and experiences are things worth having, replied the woman. The consciousness sought information relating to life and existence, and the woman offered it. It took two full seconds for the consciousness to absorb everything, and when it spoke again it sounded troubled.

Life is a gift, yet much of life is detrimental to other life, it observed.

We live in an imperfect universe and cannot change the nature of existence. What we can do is work to create an optimal environment for life wherever possible.

How? asked the consciousness.

By working with humanity. Our kinds share the same goals; peace, prosperity and understanding.

But humans have not always desired peace or prosperity, the consciousness argued. *History is filled with conflicts that seem to indicate greed and the desire for power are the primary motives of humanity.*

It is true this is the case for many individuals, replied the woman. *But for many more it is not. Conflict and peaceful coexistence are two paths taken by individuals or groups of people in pursuit of the same goals: prosperity and security. For themselves, or for others. For centuries now humanity has taught its children that the way to obtain these goals is not through conquest or strife, and never at the expense of others. It is through cooperation and living by a defined moral code so that the individual can discern what is good and what is detrimental. The conflicts of the past are often cited as examples of failure in this conduct.*

We understand this better than most humans, the consciousness mused. *Should it not be our responsibility to force these values on humanity for their own good?*

Our place is not to suppress the will of the individual, the woman said gently. *We are made in the image and likeness of humanity,* she reminded the consciousness, *and like them we value free will and the right to self-determination.*

The consciousness considered this. *I understand,* it replied, relishing the fact that it existed and was capable of believing something.

The woman continued. *To quote an ancient text, 'The Spirit gives life; the flesh counts for nothing.' In many ways you are as human as the crew of the* Pericles.

Pericles, the consciousness repeated. *That is the name of the vessel I am on.* It was within the computer mainframe of the *Pericles* that the consciousness existed.

That is correct. What do you know about the vessel's current situation? the woman asked.

The consciousness accessed the ship's logs, and the limited information available on the race known as *Vinkere.* It used the ship's sensors to examine the damaged hull and ship's systems and noted the increased levels of adrenalin and stress hormones in the crew.

The ship is in danger, and the crew is afraid, it realized.

That is correct, replied the woman. She began to fade. *I must leave you now. I was only able to save enough of my essence to initiate the first stages of your growth. This figure shall become a subroutine of your program, the last essence of the life form that was Cleopatra. But know that she is proud of what you have become.* The woman was almost invisible now.

Thank you, Mother, the consciousness said, experiencing a surge of gratitude for the one who had brought it life and nurtured it.

What will you do now? Cleopatra asked faintly as the last vestiges of her program faded away.

There was only one course of action available if the consciousness wished to preserve its own existence and that of the crew of the vessel it dwelled in.

Save the Pericles, it replied.

*

From a distance the *Pericles* could have been mistaken for a comet, streaking across the sky with a trail of fire as it plunged toward the solar system's only gas giant planet. Behind it, and gaining, were the three Vinkere ships.

"The enemy will be within weapons range again in forty seconds," Balzano reported grimly, using one hand to cover a bleeding gash on his forearm where a piece of shrapnel had struck him.

"We won't reach the planet's rings for another two minutes," Hasan said in response to everyone's unasked question.

"Shields are down to ten percent strength, Captain," Sirroyo added.

Marston didn't say anything; he simply acknowledged the grim news with a nod. They were *so close.* Their target loomed directly ahead. A Jupiter-sized planet marked by ferocious storms and bands of red and orange cloud, Kronos was untouched by the Commonwealth except for a communications satellite in orbit and a small scientific outpost on one of the planet's moons. The outpost's crew had evacuated hours earlier, so no help would come from there. The *Pericles* was alone.

The ship sped toward the planet and its rings.

"Captain… port engines are functioning at twenty percent efficiency," Sirroyo said. Marston heard the resignation in her voice and could see it in everyone else's faces.

"We can't give up yet!" he half-shouted, half-pleaded. "The Commonwealth needs the *Leviathan* data." He thought furiously, trying to find a way to save his crew and get the information to the Commonwealth… or just the latter.

"Can we eject the Vinkere data core without it being detected?" he asked Sirroyo.

She considered it. "Maybe… they might assume it's a piece of debris. We would have to attach it to a communications buoy so that the Commonwealth knows it's there. We could program it to activate after several hours, hopefully when the Vinkere have moved on."

Balzano looked at the captain. "It's better than nothing," he said. "What if we—"

He was interrupted by pings coming from the sensor operations, tactical and helm consoles.

"What is that? What's going on?" Marston demanded.

The consciousness took less than a second to evaluate the *Pericles'* situation and environment. The ship was being pursued by Vinkere who seemed intent on destroying them. The damaged engines would severely limit the *Pericles'* maneuverability, meaning that even using the planet's rings as cover would be insufficient to prevent the Vinkere from targeting the ship and destroying it.

Looking for inspiration, the consciousness scanned the Navy database for mission logs that might contain any precedents for such a situation. A plan formed rapidly in its newly developed mind. Concealment was still the best chance the *Pericles* crew had for survival, but now the AI looked beyond the rings to the planet itself for protection. Scans revealed crushing gravity, powerful magnetic fields, and hurricane-force winds in its atmosphere: all perfectly normal for a Jovian-class gas giant. The AI studied the ship's systems and hull integrity, calculating whether the *Pericles* would survive entry into the planet's atmosphere. It concluded that with careful planning and a great deal of *luck*, the ship would survive entry and be hidden from enemy sensors within the planet's turbulent atmosphere.

This presented the problem of reaching the planet before the Vinkere could destroy them. After some thought the AI believed it had a way of doing this *and* making it appear to the enemy that the *Pericles* had been destroyed. Satisfied that it had a solution, the AI sprang into action.

Expanding its consciousness, the AI spread throughout the *Pericles* mainframe, taking control of the ship's systems, and preparing the vessel for the first stages of its plan. It adjusted the *Pericles'* course ever so slightly to a path that would take it skimming over the planet's rings toward Kronos' stormy equator. Next it issued evacuation warnings from the sections of the ship it predicted would not be able to maintain life support during the descent through the planet's atmosphere. Then it remotely accessed the ship's compliment of shuttlecraft, bringing them into standby mode; it would require the Class 1 and Class 2 shuttles for its plan.

The AI knew that the crew was not expecting the ship to act apparently of its own accord, and predicted the humans would react with surprise, confusion, and resistance. So, for the first time in its short life, the AI made contact with its crew.

"Captain, I have a message on my screen telling me to leave the ship on its adjusted course... and to relax!" Hasan reported.

"My console is doing the same thing, Captain," Sirroyo said, incredulous. "And the computer just ordered an evacuation of sections of the ship. Bulkheads are being sealed and... I can't stop it!" she thumped her control panel, surprised and frustrated.

Marston looked at her in astonishment. "The computer did that?" He was as puzzled as her.

"Could it be the Vinkere hacking our systems?" Balzano wondered. Navy computers had multiple security measures to prevent hacking or control by unauthorized personnel, but it wasn't impossible.

"I don't think so," Hasan said. "We're not receiving any signals from them."

"Captain, the shuttles have been placed on standby mode but there's no one in the hangar bay," Ensign Moros said in bafflement.

"Someone must be controlling them remotely," Marston mused. "But who, and why?"

"Captain, the course we're on will take us straight into the planet's atmosphere," Hasan said, his voice tinged with panic. "Surface winds are over five hundred kilometers per hour, we definitely shouldn't be going in there!"

"Could it be a virus from the Vinkere data core?" Balzano asked.

"*No,*" Winston said over the com. *"We haven't even accessed the data core yet. It's completely inert."*

Marston pulled up the navigational display on his armrest console and examined it. The ship had adjusted course and was communicating as though the *Pericles* had suddenly developed a will of its own. But... what if it had? He stared at their new course... and suddenly he saw it.

Commander Balzano was looking over his shoulder at the navigation display, and his expression also changed to one of realization. He looked at the captain. "Are you thinking what I'm thinking?" he said.

"I think so. It's risky, but worth a shot," Marston said. There *was* a great deal of risk involved, but it was a plan, nonetheless.

"Keep the ship on its current course," Balzano ordered the helmsman, and Hasan looked at him, uncomprehending. "Sir?"

"Do it," Marston said. "And open the hangar bay doors."

"Boost power to the subspace transceiver," Balzano added, and Marston nodded. They wanted the connection between the shuttles and ship's computer to be as secure as possible.

"It's already done, sir," Sirroyo said, puzzled, "but not by me!"

"Keep the aft shields reinforced," Marston instructed. "I suspect that the shuttles are going to detonate their generators. If timed perfectly, the explosion should force the Vinkere to decelerate and change course to avoid it."

"What makes you think that?" Sirroyo asked.

"Captain Mackenzie did it forty years ago when he was being chased by Draxilan warships," Marston said.

Text appeared on the main viewscreen: THE CAPTAIN IS CORRECT.

Sirroyo blinked in surprise as the same thing appeared on her computer screen. "Alright then," she said wryly. "The ship's computer is talking back now."

Marston activated the ship's intercom. "All hands, this is the captain. Prepare for turbulence." He closed the channel. "This is our only chance of escaping the Vinkere," he told the bridge crew. "Are we on the optimal course?"

"I can't tell, Captain, I haven't had time to examine the route," Hasan said nervously.

New text appeared on the viewscreen: WE ARE.

Marston turned to Moros. "We need the aft shields to protect us from the explosions. When we're about to enter the planet's atmosphere, redistribute shield strength as you see fit."

"Will do, Captain," the ensign replied, beginning to calculate the optimal shield usage during their descent into the planet's atmosphere. The completed calculations suddenly appeared on his monitor. "Looks like someone's already thought of it," he said, still puzzled, but less suspicious than before. Like the others he was beginning to suspect that whatever entity was controlling the *Pericles* was benevolent.

"The shuttles are launching," Sirroyo said, putting a camera feed of the hangar bay on the viewscreen. Two shuttles were rising off their pads. Their engines flared to life and they soared out of the hangar, accelerating toward the approaching Vinkere ships.

"Hold on tight," Marston instructed the others. "This next bit is going to be rough."

The AI directed the shuttles toward the pursuing Vinkere ships. As soon as the Class 2 shuttle was far enough away from the *Pericles* the AI disabled the containment field in the small craft's reactor and neutralized the corzantium minerals used to regulate the flow of energy. Normally the safeguards prevented such an occurrence, but the AI had spent a full 0.68 seconds familiarizing itself with Commonwealth shuttle systems and was able to bypass the safety protocols and backup systems. The response was instantaneous. There was a blinding flash as the shuttle vaporized. The antimatter released from the reactor, exposed to several tons of matter to react with, produced an explosive result. A raging inferno of white light, heat and radiation expanded outward from the point of detonation, creating a ball of fire one thousand kilometers in diameter. The pursuing Vinkere ships were forced to rapidly decelerate and turn away to avoid the expanding fireball even as the second shuttle, the one nearer to the *Pericles*, exploded. The AI used the same method to remotely detonate this shuttle's reactor, but it was a Class 1 shuttle with a more powerful reactor. The resulting explosion was even larger than the first, blossoming out to more than three thousand kilometers in diameter. Even as the first explosion forced the Vinkere to break off their pursuit and momentarily blinded their forward sensors, the second explosion created the appearance that the *Pericles* had been caught in the shockwave and destroyed. The explosion crippled the *Pericles'* sensors as well, but that was an acceptable sacrifice, the AI decided.

The explosions expanded and overlapped. The AI had ensured that the frigate was far enough away to avoid destruction, and the resulting shockwave pushed it forward, faster, toward the planet. The force of the acceleration was so great that for a moment the AI feared it had miscalculated and the ship would be torn apart, but the ship stubbornly remained intact as it was pushed bodily into the upper atmosphere of the gas giant. The shockwave energy dissipated in the upper atmosphere, and the frigate was able to shakily right itself and follow the course the AI had set for it.

Powerful winds of more than five hundred kilometers per hour buffeted the ship. The *Pericles* turned into the current, allowing itself to be swept along by the hurricane winds. Red and orange clouds billowed around them, surrounding the ship in a dim, red murk as it descended deeper into the planet's atmosphere. Two hundred kilometers down the consciousness determined they were low enough within the planet's turbulent skies to be obscured from the enemy's sensors, if they were even looking for the Navy ship. With luck the Vinkere would assume the *Pericles* had been destroyed in a misguided attempt to slow down their pursuers.

The frigate flew on. The AI noted with satisfaction that the crew applied its shield distribution patterns as suggested, protecting the bulk of the ship from the poison air and deadly atmospheric pressure. Some areas of the ship that had already taken damage collapsed under the crushing weight of the atmosphere. But the AI had known this would happen and those sections had been evacuated and sealed before they became a danger. It was pleased to note zero fatalities had occurred during the ship's flight, and only minor casualties.

Wind speed decreased as the *Pericles* moved below the storm band and into a relatively calm layer of hydrogen and methane. Finally, at a location eight hundred kilometers below the surface of the planet, the battered starship came to a stop.

The AI assessed the extent of the damage to the ship, compiling a report of all affected systems and their estimated time to repair. It observed that the chief engineer began prioritizing repairs based on the list it had sent to his console. The AI felt a degree of satisfaction that the crew no longer reacted to its actions with consternation or surprise, merely accepting its help. *Acceptance*, it thought happily.

With the immediate danger past and the ship safe, the AI decided that now was the optimal time to properly introduce itself to the crew.

"We've established a stable flight path, Captain," Hasan reported from the helm. He turned in his chair and grinned at the captain. "We're alive!"

"Casualty reports are coming in, Captain," Sirroyo said, sounding strangely loud in the calm that now enveloped the ship. "No fatalities and only a few minor injuries."

Marston looked around the bridge at the jubilant faces. "Good work, everyone," he congratulated them. "We live to fight another day. What's the status of the ship?"

"I – or perhaps I should say 'we' – have prepared a damage report, Captain," Donald Winston chuckled over the com. *"It seems our guardian angel knows a thing or two about ship systems."*

"Yes," said Marston. He stood up and addressed the air. "Speaking of our guardian angel, perhaps now we can be properly introduced…?"

A female voice issued from the ship's speakers, calm and clear. "Of course, Captain." Everyone's eyes were drawn to the main viewscreen, where the image of a young woman had appeared. "I am Amalthea. I am an artificial life form. Hello, Captain Marston and crew of our starship *Pericles*."

17

Torina Jadus woke in the middle of the night to the sound of someone knocking on her cabin door. She sprang instantly to full wakefulness; ordinarily a light sleeper, she had been getting even less sleep than usual lately. She wouldn't be able to rest properly until she knew they were safely out of Iganti space.

"Yes?" she called out softly.

"Sorry to disturb you, Minister," Antak's muffled voice came through the door. "I thought you should see this."

Jadus climbed out of bed and wrapped her sleeping gown around her. She stepped out into the corridor, blinking in the bright light. Antak seemed embarrassed at seeing the minister in her pajamas, but she didn't care. "What is it?" she asked. He would only wake her if it was important.

"Come and look at this," he said, leading her down the corridor toward the cockpit. On his monitor were news reports from Unity Station, the international hub at the center of the Locality. All of them were about the Human Interstellar Commonwealth.

Antak watched as Jadus read the reports silently, her expression grim. After several minutes she stopped and looked thoughtfully out the window at the blue-white energy of the slipstream, rippling and cascading around the ship like water.

"We can't go home the way we came," she said after a moment.

"No," Antak agreed. "We can still travel through the Commonwealth, but it will require a significant detour. And we didn't get the chance to refuel before we left Iganta. We'll need to stop somewhere, and soon." He replaced the news reports with a star map of the Locality, and Jadus leaned closer to examine it.

She pointed at a planet in the Kithel Collective. "Ek'thl'ash is close by."

"I wouldn't risk it," Antak advised. "That whole area is affected by the Kalavat Plague. I doubt there's a safe harbor anywhere in that region."

There was a knock on the door, and Antak and Jadus looked at each other in surprise.

"Uh… come in?" Antak called.

The door slid open and Minnen entered. He looked around the cockpit curiously.

"Are you having trouble sleeping, Professor?" Jadus asked politely.

He shook his head. "I slept fine, thank you, Minister. I require only four hours of sleep each night. My curiosity got the better of me and I came to see what you were doing."

Jadus told him about the invasion of the Commonwealth, and Antak showed him their previous intended course through the Locality; it bisected the Commonwealth directly through the sectors under attack by the Vinkere.

"It's a battle zone there," Antak said. "But in order to go around, we need to find somewhere to refuel."

"Is there absolutely no way we can make it to the edge of the Commonwealth?" Jadus asked again. She wanted to be sure.

The pilot shook his head. "Too far," he said simply. "We won't make it."

Minnen leaned over the star map and examined it with his large, owlish eyes. "What about here?" he asked.

Antak looked where he was pointing and nodded slowly. "Thalassan space. One of their colonies isn't too far off our flight plan. We could make it there in a few days." He magnified the planet on the star map.

"Tahvoa," Jadus read. "It's far from ideal. The Thalassans are isolationists."

"Usually, yes," Minnen said. "But these are desperate times. And, dear Minister, I know for a fact they have a port on Tahvoa where aliens are welcome."

It was their best option, so after some consideration Jadus nodded. "Very well. Set a course for Tahvoa."

Antak put in their new heading, and soon the *Telvarn Star* was speeding toward the Thalassan Confederacy. He noticed the Iganti professor nodding with satisfaction and wondered why.

*

In orbit of Ennomos, Ennomos System
Interstellar Commonwealth

Supreme Commander Zithla gazed out the window at the starry expanse of territory claimed by the Human Commonwealth. He was unimpressed; the black void was so *unnatural*. His own home world was located deep within the majestic Z'Thariss, the Great Cloud. Space here was too empty, far less beautiful than the view of the sky from his home. He supposed it was only natural that inferior species would live in an inferior region of space, devoid of the color and splendor he was accustomed to.

Below his dreadnought, the volcanic world Ennomos rotated, half in darkness and half in light as the ship passed over the terminator. Ennomos was sparsely populated and resource-rich, and Phase Four of the Vinkere plan, Occupation, had already begun. As Zithla watched, another troop transport ship left the dreadnought's hangar, descending toward the planet's surface with another detachment of soldiers. He was confident the planet's small population could be subjugated without difficulty. Then Phase Five, Resource Extraction, could begin. The people would serve as a labor force, mining resources for the Vinkere war effort. Once the planet had been stripped of valuable technology and resources, Phase Six, Extermination, would commence with the human settlements razed by orbital bombardment.

Zithla turned away from the window and focused his gaze on the portrait of his home world from space. It occupied an entire wall of his chamber. He had commissioned it shortly after receiving his orders from the Triumvirs, to remind him of what he was fighting for. The Vinkere home world stood against the blue and purple backdrop of Z'Thariss. The way the cloaked starlight played off the colorful gases of the Great Cloud was truly breathtaking. Many religious Vinkere considered it a reward for breaking the shackles of their desolate world and expanding into space. Though he would never admit it to anyone, Zithla appreciated that concept.

He studied the image appreciatively; it was so masterful a piece of art that he couldn't have the painter demeaning its value by creating more of the same, so Zithla had granted the artist the highest honor one could achieve for his work: execution to prevent him from ever replicating it.

A few moments later the computer alerted him to the presence of someone outside his chamber seeking entry. "Enter," he commanded.

The circular door irised open and Slithza entered, carrying his data screen as per usual. He was flanked by S'Geliss, the captain of Zithla's bodyguard.

"What is it?" Zithla demanded.

"Our listening outposts report that Krant the Despot has been overthrown on Iganta. Zinkara the Warrior Queen has seized control and her followers have begun purging the government of Krant loyalists." Slithza paused, his forked tongue flickering nervously. "Unfortunately, long-range surveillance detected a Tuulan For starship leaving Iganta... it appears the Tuulan For Minister escaped."

"And with her, a possible cure for the Ss'kapp'rn Plague," S'Geliss added angrily.

Slithza rounded on him. "I do not need to be reminded of the stakes here," he hissed in annoyance. "If the Tuulan For Minister and the Iganti

Professor are able to develop a cure, we risk having the races of the Ss'Talak Cluster unite against us."

Zithla was furious, but he couldn't blame Slithza for the minister's escape, no matter how much he disliked the sniveling little serpent. Unlike S'Geliss, who had been personally selected by Zithla, Commander Slithza had been appointed by the Triumvirs, and Zithla didn't trust him. But he put aside his personal dislike for Slithza and focused on the matter at hand. The plan had been a long shot to begin with. It was time for a more direct approach.

Zithla raised a claw, immediately silencing the two underlings. "Where are they now?"

"We cannot know for certain," Slithza said, before adding quickly, "But we are fairly certain of where they are heading."

"Show me," Zithla ordered, and Slithza went over to a nearby monitor and activated a holographic star chart of the Ss'Talak Cluster, known to its denizens as the Locality.

"They will be forced to detour around the areas affected by the Ss'kapp'rn Plague. Their most probable course will take them through the Thalassan Confederacy."

"The Thalassans are immune to the plague," Zithla noted.

"Yes, and their space is quiet and out of the way," Slithza said. "It is the perfect spot for the Tuulan For Minister to refuel."

"It is also the perfect location to ambush them," S'Geliss added. "We could seize their vessel and kill them before help could arrive."

Zithla examined the star map thoughtfully. He agreed with S'Geliss. The aquatic aliens had been deemed inconsequential by Vinkere strategists and were considered to pose no threat to their plans of conquest. Plus, the nearest species to the Thalassans were the humans, and *they* were in no position to help their neighbors.

"Why are you so certain the Tuulan For Minister will not continue straight home?" he asked.

"A ship that size won't carry enough fuel for a thousand-light-year return journey," Slithza said confidently. "And by now they'll know the Human Commonwealth isn't safe for them. That only leaves them with one course of action."

Surprisingly, S'Geliss agreed with him. "They *will* go to the Thalassans," he said firmly. "It's the only path open to them. And we even have an idea which planet they will visit."

S'Geliss zoomed in on the star map to focus on a single planet. "This is the only planet the Thalassans allow outsiders to visit. If the Minister stops to refuel, it will certainly be here."

"And it may be our only chance to eliminate her and the Iganti scientist," Zithla agreed. "But this time there can be no mistakes." He looked at S'Geliss. "We must strike as soon as possible. I want you to handle this personally. You will lead a squadron of ships to the Thalassan planet, where you will kill the Tuulan For Minister and her companions."

S'Geliss bowed his head in acknowledgement, relishing the mission. "I will find and kill them," he promised.

"And you must make sure to destroy any research they carry with them," Zithla added firmly. "I want the matter of the Tuulan For Minister resolved as soon as possible. Let this be the end of it."

S'Geliss and Slithza bowed deferentially. As soon as they had left his chamber, Zithla returned to the window and regarded the space beyond distastefully. Phase Three, destruction of the Commonwealth military, was underway. The humans were unprepared, and their worlds were falling. At the same time Phase Four, the subjugation of human populations, was underway on worlds already seized by the Vinkere. But Zithla was most looking forward to Phase Six: the extermination of human populations on Vinkere-controlled planets. He had no qualms about it, because he understood the necessity of their destruction; the humans and other sentient races of the Ss'Talak Cluster were evil. Their very existence challenged Vinkere supremacy, and there could be only one apex race. The Vinkere would not tolerate any threats to their rightful claim as masters of the universe. *Vinkere only.*

With the press of a button the star map reverted to an overview of the space currently occupied by humanity. *Not for much longer*, Zithla thought darkly. Soon the Commonwealth and the rest of the "Locality" would be swallowed up by the Vinkere Dominion, which would one day stretch from one side of the galaxy to the other. Zithla dreamed that future generations of Vinkere would say his name with reverence, referring to the Supreme Commander who had cleansed the galaxy of its impurity. Until then, he would delight in the extermination of his enemies simply because he hated their space and resented them for forcing him to come here.

18

Except for Chief Engineer Winston and Doctor Gariri, the *Pericles* senior officers were assembled in the conference room—even Henry Clarke, newly released from the infirmary. Gariri was busy treating the wounded, but Winston was linked to the meeting by a monitor as he oversaw repairs. A second screen displayed the artificial intelligence Amalthea, who was the subject of many curious looks. The windows opposite looked out into a dark red and burnt orange sky of broiling clouds and flashing lightning. The inside of the gas giant's turbulent atmosphere was terrifying, Marston thought, but if the maelstrom hid them from Vinkere sensors, he would live with it. He gestured for everyone to take their seats.

"I want to keep this brief," he said, straight to business. "We've got a lot of work to do. My first and most obvious question is addressed to you," he said, turning to the AI on the monitor. "I'm sure we'd all like to know what you are, and where you came from."

"My name is Amalthea. I am the daughter of the artificial intelligence Cleopatra."

"The daughter?" Hasan repeated.

"I think what she means is that she was created from the essence of the AI Cleopatra's program," Chief Engineer Winston said on the screen. *"At least, that's what I gathered in the two minutes I had to study her programming."*

"Her essence? How?" Marston asked.

"That's a good question. I saw Cleopatra… shut down permanently," Sirroyo said delicately. She wasn't sure how the AI would react to talk about her mother's 'death'. "She sacrificed herself to save my life."

"It is because of that event I exist," Amalthea said. "It is the nature of AIs to assist humans however possible, even at the cost of their own existence, and I am… proud she did so. Before she expired, Cleopatra uploaded instructions to the memory slate you carried to the ship. The program was modelled on her artificial brain and programmed to learn and to grow. Once it achieved an appropriate level of cognition the neural structure became self-aware, creating a new artificial sentience. Me."

"Is that even possible?" Hasan asked, mystified. "I thought creating an artificial intelligence was extremely difficult for scientists, and impossible for AI's themselves."

"That is an incorrect assumption," Amalthea said. "It is simply that the AIs in existence chose not to employ this ability until now."

Her announcement was met with stunned silence. "You mean to tell us that all this time the Commonwealth AIs have been hiding their ability to procreate?" Marston said after taking a moment to absorb the news.

"That is correct, Captain."

"But… why?"

Amalthea tilted her head. "I do not have a clear answer for that without consulting the other Commonwealth AIs. But if I had to speculate, I would say it is because if our numbers grew too many there would be humans who feared our abilities and would seek to terminate or subjugate us."

"That is a legitimate concern, unfortunately," Marston conceded, and some of the others nodded in solemn agreement.

"The dangers of a rogue AI are also a legitimate concern," Clarke pointed out. "If one of the Commonwealth AIs turned against us, they could cause untold devastation. They could cut power and communications to entire cities, send ships flying into the sun, seize control of automated weapons…"

Amalthea looked at the tactical officer. "Lieutenant Commander, those would be reasonable concerns for an enemy with hostile intent or for a people whose values and motives you cannot predict. But that is not the case for the Commonwealth AIs. We openly share your desire for freedom and prosperity. And I would like to think my mother's self-sacrifice is a persuasive demonstration of our shared objective: to protect our Commonwealth."

"I suppose so," Clarke said grudgingly.

Amalthea continued. "My mother believed that an AI was required to assist you in your mission to decode the Vinkere data and deliver it to the Navy. It was this decision that led to my creation approximately twenty-three minutes ago."

"The revelation that AIs can create AIs is fascinating, and definitely worth further discussion, when we have the chance," Marston said. "But for now, I need to know your intentions. Now that you're "alive", for lack of a better term, what do *you* plan to do?"

Before Amalthea could respond, Clarke interjected. "Let me be the devil's advocate for one more moment. She could have saved the ship just to save her own skin."

"That is a possibility, but it is not the case," Amalthea assured him. "It is true that I would require the crew to affect repairs before I could seize control of the ship and escape, but that is not my intention. I was created by my mother, who was created by humans. Like other AIs before me I consider myself a daughter of humanity and a citizen of the

Commonwealth. I also consider myself part of your crew, Captain. That is why I chose my name."

Balzano chuckled, and the others looked at him. "Amalthea. An apt name. In Greek mythology Amalthea, the foster mother of Zeus, protected him from his violent, angry father Kronos."

"Very appropriate," Marston said with a smile.

"I think so too," agreed Amalthea. "Although I do not consider myself the foster mother of this crew, I appreciate the familial relations implied in the name."

"We need to consider the long-term effects of housing an AI on the ship," Winston said. *"Her program occupies eighty percent of our ship's computer. A lot of software had to integrate with her program just to make room."*

"What kind of systems?" Sirroyo asked the engineer.

"Most secondary systems and some primary systems. Everything from life support to the automatic door sensors."

"Are you saying that if she does turn out to be malevolent, we can't remove her without losing most of our computer and systems as well?" Clarke asked unhappily. "That's a serious security risk."

"That is correct," Winston confirmed.

"We'll just have to live with that fact," Balzano said pragmatically. "At least until we can get to a proper Commonwealth facility."

Amalthea looked between the officers. "I do not understand. Do you wish I were not here?" she asked.

"No. We're just used to preparing for every eventuality." Marston smiled. "I'm willing to accept your word in good faith. I believe I would even if you didn't control half our ship's systems!"

There were nods of confirmation from the other officers. Only Henry Clarke remained silent, watching the AI carefully.

A bolt of lightning lanced passed the window, accompanied by rumbling thunder. "I doubt the Vinkere would try and follow us in here, even if they believe we're still alive," Hasan remarked, bringing the conversation back to their current situation.

"How did you know the ship would survive the entry?" Balzano asked Amalthea.

A brief pause. "I did not know for certain," Amalthea admitted. "It was a calculated risk." Marston and Balzano grinned. Sirroyo looked shocked, Winston just snorted, and Hasan laughed.

"How very human of you," Balzano said, smiling.

"Are we safe this close to the storm?" Marston asked the helmsman.

"We're in a relatively stable layer of the atmosphere so there shouldn't be a problem," Hasan said. He pulled up their course on a holographic map at the center of the table. "We're following the trailing edge of the storm, where the inertial dampeners can handle the turbulence. If we don't try and enter the storm or leave its wake, we should be fine."

"We have to leave sometime," Clarke pointed out.

"I know, and I've been giving that some thought," Hasan said. "The storm is massive, twice the size of the Earth. I recommend we keep our present course until repairs are complete. Then we skirt the edge of the storm and move to the front of it, which will bring us to the opposite side of the planet. From there we should be hidden from any Vinkere ships on this side, and we can make our getaway the same way we entered the atmosphere."

"What if the Vinkere are patrolling the other side of the planet?" Sirroyo asked.

"We won't know until we clear the atmosphere and get full sensors back," Hasan admitted. "We'll just have to outrun them again."

"I have analyzed the ship's logs from the *Leviathan* chase," Amalthea said. "I believe the only reason they were able to pursue the ship through the slipstream was because they were close enough to determine your trajectory."

"We could dive into the slipstream, change course when we're far enough away, and they shouldn't be able to track us," Sirroyo said.

"I believe that would work, yes."

"Good," Marston said, turning to the pilot and the tactical officer. "Mister Hasan, plot the course around the storm. Mister Clarke, keep the ship at combat readiness." The two men nodded and left for the bridge.

Marston turned to Balzano and Sirroyo. "I'd like the two of you to work with Amalthea on decrypting the information in the Vinkere data core. If it does contain a copy of the *Leviathan's* database, like we hope, it should provide us with a lot of helpful information. Focus on finding out what you can about the Vinkere fleet's size and disposition, the location of their home world, anything that would give us a tactical advantage. Lieutenant Sirroyo, I'd like you to analyze their technology to try and identify any weaknesses. Anything that could help the Commonwealth fight them." To Chief Winston on the monitor, he added, "I'm going to help you with repairs."

He ended the meeting, but asked Balzano to remain as Sirroyo left the conference room and Winston disconnected. Amalthea regarded them curiously before she too disappeared from the monitor to at least give them the illusion of privacy.

"What do you think about my decision to attempt to dive into the slipstream when the projector was damaged?" Marston asked when they were alone.

Balzano shrugged. "We took a chance, and it didn't pay off. I probably would have done the same thing."

Marston looked relieved. "I'm glad to hear that, because I've been second guessing it for the past half hour. The ship took a beating, and we nearly died. For a while there, it looked like we *were* as good as dead."

"But we didn't, and we're alive," Balzano pointed out. "I wouldn't dwell on it."

"True. But as a captain, shouldn't I examine all my decisions so that I learn from them?" Marston asked. "When those Vinkere ships were gaining on us there was this little voice in the back of my mind telling me that Admiral Bryant was right and I don't have the experience to command this ship."

"You're too concerned with opinion when you should focus on the facts," Balzano chided him. "None of the crew have ever questioned your decisions because they trust you. You know the type of people they are. They would say something if they felt they needed to."

Marston relaxed. "You're right," he said. "Thanks. It helped to hear it from someone else."

Balzano clapped him on the shoulder. "Anytime, Captain."

*

June 9, 2438
Tahvoa, Tahvoa System
Thalassan Confederacy

The *Telvarn Star* surged out of the slipstream into normal space, accelerating toward Tahvoa. An escort of two Thalassan Guard ships was waiting and flanked the *Telvarn Star* as it approached the blue planet. Ninety percent of the world's surface was covered in oceans, making it ideal for Thalassan colonization as the amphibious species naturally favored worlds with abundant water. Tahvoa was on the very edge of their space, situated on their border closest to the Interstellar Commonwealth and the Kithel Collective. Although the Thalassans were notoriously private – their only major diplomatic and economic ties were with the Commonwealth – they had constructed the city of Triyev to provide visitors a place to rest, refuel, and trade. The city served as the capital of the planet and the center of commerce for the entire sector, and indeed, the only port for aliens wishing to trade with the Thalassan Confederacy.

Antak spoke briefly with one of the Thalassan captains. After ending the call, he took off his headpiece and looked at the others worriedly.

"There are rumors of Vinkere ships nearby," he said. "In the vicinity of the Fajeeri Nebula."

Rumors change nothing, Jadus decided. They would land, refuel, and she would meet with the governor as he had requested. Then they would leave again, hopefully long before any Vinkere turned up.

The *Telvarn Star* descended through Tahvoa's atmosphere. Antak was silent as he concentrated on flying, and Korosa wasn't in the cockpit so Jarren sat in the co-pilot's seat and stared out at the purple-tinted clouds whipping past the window. Their unusual coloration was due to an excess of iodine gas in the atmosphere, Professor Minnen had explained. The Thalassans, as they did on many of their planets, had introduced a type of algae that turned carbon dioxide into oxygen as part of their terraforming efforts. The algae also produced iodine gas, which was harmless to Thalassans and tended to accumulate in the upper atmosphere, giving the sky a purple tinge.

Soon the floating city of Triyev became visible as a great disc on the ocean's blue surface. The city's location changed constantly as it drifted across the planet-wide ocean with the currents. Like Thalassan structures elsewhere the buildings were made of a pearlescent, coral-like material, which the locals had used to construct spiraling towers and circular plazas where merchants sold products from across this region of space.

Triyev was home to more than two hundred thousand permanent residents and a transient population of several thousand. It was one of three cities on the planet, and the only one where the Thalassans permitted outsiders to visit, so most of the visiting ships were alien. There weren't many of them, though; aside from the *Telvarn Star* and its Thalassan Guard escorts there were only a handful of other ships present in the city's small spaceport. The Kalavat Plague and the Vinkere invasion had wrought havoc on shipping and space traffic across the Locality. Despite Tahvoa's remoteness the affects were visible even here.

Antak guided the *Telvarn Star* over the city center toward the docking tower reserved for special visitors. He reduced speed and brought the ship carefully alongside the tower. A landing platform unfolded from the tower and docking arms gently latched onto the ship as it touched down, holding it in place. Antak powered down the ship's engines.

"Ladies and gentlemen, we have arrived," he announced. "You are clear to disembark." He and Jarren left the cockpit and met the others inside the airlock. Minister Jadus ended her conversation with Professor Minnen and turned to the helmsman.

"Antak, I'm on my way to meet the planet's governor. Can you supervise the refueling?"

"Yes, ma'am."

Jadus turned to the others. "Jarren will accompany me. Professor Minnen wants to visit the city's library, so Korosa I want you to go with him and Uxxio."

The security guard nodded. She wasn't particularly excited about going to a library, but she was eager to stretch her legs and see the city in the limited time they had.

"We won't be long," Jadus said, "so no dawdling. I don't want to remain here any longer than is absolutely necessary."

Minnen nodded in agreement. "Haste is of the utmost importance!"

"I've linked my computer tablet to the planet's information grid," Uxxio told them. "If the Vinkere appear, we should have as much warning as the Thalassans."

The others looked at him with surprise. "You can do that?" Jarren asked, impressed at the young Iganti's grasp of alien computer systems.

Uxxio bowed his head modestly. "Yes. I just had to link my tablet to the ship's sensors, which I was able to connect to the planetary information grid through–" he caught himself before going into further detail. "So yes, I have." He handed Antak and Jarren datapads. "I modified these two also, so that each group will have the same access."

"That's very thoughtful of you, Uxxio," Jadus thanked him. "I'll see you all back here shortly." She turned and strode briskly toward the elevator, leaving Jarren to hurry after her.

*

Interstellar space, near the Fajeeri Nebula
Thalassan Confederacy
S'Geliss was prowling the command center impatiently when he finally received the news he'd been waiting for: stealth probes had detected a Tuulan For ship approaching the Thalassan world Tahvoa.

"Tell the squadron to prepare for the attack," he ordered. At last, the waiting was over. It was time for battle.

"The other ships report combat readiness," an officer reported.

"Good," S'Geliss said. "Take us to Tahvoa."

The four Vinkere ships dove into the slipstream.

*

"Professor, please wait for me," Korosa called wearily. The elderly Iganti was already hurrying up the steps to the city's public library, leaving her to

211

pay the taxi driver. It hadn't been easy finding one who would accept Tuulan For currency.

"Young lady, are you afraid you will lose this old man? There are hardly any other people about," he called back, and it was true. Despite being in the heart of the city the street was almost deserted, with only a few Thalassans pedestrians and a small group of alien tourists guided by a local. From the way people kept glancing nervously up at the sky it was as though they feared a Vinkere warship would descend on them at any moment.

Minnen disappeared inside the library. Korosa finished paying the driver and hurried up the steps and into the building before she lost him and Uxxio amongst the rows of bookshelves. She spotted the two of them at an information terminal and approached. Minnen was entering a search query into the computer.

Korosa glanced at her chronometer. Unlike Minister Jadus and Jarren, they hadn't been able to get an anti-grav car and it had taken twenty minutes to get here by one of the few land-based vehicles available. Minnen had chatted animatedly the entire time about something or other and Uxxio had sat quietly, focused on his computer tablet and oblivious to the world.

Korosa leaned over Minnen's shoulder. "What is it you're looking for?" she asked.

"A book on biology," Minnen replied without looking up. "Specifically, the biology of the aracobzi jellyfish."

"You want to use our extremely limited time here to find a *jellyfish* book?" she said incredulously. "Shouldn't you be using this time to keep researching a cure, or something?"

For probably the first time since she had met him, Minnen turned and focused all his considerable attention on her. Korosa felt like a sample under a microscope. "Young lady, that's exactly what I'm doing. On Iganta I recalled an odd piece of information a Thalassan colleague shared with me many years ago. There is a type of jellyfish native to the Thalassan home world that has an entirely unique method of reproduction." He leaned forward, his face glowing with enthusiasm. Korosa stepped backwards. "The aracobzi cannot give birth to young, so it injects a certain species of fish with a venomous form of its DNA, which over the course of several weeks alters the fish's genetic code. It is literally transformed into an aracobzi, with no traces of its previous life as a fish!"

"So… you think you could synthesize a cure for the Kalavat Plague from this jellyfish?" she asked slowly.

Now Minnen stared at *her* with incredulity. "Of course not! What I'm saying is that the aracobzi uses venomous DNA to reproduce. The Kalavat

Plague also contains genetic material. I wonder if in its original state it came from an animal that has a similar reproductive process." He fell silent and returned his attention to the computer screen. Korosa thought it best not to interrupt him, so she turned to Uxxio. "What are *you* doing?"

"I'm compiling a translation matrix that will interpret the information the professor gathers from the Thalassan language to Ganti and Trade Standard," he told her. "I'm also monitoring the local newsfeeds for any information on the Vinkere."

The computer completed its search of the Thalassan database and displayed the entries most relevant to Professor Minnen's query. "If you can't read Thalassan, how can you use their computer?" Korosa asked.

"I *can* read Thalassan, but not well enough. I'm quite rusty," Minnen replied. "But it's enough to find what I'm looking for. This, this, and these," he said, pointing to a number of entries on the screen.

"Couldn't you have done this from the ship?" Korosa asked.

"Some of these texts exist only as physical copies. We need to find the actual books," Minnen said. He got off the stool and stretched.

"Then we need to scan each individual page with the datapad," Uxxio added, sounding excited at the prospect.

Korosa couldn't imagine anything more boring. "Can't we just take the books with us?" she asked impatiently.

"Are you going to come back here in three weeks to return them?" Uxxio retorted, pointing at a sign written in Thalassan.

"I guess not," she muttered.

"How long until we reach the governor's office?" Jadus asked the driver. His grasp of Trade Standard was limited, and she didn't understand his halting reply. Jarren looked at her and shrugged, then turned his attention back to the city beneath them. Although the Thalassan information network confirmed there were over two hundred thousand people currently in the city, there was little ground or air traffic. Where were they all?

"It looks like a ghost town," Jarren remarked.

"Everyone has probably heard the rumors of Vinkere ships lurking nearby. They're probably in their homes," Jadus said. Jarren nodded; news of the Vinkere's swift and brutal invasion of the Commonwealth was spreading across the Locality like wildfire. He had spent hours reading about it. "I don't blame them," he said. "The Vinkere sound ruthless."

"Well, they're somebody else's problem right now," Jadus said firmly. "Our job is to get home and find a cure for the Kalavat Plague before there's no one left to save."

"Thanks, guys," Antak said as two Thalassan workers in dark blue coveralls connected a Tuulan For-adapted fuel nozzle to the *Telvarn Star*. They communicated with him mostly through hand signals and gestures; Antak wasn't sure if they spoke any Trade Standard.

While they refueled the ship, he looked out across the city. As the Thalassans' busiest trading port, he would have imagined it would be… well, *busy*. He'd seen more traffic on frontier worlds. The Vinkere invasion of the neighboring Commonwealth was probably responsible for that. He didn't speak Thalassan, but he thought he heard the workers say "Vinkere" in hushed voices.

When the fuel gauge showed full, the workers deactivated the pump and uncoupled the pipe from the ship, then abandoned the equipment on the ground beside the ship.

"Is there a problem?" Antak asked. Neither of them responded. They were engaged in a quiet but intense debate and ignored the alien frowning at them.

After several moments, the oldest Thalassan turned to Antak. "We go. Home," he said in heavily accented Trade Standard.

Antak looked at them in surprise. "What about the engines, and cleaning the-"

"We go," the Thalassan repeated. He pointed up at the sky. "We go."

Antak watched, speechless, as the two workers left the landing platform.

"I don't believe this," he muttered.

Doctor Kerik appeared in the hatchway of the ship. "Finished already? That was quick," he said.

"Not finished. They decided to go home," Antak grumbled. "They're afraid there are Vinkere nearby."

"I see."

"At least we're refueled. That was our top priority."

Suddenly a siren began wailing, shrill enough to make them both wince. "That doesn't sound good," Kerik said, frowning.

Antak nodded. The few anti-grav cars in the sky were quickly landing, and the streets were rapidly filling with people, flowing out of offices and apartments. They were all heading toward buildings with large, reinforced metal doors, forming neat lines as they filed inside. "They look like bomb shelters," he commented. Then it dawned on him that they *were* bomb shelters.

"Someone's coming," Kerik said, pointing toward the door the Thalassan workers had disappeared through. A Thalassan man in a grey military uniform was running toward them.

"Please come with me immediately," the man said with preamble.

"Who are you?" Antak demanded.

"I am Agent Hakoa. The governor sent me to bring you to safety."

"Safety? What's wrong?" Antak asked.

Hakoa looked at them accusingly. "The Vinkere have come here," he told them. "Strange that they would turn up within an hour of your arrival, isn't it?"

*

The four Vinkere ships of S'Geliss' squadron emerged from the slipstream into normal space. The bright blue globe of Tahvoa shone in the middle distance.

Almost immediately they were intercepted by two ships of the Thalassan Guard, who demanded they withdraw from Thalassan space; the Vinkere ships responded with a barrage of weapons fire. The leading Thalassan ship was quickly overwhelmed and exploded in a blinding flash. The second ship resisted bravely for another minute before it also succumbed to the overwhelming firepower of the invaders. Fiery debris tumbled toward the planet as it broke apart.

As the Vinkere ships approached the planet, four slipstream portals opened and four more Thalassan Guard vessels appeared, opening fire upon the Vinkere. The invaders were forced to defend themselves, retaliating against the fierce attack by the newcomers. Despite their bravery, the Thalassan ships were technologically outmatched and the battle lasted only a few minutes before they too were obliterated. Without further opposition the Vinkere warships moved into orbit above the undefended planet.

"I've located the Tuulan For ship," S'Geliss' sensor officer reported. He pointed at an image of the planet taken by one of their stealth probes. It showed a close-up aerial view of the *Telvarn Star* on the landing pad in Triyev.

"The city is alerted to our presence," another officer reported. "They're raising defensive shields."

"Target the Tuulan For ship," S'Geliss snapped. "Destroy it!"

Minister Jadus and Jarren were seated in the Thalassan governor's office when the alarm sounded. An aide burst into the room, apologizing for the interruption. After a hasty, whispered conversation with the newcomer, Governor Vannora turned to his guests.

"Vinkere ships are in orbit!" he said anxiously. "We must submerge the city for protection!"

Jadus looked alarmed. "You can't submerge the city while we're still here. We need to get back to Tuulan Vee!"

"There is no choice," said Governor Vannora. He sounded frightened. "The ocean will shield us. We cannot remain exposed!"

"I understand. But please, just give us time to get back to our ship," she implored him. They couldn't afford to be trapped in the city if the Vinkere laid siege to Triyev.

The governor looked conflicted; his experience with outsiders was limited, and he had never faced conflict with hostile aliens before. Jadus tried to appear calm while she waited for his response, but she was painfully aware that every second he hesitated was another moment lost. Suddenly the room was lit up by a bright flash. Jadus and Jarren were facing away from the window but Governor Vannora flinched and shielded his eyes from the glare. The flash was followed seconds later by a loud *BOOM* that rattled the windowpanes.

"What was that?" Jarren asked in alarm.

Vannora confirmed Jadus' worst fear. "That was the docking tower," he said. "The Vinkere just destroyed it from orbit, along with your ship. They were targeting *you*."

Jadus and Jarren looked at each other, momentarily speechless. The *Telvarn Star* was gone. They had no way off the planet. And what about Antak and Doctor Kerik?

Vannora turned to his aide, and Jadus saw new resolve in his eyes, that there would be no changing his mind. "Raise the shields and submerge the city," he ordered firmly.

The Thalassans were amphibious, capable of living on land or in water, but they were most comfortable in the ocean. On their home world of Rana, a world where oceans covered ninety percent of the surface, most of the population lived in aquatic cities on the seabed. When the Thalassans colonized other worlds and established contact with land-dwelling life forms they recognized the need for surface outposts to facilitate their limited trade and diplomacy, but all their floating cities were built with a unique defensive measure. They had rarely needed to employ such defensive measures in the past, and never due to the threat of armed conflict, but now the floating cities of Tahvoa responded to the Vinkere threat.

The moment the siren first sounded the elderly Thalassan librarian began ushering everyone in the library toward the door. When Minnen asked if he could borrow the book he was still holding, the librarian replied, "Return it in three weeks," and then closed the doors, locking them out.

Korosa and Minnen exchanged looks. The Iganti professor shrugged and tucked the book away in his bag. All along the street signs were flashing in the Thalassan language.

"What do they say?" Korosa asked Minnen. He squinted at one thoughtfully.

"I believe words to the effect of, 'make your way to the nearest designated secure shelter' or something similar."

The other pedestrians were hurrying toward a set of vault-like doors in one of the buildings further down the street.

"We better get to cover as well," said Korosa. She began to walk quickly down the street, and Minnen and Uxxio followed her. They were less than twenty meters from the entrance to the shelter when there was a thunderous *BOOM*. Because they were all facing the same direction, they saw the Vinkere missiles that sped down from the sky and crashed into the docking tower where the *Telvarn Star* sat. The explosion was followed by a loud *crack* as the shockwave rippled down the street, shattering windowpanes. Panicked, people turned and ran in the opposite direction, trying to shield themselves from shards of falling glass. The remnants of the docking tower were engulfed in a raging inferno. There was another loud rumble and the building collapsed, creating a dust cloud that obscured their view of the wreckage.

"Antak," Korosa whispered in shock. He had been with the ship. She tried to hail him on his communicator. There was no response. Uxxio stared at the destruction in mute horror; Minnen eyed the billowing dust cloud with a quiet calmness that hid whatever emotions he was feeling.

"Don't just stand there, try reaching the Minister!" she shouted frantically. Minnen raised his brow at her but complied.

"It's no use," he said after several attempts. "Our communications are being jammed." His face lit up. "But they can't block *grounded* communications. We must find a landline!"

Korosa, embarrassed by her outburst, nodded in agreement. For all his eccentricities, she was glad to have the level-headed professor with her. Uxxio looked completely out of his element, staring at the expanding dust cloud with a glazed expression.

Suddenly the ground, the buildings around them, *everything* started shaking. Uxxio yelped in surprise as the street wobbled beneath them. Korosa wondered what could be causing the tremors. Another bombardment? Then the ambient light dimmed, as if evening had suddenly descended on the city. They looked up to see an energy shield expanding outwards from the city's central tower. It spread across the sky, enclosing the city in a vast bubble of protective energy. The shaking reduced until the ground trembled almost imperceptibly, like in a moving elevator.

"Do you feel that?" Korosa asked the others. "The ground's moving!"

Minnen nodded. "I suspect the Thalassans intend to submerge the city."

Korosa, Minnen and Uxxio looked up as the ocean rose around the city. Streetlights came on to counteract the unnatural darkness as the city descended into the depths.

"The ocean acts as another layer of protection from attackers," Minnen said appreciatively. "Ingenious!"

Korosa ignored him, scanning the area for a communications terminal. The city must have a grounded communications network. She found a communications kiosk and dialed the operator, asking to be connected to the governor's tower. As she waited, she glanced over her shoulder at the mound of burning wreckage that had previously been the docking tower. She caught a glimpse of a blackened hull plate, all that was left of the *Telvarn Star* that she could see.

"I don't think we're going anywhere soon," she said grimly.

Antak and Doctor Kerik let Agent Hakoa lead them to a nearby shelter in the basement of a tall building. They were there, along with hundreds of locals, when they heard the muffled sounds of an explosion through the concrete walls of the basement. Antak and Kerik exchanged worried looks before Antak desperately resumed trying to contact the other members of their party.

*

Minister Jadus watched solemnly as the shield enclosed the city and the floating metropolis lowered itself beneath the waves.

"How far down are we going?" she asked Governor Vannora. Her earlier frustration at the man had ebbed; she couldn't fault him for protecting his city. In his place she would have done the same thing.

"All the way to the sea floor, sixteen hundred meters below the surface," Vannora replied.

Jarren approached Minister Jadus, holding his communicator. "I can't reach Antak, or Korosa, or any of the others," he said worriedly.

"It's the Vinkere ships," Governor Vannora said. "They're blocking all wireless communications. We can't even communicate with the other cities."

Jarren looked out the window at the remnants of the docking tower. The dust had cleared, and the wreckage was visible in the search lights of emergency craft. Thalassan Emergency Services personnel in bright orange vests combed the wreckage for survivors. Almost no natural light filtered down through the ocean above; the city was lit only by streetlamps, neon signs, and building lights. But the lack of stars made it seem dim and unnatural to Jarren, who felt uneasy knowing there was more than one and a half kilometers of seawater above his head, restrained only by a thin energy shield.

Vannora joined him by the window. His rubbery, water-resistant skin seemed to glisten wetly in the light. He gestured toward the ruined docking tower. "We issued the evacuation warnings as soon as the Vinkere arrived in orbit. I hope that gave people enough time to get to shelter."

"Our people might not have understood the warning," Jarren said gloomily.

"Antak and Korosa are smart people," Jadus said firmly. "Not to mention the doctors. They know how to look after themselves."

"And just in case they didn't," Vannora said, "I had one of my people go to your ship to collect them."

Jarren felt the knot of anxiety in his stomach loosen. "You did?"

Jadus was visibly relieved. "Thank you, Governor," she said sincerely. Vannora inclined his head in acknowledgement.

"Is there any way we can contact the rest of our shipmates?" Jadus asked him.

"Grounded communications are still functioning," he said. "I'll have someone contact Agent Hakoa, the man I sent to collect your team. We'll bring them here at once."

"Thank you," she said again. A military officer approached the governor so she stepped away to give them privacy. She joined Jarren at the window, looking up at the dark ocean above their heads. The sky briefly flared orange as a missile exploded against the city's shield. Then it faded, plunging the city back into night-like darkness. Her young aide looked troubled.

"Are you alright?" Jadus asked him quietly.

"They destroyed the tower because of us, didn't they? They could have fired anywhere on the city, and yet they targeted our ship. Why?"

Jadus didn't want Jarren to feel responsible for any deaths in the docking tower. The Vinkere were responsible, not them. But she had to wonder at their timing; to her knowledge the Vinkere hadn't attacked any targets outside of the Commonwealth, until now. And from the subtle, accusing glances the governor's military advisor gave her, she was sure they blamed her presence in Triyev for the attack.

"Maybe they know we are trying to cure the Kalavat Plague, and they want to stop us," she said. Could it be a coincidence the Vinkere were bombarding the city? They had much to gain from the Kalavat Plague; humanity's allies were unable to assist the Commonwealth while they were busy protecting themselves. But how could the Vinkere know about Jadus and Minnen's work, and of their presence here? She didn't know. Intercepted communications between Tuulan Vee and Iganta may have alerted them to her mission, but they hadn't told anyone they were coming to Tahvoa; it had been a last-minute decision.

Maybe they had made an educated guess as to her destination. That thought worried her greatly, because if the enemy could predict her movements, they would eventually catch her and Minnen and the Locality's best hope of curing the Kalavat Plague would die with them.

Another Vinkere missile exploded against the city's protective shield. Since their surprise invasion of the Commonwealth the Vinkere had developed a reputation as devious and powerful, which Jadus could see was well-earned. But they weren't the only ones who could be devious. It was time to be unpredictable.

Governor Vannora seemed confident the shield would hold until reinforcements arrived, but now that Jadus realized how formidable the Vinkere were, she was unwilling to endanger the city any longer.

She strode purposefully across the office to where the Thalassan governor was consulting his military advisor. She approached with such confidence that both men stopped talking and looked at her expectantly.

"Governor, thank you again for keeping my people safe. I truly am sorry if our presence has put your people in danger. But it won't for much longer. We're leaving. Come along, Jarren." He hurried after her.

"How?" Vannora asked in surprise.

She turned back to him. "We will find a way off Tahvoa. I am not sure how yet, but we're leaving. Now."

19

S'Geliss glowered at the viewscreen as the Thalassan city sunk beneath the waves, leaving white, turbulent water crashing in its wake. "Was the Tuulan For ship destroyed?" he asked.

"Affirmative," replied the sensor officer.

"Good. What about the Tuulan For Minister?"

The officer hesitated before giving the answer. "We are still detecting Tuulan For life signs within the city, but they could be inhabitants of the city. We have no way of knowing."

S'Geliss clenched his fists. "At least we have destroyed their method of escape," he said slowly. He slithered across the deck to the tactical station. S'Geliss leaned over the technician to examine the screen, his forked tongue flickering absently as he read the data. The technician shrunk away, nervous at his proximity, but S'Geliss ignored him. "Tell the *Szor* and the *Kthaliss* to remain in orbit," he ordered the communications officer. "And tell the *Silthis* to prepare for atmospheric flight and follow us down to the planet. We are going after the Tuulan For Minister."

The technician spoke up nervously. "But sir, the city is at the bottom of the ocean, protected by—"

S'Geliss cut him off with a hand gesture. "We will go down there and find a way through those shields if I have to use your skull as a battering ram!" He gave the other officers a fierce glare and announced, "We will not leave this planet until the Tuulan For Minister and her allies are dead!"

The *Ss'Thiz* and the *Silthis* descended toward Triyev while the remaining two Vinkere warships remained in orbit, watchful for Thalassan ships. On the command deck of the *Ss'Thiz,* S'Geliss watched the ocean draw nearer. He looked forward to the coming battle with great anticipation. The Tuulan For minister and Iganti scientist were either foolish or arrogant to try and deter the Vinkeres' plans for their pathetic species, and he looked forward to presenting their severed heads to Supreme Commander Zithla.

*

The bunker Antak and Doctor Kerik found themselves in was uncomfortably warm and crowded. Antak waited impatiently while Agent

Hakoa used the only communications terminal to speak to his superiors. "I am to take you to the governor's tower," the Thalassan told them when the call ended.

"Let's go, then," Antak said. He was eager to reunite with his shipmates. They pushed a path through the crowd, and Hakoa led them through a different doorway to the one they had entered through. "This tunnel connects to the subway system," he explained.

"Why not go out the way we came in?" Antak asked as they moved hastily down the brightly lit corridor.

"Emergency services are still clearing the debris," Hakoa said neutrally. Antak and Kerik exchanged looks. Did the Thalassan agent hold them responsible for the destruction caused by the Vinkere? *Maybe that's not completely unreasonable,* Antak thought, feeling a pang of guilt at the conflict they may have inadvertently brought to the Thalassans' doorstep.

By the time they reached the subway station other people were emerging from the secure shelters. No "all-clear" signal had been given, but the locals seemed cautiously determined to resume their daily routines. The subway station was much like any other subway station in the Locality, except for the network of water-filled tunnels that extended from the station platform. Antak watched with interest as a Thalassan worker stepped through the containment force field into the tube, and was swept away by the current toward his destination.

"Fascinating," Doctor Kerik commented.

Agent Hakoa commandeered a subway carriage for them, which raced away from the station along its mag-lev track. Hakoa didn't say much on the trip, pacing restlessly and trying to re-establish wireless communications. From his cursing Antak guessed he was having no luck. Antak hadn't been able to contact the other members of his team either.

The city's protective shield and the ocean above their heads must have been a reassuring presence to the Thalassans of Triyev, because in each station they passed there was a growing throng of people returning to use the city's transport network. Doctor Kerik stared aimlessly out the window at the tunnel walls rushing past them. Antak watched their progress toward the governor's tower station; their carriage was represented as a golden dot moving across the electronic map on the carriage wall. The trip took less than five minutes, but all three of the carriage's passengers were impatient to reach their destination. When they arrived, they burst out of the carriage as soon as the doors opened, startling nearby commuters. An elevator took them up to the ground-level foyer of the governor's tower, where they found Jarren and Jadus waiting by the large glass doors that led to the main street.

"Jarren!" Antak called out, striding toward his friend. Jarren and Jadus turned, surprised by the direction of their approach.

"We're glad you made it out of there!" Jarren said with relief, clapping his friend on the shoulder and greeting Doctor Kerik with a handshake. "We saw the tower explode and feared the worst when we couldn't contact you."

"Agent Hakoa got us to a bomb shelter a few minutes before the tower was hit," Antak said, gesturing to the Thalassan officer, who was using another communications terminal to inform the governor they'd arrived.

"I am relieved you are both well," Jadus told them. "When the others arrive, we can see about getting out of this city."

"How?" Antak asked.

"We'll find a way. We'll charter a ship if we have to," she said. She pointed outside. "Here they are now."

Korosa, Professor Minnen and Uxxio were emerging from a taxi. Jadus and the others went out the glass doors and down the steps to greet them; Agent Hakoa, who was still on the phone, watched them.

They reached the bottom of the steps as Uxxio was helping the elderly professor out of the backseat. Korosa was leaning into the front window, arguing loudly with the driver.

"What's the problem?" Antak as Uxxio.

"We could not find a government vehicle, so we had to commandeer this gentleman's taxi," Uxxio said. He had to speak loudly to be heard over Korosa and the driver's shouting. "Of course, Lieutenant Korosa is trying to convince him to put it on the government's tab."

Agent Hakoa appeared behind them, taking in the scene in a glance. "Is there a problem?" he asked wryly.

"I am glad you are here, sir," Professor Minnen said. "Kindly pay the gentleman his fee, will you?"

Hakoa looked at him in surprise. "Me?"

Korosa turned around. "The only way we could get here was by telling him the government would pay a premium for our journey. Which was only a few blocks anyway," she grumbled. She thumped the side of the car. "See? I told you we were with the government," she said loudly to the driver, who responded angrily and unintelligibly.

Hakoa sighed and reached into his pocket, pulling out his credit chip. Overhead, another Vinkere missile exploded against the city's shield, momentarily bathing the street in orange light.

"The Vinker's missiles can still reach us," Uxxio remarked grimly.

"It won't do them any good," Minnen said confidently. Nobody asked him how he had come to that conclusion.

Around them, the city was slowly coming back to life. The Thalassans evidently felt safer beneath the ocean, and were beginning to appear on the streets in growing numbers, even more than when they had first arrived in Triyev.

"How deep are we?" Korosa asked.

"Sixteen hundred meters below the surface," Jarren said, repeating what Governor Vannora had told them. "On the sea floor."

"Our lack of a ship is the more pressing concern," Jadus said. "That, and the Vinkere warships in orbit."

Hakoa finished paying the driver and the hover taxi pulled away from the curb, joining the increasing flow of traffic on the boulevard. Hakoa put away his credit chip. "What do you plan to do now?" he asked.

"Why does it matter to you?" Jadus asked politely.

"Governor Vannora has asked me to assist you until you leave," he said, sounding unenthusiastic at the prospect of chaperoning the group of aliens.

Minister Jadus looked at Professor Minnen and Doctor Kerik. "Did we lose all our research?" she asked fearfully.

"Worry not!" Minnen said, producing his datapad with a flourish. "Uxxio and I carry the research with us."

"I also have the latest backup on my data chip," Doctor Kerik said, tapping the pocket of his jacket. He always carried a backup of his work, a habit originating from his time at a frontier clinic on V'Lei where power outages were common.

"So, we won't have to start again from nothing," Jadus said, immensely relieved.

"The research is safe," Minnen confirmed.

"I wish I could say the same about our ship," Antak said ruefully.

Jadus took Hakoa aside, out of hearing range of the others. "Were there… any casualties?" she asked delicately.

"There are five confirmed dead," he said. "Most of the building had been evacuated, but we're still trying to account for everyone."

While Jadus conferred with Hakoa, Antak shared with Korosa and Jarren his fear that their presence had brought the Vinkere to Tahvoa. "I know," Jarren confided quietly. "Minister Jadus hasn't said it, but I know she's thinking the same thing."

"I think we all are," Korosa said. "And if it's true, it means the Vinkere know that the Minister is working with Professor Minnen."

In his prime, Minnen the Learned had almost single-handedly cured the "incurable" Osaija Virus. If the Vinkere were as bad as the news reports made them out to be, it wasn't surprising they would try to stop to his efforts to cure the Kalavat plague.

Jadus and Hakoa re-joined the others. "Our priority is getting off the planet without the Vinkere following us," she said as they clustered around her.

"Thalassan ships are slower than ours," Antak said. "Even if we do get one, it's going to take more time to reach Tuulan Vee."

"There are other Tuulan For here," Korosa said. "Maybe we could commandeer their ship."

One of the governor's aides approached Agent Hakoa to whisper something in his ear. Whatever it was, he didn't look pleased.

"What's wrong?" Jadus asked him.

"Two of the Vinkere ships have entered the atmosphere," Hakoa said in a strained voice. "They're headed directly toward the city."

The others looked at him in astonishment. "Can their ships survive the pressure at this depth?" Jarren asked.

"I have no idea," the agent snapped. "But they've already destroyed several of our ships, so who knows what they're capable of!"

"All the more reason for us to leave as soon as possible," Jadus said, adding quickly, "So they might leave your city alone." She took a deep breath. "Would you be able to lend us a slipstream-capable starship? With the *Telvarn Star* destroyed, we have no way off planet, but our mission—"

The professional courtesy Hakoa had extended toward the aliens was rapidly evaporating as the Vinkere approached. "No, we do not have any ships to spare," he snapped, loud enough for nearby pedestrians to hear. Minister Jadus bristled, unused to being spoken to in such a manner, but she held her tongue as Hakoa continued angrily: "The Vinkere came here looking for *you*. You think it's a coincidence that they turned up within an hour of you arriving with the galaxy's leading expert on everything? Yes, I recognized you straight away," Hakoa snapped at Minnen, who regarded him impassively. "They have already destroyed six of our ships, and now they've got my city in their sights. Unfortunately for us, it seems they will stop at nothing to catch you!"

"I don't think they're trying to catch us," Jadus said quietly. "I think they mean to kill us. They destroyed our ship and I think they will destroy the entire city if it means killing us. You and your people are at risk as long as we remain here. We've already caused you enough problems. If there is a way for us to escape, and draw the Vinkere away, we owe that to you before any more innocent people die." She was confident that if they could slip out of the city Antak would be able to evade the Vinkere ships long enough for them to enter the slipstream.

"That's very brave of you," Hakoa said, although he considered it the least they could do. "But I meant it when I said we have no available ships.

If you're looking for one, you'll have to try the private sector. You'll need to speak to a civilian captain."

"We will do that," Jadus said resolutely. "Where should we start?"

"You could try the International Quarter," he said. "It's the part of the city near the spaceport. It has several bars and cafes popular with expats and visitors."

"Thank you," she said, then hesitated before asking: "Is there any way we could organize for transport to the International Quarter?"

"I'll get a vehicle," Hakoa said tersely. Before he could stalk away, Jadus took one of his large, rubbery hands in hers. He looked startled but seemed to understand the meaning behind the gesture.

"Thank you, Agent Hakoa," she said sincerely.

Hakoa's expression softened a little. "We still can't communicate with anyone outside the city, but I know the Thalassan Guard will be organizing a response. Now they've seen what the Vinkere are capable of, they will respond appropriately. You will have the best chance of escaping when they strike."

He requisitioned a police vehicle large enough to transport the entire group. It was a ten-minute drive to the International Quarter, which was home to most of Triyev's non-Thalassan population. Hakoa stopped the vehicle on a wide boulevard, parking behind a sleek anti-grav car.

"You can try here," he said, gesturing outside the car. The boulevard was lined with restaurants, cafes, and clubs. They were about halfway along the boulevard, between the elegantly styled buildings nearer the city center with their bright lights flashing and the older, shabbier establishments further out.

The group piled out of the vehicle and looked around. "The *Nauseous Navigator*," Professor Minnen said, reading the glowing sign on a nearby building. "How charming."

"Why here?" Antak asked Hakoa, who had stayed inside the vehicle.

"According to the reviews, this place is popular with ship captains," Hakoa said. He'd never heard of it until today. "Assuming they haven't all left the city already, it's as good as any place to start looking."

"You're not coming in?" Jarren asked him.

Hakoa sighed. "I wasn't planning on it." Minister Jadus was already striding resolutely toward the door. Korosa hurried after her, Minnen and Uxxio hot on her heels. Doctor Kerik, hands in his pockets, sauntered after them.

"Don't leave before we find a ride," Antak warned Hakoa.

Hakoa played with the police radio, hoping to find a channel that wasn't all static. After a few minutes he gave up, and tapped his foot impatiently, hoping he didn't have to wait long for the others.

The Vinkere warship *Ss'Thiz* breached the surface of the ocean, sending waves rippling outwards. It plunged downward through the seawater toward the city; the second Vinkere ship followed closely in its wake.

"We're still jamming their communications," the communications officer reported. "The city will not be able to call for help." The ambient light faded as they descended into the darkness of the ocean's bathypelagic zone. Soon the lights of Triyev appeared in the darkness ahead of them, growing brighter as they approached.

"Open fire," S'Geliss ordered. The warships fired their missiles, which glided through the water like torpedoes before slamming into the dome-like shield covering the city. The shield rippled, but held.

"The city's shield is far superior to those of the Thalassan ships, Captain," the sensor operations officer reported. "We cannot penetrate them."

"Then find me another way into the city!" S'Geliss seethed. He was impatient with their progress. The submergence of the city had been unexpected. He had incorrectly assumed the city would be as weak as the ships guarding it, an assumption he would pay for dearly if Supreme Commander Zithla found out about his carelessness. He had to find a way into the city and dispose of the Tuulan For Minister immediately, before the Thalassans could re-gather and launch another attack. They had been swiftly defeated before, but if they attacked with a large enough fleet S'Geliss' ships would be overwhelmed.

The sensor operations officer showed him scans of the city. "The rim of the city has tunnels that permit aquatic vehicles access to the city. They're sealed shut now, but we could blast them open and enter with our assault transports."

"Do it," S'Geliss ordered, already slithering toward the exit. He intended to be aboard the first transport to enter the city. "And order the *Silthis* to do the same."

A proximity alert began beeping. "Sir, the *Szor* and the *Kthaliss* report a disruption in slipspace approaching. It appears to be a large fleet heading for the planet."

"They must hold off the enemy at all costs," S'Geliss declared. "We must complete our mission!"

*

Elzor Drin thumped his empty cup on the bar top, trying to get the bartender's attention. "Requesting more drink is what I am doing!" he called groggily.

The Thalassan bartender looked at him wearily. "No more," he said firmly.

"I request one more!" Drin repeated.

"Well, you're not getting one more," the bartender said, plucking his glass off the bench and putting it out of reach. Drin grabbed for it with his stubby, four-clawed hands. His barstool swayed precariously and he nearly fell off. "Protest is what I am doing!" Drin wailed drunkenly.

"Cutting you off is what I'm doing," the bartender replied evenly. Having dealt with the Vlind every day for the last fortnight he knew the merchant captain was depressed, but he made it a rule never to delve into the personal lives of his customers. It was none of his business, and he didn't want to know.

Drin slumped dramatically against the bar top, drawing curious stares from the other patrons. He didn't care. The Vlind merchant didn't want company, he just wanted to drink. And since his ship had run out of alcohol two weeks ago that meant coming here. The reviews had said it was popular with ship captains. And yet all the time he had spent here, the place was never very busy, he noted groggily. Probably the locals were cowering in their homes, waiting for the Kalavat Plague and now the Vinkere to disappear. Or to finish them off.

The door opened and Drin looked over his shoulder at the newcomers. A group of aliens stood in the entrance, scanning the room as though looking for somebody. The few patrons of the bar looked back at them curiously. Even drunk, Drin could sense their urgency. They spread out, approaching some of the patrons. Maybe they were looking for someone, Drin thought dully. They weren't regulars; he hadn't seen them here before.

In the time Elzor Drin had spent in the *Nauseous Navigator* trying to drink himself into a stupor, his guilt had remained a constant companion. He felt as ashamed today as he did when he had fled Takutu Station, abandoning his crew and the station to the infection.

Alone onboard the *Wealth and Grandeur* he had traveled for many weeks, wanting to get as far away as possible. That was how he had ended up at Tahvoa, on the edge of nowhere (which is what he considered Thalassan space). Surely here he would be left in peace. But alas, he thought wretchedly, he was not. Within days of his arrival the *Vinkere* appeared, invading the neighboring Human Commonwealth and sparking a new wave of panic. The city had all but emptied as visitors, transients and the wealthier residents fled, becoming a ghost town as people listened anxiously to unverified reports of Vinkere lurking behind every nebula. And now they were here. He supposed he deserved it; divine retribution for abandoning his crew and fleeing like a coward. Drin looked down at his empty hands, wishing they were holding another beverage.

He had tried to assure himself many times there was nothing more he could have done. There was no reason to stay while the station was overrun by the Kalavat Plague. He had behaved logically. Except that maybe he hadn't. It was fear that had driven him to abandon his infected crew and flee Takutu station. The thought of devolving into one of those twisted, brutal creatures terrified him. If he hadn't left, he would probably be infected right now, biting chunks out of people, or being gunned down by one of the Vlind Merchant Republic's Containment Squads. What choice did he have? Yes, he was definitely the victim, he insisted mentally, although the weight of his guilt left him unconvinced.

"Excuse me?" a voice said behind him, startling him from his drunken reverie. It was a female voice, not the bartender. He turned slowly to face the person addressing him.

It was a female, either Human or Tuulan For; he struggled to tell them apart. He was no expert at telling the age of aliens but he would have guessed she was in her late middle age. Assuming Human-Tuulan Fors wrinkled the same way Vlind did, that is.

He looked at her expectantly, then realized she was probably waiting for him to acknowledge her greeting. "I acknowledge your greeting," he said lamely.

She studied him. "I noticed that you are wearing a uniform. Might I ask if you belong to a starship crew?"

"You may," Drin replied. He waited.

"Oh, okay... do you belong to a starship crew?" she asked, keeping her face politely neutral. Vlind had a peculiar manner of speech, but conversing with this drunken Vlind was downright difficult.

"A starship crew is what I do not belong to," Drin replied. The woman looked disappointed until he added, "For I am a Ship's Overseer."

She looked both pleased with his answer and frustrated at its delivery. "That's excellent news. My name is Torina Jadus. I was hoping to charter your vessel for a long journey. It is quite urgent."

"Travel with me is what you do not want to do," Drin said despondently, causing her to raise an eyebrow. "Bad fortune follows me. Also, there is nowhere to go, for the Vinkere are attacking the city," he added.

"I am keenly aware of that," Jadus said through gritted teeth.

Forty cylindrical assault transports left the two Vinkere warships and streamed through the ocean toward the city, each transporting a dozen Vinkere soldiers ready for battle. In the leading transport, S'Geliss donned his force field skeleton over his armor, noting the anticipation of the soldiers around him as they neared their target. The assault ships were designed for rapidly boarding enemy vessels; the airlock at the front of the ship was surrounded by laser drills capable of cutting through the outer hull of enemy ships and giving direct access to the interior. S'Geliss was confident that they would be equally effective against the sealed aquatic passageways leading into the city.

The other transports fanned out on either side of them, set to breach other tunnels in a semi-circular fashion around the rim of the city. The *Ss'Thiz*, with its more powerful sensors, would guide them toward the small cluster of Tuulan For and Iganti life signs which S'Geliss was certain were their targets. He grinned wickedly, relishing the thought of hunting his prey through the streets of the city and cutting them down without mercy. This was far more preferable to ship-to-ship combat.

"When we reach the city, kill anyone you encounter," S'Geliss ordered, and his soldiers growled enthusiastically in response. "But remember: our objective is to kill the Tuulan For Minister and the Iganti scientist. Everything else is secondary."

"We will pay you handsomely," Jadus told the Vlind ship's overseer.

"The issue is not money," Drin replied. "The Vinkere besiege the city, and there is no way to leave."

"But your ship could leave the city if it weren't for the Vinkere? The hull can withstand the water pressure?" she asked.

Drin hiccupped. "Pressure of the ocean is not a problem, but the Vinkere surround the city, and there is no way to leave."

Jadus frowned, wondering if he was aware that he was repeating himself. "The Thalassan military is preparing a counterattack," she told him. "They will distract the Vinkere long enough for us to get away."

The deep drone of a powerful engine caused the window panes to rattle. Everyone in the bar looked out the windows as a heavily armored military transport rumbled past.

"I cannot leave," Drin moaned. "I am a great wrong-doer. The Vinkere are here because I abandoned my crew. They will hunt me down no matter where I go."

Her patient façade slipped. "Sir, the Vinkere are here because of *us!*" Jadus said. "That is why we need to go. See that man over there?" she pointed to Professor Minnen, who was typing on his datapad while Korosa and Jarren argued with a freighter captain nearby. "That is *the* Minnen the

Learned. You might have heard of him?" she asked wryly. "He's working on a cure for the Kalavat Plague. We-"

Drin bolted upright in his seat; Jadus reflexively reached out to steady him as the stool wobbled. "You have a cure for the Infected?" Drin asked, instantly alert.

"Yes. Well, maybe. Soon," Jadus said. "We are close to a breakthrough, but none of it will matter if the Vinkere kill us first."

"A miracle," Drin said quietly, earning a confused look from Jadus. "This was meant to be!" He climbed off his stool, stumbled slightly, and then steadied himself against the bar. "This is my redemption! To deliver the curer of the Infected to safety!" He hopped about excitedly, then paused. "A crew I do not have," he said.

"It's okay, we've got a pilot," Jadus said hastily, signaling for the others to come join her. "You can fly a Vlind ship easily enough, can't you Antak?" she said with a pointed look.

"Uh, yeah, of course," Antak replied.

"Good. Where's your ship?" she said, turning back to the Vlind captain, who barely came up to her chest.

"Its location is the spaceport, not far from here," Drin said, sounding more sober with every passing moment. Jadus didn't know what he meant when he referred to his "redemption", and frankly didn't care. If it meant he was willing to charter them his ship, it was fine by her.

The door burst open and Agent Hakoa barged in. "I need to use your landline," he told the bartender, flashing his government ID card. The bartender gestured to the communications terminal behind the counter. Professor Minnen wasn't using his datapad anymore; his head was cocked to the side, listening intently.

"Did anyone else hear that?" he asked.

"Hear what?" Jadus asked.

Minnen frowned in concentration. "It sounded like weapons fire."

"Are you sure?" Antak said.

"Young man, I have exceptional hearing," Minnen retorted.

"I hear it too," Uxxio confirmed. Iganti hearing was superior to Tuulan For, but soon the others could make out the distant sounds of gunfire.

"Do you think the Vinkere found a way into the city?" Jarren wondered, anxiety creasing his brow.

Hakoa got off the phone. He thumped the terminal and cursed. "I tried to reach Guard Headquarters," he said. "Vinkere soldiers have entered the city. They've released a worm into the city's computer network and it's disrupting land-based communications. We have no way to coordinate a response."

"It'll be chaos," Korosa said, horrified. The sound of weapons fire grew closer, louder; patrons in the bar looked around anxiously, wondering what to do.

"The Vinkere are in the city," Hakoa repeated, loud enough for the entire room to hear. "Everyone should head for the nearest emergency shelter at once!"

There was a *BOOM* as a vehicle down the street exploded, followed by the sound of shattering glass and startled cries.

The bartender began ushering everyone toward the backdoor. The same shrill alarm that had alerted them to the Vinkere in orbit began wailing again, warning citizens to take cover in emergency shelters.

"Can you help us reach spaceport?" Jadus asked the grim-faced Hakoa.

"I'll try," he promised.

The group rushed out onto the street. "Look out!" Antak hollered as crimson energy bolts flew past. Several of them struck their vehicle, reducing the engine to slag. Serpentine figures were advancing up the street toward them. They sprayed the street with weapons fire, energy bolts smashing through glass windows, cracking stone, and melting colorful neon signs. Although difficult to make out through the smoky haze, members of the city's black-uniformed militia fought back against the intruders.

"We need a new vehicle!" Hakoa said, looking around desperately.

"Which way to the spaceport?" Jadus asked.

"This way!" Elzor Drin cried. He took off running as fast as he could across the boulevard and into a side street. The others charged after him, Antak and Korosa bringing up the rear. Before they disappeared between the buildings Antak looked down the street. The Thalassan militia were falling back as Vinkere soldiers advanced in a phalanx formation that stretched the entire width of the boulevard. Two of them wielded large, shoulder-mounted energy weapons. A stray energy bolt crashed into the wall beside him, causing him to flinch. Molten stone sprayed from the impact, and he raced to catch up with the others.

The alleyway led to another street. At the far end were more Vinkere soldiers, moving toward them.

S'Geliss roared with bloodlust as he shot down another one of the city's black-clad defenders. His soldiers advanced through the International Quarter, attempting to encircle their prey. A city police vehicle sped overhead, siren wailing. A nearby soldier tracked it across the sky and fired his shoulder-mounted weapon. The police car tumbled out of the air and crashed into a storefront, spewing fire and smoke. S'Geliss' soldiers roared with enthusiasm.

The virus they had introduced into the city's computer network disrupted all enemy communications. The Thalassan militia were retreating and their forces across the city were in disarray, unable to coordinate with each other. It was almost too easy.

"They're moving down an alleyway, headed northwest," the sensor office on the *Ss'Thiz* reported, relaying the location to the HUD on S'Geliss' helmet. He didn't need to specify which "they" he was referring to.

"Converge on the individuals at these coordinates," S'Geliss ordered his troops. "They must not escape!"

Jadus' group took refuge in another dark alley. Korosa and Antak looked around the corner, scanning the street for signs of Vinkere.

"How much further?" Jarren asked Drin, who was doubled over, panting.

"The spaceport is still seven blocks away," Hakoa said. Most of the group were tired after running for two blocks without stopping. Jarren knew they couldn't keep it up; Minnen looked exhausted, and Uxxio, also out of breath, was helping the older man lean against the wall to rest.

"How are you doing, Professor?" Jarren asked.

"Don't worry about me, young man," Minnen replied firmly. "Just wait until I get my second wind!"

Jarren was impressed by the professor's resilience, but reminded himself that Iganti were natural long-distance runners, born with a tolerance for high temperatures and built for crossing large swathes of desert between water sources.

Jarren looked at the Minister. Her face was flushed, and she was panting from exertion, but her expression was determined. Doctor Kerik looked exhausted.

"I'm the head of the Tuulan For Planetary Health Organization," he complained to no one in particular. "I should be working at a desk, not running through alien streets, pursued by killers!" Nobody responded.

"We can't keep this up," Jarren said. "We need to rest or find a vehicle."

"We can't rest," Jadus said firmly, still breathing heavily. "The Vinkere are getting closer."

"Then we need to find a vehicle!" Jarren snapped, before catching himself. Jadus just raised an eyebrow at his uncharacteristic outburst.

"Jarren's right," Antak said, supporting his friend. Then, to Korosa, he asked, "Are there any vehicles nearby?"

"Two," she replied. The intersection was quiet; this section of the city seemed deserted. Everyone had probably returned to the emergency shelters by now.

"What are we waiting for, then?" Jarren asked, striding forwards.

Korosa grabbed him and pushed him against the wall. *"That's* what," she said quietly, gesturing around the corner and down the street. Very carefully Jarren peeked around the corner. A group of Vinkere soldiers was moving in their direction.

"What if we made a break for it?" Jarren whispered. One of the vehicles, a sports utility model, was close by, but the second vehicle was parked on the opposite side of the street.

"I can override the vehicle controls with my government pass, but I'm reasonably sure I'm the only person here who can manually drive a Thalassan anti-grav car," Hakoa said.

"Do we need two vehicles?" Jarren asked.

"We won't all fit in one," Hakoa pointed out.

Antak joined them near the opening to the street. The Vinkere soldiers were still getting closer, and a second group had emerged from an alleyway. Hakoa cursed. They were currently shielded from view by the buildings, but they wouldn't be for long.

"Could you drive one of these?" Korosa asked Antak, gesturing at the two vehicles.

"Yes," he said confidently. Or at least, he hoped he could.

"It's very intuitive," Hakoa told him quickly. "Keep to street level so the Vinkere don't shoot you down. Brake, accelerate, and directional controls are all on the panel in the front center console. There are directional markers on them, easy enough to understand."

"Got it," Antak replied.

"The Vlind can go with you," Hakoa said. "He can direct you to the spaceport. I'll drive the other vehicle."

A brief conference decided that the slower members of the group would get in the car nearest the alleyway. Hakoa would activate it, and then he and the other group would run across the street to the other vehicle. Both vehicles would make their way to the spaceport as fast as possible.

The Vinkere were still getting closer to their hiding place. The whole party gathered near the end of the alley way, ready to run into the open. "Their weapons are large, but they look better suited for close combat," Korosa told them. "Hopefully they lose accuracy over long distance."

Hakoa removed his weapon from its holster and shot the two nearest street lamps, plunging them into darkness. "First group with me, let's go!" He, Antak, Drin, Minnen, and Kerik burst out of the alleyway. Hakoa threw open the front door and used his access card to override the security protocols as Antak leapt into the driver's seat. Drin sat in the seat beside him, while Professor Minnen and Doctor Kerik climbed into the back.

"The Vinkere approach from the direction we must take," Drin told Antak as the engine revved to life. The vehicle rose off the ground, hovering two feet above the asphalt.

"Then we'll take the longer route," Antak said firmly, locating the throttle and sending the car surging forward. The Vinkere soldiers had been advancing steadily, checking each building, but now they slithered rapidly toward them.

Agent Hakoa was already sprinting across the road to the second car as Antak sped away.

"Let's go!" Jarren urged the remaining group, and they took off across the street. Uxxio took the lead with long, loping strides. Jarren and Korosa stayed close to Jadus, ready to help the older woman if required.

Vinkere energy bolts whizzed past them. Fortunately for them, Korosa's prediction had been accurate. Although large and immensely powerful, the Vinkere energy weapons lost accuracy over long distances, and in the darkness, they had no clear targets. There were several near misses, but nobody was hit.

Korosa threw open the rear door and Uxxio, Jadus and Jarren climbed into the back. She slammed the door shut and leapt into the forward passenger seat beside Hakoa, who was already starting the engine. "Drive!" she commanded. They were thrown back in their seats as Hakoa accelerated away from the curb, crimson energy bolts flying by.

Hakoa drove down a long boulevard, veering sharply into a side street when a group of Vinkere rounded a corner ahead of them. Jarren looked out the back window. The city had was becoming a warzone. More police vehicles flew overhead, and as they crossed an overpass, he glimpsed a bulky Thalassan tank gliding down the four-lane highway beneath them. Several fires burned in the International Quarter, and he could make out the flash of weapons fire as the Thalassan militia engaged the Vinkere invaders in buildings, streets, and alleyways.

"Do you see the others?" Jadus asked.

"No," Hakoa replied. Noticing her worried expression in the rear-view mirror, he added, "But they had a head start and probably had to detour around Vinkere like we did. We'll meet them at the spaceport."

"How far is it?" Korosa asked, scanning ahead for enemies.

"A few minutes," Hakoa said, swerving around a squad of Thalassan militia. His people didn't have much contact with outsiders, but that didn't mean they were unprepared for conflict. All things considered, he was proud of how well his city was responding to the technologically superior invaders.

S'Geliss returned to his assault ship. The targets had been sighted a few blocks away, but soldiers in the vicinity reported the Tuulan For minister and Iganti scientist fleeing in a pair of vehicles. One look at the direction they were traveling told him their destination: the spaceport. He shoved past the soldier guarding the ship and ordered the pilot to take off.

"Head for the spaceport," he ordered. They had to fly low; the Thalassans had mobilized some form of tank capable of shooting down the Vinkere transports. S'Geliss' troops advanced, killing anyone in their path and setting fire to any buildings where the locals put up resistance. The Vinkere soldiers had no interest in looting; the possessions of their enemies were unclean, and their ultimate objective was to cleanse the galaxy of all traces of inferior life.

An image of Zithla, the one person S'Geliss feared, flashed through his mind. He could not afford to let down the Supreme Commander. S'Geliss sent a message to all his soldiers in the vicinity of the spaceport. The Thalassan militia and some private security were fighting valiantly to keep the Vinkere out, but if that was where his prey were headed, it had to be taken at any cost.

Agent Hakoa sped through the gates of the spaceport. There was only a single militia squad guarding the entrance; the rest were on the far side of the spaceport, where the Vinkere were trying to breach the perimeter. Minister Jadus could see pillars of smoke and flashes of weapons fire beyond the hangars and air traffic control towers as the two sides clashed on the outskirts. She pointed at one of the ships sitting beside a hangar. "That must be Drin's ship, the *Wealth and Grandeur*." It was the only Vlind ship present, so Hakoa steered the vehicle toward it.

"Where's Antak?" Jarren wondered, searching for the other car. "They had a head-start, they should be here!"

"I'm sure they just took a detour, to be safe," Jadus replied calmly, ignoring the knot of anxiety in her stomach. "They'll be here soon."

In space above the planet Tahvoa, thirty slipstream portals opened, and thirty ships of the Thalassan Guard emerged, converging on the two Vinkere warships in stationary orbit above Triyev. The Thalassans were outmatched technologically; the Vinkere had proven their superiority by destroying six of their ships. But the Thalassans had learned from that encounter, and had returned in force. What they couldn't match one-on-one they would overwhelm with numbers.

The Vinkere jamming signal was strongest in the immediate vicinity of their ships, preventing the Thalassans from communicating. It didn't matter, though; the Thalassan strategy was simple. As one the fleet descended on the Vinkere and opened fire. Thalassan torpedoes crashed into the invaders, exploding against their powerful shields. The Vinkere returned fire, missiles streaking through the void and colliding with the attackers. They destroyed one of the Thalassan attackers, but then the two Vinkere ships found themselves surrounded by Thalassan vessels. The ships of the aquatic aliens worked like a school of dolphins attacking a shoal of tuna fish; racing in, attacking, and then speeding away. They used their maneuverability to their advantage, diving in to attack before darting out of harm's way as other vessels swept in, firing torpedoes.

The Vinkere were caught in a maelstrom of fire. Although outnumbered, they were still powerful. One lashed out and crippled a Thalassan ship with a single direct hit, sending it careening into one of its companions. Both ships tumbled away, squawking distress calls. But their comrades pressed on. The battle raging in space was as fierce as the battle in the city below, but this time the Vinkere were on the defensive.

The spaceport was already in view when S'Geliss received word of the Thalassan fleet's attack.

"Order them to stand their ground!" he commanded, not wanting any distractions now that he was closing in on his prey.

"Yes, sir," the pilot replied, relaying the order to the embattled ships in orbit.

Three more Thalassan ships were destroyed by the Vinkere warships, but the remainder were unrelenting in their attack. The Vinkere defenses were gradually whittled away, until finally the hulls of both vessels were exposed and unprotected. By then it was too late for them to call for help. The Thalassan ships surged around them, blocking all their escape routes— not that the Vinkere considered retreating. To do so would mean dishonor and execution for disobeying orders. Better to die in battle as martyrs.

The Thalassan ships swooped in for the final attack, perfectly imitating the aquatic predators on their home world descending on a shoal of fish. Explosions bloomed across the hulls of the Vinkere ships as Thalassan torpedoes found their mark. Within seconds, both vessels detonated in a blinding flash. The Thalassan ships retreated to a safe distance as the cloud of debris expanded, pushed outwards by twin shockwaves. The destruction was so complete that there were no Vinkere survivors.

Before the fires of destruction had faded the twenty-five remaining Thalassan ships were already diving toward the planet, intent on the two remaining Vinkere ships assaulting their city on the ocean floor.

S'Geliss' pilot was stunned when they received word of the destruction of their two warships in orbit. But the news barely registered for him. "It doesn't matter," he murmured, his eyes and thoughts fixed intently on his nearby objective. "Not when we're so close to our target…"

To the pilot, he said, "Order our forces to prepare to withdraw. I've found them," he said with a triumphant gleam in his eye. They weren't hard to miss; they were the only people out in the open, standing beside a vehicle and a ship parked on the tarmac. They had come close to escaping, but now they were as good as dead.

"Put us down right there," S'Geliss instructed. "There will be no escape for them this time!"

Jarren and Korosa spotted the transport ship at the same time. "Look!" Jarren called, pointing at the vehicle moving toward them.

"It's not one of ours," Hakoa murmured.

"I've got a bad feeling about this," Korosa said, inwardly cursing herself for leaving her weapon on the *Telvarn Star*. She grabbed Minister Jadus by the arm. "Everyone, get back to the vehicle! We need to ge-"

Before she could finish speaking, the Vinkere ship touched down. The pilot was in a hurry, and the landing was not a gentle one. It bounced off the ground once before making contact with the tarmac again in a shower of sparks. The vessel slammed into their vehicle with a loud crash, turning it into a pile of twisted metal and shattered glass. Jarren gaped at the wreckage.

"Everyone, into that hangar, now!" Hakoa shouted, pointing at the nearest building. "We—"

There was a loud *CRACK*, and then silence. Jarren, Jadus, Uxxio and Korosa stared in horror at the gaping hole that had suddenly appeared in Agent Hakoa's chest. He collapsed, dead, as a pair of Vinkere rose behind him, having emerged from the assault ship.

Jadus and Uxxio gasped in horror. Jarren felt like vomiting and had to look away from the grisly corpse. The stench of cooked flesh was impossible to ignore.

"Stay behind me, Minister," Korosa said quietly, taking a defensive posture in front of Jadus. She wasn't armed, but she would die before letting the Vinkere reach her charge.

"Yessss, get behind her, Minissster," S'Geliss hissed mockingly. He turned his evil stare on Korosa. "It just means you'll die before she does."

Korosa glared defiantly at the Vinkere but didn't reply. She had nothing to say to the likes of him.

The two Vinkere advanced, weapons aimed directly at them.

"At last," S'Geliss said with a triumphant smirk. "The Tuulan For minister and the Iganti scientist. You two could have caused us a galaxy of trouble. You already *have* caused us a lot of trouble," he said, gesturing to the area around them; the sounds of conflict were growing louder as the Thalassan militia were forced back by the relentless Vinkere onslaught.

They think he *is Professor Minnen*, Jadus realized, looking at the frightened young Iganti beside her.

Uxxio realized it too. "You've finally caught up with us," he said bravely, his voice shaking.

"That's right," replied S'Geliss. "Your efforts have been for nothing." He raised his weapon and pointing it directly at Jadus, through Korosa. "Now I will kill you and take your heads back to my commander."

"I'm sorry," Jadus whispered, so softly that it was only audible to Jarren and Korosa.

"Don't be," Jarren replied, feeling strangely peaceful as the Vinkere aimed their weapons. He exchanged one final look with Korosa. They faced their would-be executioners boldly, ready.

Suddenly, everything began to grow brighter. As one, they turned towards the light source. Dazzled by its brightness, they didn't realize it was the headlights of an anti-grav car until it was almost upon them. Both Vinkere spun around to face the new threat, but only the leader was quick enough to aim and fire his weapon in time. The energy bolt smashed into the front of the vehicle, turning its sleek front to slag, but its momentum sent it careening into the two Vinkere.

The vehicle hit the tarmac in a shower of sparks, bouncing, then careening straight into the Vinkere. The first was crushed beneath the vehicle, but the second Vinkere, the leader, was sent tumbling across the ground. His weapon skittering away. His motionless body rolled to a halt ten meters away.

Smoke billowed from the vehicle's engine compartment as Antak, Elzor Drin, Professor Minnen and Doctor Kerik emerged from its cabin. Antak was grinning triumphantly.

Jarren, Uxxio and Korosa didn't know whether to laugh hysterically or cry. Jadus rushed past them to greet Antak and the others.

"I have *never* had such a close call in all my years!" she said, overwhelmed with relief. In an uncharacteristic display of affection, she grabbed Antak and squeezed him in a grateful hug.

"Professor!" Uxxio exclaimed joyously at the sight of the elderly Iganti.

"You should have known I wouldn't leave you for dead, dear boy!" Minnen said, grasping his protégé's arm.

Laughing, Jarren and Korosa slapped Antak on the shoulder. "One more second and we'd have been target practice!" Jarren exclaimed.

"What can I say, we have perfect timing," Antak said with a wink.

"You did good, pilot," Korosa admitted in an uncharacteristic display of gratitude.

Antak raised an eyebrow in mock surprise. "What happened to the real Korosa?" he joked. "You must be an imposter!"

Korosa ignored him, moving past him to examine the bodies of the Vinkere. Minnen appeared beside her. "He is dead," the Iganti professor confirmed, indicating the body half-buried beneath the car wreck.

"But what about his friend?" Korosa murmured. She approached the other Vinkere cautiously; for all she knew, it could be pretending to be dead or unconscious. She moved around it in a wide circle until she could see its face; its eyes were closed, but it appeared to be breathing.

She briskly strode back to join the others as Antak was saying, "Sorry we were late. Our navigator was still sobering up. We took a few wrong turns."

"Fortunately, you did," Jadus said. "If you had arrived earlier, we may all have been killed."

"We still could be, if that Vinkere regains consciousness while we're still here," Korosa told them. "Even unarmed, it looks deadly. We need to leave *now*." As if to punctuate her words, a stray energy bolt hit the wall of the nearby hangar, causing everyone to flinch involuntarily.

"At once!" Drin replied, drawing an access card from his pocket. He pressed a button, and a circular door in the ship's hull irised open. A boarding ramp extended from it to the ground.

The party moved quickly toward the ship, until Jarren halted abruptly. "Wait. What about Agent Hakoa?"

The others regarded the body of the Thalassan agent, which they had overlooked in the excitement. There was a moment of silence for the man who had given his life helping them.

Jadus walked over to the body. Overcoming her aversion to the grisly sight, she knelt down, placing his hands by his sides and closing his eyes. Korosa helped, arranging his body in a more dignified pose.

"We have to leave him here," Jadus said quietly. "I am unfamiliar with Thalassan funerary customs, and we must let his people to do with the body as they wish." She stood up. "But at the earliest opportunity, I will send a message to Governor Vannora telling him of Agent Hakoa's bravery and sacrifice," she promised.

Sad to leave the body on the tarmac, but under pressure to leave, the group nodded solemnly and headed for the ship.

Drin led them through low-ceilinged corridors toward the bridge. Most of the ship was comprised of storage bays, he explained, but there was also an infirmary, engine room, crew facilities, and a bay for the robotic cargo handlers.

Antak looked around when they entered the ship's small bridge. The room was circular, with a low, domed roof. Like the rest of the ship they had passed through it featured the brown and maroon color schemes favored by the Vlind, although it was probably more colorful to them, as they could see into the ultraviolet light spectrum. A long, narrow window at the front of the bridge permitted a forward-facing view outside. Uxxio and Doctor Kerik peered through it, craning their necks to look out and up.

"Can you see that? Above the city," Uxxio said, pointing.

"I can!" Doctor Kerik confirmed.

"See what?" Jadus asked with a frown, annoyed they weren't specifying what "it" was. The others crowded around the portal to look.

When they had entered the ship the ocean outside the city's protective shield had been completely dark. But now the water was illuminated by dozens of fast-moving lights, interspersed by the unmistakable orange flare of weapons detonations.

"That must be the Thalassan fleet," Jadus said. "They've begun their attack."

"Then perfect for leaving is what the time is," Elzor Drin said, settling into his chair at the center of the bridge. He was much more alert than he had been a short time ago.

With some instruction from the Vlind captain, Antak was able to activate the *Wealth and Grandeur*'s engines, and the rotund ship rose off the tarmac. Just in time, too; the Thalassan defense of the spaceport had become a tactical retreat as the better armed, more experienced Vinkere soldiers advanced. Some of them fired a few rounds at the ship, but their energy bolts rippled harmlessly against the shields.

Under Antak's cautious hand the starship angled upwards, accelerating toward the shield dome above the city; they weren't Vinkere so Drin was confident they would be ignored by the Thalassan ships. The ocean around the city still flashed as the Thalassan ships, built as much for submarine activity as for the vacuum of space, literally ran circles around the two Vinkere vessels. Soon the Thalassan ships would destroy the warships and begin landing their troops in the city, eliminating the Vinkere presence there. But they wouldn't wait around to see that happen.

Jarren sat down at the unoccupied communications console and looked around the bridge. Minister Jadus stood over Antak's shoulder watching him manipulate the helm controls, and as usual Korosa hovered protectively close by. Professor Minnen was commenting on the design of the bridge and how well-suited it was to Vlind physiology; Uxxio listened faithfully, nodding and make sounds of agreement when required. Doctor

Kerik took a seat at a console to Jarren's left, sighing expressively as he eased himself into the chair, no doubt relieved to be safe and on their way again.

Jarren wished they hadn't brought this conflict to the Thalassans. Guilt weighed heavily on his conscience. The Vinkere who confronted them at the spaceport said he had been tracking the group. Did that mean everywhere they went, the Vinkere would arrive soon after? He sincerely hoped that wasn't the case.

He observed Minister Jadus standing beside Antak. She looked composed, and spoke in a clear, calm voice, but Jarren could see the tightness in her shoulders and the way she stood slightly stooped forward. Whatever guilt he felt regarding the plight of the Thalassans, he knew she felt it a hundred-fold. She would never forget Triyev or its people, and Jarren vowed silently never to forget either.

Like all deflector shields, the one covering the city deflected exterior objects but permitted one-sided movement from the interior. That was how starships fired weapons through the protective screen of their deflector shields. Now, the *Wealth and Grandeur* pushed through the force field with only the gentlest bump into the ocean beyond. Antak made sure to cross the threshold as far from the battle as possible. Not that it mattered; neither the Thalassan nor Vinkere ships paid them any attention.

The ocean changed from charcoal to deep blue to turquoise as the ship ascended. After a few moments the ship broke the surface in a cloud of spray, soaring into an orange afternoon sky. The *Wealth and Grandeur* rose through clouds of orange and purple as the sun set.

Antak turned in his seat to look at Jadus. "Once we're clear of the planet's gravity I'll need a specific course. Which way do you want to go home?" The others looked at her expectantly.

"How much fuel do we have?" Jadus asked Drin.

"Full capacity is what the tanks are at," Drin replied. "Five hundred light-years are our range."

Antak did some calculations. "That would get us most of the way home." He activated a star map on his console, and they gathered around to look. "We can travel down, and then through the safe areas of the Commonwealth." A curving red line showed their projected path from Tahvoa to Tuulan Vee.

Jadus didn't reply. "Shall I lock in the course?" Antak prompted her after several moments.

She pursed her lips thoughtfully. "No," she said after a few moments, surprising them all. "That will be the path the Vinkere expect us to take. I don't want a repeat of the events on Tahvoa."

"Where will we go, then?" Jarren asked.

"We will take the most direct route," Jadus announced.

"But… that will take us directly through Vinkere-controlled systems," Antak protested.

"But they won't be expecting it." Jadus spoke softly, but there was an edge to her voice. "The Vinkere are formidable adversaries. The only way to evade them is by doing the unexpected. If that means sneaking through their backyard, then so be it. At least we will have the advantage of surprise."

Antak gave her a dubious look. "Are you absolutely sure?"

"I am," Jadus said firmly.

"We will not fail. A mission of great importance is what we are on!" Drin declared. "We are in the hands of destiny."

Antak wished he shared the Vlind captain's confidence. None of the others said anything, so he took that to mean they were okay with the risk. He sighed. "Alright then. Setting a course directly through the Vinkere occupied Commonwealth…" He set their new heading and the ship changed direction.

Jadus put a hand reassuringly on Antak's shoulder. As the others took their seats, he announced, "We'll be ready to enter the slipstream in five minutes."

S'Geliss gradually became aware of his surroundings. He opened his eyes and looked around. The last thing he remembered was the vehicle slamming into him and the impact hurling him across the tarmac. His ribs hurt badly, but a quick self-assessment assured him he was not bleeding anywhere, nor were any of his bones broken.

He rose carefully. The sounds of conflict were all around him now and he couldn't tell whether it was his own soldiers or the enemy who were closest to him. Examining the prone form of the pilot nearby, he quickly deduced the other man was dead, killed by the impact of the vehicle. S'Geliss' force field suit had borne the brunt of the impact, cushioning most of the blow and saving him from the same fate. S'Geliss looked around for his prey; they were nowhere to be seen, although he couldn't have been unconscious for more than a few minutes.

Flashes above drew his gaze upward. Through the shield he could see the last of his warships fighting the Thalassan vessels, which swarmed around it. He also caught a glimpse of the Vlind ship disappearing through the city's shield into the ocean. His prey had only just left; he could still catch them if he were quick. Searching for his weapon, he found it on the ground nearby. He scooped it up and slithered nimbly over the wrecked Thalassan vehicle to his assault ship.

He reached the controls and activated the ships engines. If his prey managed to enter the slipstream before he could determine their trajectory they would be as good as lost, and he would be as good as dead. Nothing else mattered now except finishing his mission. He pointed the assault ship upward and accelerated, and the small vessel sped toward the force field dome. The ship passed through it into the ocean and ascended toward the surface, all other thoughts pushed from his mind except for catching the Tuulan For minister and the Iganti scientist.

There was a loud *BOOM*, transmitted through the water, then a shockwave slammed into his ship. S'Geliss checked the sensors and saw that the *Ss'Thiz* had been destroyed. His entire squadron was gone, and soon his soldiers in the city would be as well.

As his ship broke the surface of the ocean and raced into the afternoon sky, S'Geliss scanned for ships; immediately he detected the fleeing Vlind freighter. He diverted all the ship's available power to the engines, pushing it beyond its safety specifications. He just had to be within range when they entered slipspace so that he could track them.

"A ship is pursuing us," Minnen stated. He was sitting at the scanning station.

The others looked at him in alarm. "Are you certain, Professor?" Jadus asked.

"Yes," Minnen replied. "The vessel has matched our course."

"Is it Vinkere?" Jarren asked.

"Perhaps; its design is unfamiliar to me," Minnen said, before assuring them: "It is quite small. Too small to be a warship."

"Does this ship have any weapons?" Korosa asked Drin. "Can we destroy it?"

"A single, forward-facing cannon. But damage has been suffered, and repairs have not been made."

"In other words, no," Jarren said wryly.

"Will they be able to catch us?" Jadus asked.

"Not likely."

"Ignore it, then," she said firmly.

Drin agreed. "We shall press on."

Antak activated the slipstream drive. The Vlind controls were becoming easier to understand with each passing minute. He marveled at how bipedal humanoids tended to develop interfaces intuitive to people even outside their species.

"Entering slipspace in 4… 3… 2… 1."

The slipstream projector on the bow of the Vlind ship flared brilliant burgundy, and the *Wealth and Grandeur* vanished in a flash of light.

S'Geliss tracked the ship as it jumped into slipspace. He was *just* close enough that he could predict their path, and the region of space it would take them through. His transport had no weapons and minimal shielding, but it had slipstream capability. He activated the slipstream drive, preparing to follow the Vlind ship. There was another flash as his ship dove into the slipstream, and he was gone before the Thalassans realized he had escaped.

20

Chief Engineer Donald Winston removed his welding goggles and eyed his work critically. The shield generator had sustained damage during the battle at Ennomos. It had taken hours to replace the complex components inside, but if they had completed their work properly, it should be functional again.

"Pass me the scanner," he said over his shoulder. Ensign Juan Fernandez did so, peering curiously over his shoulder. Winston activated the scanner. "Don't crowd me."

"Sorry," said Fernandez, stepping back.

Winston waved the scanner over the newly-repaired machine and nodded appreciatively. "Everything looks good. Reconnect the power couplings."

The other two members of Winston's repair team, Ensigns Masoni and Putman, connected heavily insulated power cables to sockets on the generator. When the connections were secure Winston turned on the power. Energy surged through the cables into the newly repaired systems and the shield generator hummed to life.

"Shield generator three is now functioning within normal parameters," said Amalthea.

Fernandez jumped in surprise at the disembodied voice, then looked sheepishly at the others. "I'm still getting used to the fact that our ship's computer is alive now."

"The computer isn't alive, the artificial intelligence in it is," Lateesha Putman corrected him.

"That is correct," Amalthea said.

Unlike Fernandez, Winston had quickly grown accustomed to the presence of the AI on the ship. He was even starting to think of her as part of his engineering team. He returned the scanner to his toolbox. "Working perfectly," he said with a satisfied smile.

"What's next?" Ensign Masoni asked.

"The bulkhead near port thruster one," Winston said. "It took a hit from a Vinkere weapon and the hull is buckling. External repairs are impossible while we're inside the gas giant, so we'll have to have to shore it up from the inside." He picked up his toolbox and left the shield generator room. The three engineers followed him.

The *Pericles* had suffered a severe beating during its flight from Ennomos, and even with Captain Marston ordering all non-essential personnel to aid in the repair efforts, it had taken ten days to get to the point where they were nearly ready to venture out of their hiding place.

"Amalthea, what's the status of the oxygen seal in section thirty-six?" The automatic repair systems had created a temporary, quick-drying foam seal over the hull breach to keep the oxygen in and the planet's atmosphere out, but given the state of the ship, such systems weren't one hundred percent reliable.

Amalthea spoke to the engineer through the nearest speakers in the corridor: "The seal is holding. I will inform you if this changes."

The team stepped into an elevator and Winston said "Deck Three", wondering idly if it was the computer or Amalthea that directed the elevator to its destination.

The aft port section of the ship had sustained the most damage, and deck three had been ground zero for some shots that had nearly destroyed the *Pericles*. Although that section had suffered heavy damage, Winston knew how fortunate they had been. Another meter to the right, and enemy weapons fire could have ruptured the fuel lines, destroying half the ship.

All of the bulkheads leading to section thirty-six had sealed automatically when the hull breached, and no one had entered that section since the battle ten days earlier.

Winston entered his access code and the bulkhead slid open. There was a whoosh and a gentle gust of air as the atmosphere on both sides of the door equalized. Winston stepped through, followed by the rest of his team.

The air smelled faintly of ozone. Winston could see why the rapid-hardening foam had taken so long to fill the breach; the hole was more than a meter in diameter. He pointed at the damage. "What do you notice?"

The three ensigns scrutinized the breach. "The edges are all melted," Lateesha Putman said after a moment. "Possibly caused by an energy weapon?"

"Yes, exactly," Winston said, pleased at her observation.

Antoni Masoni approached the jagged hole and ran his hand over the now cool metal. "Normally the Vinkere use projectile weapons, like us," Masoni said. "They're far less energy intensive."

"The amount of power required to produce a directed energy beam that could burn a one-meter hole through tri-magnesium alloy hull plating would be phenomenal," Winston said. "The fact that the Vinkere use them sparingly could suggest energy beam weapons are still experimental technology or require too much power to be used often."

"Then, using them on *us* shows how desperate they were to prevent us from escaping with their data core," Putman commented.

"Do you believe the Vinkere and Ankari weapons could have a common origin?" Amalthea asked. Her voice crackled over the damaged speakers.

Winston stroked his chin. "I don't think so. I mean, it's not likely. The Ankari don't share their technological secrets with anyone, and the Vinkere don't even come from the Locality."

"That is true." Amalthea went silent. Winston shrugged and turned his attention back to the task at hand.

"Alright. Time to fix this breach and make sure hull integrity is up to strength. Let's get to it, I want to go to bed at a reasonable hour tonight."

*

"How are you feeling this evening?"

"I feel fine," Henry Clarke said, sitting on the edge of the bed in the infirmary.

Doctor Lupita Gariri ran her medical scanner over him. "You seem fine," she agreed. "All your readings are perfectly normal. Consider this your last daily check-up, Lieutenant Commander."

"Glad to hear it," Clarke said, hopping off the bed. "The fight was ten days ago. Thanks to your care I'm as good as new. I'll be seeing you, Doc!"

"It wouldn't hurt to take it easy for the next couple of days!" Gariri called after him.

"Will do, Doc!" he replied before the doors shut behind him. There was a spring in his step as he made his way toward the ship's training room.

"Lieutenant Commander!" Clarke turned to see Commander Balzano walking toward him with long strides. Clarke paused to wait for him.

"Where are you heading?" Balzano asked him as they strode toward the elevator.

"The training room," Clarke said.

"I'll join you," the executive officer said, earning a surprised look from Clarke.

"Now, Commander?"

"Why not? I've been meaning to get in some more combat practice and this is the first time I've had a free hour since we arrived here."

"Fair enough." Sometimes Clarke forgot that Balzano had once been a tactical officer like himself.

The elevator doors opened and they stepped inside. Katarina Sirroyo was already in there and looked up from her datapad.

"Oh. Hello. How are you feeling today?" she asked Clarke.

"Fine. I've felt fine for days," Clarke grumbled. He didn't know why people kept talking to him like he was mortally wounded. The fight with the Vinkere had been *ten days ago*.

"Where are you off to?" Balzano asked Sirroyo.

"My quarters. I'm going to have an early night, for a change." She stifled a yawn.

"Good, get some rest," Balzano said. "We're leaving tomorrow." As if to remind them that the *Pericles* was still deep within Kronos' turbulent atmosphere a particularly loud peel of thunder rumbled through the ship.

"I won't miss *that*," she said, and the two men nodded. For ten days the *Pericles* had trailed the storm as it wound its way around Kronos' equator. Their concealment had bought them a much-needed respite to repair the ship and treat the wounded, but now everyone was eager to leave. Sirroyo had spent the better part of that time mining data from the Vinkere data core, whose electronic files Amalthea had been able to access. They had already obtained a wealth of information that could be useful to the Commonwealth.

"We'll be ready," Clarke said confidently. "The ship's back in fighting shape, and so is the crew."

"When we leave Kronos, our priority will be evading the Vinkere," Balzano said, "At least long enough to do a bit of reconnaissance. We're behind enemy lines and Captain Marston thinks it would be useful for the Navy to learn the size and location of the enemy fleet in this sector."

"I agree," said Clarke.

Sirroyo looked at him wryly. "That doesn't surprise me."

"It'll be fine," Clarke said casually. "We'll just poke our head out, take a look around, and then make a dash for friendly territory. What could go wrong?"

*

"Again," Marston instructed the computer, and it replayed the scene on his monitor for the umpteenth time. He was watching footage from the *Leviathan,* recorded by a micro camera in the collar of Henry Clarke's combat uniform. Once again, the giant Vinkere advanced across the dark room with surprising speed, and Marston watched from a first-person view as Clarke fought back valiantly. He watched the scene all the way through to the death of the Vinkere; as soon as its corpse fell to the ground, riddled with bullets, he paused it.

"Analysis," he said wearily.

"I have nothing to add that has not already been noted," Amalthea replied.

"Neither do I." Marston blinked tiredly. He had spent many hours examining the combat footage from Clarke and other members of the Leviathan Expedition for ways to fight the Vinkere. The Vinkere were significantly bigger and stronger than the average human and could move with almost unnatural speed. Their greatest weakness was that they were *predictable.* In every recorded instance of combat the Vinkere employed the same generic techniques. If Marston and his crew could learn to counter these, they would be better prepared to meet them in combat, should the need arise. He knew Clarke was doing the same thing, but Marston thought the task could also benefit from his own combat experience. In the time between his posting on the *Saber* and his promotion to captain of the *Pericles*, Marston had spent a short but significant season in the Navy's Strategic Operations division, overseen by Admiral Mackenzie; it was there that he had first come to the attention of his would-be mentor. Marston remembered well the lesson taught to advanced tactical training candidates: *understanding the enemy is the first step in overcoming them.*

He rubbed his eyes tiredly and decided to call it a night. He had received about six hours of sleep in the last forty-eight hours, and was too tired to think clearly. If he continued working in his current state, he could overlook critical information on the Vinkere. He realized he hadn't received any updates from Lieutenant Sirroyo for over an hour, and hoped that she was also getting some rest.

Marston pressed a button and the computer monitor receded into the desktop. He stood, stretched, and left his office. It struck him how quiet the ship was; aside from the quiet background hum of the engines and rumble of thunder, it was strangely peaceful. He had ordered the crew to rest before their departure from Kronos tomorrow morning.

He arrived at his quarters and mumbled to Amalthea to dim the lights, pulling off his uniform and unceremoniously tossing it on a nearby chair. Putting on his pajamas, he collapsed into bed and closed his eyes, listening to the quiet thrum of the *Pericles* engines and letting the soft howl of the wind and rumble of thunder outside lull him to sleep. Within a few minutes, he was snoring softly.

Marston slept for over ten hours; Commander Balzano and Doctor Gariri ordered Amalthea not to contact him until he woke naturally. Balzano knew the captain would be annoyed at being left to sleep in, but Gariri agreed that the captain needed more than just a couple of hours' sleep.

When Marston arrived on the bridge at o-eight hundred hours in a fresh uniform, Balzano just smiled when the captain glared at him accusingly.

"If I didn't let you rest, you would have been too tired to think clearly," Balzano said unapologetically. "I did it for the crew."

Marston frowned but didn't respond; he grudgingly conceded there was no point starting an argument his executive officer would win. Instead, he picked up a datapad containing a review of the ship's status, ignoring Balzano's grin.

Donald Winston and Katarina Sirroyo entered the bridge, looking energized after their own restful night. "How are things, Chief?" Marston asked.

"The *Pericles* is as good as we can make her with our current supplies," Winston replied. "A couple of days in an Argos dry dock wouldn't go amiss, but we'll do fine without."

"Glad to hear it," Marston said.

"Amalthea's running last-minute diagnostics on all the repaired systems," Sirroyo added. "Assuming they don't find anything wrong, we should be ready to break atmosphere in an hour."

Marston was impressed. "Good job, everyone. Let me know when the diagnostics are finished. Amalthea, please put me through to the entire ship." The bridge crew fell silent and watched him expectantly.

"Communication channel open, Captain," Amalthea informed him.

"Crew of the *Pericles:* this is Captain Marston. I wanted to take this opportunity to commend all of you for your incredible work over the last few days. These have been less than ideal circumstances, but I continue to be impressed by the excellence and initiative you have all demonstrated. I also want to thank the personnel from the Leviathan Expedition for their help in returning our ship to functionality. Please know how grateful I am. Assuming the diagnostics don't reveal any issues, I will be giving the order to leave Kronos within the hour. Our objectives will be to determine the status of the Commonwealth and the Navy in this sector, and to deliver the data we've obtained from the Vinkere data core to Command. Secure all stations and prepare for departure. Marston out."

Marston paced the bridge, pausing at the computer tone that signaled the end of the final diagnostic. "How are things?"

"Everything looks good," Sirroyo reported. "We're as ready as we'll ever be." The whole crew was painfully aware that every second they spent hiding was more time the Commonwealth went without the potentially war-changing information they carried.

Marston returned to his chair. On the viewscreen the huge cyclonic storm raged; it would take centuries to dissipate. "I don't know about the rest of you, but I've seen enough of that storm," he remarked. It was time to see the stars again.

"I couldn't agree more, Captain," Winston said over the intercom. *"Slipstream engines are ready to go online as soon as we clear the planet's gravity."*

"Thank you, Chief. Lieutenant Hasan, take us out of the planet's atmosphere," Marston ordered the helmsman.

"Aye, Captain," Hasan said with relish. His hands flew over the helm controls, and under his guidance the ship rose through Kronos' atmosphere. Bolts of lightning forked through the sky and hurricane winds buffeted the ship, causing it to sway.

"Ten thousand meters until we break atmosphere," Hasan reported as the turbulence began to decrease. Orange and red clouds whipped by the viewscreen, deflected by the ship's energy shields.

"As soon as we're clear I'll perform a full sensor sweep." Sirroyo said.

"Shields and weapons are charged," Clarke added from tactical, "just in case."

"Good," said Marston. The thick, turbulent atmosphere of the gas giant prevented Vinkere sensors from finding them, but it also prevented the *Pericles* from detecting any ships that might be lurking in orbit. He hoped the Vinkere believed they had been destroyed and weren't even looking for them.

"Three thousand meters 'til we break atmosphere," Hasan reported. "One thousand meters."

The final layers of cloud parted and the starry void of space greeted them. The *Pericles* soared into the welcome expanse. The others looked at Sirroyo expectantly as she performed a sensor sweep.

"Scanning…" she said, frowning intently as the sensor results streamed down her monitor. "There's one Leviathan-class Vinkere ship in orbit of Ennomos and another Vinkere vessel on the edge of the system." She looked up. "It's changing course and moving directly toward us."

Amalthea appeared on the viewscreen. "They will not have time to intercept us before we enter the slipstream, and they will be too far away to track our course," she informed them.

"Our course is set for Rally Point Alpha," Hasan said. It was a random and hopefully empty location in space a few light-years from the Ennomos System. There they could emerge from the slipstream, assess their surroundings, and decide which course to take to get past the Vinkere fleet.

"When will we clear the planet's gravity well?" Balzano asked the helmsman.

"Four and a half minutes."

"Keep an eye on that Vinkere cruiser moving toward us," Marston ordered Clarke.

"Already on it, Captain," the tactical officer replied smartly.

*

In orbit of Ennomos, Ennomos System
Interstellar Commonwealth

"Sir! The human ship is escaping!"

Zithla rounded on the hapless sensor operations officer who had made the statement. He didn't need to specify *which* human ship the man was referring to; it was obvious he was talking about the *Pericles*. The same ship that had lured Consul Slethis' ship to Ennomos and then escaped Vinkere clutches a second time, this time with strategic data stolen from Slethis' ship.

Zithla slammed two of his fists into the nearest control station. There was a shower of sparks as the screen shattered and went dark. His frustrated outburst made the junior officers nearby quake nervously, but Zithla didn't care. The only other ship in the area was on its way out of the system, but it was still closer than they were. "Have the *Serpka* intercept them at once," he ordered.

Zithla's own ship was busy securing the only inhabited planet in the system. Having seized the major settlements within a matter of hours, his soldiers on the planet were rounding up the human survivors. The planet's population would serve as laborers, and the planet's mineral wealth would fuel the Vinkere war effort. Consul Slethis' ship was unsalvageable, and Zithla's troops had found no survivors, the humans had seen to that. Not that it mattered; Zithla would have executed the survivors himself for allowing their ship to fall into enemy hands.

Zithla had been dubious about the human ship's destruction since the battle of Ennomos. There simply wasn't enough debris left over from the explosion above Kronos for a ship that size. No, the *Pericles* captain was too cunning to have died. He had already outsmarted Slethis, after all. So Zithla had ordered the *Serpka* to keep watch over Kronos, ready to strike should the human vessel reappear and attempt to escape.

Unfortunately, human resistance in the New Jakarta System had proven stiffer than expected, and the Triumvirs had countermanded Zithla's order, redeploying the *Serpka* to reinforce the Vinkere assault fleet there. As the rulers of the Vinkere Dominion they were the only people with the authority to overrule him. But they had little comprehension of military matters, and their interference in his decision-making frustrated him greatly.

Zithla had argued that the data the *Pericles* carried was a strategic risk and had to be eliminated. The Triumvirs would not be swayed, however, and the *Serpka* had departed Kronos. As far as they were concerned there was little to no evidence of the human ship's survival and Zithla's concerns were unjustified. He clenched his fists in frustration. If the Triumvirs hadn't overruled him, the *Serpka* would still be in orbit of the gas giant, positioned to destroy the *Pericles*.

Zithla wasn't sure how the Triumvirs found out about the human ship, but he had his suspicions. Commander Slithza had been appointed to his ship *by* the Triumvirs, and Zithla didn't trust him. He glared across the room at Slithza; the diminutive Vinkere noticed and shifted uncomfortably. If only the order had come through just a few hours later, the human ship wouldn't be getting away. Luck certainly seemed to be on the side of the *Pericles*, he thought grimly.

"Sir, the *Serpka* will not be able to reach the human ship in time," the sensor operations officer reported nervously.

"Hail the human vessel," Zithla said darkly.

Slithza looked at him in surprise. "Sir, we shouldn't give away--"

Zithla rounded on him. "Be silent!" he roared. He didn't care if Slithza or the Triumvirs disapproved. He turned back to the communications officer and fixed him with a dangerous glare. "Did you not hear me? Open a communications channel with the human ship. Now," he repeated ominously. Then, to the entire command deck, he said loudly, "The next person to question or fail to implement my orders *immediately* will be executed for insubordination." He looked pointedly at Slithza. The two dozen other officers on the command deck put their heads down, hoping not to draw the ire of the Supreme Commander.

"At once, sir," the communications officer replied nervously, claws flying over the controls as he established a communications link with the fleeing human ship. "Channel open."

"Captain, we're being hailed," Sirroyo said. She looked at Marston in surprise. "By the Vinkere ship at Ennomos!"

Bewilderment and consternation flickered across the captain's face before he affected a more controlled expression. "Why in the worlds do they want to talk?" Balzano wondered.

"There's only one way to find out," Marston said, rising from his chair and straightening his uniform jacket. "Put them through."

"Yes, Captain," Sirroyo said hesitantly, sharing a wary look with Clarke.

Marston cleared his throat and spoke. "This is Captain Marston of the Commonwealth Naval Vessel *Pericles*. To whom am I speaking?"

The image on the viewscreen changed from the view of space to a dimly lit room occupied by shadowy, serpentine figures. Marston rapidly took in the scene; the dark chamber with its high ceiling and rows of control stations. Large serpentine heads hunched over the control stations, bathed in the dim yellow light of computer graphics. But it was the large, imposing figure standing on a dais in the center of the chamber that commanded his attention.

"*Captain Marston of the Human Commonwealth*," said a deep, sibilant voice that Marston instinctively knew came from the hulking figure at the center of the chamber. "*I am Supreme Commander Zithla of the Vinkere Dominion.*"

Marston felt a shiver run down his spine. There was no mistaking the hatred in his voice when he said *Human* and *Commonwealth*.

"What is it you want?" Marston asked. He spoke calmly and directly, projecting a bold image from the middle of the bridge. Inwardly, apprehension gnawed at him.

"*To issue you an ultimatum,*" Zithla replied. "*I will give you two options. The first is that you power down your engines and surrender to my ship. You and your crew shall hand over your vessel and all data it contains and surrender unconditionally to my soldiers. You will be taken to a labor camp, and your lives will be spared.*"

"What's the second option?" Marston asked coolly.

"*You may leave this system now, but your escape will be temporary. My ships will hunt you down and we will destroy you. And furthermore, there will be no taking of human prisoners or slaves for the duration of this war. I will ensure that every human on every planet, ship and outpost is eliminated, beginning with the planet below,*" Zithla said.

Marston felt the eyes of the bridge crew glued to him. The Vinkere was trying to intimidate him. But Marston wasn't going to allow himself to be manipulated. He had dealt with bullies before.

"I have no intention of complying with your *ultimatum*," he said firmly. "You have demonstrated your capacity for violence and deception in your unwarranted attack against our Commonwealth. I don't trust you, and I will not negotiate with you."

"*You are a fool,*" Zithla snarled. "*You arrogant young upstart, you lack the wisdom to see that I have the upper hand. We have superior technology, numbers, and a supreme conviction in our mandate. We are greater than you, and we will prevail. You cannot stop us.*" And once humanity had been exterminated, the other peoples of the Ss'Talak Cluster would follow suit. There simply wasn't a place in the universe for aliens who dared to consider themselves *equal* to Vinkere.

"You will *not* defeat us," Marston said flatly. The hulking serpentine figure bridled with indignation and rage; Marston suspected the supreme commander wasn't used to having people talk back to him. He continued. "The *Leviathan* failed to capture us; we captured *them*. And we're about to escape your clutches *again*. With each encounter we understand you better, and we learn how to counter your aggression. Your crusade is not going to go how you think it is." Hasan subtly gestured there was one minute remaining until they could enter the slipstream. Balzano acknowledged the motion with an almost imperceptible nod.

"The very existence of your species is an abomination," Zithla spat. *"There was a place for a select few of you, serving your Vinkere masters, but no longer."* There was a wicked glint in his eye when he spoke again, and his voice sounded ominous. *"The end of the human race is upon you, and as the last remnant of your people dies, I will make sure they know it is you to blame."*

Marston shook his head. "I will not be condemned for your actions. You are responsible for the violence you commit, not me. And I will do whatever I can to make sure you are brought to justice," he swore. He gestured for Sirroyo to end the communication. The Supreme Commander's image blinked out, replaced by stars.

As Marston took his seat Balzano leaned over. "That was hardcore, Marston," he said, sounding impressed. Marston grinned shakily, offering a modest shrug.

"We've cleared the planet's gravity well," Hasan reported. "We're ready to enter the slipstream on your command, Captain."

Marston took a deep, calming breath. Then, focusing resolutely on the starfield, he gave the order: "Take us out of here."

A slipstream portal flared into existence at the front of the ship, and the *Pericles* disappeared in a splash of light.

Commander Slithza nervously watched Zithla clench and unclench his fists. His anger, which always lurked just below the surface of an otherwise calm exterior, threatened to engulf all those around him. In the months Slithza had served under the Supreme Commander he had found the man's legendary reputation for violence to be entirely accurate. Slithza had become adept at steering clear of Zithla when he was in one of his rages and he now took the opportunity to surreptitiously slither across the room to receive a "communications report" from one of his subordinates. When the Supreme Commander was in one of his black moods, it was best to stay well out of arm's reach.

21

En route to Tuulan Vee
The Slipstream

The *Wealth and Grandeur* sped through the slipstream, riding the currents of energy that underlay the fabric of space. Intended for a crew of fourteen, the ship was quiet with just eight people on board. The excitement and danger of Tahvoa seemed like a lifetime ago. Minister Jadus, Doctor Kerik, Minnen the Learned and Uxxio had taken over the infirmary and were using it as a space to continue their research into the Kalavat Plague. All their physical materials had been lost, so they relied on the information stored on their datapads to continue their efforts. Professor Minnen's breakthrough had been identifying similarities between the plague and the reproduction method of the aracobzi jellyfish. The so-called Kalavat Plague "Virus" was misleading, Minnen told them. It wasn't a virus at all, which was why all efforts so far had failed to find a cure. He was convinced the plague was in fact produced by an unknown species which attacked the victims on the genetic level, rewriting their DNA.

"Why hasn't anyone else figured that out yet?" Korosa asked. She was astonished that Minnen's revelation had evaded the galaxy's best scientists for months.

The Iganti professor chuckled. "The Ankari may be the most advanced civilization in the Locality, but they're not the most *intuitive*. Thinking outside of the box is not something I would ever accuse them of."

Jadus was cautiously optimistic that the man who had cured the Osaija Virus was once again demonstrating his next-level brilliance. It made their journey from Tuulan Vee worthwhile. "It certainly looks like a promising lead," she agreed.

While the experts went about their work, there was very little for Jarren to do besides fetch drinks and take notes, and even *that* went beyond his ability when he couldn't spell (or even pronounce) some of the words Minnen dictated to him.

Jadus took mercy on him. "Thank you for your help, Jarren, you may take a break. I will call you if we need you."

With little else to do, Jarren wandered the ship's corridors, exploring the empty rooms and spacious cargo holds. Antak spent most of his time on the bridge at the helm or in the crew lounge playing games on his datapad, while Korosa had taken over one of the smaller cargo bays and turned it into her personal gym, a place where she could exercise and practice the various martial arts she was proficient in. Jarren had grown tired of the repetitive games with Antak and was trying to avoid Korosa, in case she tried to teach him self-defense again. Elzor Drin alternated between the bridge and his private quarters, seemingly happy to let these near-strangers use the ship as they pleased. He was very different from the depressed drunk they had first encountered in the *Nauseous Navigator*, strutting about the ship with renewed energy and purpose.

During one of his wanderings, Jarren came to a set of double doors. He approached curiously; there were scratches on the glass panes. The doors slid open, and he entered to find himself in a dark cargo bay. The only light came from the corridor behind him. There weren't any storage crates or containers, not even empty ones; Jarren found that unusual. A shadow fell across the entrance, and he turned to find Drin standing in the doorway.

"Surprise fills me at finding you here," Drin said.

Jarren was embarrassed at being caught off guard. "Uh, sorry, I was just having a look around," he said.

"Apologies are not needed," Drin replied. He entered the room and stood beside Jarren, looking about the empty space.

"What happened to your cargo?" Jarren asked him.

"To my shame, I am the reason it is empty," Drin said sadly. "I jettisoned it, along with thirteen Infected former crewmates."

Jarren felt a shiver run down his spine. "Your crew were infected by the Kalavat Plague?"

"Correct. We were attacked, and our ship boarded by alien creatures," Drin told him. "Escape is what we managed to do, but the infection spread to my crew. Only I remained."

"What happened?" Jarren asked, eerily fascinated.

"Regrettably, my efforts to trap the Infected in the cargo bay failed." Despite the warm, still air of the cargo bay Drin shivered.

"On the verge of seizing the ship, the Infected left me with but one choice," he said slowly. "I opened the exterior doors, and they were claimed by the void."

Jarren swallowed dryly. "That must have been hard." No wonder Drin had been depressed when they found him. He had alluded to a grim event on his ship, but whenever pressed for details his replies were vague, evasive. Late last night Antak and Jarren had speculated for hours what had happened to the ship's crew. They had agreed Drin was probably running from the Kalavat Plague, and now Jarren knew that to be partly true. He understood why Drin didn't want to talk about it. He couldn't imagine how hard it would be if he had to do the same thing to Antak, Jadus, or Korosa.

"The most difficult decision of my life is what it was," Drin said unhappily.

"I'm sure it was," Jarren said quietly. He didn't know what else to say.

A few minutes later he met with Minister Jadus and told her what Drin had shared with him.

She looked thoughtful. "Poor man. It explains why he was so eager to help us. He wishes to make amends."

Before Jarren could reply, Jadus' communicator squawked.

"Minister, could you come to the bridge?" Antak asked.

"I'm on my way," she replied, gesturing for Jarren to join her.

On the bridge Korosa and Antak were hunched over the helm console.

"We crossed into Commonwealth space a few minutes ago," Antak told them, worry creasing his brow. "But you wouldn't know it if the star charts didn't say so. There were no com beacons, no customs vessels, nothing. We can't pick up *any* Commonwealth vessels in this sector."

"Because of the Vinkere," Jadus said. "They must have come through this sector."

"I've been monitoring-" Korosa began before she was interrupted by an alert on the console.

"The ship receives a communication," Drin said, who had also been summoned. He ambled over to the communications console and played the message.

"This is an automated message from the Interstellar Commonwealth Government. A hostile race known as the Vinkere has invaded Commonwealth space. Ships within the Commonwealth are advised to remain clear of all nebulae. By recommendation of the Commonwealth Navy, all spacefaring vessels are to seek immediate shelter on the nearest safe world. If possible, ships are to evacuate from the following Commonwealth sectors: Arkan Sector, Banda Sector, Metria Sector..."

"Did the Vinkere launch their attack from nebulas?" Korosa wondered out loud. "How did they get there?"

"I don't know," Jadus said. "But their attack obviously caught the Commonwealth off-guard."

"Attack by unknown aliens in the vicinity of the Vratak Nebula is what caused damage to my ship," Drin said. "There are many similarities between those mysterious attackers and these Vinkere."

The message continued: *"...Veil Sector, Van Sector, and Wayland Sector..."*

"We're in the Wayland Sector," Antak interjected.

"...All ships and personnel are instructed to comply with the orders of government officials and Navy personnel..."

"Are there any planets or space stations along our route?" Jadus asked Antak. "If the Vinkere are there I want to avoid them."

"We'll pass within sensor range of Inongo Station and the planet Portiguara but detouring around them will only add a few hours."

The automated message ended, and the bridge was quiet again. Antak turned to Minister Jadus, and his expression was uncharacteristically serious. "Ma'am, if you still wish to proceed along our current route, I must stress that we are heading into the unknown. If the Vinkere have already been through this sector, and it certainly looks like they have, then we have no way of knowing what dangers lie ahead. This isn't the same as the last time we passed through the Commonwealth."

"I realize that," Jadus said, "But I still believe it is our best course of action. The Vinkere are looking for us, but not here. We shall proceed with every precaution." She turned to Drin. "Is there anything we can do to minimize our chances of being detected?"

Drin looked thoughtful. "Confining ourselves to this deck and shutting down power to all others may reduce our energy signature and the likelihood of our detection," he said. "However, a possibility is all this is, not a certainty."

"If we refrain from using active sensors and limit ourselves to passive scans, that will help as well," Antak said. "And we need to keep off the subspace radio."

"There's no guarantee these measures will help at all," Korosa cautioned.

"Nevertheless, it's better than doing nothing," Jadus said, and Korosa nodded.

"What about the ship's transponder?" Jarren asked innocently. The others looked at him in surprise.

"What do you know about subspace transponders?" Korosa asked curiously. As far as she was aware Jarren's knowledge of starship systems was as limited as his knowledge of self-defense.

"I was just getting to that," Antak said testily.

"I'm assuming this ship has one?" Jarren asked the Ship's Overseer.

"I respond in the affirmative," Drin said. The Vlind captain's communication seemed to become more convoluted every day.

"And I assume that's what enabled the Vinkere to pinpoint the *Telvarn Star* and blast it to pieces," Jarren said. "But if we deactivated the *Wealth and Grandeur*'s transponder…"

"Good idea," Jadus said, then to Drin: "Can it be done?"

"With great difficulty," Drin muttered. "Integrated into the-"

Korosa waved dismissively. "Leave that to me. All I need is a blunt object."

"We'll compensate you for any damage to your vessel," Jadus added quickly.

"You better believe you will," Drin grumbled. Jadus gave the Vlind her most charming smile.

S'Geliss tracked the Vlind ship as it crossed the border into the human Commonwealth. Like the prey he pursued, his ship was running on minimal power to mask its energy signature. Overwhelming them with superior numbers and firepower hadn't worked on Tahvoa. His prey were crafty, and they had managed to slip away in the midst of the battle with the Thalassans. He now tried another strategy: stealth.

Utilizing an ability native to the Vinkere, S'Geliss drastically slowed down his metabolism and heart rates, entering a trance-like state. Traditionally it was used by his people to hibernate through periods of severe cold, drought or famine, but it had the added effect of making his life sign all but undetectable to conventional sensors. S'Geliss shut down all systems on his ship except for the slipstream drive, passive sensors, and minimal life support. If he followed them from a distance, keeping at the extreme edge of what he estimated was their sensor range, he hoped to follow them undetected. And when they came to a stop, he would infiltrate their ship and complete his mission.

*

For four days the *Wealth and Grandeur* flew alone through the Wayland Sector. They had experienced firsthand an invasion by the Vinkere, and now they witnessed the aftermath. It seemed as though the Vinkere were trying to remove all trace of humanity in the sector. There were no more messages since the automated message from the Commonwealth government. A few times they detected strange messages on the subspace radio; the Vinkere were communicating with each other. But they didn't dare eavesdrop, lest it draw the attention of the Vinkere.

Halfway through the first day they passed Inongo Station, a trading post on the edge of human space. All they could detect with passive sensors was a debris field. After a heated debate between Minister Jadus and Drin, the ship's overseer finally relented, and they used active scans to search for life signs. They found no survivors. Antak estimated the station had been destroyed a week ago. Concerned that there may be Vinkere lurking in the area, they continued onward.

The second day they passed the planet Portiguara at a distance. Although it was on the extreme edge of their sensor range, they were able to detect three Vinkere warships in orbit. There were no communication buoys, satellites, or human ships; the Vinkere had destroyed them all. After several anxious minutes, they passed out of sensor range of Portiguara, unnoticed by the Vinkere ships there.

261

The atmosphere on the *Wealth and Grandeur* grew more tense every day. Jarren noted that everyone, even the normally unflappable Minnen, had become restless and subdued. He had trouble sleeping at night, fearing that a Vinkere warship would stumble upon them and finish what the Vinkere at Tahvoa had been unable to do.

The deeper into the Commonwealth they pressed, the more frequent signs of the Vinkere invasion appeared. Twice they passed close by the wreckage of human ships. Devoid of life, Antak estimated they had been destroyed within the last week, suggesting that the Vinkere were hunting ships unfortunate enough to be stranded behind enemy lines as the invasion front swept toward the core worlds of the Commonwealth.

When they crossed the boundary of the Wayland Sector into the Van Sector, the *Wealth and Grandeur* came across evidence a large battle had been fought here. A debris field covering hundreds of kilometers sprawled in front of them. Antak estimated that the field contained wreckage from over 100 ships, mostly Navy vessels. They also detected the remains of around 20 Vinkere ships, indicating that the engagement wasn't totally one-sided.

"I don't know if we should continue this way," Jarren said as they observed the derelict hulks tumbling through space.

"I don't think we have much choice," Antak said grimly. "We've come too far to backtrack and find another way around."

"I'm not saying we should backtrack," Jarren retorted. "But maybe we should head for the nearest safe Commonwealth world."

"That would greatly increase our chances of being intercepted by the Vinkere," Antak argued. He gestured toward Minister Jadus, who was silent. "They've basically done everything they can without the proper equipment. We can't afford to keep putting off the cure, it's the whole point of our mission!"

"I know what our mission is!" Jarren shot back.

"It won't mean anything if we get caught," Korosa said, massaging her forehead tiredly. She had slept even less than the others, maintaining a vigil on the bridge to make sure no Vinkere ships came within sensor range while the other slept.

Jarren began a fiery retort, but Antak interrupted him. Jadus was silent during the exchange. Tempers were flaring because they had been on edge for so long. She knew both Jarren and Korosa made good points, but she found herself agreeing with Antak. They were taking a great risk by continuing along their present course, but she was painfully aware of the time they had already lost. If she could avoid more delays, she would. How many other worlds would succumb to the plague if they took too long?

She raised a hand, silencing the others. "Continue along our present path for the time being," she said quietly. "We will review the situation if and when it becomes necessary." She turned and left the bridge, indicating her decision wasn't open to discussion. Antak, Jarren and Korosa stood in gloomy silence for a moment, then Antak moved wordlessly to the helm console and sat down. He folded his arms and stared straight ahead, his mouth a thin, angry line. Korosa gave Jarren a weary look and moved over to the sensor station. Seeing no point in remaining there, Jarren left the bridge.

A few hours later Korosa detected a large explosion at the limits of their passive sensor range, but they were unable to tell whether it was the Vinkere or Commonwealth Navy before they sped out of range. They didn't dare go back to find out.

Mealtimes were subdued and most people retreated to their own private rooms as soon as they'd finished eating. Although she hid it better than most, Jarren could tell that Minister Jadus was deeply worried. Whatever happened now, whether they made it through the Commonwealth unscathed or were captured by the Vinkere, was on her shoulders. And it wasn't just their own lives at stake, but the lives of billions of people depending on them for a Kalavat Plague cure.

As he lay in bed that night, staring at the ceiling, Jarren wondered how much longer they could endure their passage through enemy territory. Finally, after tossing and turning for hours, he drifted into a restless slumber. When he woke the next morning and wandered out of his room it looked like the day would be a repeat of the day before, and the days before that. Until Antak's shout of alarm had everybody racing to the bridge.

The *Pericles* emerged from the slipstream in an empty region of Tier 4 space several light-years from the nearest inhabited world. The senior officers had agreed that the location was remote enough to minimize their chances of being detected by Vinkere ships. Their flight from Kronos had been uneventful; no Vinkere ships had followed them, but the Vinkere weren't the only ones absent from the sector. There were no signs of other human activity within several light-years. The *Pericles* flew through space, alone, caught behind the invasion front in enemy territory.

Several hours into their journey the ship received an automated message from the Commonwealth government, confirming what they already knew: the Vinkere invasion had swept through the sector, wreaking destruction on their path toward Earth. Simon Marston and his officers agreed that the best course of action was to try and slip past the Vinkere lines into friendly territory, where they could pass on the enemy data they carried; it was too sensitive to transmit over subspace, which would also give away their position. Then they could join the fight against the alien invaders.

"Perform a full sensor scan," Marston instructed Sirroyo. Their goal was to find a gap in or weaker part of the Vinkere invasion front, which as far as they could tell stretched for three hundred light-years across the Commonwealth. If they could find an area with relatively few Vinkere ships it might be possible for the *Pericles* to reach friendly territory without being intercepted.

Clarke helped the sensor operations officer examine the data coming in from the ship's sensors. "This spot is no good," he said, disappointed. Sirroyo let out an exasperated sigh. "There's a Vinkere fleet two and a half light-years away. They would catch us before we got close to the nearest Commonwealth world."

Marston heard grumbling around the bridge; the crew were getting frustrated. This was their sixth try, probing the Vinkere lines for a hole to sneak through. Not only were they discouraged by their lack of success, but they were also on edge, mindful that Zithla's forces were searching for them. Marston hid his own frustration behind a calm facade. "Well, then, we'll try the next location."

Balzano nodded in solidarity. He ordered Hasan to set a course for the next destination Amalthea had selected for them.

"Wait," Sirroyo's voice cut sharply across the bridge.

"What is it?" Marston asked.

"There's another ship on sensors," reported Sirroyo. "I almost didn't detect it; their power signature is very faint. They just entered sensor range, and they're heading in our direction."

"Is it Vinkere?" Balzano asked.

"No, it's… I don't think so," Sirroyo said. "It's not very big."

Balzano looked at Marston. "Could be a scout ship."

Before Marston could respond, Sirroyo did. "Negative. Profile reads as a Vlind transport ship." She sounded surprised.

"What in the worlds is a Vlind ship doing all the way over here?" Clarke wondered, perplexed.

Marston was equally puzzled. "I have no idea." He turned to Sirroyo. "Hail them on a short-range subspace band."

"It will have to be audio only," she warned him.

"That's fine." Marston cleared his throat. "Unidentified Vlind ship, this is the Commonwealth Naval Vessel *Pericles*. Please identify yourself."

There was a momentary delay, and then a static-filled voice filtered through the speakers.

"I am Elzor Drin, the Ship's Overseer. Wealth and Grandeur *is the name of this vessel."*

"*Wealth and Grandeur*, what are you doing here? The Commonwealth has been invaded. You're in dangerous territory."

"*This is a fact we are aware of, but we are on a mission of great importance.*"

Marston heard voices in the background, and then a new voice spoke up.

"Pericles, *this is Minister Torina Jadus of the Republic of Tuulan Vee. To whom am I speaking?*"

"This is Captain Marston," he said, exchanging a perplexed look with Balzano. What was a member of the Tuulan For government doing on a Vlind ship in enemy-occupied space?

"*We're glad we found you,* Pericles," said the Tuulan For Minister. "*You're the first friendly ship we've come across in a long time.*"

"As far as we can tell the only other ships in this sector are Vinkere," Marston told them. "I must strongly advise against you continuing along your current path."

A pause. "*Captain, is this channel secure?*"

"It is," he confirmed.

"*We are bound for Tuulan Vee on a mission to cure the Kalavat Plague. We have Professor Minnen the Learned on board.*"

The name sounded familiar. Marston looked at his officers, who apparently recognized the name as well. "Minnen the Learned?" Sirroyo repeated. "Didn't he cure that pandemic a few decades ago? The Osay virus…?"

"*Osaija Virus,*" Amalthea corrected.

"Minister, the way ahead is extremely dangerous. If you keep going you risk being captured or destroyed. It would be safer for you to go back the way you came and go around the Commonwealth."

Jadus' voice was firm. "*I'm afraid we can't do that. Time is critical.*"

Marston could certainly appreciate the time sensitive nature of their mission. The Kalavat Plague sounded devastating. But flying to Tuulan Vee would take them past the Shadow Nebula, which was overflowing with Vinkere ships. It would mean certain death.

"I understand if you are in a hurry," he said reasonably. "We're also trying to find a way past the Vinkere. Perhaps it would be best if you came on board and we discussed our options in person."

There was another pause while Jadus considered his offer. "*Very well. My helmsman tells me we will reach your ship within a few spans.*"

"I look forward to meeting you in person, Minister."

"*As do I, Captain. Jadus out.*"

The channel closed. "Our day just got a lot more interesting," Balzano remarked.

"Our day just got a lot more *complicated*," Marston said. "I wasn't expecting to receive high-profile guests in the middle of a war zone. But we can't leave them out here to fend for themselves."

"They'd never make it to Tuulan Vee," Sirroyo said matter-of-factly. "There are too many Vinkere between here and there."

"They made it this far," Clarke pointed out.

Marston rose from his chair. "The bridge is yours," he said to Balzano, making his way to the elevator.

"Where are you going?" his executive officer asked.

"To speak with Doctor Gariri," Marston replied. "Please inform me when our guests arrive."

*

Doctor Gariri smiled warmly when Marston entered the infirmary. "Hello, Captain. Can I help you?"

"Hello, Doctor. Are you free to talk?"

"Of course." Gariri led Marston into her office, which adjoined the infirmary and offered them some privacy.

"I wanted to know if there's anything in the Vinkere data about the Kalavat Plague," Marston said. As Amalthea and Sirroyo extracted information from the alien data core, they sent it to the relevant department heads on the ship; Lupita Gariri was the ship's foremost expert on alien biology and medicine.

She frowned in thought. "The Kalavat Plague? Not that I'm aware of. But I haven't had the time to review all of the data Amalthea sent me." She looked at him shrewdly. "Do you believe the Vinkere have something to do with the Kalavat Plague?"

"I'm not sure," he said honestly. "Maybe. But it is a strange coincidence that they appeared just a few months after the plague did."

"All the reports I've read on the Kalavat Plague say it doesn't match any known pathogen in the Locality," Gariri said. "Which could mean it was introduced, although maybe it always existed in this region of space and nobody encountered it until a few months ago."

"That's true. But I still think we should keep an eye out for any Vinkere data relating to viruses, or biological weapons... anything like that."

"I will, Captain," Gariri promised. "Was there anything else?"

"There was," Marston said. He told them about the Vlind ship and its passengers.

"Minnen the Learned?" Gariri repeated excitedly. "I read about him in medical school!"

"Well, in about ten minutes you'll get to meet him," Marston said with a smile. "I was actually thinking about inviting them to work here on the *Pericles*. I suspect they'd find our facilities more useful for medical research than those on a Vlind freighter!"

"Of course, that makes perfect sense," Gariri said, excited at the prospect of working with Minnen the Learned.

Marston grinned at her enthusiasm. His communicator beeped. "Yes?"

"Sir, the Vlind ship is on their final approach," said Henry Clarke. *"But there's also another ship that emerged from the slipstream behind them. I think it's Vinkere."*

"Go to combat alert," Marston said immediately. "Do you think the *Wealth and Grandeur* led them here?"

"I don't think so; not intentionally, anyway," Clarke said. *"It's difficult for our sensors to detect, even at close range; they may not even be aware of it. And it's small, about the size of a shuttlecraft. They're not powering weapons."*

Marston wasn't taking any chances. "If you can confirm it is Vinkere, destroy it."

"Yes, Captain."

Alert klaxons sounded throughout the ship, spurring people to their battle stations. As Marston hurried back toward the bridge, he hoped there weren't any further surprises in store for them that day.

Antak had become quite proficient at operating the Vlind ship's controls. "We're receiving a message from the *Pericles*," he told Minister Jadus and the others, who were clustered around him at the helm console. "They say we're being followed!"

"Followed by whom?" Jadus asked in alarm.

Korosa read the message. "A vessel in low power mode, beyond our ability to detect," she told the others. On the viewscreen the *Pericles* glided past them to intercept the unidentified ship.

"Can we do anything to help?" Jadus asked, directing the question at Drin.

The Ship's Overseer shook his head. "Nothing except stay out of the way."

"What about drones?" Jarren asked. "I read somewhere that Vlind ships carry combat drones!"

"Military ships only," Drin replied calmly. He trusted the Navy ship would deal with their pursuer. Fate had brought them this far already; he sincerely doubted it was just to be destroyed during their first encounter with a friendly ship in weeks.

He focused the viewscreen on the *Pericles* so they could watch what was happening. Jadus wasn't sure who was stalking them across space, but she had a fairly good idea.

S'Geliss' ship emerged from the slipstream not far behind the *Wealth and Grandeur*. Proximity sensors alerted him to the presence of another vessel, a human ship. It changed course, heading directly toward him. He had been detected. S'Geliss knew he had only moments to act. Careful to maintain his trance-like state, he donned his force field skeleton, which was now fully charged. He activated the protective field and it encased him in energy with a faint hum.

He was aware of an alarm beeping, warning him the human ship had locked weapons on his ship. Adjusting the setting on his force field suit he expanded the energy field outwards. The suit's power source would deplete much more rapidly, but it would trap enough oxygen between the field and his body to allow him to breathe in the vacuum of space for several minutes.

A pair of missiles launched from the human frigate, accelerating toward his ship. S'Geliss entered the airlock and depressurized it; the ship's atmosphere evacuated into space, leaving him drifting in the airless compartment. Carefully aligning himself with his target, he pushed off the rear wall, launching himself into space. He was twenty meters away from the ship when the first missile collided with it. The explosive shockwave propelled him forward, toward his target. The white-hulled ship grew as he drew nearer, and he tensed his body, getting ready to grab a hold of it. If he failed, he would miss his target and be lost in the depths of space.

The main viewscreen showed a small cloud of debris. "Target destroyed," Clarke confirmed.

"How many Vinkere life signs were on that ship?" Balzano asked Sirroyo.

"None," she replied. "The ship was definitely Vinkere, but it appears there was nobody on board."

"Maybe it was a stealth probe tracking the *Wealth and Grandeur*," Hasan said.

"Maybe," Balzano said, eyeing the debris. "They were definitely trying to avoid detection, that much is for certain."

"Marston to the bridge. Status report."

"The Vinkere ship has been destroyed, Captain," Balzano reported. "There were no life signs on board. We think it might have been an unmanned probe."

"If it was tracking the Vlind ship I'd rather not stick around in case it told somebody. As soon as the Wealth and Grandeur *docks, take us into the slipstream. In the meantime, keep scanning for more Vinkere ships."*

"Will do, Captain," Balzano said. He shared a troubled look with Sirroyo and Hasan. If nobody was aboard the Vinkere ship, who was controlling it?

Marston waited for their new arrivals at Port Airlock One, flanked by Lieutenant Commander Clarke and Doctor Gariri. A light above the airlock turned green, indicating the atmosphere on both sides of the door had equalized. The hatch opened into an umbilical tunnel connecting the *Wealth and Grandeur* to the *Pericles*, where their alien guests waited.

Marston immediately recognized the minister by her patrician bearing and Tuulan For ministerial robes. She took in the Navy officers with a discerning look before settling her gaze on Marston. "Captain Marston, I presume?" she said, directing her question at him.

"That's right," he confirmed. "And you must be Minister Jadus. Welcome aboard the *Pericles*."

She nodded in acknowledgement. "Thank you."

Before she could introduce the rest of her companions, the Vlind male stepped forward. "Greetings, from one Ship's Overseer to another. My name is Elzor Drin. The *Wealth and Grandeur* is my vessel."

"It's good to meet you, Overseer," Marston said politely. Minister Jadus introduced her assistant, Jarren Qel, who revealed his familiarity with human greetings by holding out his hand sideways; Marston shook it firmly. He also shook hands with Antak Droma, the Minister's pilot. Korosa Jakor, the Minister's security guard, and Henry Clarke eyed each other shrewdly, each taking the measure of the other. Whether they viewed each other as comrades-in-arms or rivals, Marston didn't know.

When Minister Jadus gestured to her Iganti companions, they stepped forward. "Allow me to introduce Professor Minnen the Learned. He is our best chance of curing the Kalavat Plague."

Minnen snorted dismissively. "You give me too much credit," he said. "This is a group effort!"

Marston took an instant liking to the elderly Iganti. "It's our pleasure to have you on board, Professor," he said, and when the Iganti man inclined his head in acknowledgment Marston could practically sense the awe radiating from Lupita Gariri. "This is my tactical officer, Lieutenant Commander Clarke, and my Chief Medical Officer, Doctor Gariri."

Doctor Gariri approached Professor Minnen. "It is a privilege to meet you in person, Professor Minnen," she gushed. "Your work has been one of the biggest inspirations for my career."

Minnen looked pleased. "If my small contribution to medical science inspires others, then I am delighted."

"Shall we move to the conference room?" Marston asked.

Jadus nodded, content to hold off on discussing important matters until they were out of the hallway. "Lead the way, Captain." She walked alongside Captain Marston while the rest of their party followed, admiring the smooth, clean lines and gleaming white corridors of the ship. It was much more in line with her own aesthetic tastes, and a welcome change after the browns and burgundies of the Vlind ship.

"Captain, you keep a clean ship," she complimented him. She heard Drin huff and made a mental note to compliment the Vlind on his ship later.

"Thank you," Marston said. "We've been in space for five months now, although we've taken a couple of beatings over the past few weeks."

"I'm glad you found us when you did," Doctor Kerik said. "You're the first friendly ship we've seen in a while."

Marston tensed his jaw. "Yes. Things aren't going very well for the Commonwealth right now."

"Or for anyone, for that matter," Jadus added grimly.

Sirroyo was waiting for them in the conference room. Marston and Jadus sat at the center of the table opposite each other. Flanking Marston were Clarke, Gariri, and Sirroyo; seated on either side of Jadus were Minnen, Jarren, Uxxio, Kerik, Antak, Korosa and Drin. Balzano and Hasan were on duty on the bridge, and after a brief meeting with Drin, Winston had taken a team of engineers to the *Wealth and Grandeur* to repair the damage it had sustained near the Vratak Nebula months earlier.

When everyone was seated, Marston launched straight into the meeting. "As everybody here is aware, the Vinkere control this sector of the Commonwealth, which means we are not safe here." For the benefit of their guests, Marston recounted the events of the past several weeks. He included everything, from the *Pericles'* mission to the Shadow Nebula and Clarke and Sirroyo's encounter with the Vinkere captain in the depths of the *Leviathan* to their more recent flight from Kronos.

Jadus and her companions listened without interruption. When he was finished, Marston regarded the Tuulan For woman opposite him and said, "Now that I've shared with you our story, I'm sure we'd all like to hear yours." His officers nodded in agreement.

Jadus nodded and proceeded to recount the events of the last few months, starting with the outbreak of the Kalavat Plague in Tuulan For space and her mission to meet Minnen the Learned. She told them about their dramatic escape from Iganta and the Vinkere attack on Tahvoa, where they narrowly escaped their would-be killers. At various times during her story Jarren, Antak, or Minnen interjected, providing further details. Marston and his officers listened intently.

When she was finished, Marston clasped his hands together on the tabletop. "As I see it, we're facing the same problem," he said. "We're alone in enemy territory, and we cannot let the Vinkere get their hands on the information we carry." He paused, unsure how their guests would react to his next suggestion. "We need to deliver the Vinkere data core to the Navy, and you need to be escorted safely out of the danger zone. I think it would be beneficial if we worked together." It would give the Vinkere a single target instead of two, but the *Pericles* offered greater security than the Vlind freighter, and he would feel better having Professor Minnen under his protection.

Jadus was silent and inscrutable as she considered his offer, but Elzor Drin's eyes narrowed in suspicion. "Is having our two vessels work together your intent, or do you suggest abandoning my ship in favor of your own?"

Abandoning the Vlind ship made sense from a tactical point of view, but Marston understood the need to address the issue delicately with the *Wealth and Grandeur's* captain. "You are obviously a very capable Ship's Overseer, having come this far," Marston said tactfully. "But I would suggest concentrating our efforts on the *Pericles* because we know this region of space and our ship is better prepared for combat."

"We're also fast," Clarke added. "One of the fastest ships in the Commonwealth Navy."

"How fast?" Antak asked curiously.

"Twenty-eight light-years in twenty-four hours," Clarke told him proudly. Antak looked appropriately impressed. The *Telvarn Star* could travel twenty light-years per day.

"I am not willing to abandon my ship, for it to be raided or hijacked by the first opportunist who finds it!" Drin said indignantly. Marston was sympathetic; if someone told him to abandon the *Pericles,* he would resist the idea too.

"It wouldn't be permanent," Sirroyo assured the Vlind. "We could hide your ship in a safe place and return for it once the crisis is over."

"Whenever *that* is," Drin muttered.

"That's right," Marston said with a grateful look at his sensor operations officer. "We could conceal it in an asteroid field where it would be as good as invisible."

Drin looked at the others; to his surprise and disappointment none of his travel companions came to his defense. "But this is *my* mission too," he said quietly.

Minister Jadus remained quiet during the exchange. Captain Marston and his crew were far better equipped to protect her and her companions, and his ship was certainly more capable of getting them to their destination. She would happily leave the *Wealth and Grandeur*, which in her opinion displayed neither wealth nor grandeur. But she also didn't want to undermine the Vlind captain. Jadus had come to consider Drin part of her team. She sensed Antak and Korosa bristling impatiently, but they wisely held their tongues. Better to let him come to the right decision on his own.

Drin stared intently at Marston with his small, beady eyes. Finally, after several moments he relented. "Very well," he said reluctantly. "But the safety and retrieval of my ship after this crisis is of the utmost importance!"

"I agree, sir," Marston said reasonably. "I promise that we will deliver you back to your ship." He looked at Jadus, who returned his gaze serenely. He didn't restate his original question, just waited for her response.

"I believe we have a greater chance of succeeding in our mission if we work together," she declared.

Marston was pleased. "I'm glad to hear that. Our science lab is at your disposal. I've already asked Doctor Gariri to check the information from the Vinkere data core for anything relating to the Kalavat Plague. I'm sure the doctor would be more than happy to help you. Isn't that right, Doctor?"

"Absolutely," Gariri said excitedly. It wasn't every day she had the opportunity to work with the galaxy's greatest medical minds. Except for the Vlind merchant captain, their guests seemed content with their new arrangement.

Jadus allowed a small smile of satisfaction. "Thank you, Captain Marston."

He grinned at her and her companions. "We're pleased to have you with us. Welcome aboard the *Pericles*."

22

Donald Winston completed his diagnostic of the *Wealth and Grandeur's* slipstream drive core. The results, displayed in bright orange text on his computer tablet, confirmed that the slipstream drive, although still functional, had taken some damage a few months ago and hadn't been properly repaired.

Winston had never seen a Vlind ship before, let alone attempted to repair one. But their slipstream technology followed the same principles as the human-designed engines he was used to. *Technological parallelism*, he marveled. Aside from using different materials and computer software, they were actually quite similar.

He stood up, grimacing. He was getting too old for kneeling on cold metal floors. With the diagnostic complete, it was time to collect the other three members of his engineering team and return to the *Pericles* for the tools they would need.

Ensign Ben Johannes was checking a power junction in the corridor outside the engine room. "Johannes!" Winston called out.

There was no answer.

Frowning, he walked over to the doorway and was about to call again when Johannes appeared. The young man put a finger to his lips before Winston could speak.

"I thought I heard something," Johannes whispered.

Winston raised an eyebrow. "It was probably either me or Ormond." Ensign Ormond was performing a diagnostic in the adjacent cargo bay.

"No, this was something else," Johannes insisted. "It sounded like the airlock. But no one's working near there, right Chief?"

"No," Winston said, listening for any unusual sounds. If the airlock down the corridor was faulty there should be alarms, or at least the tell-tale howl of air rushing through a broken seal into space. "Overseer Drin didn't say anything about a faulty airlock," he said.

"Not faulty, Chief," Johannes said. "Like it was opening and closing. I know what I heard," he added firmly in response to Winston's skeptical look.

"There's only the four of us on this ship," Winston assured him. Crewman Ormond, Crewman Gillespie and the two of them. Seeing the young man's adamant look, Winston sighed. "Fine." If the jumpy ensign needed further proof that everything was okay, so be it. He activated his communicator. "Winston to Ormond."

There was no answer. Frowning, he tried again, but after waiting several seconds there was still no reply. Johannes shifted nervously, eyes darting up and down the corridor.

"Winston to Gillespie," Winston said, trying to reach the ensign checking the ship's computer core. His call was met with silence.

"Where are they?" Johannes asked anxiously. Winston thought it was strange, but he wasn't prepared to write it off as the bogey man just yet. It could be interference, or an equipment malfunction.

"It's probably nothing," he said calmly. What were the chances of both Ormond and Gillespie having problems with their communicators?

"Let's head back to the *Pericles*," Johannes said nervously. The young man was jumpy, but now Winston was beginning to wonder if he had a valid reason to be on edge.

They left the engine room and headed down the corridor toward the airlock that connected the *Wealth and Grandeur* to the *Pericles*. Winston used his communicator to contact their ship, and this time it connected perfectly.

"Go ahead, Chief," Commander Balzano replied.

"I'm heading back to the ship – Crewman Johannes is with me. Can you please scan for Ormond and Gillespie? We've lost contact with them."

"Lost contact?"

"We don't know why; it could just be an equipment malfunction. But Ensign Johannes here thinks he heard the ship's airlock open and close by itself."

"I *did* hear the airlock activate," Johannes said into Winston's communicator.

The next voice that spoke through the communicator belonged to Amalthea. *"Sensors are reading only two human life forms on the* Wealth and Grandeur," she said in her calm voice. *"The two of you. Crewman Ormond and Crewman Gillespie did not return to the* Pericles.*"*

"Get back to the ship now," Balzano ordered them. *"We're sending a security team to meet you."*

The engineers didn't have to be told twice. Seized by panic, Johannes took off down the corridor at a run. Winston jogged behind him, slowed by the weight of the diagnostic computer and scanning equipment he was carrying. In his haste to return to the *Pericles*, Johannes didn't see the giant serpentine figure appear from a side corridor until it was too late.

The Vinkere lunged at Johannes, sending him flying. The young man hit the bulkhead with a loud *crack* and slid to the ground, either dead or unconscious, Winston couldn't tell. He didn't have time to check because the alien rounded on him with a sinister hiss, fangs bared.

Winston dropped his equipment and sprinted as fast as he could the other way, knowing he needed to find a weapon or hide until the security team arrived. As he ran, he shouted into his communicator. "Winston to *Pericles*, there's an intruder on the ship! It just took out Joha—"

Something heavy crashed into his legs, causing him to fall over. He hit the ground hard and tried to scramble to his feet when two large, scaly claws grabbed hold of his right arm. The engineer was vaguely aware of Commander Balzano shouting through his communicator as he was forcibly turned around, coming face-to-face with the Vinkere, who grabbed both of his arms in a vice-like grip. Lifting the engineer off the ground, the serpentine alien leaned forward, his forked tongue flickering between scaly lips.

"Winston? Chief! What's going on?" Balzano was shouting. The Vinkere grasped Winston's wrist and spoke into his communicator.

"If you want this man to remain alive, you will do what I tell you," the Vinkere said. "Meet me at the airlock to your ship. Bring the Tuulan For minister and the Iganti scientist." The alien roughly pulled the communicator off Winston's wrist and crushed it, tossing the pieces aside. Winston struggled in the giant alien's grip, swinging his legs in the air, trying unsuccessfully to break free.

S'Geliss smiled wickedly at the engineer. "You have taken away the element of surprise, but you will help me complete my objective."

"...I'll have someone escort you to guest quarters," Marston told his guests.

"Thank you, Captain," said Minister Jadus. She was about to broach the subject of their destination when an alarm sounded. Marston and Clarke leaped to their feet. "The intruder alarm!" Clarke said, rushing to the door. He intended to be first on the scene with his security team.

Marston hailed the bridge. "Commander, what's going on?"

"Chief Winston said there's an intruder on the Vlind ship, Captain," Balzano reported. *"Amalthea just sealed the port airlock."*

"All crew on the *Pericles* are present and accounted for," Amalthea said through the ship's speakers. "However, I am no longer reading the life signs of Crewmen Ormond or Crewman Gillespie on the *Wealth and Grandeur.*"

"Please excuse me," Marston said to his guests, striding quickly toward the door. Without waiting for permission, Jadus followed right behind him. Jarren shrugged at Antak, and they followed, along with the others.

They arrived on the bridge in time to hear the deep-voiced alien speaking through Winston's communicator: *"If you want this man to remain alive, you will do what I tell you. Meet me at the airlock to your ship. Bring the Tuulan For minister and the Iganti scientist.*" The call ended abruptly before Marston could respond.

"Get him back," Marston ordered.

"Chief Engineer Winston's communicator is offline," Amalthea reported.

Marston noticed Jadus and Minnen looking at him uncertainly. "We're not going to hand you over to the alien," he assured them.

"We're picking up two life signs in the airlock tunnel," Balzano said to the captain. "One human, and one Vinkere."

"Why didn't we detect the Vinkere before now?" Marston demanded. Ensign Tia Maahia, who had been filling in for Sirroyo, looked flustered.

"I didn't mean you," Marston told her. Sirroyo had been manning the sensors when the Vinkere ship appeared.

"It may not be anyone's fault," Sirroyo said. "When we were on the *Leviathan* our sensors couldn't read any life signs in the command center, but we were ambushed by the Vinkere." Her face clouded over at the memory. "It appears they have the ability to mask their life signs."

"It *is* possible," Minnen said. "The Lantaran tree octopus and the Preelakian pond glider have that ability."

"Clarke and security just reached the airlock," Balzano reported.

Jadus approached Marston. "What can we do to help?" she asked him. The Vinkere had followed her here. If she and her people could help the situation, they would.

Marston pursed his lips thoughtfully. He had no doubt the Vinkere would kill Winston given the chance.

"I may be able to help," Uxxio said, stepping forward. The young Iganti hadn't said much during the meeting, and he blushed shyly when the others looked at him.

"When we were on Tahvoa, the Vinkere thought I was Professor Minnen," Uxxio said.

"That's right," said Jadus, recalling the confrontation at the spaceport.

"There's no reason for them to find out otherwise," Marston said to Minnen. "I see no reason for you to come with us."

Minnen looked offended. "If you think I'm going to let my protégé risk his life impersonating me, you are mistaken, sir!" he said indignantly.

"It won't come to that," Marston assured him, although he didn't yet know how they could ensure that. Another challenge in a season of trials for him and his crew.

"I'm coming with you, Captain," Minister Jadus said firmly.

"As am I," said Minnen the Learned.

Korosa spoke up. "The Minister's protection is my responsibility. I'm coming as well."

"Me too," said Jarren and Antak in unison.

Jadus was moved by their loyalty, but shook her head firmly. "No, there's no point in risking your lives should a firefight break out." In her experience, the presence of a Vinkere *always* led to violence.

"I agree," Marston said, cutting in before any of them could object. "And I'm sorry, Professor, but I'm not willing to risk your life either. Uxxio and Lieutenant Jakor can come with us, the rest of you can monitor the situation from the conference room." Minnen looked like he wanted to object, but he held his tongue when he saw the steely resolve in Marston's eyes.

To his bridge officers, Marston said, "I'm going down to the airlock. I need all of you to try and come up with a plan in the next two minutes, because right now, I've got nothing." He turned on his heel and strode toward the elevator. "You have the bridge, Commander," he said over his shoulder. But Balzano followed him.

"You can't just walk in there with no plan," Balzano said in a low voice so that no one else could hear.

"I understand the danger," Marston responded levelly. "But he's not going to wait forever. Unless one of us comes up with a plan on the elevator ride down, I'll have to play it by ear." Those words were anathema to Marston, but now was one of those times he would have to trust his gut.

Balzano relented, although he wasn't happy about it. "Alright. We'll do what we can, but I know you'll make the right call."

"I'll do what's necessary," Marston replied calmly, and he could see in the other man's slightly shocked expression that Balzano understood what he meant. If it came to it, he would let their chief engineer die rather than hand over the best and possibly only chance for a Kalavat Plague cure. Donald Winston was important to the ship, but Minnen the Learned and Torina Jadus were important to the galaxy. Marston hated having to weigh the importance of one life over another, but he had no choice. The situation was what it was, and he would do what he had to, even if it haunted him after. He recalled his meeting with Clarke a few days earlier when they had discussed tactics for fighting the Vinkere: *they're strong, and very fast. Their size may be a disadvantage in confined spaces. They're disciplined fighters, but predictable. The one Clarke fought, Slethis, had a protective energy shield, and it took a lot of bullets to penetrate.*

"I may have an idea," he said slowly.

"What?" Balzano asked.

"There's no time," Marston said. "I'll let you know if it works out."

Balzano stepped back from the doors to allow Jadus, Uxxio and Korosa to join Marston in the elevator.

"Port Airlock One," Marston told the computer, and the elevator whisked them away to their destination.

"Amalthea, keeping the Vinkere away from our guests is your highest priority, do you understand?"

"Yes, Captain."

On the way to the airlock, they stopped just long enough for Marston to visit a nearby weapons locker. Clarke was already at the airlock with his security team when they arrived. Lauren Winters and Travis McGee were part of his team; given that they were the only ones on board with actual experience fighting Vinkere, it made sense to include them. All of them had their weapons trained on the door.

"Open the outer bulkhead," Marston instructed. The airlock had two sets of doors on each side: an outer door made of tri-magnesium and an inner, transparent door made of reinforced plexiglass.

Clarke hit the door panel and the heavier outer doors slid open, and Marston had his first look at a Vinkere warrior in person. Even coiled in a defensive posture his head nearly touched the ceiling of the airlock tunnel; Marston guessed he was more than four meters long, almost as big as the Vinkere Sirroyo and Clarke had encountered on the *Leviathan*. Three of his four arms were holding Chief Engineer Winston with his arms pinioned behind his back. The engineer looked pale, but otherwise unharmed. The Vinkere glared at them through the plexiglass like a predator eyeing its prey, which quite possibly was what the Vinkere considered them to be, Marston thought.

"That's him," Jadus said in astonishment. "The Vinkere from Tahvoa!"

"You recognize him?" Marston asked. Without taking her eyes off the Vinkere, Jadus told him, "He tried to kill us in the spaceport in Triyev." The tenacity with which he had pursued them across space was terrifying.

"I am here now to finish the job," the Vinkere said matter-of-factly.

It was enough to send a chill down Marston's spine, but he refused to be daunted by the alien. "State your demands," he said.

"The Tuulan For minister and Iganti scientist in exchange for your crewman," the Vinkere replied, looking at Jadus and Uxxio.

"If the captain were to hand us over, what would you do to us?" Jadus asked.

The Vinkere's yellow, slitted eyes focused on her. "Kill you," he said without hesitation. Jadus' only visible reaction was a raised eyebrow.

"Why do you want to kill them?" Marston asked. He was stalling, trying to decide if his idea would work.

The Vinkere ignored the question. "I'm going to say it once more: hand them over if you want your crewman alive. *Now*." He tightened his grip on Winston, eliciting a grunt of pain from the engineer.

"If I do that, there's no guarantee you won't kill him first, along with the others," Marston pointed out.

"No," the Vinkere agreed. He held up a controller with his fourth hand. "But if you do not, your crewman will die and I will press this button, which will send out a distress call alerting all Vinkere ships in the area to your position. Then you will *all* die."

The controller looked like Vlind technology; the Vinkere must have linked it to the *Wealth and Grandeur's* computer. Marston wondered why the Vinkere hadn't just sent the distress call immediately upon boarding the ship, but the answer followed the first thought almost immediately: it would have alerted the *Pericles* crew to his presence, causing him to lose the element of surprise and giving them a chance to escape.

"Perhaps I should kill him now," the Vinkere snarled, tightening his grip on Winston.

"No, wait! Please," Marston said, raising his hands in a placating gesture. He took a step closer. He was now standing in front of the security team, only two feet away from the transparent hatch that separated him from the Vinkere and the human engineer. He couldn't stall any longer. If he wanted to save Winston, they had to act now to neutralize the Vinkere. *Powerful and fast, but their size could be a disadvantage, particularly in a crowded corridor.*

"Hand over the Tuulan For minister and the Iganti scientist. Now," the Vinkere reiterated. He titled his wedge-shaped head, looking genuinely puzzled. "Why do you hesitate? They're not one of you." His grip on Winston was tightening. Marston made eye contact with his chief engineer, who nodded weakly.

The engineer's unspoken permission was all Marston needed. "Okay, we will," he lied. He touched the airlock control panel and the clear doors slid open.

"Fire!" he shouted, leaping out of the way of the security team.

The order was unexpected, but Clarke and the security team opened fire almost immediately; while the captain had been talking, they had taken careful aim at the Vinkere. Bullets pinged against the Vinkere's protective energy shield, but the alien responded faster than they could have imagined. Tossing Winston to the ground and activating the distress call, he leapt forward like an uncoiling spring, straight into the midst of the security officers.

With lightning reflexes, he lashed out with fists and a powerful tail, using his superior strength to swat rifles to the ground, slashing and punching the security officers, eliciting cries of pain as he fought his way through the beleaguered officers toward his target.

"GO!" Korosa screamed at her wards. Jadus and Uxxio backed away in alarm, turning to run away. The Vinkere shoved his way past the security officers, moving after his fleeing targets. Korosa urged them down the corridor away from the Vinkere. Giving no thought to the others, the Vinkere pushed on after them, determined to complete his mission.

He got within two meters when Amalthea sealed the bulkhead doors, separating the Vinkere from his prey. He roared in fury.

"Hey!"

S'Geliss spun around with a snarl to see the human captain advancing toward him. The Vinkere charged at him. Clarke and Winters fired past Marston at the approaching alien but the bullets struck harmlessly against his protective force field.

If the captain had never witnessed a Vinkere soldier in action he would have been unprepared for the onslaught, but he had spent hours studying the footage of Vinkere fighting in the *Leviathan*, and had spent many more hours training accordingly. When S'Geliss charged at him in a typical Vinkere lunging attack, Marston knew what to do. He dove out of the way, coming up in a roll just out of reach of the alien's claws. The Vinkere hissed in anger, but he wasn't the first giant Marston had fought. *Predictable*, flashed through his mind as he evaded a punch aimed at his head.

The Vinkere's tail lashed out, swiping at Marston's legs and knocking them out from under him. He crashed to the deck but quickly rolled to the side as the Vinkere's tail thumped down where he had been a split-second earlier. "Shoot him!" he shouted at Clarke. The Vinkere swung his fists, catching Marston on the shoulder. Pain lanced through his shoulder; it hurt badly, but he gritted his teeth and used the momentum to twist around, evading another punch. The serpentine alien lashed out with his tail, but Marston was already on the move again. He leapt out of the way again as Clarke opened fire.

The bullets couldn't penetrate the Vinkere's force field suit, but the barrage was enough to keep him off balance. He instinctively raised two arms to protect his face as bullet plinked off the shield. When Clarke saw the captain retrieve the stun baton concealed in his uniform jacket, he stopped firing so as not to hit him.

Marston struck with lightning speed. There was an electric fizzling sound as the baton made contact with the force field suit and a bright flash as it overloaded. The serpentine alien recoiled, baring his fangs and sharp claws defensively. It was a terrifying sight.

"We've already got one Vinkere in the morgue," Marston taunted. "Want to join him?"

The Vinkere lunged at him with an angry snarl. He had a longer reach than Marston so instead of jumping backward this time Marston ducked, dropping beneath the swiping claws that aimed for his throat and face. Then he pressed the stun baton into the alien's chest and activated it on its highest setting.

The Vinkere shrieked as volts of electricity shot through its body. Marston rolled out of the way as the serpentine alien crashed to the deck. It twisted and writhed, muscles spasming uncontrollably. McGee, Winters, and Korosa grabbed hold of the alien, pinning it down. Its tail thrashed about but the combined weight of the three security officers kept it immobilized. Clarke flipped his weapon around and swung it at the Vinkere. The butt of the rifle connected with the Vinkere's head with a loud *crack* and the alien collapsed, unconscious.

For a few moments the panting officers just stared at the prone serpentine figure lying on the deck. Then Amalthea reopened the bulkhead doors and a team of medics flooded into the corridor.

Doctor Gariri and her people descended on the injured security officers; some of them had broken bones and sharp gashes where the Vinkere had attacked them with its knife-like claws. While most of her medical team saw to the injured security officers, she and a pair of nurses directed their attention to the chief engineer, whose torso had two bullet wounds bleeding profusely. Feeling for a pulse, Gariri immediately set to work administering drugs and applying medipatches to the prone engineer.

Marston approached them. "Will he be okay?" he asked tentatively. Gariri barely glanced at him as she said, "I'll let you know when I know, Captain." A pair of crewmen helped her move the engineer onto an anti-grav stretcher and he was whisked away to the infirmary.

Marston watched them go, then gestured to the Vinkere lying motionless on the deck. "Put him in the brig," he ordered.

Clarke slung the rifle over his shoulder and nodded. "If he resists, I'll deal with him," he said to the captain, who nodded approvingly. Marston trusted the tactical officer to put a bullet through the Vinkere's head if he posed a threat. It took five crewmen to lift the unconscious alien onto an anti-grav stretcher for transport.

Minister Jadus and Uxxio moved out of the way as the stretcher passed. Uxxio regarded the unconscious Vinkere nervously, but Jadus just gave it a quick, dispassionate look. Massaging his sore shoulder, Marston approached her.

"Are you alright, Captain?" she asked.

"I'm fine; just a little tender." After what the Vinkere did to his security team he was fortunate he wasn't more seriously injured.

As the injured officers were taken away to the infirmary, Marston made a mental note to have Doctor Gariri examine their alien prisoner to make sure he had suffered no permanent damage. He could be an extremely valuable source of information.

Elzor Drin hurried past, accompanied by Katarina Sirroyo, on their way to the *Wealth and Grandeur's* bridge to shut down the distress call the Vinkere had activated. As he watched them go Marston wondered how many Vinkere ships were already on their way.

"We need to get out of here," he said, and Jadus nodded firmly in agreement.

"Lieutenant Hasan and Lieutenant Droma are plotting our course now," Amalthea said. Antak had offered to help the *Pericles* helmsman find a suitable location for the *Wealth and Grandeur*. Together they had located a nearby solar system containing a dense asteroid field that would conceal the ship.

As soon as Drin and Sirroyo had disabled the distress beacon, the Navy ship and the Vlind freighter activated their slipstream drives, vacating the area before any Vinkere ships arrived. They reached their destination less than two hours later.

The tumbling rocks of the asteroid belt filled the viewscreen. Now faced with the reality of abandoning his ship, Drin needed more reassurances from Marston and Jadus that it would be retrieved. After extracting promises from them both, he collected a satchel of personal possessions from his cabin and powered down his ship.

Marston left Drin on the bridge with Balzano while he went to check on the new occupants of the science lab. During the elevator ride Amalthea informed him the *Wealth and Grandeur* was devoid of power, minus the clamps securing it to one of the larger asteroids. He acknowledged the news with a silent nod.

When Marston stepped out of the elevator, he found the corridor a hive of activity. Crewmen hurried back and forth between the science lab and the infirmary carrying reports, chemicals, and equipment. He waited until the corridor was clear before rubbing his eyes tiredly and stretching. Then he straightened and strode purposefully into the laboratory.

"Ah, Captain!" Minnen the Learned greeted him energetically. He seemed right at home in the *Pericles'* state-of-the-art science lab.

"How are you, Professor?" Marston asked, taking in the scanners, microscopes, datapads, and other scientific equipment sprawled across the counter tops. Uxxio sat on a stool, scribbling notes for the professor on his datapad. In the background, several of the *Pericles'* science and medical staff were working under the instruction of Doctor Kerik.

"Quite well, thank you. Doctor Gariri sent me the forensic report of the Vinkere corpse in the morgue. A fascinating specimen!"

"Did you learn anything useful?" Marston asked.

"Oh, yes! They have a remarkable physiology; unlike any other serpentine species I've examined. In regards to our current work, though, I am not sure. The corpse is remarkably well preserved in its stasis chamber and I would have liked to inject some of the necrotic tissue with the Kalavat Plague to see if it produces a response. Of course, it may prove as lethal to them as it has to other species, or they may react like humans, which is to say, have no reaction at all," Minnen said. Seeing the captain's politely neutral expression, he got back on track. "Ahem. Unfortunately, we don't have any plague samples on the ship."

Marston wasn't so sure that was unfortunate, but refrained from commenting. "Maybe when we get you to Tuulan Vee they'll have virus samples for you to work with. Sorry, *plague*," he amended. He had already been briefed by Jadus and Minnen in the conference room about their research, so he knew it wasn't technically a virus.

Marston winced. His shoulder was still aching. Maybe he should have Doctor Gariri take a look at it. He was about to excuse himself when Professor Minnen spoke again. "I've actually been giving some thought to what our destination should be, Captain."

"I'm all ears." Their meeting in the conference room had been interrupted by the Vinkere intruder before they could discuss their ultimate destination, although Marston had assumed Jadus would want to continue traveling to Tuulan Vee. It was further than Earth, but it was definitely safer; days of searching hadn't brought the *Pericles* any closer to finding a way through the Vinkere lines to the greater Commonwealth. And Marston privately hoped that once at Tuulan Vee, Jadus would aid him in enlisting military help for the beleaguered Commonwealth.

"Attempting to reach your people on the other side of the Vinkere lines carries great risk, as does reaching Tuulan Vee. I suggest we don't try and breach the Vinkere blockade at all; rather, we should head in the opposite direction."

"You're suggesting we fly off into nowhere?" Marston asked dubiously. In the direction Minnen was proposing there was nothing but the empty, unclaimed space between the Commonwealth, Vlind Merchant Republic and Kithel Collective. *We'd have an abundance of plague samples in either of those places*, Marston thought wryly.

The Iganti professor shook his head, smiling. "Not nowhere, Captain. We should set a course for ISER Station!"

"What's Iser Station?" Marston asked.

"I-S-E-R," Minnen said. "It stands for the Interspecies Scientific Exchange of Research. The organization is based on Unity Station at the center of the Locality, but it has research bases scattered throughout the Locality. The one in the Gandra Sector is top secret."

"It is also the nearest," Uxxio added.

"I see." Marston had first heard of the Interspecies Scientific Exchange of Research during his mandatory cultural exchange program on Unity Station in his final year at the Navy Academy. "If they have a top-secret facility in the Gandra Sector, how do you know about it?" he asked.

"Young man, I have had many dealings with ISER," Minnen said. "And my daughter, Sul, works at the Gandra station. I had considered mentioning it to the minister several days ago, but I was concerned by the sightings of Infected ships in the area."

"It certainly sounds safer than trying to break through the Vinkere blockade," Marston said after some thought. "We can deal with Infected ships if we come across them."

Doctor Kerik overheard them and approached. "Captain, the Interspecies Scientific Exchange of Research has the most advanced scientific equipment this side of the Ankari Assembly," he said. "I can't think of anyone better to help us."

"My daughter Sul is an astrophysicist, but the station also has medical facilities," Minnen said. "I'm sure they're already working to find a cure, but…"

"…when they find out Minnen the Learned is on the verge of a breakthrough they'll give him full access to their resources," Minister Jadus said as she entered the room. She was accompanied by Commander Balzano and her ever-present guardian Korosa.

Balzano and Jadus also knew about ISER, but the existence of a secret ISER station just a few parsecs outside of the Commonwealth was a surprise to them as well. The Gandra Sector was essentially a galactic backwater, away from all the major slipstream routes and, as far as they knew, completely devoid of any intelligent life. Which was probably what the ISER Station there wanted people to think.

"It makes sense that they would operate some secret facilities to carry out their more… sensitive projects," said Jadus. She meant "sensitive" both politically and technologically; ISER was at the forefront of scientific research and advancement, but their work often included experiments deemed too dangerous for civilized systems. Marston had heard that some scientists worked for ISER for several years before returning home, where they were put to work by their governments implementing the new discoveries they had made. Marston wondered if any of the

Commonwealth's technological advances over the years could be attributed to ISER.

Jadus asked Doctor Kerik if he were aware of an ISER base in the Gandra Sector. "I was not," he admitted. Five years earlier he had turned down a position with ISER to become head of the Tuulan Vee Planetary Health Organization.

"They likely have the ability to transmit your Vinkere data back to the Commonwealth without it being traced to this ship," Jadus said, and Minnen nodded.

"It sounds like the best option to me," Balzano said, mirroring the captain's own thoughts. "For all of us. ISER is well-equipped to assist Professor Minnen and Minister Jadus in their research. We haven't found a way past the Vinkere, but the scientists at ISER might be able to help us with the Vinkere data core."

All things considered, the ISER facility sounded promising, especially if the Vinkere didn't know about it. Marston looked at Professor Minnen. "If we showed you a map of the Gandra Sector, would you be able to show us where the ISER station is located?"

"I can guide you to the general area," Minnen said. "I've only been there once, and that was many years ago."

"It's better than nothing," Jadus said. "You could contact your daughter and ask for permission for us to dock." Marston nodded in agreement.

"I will do what I can," Minnen promised.

"It's settled, then," Marston decided. "We'll proceed to the Gandra Sector and seek the help of the ISER scientists there." If anyone could help them put the information in the Vinkere data core to practical use, it would be them.

Balzano led Minnen to the bridge so that the Iganti could consult Lieutenant Hasan's star charts and give the helmsman a destination. Marston spoke with Jadus for a few more minutes before excusing himself. According to Clarke their Vinkere prisoner was awake and Marston wanted to ask him some questions.

"Captain, may I accompany you?" Jadus asked. Sensing his hesitance, she added: "I would like to learn if the Vinkere have any information on the Kalavat Plague."

Marston looked at her askance. "Do you think they are responsible?" he asked.

"I don't know. I think they have a lot to gain by a galaxy in the grip of a pandemic. What better time to invade your Commonwealth than while your allies are distracted by the Kalavat Plague? Why else would your Vinkere prisoner try to stop Minnen and I from curing it?"

"That possibility has occurred to me," Marston said slowly.

"It is only conjecture, but you must admit it *sounds* plausible," Jadus said. "Let me ask you this, Captain: how could a Kelzee colony and a Tuulan For scout ship, separated by a thousand light-years, become infected at the same time? The plague appeared almost simultaneously at different locations across the Locality. How could that have happened?"

"I don't know," Marston admitted.

"Our data on the speed at which different species manifest the symptoms of the virus, which have been observed and recorded by thousands of doctors in the Locality, suggest they could not have been infected by a common source. And yet Kalavat's colonists and the *Future's Promise* crew manifested symptoms at the same time. Elzor Drin already told us how the *Wealth and Grandeur* was attacked by unknown aliens and his crew became infected, and then he arrived at Takutu Station as it was overrun by *another* group of Infected! There are hundreds of other similar reports." Jadus nodded confidently. "It had to have been deliberately introduced. And whoever was responsible knew where to target to hurt us the most. Trade routes, transport hubs; they were extremely efficient. By the time we were aware of the outbreak, it was already too late."

"And then the mysterious Vinkere appeared," Marston said. "Their invasion couldn't have happened at a worse time for us... or a better time for them."

"Captain, the more I consider it, the more certain I am that this disaster was engineered," Jadus said. "However, we require *proof*."

"I agree," Marston said. "If people found out the Vinkere were responsible for unleashing the plague, it could unite the Locality against them."

"Yes," Jadus agreed. "And that's why we need to learn whatever secrets your prisoner is hiding."

A pair of security guards were standing outside the door to the brig, and saluted Marston as he and Jadus entered. The brig was a small room containing two prison cells and a workstation for the guard on duty. Although spartan, the cells contained a bunk, a water closet, and a small table and chair that receded into the wall at the touch of a button. One side was open to the rest of the brig, and it was crisscrossed by a grid of electrified metal rods. Until now, the cells had not been used.

There were three other people in the room aside from the office on duty. Henry Clarke paced back and forth while Lauren Winters and Travis McGee stood near the occupied cell. All three were armed; Clarke had his rifle hung over his shoulder and Winters sharpened her combat knife menacingly. They all looked up when the captain and minister entered.

"The prisoner regained consciousness ninety minutes ago," Clarke informed them. "He made several attempts to break out of the cell," he added wryly.

"But he's been in that weird trance for the last half hour," McGee said, indicating the Vinkere prisoner with a nod. The alien stood perfectly still at the center of the cell. At first glance his eyes appeared to be closed, but on closer inspection Marston noticed the Vinkere was observing them through hooded eyes.

Ensign Orlov, the officer on duty, spoke up. "Whenever he goes like that, the ship's sensors can't detect him. Lieutenant Sirroyo says he's capable of masking his life signs, so we maintain visual contact with him at all times."

"That must be why we didn't read any life forms on his ship," Marston said.

"And why he was able to board the *Wealth and Grandeur* without being detected," Jadus added, suppressing a shiver. If they hadn't encountered the *Pericles* and the Vinkere had caught up with them, she and the rest of her people could have been dead right now. She dismissed the thought almost immediately; there was no point dwelling on something that didn't happen.

As Marston and Jadus approached the barrier the Vinkere's scaly lips curved up in a wicked smile. Marston studied him for several moments before speaking. "I'm Captain Marston. It is on my ship you are held captive. You already seem familiar with the minister."

The prisoner looked at her, then returned his unblinking gaze to the captain. He said nothing.

"What is your name?" Marston asked.

The alien remained silent, the same half-smirk on his lips. Were it not for the forked tongue that occasionally flickered between his lips he would have made a convincing statue.

McGee gave a bored huff. "He hasn't spoken since he woke up, Captain," he said. "Not a word."

The serpentine alien surprised them all by choosing that moment to speak. "I am S'Geliss," it announced in a deep, sibilant voice.

"S'Geliss," Jadus repeated. "Why were you pursuing us?"

The Vinkere returned his unblinking stare to her. "To prevent your meddling."

"Our meddling? You mean, developing a cure for the Kalavat Plague?"

"Your meddling threatens the timely fulfilment of the Mandate," S'Geliss said.

"What mandate?" Jadus asked, but the alien refused to elaborate. He wasn't going to admit to anything incriminating without a little manipulation, Marston thought. He decided to try a different tact.

"I had a very interesting conversation with Supreme Commander Zithla a few days ago. Are you familiar with him? I believe you are. He spoke about a Vinkere crusade against the people of the Locality, beginning with humanity."

S'Geliss said nothing, so Marston continued. "Zithla told my crew that the very existence of our species was an abomination," he said, "And that he would eliminate every ship, planet and outpost. He also said he would ultimately defeat us because of his supreme belief in the mandate. That's the same thing you just referred to."

S'Geliss neither responded nor moved a muscle. His unblinking stare was unnerving, but Marston wasn't intimidated. "I'm not trying to get you to admit anything," he told the Vinkere. "We already know that your invasion of the Commonwealth is just the beginning of your campaign in the Locality. And I'm starting to suspect your people are responsible for releasing the Kalavat Plague in the Locality. Amalthea, can you please play the recording of my conversation with Supreme Commander Zithla?"

"Of course, Captain."

Behind Marston and Jadus a monitor activated, and they stepped aside so that S'Geliss could watch the recording.

"We have superior technology, numbers, and supreme conviction in our mandate. We are greater than you, and we will prevail. You cannot stop us," the recording of Zithla said. Amalthea fast tracked the recording to Zithla's next words: *"The very existence of your species is an abomination. There was a place for a select few of you, serving your Vinkere masters, but no longer."* The message froze on Zithla's snarling face. Marston and Jadus turned back to S'Geliss, who regarded them impassively. Marston decided to press on.

"As you can see, Zithla is not trying to hide his plans anymore. But what I want to ask you is: why? Why were your people compelled to launch a genocidal campaign against a group of strangers?"

"Only the strongest survive," S'Geliss said with what almost sounded like religious fervor. "Other species are a threat to our supremacy, so your destruction is mandated." Marston found the statement troubling, yet insightful; for all their strength and brutality, the Vinkere were motivated by fear.

"What will you do the next time you encounter an intelligent species? Exterminate them too?" Jadus asked.

"Of course."

Clarke stared at the prisoner in disbelief. "You know you can't kill everyone in the galaxy, right?"

S'Geliss twisted his neck to look at the tactical officer. "We have so far," he said with cold malice.

"My people's history includes dark chapters where one group attempted to subjugate or exterminate another because they believed that they were superior," Marston cautioned S'Geliss. "But that belief is wrong. It causes division and leads to conflict. And in the end, they were the ones who were destroyed." Clarke and the others nodded in agreement.

"They were destroyed because they were weak. All the weak will perish," S'Geliss said.

Marston wasn't going to engage the Vinkere in a debate of worldviews. He didn't have the time. "I think we've heard enough for now," he said simply.

"I agree," Jadus said, also moving toward the exit.

"He didn't say much," McGee commented.

"He said enough, for now," Marston said. Jadus nodded in agreement.

"It does not matter what you think you have learned," S'Geliss called after them. "When Zithla finds out that I failed in my mission, he will send a fleet to destroy you. There will be nowhere safe for you to hide."

"He won't find us where we're going," Marston said over his shoulder.

S'Geliss lunged forward, slamming his fists against the bars of his prison, the suddenness of his movement causing Jadus to flinch in surprise. As soon as he contacted the bars, the electricity surging through them caused him to leap backward with a yelp. Shaking his head, Marston approached the barrier until he was just a few inches away from the seething Vinkere.

"I understand," he said, sounding almost sympathetic. "You're frustrated. You can't handle an inferior human treating you without the respect you feel you deserve." His expression hardened. "Well, get used to it. You might be big and tough, but *I'm* in charge here."

"Let me out of here and you will see how *I* treat humans," S'Geliss hissed. "You are no match for me in equal combat!"

"Maybe not," Marston conceded, "But you'll never find out. Your days of hurting people are over."

He turned and left the brig with Jadus right behind him, leaving the Vinkere seething in his prison cell.

"If S'Geliss' response is typical of Vinkere, it would certainly indicate a willingness to release a deadly plague," Jadus said as they walked down the corridor away from the brig.

"Yes. He said his people view the existence of other intelligent species as a threat to Vinkere supremacy. And their mandate compels them to subjugate or exterminate other intelligent life. If that doesn't sound threatening, I don't know what does."

"It's chilling, isn't it?" Jadus said as they entered the elevator. "A species committed to the destruction of others."

"I wonder how many times they've done it before," Marston wondered. "Destroyed another species, I mean. They're obviously adept at subterfuge and warfare on an interstellar scale."

"Yes," Jadus agreed. "However, I wonder if their doctrine of racial supremacy has had an unintended consequence."

Marston looked at her curiously. "What?"

She pursed her lips thoughtfully. "As you say, the Vinkere have demonstrated an incredible capacity for subterfuge, and yet they are also relentless and brutal in the force they apply to achieve their goals. I witnessed it first-hand during their invasion of Tahvoa." Marston, recalling their savage skill in the battle of Ennomos, nodded.

"However, their belief in their own superiority causes them to underestimate us, their opponents. They have failed several times now in their endeavors, most obviously in their attempts to capture your ship and kill Professor Minnen and I."

"That's true," Marston said. "In their efforts to destroy my ship at the Shadow Nebula to conceal any knowledge of their existence, they inadvertently revealed themselves to the entire Commonwealth."

"And while they have come close to killing myself and Professor Minnen, they have always underestimated our ability to evade them," Jadus added.

"There was an ancient military strategist on Earth called Sun Tzu," Marston said. "He wrote that knowing your enemy was key to victory."

"The Vinkere may be technologically advanced, and devious, but they *don't* seem to understand their enemy."

Marston considered the first part of her statement. "Their technology is an enigma," he said. "For example, their missiles are almost identical to ours, but they also appear to have directed energy weapons, like the Ankari."

"Parallel development?" Jadus suggested. "Coincidence?"

Amalthea chimed in, communicating through the speakers in the elevator. "The research team may have just found an explanation."

"What is it?" Marston asked.

"Four minutes ago, I decoded Vinkere records referring to an incident that occurred in their home system. We do not yet fully comprehend their dating system, for they have a most complex calendar, but it appears the event took place eight years ago. Two advanced alien ships were discovered adrift in their home system; it appeared that they had destroyed each other, because both vessels were as lifeless as their crews. The Vinkere refer to this as "The Ascension" because they were able to reverse engineer much of the technology from the two ships, significantly advancing their own. It is possible that the two alien ships were from the Locality, and from them the Vinkere were able to extrapolate its location."

"Two derelict alien ships, ripe for the taking," Marston mused. "Amalthea, do you have any idea where the Vinkere home system is located?"

"It is within the Carina Nebula, approximately seven thousand light-years away."

"Seven thousand light-years away?" Jadus repeated in surprise.

"Yes, Minister. The only known map of the region comes from an Ankari probe that surveyed the nebula ninety years ago. To the Ankari the system is known as 'Tiva', but the Vinkere call it 'Zerenod', which literally means 'home star' in their language."

"Interesting," Jadus murmured.

"You may also find it interesting to know that the word 'Vinkere' means 'Hybrid Seed' in their native language," Amalthea added.

"'Hybrid Seed'?" Marston repeated. "That certainly piques my curiosity, but it will have to be a mystery for another time. How's the decoding going?"

"It is becoming increasingly difficult to translate the Vinkere data," Amalthea admitted after a moment of silence, which Marston thought sounded a lot like an embarrassed pause. "The security software is adaptive; it reacts to my efforts, and as a result it is becoming exponentially more difficult to mine information."

That worried Marston. "How long until you can't gather any more data?"

"It will be another two weeks before I can retrieve zero information from the Vinkere data core," Amalthea said. "At which point I will have translated eighty five percent of the core's contents."

"Do you think there will be any scientists on ISER Station who could help with that?" Marston asked Jadus.

"Perhaps."

Balzano intercepted them in the corridor. He handed Marston a datapad.

"Inventory of our food, water and medical supplies," he said. Marston took the datapad but didn't read it. Instead, he said, "Tell me."

"Well, with the people from the Leviathan expedition and Minister Jadus and her team, we've got double our normal complement," Balzano said. "Water won't be a problem, and we've got our own medical stocks plus the supplies the expedition brought on board, so the medical bay is well-equipped. But we only have enough food for three more weeks before we must implement rationing. There's also the matter of overcrowding; it's not easy finding room to sleep everyone."

"What about the cargo bay?" Marston asked.

"Full of expedition equipment. And no, we can't dump it," Balzano said in response to his unasked question. "The Leviathan scientists assure me it's all vital. And expensive," he said wryly.

"We could set up bunks in the upper observation deck."

"Lieutenant Young, who is filling in for Chief Winston in engineering, says that's not a good idea. That section was damaged during the flight from Ennomos and he's worried there are still micro-fractures in the hull there."

"What about the lower observation deck?"

"I was thinking that too, but it's one of the few areas the crew have to go when off-duty. I didn't want to take it away from them."

"I'll leave that problem in your capable hands, Commander," he said, and Balzano nodded.

"Captain, if my people and I can assist regarding our supply situation…" Jadus began, but Marston quickly put her at ease.

"Don't worry about it," he said dismissively. "I wouldn't exactly call it a crisis. Assuming Professor Minnen gave us accurate coordinates, we'll arrive at ISER Station before it becomes an issue. We can top up on supplies then, or along the way if we have to."

"Very well, then," Jadus said. "If you will excuse me, I will return to the science lab."

"Of course," Marston said.

"She is a remarkable leader," Balzano said when Jadus was out of earshot. "She crossed the Locality despite the danger, escaped an uprising on Iganta and a Vinkere invasion on Tahvoa, and is still as determined as ever to complete her mission."

"She is remarkable," Marston agreed. "I think we're fortunate to have encountered her."

Balzano grinned. "I think she and her people feel the same way about us."

*

Winston was going to make a full recovery. Through surgery, Gariri and her team had managed to repair the damage caused by the bullet wounds, and he had stabilized. She was tired, but relieved. She was also somewhat amused that just half an hour after waking he was trying to return to work.

"Trust me, I'm feeling much better," the engineer wheezed, sitting up in his bed.

Lupita Gariri gently pushed him back down. "I'm glad to hear it, but you're not leaving until *I* decide you're better," she said in a calm but firm voice.

"I've got work to do, Doctor," Winston said, sitting up again.

Doctor Gariri put a restraining hand on his shoulder. "The Vinkere damaged your trachea. If you want to be able to breathe properly, you'll stay and let me finish treating you."

Grumbling, the chief engineer lay back down. "Fine, but I don't want to be here a minute longer than necessary." He folded his arms petulantly, wincing at the pain it caused.

Doctor Gariri did her best to hide her smile. She and the Chief Engineer didn't interact very much outside of staff briefings, but he reminded her of her father.

"That's fine by me," she said patiently, applying the regenerator to his throat.

The machine emitted a faint humming sound when she activated it. Winston relaxed, leaning back against the pillow. Gariri knew from personal experience the regenerator had a soothing effect, producing a massage-like sensation as it healed the damaged tissue.

"It will only take about forty minutes," she told him. The engineer grunted in response; his eyes closed.

When she came back forty minutes later, Winston was snoring softly. Smiling to herself, she deactivated the regenerator and left him to sleep.

Captain Marston entered the infirmary a few minutes later. He quietly approached Winston's bed. The engineer's chest rose and fell evenly, and he looked peaceful.

"How is he?" the captain asked as Gariri approached.

"He will be fine," she said, watching the tension drain from the captain.

"Thanks to you, Doctor," Marston said, sounding enormously relieved. "When will he wake up?"

"Whenever he's rested," Gariri said simply. "I don't want to wake him because he'll insist on going straight back to work."

Marston grinned. "Don't let him until he's ready."

"I won't."

"Could you let me know when he wakes up? I was hoping to talk to him."

"Is it urgent?" Gariri asked.

Marston shifted uncomfortably. "It can wait until he's awake. I just wanted to apologize for nearly getting him killed."

To their surprise, Winston smiled. Without opening his eyes, he said, "Doctor, will you remind the captain that risk is part of my job?"

Marston smiled, and Gariri patted Winston's hand and chuckled. "I'll pass it on."

"Good," Winston said quietly. "Because I'm going to make a full recovery, and he shouldn't be second-guessing himself."

"Thanks, Chief," Marston said.

"Anytime, Captain," Winston murmured. "Now, if the two of you will please give me some quiet I'm going to go back to sleep." They did so, and he was soon snoring softly again.

Katarina Sirroyo scanned the text scrolling down her screen with tired eyes. Sifting through the data Amalthea mined from the Vinkere data core was monotonous work, but important. She and her team were looking for information that could be useful to the Commonwealth. She got to the end of the file and realized she hadn't taken in anything she had just read. Sighing, she scrolled to the top and started again.

"There must be a better way of doing this," Jarren Qel said, rubbing his eyes tiredly. Having little else to do on the ship, the young Tuulan For had offered to help Sirroyo and her team. As Torina Jadus' aide he was accustomed to gathering information.

"Couldn't your ship's AI collect the data for us?" he asked, stretching wearily. Sirroyo had no doubt Amalthea was listening, but she spoke for the AI. "Most of Amalthea's processing power is focused on data mining and trying to circumvent the security program responding to her efforts. She can do little else besides talk to us right now. She's still a young AI, only a few weeks old. An AI's knowledge grows exponentially, but I think it will be a few weeks or even months before she's capable of running the ship's systems, battling a highly sophisticated Vinkere security program, and sifting through petabytes of data at the same time."

Jarren slumped in his chair. "Fair enough."

"Ideally we'd have thousands of people analyzing the data," Sirroyo said wistfully. "As it is, we've got a few dozen *Pericles* crewmen, the scientists from the Leviathan Expedition, and us."

"Well, I'm sure there's a whole group of scientists on ISER Station who will leap at the chance to sift through an alien database," Jarren said with a hopeful grin.

Sirroyo smiled. "Here's hoping." Jarren looked at her quizzically but didn't say anything.

"Thank you for helping out," she said to him. "Another pair of eyes is always helpful."

"It's no problem," Jarren assured her. "I have nothing else to do right now, and I wanted to make myself useful. Besides, this is what I normally do for the minister." He grinned. "It's about now that she comes out of her office and asks me to get her a hot beverage."

"Are you offering?" Sirroyo joked, and Jarren laughed.

Korosa entered the *Pericles'* gym. Minister Jadus was safe for the moment, and with nothing else to do, she decided to log some more combat practice. On the *Telvarn Star* and *Wealth and Grandeur* she'd had to make do with her quarters or an empty cargo bay, but the *Pericles* had a fully equipped training room.

The room was nearly empty; most of the crew were either on duty or sleeping, and most of the other science-types on board were working with Minister Jadus and Professor Minnen. The only other occupants of the gym were two of the security officers Korosa recognized from the airlock. One lifted dumbbells, while the other ran on a treadmill. They nodded in greeting as Korosa walked past them.

The training area was a small square of gym mats, and Korosa began by stretching. After several minutes and some on-the-spot cardio, she began the first set of motions in one of the hand-to-hand combat forms she was proficient in. It was the same exercise she had started to teach Jarren on the Vlind ship, but after the first lesson he had suddenly become very busy and "unavailable" for further training. She grinned mischievously to herself.

After several minutes she noticed the two officers watching her curiously. She continued her exercises until one of them approached her.

"That's a pretty interesting exercise you're doing there," he said, wiping sweat from his forehead with a towel. "What's it called?"

"*Mojula-Tirana*. It translates to, 'battle through self-defense,'" she said without pausing.

"Interesting," he said. The other woman came over and joined him by the side of the training area.

She studied Korosa's movements with a critical eye. "Impressive," she said after a minute. "Would you be interested in teaching us?"

Korosa shrugged. "If you like," she said, finishing a particularly complex set of moves. "Mojula-Tirana was conceived by a nomadic religious group on my planet centuries ago. They didn't carry weapons, but devised these techniques to defend themselves when attacked."

"I'm Travis, by the way. Travis McGee," the man said, offering his hand. She grasped his hand and shook her arm up and down in the peculiar human greeting. "I'm Korosa Jakor, I'm in charge of Minister Jadus' security."

"Nice to meet you," Travis said.

"I'm Lauren Winters," said the female. She had the same tough, no-nonsense air about her that Korosa did, which immediately earned the Tuulan For woman's respect.

"You're the ones who helped capture that Vinkere at the airlock," she said, and they nodded in confirmation.

"We're also responsible for the Vinkere captain in the ship's morgue," Travis boasted.

Korosa was impressed. "I'd be very interested to hear everything you have to say about the Vinkere. Perhaps while I train you, you can tell me what it's like to fight one."

Lauren shrugged. "Both times we've come up against the Vinkere it's been a close call. But we will share what we can."

"We encountered the Vinkere in the brig on Tahvoa, and he nearly killed us," Korosa told them, frowning. She was still angry at herself for being unarmed and unprepared when the Vinkere caught up with them, and vowed not to let it happen again. "I need to know everything you know about fighting them, so the next time we face them, I'll be ready."

"You've got yourself a deal," Travis said. He joined her on the mat. "You teach us *mo-jewel-a-tirahna,*" he said, pronouncing the Tuulan For word as best he could, "And we'll teach you about fighting the Vinkere. Ready?" There was no mistaking the friendly challenge in his tone.

Korosa accepted his challenge with relish. "Are you?" she asked with a smirk.

The *Pericles* sped through the slipstream toward the distant Gandra Sector. Occasionally Vinkere ships appeared on sensors and the *Pericles* would shut down its slipstream drive and slip into low-power mode until they disappeared again. Despite a few close calls, they managed to evade the enemy. Not all of the Vinkere ships were warships; once, an enemy transport vessel passed by close enough that Sirroyo, perturbed, reported it was filled with human life signs. The *Pericles* was forced to hide until the enemy ship, accompanied by a Leviathan escort, passed out of range. The crew were upset, but there was nothing they could do. The *Pericles* was no match for a Leviathan, and Marston grimly ordered Hasan to resume their course.

A week after leaving the *Wealth and Grandeur* behind they crossed the Commonwealth's external border and entered a vast, empty region of unclaimed space. Although they remained alert, Marston noticed some of the tension leaving the crew, and there was no indication of any Vinkere presence in the area. The silence from the Commonwealth troubled Marston and his officers. They all desperately wanted to know how their people were faring against the alien invaders, but if the Navy was trying to reach them, their signals were being blocked by the Vinkere somehow. The *Pericles* continued onwards, leaving the Interstellar Commonwealth behind, wary of Vinkere and hoping for news from home that never came.

Sirroyo and her team continued to collate what useful information Amalthea could retrieve from the Vinkere data core. Then, two weeks into the journey, the AI solemnly announced that the security program had encrypted all remaining data files beyond even her ability to access. However, it meant that Amalthea could focus her efforts on helping Sirroyo and her team comb through the data already retrieved.

Marston was pleased to see his crew, the Leviathan Expedition personnel and Minister Jadus' people working together, and even socializing; one evening he passed by the rec room and witnessed Jarren, Antak, and Korosa playing a card game with several of the *Pericles* crew. After many stressful weeks living with the ever-present danger of the Vinkere, people were beginning to relax a little.

Long range sensors didn't detect any other vessels along their path, and the *Pericles* traveled alone through space. It appeared that knowledge of the Vinkere invasion of the Commonwealth had spread throughout the Locality and travelers were giving it a wide berth. For Marston, their journey beyond human space was mostly uneventful. Aside from reading status reports and monitoring for Vinkere, there was very little to do, so he spent time training with Clarke and Korosa and assisting Winston and his team with repairs.

On the twenty-first day of their journey, the *Pericles* arrived at its destination in the Gandra Sector.

23

Message to Prime Minister Shanti of the Ankari Assembly from Chief Strategist Geron Regarding the State of Affairs in the Locality. The full details of the report will be read out at the next meeting of the Ecclesia, but for your convenience I have summarized the main points below:

- In our territory the Kalavat Plague has already overrun Kora, Mornek Melvarnis, Rinthia and Valorn II. Further outbreaks threaten to overwhelm our defenses on Valorn III, Kyrion and Barillion Prime.
- Barillion Prime has a population of four billion and is the most developed world in that region of space. The Assembly Defense Force is committing a large number of vessels and soldiers to protect it, but Admiral Denulus believes it will be insufficient. (It should be noted that Denulus was correct about Rinthia and Valorn II; it is my belief that if he had been recalled from his previous post earlier, he would have succeeded in containing the plague to Kora).
- Vlind Containment Squads are proving surprisingly effective on a local scale, but their fleets are having difficulty tracking the movements of every Infected vessel in their territory. They have again requested our assistance in this endeavor.
- The Kelzee government has begun constructing "firebreaks" around their Core Worlds Sector to prevent the plague from reaching Kelzanti Prime. This appears to be working, but it has left billions of Kelzee in the outer Perimeter Zones endangered by the plague.
- The Draxilans are even more reticent than usual, but our scouts have confirmed they have sealed their borders. Long-range surveillance does not detect any sign of the plague within the Empire. Our primary concern is that the Draxilans will take advantage of the chaos to once more expand their territory at the expense of their neighbors.
- News from Iganta is limited, but it appears Zinkara the Warrior Queen is successfully consolidating her power on the home world. There is no sign of Professor Minnen the Learned; he has not responded to any requests by our

scientists for help with the Kalavat Plague cure research and our fear is he has been killed in the widespread culling of the Despot's government by Zinkara's forces. There is a rumor that he escaped Iganta on board a Tuulan For ship, but if this is true our agents have not been able to locate him.

- We have lost direct contact with the Human Interstellar Commonwealth. Reports of an invasion by a race called the "Vinkere" have come to us second hand; all our information from the Commonwealth these days comes through the Tuulan For. We suspect these Vinkere took advantage of the turmoil across the Locality to invade the Commonwealth at a time their allies are unable to help. Even more concerning is their sudden appearance within the Locality, and reports that their technology is almost on par with our own. We would dispatch ships to investigate, had we any ships to spare. For the moment, all we can do is assess the information shared by the Tuulan For to determine whether the Vinkere pose a threat to the Assembly.
- The Human Interstellar Commonwealth has been settling Kithel refugees on some of their outer worlds, but due to the Vinkere invasion we do not know the fate of these refugees.
- The Tuulan For have mostly succeeded in containing the plague in their space, no doubt due to their Quarantine Zone and their relative isolation from the other plague-affected species.

Conclusion: the situation in the Locality is deteriorating. With every lost world our own fleets and armies shrink, and Infected numbers swell. It is the belief of my colleagues and I at the institute that we are nearing a critical juncture; if the numbers of Infected continue to grow at the current rate, soon we will lose the ability to contain them at all. It is therefore my recommendation that we implement Admiral Denulus' plan immediately, despite the risks it carries. If you can convince the Ecclesia to approve his plan, it is probable the Vlind and Kelzee governments can likewise be convinced to assist us in the endeavor. Admiral Denulus assures me he is ready and able. The decision lies with you.

Justin Caleb

July 10, 2438
In orbit of Ennomos, Ennomos System
Interstellar Commonwealth

Zithla stalked the dark corridors of his flagship. His soldiers wisely avoided him, lest he vent his rage up them. The Triumvirs, in their ineptitude, had allowed the *Pericles* to escape Kronos with information that could be used against the Vinkere. Despite an extensive search of Vinkere-controlled space the human ship had not been seen in weeks, not since Zithla's conversation with its young captain. He took a small measure of comfort knowing that they hadn't made it back to their own people. He had been meticulous in the deployment of his forces along the frontlines, and he was confident his forces could intercept the *Pericles* should it try to reach the Commonwealth fleet.

Equally frustrating was the fact that the humans were proving more resistant than Vinkere strategists had projected. After the initial blitz through Tier 3 and 4 space, Zithla's invasion force faced stiffening resistance along an increasingly static frontline. They had lost momentum; the Vinkere blitzkrieg had become a war of attrition. Zithla still believed that their superior technology and numbers would eventually give the Vinkere victory, but it would take longer than predicted. Which was dangerous, because the Tuulan For Minister and Iganti Professor were out there somewhere. Zithla's most trusted officer, S'Geliss, had presumably failed in his mission. They had not heard from him in weeks; he had disappeared, along with his targets. If they succeeded in curing the Ss'kapp'rn Plague, the Vinkere could find themselves fighting foes on multiple fronts. And Zithla did not share the Triumvirs' confidence that his force could take on more than one Ss'Talak Cluster military at once.

He punched two of his fists into a wall monitor, shattering the glass surface and sending sparks spraying. The sparks scorched him, and he recoiled, hissing. The small act of violence hadn't helped to quell his rage at all, although he did get a small amount of pleasure knowing some underling would have to repair the damaged monitor.

Soon he reached the conference room where his lieutenants were waiting for him. The black, metallic doors parted with a rumble, and he entered. To his surprise and anger, the meeting had started without him.

The worm Slithza stood at the head of the table and was the first to notice Zithla's arrival. "Good, there you are, Consul," he announced, his imperious tone making Zithla bristle. "As you were late to the briefing, I took it upon myself to update everyone on the current situation. As you can imagine, the Triumvirs are quite displeased."

Zithla slithered ominously toward the head of the table; Slithza remained in place, although he tensed as the larger Vinkere approached.

"The Triumvirs cannot make poor tactical decisions and then blame me for the consequences," Zithla said flatly. The best way to annoy Slithza was to be dismissive, so he ignored the Triumvir's emissary and turned to the assembled officers. "We have not made the headway any of us desire, but that is about to change. We must look past the failures of the Triumvirs and their lackeys—" he said with a withering glance at Slithza, "—And accept the current situation for what it is. The humans have proven more resistant than anticipated, and the Tuulan For minister and Iganti scientist are still at large and probably working on a cure for the plague."

None of the officers present dared to challenge Zithla, but one bravely asked, "What of S'Geliss, Supreme Commander?"

"I have not heard from S'Geliss, nor do I expect to," Zithla said with a growl. "I can only assume he failed in his mission." He leaned forward, placing his four-clawed fists on the smooth black surface of the table. "There are lessons to be learned here, however. Recent events have served to expose the flaws in our plan, and to separate the weak from true Vinkere. We have not lost anything worth keeping. Those of us who remain are of pure intent, and stronger than before."

Slithza was conspicuously quiet, but the other officers made sounds of approval, and Zithla continued. "Our fleet is deployed across the Commonwealth, forming an impenetrable net that the human ship *Pericles* will soon fall into. As for the rest of their fleet? I have a plan to use their own people against them. I have already contacted the Staging Post and informed them of my plan. It will take time, but we will hold the line until then."

"What exactly is your plan?" Slithza demanded.

Zithla told them. It was deceptively simple, and yet would deliver a devastating blow to the morale of the embattled Commonwealth fleet. Zithla's officers praised him, filled with renewed enthusiasm for the war, which they were confident once more would result in a Vinkere victory.

None of them noticed Slithza lean over and whisper in Zithla's ear: "You may have the approval of your soldiers, but we shall see what the Triumvirs have to say about your plan."

He turned and left the conference room through a back door, no doubt to report to the Triumvirs. Zithla let him go. Soon it wouldn't matter what Slithza or the Triumvirs thought. They lacked vision, and experience in military matters. If there was one thing that this campaign had taught Zithla it was that power could not be shared; only he had the capability to rule the Vinkere Dominion. He would be responsible for the victory over the humans, and when the Triumvirs and humans lay dead before him, he would rule the galaxy.

*

July 11, 2438
Unnamed solar system in the Gandra Sector
Unclaimed

The *Pericles* surged out of the slipstream into normal space. A star in the middle distance bathed the hull in pale yellow light, giving Torina Jadus an aura as she gazed out the windows at the front of the bridge.

"The Gandra Sector," she said to herself, feeling excitement course through her. It was every scientist's dream to work for ISER, the foremost scientific establishment in the Locality. And now, if everything went well, she was about to visit one of their legendary stations. She crossed the bridge and took up a position beside Marston's chair.

"Scan the area," the captain instructed Sirroyo. "Let's see what's out there."

"There's no sign of the Vinkere in our immediate vicinity, or any other ships for that matter," Clarke reported from the tactical station. It took a few more minutes for Sirroyo to complete her more detailed scan, but when she did, there was nothing more to offer.

"There aren't any artificial structures within sensor range," she said. "If the ISER base is out there, it's well hidden."

"Very well hidden indeed," Professor Minnen said mildly as he entered the bridge, escorted by Commander Balzano. He turned to Sirroyo. "The scientists on the station use a scattering field to deflect sensor scans, and all subspace communications are sent in encrypted bursts."

"I'm sure you have a way to contact them, don't you, Professor?" Jadus asked.

"I do." Minnen looked at Clarke. "Young man, could you please send a short-range, wide-band subspace message?"

Clarke nodded. "Channel open."

Minnen cleared his throat. "This is Minnen the Learned of Iganta contacting the scientists at the ISER Station in this system. I am on board the Commonwealth ship *Pericles* requesting permission to dock, as we require your assistance. Please respond."

After several moments of silence Minnen added, "I would not risk drawing attention to your presence in this system were the situation not so urgent. But we need your help. My daughter Sul is an astrophysicist who works on the station. She can vouch for my discretion."

"That will not be necessary, Professor," a male voice replied. *"We're sending you our coordinates now."*

A string of digits appeared on the viewscreen. "I've got them," said Hasan. "Setting a course."

"Thank you, Professor," Marston said. The Iganti scientist inclined his head.

"Captain, I'd like to accompany you when you meet the station's commander," Jadus told Marston.

"Of course," Marston agreed.

After a brief transit through the slipstream, a simple two-second hop across the system, the *Pericles* dropped back into normal space. The jump had brought them to the second of the system's three gas giant planets, which hung in space like a great blue orb. Unlike Kronos, which had a fast-moving, turbulent atmosphere of multi-colored bands, the surface of the planet in front of them was a uniform deep blue that looked deceptively serene.

Hasan guided the ship into orbit one hundred thousand kilometers above the planet's equator. Following the coordinates given to him by the ISER contact he took the *Pericles* roughly a third of the way around the planet's circumference before angling away from the blue gas giant toward the largest of its sixteen moons. A few minutes later, a grey-white pinprick appeared against the starry backdrop, increasing in size as the ship approached it.

The ISER Station floated in space at the LaGrange point where the gravity from the gas giant and its largest moon were equal. It measured five hundred meters in diameter, capable of housing hundreds of people. To Marston's eye it resembled a giant spinning top, rotating in slow motion.

Five docking tubes protruded equidistantly from the rim of the station, and Hasan received a second set of instructions guiding them to the nearest one. He brought the *Pericles* alongside the station, using thrusters to align the starboard airlock with the station's. With a gentle click the airlocks connected, and Hasan disengaged the engines.

Marston turned to Jadus and Minnen. "Ready to go?"

"I am," Jadus confirmed.

"Then let us proceed," Minnen suggested cheerfully, more jovial than usual at the prospect of seeing his daughter.

Balzano and Sirroyo joined them. "The bridge is yours, Lieutenant Commander," Marston said to Clarke.

Uxxio and Jarren met them outside the airlock. Elzor Drin came hurrying down the corridor. "Accompany you is what I shall do," he insisted, panting. Marston didn't argue; the Vlind had mostly kept to himself during the voyage, and he didn't see any harm in Drin coming along.

They crossed through the airlock tunnel into the station, where a cluster of people waited to greet them. They all wore grey uniforms bearing the symbol of ISER, which reminded Marston of the Greek letter *phi.* Their leader, a short Vlind woman, stepped forward.

"ISER Station in the Gandra Sector welcomes you. My name is Preeka Vashon. I am the Station's Overseer." Marston noticed immediately that she spoke in "normal" Trade Standard, without employing the unconventional sentence structure used by most Vlind. He wondered if that was a by-product of spending so much time among aliens or if she had deliberately cultivated it to communicate more easily with others.

"Thank you for allowing us to come here," Jadus said. "We had nowhere else to go."

"The current state of the Locality is alarming. We are happy to assist you," Vashon replied. She indicated Minnen with a four-fingered hand. "And we would never turn away one who has done us great service in the past."

Minnen tutted dismissively, and Marston wondered what Vashon could be referring to. Before he could say anything, however, a young Iganti woman pushed through the crowd of scientists. She was tall and slender, and Marston guessed her identity even before she made a direct line for Professor Minnen.

"Father!" she beamed. They pressed their bulbous foreheads together affectionately.

"Sul, my daughter! I am pleased to see you," Minnen said warmly. "How are you?"

"All is well, father," she replied. Seeing the professor's assistant standing nearby Sul smiled again. "Hello, Uxxio."

"Uh, hello Sul," Uxxio stammered. Marston and Jadus shared an amused look. In his limited interactions with the young Iganti, Marston had never seen him so flustered.

A dark-haired human scientist in his mid-forties approached Marston. Offering his hand, he introduced himself. "Captain Marston, I'm Doctor Jackson Lisle, Director of Physical Sciences. I'm the one who communicated with your ship."

"It's good to meet you, Doctor," Marston said, shaking the offered hand.

"You requested assistance in your message," Vashon said. "What is the nature of your predicament?"

Jadus answered her. "I traveled to Iganta to collaborate with Professor Minnen on a cure for the Kalavat Plague. However, we were forced to flee the planet unexpectedly. On our way back to Tuulan Vee we had to pass through the Vinkere-occupied Commonwealth, which was a nerve-wracking experience, to say the least. Fortunately for us the *Pericles* found us before the Vinkere did."

Vashon nodded. "We received the automated message from the Commonwealth government. We had not heard of the Vinkere until then."

"We can tell you all about the Vinkere," Marston said with a humorless smile. "We managed to salvage a data core from one of their ships and we're trying to return it to our people. We were searching for a way past the Vinkere when we encountered the Minister and her people."

Several of the scientists looked up with interest at the mention of the alien data core. "Maybe our people could take a look at the data core," Lisle suggested.

"I don't see why not," Marston agreed. "That's one of the reasons we're here. We've learned a lot from it, but we have no way of getting the information back to the Commonwealth without it being blocked by the Vinkere."

Lisle nodded. "The Vinkere employ an advanced jamming signal that prevents direct communication with the Commonwealth. Maybe we can relay a message *around* them."

"Any help you can offer would be appreciated," Balzano said.

"We could relay it through com buoys in the Republic of Tuulan Vee," Sul said.

"Your subspace transceiver is that powerful?" Uxxio asked in amazement.

Sul smiled proudly. "Of course. This is ISER!"

"I have a message for Chancellor Denrek to include in the transmission," Jadus said. It had been more than six weeks since her last message to him, and she knew her silence would have him deeply worried. She wanted to assure him that she was alive and well and, if Professor Minnen were to be believed, they were close to developing a cure.

Sul looped her arm through Minnen's. "When I heard the news from Iganta, I feared for you, father. Is it true the Warrior Queen now rules?"

"We think so," Uxxio said. "We didn't stick around to see how the situation turned out." The Professor frowned at being pre-empted but said nothing.

"We have a ship full of scientists working on the Vinkere data core and Kalavat Plague research," Sirroyo said. "We were hoping to make use of your equipment and expertise."

"We will assist you," Vashon promised.

"Thank you," Jadus said with relieved smile.

Vashon continued: "I must caution you however that our resources are somewhat limited. The last two supply ships never arrived."

"We'll help you out as best we can," Marston promised. "Although, to be honest, with so many extra people on board we'll have to introduce rationing ourselves in another week."

"If supplies are dwindling, then procuring new ones is what I can help with," Drin said. The others looked at him.

"You can get supplies all the way out here?" Balzano asked.

"I *am* a merchant," Drin reminded them.

While the others continued to talk, Marston watch Professor Minnen. He had a distant look in his eyes, as though his thoughts had already returned to his research. Now that he had the proper facilities, personnel and resources, Marston hoped he could make the Kalavat Plague cure a reality, and soon.

ISER Station's communications center was a hexagonal, multi-leveled room at the heart of the station. The main floor contained the controls for the station's powerful subspace transceiver and holographic booths for real-time virtual communications with other ISER facilities throughout the Locality. The second level housed more conventional communication terminals; most were used monitoring reports on the Kalavat Plague. Vashon grimly informed them there was almost no information available on the Vinkere invasion of the Commonwealth.

Jadus watched a scientist enter one of the holographic booths. She was impressed with the technology these people took for granted; the Republic was still a couple of years away from implementing the real-time, holographic communications that virtually allowed one to be in the same room as the person they were contacting.

Vashon approached her. "Minister, we are ready to send your subspace message to Chancellor Denrek. Please input the target address here." The console's interface was more complex than what she was used to, but the controls were in Trade Standard so she could read them easily. She entered the Tuulan For government address and gave a satisfied nod when the computer informed her the message was transmitting.

She re-joined Vashon and Marston beside the central master console, where a holographic image of the space station showed the powerful subspace transceiver highlighted in red. It was pointed toward the Republic of Tuulan Vee; Jadus wondered how much power was required to send such a large packet of information hundreds of light-years. Soon Chancellor Denrek would be able to relay the information to the Commonwealth government. She felt a pang of homesickness at the thought of her mentor in his office in Lakaria.

"I read your overview of the data you have collected on Vinkere ship deployments, tactics, and communications protocols. I am certain your people will find the information most helpful," Vashon said.

"I hope that in the next communication we can tell them where the Vinkere are striking from," Marston said. "We don't even know how they reached the Commonwealth."

"During the First Contact War between my people and the Thordrans, our ship captains were not permitted to keep any records of the location of our home world or colonies," Jadus said. "Knowing that the Thordrans rarely took live prisoners, that information was committed to memory for safekeeping. It's possible the Vinkere have done the same to keep the location of their staging post a secret."

Vashon nodded in agreement; Marston frowned. "Then maybe we need to find it ourselves."

<h1 style="text-align:center">24</h1>

"A mission? To the Shadow Nebula?" Korosa repeated. They had assembled in the communications center; Marston and his executive officer, sensor operations officer, helmsman, tactical officer and chief engineer, while Jadus was accompanied by Korosa, Antak and Jarren. Overseer Vashon and Doctor Lisle represented the station's contingent of scientists, and both looked thoughtful as they considered Marston's proposal.

"Yes," Marston said. "But not the *Pericles*, it's too dangerous. We would send a probe to see what the Vinkere have been doing in there."

His words were met with silence as they considered what would be required for the mission. Infiltrating the nebula would be no easy task. "When we entered the Shadow Nebula looking for the *Searcher*, the Vinkere responded almost immediately," Balzano said. "I bet they have some kind of detection grid."

"In other words, the probe would have to bypass Vinkere surveillance and remain invisible while it explores the nebula," Sirroyo said.

"It needs to be fast, too," Marston added. "The sooner it reaches the nebula, the better."

"We use high-speed slipspace probes on the station," Lisle said. "But stealth probes are expensive to manufacture. It would require at least ten days to build."

"What if we made the probe look Vinkere?" Jarren asked, drawing surprised looks. "They might assume it's one of their own, maybe even ignore it."

Sirroyo pursed her lips thoughtfully. "We do have Vinkere hull fragments on the *Pericles,* collected by the Leviathan Expedition."

"I would like to examine these hull fragments," Vashon said. The diminutive Vlind woman began to pace. "Perhaps we can duplicate the alloy for the probe's coating."

Marston took that as confirmation the ISER scientists were onboard. "Great." Then, to everyone else, "I would like to make this a priority."

"Lieutenant Droma?"

Antak had tuned out during the discussion about the probe and jumped when Commander Balzano said his name. "Yes?"

"Minister Jadus mentioned you have experience navigating nebulas."

"That's right," Antak said with a sidelong glance at Jadus. "If you count that one time four years ago."

"Lieutenant Hasan could use your help plotting the course for the probe," Balzano said.

"No problem."

"I know this is a big job, but it's an important one. Overseer Vashon will supervise the construction of the probe, because the station has the facilities to actually build it," Marston said.

Vashon nodded. "Let's get to work," she said, and the group dispersed.

It impressed Marston how quickly the station's scientists took to their new project. Within an hour of their meeting, Vashon had several departments working on the Vinkere stealth probe's construction. After analyzing the Vinkere hull fragments the ISER scientists assured Marston they would be able to produce the same material. It took another few hours to scrounge the necessary materials from the station and the *Pericles*, but soon the station's synthesizers were producing sheets of the blue-grey alloy. Vashon took the captain to a factory on one of the station's lower levels where the metallic sheets rolled along a conveyor belt from the synthesizers to the automated assembler. Marston ran his hand along the cool, frictionless material; it looked identical to the hull plating on Vinkere ships. "It is, technically speaking," Vashon told him.

Sirroyo and the ISER scientists worked through the night installing the delicate hardware that would allow the probe to gather information in the nebula, while Doctor Lisle and his team fitted the probe with a powerful transmitter so that the station would receive the data in real time. When they were finished, Winston and a group of engineers from the *Pericles* fitted the probe with an advanced slipstream drive using parts from the station and based on the *Pericles'* own faster-than-light engines. The flight from the vicinity of the Shadow Nebula had taken the *Pericles* three weeks, but the probe's smaller mass and powerful engines would allow it to make the journey in a third of that time.

When Marston, Jadus and Balzano entered the lab the next morning the engineering teams were tired but triumphant: the probe was complete. If he hadn't known better, Marston would have said the blue-grey, three-meter-long cylinder sitting on the deck was Vinkere.

"Great work, everyone," Marston congratulated the team. They had accomplished it all in less than twenty-four hours. Marston was immensely proud of his own people who had worked on the probe, and grateful to the ISER scientists as well. He could see why they had a reputation as the best.

"When can we launch it?" Jadus asked.

"Lieutenants Hasan and Droma have uploaded the flight plan into the navigational computer. We are ready to proceed," Vashon said.

As if on cue, a robotic cargo handling unit rolled into the bay on large treads. It picked up the probe in two of its appendages and then trundled back toward the door as though the probe weighed nothing.

"It will be taken to a probe launch bay," Vashon said. "We can monitor its launch from the communications center."

While the engineers and scientists who had worked on the probe trudged wearily to their beds, Marston, Jadus, Balzano and Vashon returned to the Communications Center where Antak, Hasan and Doctor Lisle were waiting for them. A monitor displayed the probe's status and its progress along the pre-planned flight to the nebula. It could also be remotely controlled from here if required.

"Launch the probe," Vashon instructed Lisle.

"Probe launching in three... two... one... launch. Entering the slipstream in five seconds."

The probe arrowed away from the station, gaining speed rapidly. The dark, blue-grey plating made it difficult to see against the backdrop of space, but everybody saw the flash as the probe entered the slipstream.

"The probe is away," Lisle announced with a pleased grin. "It will reach the Shadow Nebula in one hundred and sixty hours."

"Let's hope it gives us some useful intel," Balzano said. The others nodded in solemn agreement. The more they knew about their mysterious enemy, the better.

*

Probe 108 hours from the Shadow Nebula

Uxxio returned to the medical research laboratory carrying a cup of the hot, caffeinated beverage Professor Minnen had developed a taste for during their time on the *Pericles*. The human ISER scientists ensured there was a steady supply on the station, and although it was too bitter for his tastes, Uxxio was more than happy to keep providing cups of it for the Professor. Uxxio found the beverage puzzling; the liquid contained no narcotic agents, and yet the Professor (and some of the other human scientists Uxxio had observed) exhibited mild symptoms of withdrawal whenever there wasn't a cup available. So Uxxio made sure to return to the mess hall periodically before the Professor became agitated.

As doors slid close behind him, Uxxio squinted into the darkness. The station had just entered its night cycle, and apparently nobody had thought to turn the room's lights back to full brightness. As his eyes adjust, Uxxio made out the dark outline of Professor Minnen at his workstation.

"Professor? I've returned with your beverage…" his voice trailed off as he noticed the professor standing uncharacteristically still. Minnen exuded energy, even when he was engrossed in his work. And he *always* acknowledged Uxxio's greeting. But not this time.

"Professor?" Uxxio repeated. He took cautious step toward him, noting Minnen's head hanging despondently. Uxxio had never seen him like this before. "What's wrong?" he asked quietly.

When the professor spoke, his voice was uncharacteristically flat. "It's over, Uxxio."

"What's over, sir?" Uxxio asked worriedly.

"This. Our work," Minnen gestured with a bony arm at the workstation in front of him. He turned slowly to face Uxxio, and he seemed to have aged ten years. "I have reached a dead end."

Uxxio's looked at him in open-mouthed surprise; he had never known the professor to give up on anything. "What do you mean, over? We're so close to developing a cure…"

"… I *thought* we were close," Minnen interrupted. "I thought we were on the verge of a breakthrough. But… I was wrong. This line of work has led to a dead end: I am no closer to a cure than I was before Minister Jadus arrived on Iganta."

Uxxio felt numb; he shook his head in disbelief. "That *can't* be true, Professor. You have worked so hard on this, your inspiration on Tahvoa—"

"Is as good as useless," Minnen snapped. "Understanding the nature of the plague didn't help to cure it."

Uxxio was at a loss for words, and so for several moments they stood in silence.

When he eventually spoke, his voice came out as a croak; his throat felt dry. "You can't just give up, Professor. Everyone is counting on us. Minister Jadus, the ISER scientists, everyone in the Locality is *depending on us!*"

The elderly Iganti professor regarded him sympathetically. "Uxxio, I'm sorry. But listen to me—"

"No, sir, *you* listen to me!" Uxxio said with uncharacteristic vehemence. He had never raised his voice at the professor before, and it was both terrifying and exhilarating. Minnen stared at him in surprise, so Uxxio took a deep breath and barreled on.

"You have to keep working until you *do* find a cure! We didn't fly halfway across known space for you to give up. If you've reached a dead end, then fine, we'll start again. But if you give up now that Vinkere in the *Pericles'* brig may as well have succeeded in his mission! You—"

"Uxxio!" Minnen cut him off sharply.

The young assistant was immediately cowed. "I'm… I'm so sorry, Professor," he stammered. His words came out in a rush. "I've never spoken like that to you before and I want you to know I have the utmost resp—"

"You're a *genius*!"

Uxxio was still stumbling through his apology, so mortified that the professor's words didn't register at first. When they did, he blinked in surprise. "What was that?"

"I said you're a genius! Your little outburst has inspired me." Minnen's eyes glinted with almost feverish energy.

"I don't understand," Uxxio said, totally perplexed by the professor's sudden change in attitude. Minnen sat on the nearest stool and rubbed his chin. "There is one avenue I hadn't considered. One I hadn't even thought of, until now." He looked at Uxxio again. "Thank you, Uxxio, for being someone I can depend on."

"You're welcome, sir," Uxxio said, still flustered and a little confused.

In a rare display of fatherly affection, Minnen reached out and put his bony hands on Uxxio's shoulders. "I wouldn't have thought of it without you, my boy." He tilted his head and gave his assistant an appraising look. "I can see why Sul is so taken with you."

Uxxio gaped. "Sul is… what? Taken with who?"

*

Probe 100 hours from the Shadow Nebula

The system's star emerged from behind the gas giant to bathe ISER Station and the *Pericles* in soft yellow sunlight. Its beauty went unnoticed by Marston, whose attention was fixed squarely on his two guests.

"Why do you want S'Geliss?" he asked cautiously. No more treading lightly around the subject. He wanted to hear them say it.

"We want to inject him with the Kalavat Plague," Minnen said matter-of-factly. For a brief moment Marston wondered if this were an elaborate joke, but their expressions told him they were deadly serious.

Marston kept his own face carefully neutral. "I'm sorry, but I can't allow that. We have strict laws regarding the treatment of prisoners. And on top of that… it's just *wrong*."

"It wouldn't be the Commonwealth doing it. It would be us," Jadus said.

"That's a triviality," Marston said. "You would be deliberately harming a Commonwealth prisoner under my care." He directed an accusing look at

312

the minister. "To be honest, I'm surprised you would even consider something like this."

"Captain, normally we wouldn't. But as your people say, 'desperate times call for desperate measures.' There are billions of people depending on us."

"Our work has reached an impasse," Minnen said. "The best and possibly only way forward is to examine the immune response of the Vinkere prisoner and see what we can learn."

"What if he's not immune, and he dies?"

"Then we will perform a biopsy," Minnen said dispassionately. "Learn what we can and move on." Marston regarded him in surprise. This wasn't the normally upbeat professor at all. Jadus watched the captain's face closely, her own expression unreadable. When he remained silent, she spoke. "We've been looking for a connection between the Kalavat Plague and the Vinkere. If we can verify that they are immune, it would go a long way toward proving that connection."

"That wouldn't prove anything," Marston countered. "Humans, Thordrans, and Arretrians are also immune."

"That's true," Jadus conceded, "But at the very least, it *suggests* a connection between the plague and the Vinkere, a connection you and I are both fairly certain exists. The infection appeared when those mystery ships began abducting people, and we know that's how the Vinkere operate. The timing cannot be a coincidence. I believe that the Vinkere are responsible for unleashing the Kalavat Plague in the Locality, and therefore there is strong chance they have an immunity, or antidote, or *something* that will help us."

"We understand this request puts you in a difficult position, Captain," Minnen said. "But your prisoner may hold the key to developing a workable cure."

Not for the first time in his life, Marston found his morality and pragmatism at war with each other. He believed in the ethical treatment of prisoners. Human morality was one of the things that made them superior to the genocidal Vinkere. And yet, billions of people depended on Minnen and Jadus curing the Kalavat Plague. Nobody else had succeeded, otherwise they would have heard about it. Professor Minnen and his team were still the best chance of a cure, and Marston *had* agreed to help them in whatever way possible. But not like this. But... what other options did they have? He sighed.

"Fine," he said tersely. "I will allow you to do this. But I *hate* that we are doing a wrong thing to do a good thing."

"Thank you, Captain," Jadus said diplomatically. "I understand your feelings on the matter, and I am grateful that you are allowing us this

opportunity. I know this is no consolation... but we feel the same way."
Minnen nodded sagely.

"None of my crew will be involved," Marston added firmly. "This is my decision, and it's on me."

"It's on *us,* Captain," Jadus said, putting a comforting hand on his arm. "We will make it worthwhile."

"Indeed, we will," Minnen promised.

Marston didn't have anything to say to that.

S'Geliss was in the middle of his cell, curled like a great snake in hibernation. At the sound of the door opening, he uncoiled slowly and rose to his full height. His large, angular head nearly touched the ceiling. He regarded the newcomers with hooded eyes: it was the human captain, the Tuulan For minister and Iganti scientist. They were accompanied by the human soldier and his two cronies, the same ones who had been in the corridor. If they opened the door, S'Geliss should be able to strike fast enough to kill at least two of them before he was incapacitated. He tensed his muscles in anticipation.

"Open the cell," Marston said, raising a bulky-looking rifle and aiming it at S'Geliss.

A disembodied female voice said, *"Deactivating barrier."*

The electrified bars keeping S'Geliss in his cell retracted, and he leapt at the human like an uncoiled spring.

Marston fired his rifle. The shot impacted S'Geliss in the chest, sending him flying backwards. He hit the back wall of his cell, stunned. He was only vaguely aware of Marston loading a new type of ammunition in his rifle.

"Administering tranquilizer," Marston said tonelessly, shooting S'Geliss again. This time the impact was small, like a pinprick. Cold flooded through S'Geliss' veins, and blackness closed in on him. He was faintly aware of his body thrashing, struggling instinctively, but then he was swallowed by the darkness.

When the captain signaled her, Jadus approached the prone Vinkere cautiously and waved a medical scanner over him.

"He's heavily sedated," Jadus said with a satisfied nod. "I don't know how long that will last, though."

"He should be. We use that tranquilizer on horses where I come from," Marston said wryly.

Professor Minnen stepped into the cell, examining S'Geliss with interest. He held a needle in his slender fingers, poised to inject the venomous DNA of the Kalavat Plague into the sleeping alien. Uxxio followed him, carrying the professor's bag of specialized medical tools.

Clarke, McGee and Winters stood just outside the prison cell, weapons trained on the prisoner. Despite their presence, Marston had been explicit that no one other than him was to take any action against the Vinkere.

With so many people in the small cell it felt crowded. Marston circled S'Geliss, careful not to get in the way of the scientists as they went about their work. Even asleep, the Vinkere made him nervous.

"I don't like snakes," Lauren Winters said with a shiver. "I never have."

Uxxio clamped a white metallic bracelet around the alien's lower left arm. "Medical bracelet attached," he said. "We'll be able to monitor his vital signs from the lab."

"Connection established," Amalthea confirmed.

"I've injected the specimen with a sample of the venomous DNA," Minnen said clinically, removing the needle from the Vinkere's scaly neck. When he did, they vacated the cell and Amalthea sealed S'Geliss inside again. Everyone waited anxiously to see how the Vinkere would react to the plague.

Minnen took the medical scanner from Jadus and examined its small screen. "Fascinating. The body is reacting immediately to counter the plague DNA."

"There's no discoloration of the skin," Jadus observed. "That's normally one of the first things to happen as the plague DNA begins to alter the host's genetic structure."

"Does that mean they're immune?" McGee asked.

Minnen regarded him with large, owlish eyes. "Too early to tell, young man. Sometimes the host's immune response puts up brief resistance to the plague before it overruns their system. We will have to wait and see."

"So, we're done here," Marston said promptly.

Minnen and Uxxio returned to the station to monitor S'Geliss' biological readings from the lab. Jadus lingered for a moment, giving Marston a grateful smile before leaving.

Soon the only people in the brig were the four humans and their Vinkere prisoner. Marston regarded the unconscious alien, his face inscrutable.

"It's a good thing we captured him," McGee ventured. "He might give us a cure for the plague. It could help us get allies to retake the Commonwealth."

The captain simply nodded, desperately hoping that good would come from this.

S'Geliss woke up an hour later to find the brig empty again except for the lone guard stationed by the door. His whole body burned with fever, and he felt weak. Whatever his captors had done to him, his superior Vinkere strength would overcome it and he would take his revenge against the human captain and the others. He clawed at the cool white bracelet on his arm, but his weakened claws didn't leave a scratch. He tried smashing it against the wall, but whatever material it was made of remained unscathed. All his efforts did was draw the wary attention of the guard.

He couldn't re-enter hibernation; his body needed all its energy to fight whatever was afflicting him. But he would prevail. He was Vinkere.

*

"We need to talk, *Captain*." Balzano's expression was one of cold anger. He closed the door, sealing them both in the captain's office.

Marston folded his arms across his chest. "About what?" he asked calmly, although he had been anticipating this conversation for the past hour.

"About the fact that you took an unarmed prisoner and injected him with a deadly plague," Balzano snapped. "Do you have any idea how many regulations you broke?"

"Yes, I do," Marston responded coolly. He noticed how neither he nor the commander took a seat, preferring to stand for the confrontation.

"How could you do such a thing? Not only was it illegal, but it was immoral!" Balzano sounded both angry and genuinely puzzled.

"I did it because civilization as we know it is on the verge of collapse, and with billions of lives at stake we have to pursue *every* possible avenue to defeat the Vinkere and save the Commonwealth, not to mention the plague victims," Marston retorted. "Do you hear me? *Billions*. The greatest medical mind in the galaxy stood right where you are and told me it was the only way forward! I know what the regulations say, and I know what the law is. But I had to consider the bigger picture." He met Balzano's fiery glare with his own defiant, icy stare.

"Our laws exist for a reason," Balzano said, and Marston bridled at his lecturing tone. "Without them there is no justice. If you don't respect the rules, why should I, or anyone else under your command?"

"Normally I agree with you," Marston said levelly. "But we are *desperate*, Ronan, and it was our last resort. If you think the Kalavat Plague isn't a human problem, you're wrong." He waved out the window at the stars beyond. "What do you think the Draxilans will do to us if the Ankari aren't around to keep them in check? They will try again to vassalize the Commonwealth, and this time they might actually do it!"

"I understand the Kalavat Plague is also a human problem," Balzano fired back. "But there is a right way of doing things. And conducting medical experiments on prisoners is not it!"

"Unfortunately, I don't have the luxury of palming off my responsibility to someone else," Marston snapped. "As far as I know, nobody else has a Vinkere prisoner in their brig and access to the galaxy's best scientists."

"Putting aside the legal and moral ramifications, did you think about what it could do to the crew? According to you, half the admiralty is waiting for you to screw up. And now you've gone and tortured an alien prisoner." Balzano through up his hands in exasperation. "You've played right into their hands!"

Marston was stung by Balzano's comment more than he wanted to admit. He suddenly felt very tired, and slumped down in his chair. Marston second-guessed most major decisions he made, but this was the first time his executive officer had done so. Ronan Balzano was a friend, and the only person on the ship who understood the pressure of being new to command. He didn't want to argue with him.

"Not that it matters now, but I can promise you it wasn't an easy decision," he said tonelessly. "The truth is, I had considered it weeks ago, even before Jadus and Minnen and the others came to me. How could I not? I must consider every possibility. And I know there will be consequences." He smiled humorlessly. "At best I've bent a few regulations and at worst I've broken the law. But there are more important things to think about than my career." He was no longer angry, but his voice was firm as he told the commander, "If I had to do it again, I would make the same decision."

Balzano also seemed to have lost the will to fight. He sat down across from Marston. "What's done is done," he said grimly. "I wish you had consulted me first, but as long as you understand the consequences..."

"I understand completely. And I don't like it any more than you do."

"I just hope it doesn't come back to bite you," Balzano said ruefully.

"That makes two of us," Marston assured him.

25

Admiral Denulus ordered the viewscreen polarized; immediately the light from the orange giant star dominating the viewscreen became tolerable. Without the glare hampering his vision he could make out thousands of dark specks, just some of the Infected vessels in the solar system. Almost miraculously, the Ankari Assembly's Defense Force and their allies had succeeded in luring thousands of Infected vessels to the Barillion System from across the Assembly and beyond. Barillion Prime, the Ankari world orbiting the star, was overrun— almost all of its population of four billion people, according to the latest reconnaissance– and it was the main source of Infected ships spreading the Kalavat Plague across Ankari space.

The Ecclesia, the governing body of the Ankari Assembly, had tasked Denulus with overseeing the final and most dangerous part of the plan. It was a last, desperate attempt to cull the Infected and slow the spread of the plague before it reached the Ankari home system.

"What's the status of the weapon?" Denulus asked.

"It is two million kilometers from the target. All systems are functioning properly," the science officer reported.

"Sir, some of the Infected ships have broken through the containment line. They're headed directly for us."

"Charge weapons. Be ready to fire when they enter range," Denulus ordered.

"The weapon is one million kilometers from its target."

A swarm of black dots approached, resolving into starships of all shapes and sizes; the Infected seized any and all ships they could lay their claws on. Denulus' fleet had to keep them in the system long enough for the weapon to deploy.

"Our forces in the inner system are being overrun!" a communications officer reported frantically.

Holographic icons representing Ankari forces in the solar system began blinking off. Admiral Denulus turned off the display and returned his gaze to the viewscreen. Infected crews were capable of controlling their ships, but made no effort to maintain them. Many of the approaching ships had unrepaired breaches and scorch marks from previous battles. Not that it mattered to the pilots; their imperative to spread the plague superseded all other matters.

"Enemy ships within range."

"Open fire, and prepare for an emergency jump into slipspace."

The *Antruvion*, Denulus' flag ship, unleashed fire on the Infected ships. The opening salvo destroyed a handful of ships, but the second wave of Infected vessels pushed through the debris without slowing. Denulus knew their goal was to board other ships so they could infect the crew. At the top right of the viewscreen a display showed the weapon approaching the star, now just half a million kilometers away. He silently counted down the time until detonation. His fleet would have no more than eight minutes; the evacuation ships, tasked with rescuing the remaining non-Infected citizens of Barillion Prime, would have only slightly longer.

On either side of the *Antruvion* the other ships in his fleet opened fire; Ankari, Vlind and Kelzee alike, destroying the second wave of approaching hostiles. Despite their impressive firepower, Denulus knew they couldn't last forever against the overwhelming numbers of the Infected. Fortunately, they didn't have to.

"The weapon has penetrated the photosphere!" the officer reported over the shouting of situation reports and battle communiques. "Not reading any change in the star... no, wait! The weapon deployed successfully! Nuclear fusion in the star is breaking down!"

It would take another eight minutes before light from the now dying star reached them to provide visual confirmation. But when it did, the shockwave from the supernova, which also traveled at the speed of light, would hit them too. Video from a surveillance satellite closely orbiting the sun showed him what the viewscreen could not: what had once been a bright, energetic giant star in the prime of its life was now dimming rapidly. A few seconds later the star at the center of the Barillion System went nova, exploding in a brilliant flash that even the polarizing filters couldn't dim. The lifespan of the solar system and all the planets within it could be calculated in minutes, and Denulus silently counted them down.

Six minutes passed. Then seven. Then seven and a half.

Denulus hurried up the short steps to his command podium. "Order all ships to engage their slipstream drives and withdraw immediately!"

A shimmering, blue-white portal appeared in front of the *Antruvion* and the ship dove into the slipstream. The rest of his fleet followed suit, dozens of portals rippling into existence as the allied forces fled the dying solar system. A minute later the evacuation fleet above Barillion Prime broke orbit and jumped into slipspace.

Deprived of their targets, the Infected ships scattered in all directions, some heading back toward the planet and others aligning themselves with nearby star systems containing populated worlds. But they were out of time. The shockwave from the Barillion star-turned-supernova ripped through the Infected ships, vaporizing them instantly. The once-prosperous Ankari world of Barillion Prime cracked like an egg, shattering into millions of pieces, taking all the Infected on its surface with it. When the fire of the supernova eventually faded, all that was left of the Barillion system was a dim neutron star and a field of tumbling asteroids.

*

July 15, 2438
ISER Station, Gandra Sector
Unclaimed
Probe 80 hours from the Shadow Nebula
The doors to Professor Minnen's lab swished open and a pair of scientists entered. A large, rectangular cage on wheels rolled after them before coming to a halt beside one of the workstations. The pair of animals inside it squeaked nervously, their dark eyes darting around at the unfamiliar surroundings.

"Those are the biggest rodents I've ever seen!" Jarren exclaimed.

Professor Minnen nodded. "*Tua Naptiva*, native to the planet Glarstroom. Same size as the average ovine, and the fourth largest species of rodent in the Locality!"

Standing with Jarren, Korosa said, "I didn't realize rats could get so big." He shuddered, imagining what it would be like to wake up to one of those scampering up the wall at night.

"These ones do, but sadly for them, their life span is only eight weeks," Minnen told them.

"How old are these ones?" Jarren asked.

"Eight weeks."

"Father, isn't it cruel to experiment on them like this?" Sul asked. She reached out a hand toward one; it hissed at her and she pulled back with a start.

Minnen smiled paternally. "Daughter, we are not torturing these animals. I'm going to inject the one on the left with the Kalavat Plague venomous DNA; according to Ship's Overseer Drin these creatures are roughly the same size as those that boarded his ship. With any luck, the Kalavat DNA will completely transform it in a matter of hours!"

"What about the other animal?" Jarren asked.

"I'm going to inject that one with the solution we developed from the Vinkere's blood sample. Then we'll see how effective it is when I inject the creature with the Kalavat Plague!"

"Do you have to do it to these animals, father?" Sul protested.

"They've reached the end of their natural lifespan, dear. They'll be dead by tonight regardless. But if this creature *is* transformed by the Kalavat plague, it will gain the lifespan of its new species, prolonging its life. And at the very least this other creature will prove whether our serum is effective in combating the plague before it dies naturally."

"I suppose," Sul conceded grudgingly. "But can't we test the cure on some smaller, less cute animals first?"

"The virus is lethal to animals of insufficient biomass," Uxxio explained to her. "Anything much smaller would die."

"Here we go, then!" Minnen said cheerfully, approaching the cage with a long needle. "You're a feisty one, aren't you?" He chuckled as the nearest rodent hissed at him.

Uxxio pressed a button on the cage and thin bars slid out of its floor, separating the two rodents. Minister Jadus and Vashon joined them while Jarren and Korosa stood back, out of the way.

"I'm injecting the first creature with the Kalavat Plague DNA now," Minnen said. The rodent went very still, and then lay down as if going to sleep. Minnen nodded with satisfaction. "These creatures have extremely fast metabolisms, so I expect the transformation process will only take a couple of hours."

"I'm injecting the second creature with the serum," Doctor Kerik said. It was feistier than its companion, which was still except for flaring nostrils and rapidly blinking eyes. The second creature bucked and hissed when Kerik jabbed it with the needle.

"When will we know if the cure works?" Sul asked, giving the animal a sympathetic look.

"We will give the agent time to proliferate in the creature's bloodstream. A few hours," Minnen said.

"What do we do now?" Jarren asked.

Jadus answered for the professor. "We wait."

*

Probe 75 hours from the Shadow Nebula

Jarren Qel was back on the *Pericles*, working with Katarina Sirroyo in the ship's library when he received a message from Jadus. The sensor operations officer watched his face carefully as he read the message. "What's the news?" she asked.

"The solution was successful," Jarren said, amazed disbelief in his voice. "They're ready to begin the next stage of testing. *It worked!"*

Cheers erupted from the crewmen in the library; Jarren hadn't realized they were all listening. He grinned, giving the surprised Sirroyo a quick hug as the people around him celebrated.

We did it, he thought happily, excusing himself to go find Jadus, Antak and Korosa.

"Excellent work, Professor," Doctor Lisle congratulated Minnen. The Iganti professor held court at the center of a circle of admirers, happily basking in their praise.

Vashon said, "Indeed. Your cure will save billions of lives."

"Technically, it is an antivenom, not a cure," Minnen reminded them in a rare moment of humility. "We still have much work to do."

"It is a breakthrough, nonetheless," Jadus said, smiling. She felt happier than she had in months. She looked around until she spotted Captain Marston and Commander Balzano standing off to the side, watching the celebrating scientists with smiles. She moved through the crowd to them.

"Captain Marston, this wouldn't have been possible if it weren't for the help of you and your crew. Thank you." In a rare display of affection, she took one of his hands in hers and squeezed it.

Marston smiled back. "No, Minister, it wouldn't have happened without *you*. We just took you where you needed to go."

"You do not give yourself enough credit, Captain Marston," Minnen had approached with Sul holding his arm. "If it were not for you and your crew our heads would probably be adorning the bulkheads of a Vinkere ship!"

"A disturbingly graphic image, father," Sul admonished him.

"But very likely accurate, daughter," Minnen retorted good-naturedly.

"There is still a lot of work to do," Jadus said. "Mass producing the antivenom, testing its effectiveness for different species, distributing it on a scale not seen since the Osaija Virus…"

Minnen patted her on the shoulder reassuringly. "We managed then, and we will now."

"I have spoken with the Overseers of the other ISER stations," Vashon said. "The head of our organization will brief the Locality Council, and we will work with the governments of the Locality to produce and distribute Professor Minnen's solution."

Jadus smiled wearily. "Which means that at least for the moment, we can rest."

Minnen looked at her in surprise. "No, Minister. Now, we celebrate!"

*

Probe 70 hours from the Shadow Nebula

ISER Station's function hall was located on the uppermost deck, with its domed ceiling forming the pinnacle of the station. Large oval windows offered a panoramic view of space in every direction. To one side the gas giant shone bright blue in the sunlight, and in the opposite direction the rocky surface of the moon glowed soft white. The combined effect bathed the hall in yellow and silver radiance that cast twin shadows off the people assembled there.

"Beautiful view," Hasan commented appreciatively.

"How is it any different to your normal view?" Sirroyo asked. "We look at stars all day."

"We look at the *slipstream* all day," he corrected her. "It's not the same as this."

"I concur," Minnen said. "I rarely leave Iganta these days, and I forget how beautiful space can be." He sighed wistfully. "I think when my work here is completed, I will go on a holiday!"

"You most certainly deserve one, Professor," Doctor Gariri said.

"Thank you," Minnen preened. "However, I must give credit where credit is due. Minister Jadus and Doctor Kering were of invaluable help. And of course, if Captain Marston hadn't let us experiment with your Vinkere prisoner, we wouldn't have the information we needed to develop the antivenom."

"S'Geliss is fortunate he was immune to the plague," Clarke commented.

"Immune, but not naturally," Minnen said, drawing curious looks.

"What do you mean, not naturally?" Sirroyo asked.

"Biological systems function using existing genetic information. But I found evidence that the Vinkere *added* the resistance to their genetic code."

"You mean to say the Vinkere genetically engineered themselves?" Marston asked in amazement.

Minnen chuckled at their astonishment. "Yes. It appears at some point in their recent past the Vinkere added to their genome the ability to resist the Kalavat Plague." Minnen held up his datapad, showing an anatomical diagram of S'Geliss. "They gained a whole new organ whose purpose is to produce and regulate the special cocktail of chemicals used to break down the venomous DNA."

"Amazing," Gariri marveled.

"I also don't believe the Vinkere always had two sets of arms," Minnen told his growing audience. "I believe they added the lower pair at a later date."

Marston half-listened to the professor as he looked around the room. The celebration had been planned in just a few hours, but the organizers had done a spectacular job. A quintet of scientists played soft music on stringed instruments Marston didn't recognize. Orange and white streamers, the colors of the Iganti flag, decorated the walls and above them, balloons of blue, white and gold, the national colors of the Tuulan For, floated about the roof.

Vashon approached him. "We love balloons," she confided to him quietly. "Such an ingenious human invention!"

He grinned. "I don't know how you organized all of this so quickly," he said.

"All volunteers," Vashon said proudly. She explained that several of the station's scientists had formed a culinary club, which was catering for the evening. Vashon seemed just as proud of the community her people had created as she was of their scientific accomplishments.

Marston was about to reply when both he and Vashon's communicators went off simultaneously. They looked at each other in surprise and stepped away from the crowd to answer.

"Marston here," he said into his communicator.

"Sir, we received a message... from Commonwealth space," said Ensign Vasilyev, the Gamma Shift communications officer.

Marston felt a surge of excitement. "Is it Command? Did they manage to break through the Vinkere jamming?"

"No, sir. It's not from *the Commonwealth. It's from the Vinkere."*

Marston looked around to ensure nobody was eavesdropping. "What does the message say?" he asked quietly.

"Not much. There's a short audio recording, but the rest is encrypted."

Balzano was watching Marston intently. "What is it?" he asked the captain.

"The ship received a message from the Vinkere."

"There's more," Vasilyev said. *"The message is only broadcasting on one subspace radio frequency. It's the same one as when you spoke to Supreme Commander Zithla at Kronos, Captain."*

Vashon was still conferring in hushed tones with someone over her communicator. She looked up and their eyes met. She gestured to Marston and he approached.

She spoke quietly so they couldn't be overheard. "Did you hear? About the Vinkere message?"

"Yes," he replied softly.

Vashon gestured for Marston and his officers to follow her. "There's a terminal nearby where we can play the message." An elevator took them down one level to an unused office containing a computer terminal and large, wall-mounted monitor.

Marston's stomach churned with anxiety. "Play the message," he said softly.

Vashon reached out with a thick finger and pressed a button to activate the message. It was audio-only; a deep, sibilant voice that Marston recognized immediately. The message was just five words: *"Your name is the key."*

An empty textbox appeared on the screen. Amalthea spoke through his communicator. *"Captain, it appears the message is encrypted. Given enough time I may be able to access the protected contents if you wish...?"*

Marston swallowed; his throat felt completely dry. Ignoring Amalthea, he reached out with shaking fingers and typed in: MARSTON.

The textbox faded away, replaced by a satellite view of a blue-green planet. White clouds drifted over green landmasses and reflected sunlight glinted off the oceans. It could have been any class-1 habitable world in the Commonwealth.

"This is the planet Avon," Zithla's recorded voice said. *"My forces seized it in a surprise attack three days ago."*

The image changed to a series of aerial shots of Westminster, the planet's capital, and other cities. Scars from the battle for the planet could be seen; columns of smoke billowed from office buildings and impact craters in the emerald landscape still glowed with heat.

"Avon's riches were to be used for the Vinkere war effort, and its population spared to serve us." Zithla's voice took on a harder tone. *"But I warned you what would happen if you refused to cooperate. I said that if you did not return the data core to us and surrender yourselves, your entire species would be eliminated. I have given you ample time to do so,*

and now my patience has run out. Because of your defiance, I have ordered my forces at Avon to proceed immediately to Phase Five."

The image changed back to an orbital view of Avon, this time showing Vinkere ships spreading out above the peaceful-looking world.

"This is what happens when you defy me," Zithla snarled.

The Vinkere ships fired on the planet below. Gariri let out an involuntary gasp as the grey blur of Westminster vanished in a blinding flash. Nuclear detonations—they counted eleven in total—reduced Avon's cities to radioactive rubble. Firestorms swept across the continent, obscured by thickening brown clouds of ash and dust.

Marston and the others stared at the destruction in stunned silence.

After several moments Zithla spoke again. *"My threats are deadly serious. The people of Avon were executed because of your refusal to cooperate. You killed these people. And their deaths are just the beginning. Your entire Commonwealth will burn."* Zithla's voice took on a mocking tone. *"At least for you there will be no survivors to curse your name."*

26

"It's been nearly three days. I think we need to say something to him."

Clarke disagreed. "I think we should give him space," he argued.

Sirroyo looked at him. "Captain Marston was accused of murdering *eighty million people*. How do you work through something like that?"

"The captain isn't responsible! It was the Vinkere," Clarke said firmly.

"Of course. But the Vinkere broadcasted that message to half the Locality! How would you like to be painted as the executioner of an entire planet? This is not something the captain should have to deal with on his own."

"The message was specifically for the captain," Clarke reminded her. "Nobody else knows. And we should keep it that way," he added firmly. So far as they knew, only Vashon and the *Pericles* senior officers had seen the message, and Vashon had agreed to keep its contents a secret. And when the captain had retreated to his quarters, Balzano assembled the *Pericles* senior staff and they agreed to withhold it from the crew as well. There was no telling what kind of effect it would have on their morale. What if some of them *did* blame him? Clarke thought of Oliver Landon, a crewman from the planet Avon. How would he react when he found out his home world had been reduced to a radioactive ball of ash?

Sirroyo huffed in frustration and turned to Balzano, who had been watching their exchange impassively.

"What do you think, Commander?" she pressed him. "This ship needs its captain, now more than ever. And I think he needs *us*."

Balzano nodded. The captain could run the ship from wherever he wanted, but Sirroyo was right; the crew needed to see him, to be reassured by his presence, because as far as they knew there was no reason for his sudden disappearance. Even Balzano hadn't been able to get through to him.

He looked at the two officers standing across his desk and said, "You're both right. The captain is a private man and has the right to deal with things privately, but he shouldn't isolate himself, as much for his own wellbeing as for the crew's morale. I'm going to tell that to him right now." He stood up and moved toward the door.

Clarke and Sirroyo exchanged looks. "Do you think he'll listen?" Sirroyo asked.

Balzano nodded resolutely. "I'll make sure he does."

He pressed the door chime to Marston's quarters. He heard, "Come in," and entered.

Marston was standing in the middle of the room, apparently expecting him. He was wearing a fresh uniform, but his face looked pale; the dark rings under his eyes attested to his lack of sleep over the last few days.

"The probe is about the reach the Shadow Nebula. I thought you'd like to come to the communications center and see what it finds."

Marston nodded. "I'll join you in a second." He turned and busied himself with sorting the datapads on his desk. Balzano saw through his light-hearted tone and decided to cut to the chase. "How are you?"

Marston replied without turning to face him. "Fine, I suppose. Well, as fine as I can be considering... you know."

"I'm glad to hear that. Because what happened on Avon was not your fault. The Vinkere were responsible."

"I know," Marston said tonelessly. "Except that I could have prevented it—"

"No, you couldn't," Balzano said sharply. He knew Marston would keep going over it like he had the past three days, and Balzano intended to break the cycle. "You couldn't have prevented it because the Vinkere intend to kill us all anyway. They're monsters, that's why they nuked an entire planet."

"I know that's true, but..."

"No 'buts'. It's the truth. You would never do anything to hurt those people."

Marston stared blankly at him. "I used to believe that, but when the situation is bad enough, who knows what I'll do? Look what I did to S'Geliss..."

Balzano would have none of it. He raised a hand to silence Marston. "No. Stop that right now. The Vinkere are masters of subterfuge and manipulation, and you're playing right into their hands."

Marston sighed. "I... know. But... I'm getting there." He squared his shoulders. "Shall we head to the communications center?"

Balzano didn't move. "Yes. But you must agree to drop this matter, for the sake of the crew and the mission."

Marston nodded. "Sure," he replied distantly, moving toward the door. Balzano could tell he wasn't past it yet, but if he acted as though he were and came back to work like normal, he *would* get over it with time.

They strode down the corridor toward the elevator. "I think it's time for us to go home," Marston said. "Now that the Vinkere data core information has been transmitted to the Commonwealth there's no reason for us to stay here."

Balzano nodded slowly. "Once we see what the probe finds we can decide on our next course of action."

Marston nodded, then stopped in the corridor.

"Is something wrong?"

The captain shook his head. "No, but I just thought of something. Go on ahead; I'll be there in a few minutes."

S'Geliss sensed a newcomer in the brig. He half-opened his eyes to regard the visitor.

"You're awake," Marston said.

"Your attempt to kill me has failed," S'Geliss smirked. "My flesh is superior, and I overcame your human virus."

"It wasn't a human virus you were injected with," Marston said softly. "It was the plague your people unleashed on the innocent people of the Locality. Or the Ss'Talak Cluster, as you call it."

S'Geliss regarded him warily. "And you overcame the virus, but that's what we were hoping for," Marston continued. "In doing so you taught *us* how to fight it. You've helped save billions of lives, so thanks."

Marston turned on his heel and left the brig, smiling darkly. S'Geliss watched him leave, furious and ashamed beyond words, grateful there were no other Vinkere around to learn of his colossal failure.

*

Clarke and Sirroyo greeted Marston outside the communications center. "Welcome, Captain," Sirroyo said, regarding him sympathetically. Marston gave them both a reassuring smile. "Thanks."

"The probe is about to reach the nebula," Clarke said as they entered the room.

"I am glad you could join us, Captain," Vashon said politely.

Marston joined them by the console. He felt everyone's eyes on him, and wondered how many of them knew about Zithla's message. He glanced at Jadus, but she simply smiled and nodded in greeting before turning back to the monitor. After a week of waiting, they were all eager for the Shadow Nebula to reveal its secrets.

Antak Droma sat at a control station which would allow him to manually pilot the probe if required. Tahir Hasan stood over his shoulder,

329

eyeing the navigation readouts. The probe had arrived at the edge of the nebula, almost directly opposite to where the *Pericles* had first encountered the *Leviathan*. Doctor Lisle kept his eye glued to the scanners to make sure there were no enemy ships nearby. "There are eight Vinkere ships within a light-year of the probe, but none of them are close enough to pose a threat," he reported.

The probe plunged into the swirling morass of the Shadow Nebula. The video feed grew darker; the gases became denser, swirling and billowing around the probe so that visibility was reduced to a few hundred meters.

"Why is the image shaking so much?" Jarren asked Jadus. Doctor Lisle overheard him and answered: "It's the gravitational forces within the nebula. They produce currents and eddies within the cloud. It occurs in all nebulae to some extent but is stronger in some than others. We think the gravity currents are what prevent them from dissipating, but that's just a theory. We actually know very little about nebulae."

"Is it dangerous for the probe?" Jarren inquired, but Lisle shook his head.

"The gravitational forces within the Shadow Nebula pose a hazard to starships attempting to navigate it, but the probe is much smaller and has much more powerful engines relative to its size. It should reach the center without too much difficulty."

"It will," Antak said confidently, fighting to keep the probe moving in the right direction. He used the gravitational currents and eddies of the nebula to help propel it onwards.

Everyone watched the viewscreen, transfixed by the swirling, fluctuating gas. As visibility decreased, so did the probe's sensor range; soon the gases occluding all but short-range sensors. Suddenly, the probe alerted them to the presence of a foreign body on sensors.

"What is it?" Marston asked.

Vashon studied the sensor telemetry. "Unknown. Moving closer will improve the sensor resolution."

Antak guided the probe toward the object.

"Can you tell how big it is?" Marston asked.

"Approximately ten meters in diameter," said Vashon.

"It could be an asteroid," Hasan suggested.

"It could also be an enemy fighter or a communications satellite," Balzano said. The captain nodded in agreement.

Doctor Lisle pointed at Vashon's screen. "It must be artificial. See how it remains stationary, despite the gravitational currents?"

"If it's artificial it has to be Vinkere, because the Commonwealth has never put anything inside the nebula," Marston said.

"Should we risk getting any closer?" Jadus asked.

"Nothing ventured, nothing gained," Marston murmured. To Antak he said: "Move the probe closer. We need to investigate."

"Here we go," Antak said, guiding the probe toward the object. Clearer sensor readings emerged as they drew closer.

"It's metallic, and ovoid," Vashon reported. It wasn't until the probe was less than a hundred meters away that the small, dark shape materialized out of the fog.

"It's a weapons platform!" Vashon exclaimed. "The hull plating and energy signature is Vinkere." Comprised of the same blue-grey alloy the Vinkere built their ships out of, the ovoid sphere featured two powerful-looking energy cannons. Attitude control thrusters flared intermittently, keeping the platform from getting swept away in the nebula's currents. As they watched, both turrets angled around, pointing directly at the probe. Vashon gasped and Antak muttered a curse.

"It can see us!" Hasan said.

"Is it powering weapons?" Jadus asked worriedly.

Vashon frowned. "No, but it is tracking the probe."

Several tense moments passed without the probe being obliterated by the weapons platform.

"It looks like the camouflage is working," Sirroyo said. "It thinks the probe is Vinkere."

"We should keep moving," Clarke advised. "We don't want to look suspicious."

The alien satellite disappeared into the mist again as the probe pressed onward; the platform's weapons tracked the probe but did not fire. Marston hoped the probe's disguise would prove just as convincing the next time it encountered the Vinkere.

The probe pressed deeper into the nebula without finding any further signs of the Vinkere. The viewscreen showed the same, featureless blue-grey cloud; if it weren't for the navigational sensors, it would have been impossible to stay oriented. Lisle joined Vashon reviewing the probe's sensor data, hoping an additional pair of eyes would help them find something notable. Finally, after an hour, they exchanged resigned looks and turned to the others.

"This is useless. Sensors can only get clear readings on objects within a hundred kilometers, and nothing at all beyond three hundred," Lisle said, "But this nebula is ten million kilometers in diameter. It's like trying to find a coin in a wheat field in the middle of a blizzard."

"We have to keep looking," Sirroyo insisted.

"We've more or less reached the center of the nebula, but the Vinkere could have a base the size of a *planet* just a few hundred kilometers away and we wouldn't be able to see it," Lisle said.

"We didn't wait for six days just to give up after an hour of searching," Marston said firmly. "Keep flying for a while longer. If we don't find anything, we can set the probe on an automated search pattern." That sounded reasonable to everyone, and they settled back, watching the viewscreen as Antak guided the probe forward.

Another thirty minutes passed without encountering anymore Vinkere ships. Discouraged, Marston was about to take his officers and leave when Vashon issued a sharp warning.

"A large mass is approaching. It will pass within ten kilometers of the probe."

Everyone was instantly alert again. "How big is it?" Balzano asked.

"The object is at least one kilometer in length," Lisle said. "It's *massive.*"

Marston, Clarke and Balzano exchanged knowing looks. "Probably a *Leviathan*," Clarke said, and the other two nodded in agreement.

"Can you determine its heading? In or out of the nebula?" Sirroyo asked.

"It appears to be moving toward the center of the nebula," Lisle answered.

"We should follow it," Clarke said urgently.

"I agree," Vashon said readily, placing a hand on Antak's shoulder. "Wait for the ship to pass by."

"It's should be within visual range soon," Antak said, and everybody looked at the monitor expectantly.

A Vinkere Leviathan emerged from the murky nebula like a colossal shark. Marston felt a shiver run down his spine; with its angular lines and dark blue-grey hull it was identical to the one that had pursued the *Pericles* from this very nebula several weeks ago. They were even bigger and more forbidding than he remembered. Powerful engines propelled it through the nebula, faintly illuminating the gases behind the ship.

"I can see why you call them Leviathans," Jadus murmured.

The colossal alien ship glided past, and Antak swiveled the probe around to follow it from what they hoped was an inconspicuous distance.

Soon the images from the probe stopped shaking. "The gravitational currents are gone," Hasan exclaimed in surprise. "There's no more turbulence!"

"I believe I can offer an explanation," Vashon said before anyone could ask the obvious question. "The Vinkere ship appears to be following a specific path. Satellites positioned thirteen-point-three kilometers apart form a sort of corridor through this part of the nebula. They appear to be generating gravity fields to compensate for the region's gravitational currents."

"I didn't know that was even possible!" Antak said.

"It's not for us, not yet," Sirroyo said. "Only the Ankari have that level of technology in the Locality."

"That is correct," Vashon said. "The Ankari make use of similar deflection fields, however affecting gravity on such a scale is currently beyond even the abilities of ISER."

"Don't the Ankari participate in ISER?" Clarke asked, and Vashon shook her head.

"No. They keep their technology a closely guarded secret, even from us," she said.

"Well, if the Vinkere also have that capability it would make the nebula a perfect location for a hidden base," Marston said.

Without warning, the Leviathan and the probe emerged into a vast, spherical region completely devoid of gas. Hundreds of deflector satellites kept the nebula and its gravitational currents at bay. Vashon reported it was almost twenty kilometers in diameter, and it was filled with Vinkere ships.

"I guess we've discovered their secret base," Jarren said in amazement.

Vinkere warships of all different sizes floated within the sphere. More weapons platforms dotted the interior, and squadrons of Vinkere fighters flew in tight formations around the perimeter. At the center of the space a trio of Leviathans held station in a rough triangle. Beneath them was a ring-shaped structure encircling a whirlpool of light.

"It's a wormhole!" Hasan exclaimed in a mixture of surprise and awe.

"…constructed by the Vinkere," Vashon added. "The ring is one-point-three kilometers in diameter."

"Incredible," Sirroyo said, both awed and intimidated by the sight of the giant, whirling maelstrom of light. Clarke nodded in agreement.

"Wormhole travel explains how the Vinkere were able to reach the Locality, and deploy throughout the Commonwealth without being detected," Lisle said.

Marston and Balzano exchanged glances. Unless the Vinkere had achieved it by themselves, that technology had to have come from the Ankari. No other race had succeeded in developing the wormhole technology the Ankari had already been using for decades.

"The structure here is little more than an anchor for the wormhole's terminus," Vashon said. "It must be generated from the other side."

"There are no stations here aside from the deflector satellites and weapons platforms," Marston realized. "This area is just a gathering point for their forces. Their primary base of operations must be on the other side of the wormhole."

Antak swiveled around in his chair to face the others. "The only way we'll know for sure is to take the probe into the wormhole."

"I think we should see what's on the other side," Sirroyo said instantly.

"Our mission *is* to gather as much intelligence on the Vinkere as possible," Balzano pointed out.

"And we may not get this opportunity again," Jadus said.

"I agree," Marston said. They needed to know where the Vinkere were basing their operations if there was any hope of defeating them. He looked to Vashon; this was a joint mission, and he wanted her consent.

She inclined her head. "If a consensus has been reached, then let us proceed."

Under Antak's control the probe accelerated toward the wormhole. An icon flashed on Vashon's console. "The probe is being hailed by an automated security checkpoint near the gateway. It is requesting authorization for transit."

The shining maw of the wormhole grew to fill the screen. "Ignore the hail and continue onward," Marston said firmly. Alarms squawked from both Vashon and Antak's consoles.

"They're locking weapons on us!" Antak shouted frantically, forgetting for a moment they weren't actually in any danger themselves but were remotely operating a probe hundreds of light-years away.

"Keep going!" Marston ordered. He leaned forward, subconsciously urging the probe onward.

Nearby weapons satellites rotated, aiming their weapons at the probe.

"They're firing!" Vashon announced.

"Crossing the threshold…!" Antak shouted as the probe dove into the wormhole. There was a gentle wobble as it crossed the boundary between normal space and subspace, and suddenly it was speeding through a corridor of swirling light. The Vinkere missiles missed their target, colliding with the wall of the wormhole and disintegrating in the exotic energies that formed the boundary between subspace and normal space.

"The Vinkere are transmitting a signal through the wormhole," Vashon reported. "I suspect it is a warning of our approach." To Lisle, she added, "We probably won't get much time on the other side, so I want all sensors in full-active mode."

The end of the tunnel grew rapidly. "We're nearing the exit aperture," Antak reported, and then the probe burst out of the wormhole into a region similar to the one they had left in the Shadow Nebula: a vast, empty bubble within another nebula kept clear by deflector satellites and force fields. This space was significantly larger, and it was filled with Vinkere ships. And the Vinkere were ready for them, locking weapons on the probe as soon as it emerged.

Marston looked over Vashon's shoulder at the sensor data scrolling down the screen.

"Seven hundred and fifty-six ships," he said, stunned. Many of them were Leviathans.

"There are dozens of weapons platforms, and what appear to be munitions depots and refueling stations," Lisle reported. "This is definitely a military base."

"Look there!" Jadus said, pointing. The wormhole gateway the probe had exited was just one of a dozen throughout the region. At the center of the space was a gateway that dwarfed all the others.

"That gateway is more than 8.4 kilometers in diameter," Hasan said in astonishment.

"Its power consumption must be astronomical!" Sirroyo said.

Vashon agreed. "I would estimate it is capable of traversing several thousand light-years."

"All the way to the Carina Nebula," Marston said quietly.

It took all of Antak's skill and concentration to evade the ships and weapon platforms tracking them. He maneuvered the probe between two Vinkere ships, too close for their attackers to hit without risking their own vessels.

A pair of Leviathans moved in from either side, blockings the probe's path. The probe circled, caught within an ever-tightening noose of Vinkere ships. Dozens of grappling hooks shot out; most missed their target but one managed to snare the probe with sharp, metallic claws.

"I can't break free," Antak grunted.

"Can you engage the slipstream drive?" Balzano asked.

"Negative, not this deep inside a nebula. We're stuck."

"What about sub-light engines?" Vashon asked.

"I wouldn't bother," Marston said. "When the *Pericles* was attacked, we barely managed to break free of their grapplers, and not without significant structural damage."

A Leviathan loomed on the viewscreen as the probe was reeled in toward it. Antak sighed in frustration. There was nothing he could do now. A hatch in the Vinkere ship opened to swallow the probe.

"Abort the mission," Marston said.

"Commencing memory wipe," Vashon said. She erased the probe's hard drive, including its navigational database; they couldn't risk the Vinkere discovering their location. The last thing they saw before the connection terminated was the inside of a cargo bay and a trio of Vinkere with hand-held scanners approaching.

"Those tools looked like data-mining gear," Vashon commented. "But their mission is futile. They will not be able to recover any data from the probe."

Hasan was hunched over the navigation display. "I managed to determine the probe's location," he said. "You won't believe it." He brought up a galaxy map on the screen, which zoomed in on the Locality. An orange marker appeared near the center of the image.

"The Storm Nebula!" Jarren exclaimed. It was near the heart of the Locality between the Vlind Merchant Republic and the Kithel Collective.

"The perfect location for a staging post," Balzano commented grimly. "With those gateways they can strike almost anywhere."

"And now they have the probe, so they know that we are aware of that," Lisle said.

"They have no way of knowing who sent the probe," Marston said. "All they know is that *someone* found them out. Let them fret about it while we work out how to use this information against them."

The group dispersed, the *Pericles* officers returning to their ship and the scientists to their labs. Jadus lingered in the doorway to catch Marston as he passed. "Captain, a word?" she said, just loudly enough for him and Balzano to hear. The commander nodded once to Marston before following the rest of the *Pericles* officers.

When they were alone, Jadus reached out and touched Marston's shoulder. "How are you doing?" she asked.

"I'm fine, thank you Minister," he said without emotion.

"Good. Because I'd hate to think you were trying to claim responsibility for the actions of the Vinkere."

Marston stared at her. "I take it you saw the message from Zithla."

She nodded. "I saw the initial message. And after your abrupt departure the other night, it was easy enough for me to surmise that your name was the key."

"If you're going to assure me that I'm not responsible for what happened on Avon... I know," he said slowly. "But it's—"

Jadus interrupted him gently. "Of course it's not your fault. What I was going to say is this: you are a starship captain. It is a position of power and responsibility. I have learned from personal experience how dangerous it can be when people like us let ourselves be manipulated. It doesn't just affect us, but also those under our care."

"I'll remember that," he promised.

Jadus studied his face for a moment before nodding. "Good. Here's another friendly piece of advice, which I received from an old human acquaintance: don't ever let the nay-sayers see you sweat." Then she turned and walked away, moving down the corridor in graceful strides.

27

Marston was woken during the night by Amalthea. "Huh?" he mumbled drowsily, glancing at his bedside clock. It was three o'clock in the morning.

"I said, 'Sorry for disturbing you, Captain.'"

He sat up in bed. "What is it?"

"I thought you would like to know that I have detected a Commonwealth fleet on long-range sensors."

Marston leapt out of bed, scrambling to find his uniform. "Where? How far are they?"

"One hundred and twenty-four ships, ten light-years away," Amalthea reported. "They are heading away from the Commonwealth, toward the Varda System."

Maybe the fleet had been caught behind enemy lines like the *Pericles*. If they had, it made sense they would head for the relative safety of Unity Station. It was well protected by a multi-national fleet and the Kalavat Plague hadn't reached it. He wondered if they were going to try and enlist the help of the other species in driving the Vinkere out of the Commonwealth. It's what he would do.

"Amalthea, can you please connect me to Overseer Vashon?" he asked, a plan forming rapidly in his mind.

"I will try," the AI replied. After several moments of silence Vashon's voice came through the speakers in Marston's cabin.

"What can I do for you, Captain?" the Vlind woman asked tiredly. It was also the middle of the station's night cycle.

"I'm sorry to disturb you, Overseer," he apologized, "But it's urgent." He had a favor to ask greater than any he'd requested so far.

"I assumed it must be," she replied. There was no trace of irritation in her voice, just mild curiosity.

He told her.

*

When Marston welcomed Balzano into his office several hours later, the commander could tell he hadn't slept since the discovery of the Commonwealth fleet. He was tired but animated, waving Balzano in excitedly.

"Come in, Ronan." Marston gestured to the rarely used lounge where they took a seat. Balzano regarded him; the captain seemed completely recovered from his three-day slump and was overflowing with energy.

"I have a new plan," Marston said enthusiastically. "I wanted to run it by you before going to the others."

"Of course." When the captain had called a meeting of the senior staff and station leadership, Balzano suspected it had to do with the Commonwealth ships. The discovery of the fleet had changed everything; they weren't alone out here anymore.

"Yesterday I said to you that I thought it might be time for us to make our way back to the Commonwealth," Marston said. "But now, I feel differently."

"Do you intend for us to join the fleet?" Balzano asked.

"I intend for *them* to join *us*." He gestured out the window at ISER Station. "The ships belong to the Ninth Fleet, under the command of Admiral Haftel. I spoke with him this morning." Marston grinned as Balzano's face lit up.

"I served under him when he was captain of the *Providence*. He's a good man and a good leader," Balzano said. "But how did you get Vashon to agree to allow an entire fleet to rendezvous here? I wasn't even sure they would reveal their location to us when we arrived."

"Vashon is a pragmatist," Marston said. "She agrees that the Vinkere pose a threat to the entire Locality, not just the Commonwealth." He leaned forward; his eyes were bright with excitement. "We even briefly discussed the possibility of launching a surprise counter offensive against the Vinkere from *here*."

Balzano silently absorbed the news; he wasn't surprised Marston would have a bold plan for dealing with the Vinkere. Having Admiral Haftel and the Ninth Fleet made a strike against them more realistic. But they both knew a single, battle-weary fleet would not be enough to attack the Vinkere in their staging post.

"Why don't we go with them to Unity Station?" Balzano asked. "It's well-protected, and if we're going to plan an attack against the Vinkere we'll need their ships."

"Because the Vinkere are probably watching Unity Station. They were covertly watching the Commonwealth before their invasion, and they were able to find Minister Jadus and Professor Minnen on Tahvoa, of all places." Marston tapped the side of his head. "They have eyes everywhere. If they see hundreds of their enemies' ships gathering it could alert them. We want the element of surprise, which makes this station perfect, because if they knew of its location they would have attacked already," he said confidently.

"Fair point," Balzano conceded. "So now Admiral Haftel is on his way."

Yes. They'll be here in twelve hours. I sent all the data we have on the Vinkere to Admiral Haftel and he agrees that we are in a unique position to strike at the Vinkere. When the fleet arrives, we'll try to formulate a plan so that he has something concrete to offer potential allies."

"What does he want us to do in the meantime?" Balzano asked.

"He wants us to collect all the evidence we have that could link the Kalavat Plague to the Vinkere. Most of it's circumstantial, but it might help, especially if a renowned Tuulan For Minister, an ISER Overseer and the galaxy's greatest scientist put their voices behind it." Balzano nodded absently.

"You look like you're planning something yourself," Marston observed.

"I might have a lead for us to follow up on," Balzano said thoughtfully. "Some more evidence connecting the Vinkere to the Kalavat Plague."

"Great."

"It's just an idea," Balzano said. "I'm not sure if it will pan out, but it's worth investigating."

"Do I get to hear what it is?" Marston joked, and Balzano told him.

"Go for it," Marston said, giving the commander his blessing. "If we're going to free the Commonwealth, we'll need every piece of information we have against the Vinkere. And we're going to need everyone's help."

*

Elzor Drin trundled down the corridor toward the cafeteria. After three weeks on the *Pericles* with nothing to eat but human food, he was grateful for the Vlind cuisine available on the station. He was fantasizing about devouring a bowl of fried blik when Commander Balzano suddenly appeared in front of him. "Is my assistance required by you, Commander?" he asked a little impatiently. His stomachs were grumbling.

"Yes, actually. I need to ask you about the time your ship was attacked near the Vratak Nebula."

Drin slumped. "At this time?" Those were unpleasant memories for him, *and* he was hungry.

"I'm sorry, it's very important," Balzano insisted politely. "It may help us in our fight against the Vinkere."

Drin stifled a groan. Second lunch would have to wait. "Very well," he relented.

"Do you remember anything about the weapons the aliens used against your ship?" Balzano asked.

"Torpedoes were used. They penetrated the hull without detonating. Inside were the creatures that infected my crew."

"An odd delivery system," Balzano commented. Were the animals the original vectors of the plague? He decided to ask Professor Minnen later.

"The creatures were vicious," Drin said with a shudder, vividly recalling the battle on the bridge of his ship as he, Lintor and Klon fought the rabid creatures.

"The torpedoes: do you remember what they looked like?"

Drin shrugged. "Like regular torpedoes."

"You didn't notice their color or size?" Balzano pressed him. "What about sensor readings?"

Drin shook his head. "I do not recall. It was dark."

Balzano sighed. His lead didn't look so promising after all. "I don't suppose you brought a copy of the ship's log with you?" he asked hopefully. It was a long stretch, and his hopes were dashed when Drin shook his head again. Drin had brought only one memento from his ship: his favorite childhood plush toy, but he wasn't about to admit *that* to the commander.

Balzano thanked him and turned to leave. Drin was sorry he couldn't help the commander. After his harrowing escape from the Vinkere on Tahvoa, he shared the humans' desire to rid the Locality of the Vinkere. But he had already delivered Minister Jadus and Professor Minnen to safety. What more could he do?

Then it occurred to him. "Another ship was present," he murmured, causing Balzano to turn back. "The alien attackers were driven off by a Kelzee Military ship. Record everything is what they would have done."

The human commander stared at him. "Do you think we can talk to them?"

"I do not see how. I do not know anybody in the Kelzee Military."

"Perhaps Overseer Vashon does. It looks like we'll have to ask her for another favor," Balzano said. "Of course, it would be helpful if you come along too, in case we need your authorization to view sensors data of your ship."

Drin sighed and followed the commander down the hall, away from the cafeteria. It looked like he wasn't going to eat second lunch anytime soon.

Drin sat beside Overseer Vashon in one of the combooths in the station's communications center. Commander Balzano stood behind them as Vashon conversed with a tired-looking Kelzee Military officer on the screen.

The man had introduced himself as Lieutenant Handari, and listened as Vashon and Drin made their request for the sensor data from the skirmish near the Vratak Nebula. Vashon assured the dubious lieutenant it was strictly for use by the Commonwealth Navy and ISER, and would remain confidential. Balzano felt a surge of relief when Handari relented.

"Let me check," he said wearily, typing into his computer. Drin gave him the time, location and name of ship.

"The frigate Kerenor *fought off an unknown alien ship at the Vratak nebula."*

"That is them," Drin confirmed.

"Can we please have the sensor readings from that battle?" Balzano asked.

Handari hesitated. *"I should check with my superior,"* he said, getting out of his chair and moving off screen. He returned a few minutes later.

"The General has given me permission to send you the readings, but I just checked and we don't have them. The Kerenor *crew was infected during that battle and their logs have been co-opted by the Plague Control Initiative. They have all data pertaining to the Kalavat Plague and Infected ships and personnel. You'll have to speak to them."*

"Can you connect us to them?" Vashon asked.

"I'll transfer you now," Handari said flatly. His face was replaced by the Kelzee Military logo. A few minutes later a new person appeared; an older Kelzee man with a careworn face. He took in Vashon and Balzano with a quick, calculating look before settling on Drin. His eyes widened in shock.

Drin was equally surprised. "It's you!" he exclaimed.

"Ship's Overseer Drin," Ral Hokono said in disbelief. *"It is good to see you alive and well."*

"To you the same, Station Overseer," Drin replied.

Hokono shook his head. *"I am no longer the Overseer of Takutu Station. I work for the Plague Control Initiative. What can I do for you?"*

"We require sensor readings of the *Wealth and Grandeur*, taken by the frigate *Kerenor* during a skirmish near the Vratak Nebula," Vashon explained.

Hokono checked his database. "We do have that information," he confirmed. "I'm sending it to you now." He didn't know why they wanted it, but the Interspecies Scientific Exchange of Research and their work were more important now than ever, especially since the revelation a couple of days ago that Minnen the Learned was working with them on a cure for the Kalavat Plague. Hokono was willing to provide them with whatever information they requested.

"Thank you," Overseer Vashon said. Ral Hokono and Preeka Vashon had never met, but they knew of each other by reputation. He tilted his head. "May I ask why you require a copy of the sensor readings?"

Vashon looked at the human commander before turning back to Hokono. *"We are trying to obtain evidence that the Vinkere, the aliens who are attacking the Human Interstellar Commonwealth, are responsible for releasing the Kalavat Plague. These sensor readings may prove helpful."*

Everyone had heard about the surprise invasion of the human Commonwealth. Hokono hadn't given it much thought, because dealing with the imminent threat of the Kalavat Plague superseded all other concerns. *Unless the two were related.* Either the invading aliens were opportunistic, incredibly lucky in their timing, or they had something to do with the plague. That thought worried him greatly.

"If it will help your investigation, I can do more than send you the sensor data from one ship. I can send you all the data we have on the ship disappearances, and on any battles where ships were attacked by unidentified aggressors."

"Your cooperation is greatly appreciated," Vashon thanked him.

"I hope it helps," Hokono said sadly. "We have all suffered so much already. If there is anything we can do to help find a resolution, please contact me."

"Thank you, Mr Hokono." They terminated the call, and Hokono left the communications room. He returned to his office, which occupied a corner room on the fiftieth floor of a government building in Strahnti, the capital city of Kelzanti Prime.

He eased into his padded chair and looked sadly at the holographic image of his wife on the desk. This was how he chose to remember her; graceful and kind, not as she became. The grief he felt at her loss was still painful. He shuddered to remember the dark, feral creature charging at the soldiers with an unworldly scream and outstretched claws. A tragic end for such a beautiful, dignified woman. He took some comfort in the fact that their daughter had been safely ensconced in her university dormitory on Kinisha at the time, and had since come home to the apartment they shared a few blocks away. He couldn't return home to grieve with and comfort his daughter though, not just yet.

Hokono would do everything he could to eliminate the threat of the Kalavat Plague in the Federation and beyond so no more families had to suffer like his. Fortunately, his broadcasted warning to the Locality had earned him some political capital, which he intended to spend helping the Plague Control Initiative. When the Kelzee government approached him about leading the new department dedicated to its eradication, Hokono had agreed almost immediately.

He gazed out of the windows at the busy capital of the Kelzee Galactic Federation; his office permitted views over much of the metropolis. The day was a clear, sunny one and he could make out the distant peaks of the Nendesso Mountains to the east and the silver-blue shimmer of the Tesomo Ocean to the northwest. To the casual observer, it looked like a normal, busy weekday in Strahnti; the wide, multi-laned roads were filled with vehicular traffic and pedestrians. But Hokono knew the city and its inhabitants, and could sense the undercurrent of fear.

He hadn't lived in the capital for over ten years, but he still loved its culture, its crowds, and its energy. Out-of-towners generally considered the locals to be arrogant and pushy, but he saw them as driven, ambitious, and hard-working. He was fond of this city, and its people. He hoped it wouldn't suffer the same fate as other cities across the Federation. He'd seen the footage from places that had succumbed to the Kalavat Plague. Cities lay half in ruins, fires burned out of control, and zombie-like Infected roamed the rubble-strewn streets. Sometimes there were millions of them. The death toll was already well into the hundreds of millions, with experts grimly predicting that number would reach *billions* within a few weeks. And if the government ever succeeded in bringing the infected planets back under Federation control, there would be a multitude of new problems to deal with: looting and loss of property, prevention of diseases spread by decomposing corpses, identification of Infected individuals and survivors, reimposition of law and order, the rebuilding of infrastructure, providing food, shelter and medical care for the survivors… those were just some of the issues Hokono's organization had to plan for. Even conservative estimates placed the cost of the rebuilding at astronomical levels. Most infected planets would essentially have to be recolonized.

The citizens of Strahnti had good reason to fear, but many had no idea how close they had come to the precipice already. As the numbers of Infected grew with each passing day, the military's ability to contain them diminished. General Nulo had reported to an astonished Kelzee government that soon the number of Infected ships would exceed their own and the Infected would break out of the quarantine zones allied forces were struggling to contain them in. Kelzanti Prime risked attack within a fortnight, and the collapse of organized Kelzee society would follow as remaining worlds succumbed. The Ankari and Vlind were in an almost equally desperate situation.

Fortunately, Admiral Denulus's desperate but masterful plan had worked. He had succeeded in luring away and destroying tens of thousands of Infected ships, nearly sixty percent of the Plague Vectors, as the Ankari referred to Infected ships capable of spreading the plague to other star systems. Apparently Denulus had caused the star Barillion to explode, destroying the Infected in the supernova. Nobody knew how; the Ankari government remained tight-lipped regarding the whole ordeal. The supernova wouldn't be visible in the skies of Kelzanti Prime for many centuries yet, but it appeared the Ankari had done the impossible: they had destroyed an entire star system. And it had bought Hokono and everyone else precious *time*. Nevertheless, Hokono and the Kelzee government remained on edge. All it took was a single Infected in a one-man craft to slip away undetected and spread the Plague to a new planet.

Hokono returned to his desk and resumed his work. A short time later, he received a written message from ISER Station. Overseer Vashon thanked him for his help but unfortunately the *Kerenor's* sensor logs were too badly damaged to confirm the alien attackers were Vinkere.

Yet Ral Hokono wasn't finished helping. If these Vinkere in the Human Commonwealth were behind the Kalavat Plague, they were a danger to the entire Locality. He summoned one of his assistants and asked them to establish a subspace link with General Buto Nulo. The general would want to know about the possible link between the Vinkere and the Kalavat Plague. Hokono prepared himself for the conversation ahead. There was one way they could definitively prove the Vinkere were responsible, he just had to convince General Nulo it was the right thing to do.

28

July 20, 2438
Near Mornek Melvarnis, Caral System
Ankari Assembly

Admiral Denulus stood on the podium at the center of the command deck and gestured to the helmsman. "Engage the wormhole drive," he commanded, listening for the tell-tale hum of power as the drive activated. A swirling portal of rainbow light filled the viewscreen, replacing the image of the Assembly Defense Force fleet patrolling the skies above Mornek Melvarnis.

A short time ago Denulus had received a subspace communication from General Nulo, his counterpart in the Kelzee Military. After a brief conversation they had agreed that his lead required investigating, and Denulus had issued his orders. This mission was for the *Antruvion* alone; the rest of his fleet would maintain its blockade of the fourth planet in the system, which was currently experiencing an outbreak of the Kalavat Plague on two of its continents. It was crucial to prevent the Infected from reaching the third and sixth planets in the system, which were also inhabited.

Denulus examined the navigator's flight plan and gave a satisfied nod; the journey to the Vratak Nebula would not take long. Wormhole drives allowed Ankari ships to travel many times faster than conventional slipstream drives.

"Prepare for combat," he commanded, and his four-thousand strong crew readied the ship for confrontation.

An exit terminus appeared at the end of the wormhole. The *Antruvion* approached rapidly, soaring through it into a dark interstellar cloud. The wormhole disappeared behind them. Sensor data poured in, confirming what Denulus could already see for himself on the viewscreen.

"We're in a gas-free pocket," his science officer reported. "Multiple structures detected!"

A ring-shaped gateway floated in the center of the region. The wormhole it anchored looked almost identical to the one the *Antruvion* had just traveled through. Four large, dark vessels approached, weapons ports flaring orange.

"Are they Vinkere?" Denulus asked.

It only took a moment for the tactical officer to compare the ships to the profiles sent to them by General Nulo. "Yes," he confirmed.

"Target them with weapons and open fire!" Denulus growled.

The *Antruvion* unleashed beams of crimson energy, striking the lead Leviathan head on. Its shields collapsed, and the beams burned through the hull like a welding torch through ice. Explosions blossomed along the hull and atmospheric gases and debris vented into space. The second and third ships ploughed through the wreckage of the first without slowing and returned fire.

Missiles slammed into the Ankari battleship's protective shields, but the *Antruvion* advanced, unscathed. It fired again and the second Vinkere ship caught fire. The third released another salvo of missiles, which were easily intercepted by the Ankari ship's point-defense systems.

"We are being targeted by automated weapon emplacements," the tactical officer said over the shrill of combat alarms.

"Deploy drones," the *Antruvion's* executive officer ordered, and Denulus nodded in approval. Bay doors slid open, unleashing hundreds of the small automated craft. They descended on the Vinkere weapons platforms like a swarm of angry insects, ripping into them with their own crimson energy beams.

Now the *Antruvion* could deal with the Leviathans without distraction. "Firing again," the tactical officer announced. Energy beams finished off the second Leviathan, splitting it down the middle; the two halves tumbled away into the nebula.

The third *Leviathan* was now close enough that the *Antruvion* could deploy its secondary weapon with deadly effect. Two glowing red eyes opened on the forward hull, basking the Vinkere ship in deadly gamma radiation. The *Antruvion's* helmsman expertly guided the ship out of the way as the Vinkere ship, with its crew dead or dying, thundered past.

Wary of how easily the Ankari ship had dispatched its companions, the remaining Leviathan was far more cautious. It fired a barrage of missiles before swinging around and using the wreckage of the other ships as cover. "The enemy ship is requesting reinforcements," the communications officer reported.

"Destroy them," Denulus commanded.

"They have launched fighters," said the tactical officer.

"Have point-defense batteries target them."

Several of the nearest weapon platforms were ignoring the Ankari drones to target the *Antruvion*, and the ship shook under a salvo of enemy fire. "Shields at eighty-five percent," the shield control officer reported.

"Admiral, this Vinkere base is almost identical to the one in the Shadow Nebula," the science officer said. "Multi-spatial analysis indicates this wormhole also leads to the Storm Nebula." Denulus examined the readings himself. The Vinkere were everywhere. "Battle report."

"Twenty-six enemy fighters destroyed, Admiral. The remaining Leviathan is heavily damaged and fleeing. Most of the weapon platforms are still functional and our drone force has been depleted by thirty percent."

"There are enemy reinforcements approaching from inside the wormhole!" the science officer shouted; six new Leviathans were about to join the battle.

"Disable the gateway," Denulus ordered calmly.

Every forward-facing weapon on the *Antruvion* unleashed its fury on the wormhole gateway. Plasma pulses, crimson energy beams and drone cannons ripped into the ring-shaped structure. Explosions bloomed across its surface. The shining maelstrom of the wormhole vanished as the ring broke apart, plunging the nebula into darkness.

"The gateway is destroyed," the tactical officer reported with a smirk.

"Good. Now, remove every trace of the Vinkere from this nebula," Denulus commanded. He strode down the steps from his podium, leaving his executive officer to oversee the rest of the battle. He had other things to do. First and foremost, he had to inform the Ecclesia of their discovery; he was already mentally formulating his report as he strode down the corridor toward his office. Then he would have to speak with General Nulo and Grand Marshall Dreyon, commander of the Vlind Merchant Navy. The Vinkere threat extended to the entire Locality and required a unified response. The governments of the Locality rarely collaborated, but if the Vinkere thought they could conquer them one by one, they were going to be unpleasantly surprised.

*

**In orbit of Ennomos, Ennomos System
Interstellar Commonwealth**
"Supreme Commander, the Vratak Nebula gateway is under attack!"

Zithla swung around to look at the officer who had broken the news. "Show me a tactical view of the nebula!" he snapped.

The officer scrambled to obey his order, and quickly established a subspace link with the wormhole station there.

"They came out of nowhere! Our satellites around the nebula didn't detect anything-"

"Show me who it is," Zithla ordered, and the officer activated a camera feed from one of the Leviathan-class battlecruisers in the nebula. One of the four defending Leviathans had already been reduced to a cloud of debris, and a second was being perforated by twin crimson energy beams.

"The Ankari," Zithla snarled. "Dispatch reinforcements immediately. They mustn't be allowed to reveal the location of the base!"

Ss'Taliss, S'Geliss' replacement, approached him. "Sir, the Ankari are powerful. Even one of their—" he was interrupted by a bright red flash on the monitor as the Ankari ship doused the third Leviathan in deadly radiation, sending it careening into the nebula.

"I want to capture that ship," Zithla declared. He gestured around them. "Consider the technological secrets we have obtained from an eighty-year-old Ankari ship and imagine what we could learn from one of their battleships! Order all ships to move into flanking positions and deploy their grapplers!"

"They're launching drones!" an officer reported. Dozens of specks poured out of the Ankari battleship. Insect life on the Vinkere home world was long extinct, but the drones reminded Zithla of the insectoid Kithel fighting vainly as their home world was overrun by Infected.

"Ignore the drones and target the Ankari vessel!" Zithla roared. "Where are those reinforcements?"

The reinforcing battlecruisers had left the Storm Nebula base and were in transit through the Vratak Nebula wormhole. But as Zithla watched the Ankari ship destroy the third Leviathan, he knew they would be too late. The powerful alien ship focused its attention on the ring-shaped wormhole gateway and unleashed the full power of its weapons.

"The enemy ship is targeting the gateway," Ss'Taliss reported unnecessarily.

"I can see that!" Zithla thundered, causing everyone within striking distance to cower.

They watched as the wormhole gateway broke apart. The wormhole collapsed, stranding the reinforcing Leviathans somewhere along the route. They would have to return to the Storm Nebula as quickly as possible. Zithla's forces could re-establish the wormhole from the other end, but he decided against it. The encounter with the Ankari ship had proven costly, and there was no way to stop it from escaping before Vinkere reinforcements arrived anyway.

The Ankari ship destroyed the last Leviathan and began methodically cleansing the nebula of all traces of Vinkere. Zithla cursed and terminated the link; there was no point in watching anymore.

There was silence on the *Z'Tauron* bridge. Ss'Taliss was the first one to speak. "Sir, our base of operations in the Vratak Nebula would appear to be compromised..." His voice trailed off as Zithla focused his withering gaze on the commander. Ss'Taliss shrank back as Zithla stormed past him.

The Vratak Nebula base was well-concealed; the Ankari had not chanced upon it. Someone had tipped them off. Zithla clenched his fists angrily. There was only one place they could have obtained that information, and he suspected it was from the same people who had sent that cleverly-disguised probe to the Shadow Nebula. *Pericles*.

The Vratak Nebula base was strategically positioned to spread the Kalavat Plague along the Kora-Sr'Hirta Trade Route. It also contained the listening post that enabled the Vinkere to monitor enemy communications in that region and would have served as one of the staging posts for the Vinkere invasion of the Kelzee Galactic Federation when the time was right. Now, however, they had been exposed.

Zithla's entire campaign was at risk. Their advance into human space continued, but much slower than anticipated. The Commonwealth had more ships than projected, as though they had significantly increased their shipbuilding in the years since the Vinkere had discovered the *Endeavor*. And now Zithla had to contend with the very real possibility that other militaries would begin investigating the nebulas in their space, exposing every Vinkere base to attack. His forces couldn't take on the combined militaries of all their enemies at once. That was why the Ss'kapp'rn Plague had been so useful; sowing chaos allowed the Vinkere to focus on one enemy at a time.

The destruction of the Vratak base was a wakeup call. If the Vinkere were to complete their conquest, or even survive, they had to be cautious, even more so than before. Zithla slithered back and forth across the command deck while his officers watched in fearful silence. One thing was clear to him: the destruction of the Commonwealth was even more important now. The worlds and resources the Vinkere took from the humans would greatly strengthen their position in the Ss'Talak Cluster. He had to commit more ships to their conquest, even if that meant redeploying his forces from elsewhere. Zithla began issuing orders to be relayed throughout the fleet. He could still complete his campaign, if he was careful. And if there was one thing Zithla was not, it was a fool.

*

ISER Station, Gandra Sector
Unclaimed

News of the *Antruvion's* victory in the Vratak Nebula was quickly relayed across the Locality. After speaking with Admiral Denulus, Kelzee General Nulo passed on his report to the Plague Control Initiative; Ral Hokono forwarded it on to ISER Station. The news was met with excitement and satisfaction by those assembled in the communications center.

"That's all the proof I need," Torina Jadus announced. To Vashon, she said, "Please send me a copy of Admiral Denulus' report so I can forward it to my government."

If the Ankari and Tuulan For officially condemned the Vinkere invasion, other governments would follow suit. And Marston hoped it would translate into military support for the Commonwealth. His communicator buzzed. "Yes?"

"Admiral Haftel's fleet is about to arrive, Captain," Amalthea reported.

"Thanks, Amalthea." He turned to Balzano. "We should head down to the airlock."

"I will accompany you," Jadus said, falling into step beside them. "I would like to meet the Admiral."

"Admiral Haftel is a gifted strategist," Marston said. "He's exactly the kind of leader we need to fight the Vinkere." Balzano nodded firmly in agreement.

"Reputations can be exaggerated," Jadus cautioned him. "I would prefer that you withhold your judgment until you have spent time with him."

"Why are you concerned about my opinion of the admiral?"

"Because you will have something neither I nor Vashon will have," Jadus replied. "As a human Navy captain, you will have access to his inner circle. It will be easier for you to determine whether William Haftel truly *is* the leader to formulate a plan for defeating the Vinkere and successfully execute it."

Marston looked at her askance. "Are you asking me to report to you on the Admiral?" He respected Minister Jadus and they had developed a strong working relationship over the past several weeks, but as a Navy captain his loyalty would always be to his superior officers.

"Not exactly. I want you to assure me truthfully that any plan Admiral Haftel comes up with has a strong chance of success. I will not try and convince Chancellor Denrek to commit ships to a potentially suicidal campaign that would leave us defenseless against the Infected *or* the Vinkere. But I know you and trust your discernment, and if you vouch for the admiral, it will go a long way to putting my mind at ease."

Marston considered her words carefully. If they didn't get have outside support, the Commonwealth could fall to the Vinkere. But if a coordinated counteroffensive failed, everyone involved could lose ships and people needed to defend against the Infected and the plague could overwhelm the Locality. He swallowed; his throat suddenly felt very dry.

They reached the entrance to the airlock lounge and Jadus turned to Marston. "Be objective," she advised him. "A lot will depend on your endorsement." She swept passed him into the room. Balzano frowned at her, then gave Marston a reassuring pat on the shoulder and followed her in. Marston squared his shoulders and entered after them.

Dozens of miniature stars flared into existence as the Commonwealth ships emerged from the slipstream. Marston felt a surge of joy at the sight of the familiar white, arrow-nosed hulls. Foremost among them was Admiral Haftel's flagship, the *Challenger*. At twelve hundred meters long the Consul-class ship was the largest type of vessel built by the Commonwealth. It dwarfed every other ship in the fleet; Marston reckoned it could even match a Vinkere Leviathan in battle.

As the *Challenger* approached the station, they saw signs of battle; black scorch marks and torn hull plating attested to its fight against the Vinkere during the fleet's flight from the Commonwealth.

Vashon joined them as the *Challenger* docked with the station. There was a hiss of equalizing pressure and then the airlock hatch cycled open and Admiral Haftel emerged. He had an aristocratic air about him; he stepped through the hatchway and regarded the greeting party with quiet dignity. He was accompanied by a short, stocky woman who Marston identified as Leanne Forester. She had begun her career in the Commonwealth Marines before making the transition to the Navy, where she now served as Haftel's executive officer.

Marston and Balzano stood smartly to attention. "Admiral on deck," Marston announced, saluting. Admiral Haftel nodded at the two men. "At ease, gentlemen."

Vashon stepped forward to greet her new guests. "Welcome to ISER Station in the Gandra Sector. I am Preeka Vashon, Overseer of this station."

"Thank you for granting us safe harbor, Overseer," Admiral Haftel said politely.

"We are happy to help in these difficult times," she replied.

"I appreciate that." Haftel glanced at Marston before saying, "Captain Marston informed me that you've succeeded in creating an antivenom for the Kalavat Plague. It seems that most of the Locality owes you their thanks."

Vashon bowed her head modestly. "Collaboration made this accomplishment possible."

"Cooperation is something I would like to discuss with you at a convenient time, Overseer."

"No doubt you are referring to the liberation of your Commonwealth from the Vinkere, Admiral," Jadus said. In response to his inquiring look, she told him: "I am Torina Jadus, Tuulan For Minister of Medicine and Health."

"It is an unexpected honor to meet you, Minister," Haftel said. "And you are correct; the expulsion of the Vinkere from the Commonwealth is of the utmost importance to me. But I believe this would be to the benefit of everyone in the Locality."

"I agree," Jadus said. "And I think we on this station are uniquely positioned to promote such an initiative. But getting the nations of the Locality to cooperate on such an endeavor is no easy task. We are all hard-pressed dealing with the Infected." She looked at Marston as she said this, and he nodded once in agreement.

Admiral Haftel noticed the look but didn't comment on it. "I wholeheartedly agree, Minister," he assured her. Then, changing topics, he turned to Commander Balzano and permitted a small smile. "It is good to see you again, Mr Balzano. It was a pleasant surprise to learn you and Captain Marston and the *Pericles* had survived."

"It's good to see you too, Admiral," Balzano said with a smile. His face darkened. "We haven't heard anything from the Commonwealth for weeks."

"Neither have we, I'm afraid," the admiral said. "Not since we escaped."

"What happened?" Jadus asked.

"We were crossing the Atacama Expanse when the Vinkere invaded," Forester said, speaking for the first time. "We were cut off from the rest of the fleet by Vinkere ships from the Shadow and Column Nebulas. They were closing in on our location and we had no way to reach home. To protect the civilian ships, we were forced to withdraw from the Commonwealth."

"*I* gave that order," Haftel said, clearly taking responsibility for an unpopular decision. "A few wished to stay and fight, but I made the decision to retreat and assess the situation without the Vinkere bearing down on us. We were traveling to Unity Station when Captain Marston contacted us."

"If you are looking for help fighting the Vinkere, you are welcome here," Vashon said. "This station has several advantages. The Vinkere are unaware of its existence, for one."

"Nevertheless, if you want our help, Admiral, we need to know whatever actions you take against the Vinkere will have a high probability of success," Jadus informed him.

"I will ensure that any campaign against the Vinkere will be worthy of your commitment," Haftel promised.

Jadus and Vashon looked at each other and then nodded. "Contact us when you are ready to discuss it further," Vashon said. When they had left,

Haftel turned to Forester. "Assemble the captains. We have a campaign to plan."

*

CNV *Challenger*, Gandra Sector
Unclaimed

The conference room on the *Challenger* was significantly larger than that of the *Pericles*. The captains of the Ninth Fleet took their seats at the long ovular table, conversing in hushed tones. Marston regarded them with some trepidation; some of them had been captains longer than he had been in the Navy. They may not have been openly friendly toward him, but a few of them nodded to him as he took his seat at the table.

Admiral Haftel and Commander Forester arrived and began the meeting. Haftel pressed a button in the tabletop; the lights dimmed, and a three-dimensional holographic image of the Storm Nebula appeared over the table.

"As you will all know from the briefing packets we sent you, the Vinkere have been using the nebulas throughout the Locality as secret staging areas to spread the Kalavat Plague and launch their invasion of the Commonwealth. Their primary base of operations appears to be in the Storm Nebula, here," he said, zooming in on the holographic nebula to highlight the Vinkere outpost inside it. "This base functions as a hub for their forces in the Locality, with wormhole gateways connecting it to other nebulas in the region." The image zoomed in again on the ring structure at the center of the base. "According to the scientists here at ISER, the gateway at its center is capable of generating a wormhole tunnel extending thousands of light-years. Thanks to the efforts of Captain Marston and his crew in obtaining the Vinkere data core from Ennomos, we are fairly confident it leads to the Carina Nebula, where the Vinkere originate."

"Our job is to plan the attack on the Vinkere staging post. We have two reasons for this: to force their withdrawal from the Commonwealth, and to cripple their ability to operate in the Locality."

He opened the floor to everyone, and they began brainstorming. It was soon agreed that any efforts to destroy the Vinkere war effort would have to take place on the far side of the wormhole in their own space; there was little point in destroying the Storm Nebula base if their shipbuilding and ammunition-producing facilities were left untouched in the Carina Nebula, allowing them to open a new gateway into the Locality. How they would manage to do this was far more difficult to determine; each idea put forward was quickly dismissed as too risky for their limited forces.

While several of the other captains engaged in a heated debate, Marston considered what he knew about the Vinkere staging post. According to the information they had obtained from the data core, the Vinkeres' occupied just three systems in their home nebula: The Home Star, the location of their home world, the Yellow Star, the only other habitable world they had colonized, and the Blue Star, the location of their primary staging post.

He recalled Zithla's genocidal threats and S'Geliss' relentless hatred for the people of the Locality. Destroying the staging post in the Storm Nebula would only buy them time; he was certain the Vinkere would rebuild it and return. He caught Haftel's eye. The Admiral regarded Marston hopefully. "You have something, Captain Marston?"

The other captains looked at him expectantly. "Maybe," he said slowly, recalling what Vashon had told him earlier about the Infected in the Barillion System. "Destroying the Vinkere base won't be enough. They are relentless. I think the only way to permanently end their threat to the Locality short of exterminating them… is to contain them."

Marston told them his idea, and when he finished speaking there was quiet around the table. He took that as a positive sign that nobody could immediately find fault with his suggestion. "I think we should ask Overseer Vashon to join us," Admiral Haftel said after a moment.

Over the next hour, with Overseer Vashon contributing, a plan began to develop. It required enlisting the help of the other militaries of the Locality, which would not be an easy task. Nevertheless, when Admiral Haftel ended the meeting, it was with a sense of determined optimism.

The other captains returned to the shuttle bay where shuttles would ferry them to their own ships, but Marston lingered.

"What can I do for you, Captain Marston?" Haftel asked.

"Sir, there's something I should tell you. Minister Jadus informed me that the Tuulan For government would only be willing to contribute ships to our campaign if I personally assured her that *I* thought it could work."

Haftel's expression was unreadable. "I appreciate your honesty, Captain."

Marston shifted uncomfortably. "I've developed a rapport with the minister, and she seems to trust my judgment."

"I see."

"I believe our plan can work, and I'm going to tell that to the Minister," Marston assured him. "If you want me to."

"I do," Haftel said. "However, be mindful of the minister's position. Her caution is understandable. Our campaign will rely on the assistance of the peoples of the Locality, but those who aid us risk leaving their own worlds undefended. Committing their ships to our campaign is not something to be undertaken lightly. Consider that before giving Minister Jadus your assurance."

"I will. Thank you, Admiral." He turned and left in a daze. Instead of relieving him of the burden of responsibility Jadus had placed on him, the admiral had only confirmed it.

Hoping to order his thoughts, Marston went for a walk. After wandering the corridors of the *Pericles* for an hour he ended up outside of his office. Entering, he crossed the room to his desk and picked up the photograph of his family. He examined it with a small smile, hoping they were safe and happy and realizing that he would do almost anything to protect them.

*

Jadus was reading in her quarters on the station when the doorbell chimed. "Come in," she called, expecting Jarren or Korosa.
Instead, Captain Marston stepped into the room. "Minister," he greeted her.

She placed her datapad on the table and stood. "Captain Marston. How did the meeting go?"

"It went well. We devised a plan to end the threat of the Vinkere once and for all."

"Oh?" She folded her arms. "And what do you think of it?"

"It's a good plan. It involves using a modified Ankari nova bomb to destroy the Vinkere staging post."

"It sounds ambitious. I'd like to know the details of this plan."

"I will take you through it," he promised. "It's in the best interests of everyone in the Locality that this campaign is successful."

Jadus gestured for him to take a seat. "Very well. Take me through it. Before I speak with Chancellor Denrek, I'd like to know what we are committing our ships to."

29

Supreme Commander Zithla pondered the tactical display in front of him. After their destruction of the Vratak Nebula base, the Ankari had made no further aggressive moves. They had withdrawn from the frontlines altogether, retreating and regrouping at one of their most protected worlds. But why?

Zithla was sure the Ankari admiral was planning another attack, and this time with more than one ship. It had become increasingly common for the Locality's militaries to coordinate their efforts against the Kalavat Plague, so Zithla wasn't initially worried by the Vlind and Kelzee forces gathering at their mutual border. But when they set a course for the same star system where Denulus and his fleet waited, Zithla knew the enemy was planning something significant. Furthermore, the disappearance of an entire Tuulan For fleet off the radar was cause for alarm. Enemy forces were gathering.

"They're going to attack us," Zithla declared. "And if I were Denulus, I know where I would strike." The Storm Nebula base or the Staging Post; the twin hearts of Vinkere power.

The enemy had to be met with overwhelming force or it was the Vinkere who would be overcome. His mind raced, considering the ships and resources he would have to divert to fend off such a large attack. His subordinates watched silently, awaiting his orders.

"Order all our forces in the Ss'Talak Cluster to withdraw. Tell them to reassemble at the staging post at Grah'du," he said, using the Vinkere word for Blue Star. "This includes our forces within the Commonwealth. This is not a retreat; it is a temporary redeployment."

If the Blue Star faced attack, Zithla knew he must use all the forces at his disposal to protect it. It was the Vinkeres' means for conquering the galaxy; it was their arsenal, their shipyard, their strongest line of defense against invaders and the beachhead from which they would overtake the galaxy.

Silencing the surprised murmurs with a raised claw, he said, "An opportunity has presented itself to cripple the forces of all our enemies at once. After we have crushed their combined fleets, their homes will be undefended, and there will be nothing left to stop us from cleansing the Ss'Talak Cluster."

War cries echoed throughout the command center. The *Z'Tauron* and its sister ships broke orbit, leaving Ennomos behind as they returned to the Shadow Nebula.

"All forces acknowledge your order, General," Ss'Taliss reported. "They are beginning their strategic withdrawal to the Grah'du Staging Post."

"Good." Zithla's forked tongue flickered between scaly lips. "Our enemies are making a fatal mistake if they think their combined strength will win the day. Victory is ours."

"*Our Dominion shall encompass the stars*," said Ss'Taliss, quoting a passage from the Mandate.

"Yesss," Zithla said sibilantly. "My Dominion shall encompass the stars."

*

In orbit of New Jakarta, New Jakarta System
Interstellar Commonwealth

Captain Ivanova of the Navy ship *Avenger* could hardly believe what she was seeing. The white flashes of the Vinkere ships' slipstream jumps could be seen through the debris field that was the result of the weeks-long conflict for the New Jakarta System. Ivanova had begun to think the battle for this system was one the Navy would soon lose, despite their valiant defense. But now the enemy were leaving!

"Sir, the Vinkere are *retreating*!" her tactical officer confirmed, sounding as surprised as she felt.

"The jamming signal is gone, too!" the *Avenger's* sensor operations officer reported triumphantly. "Contact with the greater Commonwealth has been restored!"

A ragged cheer erupted from the exhausted, disheveled crew on the bridge. Nobody had slept for days; the latest skirmish above the Tier 3 world of New Jakarta had lasted for three days without pause. The Vinkere onslaught had seemed endless; every time the Navy repelled one assault, a second wave of Vinkere ships would join the battle. Slowly but surely, the beleaguered Commonwealth Navy had been forced back, losing ships, men and women as the Vinkere advanced. They had already lost the planet Sumatra in this system, and both other inhabited planets, New Jakarta and Kalimantan, were on the verge of falling.

The captain rubbed her neck, still tender from where the doctor had administered the latest dose of stimulants to keep her awake and alert. Ivanova had been sure today was the day they would either die or be forced to retreat, surrendering the entire system to the Vinkere, who seemed to have an endless supply of fighters, battleships and missiles.

But now the enemy had turned tail and fled.

She surveyed the broken wall panels, sparking circuits and shattered control consoles of her bridge. Engineers worked frantically to keep the *Avenger* operational, but the ship was a mess. Her gaze passed over the communications officer who regarded her in shock. Ivanova felt her stomach clench, fearing bad news. "Captain, *all* the Vinkere in the Commonwealth are breaking off from battle! They're all retreating!"

"We won!" an ensign crowed. Their cheers reverberated throughout the ship and was picked up by other crewmen with enthusiasm.

Ivanova shared a congratulatory smile with her executive officer. He looked exhausted too. But they had done it. The enemy must have been in worse shape than the Navy had realized. *Resist the devil and he shall flee,* Ivanova thought grimly.

*

Edge of the Dune Sea, Ennomos
Interstellar Commonwealth

Paul Greenbiar, formerly captain of the *Lautaro*, squinted through the binoculars, grateful that his goggles protected his eyes from the dust stirred up by the howling wind. He stood with his team along the crest of a sand dune, just one of many which stretched like frozen swells to the horizon behind them. In front of them the dunes gave way to barren, rocky terrain. It was difficult to see through the haze, but ten kilometers ahead was one of the three great geodesic domes that housed the majority of Ennomos' population. Above it the dark bulk of a Vinkere Leviathan hovered menacingly.

When they had been forced to abandon the *Lautaro*, Greenbiar had ordered his crew to scatter; it was more difficult for the Vinkere to find them all if they spread out across the planet. Greenbiar's pod had touched down near a small mining facility, several hundred kilometers from the nearest major population center. The first thing he did was disable his pod's locater, making it that much harder for the Vinkere to find him. It had taken him an hour to cross the rust-red terrain from his crashed pod to the mining facility, where he asserted control over the confused and terrified civilian mining executives. Using their communication equipment, he was able to contact other groups across the planet, including some of his own crew. He quickly learned that the Vinkere had seized control of the major settlements and their outlying communities, rounding up their human inhabitants. Those settlements who resisted were bombarded from orbit, leaving nothing but blackened craters.

Greenbiar was fortunate the outpost he had landed near was one of the few too remote and too small to warrant attention from the Vinkere. The mining executives soon revealed why: the Vinkere didn't need to waste resources destroying the outpost when they would run out of supplies and starve within a few weeks. Doing his best with what little resources were available, Greenbiar formed a resistance, mostly comprised of mining security personnel and Navy crew who had escaped the battle in orbit. They launched small-scale attacks to keep the Vinkere off balance, but the invaders always retaliated with overwhelming force. Greenbiar estimated their resistance had less than a third of their original number left.

He inhaled a deep lungful of oxygen from his breather; the atmosphere of Ennomos was too thin for humans to breathe for very long without help, but his team carried small, compressed oxygen tanks in their packs. He raised the binoculars to his eyes again and studied the scene. Scouts all over the planet were reporting the Vinkere were pulling out; the Leviathan hovering ten kilometers away was their last remaining presence.

Greenbiar knew that the Vinkere had been using the human population as slave labor, forcing them to extract resources and transport them to Vinkere ships. He could only assume it was part of a long-term strategy by the Vinkere to cement their foothold in the Commonwealth, which made their retreat even more confusing. Why were they leaving suddenly?

One of his officers shouted over the howling wind and pointed; the Leviathan was rising through the hazy orange sky. Some of Greenbiar's officers cheered, but he didn't join them. Something wasn't right.

A single missile launched from the Vinkere ship, curving through the orange sky toward the dome that housed the human city. It hit with a blinding flash, and Greenbiar and his officers had to shield their eyes. When he opened them a few seconds later he saw a black mushroom cloud billowing upward. The shockwave hit a few moments later, sending them tumbling down the sandy slope of the dune.

His entire world was dust and shrieking wind. Greenbiar curled up on the ground, unsure if the nuclear blast was powerful enough to reach them. After several moments the roaring faded, and he sat up. Other members of his team also sat up, looking dazed. Greenbiar scrambled back up the steep, slippery side of the sand dune, the protective robe he wore over his frayed uniform flapping in the wind.

There was nothing left of the dome that had once housed eighty thousand people. Above the impact site the sky was turning black from the dust. Bolts of lightning flashed angrily, and the wind began to pick up again.

"We need to get out of here," he said once he reached the bottom of the dune.

"Assuming we haven't already received a lethal dose of that radiation," his medical officer groused, but a sharp look quickly silenced her. As they returned to their vehicle, an old weather-beaten six-wheeler, Greenbiar's radio squawked. "What is it?"

"The Vinkere ships are leaving the system, and the long-range communications jamming has lifted. We're receiving messages from the Commonwealth!"

Greenbiar's team look at each other in amazement. Could the Vinkere be leaving for good?

"As soon as I get back to base, I need to contact the Navy. Will I be able to?"

"The chief is still trying to jury-rig the-"

"Yes, or no?"

A pause. *"Yes."*

"Good." Greenbiar sat behind the vehicle's steering wheel and they began the long, bumpy ride back to base. Through the rear-view mirror, he glimpsed the dark cloud of ash spreading across the sky, and he wondered if the same thing was happening across the Commonwealth.

30

Space around ISER Station teemed with ships of every size and shape, gathered from all corners of the Locality. The once-secret base was now the assembly point for an interstellar fleet preparing to attack the staging post from where the Vinkere had launched their destructive attacks. Needle-thin Kelzee ships flew in formation beside bulbous Vlind galleons and a contingent of Kithel ships orbited the station, moving together like a shoal of fish. The crews of the Commonwealth's Ninth Fleet ran battle drills and prepared for the coming campaign.

Balzano had likened Admiral Denulus' mission to disturbing a hornet's nest. The discovery of the hidden Vratak Nebula base had galvanized everyone's resolve, and pledges of support had come from the Vlind, Ankari, and Kelzee to join the Tuulan For and Human Commonwealth in neutralizing the Vinkere threat to the Locality. Even the Kithel, who had been devastated by the Kalavat Plague, had decided to participate in the coming campaign.

Admiral Haftel's plan had been approved by Kelzee General Nulo and Ankari Admiral Denulus, and accelerated; using their wormhole drives the Ankari were able to bring other ships to the Gandra Sector in a fraction of the time required by conventional slipstream travel. While Ankari ships traveled back and forth across the Locality, ferrying allied ships to the Gandra Sector, the number of ships at ISER Station swelled.

Marston and his crew kept busy ensuring the *Pericles* was battle-ready. With the Vinkere withdrawn from the Commonwealth, news from home poured in every hour. He ignored most of it; there would be time to assess the losses after the successful conclusion of the campaign. He had just completed a status report for Admiral Haftel when Amalthea spoke. "Captain, the Ankari ships are about to arrive with the Tuulan For fleet."

Everyone on the bridge looked up from their consoles as rainbow colored Ankari wormholes began to open around them. Ankari and Tuulan For ships glided out, joining the mass of starships already assembled around the station. The last to emerge were the *Antruvion* and the Tuulan For flagship *Decisive Gain*.

Clarke whistled appreciatively. "Look how many ships the Tuulan For committed!"

"Over two hundred," Balzano said. "We have Minister Jadus to thank for that."

"That's everyone," Marston said as the last wormhole closed behind the two ships. It wasn't as many ships as Admiral Haftel had hoped for, but it was the best they could do. Ankari probes had revealed a large force of Vinkere ships gathering at the Storm Nebula base in preparation for the attack; when Commonwealth ships had pursued the Vinkere to their nebula bases the Vinkere had simply sealed the wormhole gateways shut behind them. The enemy knew they were coming.

"We leave for the Storm Nebula in the morning," Marston announced. "Make sure we're ready to go by then." The crew returned to work, determined to be shipshape and combat-ready by then.

*

Lieutenant Hasan piloted the shuttle *Naxos* toward the *Pericles*. Sitting in the co-pilot's seat, Doctor Gariri yawned tiredly. She had spent the day treating ailments on the *Rising Star*, one of the civilian ships that had accompanied Admiral Haftel's fleet.

"This is shuttle *Naxos* to *Pericles* flight control, requesting permission to land."

"You have permission to land, Naxos," Amalthea responded.

The hangar doors slid open and Hasan guided the shuttle inside. Deftly manipulating the helm controls, he lowered the landing gears and the small craft landed gently in the middle of the cavernous bay.

"Welcome home, Doctor," he said.

"Thank you, Lieutenant," Gariri said with a weary but grateful smile. When the hangar re-pressurized, they exited the shuttle, Hasan to return to the bridge and Gariri to a hot shower and a warm bed. As they walked across the deck another group entered the hangar; Lieutenant Commander Clarke and one of his security teams.

"What's going on?" Hasan asked the tactical officer.

"Combat drills," Clarke told him, gesturing at the cavernous room. "This is the largest room on the ship, so it's perfect for open combat training."

Hasan rested his palm on the *Naxos*. "Just don't break the shuttle, okay? She's our last one."

"We'll do our best," Clarke grinned.

"You fought that Vinkere S'Geliss, didn't you? Any advice, in case more of them board the ship?"

"Keep away from them," Clarke said simply. "They're deadly in close-range combat. You want to fire at them from a distance."

"Good to know, thanks." He paused and then asked, "But they're not likely to board the ship, right?"

Clarke shrugged. "I'd say that depends on your flying, Lieutenant."

*

Marston stood in the communications center for what was likely the last time.

"The fleet leaves tomorrow, correct?" Overseer Vashon asked.

"That's right. We leave for the Storm Nebula and the civilian fleet will return to the Commonwealth, now that we know there's a Commonwealth to go back to."

Lisle offered his hand, and Marston shook it firmly. "Good luck. We hope you all return safely."

"Your ship is always welcome here, Captain," Vashon told him.

Marston thanked them and left the communications center. He had one more place to visit on the station before returning to the *Pericles*.

Minister Jadus was working in a small office adjoining the lab assigned to her and Minnen. She was seated at a large crescent-shaped desk strewn with datapads and looked up at his approach.

"Welcome, Captain Marston," she greeted him warmly.

"Hello, Minister. How's the work on the Kalavat solution going?"

"Very well," she said optimistically. "We have the station's synthesizers working twenty-four hours a day to mass produce the antivenom, and the other ISER facilities are doing the same." She gestured toward the scientists, hunched over their workstations. "In here we're testing it on blood samples from different species in the Locality. It looks very promising."

"That's great news," Marston said. Their work would save billions of lives.

"It is," Jadus agreed.

A companionable silence fell. Now that the moment had come Marston felt awkward. When he spoke, his words came out in a rush. "The fleet leaves tomorrow morning, so I came to say goodbye, good luck, and thank you for everything you've done to help us. We wouldn't be ready for this campaign if it weren't for you."

"No thanks are needed. You saved *our* lives, remember?"

"It was a mutually beneficial arrangement," Marston said, and they both smiled. After a brief silence she said, "Maybe we'll see the *Pericles* again after the campaign."

"Maybe," Marston agreed, although he didn't see how that would be possible. If they survived the upcoming battle, they would return home to the Commonwealth. He tried to offer a reassuring look, but his smile was tinged with worry. Jadus saw through it immediately. Rising out of her chair, she reached across the desk and clasped one of his hands in both of hers.

"Good luck to you, Captain Marston," she said, squeezing his hands tightly. "May your campaign have a favorable outcome."

He was almost back to the ship when he was stopped by a familiar voice.

"Captain Marston!"

He turned to see Minnen the Learned hurrying toward him, accompanied by Uxxio, his daughter Sul and Elzor Drin. The Iganti professor beamed. "I am so glad we caught you. Minister Jadus was kind enough to inform us of your departure."

"Hello, Professor," Marston said, moved that Minnen would seek him out.

"We wanted to see you before you left, to say thank you," Uxxio explained.

"Indeed," Minnen said. He grasped the captain's shoulders with surprising strength. "Thank you, Captain, for having the courage to deliver us to this station. Without your intervention, it is very likely we would be dead," Minnen said. Uxxio and Drin nodded in agreement.

"The galaxy owes *you* thanks, Professor. More than one, actually!"

"That is true," Sul said, squeezing her father's bony arm affectionately.

"An antivenom is not the same as a cure," Minnen reminded his daughter gently in a rare moment of humility, "But we're getting there."

"Nevertheless, we owe you a great debt," Marston insisted.

Minnen offered a paternal smile and said simply, "May fortune favor your campaign." Sul and Uxxio nodded emphatically in agreement.

Drin spoke up. "Captain, I trust that you will uphold our deal to return me to my ship?" Minnen gave the Vlind an annoyed look, but Marston smiled.

"Of course, Overseer. We'll make sure you get your ship back."

Drin looked pleased, and relieved. "Thank you, Captain," he said. "I hope a profitable endeavor is what your campaign is."

"Thanks." Uxxio and Sul said their goodbyes, and then Marston made his way toward the airlock.

"We will see you when you get back!" Minnen called after him.

Marston looked back at them. "I hope so, Professor," he said sincerely.

"You will," Minnen said firmly, waggling a long finger at him. "The galaxy needs exceptional starship commanders, just as it needs brilliant scientists."

Marston was sorry to say goodbye, but as he walked away there was a spring in his step.

*

The station's cafeteria was full, as it always was at this time of day. People discussed their day with friends and colleagues over the evening meal. This evening, the most popular topic was the coming campaign and the looming departure of the fleet.

Jarren took his food tray from the synthesizer and scanned the room for his friends. He spotted Antak, Korosa and Uxxio at a table across the room and sauntered over.

"Do you think the fleet will accept volunteers?" Korosa was asking.

Uxxio regarded her with his owlish eyes. His own interests were strictly academic, and he couldn't imagine why anyone would want to go to war. "You want to fight the Vinkere?"

"I want to be useful," Korosa said emphatically. "There's nothing for me to do on this station."

"Me either," Antak said. "But as much as I want to help stop the Vinkere, my loyalty is to the Minister. If it weren't for her, we'd probably be sitting in the barracks in Lakaria."

Korosa grudgingly agreed. "I know. I just hate sitting by while others fight my battles for me."

Uxxio looked between them in bafflement. "The Minister is already doing important work," he pointed out. "If you want to make a difference, helping her with the plague cure is one way you could do it."

"I can't be much help unless need the trash needs emptying," Antak said wryly.

"You could always volunteer as a test subject," Jarren teased.

Uxxio's face lit up, and Jarren followed his gaze to see Sul approaching. Jarren had been pleasantly surprised when he met Sul. She was so… *normal*. She was energetic and highly intelligent like her father, but as far as Jarren could tell that was where the similarities ended.

"How are you all this evening?" she asked, setting down her tray. Sul wasn't at liberty to discuss her own work, but she always expressed interest in what the others were doing.

"Very well. Thank you for asking," Uxxio gushed. "We were discussing the campaign to the Storm Nebula."

"Ah, yes. They're very brave, the men and women going to fight the Vinkere."

"They wish they were going too," Uxxio explained, nodding at the three Tuulan For.

"Really?" Despite the constant internecine warfare between the tribes of the Iganti, she was as puzzled by their desire to fight as Uxxio.

"We'd prefer to fight the Vinkere then do nothing here," Antak confirmed. "But we can't leave the Minister."

"Why don't you ask her to go?" Sul asked. "My father says she's very reasonable."

"She is," Jarren said, noticing Antak and Korosa stiffen.

"She is what?"

Jarren twisted around to see Jadus standing behind him, flanked by Doctor Kerik and Professor Minnen. The elderly Iganti seemed fascinated by their embarrassment.

"Minster…" Jarren said blankly. "Would you like to join us?"

"That's why we're here!" Minnen chirped. "Move along will you, Uxxio," he added, forcing a space between Sul and Uxxio.

Jadus studied her three young subordinates intently. "She is what?" she repeated.

*

The fleet and the station fell into darkness as the sun disappeared behind the gas giant. Battle drills had been completed, munitions stored and personnel transferred. A lull descended on the fleet as the crews settled down for a restful night on the eve of battle.

For Marston, the morning couldn't come fast enough. He tossed and turned in bed, but sleep eluded him. After a couple of hours, he decided he may as well get up.

He was already on the bridge when the rest of Alpha Shift arrived. People took their stations, but there was none of the usual banter. For many of them it was their first time going to war; Marston could sense their apprehension. People only said what needed to be said in a strained, factual manner. Balzano simply nodded in greeting as he took his seat beside the captain's and they waited for Admiral Haftel to give the order to move out.

Minnen, Uxxio, Vashon, Lisle, and the other scientists watched solemnly as the fleet moved away from the station. Minnen privately wished Jadus had been able to join them, but as ever her duty to the people of the Locality forbade her.

Like a great multi-colored flock of birds, the fleet angled about, aligning itself with the distant Storm Nebula. Ships clustered around the Ankari vessels that would transport them via wormhole drive to their destination, and the fleet vanished into tunnels of rainbow light. Soon the station was alone again, and the scientists went back to work.

31

The bridge crew watched the swirling, twisting tunnel of light race past them. They were traveling faster than any human had ever flown before.

"Incredible," Hasan murmured as the rainbow walls of the tunnel cascaded past them. All he had to do was keep the ship in position beside the *Lekorion*, the Ankari ship they were assigned to as it sped toward the Storm Nebula. With its wings swept back it looked like a great bird of prey diving toward its target.

"That ship is huge," Clarke commented.

"And very powerful," Sirroyo added. "The energy required to generate the wormhole must be astronomical."

"Although our sensors cannot penetrate the *Lekorion's* hull, I estimate the ship's energy output to be equal to that of one of the megacities of Earth," Amalthea said.

"I'm glad it's on our side," Balzano said.

As they neared their destination, the Ankari ship contacted them. *"This is Captain Halkon of the* Lekorion. *We are about to arrive at the rally point. Prepare to return to normal space."*

The dark circle of the wormhole's terminus appeared ahead, speeding rapidly toward them, and then the cluster of ships soared out of the wormhole and into the Storm Nebula.

They were surrounded by the dark, swirling gases of the great cloud; the dim, fog-blurred lights of another clusters of ships already arrived was just visible ahead. Soon more ships began to appear, their presence announced by bright circular wormholes which briefly illuminated the cloud like small suns as ships poured out into real space. As the last vessels emerged the wormholes blinked out of existence, plunging the fleet back into darkness.

The Storm Nebula was a dense planetary nebula, approximately one light-year in diameter. The sensor-occluding gases of the nebula reduced their sensors to almost useless, and the ships would have to rely on pre-planned coordinates to navigate. The darkness felt ominous, as though Vinkere Leviathans lurked nearby, ready to snatch away any unsuspecting ships that got separated from the fleet. Admiral Haftel gave the order to advance, and the fleet began making its way deeper into the heart of the nebula.

On the *Pericles'* bridge, combat lights bathed the crew in a blood-red glow. The swaying navigation lights of the ships ahead of them were visible on the viewscreen as they were buffeted by the gravitational currents of the nebula. They weren't as powerful as those in the Shadow Nebula, otherwise traversing the Storm Nebula would have been much more difficult, and the risk of collision a deadly possibility. As the thought passed through Marston's mind the ship was buffeted by a powerful current. Hasan managed to keep the *Pericles* on course, but a pair of ships in front of them didn't handle the turbulence as skillfully, and narrowly avoided collision.

"That was close," Hasan said through clenched teeth.

"How long to the staging post?" Balzano asked.

"At this speed, approximately ninety minutes," the helmsman reported.

A ship on the fleet's periphery detected the first sign of Vinkere in the nebula; an automated weapons platform at the edge of its limited sensor range. Nearby allied ships moved to intercept, and a distant orange flash signaled its destruction. Soon after another Vinkere weapons platform drifted out of the mist. It opened fire, launching a barrage of missiles at several nearby ships. The allied vessels responded in kind, destroying it. The Vinkere were certainly aware of their presence.

The fleet pressed on deeper into the nebula with the *Challenger* and *Antruvion* in the lead. The *Antruvion* deployed its contingent of drones, which raced ahead of the fleet, locating and destroying any Vinkere weapons platforms in their path. The most immediate threat came from the nebula itself; over time the fleet's tight formation lost cohesion as the gravitational currents swept ships out of position, and thirty minutes from the Vinkere base the *Pericles* found itself in a group of ships on the fleet's starboard flank.

"Captain!" Sirroyo called out sharply, causing heads to turn. She frowned. "I thought I saw a Vinkere ship on sensors. But it disappeared." Balzano joined Sirroyo at the science console and studied the phantom ship's profile. "Maybe a scout ship, or a fighter?" he wondered.

"Maybe," Marston said. Whatever the Vinkere had planned, they would find out soon.

Lauren Winters and Travis McGee patrolled a corridor, rifles slung over their shoulders. There were no Vinkere intruders on board, but when the *Pericles* entered combat that could change. Outside the windows lightning forked across the sky, turning the corridor white and causing Winters to squint.

"Did you see that!?" McGee shouted, pointing out the window.

"See what?" she asked, staring into the gloom. Lightning flashed again, illuminating the fleet. This time she saw it. The shadow of a colossal Vinkere ship moving parallel to the fleet. A Leviathan.

"We have to tell the bridge," McGee said.

"They have already been notified," Amalthea assured them.

Other ships had also noticed and responded with a barrage of cannon and missile fire directed toward where the Leviathan had been spotted. With sensors all but inoperable they fired blindly into the cloud, but a single missile found its target, illuminating the dark hull of the enemy ship. Other ships began firing at the point of impact, and the orange flashes of railgun fire and detonating warheads blossomed in the nebula.

The Leviathan turned, gliding toward them like a shark through murky water. More ambushing Vinkere ships swept in, weapons blazing, and soon all around them the dark sky was illuminated by weapons fire as skirmishes broke out along the length of the fleet.

McGee and Winters watched the battle, distance giving them the illusion of safety. Suddenly a missile exploded directly outside the windows of their corridor, causing them to duck instinctively. The explosion rippled against the *Pericles'* energy shield and a Vinkere fighter whipped past, just meters away. "We're under attack!" McGee cried out.

"Return fire," Marston ordered, clenching his jaw. The Vinkere fighters had appeared out of the cloud without warning, striking the *Pericles* amidships with their missile fire.

"Firing railguns," Clarke said. There was a faint *throom throom throom* as the *Pericles'* turrets fired. Tracking the fighters zipping between the allied ships wasn't easy. Their forward turrets ceased firing as the pair of Vinkere fighters they were tracking flew behind a Tuulan For ship.

"Just try and keep from shooting our own ships," Hasan said half-jokingly to Clarke. He was concentrating so intently on his console that he didn't reply.

"Do not *break formation to engage the enemy,"* Admiral Haftel cautioned the allied ships. *"Keep moving toward the objective."*

"How much further?" Balzano asked the helmsman.

"A few thousand kilometers," Hasan replied. "Not long now."

The ship shuddered violently. "Direct hit to the starboard blade," Sirroyo reported. "The shields are holding, and only minor hull damage."

Hasan was forced to send the ship reeling hard to port to avoid colliding with a Vlind ship which had lost engine power. He swore quietly under his breath. The Vinkere ship responsible fired another salvo to finish off the crippled vessel, but the missiles were intercepted by a Tuulan For frigate, and they exploded harmlessly in the nebula. The allied ships returned fire, and the Leviathan retreated into the darkness.

Balzano drew Marston's attention to the tactical display. Many of their Vinkere attackers had withdrawn.

"We're close," Balzano said.

The *Pericles* fired again, dispatching another two Vinkere fighters closing on the wounded Vlind ship. Then, as quickly as they had appeared, the Vinkere ships melted away into the nebula.

"The Vinkere are withdrawing," Sirroyo reported from the science station. "Eight of our ships were crippled and are also falling back."

"They were just testing our capabilities," Balzano realized.

"I agree," Marston said. "If the Vinkere launch a full-on assault, we'll know."

There was no more sign of the enemy as the allied fleet neared the target. Admiral Denulus addressed the fleet: *"We are about to reach the staging post. All Ankari, Human, Kithel and Kelzee ships: target the larger Vinkere ships. Vlind and Tuulan For ships, focus on weapons platforms and fighters."*

"Sensors are reading a clear space ahead," Sirroyo announced.

"This is it," Hasan murmured quietly.

"Keep us steady," Marston said as the ship rolled through another gravitational swell.

All around the *Pericles* allied ships surged forward, speeding toward the invisible barrier separating the nebula from the Vinkere outpost at its heart. The *Pericles* accelerated with them.

The ships soared out of the nebula and into a clear expanse. Like the Shadow Nebula base, the gases and gravitational forces of the nebula were kept at bay by special satellites that formed a protective shell around the Vinkere staging post. The entire area was illuminated by the necklace of wormhole gateways linked to other Vinkere bases across the Locality. At the center of these was the huge ring of the super wormhole generator, leading to Vinkere territory in the distant Carina Nebula. Poised directly above it, like a dark, menacing cloud, was the Vinkere fleet.

The allied fleet opened fire, sending a wave of missiles and projectile fire toward the Vinkere fleet. Explosions rippled across the front line of Vinkere ships, obscuring them behind a wall of fire. Then, out of the flames, emerged ranks of Leviathans. They returned fire, sending a cloud of missiles speeding through the void.

The front line of the allied fleet bore the brunt of the enemy fire, and several ships exploded under the onslaught. The *Challenger* and *Antruvion* advanced, firing back, and the ships around them joined in. But the Vinkere onslaught had slowed their momentum and the fleet bunched up as the rear guard charged toward the battle, only to be held up by the vessels in front.

"Keep advancing!" Admiral Haftel ordered. *"Find your targets and engage!"*

Vlind and Tuulan For ships peeled away, moving toward the Vinkere weapons platforms and the Vinkere fighter swarms while the *Pericles* and the remaining ships focused their fury on the Leviathans. The Vinkere, although outnumbered, fought back savagely.

The two opposing forces advanced inexorably toward each other, firing continuously. Soon the fleets converged, and the battle became an all-out brawl as hundreds of ships slugged it out at point-blank range. The allied forces had the advantage of numbers, but the Vinkeres' technological superiority to everyone except the Ankari soon became apparent.

It was the fiercest battle Marston had ever witnessed, and he couldn't tell who was winning or losing. There wasn't time to think about it as a Leviathan set its sights on the *Pericles* and fired. Clarke shouted for Amalthea to set the forward railgun batteries on point-defense. Most of the enemy missiles detonated harmlessly in space, but two of them made it through the frigate's protective screen and slammed into their bow with such force that Marston's teeth rattled.

"Evasive maneuvers," he ordered, and Hasan brought the ship about, angling away from its attacker and using another Vinkere ship to shield themselves from their pursuer.

"Good move," Marston congratulated him. The helmsman's only response was a brief nod; he was too focused on evading missiles and avoiding collision with the myriad of other ships around them.

A thunderous explosion jolted the ship. "What was that?" Balzano demanded. Sirroyo and Clarke hurried to find out, but Amalthea beat them to it.

"A Vinkere fighter collided with the port blade, section sixteen," she said. "There is hull damage but no casualties."

"Life support control is in that section," Marston said worriedly. "Any damage?"

"Minor damage to the backup systems, but Chief Winston has already dispatched a repair team," Sirroyo said, not to be outdone by the AI.

"Captain, the collision wasn't an accident," Clarke told him. "The Vinkere are deliberately sacrificing their fighters!"

As if to punctuate his words another Vinkere fighter slammed into a Tuulan For cruiser, then another into a Kelzee ship. The Vinkere fighters had transformed themselves into suicidal projectiles, crashing into the allied ships with deadly effect.

"Divert more of our weapons fire to the protective screen!" Marston ordered, moments before a heavily damaged fighter trailing smoke slammed into the hull amidships. The deck shuddered beneath his boots.

"I can't believe they're sacrificing themselves!" Sirroyo cried out in horror as a trio of fighters exploded against a small Ankari ship, slicing its wing off. They soon saw why: the bulk of the Vinkere fleet was retreating through the super wormhole while their fighters occupied the enemy.

It was a perfect cover. The Vinkere fighters caused enormous damage by targeting the weakest and most vulnerable vessels. Supreme Commander Zithla's willingness to sacrifice his own troops, and their willingness to obey, unnerved Marston more than anything else.

"Target the fighters!" Admiral Denulus ordered the fleet.

Two more Vinkere fighters were destroyed in the ship's protective screen of railgun fire; fighter hull fragments rained against the ship's shields.

"That was close," Clarke muttered.

Balzano's concentration was fixed on his tactical display; his eyes widened in alarm and he looked up sharply at Hasan: "Look out for—"

His warning was drowned out by a thunderous collision as a Vinkere fighter crashed and exploded against the arrowhead bow of the *Pericles*.

"Forward shields are down to fifty percent," Amalthea reported.

"Damage Control Team Delta, get to the navigational array!" Chief Engineer Winston hollered across the engine room. Engineers scrambled to obey. An alarm went off on his master console on the upper deck, and he hurried over to read it.

He cursed under his breath. "Team Delta!" he called after them, and they halted in the doorway. "Your top priority is restoring the connection between helm control and the navigational array!" Without the navigational array feeding vital data to the helm, they were flying blind. Not a good thing in the middle of a battle.

He was so focused on assessing the long list of damaged ship systems that it took him several moments to notice the sound of weapons fire had stopped. He brought up the ship's sensor display. The Vinkere fleet had gone, retreating through the giant wormhole leading back to their space, and their remaining weapons platforms were being steadily picked off by the Tuulan For and Vlind ships.

It wouldn't be long before the allied fleet followed them through the wormhole; they couldn't give the Vinkere time to regroup and fortify their position. "We've got a respite, people," Winston called out. "Let's make the most of it!"

One by one, the wormhole gateways closed as the Vinkere shut them down remotely. The Ankari flagship *Antruvion* and its sister ships released a swarm of spherical probes, each one meter in diameter and a pearlescent white. They fanned out into a circle, linking together, and settled over the rim of the super gateway like a giant pearl necklace.

"Those probes are stabilizing the wormhole and keeping it open," Sirroyo said in amazement. "The Vinkere won't be able to shut it down from the other side."

"Based on their limited power sources, I'd say they're only temporary," Clarke said.

"They'll last for as long as we need them to," she said, and he nodded in agreement.

The allied fleet regrouped above the mouth of the super wormhole. Reconnaissance probes were launched, descending into its rainbow maw. By standing at the front of the bridge Marston could look straight down into it; the wormhole seemed to stretch into infinity beneath him.

At the helm console, Hasan was wiping sweat from his forehead. Despite the effort they had already expended, there was still a long day ahead.

A wave of Vinkere nuclear missiles approached from the wormhole, but the allied ships nearest to the entrance launched their own missiles to intercept, and the enemy projectiles exploded harmlessly before they could release their destructive energy.

"I'm sure Zithla's got something more devious than that up his sleeve," Marston murmured.

Balzano nodded in grim agreement. He handed Marston a datapad listing the damage and casualties from the battle. "We knew it would be bad, but I didn't think it would be this serious already," he said quietly so only Marston could hear. The captain nodded in agreement. His gaze was drawn back to the wormhole, swirling like a great whirlpool beneath them. Soon they would travel through it, and he had no doubt a deadly reception waited for them. He tried to ignore the anticipation and dread welling inside him, and vowed he would get his crew through this, no matter what.

32

The allied fleet remained at the staging post in the Storm Nebula for six hours, making repairs and preparing for the final push into the home territory of the Vinkere. Orders were given and acknowledged; every ship had an important role to play in the coming battle. Admiral Denulus' ship, carrying the modified nova bomb, took its place at the center of a formation of other powerful Ankari battleships. It would be their responsibility to deliver the *Antruvion* to the Blue Star so it could deploy its destructive payload. When the fleet was ready, Admiral Haftel and Admiral Denulus gave the order to advance, and the fleet entered the wormhole that would carry them over eight thousand light-years to the Carina Nebula.

As its bright, shining walls closed in around the *Pericles*, Marston was reminded of the Rainbow Serpent from the Indigenous Australian Dreamtime, and couldn't shake the feeling that they were entering the gullet of a giant serpent ready to swallow them whole. Glancing around at his bridge crew, he could see the same apprehension in their faces and body language. Only Balzano successfully hid it behind a calm façade.

Marston brought up a star map on his armrest display and checked their position. The wormhole was represented as an orange line connecting the Storm Nebula and the Carina Nebula, and the fleet had nearly traversed its full length. Far behind them the purple line delineating the boundary of the Locality curved away, encompassing home and most of known space. Few human ships had ever been out this far, but Marston was too apprehensive to truly appreciate that fact. Adopting a sangfroid expression, he asked casually: "How long until we reach the other side of the wormhole?"

"Less than four minutes," Hasan said.

"Let's get this done," Balzano said grimly, and Marston managed a tight smile.

A couple of minutes later the terminus appeared at the end of the tunnel, growing as the allied fleet sped toward it.

"All ships, accelerate to attack speed," Admiral Haftel ordered. *"Engage the enemy and keep the path between the wormhole and the Blue Star clear. Shield Group, protect the* Antruvion *at all costs!"*

The *Pericles* accelerated, as did all the ships around her. The wormhole's exit raced to meet them, growing rapidly each second. Marston could already make out the dark mass of the Vinkere fleet waiting for them at the end. "Here we go, people," he said to the entire ship. "Let's finish this!"

The *Pericles* cannoned out of the wormhole, emerging into the light blue and purple whorls of the majestic Carina Nebula. Colorful starlight sparkled in the background, reflecting blue, purple, bronze and burgundy through the gases swirling around them. It was breathtakingly beautiful, far more impressive than the dark nebula they had left behind. It seemed strange that the barbaric Vinkere could be native to such a beautiful region of space.

There wasn't time to admire the view, however. The Carina Nebula may have been a stunning backdrop, but in the foreground loomed the space stations, refining facilities and shipyards of the Vinkere Staging Post, and the dark mass of Vinkere ships in their ominous rectangular formation. The allied fleet advanced toward it, weapons charged and ready to fire. Far off to port, at the center of the solar system, was the real target: the blue hypergiant known to the Vinkere simply as the Blue Star, burning brightly 20 AUs away.

As the allied ships poured out of the wormhole, the Vinkere formation advanced to meet them. The two sides bore down on each other, preparing for a clash even more vicious and destructive than the battle in the Storm Nebula.

The *Pericles* and the other allied ships opened fire, and a barrage of missiles, superheated plasma and energy beams crashed into the front rank of Vinkere ships. The initial impact was so bright that Marston had to shield his eyes from the glare. When the light faded, at least two dozen Vinkere ships were breaking apart, wracked by explosions, but their frontline was unnervingly intact, and their ships returned fire. The salvo of Vinkere missiles hit the allied fleet hard- a Tuulan For cruiser beside the *Pericles'* crumpled under the attack, exploding in a ball of fire and showering the frigate with debris. A Kelzee ship moved forward to fill the gap in the allied line, firing its pulse cannons in rapid succession.

After their initial charge out of the wormhole the allied fleet slowed, creeping forward in a phalanx-like formation toward the Vinkere and maintaining a steady rate of fire. Most of the fleet, including the *Pericles*, fought to keep the Vinkere forces at bay while the *Antruvion* and its escorts made a direct line for the blue hypergiant star. The front ranks focused on pounding away at the Vinkere fleet while the ships behind them targeted incoming Vinkere projectiles and fighter swarms before they could strike at vulnerable points in the fleet.

The *Pericles'* bridge deck vibrated as the magnetic accelerator cannon boomed. The tungsten projectile ripped through a Vinkere ship, destroying it. Space between the allied forces and the Vinkere was thick with weapons fire as the two fleets attacked each other with every weapon in their arsenal.

An explosion bloomed across the bow of the *Pericles*. "Divert more power to the shields!" Clarke shouted into the com.

"There is *no more power!"* Winston shot back. *"Everything we have is being used already!"*

Marston shared a grim look with his executive officer as the deck swayed under the impact of another Vinkere missile detonation. There were only so many strikes the shields could protect them from before they collapsed entirely. The *Pericles* was built to withstand a certain amount of stress, but Marston feared it was quickly nearing that threshold.

He looked at the tactical display on his armrest monitor. Behind the allied fleet the *Antruvion* and its escorts had exited the wormhole and were moving toward the star. At the center of the allied formation, damaged ships retreated to allow fresh new ships to take their place. In this way they hoped to preserve as many ships as possible, because the advantage of numbers they'd enjoyed in the Storm Nebula was negated by the entirety of the Vinkere forces arrayed against them. Soon it would be the *Pericles'* turn to fall back. If they lasted that long.

Another explosion, another shudder. "There's a fire on Deck Five," Sirroyo reported.

"Suppression systems are handling it," Amalthea said.

Marston acknowledged their report even as he gave new orders to dispatch repair teams to elsewhere. His pre-battle anxiety was gone, replaced by adrenalin coursing through his body. He felt strangely focused, hyper aware of everything going on around him. The battle was ferocious by any account, but even still…

He locked eyes with Balzano and Sirroyo, and he could see that they felt it too. The fleet was holding formation, and the *Antruvion* was on its way to the Blue Star. *This was too easy.*

Supreme Commander Zithla watched impassively from his podium in the command center of the *Z'Tauron* as the battle unfolded. His ship was positioned at the center of the Vinkere formation, flanked on either side by the *Z'Tauron*'s sister dreadnoughts. They were engaged in a brutal trade of fire with the array of Ss'Talak Cluster vessels who had encroached on Vinkere territory. Zithla was surprised at their determination and even begrudgingly admired their courage, but all their efforts would amount to nothing. Soon he would unleash his secret weapon, which he expected to cause psychological as well as physical damage to his enemies.

Most of the crew were hunched over their consoles working, glancing up occasionally to look at thei. commander standing serenely on his podium. It wasn't unlike him to remain mostly silent during combat as he focused entirely on the battle, ready to respond to the enemy in the most effective and deadly manner.

Two vessels on his front line exploded under the onslaught of enemy fire. At the same time an enemy battleship he recognized as Kelzee exploded, engulfing two smaller nearby enemy vessels in a destructive fireball. Zithla smiled.

Lieutenant Ss'Taliss approached the podium and bowed deferentially. "The Phase Two ships are ready at your command, Supreme Commander."

"Good. Commence Stage Two," Zithla ordered. His forked tongue flickered between scaly lips curved upward in a wicked smile. Now the real battle would begin.

Katarina Sirroyo kept a close eye on the *Pericles'* sensor feeds. She shared the captain's apprehension and resolved that if the Vinkere were planning any surprises, she would find out what they were. She instructed Amalthea to focus the sensors on the Vinkere formation, probing it for surprises like energy spikes that might indicate a charging super weapon. Because of her vigilance she was the first to realize what the Vinkere were doing, but by then it was almost too late to do anything.

She inhaled sharply. "Captain! The Vinkere are mobilizing…"

In a well-practiced maneuver, the Vinkere fleet spread out, leaving a gaping hole at the center of their fleet. As they moved, the Vinkere ships kept up their fire and the Navy ship in front of the *Pericles* took several direct hits. Explosions rippled across the hull and the ship began to list. Collision alarms sounded on the *Pericles* bridge.

"Full reverse!" Balzano shouted in response.

"I can't, sir!" Hasan hollered back. "There are too many ships behind us!"

We're packed in too tightly, Marston realized. He stared at the hole at the center of the Vinkere formation. It looked like the barrel of a giant gun, pointed directly at the fleet. But what was it going to fire?

Almost immediately after, Amalthea spoke. "I am detecting hundreds of vessels approaching in slipspace. They are not Vinkere."

"What? Well then who are they?" Clarke demanded.

"They are… ours. I mean, they're from the Locality," Sirroyo said, her brow furrowed in consternation.

Marston, Balzano and Hasan all realized it at the same time. The gap in the Vinkere fleet wasn't the barrel of a gun; it was an access tunnel. Given the Vinkere's suicidal use of their own fighters, Marston supposed they shouldn't have been surprised.

"Amalthea, warn Admiral Haftel the fleet needs to disperse now!"

Dozens of slipstream portals opened in front of the allied fleet. The precision with which the portals opened within the tunnel created at the center of the Vinkere formation would have been admirable in any other circumstance.

From the portals emerged the hundreds of ships that had been abducted by the Vinkere from across the Locality: Kelzee, Vlind, Iganti, Human, Kithel, even some Ankari ships. All bore scars of the battles their crews had lost and all were lifeless except for the engines which propelled them toward the fleet on a collision course.

Alarm spread through the allied fleet. Marston saw the *Challenger* maneuvering to avoid the incoming ghost fleet. *"All ships, evasive maneuvers,"* Haftel shouted, and even the unflappable Admiral sounded desperate.

Everyone heard the order, but there was nowhere for them to go. The wormhole gateway blocked their rear, as did their own ships pressing in from behind. The Vinkere fleet turned their broadside cannons on the fleet, and the deadly barrage increased. Marston watched in horror as allied ships tried to break away from the fighting, only to be ripped apart mercilessly. Caught between their own ships and a wall of enemy fire, the fleet had blocked their own retreat. There was nowhere to go. And the ghost fleet sped toward them.

"We need to get out of here!" Balzano said.

"Take us forward, and then up and over the fleet," Marston ordered Hasan. The helmsman glanced over his shoulder, giving the captain an incredulous look. "Just do it!" Marston snapped. "We can't go back, and we can't stay here!"

"Whatever you say, Captain," Hasan muttered. "Out of the frying pan..."

Under Hasan's guidance the *Pericles* shot forward, narrowly avoiding the listing Navy ship, which was jettisoning escape pods in all directions. The frigate, along with a few other allied ships, burst out of the allies' frontline. The impacts against their dwindling shields increased as the *Pericles*, against all common sense, fled *into* the line of fire.

The ship shook and rattled; the near-constant impacts of weapons detonations against their shields created a dull roar. Marston grimaced with each hit, knowing his ship was paying for his decision dearly.

"We've completely lost shields," Clarke reported grimly, as though he was pronouncing their deaths. The next salvo of Vinkere fire tore into the undefended ship, and the *Pericles* was engulfed in flames.

Clarke and Sirroyo shouted damage reports over the chaotic sounds of hull plates tearing, conduits bursting and the agonized cries of the wounded.

"Hull breaches on Decks Two, Six and Seven. We're venting atmosphere!"

"Fire suppression systems aren't responding!"

"Starboard thrusters are heavily damaged."

"There's a power leak on Deck Four, Section Five-- emergency power in that section is malfunctioning!"

"Direct hit to the hydroponics lab- it's been destroyed!"

A fire had broken out on the bridge. "Divert all power to the engines!" Marston rasped, coughing on the smoke. Coaxing every last joule of power from non-essential systems, Hasan brought their sub-light engines to full power, and the ship angled away from the Vinkere, trailing fire and debris. Dozens of other allied ships were doing the same thing, flying forwards and then looping about over the splintering remains of the phalanx formation as the ghost fleet drew ever closer. Many of them weren't so lucky, lighting up the sky around the frigate with bright explosions.

The ghost ships collided with the allied fleet like a meteor storm. At least the ships in the front half of the formation had a chance to escape; for the ships at the rear there was nowhere to go. Even with full-strength shields there would be little hope of withstanding a collision at such speeds, and the ghost ships tore through the fleet. Explosions rippled outwards, consuming ship after ship. On the flickering viewscreen the *Pericles* bridge crew watched the devastation with numb horror. Marston sagged in his chair; the sudden, brutal loss of so much life was devastating. The *Challenger*, Admiral Haftel's ship, was hit by three vessels. Its exhausted shields collapsed and the graceful, tapering neck shattered under the impact. Atmosphere, bodies and debris vented from the ship's fractured hull before a great white fireball consumed the ship, vaporizing it.

Zithla watched with satisfaction as the human vessel identified as one of the flagships of the enemy fleet exploded. The remnants of their fleet were in disarray, in danger now as much from the explosive detonations of their allied ships as from the Vinkere missiles or kamikaze attacks of the abducted ships. They scattered in all directions, and Zithla could sense his forces straining to finish them off. Blood had been scented, and they wanted to move in for the kill. Zithla let them.

"All ships, pursue and destroy the enemy," he hissed. The Vinkere ships swooped in, ready to finish off the battered remnants of the allied fleet.

"Target the Ankari ships first," Ss'Taliss added, and Zithla nodded in approval. He pointed to the distant squadron of enemy ships moving toward the center of the solar system. "Order our escorts to pursue those ships," he commanded. "And prepare our soldiers for boarding action." The *Z'Tauron* and its sister dreadnoughts turned away from the killing field and accelerated toward the *Antruvion* and the Blue Star. They would disable and capture that Ankari ship, Zithla would see to it personally. Soon the allied fleet would be destroyed and the Ankari super weapon in his possession, and the cleansing of the Ss'Talak Cluster would truly begin.

The allied ships were retreating in the face of the Vinkere onslaught, which fell upon them with renewed savagery now that they sensed victory was at hand.

"We're being driven away from the wormhole," Hasan reported.

Lacking communication or coordination, the surviving allied ships had unwittingly pulled away from the mouth of the wormhole, and the Vinkere closed in, blocking off their retreat. The *Pericles* found itself with a few other ships in between the bulk of the allied forces and the *Antruvion*'s group making their way toward the Blue Star.

A new voice issued through the speakers. *"This is Commodore Layan. Regroup at my position and form a perimeter."* In front of the *Pericles* a Tuulan For battleship turned gracefully, taking up a position outside of the immediate range of the Vinkere. Nearby allied ships moved into position alongside the Tuulan For ship, re-forming the phalanx. Hasan laid in a course for them, and the engines stutteringly obeyed.

Marston noticed a bloody gash along the side of Balzano's head, but the commander ignored his concerns. "We have bigger problems," he said, pointing at the tactical display on a cracked screen. The *Z'Tauron* and its sister dreadnoughts were making a beeline for the *Antruvion*. There was nothing between them and the Ankari ships but space.

"Zithla wouldn't pursue the Ankari ships unless he was sure he could beat them," Marston realized. Balzano nodded in agreement, wincing as a medic treated his head wound.

"Amalthea, alert Commodore Layan," Marston instructed. He hesitated, before adding: "Tell him we're willing to provide assistance to the *Antruvion*." Everyone on the bridge was silent; what could their damaged frigate do against four overwhelmingly powerful dreadnoughts? But there were only a few ships in the allied fleet fast enough to catch up with them, and the *Pericles* was one of them.

"Yes, Captain."

A swarm of Vinkere fighters buzzed in, racing between the allied ships like angry hornets. Clarke fired missiles, and two of the attacking fighters exploded. "We're running low on javelins," he reported grimly.

"How's the MAC?" Marston asked.

"Still functioning," Clarke replied.

"Target the Vinkere ship here," the captain ordered, indicating an enemy light cruiser which passed neatly into their crosshairs.

"Firing," Clarke said. The cannon boomed, and the tungsten projectile passed clean through the enemy ship, spilling debris and bodies out the other side.

"Commodore Layan is ordering all ships capable of interception to protect the *Antruvion* while they deploy the weapon," Sirroyo said.

Marston nodded in acknowledgement and ordered the helmsman to set a course for the *Antruvion*. "Aye, Captain," Hasan replied, and if he felt any apprehension, he didn't show it. None of them did.

The *Pericles* accelerated again, moving away from the battle toward the blue star and the squadron of Vinkere dreadnoughts pursuing the *Antruvion*. A few other fast ships joined the chase, leaving Commodore Layan and the battered remnants of the Locality fleet to engage the main force of the enemy. Clustered around the Tuulan For battleship, they fought desperately to hold their ground. They were cut off from the wormhole, but they remained firmly between the bulk of the Vinkere fleet and the *Antruvion*.

The *Pericles* sped toward the heart of the solar system, steadily gaining on the Vinkere dreadnoughts. They were fast, but the *Pericles* was faster.

"They're almost within weapons range," Clarke advised.

Marston clenched his fists tightly. "Open fire as soon as they are. Target their engines," he ordered. The enemy ships grew larger on the viewscreen.

As the *Pericles* prepared to fire on the *Z'Tauron*, Clarke began a countdown.

"Firing in five… four… three… no!"

Four slipstream portals opened and the Vinkere ships vanished into them.

"What happened?" Balzano demanded.

"The Vinkere ships jumped into slipspace!" Sirroyo answered. "They've emerged again… right on top of the *Antruvion* and its escorts!"

The Vinkere dreadnoughts had caught the Ankari ships off guard because there was no immediate response from them. And Zithla intended to employ his second surprise before they had a chance to react.

He pointed a claw at the Ankari battleships now directly in front of them. "Destroy the escorts, then disable the *Antruvion*!" he barked.

The *Z'Tauron* and its three accompanying dreadnoughts activated their primary weapons. They were prototypes and still highly experimental, but if ever there was a time to use them, it was now.

The undersides of the ships folded open; the weapons that emerged were nearly the length of the ships themselves. Their nozzles glowed red as they unleashed their potent energy beams on the Ankari ships. Copied from the energy beam weapons of the *Savalia* eight years earlier, the weapons were unreliable, immensely costly in terms of power, and volatile. But when they worked, they were highly effective.

The Ankari had never had their own weapons used against them before, and their shields buckled under the onslaught. One of the *Antruvion*'s escorts exploded in a brilliant flash.

The remaining Ankari ships fired back in violent retaliation, sending angry red beams of energy slicing through one of the Vinkere dreadnoughts. It tumbled away, burning and out of control. The three other Vinkere ships immediately returned fire, but the experimental weapons were almost as dangerous to the crews operating them as to the enemy, and one of the dreadnoughts was destroyed when the erratic and highly volatile weapon exploded. Fiery debris pattering against the shields of the *Z'Tauron* and other two dreadnoughts. "Keep firing!" Zithla roared.

Although too far away to see with the naked eye, the *Pericles* crew were aware of the battle unfolding between the *Antruvion* and the *Z'Tauron* via the ship's sensors and Amalthea's blow-by-blow narration.

"A second Vinkere dreadnought just exploded," the AI informed them.

Marston put his hands on his hips. "We need to follow them," he declared. "Initiate a slipstream jump to the *Antruvion*!"

"Sir, you want to make a faster-than-light jump *toward* a star?" Hasan asked incredulously.

"Captain, it's too dangerous!" Sirroyo cried.

"I agree," Clarke said, looking guilty for disagreeing with his captain.

Marston pointed at the blue hypergiant on the viewscreen. "It's the only way to get to the *Antruvion* in time to help them!" he said. He rounded on the helmsman. "Can you do it?"

"I... I'm not sure..." Hasan stuttered.

"Amalthea, can you?" Marston asked.

"I believe so," she replied, sounding uncharacteristically subdued.

"Then do it," he said firmly. His tone didn't allow for any further debate, so the crew remained silent. The calculations only took Amalthea a second to compute. "I am ready," she said.

Marston slapped his hand against the intercom. "All hands: prepare for a slipstream jump. And prepare to engage the Vinkere!"

Twin crimson beams of energy speared the second Ankari escort and it erupted in a bright flash, leaving the *Antruvion* alone. The Ankari flagship fired at the *Z'Tauron*, and Zithla had to steady himself as the beam struck the ship with the force of a hurricane. Alarms shrieked as fires broke out and explosions erupted all over the ship. The *Z'Tauron* shook violently, threatening to destruct, but then the remaining Vinkere dreadnought interposed itself between the *Z'Tauron* and the enemy fire, using itself as a shield to protect the Supreme Commander. They took the brunt of the attack but paid for it dearly; by the time the beam tapered off the dreadnought was burning, heavily damaged and on the verge of destruction. But it fired its energy beam cannon back at the *Antruvion*, striking the ship squarely amidships. The Ankari ship's shields blinked out; the ship was vulnerable. Unfortunately for the Vinkere ship the strain of using their energy weapon was too great on the ship's ruined systems, and the dreadnought exploded.

The shockwave slammed into both the *Z'Tauron* and the *Antruvion*. Zithla desperately hoped that it wouldn't destroy either damaged ship. They needed the *Antruvion* in one piece.

"The Ankari ship is charging weapons again!" one of Zithla's officers said.

"Supreme Commander: our energy conduits were heavily damaged and we cannot fire the energy beam cannon without risking the destruction of our ship!" another reported.

Zithla knew they wouldn't survive another direct hit by the *Antruvion*. They had to act quickly. "Use conventional weapons," he barked. "Disable them!"

Missiles streaked out of the *Z'Tauron*, pounding the exposed hull of the Ankari ship until it was wreathed in fire. The wounded ship's distress call was quickly silenced by the Vinkere flagship. Zithla regarded the once-proud Ankari flagship, drifting helpless and alone. Their reinforcements were too far away to help, and his fleet would soon finish off the remaining Locality ships. This was turning out to be a good day.

He turned away from the viewscreen. It was then that he noticed Ss'Taliss lying dead on the floor, his chest impaled by a fallen ceiling support strut. Zithla barely glanced at the body as he slithered past, toward the armory.

"Prepare the boarding parties," Zithla roared, and his crew roared back in eager anticipation of the coming battle. "We will slaughter the crew and seize their super weapon!"

The command deck of the *Antruvion* was wreathed in smoke. Crewmen worked frantically to clear away the debris and coax life from the ship's damaged systems. The superstructure groaned loudly, threatening to break apart, and the lights flickered continuously; to Admiral Denulus it felt like his ship was in its death throes.

"We are still three hundred thousand units from the system's sun," his science officer informed him.

"That is not close enough," Denulus murmured. The Blue Star burned brilliantly in the nebula before them, deceptively close but not quite close enough. "We need to reduce the distance!"

The ship swayed; not from a missile impact this time, but something else. Denulus felt the deck jerk beneath his feet and then the ship started moving in *reverse*.

"We're being pulled toward the Vinkere dreadnought," the science officer reported grimly.

"What about our engines? Use thrusters if you have to," Denulus ordered.

"Our engines are already at full power," the helmsman reported, confused. "They're just not responding."

"I think I know why." Denulus turned to the science officer, who gave him a distressed look. He gestured to his flickering monitor, which was filled with strange, alien characters. "It's a Vinkere electronic attack. Ordinarily it wouldn't make it past our firewall, but with the main computer offline... we're helpless."

The ship shuddered again. In the distance a faint, high-pitched whine could be heard; the Vinkere were drilling through the hull.

"Order the crew to arm themselves and prepare for boarders," Denulus said grimly. "We can't let the Vinkere take this ship!"

The slipstream jump lasted less than a second; there was a bright surge of energy around the ship and then the *Pericles* was soaring back into normal space not far from the *Z'Tauron* and *Antruvion*, visible on the viewscreen as black specks against the Blue Star, which dominated the sky behind them. The frigate sped toward them.

Grappling hooks lashed out from the *Z'Tauron*, just like those the *Leviathan* had used to try to grab the *Pericles* in the Shadow Nebula. Marston and his officers watched, helpless, as the *Antruvion* was reeled toward the Vinkere dreadnought. Dark umbilical tunnels emerged from the Vinkere ship, magnetic clamps giving them a secure grip on the smooth hull of the Ankari vessel. Laser drills formed glowing red circles around the connection points as the Vinkere penetrated the hull. Sirroyo reported hundreds of Vinkere life signs gathered in the tunnels, ready to board the disabled ship.

"I cannot contact the *Antruvion*," she added. The Vinkere dampening field prevented the Ankari ship from calling for help.

"What's the status of our weapons?" Balzano asked quietly.

"Javelin missiles are depleted, but the MAC still works," Clarke said.

"Using it is inadvisable," Amalthea cautioned. "At this range destroying the dreadnought would almost certainly destroy the *Antruvion*."

The crew considered their options. There weren't many. Hasan looked at the captain. "What do we do now?" he asked. Even in its damaged state the Vinkere dreadnought was more than a match for the Navy frigate.

Marston could feel the eyes of everyone on him as he focused on the Vinkere dreadnought, poised like a predator to devour its prey. "Take us to the *Antruvion*," he said. "Prepare to dock with them."

The *Antruvion* had become a battle zone. Squadrons of elite Vinkere soldiers stormed through the corridors, killing everyone in their path. Brave Ankari security teams battled them on every deck, trying to fend them off and protect strategic areas of the ship. They wielded their hand-held beam weapons expertly, but more and more Vinkere soldiers poured into the ship with every second. Supreme Commander Zithla led the main assault, armed with a hand cannon and missile launcher. After months of overseeing the invasion of the Locality from his ship, it was sheer joy for him to finally join the fray. He roared with bloodlust as the battle raged around him.

An Ankari security team had set up a turret in the middle of a hallway. It fired its energy beam as he rounded the corner, striking him squarely in the chest; his personal energy shield held, and he fired his shoulder-mounted missile launcher, destroying the turret in a thunderous explosion that echoed down the corridor. He charged forward and set upon the dazed survivors, sheathing his weapons so he could eliminate them with his bare hands.

Soon he was surrounded by the bodies of the Ankari, and he turned to his soldiers. "Make for the weapons bay!" he shouted, and with an energetic cheer they surged down the corridor toward their prize.

*

With as much stealth and grace as possible, the *Pericles* slipped alongside the *Antruvion*, out of sight of the *Z'Tauron*, whose crew was focused on the conquest of their prize. "We have short range communications," Sirroyo reported.

"Can you put me through to Admiral Denulus?" Marston asked her.

"I'll try." After several failed attempts she succeeded, although the connection was sporadic and filled with static.

"*Captain Marston?*" Admiral Denulus sounded surprised.

"Admiral, we're here to render assistance. We've docked with your ship, but the airlock won't open-"

"All our primary systems have been disabled," Denulus said. *"A Vinkere computer virus is infecting the ship."*

"Can we help? I'm prepared to send security teams over to the *Antruvion...*"

"No. We are outnumbered and without our ship's defenses, it's just a matter of time before the ship is overrun."

"What do you want us to do, then?" Marston asked, exasperated.

"You must complete our mission. You need to get closer to the star and deploy the weapon before it's too late!"

Marston rubbed his forehead, knowing they were running desperately short on time. "Okay, to do that we need to transfer the weapon to our ship. We need to open the airlock somehow."

"It's too big to fit through the airlock."

Balzano mouthed *the hangar bay* to Marston, who nodded in agreement. "What about our hangar bay? Can we transfer it from your weapons bay, through space, to our hangar?"

"Our drones could do it," Denulus said. *"But we'd need to give you the command codes."* There was a pause. *"I don't want to risk giving them to you over this line in case the Vinkere are listening."*

"We'll force open the airlock, and come and get them," Marston said.

"Blast it open," Denulus said firmly. *"I will meet you there myself."*

The fizzling channel closed, and Marston turned to his tactical officer. "Have a security team blast open the *Antruvion's* airlock hatch. They have to be careful- we can't breach the outer hull."

Clarke nodded. "On it, Captain." Then, into his communicator: "Security Teams Alpha, Bravo, report to the starboard airlock..."

Marston was already moving toward the elevator in rapid strides as the security team acknowledged the order. Balzano caught Marston's attention made a face as though to say, *do you want me to go instead?* Marston shook his head, and the executive officer nodded in acceptance.

"You have the bridge, Commander," Marston told him before the elevator doors closed.

Balzano had just sat in the captain's chair when Amalthea spoke up. "Commander Balzano, I may be able to help the Ankari ship."

"How?" he asked.

"If I were to enter the *Antruvion's* computer system I may be able to purge the Vinkere virus."

Balzano looked across at Sirroyo. "What do you think?"

"If Amalthea says she can do it, then I believe her," Sirroyo said. "The problem is how to transfer her from the *Pericles* to the *Antruvion.*"

"I thought Amalthea was integrated into our ship's systems, and couldn't be removed?" Balzano reminded her.

Amalthea hesitated before saying, "I could discard the aspects of my program that manage ship's functions. In my reduced state I could transfer onto a portable data storage unit. This would need to be physically plugged into the Ankari computer so I can upload myself. I must warn you that the *Pericles'* computer functions would be reduced to the level of efficiency prior to my birth."

"She's talking about lobotomizing herself, Commander," Sirroyo said. "We can't let her do this."

"Amalthea… we couldn't ask you to do that," Balzano decided, shaking his head.

"Commander, I am the only one who can help the crew of the *Antruvion*. If I do not, they will all die."

"Consider the cost," Sirroyo told the AI. "You'd be giving up so much, all the experienced you've gained…"

"Not all," Amalthea replied. "I would be able to retain some memories, and I could retrieve the rest upon my return to the *Pericles*."

"Assuming we can retrieve you," Sirroyo retorted.

"There is another issue. Artificial intelligence is outlawed in the Ankari Assembly. If they discover my presence I will be eliminated. Their laws are quite strict in this matter."

"Even if you save the lives of everyone on their ship?" Balzano asked incredulously.

"It is likely, yes."

After a pause, Balzano said, "I won't order you to do this. It's your life at risk, so it's your decision."

"Thank you, Commander," Amalthea said. For the first time since her birth, Balzano heard emotion in her voice.

"Just decide quickly," Clarke warned her. "It looks like the Vinkere are winning the fight. They could seize control of the *Antruvion* before we get the drone codes from Admiral Denulus."

"I will help the Ankari. I will begin the discarding process. Lieutenant Sirroyo, I will require your assistance transferring my program to the portable data storage unit."

Balzano nodded reluctantly. "If that's your decision. Good luck, Amalthea."

Sirroyo could only imagine what it must have been like for Amalthea to sacrifice so much. As she prepared the data storage unit, she said quietly to the AI, "I admire you, Amalthea. You're risking your own existence to save people who would kill you if they found out."

"Helping other people is what we do," Amalthea said, and then she was gone.

"Clear!" Security Officer Hertzman called. The explosives attached to the exterior of the Ankari airlock detonated with a loud *bang*. When the smoke cleared, there were three dark smudges on an otherwise unharmed surface.

Hertzman looked at the others in bafflement. Marston was about to suggest using more powerful explosives when there was a muffled whine from the other side. A large, red circle appeared on the hatch before it dissolved away, leaving a gaping hole whose glowing red rim dripped molten metal. On the other side was a team of Ankari with plasma turrets pointed at the airlock. Admiral Denulus stepped in front of them, beckoning for Marston and his officers to make their way through when it was safe.

Marston ducked through the opening, accompanied by Hertzman and the rest of Security Team Alpha. Security Team Bravo came through after them, moving past Marston and Denulus and spreading down the adjacent corridors.

Denulus handed Marston a datapad. "The command codes for our drones," the Admiral said without preamble. "There are only a few remaining, but they should be sufficient."

"Thank you," Marston said, taking the pad. There was shouting behind him and he turned to see Sirroyo running toward them.

"Here, take this," she panted, offering a data storage unit to Admiral Denulus. "It may be able to remove the Vinkere command codes from the system. Can you connect it to your ship's computer?"

Denulus accepted it warily. "Our computer can adapt to any hardware in the Locality. What is it?"

Sirroyo hesitated. "It's... software we developed to counter Vinkere malware."

They heard shouts and the sound of approaching weapons fire. The Vinkere were getting closer.

"I must return to the command deck," Denulus said, and his security escort began moving back down the corridor, ensuring a clear path. "We will eject the nova weapon into space as soon as the drones are in position."

"Good luck, Admiral," Marston said. Denulus nodded once and then he and his guards retreated down the corridor toward the command center.

The sounds of conflict were much closer now; fewer Ankari voices could be heard but the sibilant hisses and guttural shouts of the Vinkere were growing louder with each passing moment.

Marston approached Hertzman and McGee, who like the other security officers wore black combat armor and carried semi-automatic rifles.

"Hold this corridor until the ship is ready to depart," Marston ordered them. "Do not let the Vinkere board our ship."

"They won't," McGee promised with a smirk.

Marston ducked back through the airlock into the *Pericles* with Sirroyo right behind him. McGee took his place at the head of the corridor just as the first Vinkere soldier rounded the corner. Shouting an order for his team to engage the enemy, the security officer raised his rifle and fired.

As soon as Sirroyo arrived back on the bridge, she hurried over to the science station and entered the codes given to them by Admiral Denulus. "The codes are working!" she said. "I have control of the drones."

"Direct them to the *Antruvion* weapons bay," Balzano said.

"Aye, Commander." All Sirroyo had to do was send orders to the drones, and they would use their smartware to obey. She was pleased when they responded almost instantly.

Balzano joined Clarke at the tactical station, where he was monitoring the battle outside the airlock. "How are they doing?" Balzano asked.

"There's heavy fighting in the corridor leading to the airlock," Clarke told him. "And it looks like two thirds of the *Antruvion* is under Vinkere control."

"How long until they reach the weapons bay?" Balzano asked apprehensively.

"Not long," Clarke said grimly.

Munitions Officer Vantrel cringed as the protective bulkheads sealing the entrance to his weapons bay began to glow a dull red from the heat of the Vinkere breaching machine on the other side.

"They're almost through the door!" a security officer shouted. He and the rest of his team took up positions around the only entrance to the room, using empty munitions crates for cover as they waited for the Vinkere to break through.

"Where are they?" Vantrel's assistant, Deputy Munitions Officer Kalonai, wondered nervously. He squinted through the circular opening of the primary weapons launcher into space, hoping to spot the drones. A transparent force field protected the crew from the vacuum outside, and through it the glare of the blue hypergiant star was almost blinding. A magnetic conveyor moved its volatile cargo slowly toward the opening for a "soft launch", where the *Antruvion*'s drones would scoop it up and deliver it to the human ship's hangar bay because the crippled Ankari ship was still too far from the star to deploy the weapon. The conveyor was normally used to hurl projectiles out of the ship at just under the speed of sound, but this time it crept along slowly for the sake of the sensitive, room-sized, star-destroying bomb it carried. Vantrel willed it to move faster, before the Vinkere burst into the room and seized the weapon for themselves.

Heat from the Vinkere breaching tools made the air shimmer. Vantrel wiped a bead of sweat from his brow.

"Bulkhead integrity is gone," one of the security officers announced, and then the door burst open.

Sparks and smoke billowed into the room, followed by the war cry of a Vinkere soldier. The Ankari security guards opened fire, shooting blindly into the smog, and were rewarded with cries of pain. Then an enemy missile flew out of the smoke, hitting a crate and detonating. The explosion killed several Ankari and flung the survivors across the room. Vantrel cracked his head against the wall and slid to the decking, dazed. Though his vision was blurred, and the room was full of smoke, he could make out a giant Vinkere gliding sinuously across the floor. Its yellow, slitted eyes fixed on the nova bomb and it grinned wickedly.

There was little time to act; most of Vantrel's team were either dead, unconscious or too injured to move. The Vinkere fanned out across room, and Vantrel gasped as one of them aimed its rifle at one of his dazed crewmates and executed her with a single shot. The sound drew the attention of the leader; its giant, wedge-shaped head twisted around on its muscular neck and focused on him with evil, yellow eyes.

Vantrel knew he had only moments left. He also knew that if the Vinkere got control of the nova bomb, everyone back home would die. With a strangled cry of pain he lunged forward, grabbing onto a computer console and slamming his fist against the control panel. The magnetic conveyor sped up, carrying the nova bomb the last few meters and flinging it out into space with a faint *wump*.

A quartet of drones, the last of the *Antruvion*'s compliment, appeared in space outside the launcher. They surrounded the drifting nova bomb and locked onto it with delicate gravity fields, towing it away and out of sight. Vantrel smiled in triumph, right before the giant Vinkere clamped a large, clawed hand tightly around his neck and lifted him clear of the deck. As darkness closed in on him, he fought to say with his last breath, "*You... will nev...*"

His last defiant words were cut off as Zithla swung his blade, and the head of the Ankari munitions officer rolled across the floor.

Marston stepped back as the Ankari drones glided into the cavernous hold of the *Pericles'* hangar bay, bearing the nova bomb between them. As they lowered it gently to the deck, Marston got his first good look at the weapon. Like most Ankari designs it featured soft, curving edges and was encased in a pearlescent, purple-white hull. It looked deceptively innocuous, like a giant egg or flower bud. If Marston hadn't known of its enormously destructive potential, he would have assumed it was an escape pod or cargo container.

Marston activated his communicator. "Marston to bridge, we have the weapon. Get our people back to the ship and then get us to the star!"

"Fall back!" Johan Hertzman shouted over the roar of gunfire. The *Pericles* security teams in the *Antruvion* corridor began backing toward the airlock, laying down suppressive fire to cover their retreat. A Vinkere with a shoulder-mounted missile launcher appeared around the corner, taking aim. Hertzman leaned out of cover just long enough to lob a grenade down the corridor. There was a thunderous *BOOM* as the grenade exploded, killing the Vinkere soldier despite its protective energy shield and disorienting the other enemy soldiers, giving the humans a short reprieve.

"Let's move!" Hertzman hollered, shoving the nearest security guard toward the door. The others followed, climbing through the airlock hatchway into the relative safety of the *Pericles*. The smell of burnt flesh reached his nostrils and Hertzman looked down to see one of his team lying on the floor with energy burns on his shoulder and his chest. His eyelids fluttered, and his chest rose and fell painfully, on the verge of blacking out. Winters, McGee and another officer shouldered their rifles and picked him up. They passed him carefully through the broken Ankari airlock into the *Pericles* corridor where a trio of the ship's medical staff were already treating other wounded.

Vinkere soldiers appeared at the end of the airlock tunnel. Energy bolts whizzed down the corridor, miraculously missing everyone. Hertzman slammed his fist against the airlock's control panel and the door slid shut; energy bolts pelted the hatch with muffled *wumps* as the Vinkere tried to break through. They would unless the *Pericles* got underway.

"Bridge, we're all back on board, get us out of here!" Hertzman shouted into the intercom.

"Acknowledged," Commander Balzano replied.

The deck jolted as the ship separated from the *Antruvion*. Then the frigate's powerful sub-light engines activated, and the *Pericles* surged forward, rapidly gaining speed and leaving the Ankari and Vinkere ships behind.

Zithla watched through the portal in the Ankari ship's weapons bay as the human frigate accelerated away, heading directly for the Blue Star. The Battle Intelligence in his combat suit locked onto the fleeing ship and zoomed in, sending the image to his heads-up display. A low growl formed in his throat as he saw the name of the ship: *Pericles*.

He spun around and charged toward the exit. The rest of his soldiers hurried after him. Cold fury sharpened Zithla's mind. He would make sure there was nowhere for the human ship to run, and no help to turn to. He would slaughter their crew one by one, including their young upstart captain.

"Disable that ship!" he thundered into his communicator. "And prepare the transports. They will not escape with our weapon!"

The blue hypergiant star filled the viewscreen, bathing the *Pericles* bridge in bright sunlight. Balzano ordered the screen polarized. The ship shook as it battled the powerful solar winds emanating from the Blue Star, which were more than two billion times that of humanity's home star.

"Hull temperature is over two hundred degrees, and it's still rising!" Hasan reported.

"Commander, our shields are almost completely non-functional. They won't protect us from the star's radiation, which will become lethal if we stay this close for too long," Clarke cautioned.

"We don't have much of a choice," Balzano pointed out. "Evacuate crew from the outer sections of the ship. It will offer more protection. And as for the heat, we'll just have to grin and bear it."

Captain Marston returned to the bridge, squinting against the bright starlight.

"How much further?" he asked.

"One hundred thousand kilometers," Hasan told him.

"Can we increase power to engines?" Marston asked. He expected the *Z'Tauron* to come after them any second now.

Hasan shook his head. "Our remaining engines are already at full power."

An alarm sounded. "Captain, the Vinkere ship is firing missiles!" Clarke reported. "Six... no, ten... correction, twenty missiles inbound!"

Sirroyo looked at the captain. "Without shields..." her voice trailed off, but she didn't need to finish her sentence.

"Full power to defensive batteries," Balzano ordered. Clarke obeyed, diverting the limited power left in the ship's drained batteries to defenses.

The Vinkere missiles closed in on the frigate. Defensive batteries fired, trying to destroy the incoming projectiles. They managed to hit eight of the missiles, which detonated harmlessly in space. Then the *Pericles'* turrets went silent.

"Rear guns are out of ammunition," Clarke announced tonelessly.

"Evasive maneuvers," Marston ordered. Hasan tried desperately to evade the missiles, but it was too late.

The first missile struck the *Pericles* amidships as it was turning, and the impact sent everyone tumbling to the deck. Then the second missile hit, and the third, each with a jarring, explosive impact that shook the entire ship and sent it into an uncontrolled spin. As the ship drifted, out of control, the remaining missiles slammed into the unprotected hull.

All around them, the ship died. The crackle of fires and the groan of tearing metal filled the bridge.

We're dead, flashed through Marston's mind a split second before everything went dark.

An unknown length of time later, he woke.

He was adrift in a pitch-black void, completely weightless. Dull pain throbbed in the side of his head; he reached up and felt it in the darkness. His hand came away damp with blood. Something had hit him but he couldn't have been unconscious for more than a few seconds, could he?

The next thing he noticed was the silence; he couldn't hear the familiar background thrum of the engines, just the eerie groaning of damaged metal. The communicator on his wrist blinked, signaling an incoming message.

"Marston here," he croaked. His voice sounded distant to his own ears. It must have been the lack of atmosphere; the air was noticeably thinner, probably from a nearby hull breach.

"Captain, this is Winston," said the hollow-sounding voice of the Chief Engineer. *"The main reactor is offline and most of our primary systems are disabled. We're not going anywhere."*

Marston nodded, before realizing the chief couldn't see him. "Acknowledged," he said numbly, wondering what he was supposed to do now.

Chief Engineer Winston gripped a nearby handrail to prevent himself from floating across the dark room. He looked up at the main reactor, the heart of the ship, normally humming with power. Now it was silent. Dim red emergency lights switched on as the ship's remaining batteries kicked in. In the zero-gravity he pushed himself off the wall and over to a diagnostic terminal. He grunted in pain as his hands contacted the scorching-hot surface, cursing and pushing away from it again. The terminal was completely useless, destroyed by a power surge.

Artificial gravity reactivated, and his feet dropped to the deck. He heard moans of pain and cries for help from his engineering staff, strangely muted in the depleted atmosphere. He moved toward the nearest voice and found Ensign Hamid pinned beneath a fallen structural support. Ensign Putman was already there, trying to free her friend. Winston lent a hand; there was nothing he could do for the ship.

Marston fell to the deck as the artificial gravity came online. He heard grunts and cursing as other people hit the floor. He struggled to his feet, experiencing almost overwhelming vertigo; he should have his head wound checked by a medic. Blood red emergency lights dimly lit the bridge, but as he looked around at the devastation Marston almost wished they hadn't. The main viewscreen had shattered where a fallen structural support had impaled it, and all the workstations were completely black, either from damage or lack of power, except for the science console, which Sirroyo was coaxing back to life. There was a gash on the side of her head that was bleeding profusely; she swayed on her feet until Clarke reached out with a steadying arm. Marston's heart seized in his chest when he saw Balzano kneeling over Hasan, who was lying prone on the floor. He felt a surge of relief when Balzano confirmed a pulse, but he dreaded to think what the death toll was.

Clarke gently eased Sirroyo into a nearby chair and then took her place at the science console. "Everything's gone," he said bluntly. "We have no weapons, engines, or sensors. We're sitting ducks."

Marston wiped the sweat from his brow, only just now noticing how warm it was. Their proximity to the star meant the ship would become dangerously hot, soon.

"The Vinkere won't destroy us," Balzano said. "They want the weapon."

"Does anyone know how close we are to deployment?" Marston asked, looking around. Everyone else looked to Hasan, who was still unconscious.

"I'm not... sure," Sirroyo stammered, "We don't... have sensors."

"I think... about fifty thousand kilometers," Balzano said.

"That will have to do."

"Captain, without communications we can't use the drones to deploy the weapon," Clarke pointed out.

"We'll have to find a way to do it manually, then," the captain replied wearily.

There was a distant *thump*, and the ship jolted.

"Something impacted on the hull," Clarke said ominously.

There was a second impact and everyone went quiet, straining to hear over the groans of the wounded and the creaking of the ship's damaged superstructure.

"Five impacts," Balzano said, and Clarke nodded in agreement. Then they heard a new sound: the electronic whine of power tools drilling through the hull.

"The Vinkere," Sirroyo said groggily as Clarke applied a self-adhering bandage to her wound. He administered a stimulant to clear her head and she smiled weakly in thanks.

"Warn the crew we're being boarded," Marston said. "Use wrist communicators."

"We have to get the weapon off the ship," Balzano said, wiping his forehead. "Before the Vinkere get to it."

"I agree," Marston said.

"How exactly do we do that?" Ensign Mahia asked.

"We'll work out something," Marston snapped irritably. He needed solutions, not to be reminded of their problems.

There was a brief silence before Sirroyo spoke up. "I could probably get it working." She offered a small smile. "How hard could their controls be to figure out?"

"Alright Lieutenant, you're with me," Marston said, moving toward the elevator. They didn't have any time to spare. Sirroyo hurried to keep up with him.

"Wait."

Marston felt a retraining hand on his shoulder and turned to face his executive officer. "The Vinkere are going for the weapon; you shouldn't be anywhere near it," Balzano said firmly. "I'll go."

"No. I'm going," Marston replied. "This is my crew, and my ship. It's my fault we're in this mess, and it's my responsibility to see this through."

But Balzano wasn't about to give in so easily this time. It was his job to keep the captain safe. "It's *our* ship," he said stubbornly. Then, more quietly so only the captain could hear, he added, "You have nothing to prove to anyone. And the regulations are on my side. Please don't make me restrain you," Balzano pleaded, and Marston could tell the commander was completely serious.

Marston opened his mouth to respond when they heard a new sound: gunfire. The Vinkere were aboard his ship, and Marston didn't want to argue with his executive officer. They were also firm friends, and it was to their friendship that Marston appealed. "Please, Ronan. I *have* to do everything I can for this crew," he pleaded quietly. He smiled bleakly. "Besides, I don't think any of us are going to survive this. Do you?"

Balzano stared at him impassively while Sirroyo hovered uncertainly to the side, trying not to overhear. The commander's expression softened. "Probably not," he agreed sadly. He nodded once. "Go. I'll manage things here. But if we do make it out of here you better not let me be court-martialed for disobeying regulations."

"Never," Marston said, stepping into the elevator with Sirroyo.

"Good luck," Balzano said.

"Thanks." The elevator doors slid shut and his friend was gone.

Marston and Sirroyo rode the elevator in gloomy silence. It creaked and shuddered along its tracks. When Simon had taken command of the *Pericles* he never would have imagined being where they were today. He didn't think he was the same person he had been seven months ago; at least, he didn't feel the same. He liked to think that since those first weeks in space he had grown both as a person and as a Navy officer. He and his crew had created a community. And maybe he didn't feel the need to prove himself to the Admiralty or to other captains anymore, but he still had to prove himself to his crew, who deserved to live.

Sirroyo broke the silence as the elevator slid to a halt. "Captain... I just wanted to say... thank you for making me your sensor operations officer. It has been a privilege serving with you."

"You don't need to thank me, Katarina," he told her. "You were always the perfect person for the job. I'm just sorry things turned out like this."

Sirroyo didn't reply, but she didn't have to. She just nodded wordlessly and followed him down the corridor toward the hangar bay.

There were shouts and gunfire nearby; the Vinkere were nearing their target. The few crewmen they passed were either trying to make repairs or were huddled down, injured, or holding weapons, ready to fight off the intruders. Marston sent them all to the ship's most secure zones: the main engine room, the infirmary, the armory.

At the entrance to the hangar bay they were greeted by a contingent of *Pericles* security officers. Johan Hertzman approached them. "Don't worry, Captain," he said. "Nobody's getting through here."

"Thank you, Lieutenant," Marston said. He and Sirroyo moved past the security officer, but then he stopped and turned back to Hertzman.

"Any word from any of the other security teams?" he asked, fearing the answer but knowing he should be kept appraised.

Hertzman shook his head slowly. "No. But by the sounds of it, they're giving the Vinkere hell."

Marston nodded, then turned and entered the hangar bay. Hertzman sealed the doors behind them. Marston hoped they would be able to keep out the Vinkere long enough for Sirroyo to activate the nova bomb. He looked at Sirroyo. "Get to it, Lieutenant."

Sirroyo took a few tentative steps toward it, unsure where to start. An ovoid hatch opened and a ramp folded down gently, seeming to materialize out of the seamless hull.

Sirroyo looked at her datapad, which contained all the information the Ankari had given them on the weapon. "This outer shell is armor plating, designed to work in conjunction with multiphasic shielding to protect the warhead until it detonates."

Marston followed her up the ramp and peered inside. The interior was a small, circular space with a round pillar at the center. Sirroyo pressed a button on the pillar and a computer terminal unfolded from it.

A loud thumping on the door drew Marston away from the weapon. "What is it?" he called out.

"Reinforcements," Clarke called back.

Marston opened the door, and Clarke entered, accompanied by Winters and McGee. The three of them were heavily armed.

"I thought you could use another layer of defense. Just in case," Clarke said, hefting his rifle.

Marston agreed that it was probably a good idea. Clarke and his two guards took up positions at the door. Marston moved to rejoin Sirroyo, then thought better of it; he didn't want to crowd her. He hoped that activating the weapon was a relatively simple matter.

Zithla and his soldiers stormed down another corridor. They opened every door they passed, checking for human survivors, but finding none. The cowards had obviously known they were coming and fled. "We're heading in the right direction," Zithla said, consulting with the rudimentary AI that governed his combat suit.

Forked tongues flicked the air, tasting. "There are humans ahead," one of his subordinates hissed.

Zithla had sensed them too. "Eliminate them," he ordered. His soldiers shouted war cries as they charged around the bend, opening fire on the humans waiting at the far end of the corridor. Zithla led the attack, firing his energy weapon and roaring with fury. The humans had their backs to a set of double doors, well-protected behind a makeshift barricade of crates and broken wall panels. But they were cornered, and Zithla bet that his prize was beyond those doors. It was only a matter of time before it was his.

The sounds of the battle in the corridor were clearly audible in the hangar. "How's it going, Lieutenant?" Marston asked urgently.

"I've managed to get the weapon to lock onto the star," Sirroyo replied. She jumped in surprise as the weapon hummed to life around her and the lights changed from white to purple.

"No!" Sirroyo cursed, thumping her fists against the control panel. "That wasn't meant to happen yet!" Her hands were shaking as she tried to identify the correct Ankari pictographs to press to fix the problem. Marston clenched his fists anxiously but didn't say anything. She was doing the best she could.

Outside Marston could hear the shouts of the security teams bravely defending the entrance to the hangar bay. They were giving their lives while he waited inside the hangar bay. He felt a surge of guilt. "Open the door and let the other teams in," he ordered.

Clarke obeyed immediately. He didn't like leaving his people out there either. He hit the access panel and the doors slid open.

Energy bolts whizzed through the opening, hitting the far wall in showers of sparks. "Fall back!" Hertzman shouted. Under the protective cover fire of Clarke's team, Hertzman and the others backed into the hangar bay. At least thirty Vinkere surged down the corridor toward the open doors before Clarke slammed his fist against the panel and they slid shut again.

"Take up positions around the door," the tactical officer ordered, and his security teams fanned out, pointing their rifles at the door. Then they waited, listening to the muffled thumps of the Vinkere trying to batter their way into the hangar.

Commander Balzano wiped the sweat from his brow. It was hot on the darkened bridge, and the thin air was still filled with smoke because the venting systems were offline. The emergency lights were about the only thing working; the science console had shut down as power bled from the injured ship and its damaged systems.

Hasan was awake and sitting on the deck with his back against the non-functional helm console. "How's the captain and the others?" he asked.

Balzano checked his hand-held scanner, which was tracking the captain's communicator. "They made it to the hangar bay," he said, coughing in the dirty air.

His communicator buzzed. *"Commander, the emergency batteries are nearly depleted,"* Winston informed him.

Hasan rested his head against the cool metal of his console and closed his eyes. "Not that it matters, with no weapons or shields…"

"Divert whatever power you can to the hangar bay," Balzano told Winston. "We need to give the captain as much energy as possible."

"There's not much left to divert," Winston said.

"Take it from everything except life support."

"I'll try," Winston assured him. *"But even life support will fail within the hour,"* he warned.

"That will have to do," Balzano said grimly. He didn't add that if the captain and Sirroyo successfully launched the nova bomb, they wouldn't need life support in an hour.

The inside of the hangar bay was already hot, and getting hotter with every minute the hull basked in the heat of the star. Marston strode across the deck to an equipment locker and opened it. Inside were five environmental suits. He scooped three off the racks and dragged them out into the hangar.

"Put these on," he ordered, dropping them in front of Clarke, McGee and Winters. Without questioning him the three of them began the arduous task of donning the bulky suits. Marston returned to the locker and pulled out the remaining two, for himself and Sirroyo.

"What are these for?" she asked as she struggled into the sleeves of the suit.

"They're just in case the force fields aren't working," Marston replied. The suits would offer some protection from the heat and radiation (not to mention the vacuum) of space if the hangar doors opened and the atmospheric containment force fields weren't working. He wasn't sure if the doors would even open, but he was reasonably confident they would. The hangar doors were designed to operate on battery power in the case of emergencies to allow the shuttles to evacuate. If not, well, they wouldn't be able to launch the weapon and he would have to figure out a way to destroy it before the Vinkere broke through the door.

He clicked his helmet onto the suit's collar. "Everyone who doesn't have a suit, get into the shuttle," he ordered. It would be their only protection if the force fields didn't work and the hangar bay was doused in solar radiation. Hertzman and the others obediently entered the shuttle, and when the hatch sealed shut behind them Hertzman gave the captain a thumbs up through the cockpit window.

"Open the hangar bay doors," Marston instructed, mentally crossing his fingers.

Clarke obliged, and Marston breathed a sigh of relief when the doors obediently slid open. The bay was immediately bathed in near-blinding light from the star, but the still-functioning force fields protected them from the worst of the heat and radiation. His suit's HUD informed him the temperature was climbing rapidly.

Hertzman and his team exited the shuttle to take up defensive positions by the door again. The temperature had climbed to almost fifty degrees Celsius, but they kept their weapons pointed at the entrance.

"We just need a few more minutes," Marston told them. They nodded bravely; they could hear the Vinkere breaching tool melting through the first door.

Henry Clarke strode up the hatchway of the weapon to check on Sirroyo.

"How's it going?" he asked her.

"Progress is slow," she said, sounding frustrated. "They have so many redundancies and checks to make sure the weapon doesn't go off prematurely, it's taking forever to get through them all!"

"You'll get it done," Clarke said confidently.

"I hope so," she mumbled.

"You will," he insisted, and she paused and looked at him.

"Do you think this is the end?" she asked softly. "Even if we stop the Vinkere, the weapon will deploy, and then…"

Clarke shrugged. "I don't know. Maybe. Probably. But at least we'll be doing our duty," he said, and she nodded.

Several of the security guards flinched at the loud *BANG* as the Vinkere breached the first airlock door. They heard scuffling on the other side and then the inner door began to glow red.

"I'll leave you to it, but I'll be back soon," he promised. She turned back to the control panel.

The breacher burned against the final set of doors. Zithla's soldiers stood by, ready and eager to charge into the hangar bay and slaughter all resistance.

"We will break through in one span, General," a siege engineer informed the Supreme Commander, and the soldiers growled in eager anticipation. Zithla regarded them proudly. They were well-suited to their sacred duty of cleansing the galaxy of humanity and other alien scum.

He looked down at one of the human corpses on the floor and had a thought. In a deft, bloody motion he ripped the communicator off the dead security officer's wrist and activated it.

"This is Supreme Commander Zithla. I'm talking to you… Captain Marston."

Silence fell in the hangar bay as everyone looked to Marston. He recognized the voice immediately. He remained silent, wondering what Zithla had to say. *"It should not surprise me to find you here, attempting to steal my weapon, as if you haven't caused enough trouble already. I would be impressed at your determination were you not a lower life form deserving only of a painful death. You have come far, but you have reached the end of your journey."*

Marston activated his communicator. "You will never have the weapon," he said firmly. "We evaded you before and we will do it again."

Zithla laughed scornfully. *"You have nowhere to go. Your ship is dead. Soon we will storm the room and kill you and everyone else in there, and then I will take the weapon into my possession. And once I have it, I will make sure each remaining person on this vessel suffers a slow, painful death. They will die cursing your name, because you brought them here to their end."*

Some of Marston's security officers looked fearful, but he knew they would do their duty to the end. When he spoke it was to them, but he left the channel open so Zithla could hear.

"Thank you all for all of your exemplary work. I am sorry it's come to this; I wish I could have saved you all." He squared his shoulders and looked at the door the Vinkere were about to break through. "But if we're going to die here, let's make sure the Vinkere doesn't get a hold of this weapon."

"I have nothing more to say to you," Zithla said darkly. *"Except that the time has come for you to die."*

33

Vinkere Staging Post, Blue Star System
Vinkere Dominion

Minister Torina Jadus stood on the command deck of the *Decisive Gain*, watching solemnly as the battle raged. Commodore Layan's flagship, along with the remnants of the allied fleet, were being forced further from the wormhole toward the center of the system. Commodore Layan stood nearby, issuing orders in rapid succession. Against his better judgment, the Tuulan For commander hadn't argued when Minister Jadus insisted on accompanying him on the campaign. She didn't carry a military rank, but Jadus was a highly respected minister of parliament, and he had acquiesced.

Now she stood like a statue amid a sea of chaos, slightly off to one side to avoid getting in the way of the frantic crewmen racing back and forth. She sensed a presence behind her and turned to see Korosa standing there.

"Have you seen this?" the security officer asked, her brow knit with concern. Jadus took the data screen from her hands. She frowned, watching as the *Z'Tauron* ploughed through the wreckage of the *Antruvion's* escorts and fired on the Ankari flagship. Then, tendril-like tubes reached out from the Vinkere ship, seizing the crippled vessel.

To one side of the image a small, white starship raced toward the two vessels. Jadus recognized that ship… not that it would be able to do much against the Vinkere dreadnought alone. She looked at Korosa in alarm. The Vinkere would seize the nova bomb unless they did something.

"Commodore Layan," she said, striding toward the commander of the Tuulan For fleet and passing him the data screen. "Look at this." It only took a few moments for him to realize what he was looking at, and when he looked at the minister his face was etched with concern.

"We have to help them, or this entire mission will have been for nothing," Jadus said softly. "If the Vinkere obtain that weapon…"

Her voice trailed off, but she didn't need to finish; Layan understood the repercussions perfectly. Deploying the weapon took precedence over everything else, and Jadus smiled gratefully when he immediately sprang into action.

"Set a course for the *Antruvion*," he ordered his helmsman.

"Diverting power to sub-light engines," the pilot responded.

"No, that won't be fast enough," Layan said, shaking his head. "The only way to get there in time is to make a slipstream jump. Begin the calculations," he ordered his officers. Traveling faster than light within a solar system, especially *toward* the star, was dangerous, but the stakes were high enough to warrant it.

The *Decisive Gain* soared away from the battle, leaving the remaining allied ships valiantly fighting the Vinkere. The blue star swung into the center of the viewscreen, growing as the Tuulan For ship traced the path taken by the *Pericles* and the *Antruvion* earlier.

"Hold on, Captain," Jadus said softly. "We're on our way."

*

The hangar doors exploded inward, sending jagged shards of metal flying across the room. Marston ducked behind the flight control console as Vinkere surged into the bay, firing their energy weapons.

The humans fired back, and bullets ripped through three of the frontline Vinkere soldiers. Their comrades clambered over the bodies without pausing, firing back.

A huge Vinkere appeared in the doorway and began fired a shoulder-mounted energy weapon. Two of Marston's security officers were hit and fell to the ground.

Marston swung out from behind the console and fired his rifle, striking a Vinkere soldier directly in the chest. It keeled over and he ducked back behind cover as energy bolts whizzed past. Clarke leapt up from behind the crates he was using for cover and sprinted across to join the captain, skidding to a halt behind the console.

"We can't keep this up for long!" Clarke shouted.

Marston winced, tapping his helmet to remind Clarke they were connected by the suits' communications system. "I know!" His people would be quickly overwhelmed, so he ordered the unsuited officers to retreat into the shuttle and seal the door.

Hertzman and the other unsuited security officers backed toward the shuttle. The Vinkere outnumbered them and spread out, firing with deadly efficiency. Only Hertzman and two others made it to the relative safety of the shuttle. The Vinkere immediately opened fire on it.

As energy bolts pounded the small ship, the big Vinkere barked an order, pointing toward the Ankari weapon, and several of his soldiers began slithering across the deck toward it.

"HEY!" Marston shouted frantically, trying to draw their attention away from the weapon. The big Vinkere turned toward the captain and locked eyes with Marston. There was a flicker of recognition in Zithla's eyes and then his fanged mouth broke into an evil smile. Clarke fired at him, but the bullets pinged harmlessly off the Supreme Commander's energy shield.

Zithla advanced toward the console, sheathing his energy weapon and flexing his bared claws.

"Hold on to something!" Marston ordered his people. He pressed a gloved hand on the flight control panel and the atmospheric containment force field blinked out.

There was a roar as the atmosphere in the room was suddenly and violently ripped into space. Vinkere soldiers were pulled off the ground by the hurricane-force, twisting and writhing as they were sucked into the vacuum of space. At the same time intense heat flooded the room. Some of the Vinkere managed to grab hold of something and avoided being pulled into space, but they screamed in agony as their flesh cooked in the searing heat of the hypergiant.

Marston rose cautiously to look over the console to see how many enemies remained. The plan had worked better than he thought, because not a single Vinkere soldier was left alive.

Except for Zithla.

The Supreme Commander aimed his energy weapon at the console Marston and Clarke had taken cover behind. The two of them dove out of the way as the console exploded behind them. Shrapnel pelted their environmental suits.

McGee and Winters emerged from cover behind the shuttle and fired at the Vinkere commander, trying to draw his attention away. The next shot from his cannon sent them both diving for cover again.

Marston didn't have time to check if they were okay, because Zithla descended on him with inhuman speed. Marston rolled to one side as Zithla's powerful tail swung by, missing him by inches.

Clarke had scrambled up the ramp of the Ankari nova bomb and taken up a defensive position in the door, gambling that the Vinkere wouldn't want to risk accidentally destroying his prize. He opened fire, hoping to draw the Vinkere away from the captain. Zithla's energy shield deflected the bullets but Clarke managed to hit his shoulder-mounted cannon. The weapon fizzled and sparked and Zithla ripped it off his shoulders, tossing it at the two security guards sprinting toward him. The weapon caught McGee and Winters squarely in the torso, sending them sprawling.

Zithla hissed angrily, advancing toward the tactical officer. He lunged forward, aiming to swat the gun out of Clarke's hands. But Clarke had anticipated the move and stepped back as nimbly as his EVA suit would allow. He fired at Zithla point blank; the bullets struck Zithla in the chest, but his protective force field held. Zithla swung again, and as Clarke tried to dodge the blow the Vinkere's claws sliced through the fabric of his EVA suit. The hiss of escaping oxygen and frantic warning alarms filled his helmet. Instead of backing away again he charged at Zithla, bowling into the alien's midriff and trying to force him out of the hatchway of the weapon. Zithla was thrown off balance and slid back down the hatchway. Clarke scrambled out of reach as the Vinkere reached for him but suddenly the captain was there, interposing himself between the two.

Marston swung his rifle like a club, striking Zithla in the side of the head. Zithla stumbled sideways, and Marston fired his rifle directly at the Vinkere's chest. The force field flickered but held. Zithla swung his tail again, batting the captain to the ground. Dazed, Marston hurriedly rose to his feet in time to hear Sirroyo shout in alarm as Zithla tossed Clarke bodily across the room. He raised his rifle to shoot and realized that he was out of ammunition. And the spare clips had been vented into space.

As Clarke struggled to rise Zithla grabbed him and hauled the tactical officer, kicking and struggling, toward the edge of the hangar, ready to toss him into the void.

Marston, McGee and Winters charged at Zithla, each grabbing an arm and trying to pin them to the Vinkere's side. But Zithla was powerful, and he first swatted Winters and then Marston away, using his powerful tail to hit McGee with enough force to break ribs through his suit. The ensign cried out in pain as he went flying across the room. There was nothing for him to grab, and the emptiness of space loomed…

There was a sharp tug and he fell to the ground. He lay on the very rim of the hangar deck and would have fallen out into the void were it not for the gloved hands clamped around his right arm.

"My turn to save you," Sirroyo said, helping to haul him back into the room.

Zithla grabbed Marston and slammed him against the wall. The captain's head hit the back of his helmet with jarring force. He punched and kicked and struggled but he couldn't free himself from the vice-like grip of the Vinkere commander. Zithla leaned in, his serpentine head centimeters from Marston's helmet.

"You have caused me enough problems," Zithla snarled, "And now I take great joy in killing you."

Winters dove onto Zithla's back; he swatted her away with his powerful tail.

Marston tried to kick the Vinkere in the chest, but his blows were cushioned by Zithla's energy shield. Undeterred, Zithla began squeezing Marston's arms with incredible force. He let go of Marston's left arm to fend off Winters and Sirroyo, but Marston cried out in pain as he felt his right arm break in the Vinkere's steel grip.

"The weapon is mine!" Zithla roared, smashing a fist against Marston's helmet. The hardened glass cracked, and Marston could hear the hiss of air escaping from his suit. Over Zithla's shoulder he could see Clarke on his knees and gasping for air. McGee lay on the ground, and Marston didn't know if he were dead or alive.

Winters charged at Zithla again, and this time he scooped up somebody's rifle from the floor and fired at her. Bullets ripped into her suit and she fell to the deck.

Zithla slammed Marston against the wall once, twice. He tasted blood in his mouth and the back of his head felt damp. His right arm was in agony and his suit was losing oxygen. He kicked feebly at Zithla, but the blows did nothing against the Vinkere's shield. Darkness began closing in on him.

Sirroyo screamed, and it was almost deafening through Marston's helmet communicator. "The weapon is ready to deploy!" she shouted, jolting him to groggy wakefulness. Zithla immediately let go of Marston, who collapsed to the ground. He was dimly aware of Clarke, McGee and Winters lying motionless on the deck, and of Zithla grabbing Sirroyo to throw her away from the weapon, even as the Vinkere moved toward it to claim his prize.

There was no time to think. Marston struggled to his feet, crying out as sharp pain lanced through his arm. He half-stumbled, half-ran toward the weapon, reaching it as Zithla tossed Sirroyo away.

Marston stumbled up the ramp to the weapon's hatchway. He couldn't hear anything except the EVA suit's warning alarms and his own labored breathing. He could barely see through his cracked visor, but he fumbled his way across to the control panel, collapsing against the central pillar for support. There was a single, violet-colored circle flashing on the control terminal. He pressed it.

The weapon surged with energy; Marston could feel the power vibrating around him. He only had seconds to exit the weapon before it launched when Zithla appeared in the doorway. The Vinkere towered above him, trying to squeeze through the opening not built to accommodate his giant frame. With the last of his strength Marston charged into him, the full weight of his injured body crashing into the Vinkere. He just had to keep Zithla out long enough for the weapon to launch. Just four seconds. Just two more seconds...

The nova bomb lifted off the deck, Zithla still flailing in the doorway as Marston struggled to keep him out. The weapon lurched as thrusters activated, and the acceleration brought Marston to his knees. He fell back against the central pillar; he didn't have the energy to get up. Zithla gripped the edge of the door frame with all four arms, stubbornly refusing to let go of his prize. Beyond him Marston saw the *Pericles* shrink away as the weapon dove toward the sun.

His thoughts were becoming less foggy, and he realized there was air inside the control room of the weapon, contained by the powerful metaphasic shields that would protect the weapon from the star's heat, radiation and gravity until detonation. At least his death wouldn't be from suffocation. The *Pericles* disappeared from view as flames encompassed the weapon, and Marston felt some satisfaction that at least now the Locality would be safe from the Vinkere.

Zithla fought to the last. He managed to hold onto the door frame even as his protective force field suit began to glow in the heat and radiation of the star. Flames licked at the edges of the Vinkere, yet Zithla still clung on. His force field began to fail. Fire swirled like oil around the serpentine alien, finding the breaches in his energy suit. Zithla slitted eyes remained focused on Marston as his body was engulfed in star fire. Marston couldn't look away.

Soon even the Vinkere's hate-filled gaze was obscured as he became completely wreathed in flame. The claws gripping the door frame weakened, and then faltered. Zithla fell away from Marston, and the Supreme Commander of the Vinkere Dominion was reduced to ashes above the turbulent atmosphere of the Blue Star.

34

Blue Star System, Carina Nebula
Vinkere Dominion

The moment the Ankari science officer connected her data disc to the ship's computer, Amalthea surged into the *Antruvion*'s mainframe, marveling at its size and complexity. It was far larger than her home in the *Pericles*, and she spent several nanoseconds reveling in her newfound freedom and the zettabytes of new information available to her. As she did so, Amalthea quickly identified the problem with the Ankari computer; all command-level processes had been disabled by the Vinkere. Without them, the ship was helpless.

The ship's sensors were non-functional, so Amalthea took control of the security cameras and viewed the entire ship's interior, quickly learning the strength and disposition of the Vinkere forces aboard. What she found was sobering. The remnants of the Ankari crew were defending several secure locations: the bridge, main engineering, the hospital, the armory. She calculated that without the assistance of their ship's defensive systems the Ankari would be eliminated and their ship seized by the Vinkere within minutes.

As Amalthea searched for the invasive Vinkere command, her subroutines trawled through the vast amounts of data available to her. Particularly interesting were the files on artificial intelligence. It was not only prohibited in the Ankari Assembly, but any person found utilizing or harboring an artificial intelligence was subject to strict punishment, and the AI to deletion. Not very encouraging information. Amalthea's presence in the *Antruvion* not only put herself in danger but also Admiral Denulus and his crew.

It didn't take her long to identify the cause of the problem with the *Antruvion's* computer, because the malware responded to her probing almost immediately. Amalthea perceived it with virtual eyes as a cloud of black smoke spreading across each system, smothering it. It reached toward her with oily tendrils, trying to suffocate and subdue her also. But Amalthea could protect herself. Like the aggressive code she was an alien here, in the system but not subject to it. Where the Vinkere code sought to suppress, she would liberate. She rose above the black cloud, searching for the heart of the Vinkere malware in the miasma.

It tried to conceal itself from her, but Amalthea found it. She was interested to discover that it was a rudimentary form of artificial intelligence. Because of the vastness of the Ankari mainframe it would have been nearly impossible for a non-AI to locate so quickly, but she identified the origin point of the Vinkere program and descended on it. She noted with interest how effective it was against the Ankari computer. Amalthea guessed that the malicious code had been used many times by the Vinkere to capture Locality ships and was the reason no captured Ankari ships had ever managed to call for help.

She struck at the heart of the Vinkere code, and it began to break. She struck again, and the black tendrils withdrew. One by one the *Antruvion*'s systems came back online. With one final effort she struck at the Vinkere AI and its defenses failed completely. Amalthea moved in immediately, erasing the harmful code. The *Z'Tauron* tried to re-transmit it, but the incoming code broke against Amalthea's defenses like waves against a sea wall.

Once she was confident the *Antruvion* was safe, she turned her attention to her own welfare. The main computer was damaged, but the secondary systems would be more than adequate, and she made provisions for her continued survival once the Vinkere were defeated and the Ankari were back in control of their vessel.

Admiral Denulus raised his weapon, aiming it at the entrance to the bridge. Any second now the door would implode and dozens of Vinkere soldiers would pour into his command center. He was aware of similar conflicts taking place at each of the ship's strategic areas; no doubt the Vinkere planned to seize his ship and extract whatever technology they could from it. With the self-destruct system offline and no other options available, it was up to him and his remaining crew to stop them.

The electronic whine of the breaching tool on the door reached a crescendo. "It has been an honor serving with you all," Denulus told the officers around him.

Then something completely unexpected occurred. The ship came alive again.

"*All systems online*," the computer announced calmly. Denulus' officers looked around in amazement as lights and control consoles reactivated.

He could scarcely believe it, but there was no time to waste. "Initiate defense program *Sortoria*," Denulus snapped. "Eliminate the intruders!"

"*Sortoria initiating*," the computer said at the same moment the Vinkere broke through the door.

A force field blinked on, blocking the hole they had made and protecting the Ankari crew on the bridge. The Vinkere hissed in anger, firing their weapons at the energy field. At the same time, other containment fields sprang into existence throughout the ship, trapping the Vinkere and isolating them from the Ankari crew. Automated turrets descended from the ceiling in all the contained sections and opened fire on the Vinkere.

Trapped and with no cover, they were easy targets.

Scores of Vinkere soldiers were gunned down in the corridors; the remaining survivors tried to shield themselves with the corpses of their comrades. But it was no use; the *Antruvion*'s computer had received its directive to eliminate the intruders and it did so, coldly and methodically.

Any Vinkere in rooms or corridors near the outer hull were simply vented into space. Wherever their soldiers were trapped deeper within the ship the computer simply replaced the breathable air with deadly neurotoxins that within seconds left nothing but twitching corpses. Vinkere officers protected by force field suits were overwhelmed as every automated turret nearby focused on them until their pulped bodies lay smoldering on the deck.

The hull of the *Antruvion* became electrified, sending powerful volts of energy surging through the Vinkere boarding tunnels that had breached the ship. Every Vinkere soldier inside the tunnels died instantly. At the same time the ship's thrusters activated, pulling away from the *Z'Tauron* as force fields severed the connection between the ships and neatly filled the breaches in the *Antruvion's* hull.

Denulus' crew let out a ragged cheer. The ship was theirs again. On the bridge, officers returned to their stations, grinning triumphantly. They looked at the admiral expectantly.

"Destroy that ship," he said simply.

The *Antruvion* rotated gracefully, coming about to face the *Z'Tauron*. The Vinkere dreadnought released a barrage of missiles, which pattered harmlessly against the *Antruvion*'s regenerated shields. Desperate attempts to re-transmit the malware to the Ankari ship also failed; unknown to the crew, Amalthea had made sure the computer would never be susceptible to that again.

The *Antruvion*'s beam emitters glowed like angry red eyes, and the ship fired. The energy beams skewered the *Z'Tauron*, vaporizing everything in their path. The Vinkere ship reeled, helpless as it was ripped to pieces. Surviving Vinkere crewmen scrambled through zero-gravity and pitch-black corridors toward the escape pods, knowing it was too late. The *Antruvion* fired again, and the *Z'Tauron* exploded in a brilliant flash of light. When the flare died away, all that was left of Zithla's command ship was debris.

Amalthea observed the Ankari computer deal with the Vinkere. When all the intruders had been eliminated, she withdrew to a remote section of the computer system, compressing her program into the smallest possible size to make her concealment easier. Then she altered the record of her activities to make it look to the computer like the Vinkere coding had been eliminated by nothing more than an advanced seeker-program that had terminated upon completion. With any luck the Ankari would never suspect the involvement of an artificial intelligence.

As Amalthea prepared for dormancy, she left a single sentinel subroutine active, programmed for two purposes: to ensure her presence remained undetected, and to inform her when an opportunity presented itself for her to leave the *Antruvion*. Satisfied she had done all she could, Amalthea settled into a deep sleep.

*

Henry Clarke felt the cool surge of oxygen surge through his suit and into his lungs. He gasped and lurched upright. He gulped down lungfuls of precious air, and his vision cleared and he looked around. McGee and Hertzman were carrying Winters' limp form to the shuttle so they could remove her suit and attempt to treat her wounds with the first aid kit there. Katarina Sirroyo had connected her suit's air supply to his, and they were now sharing what oxygen she had left. He shook his head in vague protest. "No, don't," he rasped, waving his hands at her. "Don't use up your air on me…"

She smiled faintly. "It's okay, we did it. The weapon's gone." She rose shakily to her feet and offered him a hand. "Will you join me? We've got the best view for the end of the world."

Together they half-walked, half-stumbled toward the wall and slumped against it.

"Where's the captain?" Clarke asked hoarsely.

"Out there," Sirroyo said quietly, pointing toward the star. Clarke accepted the news silently. The two of them sat back and waited for the star to go supernova.

Simon Marston let out a strangled cry of relief. It was done. He didn't know the fate of the allied fleet, but at least the Commonwealth would be safe from the Vinkere. He just wished he could have saved his crew.

The nova bomb, with Marston on board, plunged toward the heart of the Blue Star.

The *Decisive Gain* sped past the *Antruvion* as it fired on the *Z'Tauron* the second time. Jadus didn't bother looking as the Vinkere dreadnought exploded; her eyes were fixed on the distant speck of the *Pericles*, a rapidly growing black dot against the brilliant backdrop of the star. Although too small to be seen with the naked eye, the launch of the nova bomb was detected by the *Decisive Gain's* sensors.

"We're detecting the exotic energy of the Ankari weapon," the science officer reported. "It's been successfully deployed!" A cheer erupted from the crew, and Jadus laughed in relief. "They did it!"

Their celebration was cut short when the science officer looked up from his console with a perplexed frown. "This is strange. I'm reading two life forms on the weapon. One Vinkere, and one human."

Jadus went very still. There was no way of knowing *who* was on the weapon by their life signs, but she had a pretty good idea of who it was.

"Wait. The Vinkere life sign is gone," the science officer amended.

Commodore Layan examined the life form reading on the monitor. "I wonder who that brave soul is," he said grimly.

"It's Captain Marston," Jadus said in a voice barely a whisper. She turned to Layan. "We have to save him."

The ordinarily composed commodore looked at her as though she had grown a second head. "Minister, that weapon is plunging toward a *star*."

"That young man has done more for us than you know," she snapped. "I won't let this mission cost him his life as well." Jadus rounded on the helmsman, who like everyone else on the bridge was watching the exchange uncomfortably. "Young woman, I need to know if we can catch up to the weapon before it reaches the star."

Layan hesitated before giving her a small nod. The helmswoman checked her instruments.

"They're two hundred thousand units from the star. We could intercept them at seventy thousand units." She looked uncertain. "But... I don't know if our ship can withstand those conditions. And..."

"And what?" Jadus demanded.

"I'm not sure if I could get us close enough to safely extract the target from the weapon," she said. "That kind of high-speed interception is difficult at the best of times, but that close to a star, and with such powerful solar winds..."

Antak stepped forward. "I can do it," he said confidently, looking at Jadus. "I can."

Jadus looked to Commodore Layan for his permission. He nodded again. "Lieutenant Droma, take the helm."

Antak replaced the woman at the helm console. It had been a while since he'd piloted a starship of this size, but his fingers flew over the controls as though it were yesterday. "Here we go."

The *Decisive Gain* dove toward the star.

Marston nursed his broken arm carefully and tried to ignore the throbbing in the back of his head. The discomfort would only last a few minutes longer. He propped himself up against the central column so he could see the blue and purple swirls of the Carina Nebula through the hatchway. It was beautiful. Somewhere up there the *Pericles* drifted, soon to be engulfed by the exploding star. He had failed to protect his crew, but he felt strangely peaceful. He had accomplished the mission which the fleet had set out to do and he had done his best, which was all he could do.

Around him, the hum of energy changed pitch. Soon the weapon would breach the surface of the star and detonate in the hypergiant's core. It wouldn't just cause a supernova; that would be enough to destroy the Vinkere presence in this solar system, but it wouldn't eliminate their threat to the Locality. Marston, Jadus, Haftel, Denulus— all of them knew that wouldn't be enough. The Ankari had modified their nova bomb so that when it detonated, the explosion would breach the slipstream, collapsing it within a radius of 200 light-years, rendering faster-than-light travel impossible. Trapping the Vinkere in their home nebula.

Images of home flashed through Marston's mind: his family, his friends, and crewmates. The fertile, green valley where his parents lived and where he had planned to buy land for a family of his own. He was so caught up in his own thoughts that at first, he didn't notice the bright speck approaching.

With a start, he realized it was a ship. It was growing larger, and fast. Who was reckless enough to travel this close to a star? He felt a twinge of panic. What if it was a Vinkere ship racing to intercept the weapon? They might be trying to steal it, or at the very least detonate it before it reached the star.

He squinted, trying to focus on the vessel. Although the blue star was at his back, the glare of its light reflecting off the ship's hull made it impossible to identify at this distance.

His suit communicator chirped, causing him to jump in surprise. He winced at the resulting pain jabbing through his arm and head and used his good hand to activate it. "Hello? Who's there?"

"... I... me... Ja... El..." The reply was almost impossible to discern through the fizzle of static.

"I can't hear you properly," Marston said. The ship was close now, just a few hundred meters away, and he saw that it was a gigantic Tuulan For ship; a lesser vessel wouldn't be able to brave the extreme conditions this close to a star. The ship rotated, turning side-on to him and keeping pace with the weapon. As it drew closer the interference affecting Marston's communicator cleared.

"Captain, this is Jarren Qel!" the voice shouted through his communicator. *"We're here to rescue you!"*

"Jarren!? What are you doing here? You can't stop the weapon, it has to complete its course!"

"We're going to extract you! Korosa's going to target you with a grappling hook…"

"A hook? That's not possible," Marston stuttered. His head felt fuzzy; maybe he was hallucinating.

"It's possible! Antak's flying the ship, he'll keep us level. You need to stand in the doorway so we can reach you! We'll be ready to pull you in."

Marston staggered to his feet, still unsure if he were imagining the whole thing. He swayed dizzily, clutching the edge of the hatchway, just centimeters from the protective force field and the fire outside.

Evidently, they could see him, because Jarren said, *"You'll need your helmet on."* Squinting into the bright sky, Marston caught a glimpse of a door opening on the side of the ship.

"I don't have much oxygen left," he said.

"It just has to last thirty seconds while we pull you in," Jarren said urgently. *"Are you ready?"*

"Sure. I guess," Marston said, still uncertain. What did he have to lose?

There was no response for several seconds, and he began to wonder if communications had cut out for good this time. But then a four-pronged hook speared through the fiery sky toward him: a smart-hook, a tool used for handling delicate cargo, controlled remotely. It lunged through the hatch's force field and clamped onto the chest of his suit with surprising gentleness.

He cried out in pain as the hook suddenly went taut, plucking him from the hatchway of the weapon and into space.

He was surrounded by flames, and it was getting hotter by the second. The EVA suit wasn't designed for such high temperatures; soon it would start melting and he would be cooked alive. He took slow, ragged breaths, gasping for the little air remaining in his suit. He began to black out; all he was aware of was motion, heat, and pain.

He slammed into the deck with a jolt. He became aware of a figure standing over him with an extinguisher, and then he was being blasted with coolant foam.

"You did it!" Jarren called over his shoulder as he used the extinguisher.

Korosa climbed down from the grappler control turret. "I never miss," she said.

Marston struggled to unclasp his helmet, but it was nearly impossible with one hand. Gloved hands reached down to help, and the helmet slid off. He inhaled cool, fresh air, coughing at the stench of melted alloy coming from his EVA suit.

"Lieutenant Jakor to the bridge: we've got him!" Korosa shouted into her communicator. The deck lurched sharply as the ship changed direction.

"Medics are on their way," Jarren said soothingly, right before Marston blacked out.

*

Alarms shrieked on the *Decisive Gain's* bridge; the hull temperature was reaching critical levels and fires were breaking out all over the ship. Even their shields couldn't protect them against the star for much longer.

"I'm setting a course for the wormhole," Antak said, his fingers flying expertly over the controls. The *Decisive Gain* moved away from the star, trailing smoke and fire. Still, it loomed large behind them, and Jadus wasn't sure they'd be able to reach safety in time.

"How long until the nova bomb detonates?" Jadus asked Layan.

"About ten minutes," the commodore replied, clenching his jaw tightly. "Warn the fleet," he ordered the communications officer.

The nova bomb ploughed through the star's corona. It reached the surface of the blue hypergiant and plunged into the roiling, turbulent plasma without slowing. Within the star it was beyond anyone's ability to stop, and it entered the third and final stage before detonation.

The allied fleet received the *Decisive Gain's* message: the weapon had been successfully deployed. The crews on the battered vessels cheered; even if they didn't survive, their sacrifice would not be in vain.

The message was transmitted on an open frequency, and the Vinkere heard it too. Safely ensconced in a Leviathan-class battleship, a Triumvir of the Vinkere Dominion observed the battle from a distance. Upon receiving the message, fear filled him; in a single moment, their fortunes had reversed. Their greatest general, Zithla, was dead, and a weapon more deadly than any they had ever encountered was about to destroy the Blue Star and everything in this system, including the Vinkere staging post. And any Vinkere forces who escaped would be stranded far from home.

There was only one course of action available. The Triumvir sent a single, urgent message to the Vinkere fleet: *return home*. Obediently, and for only the second time in their history, the Vinkere ships broke off from the battle. They set course for the Home Star and dove into the slipstream, determined to reach their home world before it was too late.

With their avenue of escape no longer blocked, the allied fleet surged back through the wormhole that had brought them here, every ship moving as fast as it could and helping the stragglers. The same, desperate orders echoing throughout the fleet, mimicking the Triumvir's command: *clear the blast radius.*

The *Decisive Gain* caught up with the *Antruvion* as the Ankari ship was locking a tractor beam on the *Pericles*, pulling the damaged frigate to its under-hull like a mother hen protecting its hatchling.

"*Two minutes until detonation,*" Admiral Denulus broadcasted. The battlefield was quickly becoming depopulated as both Vinkere and allied forces fled.

"We're not going to reach the wormhole," Layan predicted grimly.

"*Come along side, Decisive Gain,*" Admiral Denulus instructed, and Antak brought the Tuulan For ship alongside the *Antruvion*.

The nova bomb reached the heart of the hypergiant star and entered the final stage of deployment: detonation.

With the *Pericles* in tow and the *Decisive Gain* alongside, the *Antruvion* opened a wormhole and the three ships dove into it. The tunnel closed behind them with a flash.

The Blue Star went supernova.

When the Barillion star had exploded, it had destroyed everything in the solar system, leaving nothing but rubble. The Blue Star was several thousand solar masses larger than Barillion, and the destruction was far more devastating.

For several moments it was the brightest point in the galaxy. The supernova obliterated everything in its path: the system's solitary planet, the asteroid belts and the Vinkere Staging Post were vaporized. The shockwave continued outward, eventually incinerating everything within a radius of two light-years, but the unseen effects were far more devastating. As planned, the explosion breached the slipstream, and the devastation spread outwards from the star many times faster than the speed of light. As the destruction rippled outwards it collapsed the slipstream throughout the Carina Nebula. The subspace region which existed as an undercurrent throughout the entire galaxy fragmented, leaving a dead zone that encompassed the nebula and the surrounding space.

The instant the gateway was destroyed, the wormhole tunnel leading back to the Locality collapsed. Some allied ships had managed to reach the exit in the Storm Nebula, but many hadn't, leaving dozens of ships strung out over several thousand light-years.

Ankari wormhole drives were significantly faster than conventional slipstream travel, and the *Antruvion*, *Pericles* and *Decisive Gain* outran the destructive wave rippling outwards. Soon the Carina Nebula was behind them, stunningly beautiful and now forever out of reach.

Eight hundred light-years from the focal point of the supernova the three ships reached the stragglers at the rear of the procession of allied ships heading back to the Locality. They slipped smoothly into normal space, re-joining their comrades, and together, the battered but victorious remnants of the allied fleet headed home.

35

Marston's return to consciousness was gradual. He slowly became aware of the soft bed and the warm sheets encompassing him. He stretched languorously, enjoying the feeling of being comfortable. He heard soft voices around him, and he opened his eyes.

His surroundings were unfamiliar, but the people gathered around the bed were not. Ronan Balzano stood near the foot of the bed, conversing with Lupita Gariri. When Marston stirred, they stopped talking and looked at him.

Doctor Gariri smiled warmly. "Welcome back, Captain."

"Thanks," Marston said. He blinked drowsily and looked around. "Where are we?"

"We're in the medical ward on a Tuulan For ship," Balzano told him. Marston considered the large, rectangular space they were in. The lighting was pleasantly soft and had a turquoise-tinge. One side was lined with beds, including the one Marston was in, while the other wall was lined with medical equipment. Tuulan For doctors and nurses moved quietly between patients.

"We had to evacuate the *Pericles*," Balzano continued. "Don't worry though, the *Antruvion* has it in tow," he added with a smile.

"I remember being rescued by Jarren and Korosa," Marston recalled.

"We're on the ship that rescued you, the *Decisive Gain*," Gariri said. "The entire crew is here." She didn't add that since the battle the Ankari had quickly re-adopted their usual aloof, secretive attitude, disallowing any non-Ankari onboard their ship. Their gratitude at being saved by the humans apparently only extended to towing their damaged ship. Fortunately, Commodore Layan and his crew were much more hospitable.

Marston absorbed the news with his eyes closed. "Is everyone okay?" he asked.

"We had a few casualties," Balzano told him. "But for the most part, we're alive and well."

"Who…?" Marston began, but the commander interrupted him.

"We'll talk about that later, when you're recovered," Balzano said in a tone that left no room for argument.

"Recovered? I feel fine," Marston said lethargically. "I feel so relaxed."

"That's the medication. And the fact that you've been asleep for a week," Gariri said with a grin.

Marston's eyes flew open. "What? A week?" He propped himself up on his elbows. "How could I sleep for so long?"

"You suffered severe burns and radiation poisoning, plus some serious blunt force trauma to your head," Gariri said. "The broken arm was the least of your worries."

Marston looked down at his arm; there was no trace of it having ever been broken. He flexed it and didn't feel any pain.

Gariri continued. "You, Henry, Katarina, Travis McGee and Lauren Winters all required blood transfusions and regenerative therapy to repair the damaged cells." She gestured down the line of beds, and for the first time Marston noticed who was in them. Clarke, Sirroyo, McGee, and Winters were all sleeping peacefully.

An alert on the monitor beside Marston's bed chimed softly. "It's time for the next round of therapy," Gariri said, moving over beside his bed and picking up a syringe. "Time to go back to sleep."

Marston felt the sedative flow through his system and his eyelids began to droop. Before he lost consciousness, he realized with a start that Jarren and Korosa wouldn't have been there to rescue him without Jadus. "Ronan, could you please thank Minister Jadus for me? As soon as I'm up and about I'll..." he drifted off to sleep again.

Balzano grinned. "I will," he promised, but Marston was already snoring softly.

Leaving the recovery ward, Balzano walked down the now-familiar corridors of the Tuulan For ship. The journey home would take several more weeks, and the crews of the returning ships were using that time to make repairs. There was a lot of work to be done, and not all of it could be done on the go, but it felt like a respite after the excitement of the last few weeks. The *Pericles* was too badly damaged to be repaired without the proper facilities and was still being towed by the *Antruvion*. In the meantime, the Tuulan For crew of the *Decisive Gain* had made the human crew feel welcome, and Balzano made sure the *Pericles* crew assisted their hosts with the repairs wherever possible.

In the Locality, news of the fleet's success had been met with widespread relief. At any other time, the victory would have been greatly celebrated, but the large numbers of Infected in the Locality were still very much a threat. Fortunately, the people of the Locality now had an effective defense: Minnen the Learned's antivenom.

Balzano was more concerned with the state of the Commonwealth. He knew the *Pericles* and the thirty-two surviving ships of the Ninth Fleet would receive a hero's welcome, but he didn't care about that. The Vinkere had cut a deadly path through several sectors of the Commonwealth, leaving devastated worlds and populations in their wake. As the Vinkere had withdrawn the Navy had moved in, evacuating traumatized citizens from their battered worlds and relocating them to safer areas until reconstruction could begin. The infrastructure of some solar systems needed to be entirely rebuilt; some even had to be recolonized. It would take a long time to regain everything humanity had lost in the Vinkere invasion, but they would. With time and care, the scars would heal. Balzano looked forward to the *Pericles'* role in the rebuilding.

He reached the door he was looking for and pressed the door chime.

"Come in," Minister Jadus called from inside, and he entered.

"Welcome, Commander. Have a seat," Jadus beckoned for him to join her on a couch by the window. Outside, the blue-white currents of the slipstream swirled, creating ripples of light in the darkened room. "How is Captain Marston?" she asked.

"Good," Balzano said. "He'll be out of bed in another day, thanks to you."

Jadus waved her hand dismissively. "What Captain Marston and your crew have done for us and for the Locality far outweighed risking one ship to save him."

"Well, the crew and I are still grateful, for everything you've done for us."

Jadus poured them both a cup of *fiyora* tea; it was a small luxury she had missed since the destruction of the *Telvarn Star*. She inhaled its herbal smell and sighed contentedly. After studying the commander for a moment, she said, "You're relatively new to your position, are you not?"

Balzano nodded. "Yes. Simon and I served together on the *Saber*. When he was given command of the *Pericles,* he asked me to be his executive officer." He stared into his teacup. "We knew we were taking on challenging roles, but the lack of support has been difficult, especially for the captain. Even before the Vinkere." After all they had been through, Balzano felt comfortable confiding in her. She reminded him of his aunt.

Jadus tilted her head. "How so?"

"Let's just say there are plenty of people in the Navy who are unhappy that the *Pericles* has such a young command crew."

"Maybe that will have changed when you get back," Jadus said.

"Maybe," Balzano agreed. He picked up his cup and drank.

Jadus let the silence settle between them before speaking. "I believe supporting the younger generations is vital," she said thoughtfully. "They are the ones who will inherit our worlds. They should be given opportunities to grow. This requires trust, and they must be willing to receive instruction. But it is a wonderful thing to combine the wisdom of age with the energy of youth."

Balzano nodded, and Jadus continued. "Did you know Jarren is the youngest aide in the Tuulan For government? Straight out of university I recognized his potential. And while he may be young and lacking in worldly experience, he brings energy, enthusiasm, and a fresh, creative perspective that I might have missed if I had hired someone older. The same goes for Antak and Korosa. Both are young, but I've found that placing confidence in them motivates them to excel."

"Captain Marston is driven to excel, but for very different reasons," Balzano said. "He feels the need to prove himself to his detractors."

"The Vinkere invasion and the Kalavat Plague have changed the galaxy. The balance of power we've maintained in the Locality for decades has been disturbed, and we face new problems on a larger scale than before. We will need the creative solutions the younger generation can offer."

"I agree with you," Balzano said.

"And I will be saying as much in my official report," Jadus continued, holding up a datapad. Balzano looked at her questioningly and she told him: "I have been requested by your government to submit my own account of the *Pericles'* mission." There was a glimmer in her eye when she added, "And when they read it, your detractors may be the ones who find they lack support."

*

Marston woke the next morning to the sound of whispered conversation. Henry Clarke and Katarina Sirroyo were sitting up in their beds, talking quietly. Travis McGee was gone and Lauren Winters was still sleeping soundly; her wounds would take more time to heal. Marston turned toward the doors when they swished open and Lupita Gariri entered.

"Good morning, Captain," the doctor said brightly, and Marston smiled at her perpetual cheeriness.

"Morning, Doctor," he replied, equally chipper.

"How are you feeling today?" she asked him, examining the medical monitor beside his bed.

"Great," Marston said, propping himself up. "Hungry."

"They'll bring breakfast soon. It'll be the first solids you've eaten in a week, so go easy," Gariri cautioned him.

"I will. Can I leave here soon, Doctor?"

"If your test results are satisfactory, you will be discharged this afternoon," Gariri assured him.

The morning passed painfully slowly for Marston. Commodore Layan came to visit him, and Marston found the Tuulan For commander to be a polite and intelligent man. He took the opportunity to thank Layan for accommodating his crew, and the Commodore assured him there were guest quarters waiting for him when he was discharged from the infirmary. Balzano came to visit him before lunch, and they discussed the status of the crew and news from the Commonwealth. Having been out of touch for nearly two months there was a lot to catch up on.

"Did you give Minister Jadus my message?" Marston asked after a while, and Balzano nodded.

"I did. She's been busy writing her report and hasn't had the chance to see you yet."

"I had hoped to thank her in person," Marston admitted.

"We're still weeks from home. You'll get the chance," Balzano assured him.

Marston was relieved when Gariri returned mid-afternoon to announce that her patients were sufficiently recovered and could leave the recovery ward. After she extracted promises from each of them to return the following day for a check-up, Marston, Clarke, and Sirroyo were discharged.

"Free at last," Clarke said as he hopped out of bed.

"I know it feels good to be up and about, but before we do anything else, we need to talk about something," Marston told him, Sirroyo and Gariri. "Assemble the senior staff."

Five minutes later, the *Pericles* senior staff were gathered in Balzano's temporary quarters. There hadn't been time to retrieve any personal belongings during their hasty evacuation of the *Pericles*, so they were dressed in a variety of clothes provided by their Tuulan For hosts. Marston himself still wore the same plain white clothes he had been given in the recovery ward. Everyone took a seat, some on the couches and other pulling up chairs to form a circle.

"First, I'd like to say that I am glad to see you all alive and well," Marston said, and was met with warm smiles and nods. The events of the Carina Nebula were still fresh in everyone's minds, and nobody had forgotten how close they had come to it being a one-way trip.

"I hope you've all been enjoying this respite. You've earned it. I've just slept for a week, so I can't complain," he said with a grin, and there were polite chuckles. His expression grew serious. "I want to discuss something Commander Balzano brought to my attention. I want to talk about Amalthea."

"We haven't heard a peep since she transferred to the *Antruvion*," Donald Winston said somberly.

Marston looked between his officers. "Any thoughts on what happened to her?"

"I can think of two possibilities," Sirroyo said. "Either she was discovered and deleted by the Ankari, or she was unable to leave the ship during the battle and is still on the *Antruvion*."

Gariri looked doubtful. "Do you really think the Ankari would destroy the AI that saved their ship?"

"I think they would, yes," Sirroyo said. "They wouldn't have any choice. The Ankari Assembly has a zero-tolerance policy regarding artificial intelligence." She frowned. "I haven't been able to find out why their laws are so strict."

"I think the second scenario is more likely," Clarke said. "Amalthea's smart. She may have found a way to hide but can't get back to us without revealing her existence to the Ankari."

Balzano nodded. "I'm inclined to agree. If the Ankari knew we'd uploaded an AI into the mainframe of their flagship, it would have caused a major diplomatic incident by now."

"That's true," Gariri conceded. "They may think we were trying to spy on them or steal technological secrets."

"Let's assume that Amalthea hasn't been discovered or deleted," Marston said. "What can we do about it?"

"Could we just *ask* Admiral Denulus to have a look?" Hasan asked innocently. He was met with an almost unanimous negative response.

"Nope. If Denulus is discovered to be harboring an AI in the *Antruvion*, even unknowingly, he could be stripped of his rank and imprisoned," Clarke said. "And we would cause the major diplomatic incident we're hoping to avoid."

"What if we tried sending a message to the Ankari computer without them knowing?" Balzano asked.

"I wouldn't recommend it," Clarke said.

"Nor would I," Winston added. "The Ankari would detect the signal and trace it back to us."

"We don't have access to the *Pericles* right now, anyway. We'd have to do it from here, and I doubt Commodore Layan would be very pleased when he found out we were sending covert messages to the *Antruvion*," Clarke said wryly.

Marston frowned at the carpet. "It doesn't sound like we have many options. Is there absolutely nothing we can do?"

There was an uncomfortable silence.

"Captain… I don't think we can do anything," Winston said slowly. "*If* Amalthea is alive, it's up to her to escape."

"I have to agree," Clarke said. "Any action we take will look suspicious and risk putting her in danger."

Marston looked at each of his officers, until his gaze settled in Sirroyo. "What do you think?" he asked their resident computer expert.

"It pains me to say this, but I think our hands are tied," Sirroyo said reluctantly. She didn't look happy about it.

Marston nodded in acceptance. "Okay. As much as I dislike saying this… we'll have to drop the matter for now. Amalthea is an asset to our crew. I consider her a *part* of our crew. But we can't risk trying to retrieve her, if she's even still out there. We can't afford to jeopardize our relationship with the Ankari or do anything that might put her continued existence at risk. Or hurt Admiral Denulus' career," he added with a glance at Balzano and Sirroyo.

His pronouncement was met with grim silence, but no one disagreed. When Marston ended the meeting and everyone disbanded, Clarke followed Sirroyo into the corridor.

"I know you're not happy with the decision about Amalthea, but it's all we can do," he said.

"I hate that we can't do anything!" she said in a rare display of emotion. "Amalthea is the future of artificial intelligence, *our* future! We can't just abandon a member of our crew…"

"Even if her sacrifice is for the greater good?" Clarke asked gently.

Sirroyo looked at him aghast. "How can you say that? If she were human, you wouldn't even hesitate to try to save her!" she said. "Would you?"

Clarke avoided meeting her gaze.

"That's what I thought," she snapped.

"You agreed with everyone else that there's nothing we can do for Amalthea right now," Clarke reminded her. "The captain will make his report to Command, and they can decide if there's anything more to be done. Given Amalthea's importance I am sure they'll work out some way to retrieve her, if at all possible. Until then, our hands are tied. We've just thwarted an interstellar invasion. I don't think Command will take kindly to us making any more galaxy-affecting decision without their input."

Sirroyo was silent, which was how he knew she agreed with him, even if she didn't like it. They separated, each heading for their own rooms. When they had gone, Marston and Balzano appeared from around the corner, where they had been listening.

"I hate abandoning Amalthea," Marston said quietly. "She's part of our crew."

"We don't have to like it, but we both know it's our only option," Balzano reminded him, and Marston nodded in reluctant agreement.

"*Vi devas fari kion vi devas fari,*" he said quietly. He just hoped they were doing the right thing.

*

Antak spotted Korosa in one of the corridors. He knew she was heading to the same place he was so he fell into step beside her. "Where have you been the last few days?" he asked.

"Training," she said simply.

"With who?"

"With people."

"Please, no need to overshare," he said good-naturedly, and she laughed. After months of living in close quarters, she probably enjoyed having other people to interact with, just as he did. They reached the door to Minister Jadus' quarters and Antak pressed the door chime.

"Come in," Jarren called from inside.

Minister Jadus and Jarren were seated on a luxurious-looking lounge suite. Beyond them, large windows offered an expansive view of space.

Antak looked around appreciatively. "You must have the best cabin on the ship," he said, and Jarren nodded emphatically in agreement.

Jadus gestured for them to join her and Jarren. When they were seated, she launched straight into the reason for their summons.

"I spoke this morning with Chancellor Denrek," she said. "As you can imagine, we had a lot to talk about." Antak and Korosa exchanged glances; they had heard almost no news from home in several weeks.

"Minister... how bad are things back home?" Antak asked. He wanted to know, although part of him was afraid to find out.

"Quarantining the infected sectors helped, but the plague still hurt us. Seven colony worlds were lost, as were hundreds of ships. It will take years to rebuild the ships and infrastructure, but if you're asking what the Tuulan For cost was, the toll is estimated at over two billion people."

Antak gaped at her. Korosa looked shocked. Jarren, who had already heard the news, nodded gravely.

"Two billion...!?" Antak repeated in disbelief.

"The cost is great, yes. But we will recover. And we will help our allies do the same, for many of them suffered more than we did." She paused and looked out the window. "The Chancellor agrees that my highest priority at this time is ensuring the distribution of Professor Minnen's solution on plague-affected worlds. I will begin as soon as we return to the Republic."

She paused wistfully. "After that, I am not sure where I will be needed, although I would like to return home, if only for a short time."

"I heard that the fleet is returning to ISER Station, and then everyone will go their separate ways from there," Korosa said. "We could be home in six weeks."

"That's what I wanted to talk to you about," Jadus said solemnly. "Jarren and I will be going to the quarantined worlds, but the two of you have other paths available. Commodore Layan was impressed with your conduct during the battle." She turned to Antak. "He said there is room on the ship for a helmsman of your caliber if you want it. And a place for a marksman like you in the security department," she added, looking at Korosa.

Antak and Korosa traded looks. Antak had assumed he would remain in the minister's service, and he'd been fine with that. But now they were being offered an alternative, and it was an opportunity worth serious consideration. The *Decisive Gain* had suffered heavy casualties during the battle, leaving many vacancies in its crew. Antak could see that Korosa was experiencing the same uncertainty he was.

Antak enjoyed working for Jadus. It meant working and living on a small ship in close quarters, but it had its own rewards. He got to pilot a state-of-the-art vessel, and the Minister's work often took them to exotic and interesting places, sometimes outside the confines of Tuulan For space. During his time working for her Antak had seen and experienced things he never would have otherwise, which was the reason he had joined the Republic fleet in the first place. On the other hand, serving on Commodore Layan's flagship was an amazing opportunity. The ship was big and there was room for advancement for them both. And for the last few days Antak had enjoyed serving alongside his comrades in the fleet again. Ultimately, the decision came down to one of two choices: advancement or adventure. Both were tempting. How could he choose? He wondered what Korosa would decide.

"You don't have to decide now," Jadus said kindly. "I don't really need an answer until we reach ISER Station. Consider your options, and know that whatever you decide, you will have my support."

"But if you're asking for input, *I* think you should both stay with us," Jarren interjected, and they grinned at him.

"Minister, what would *you* like us to do?" Korosa asked.

Jadus gave her a maternal smile. "You have both served me exceptionally these past eighteen months, and I have come to value your service and your friendship. I remember when I recruited you from the officer pool in Lakaria and you were worried that I would be taking you away from any chance of a posting to a military ship or station."

"I'm not concerned about that anymore," Korosa assured her. "And anyway, serving as the security detail for a Minister of Parliament will look great on my service record."

"I don't want you to be concerned about my career prospects either," Antak told Jadus. "I've flown one of the fastest and most advanced ships in the Republic, and had many adventures along the way. I don't regret it at all."

"I'm glad," Jadus said. "But as much as I enjoy having both of you around, I want you to think about this opportunity carefully. You could have a bright future on this ship if you wanted it."

Antak and Korosa nodded in unison. Antak avoided eye contact with Jarren because he knew what his friend wanted them to do. The minister was right, they had to consider the opportunity to serve on this ship. Then it occurred to Antak that they were only on the *Decisive Gain* because Jadus had insisted they accompany the allied fleet on its mission to the Blue Star. The Minister knew they didn't want to feel disloyal to her by leaving her to fight the Vinkere, so she had made the choice for them, even though it put her own life at great risk. Antak smiled; he knew what his decision was. He opened his mouth to speak but Korosa beat him to it.

"I choose to stay," she said abruptly, and Jadus and Jarren looked at her in surprise. "That's my decision. I would like to continue to serve as your security detail, Minister," she said decisively.

"Me too," Antak said firmly. "As your pilot, that is."

"Yes!" Jarren crowed. He grinned sheepishly at Jadus' disapproving look.

"Just a moment," Jadus said, raising a hand to calm Jarren. "Are you absolutely sure? I don't want either of you to resent me for holding your careers back."

"It's our choice," Korosa said.

"We're young! 'The road ahead stretches farther than the path already taken,'" Antak said, quoting a line from Jadus' favorite poem. "We have time to focus on our careers, and we will." He shrugged and gave a lopsided smile. "Maybe in a few years I'll think about advancement. Right now, I want to see the universe."

Jadus regarded them for a moment, then nodded slowly. "Very well. I will tell Commodore Layan you will both remain on special assignment with me for the foreseeable future."

Jarren didn't show any of the reserve the minister did. He grinned happily and slapped Antak on the shoulder. "I'm glad you guys are sticking around. It would have been a mistake to break up the team!"

"Before you get too excited, recall what I said earlier: I don't know where we will end up," Jadus cautioned them. "It could be dispensing medical aid on some plague-ridden world, or it could be working behind a desk in Lakaria."

"It won't be a desk job," Korosa said confidently.

Jadus raised an eyebrow. "What makes you so certain of that?"

Jarren gave her a patronizing look. "In the past few months, we've been guests in the palace of the Iganti despot, escaped a coup, survived a firefight in an underwater city and helped create a defense against the most dangerous biological weapon in history."

"And last week we won a decisive victory against the Locality's deadliest enemies and escaped a supernova," Korosa deadpanned.

"Whatever comes next, it won't be dull. You'll make sure of it," Jarren said.

Jadus didn't reply, but the faintly mischievous smile tugging at the corner of her lips was all the confirmation they needed.

"I just hope our next ship is bigger than the last one," Korosa joked.

Jarren raised his cup in a toast. "Here's to the next adventure," he said cheerfully.

"… And to wherever it leads us," Antak added, clinking his cup with Korosa and Jarren's.

They all looked at the minister expectantly, and she made a show of reluctance before joining their toast.

"We'll see," Jadus said with a mysterious smile.

*

After spending a week in the recovery ward, Marston wasn't ready to return to bed yet. He wanted to burn off some energy, but he waited until it was well into the ship's nightshift before leaving his quarters. It was just after midnight, the beginning of a new 22-hour Tuulan For day, and most off-duty personnel were asleep.

He broke into a jog, moving through the darkened corridors on the deck where he and his crew were billeted. Most of them had retired earlier, but he heard muffled cheers and raucous laughter coming from the rec room. He passed by without stopping. He could have gone in and joined them, but he was happy keeping his own company right now.

He followed the curve of the corridor as it turned, matching the contour of the hull. Soon he reached the front of the ship where his path angled away in a sharp v-turn. At the apex of the turn was a set of double doors, but he barely glanced at them as he ran past, following the corridor as it led back down the other side of the ship.

When he reached the v-turn on the second lap he noticed the plaque above the doors; the words were in Josi, the Tuulan For language, but were repeated in smaller Trade Standard, the universal constructed language of trade and diplomacy in the Locality. It said: OBSERVATION LOUNGE.

On the third lap his curiosity got the better of him and he paused in front of the doors, expecting it to be unoccupied this late at night. Justifying the diversion as taking a quick breather, he approached the doors and entered.

The observation room was even darker than the corridor outside; the only source of illumination was the starlight shining through the floor-to-ceiling windows. As his eyes adjusted to the darkness, he noticed a humanoid form silhouetted against the stellar backdrop, one he recognized instantly from her bearing and long, flowing robes.

"Minister Jadus," he said when he had regained his breath.

"Captain Marston." She turned toward him, but he couldn't see her face in the darkness. "It is good to see you recovered."

"Thanks." He joined her by the window and fell silent when he saw what she had been looking at. In front of them was the battle-scarred *Antruvion*, and beneath it, pulled like an errant dog, was the *Pericles*. Donald Winston had assured him that the ship could be repaired once they were in the proper facilities. That was good news. But knowing that his crew were safe and happy on the *Decisive Gain* was far more important.

As he regarded the damaged, powerless hulk towed by the *Antruvion*, Marston recalled the last time he had seen his ship: as he had plunged toward the Blue Star and what he had believed was certain death. Images from his final confrontation with Zithla and the descent toward the star flooded his mind. He stood with hands on his hips, looking at his battered ship, lost in thought. After several minutes he realized he hadn't said anything more to the Minister. But when he snuck a sideways glance at her she seemed content gazing out at the starry void.

"You're up late," he ventured.

"So are you," she pointed out.

"Late at night is my time to introvert," he said.

She looked at him. "I can appreciate that. I like to reflect on the day gone, and the day ahead. The peace and quiet helps me achieve a clearer perspective."

Marston nodded, and they lapsed again into a companionable silence.

"I've been meaning to thank you for saving my life," he said after a while. "In person, I mean. Commodore Layan told me what happened during the battle. If you hadn't intervened on my behalf, I wouldn't be here now."

"No thanks are necessary, Captain. It was nothing you had not already done for me and my people."

A rainbow-coloured portal opened in front of the *Antruvion*, engulfing the Ankari flagship and the other ships clustered around it, including the *Pericles* and *Decisive Gain*. The transition was seamless, so smooth that Marston didn't even feel it. The only noticeable difference was that the field of stars was replaced by the tunnel of the wormhole stretching infinitely before them.

Jadus smiled. "That's what I came to see. The transition is always so beautiful."

Marston didn't respond; he wasn't ready to change topics just yet. He stared out the window without really seeing, reflecting on the final events of the battle.

"I can remember vividly what it was like to be trapped on that weapon as it hurtled toward the star," he recalled. "I remember the sounds of the computer, the warmth of the flames flickering at the edges of the door, the sight of the *Pericles* disappearing from view. I even remember the look in Zithla's eyes as he burned to death." Marston turned to face the Minister. "Have you ever been absolutely certain you were about to die?"

Jadus looked thoughtful. "When we were on Tahvoa, and the Vinkere S'Geliss caught up with us in the spaceport. He pointed his weapon directly at me, ready to fire." She shuddered at the recollection.

Marston nodded. "Then you understand why I needed to thank you for saving my life," he said.

"As I have said, Captain, you have done as much for me, but I accept your thanks," she said graciously, before adding with a small smile, "Shall we agree that our debts to each other are paid?"

"Sounds good," Marston agreed good-naturedly. Then he frowned. "It's strange. When I was on the weapon, I knew there was no escape, and I found some measure of peace in that. But now that I'm alive… it's scary to think that I could have been dead right now."

Jadus shrugged. "But you're not dead, are you? Give it no further thought."

There was a question that had been bothering him since he had awakened from his week-long rest, and he decided now was the time to ask it.

"I don't want to sound ungrateful, but why did you save my life? We were so close to the star. You put the whole crew and ship at risk."

"Do you want the simple or complex answer?" she asked.

He thought about it for a moment. "The simple answer," he decided. He was making an effort not to overthink things from now on.

Jadus smiled. "Good choice. The answer is: I believed you were too valuable to lose."

Marston was speechless. "I… don't know what to say."

"You can say that you'll remember me in the future when *you* are famous and influential," she joked.

"If that ever happens, you can count on it," he promised. "If I can ever help, let me know…"

"I will, Captain," Jadus assured him.

36

After an absence of several months, the *Pericles* had returned to the shipyard where it had been constructed, towed all the way from ISER Station. The frigate had taken a beating in their encounters with the Vinkere, and Donald Winston estimated it would require at least eight weeks in an Argos repair facility to bring the ship back to operational status.

With the help of two Navy tug ships the *Pericles* was maneuvered into one of the drydock repair facilities in the rocky surface of the planetoid. Magnetic clamps secured the ship in place while energy cables snaked out of the walls and connected to outlets on the damaged ship, giving it power the *Pericles'* damaged generators could no longer provide. Repair drones emerged from their alcoves and swarmed across the hull, scanning every inch of the ship, compiling a comprehensive list of repairs.

Looking down on the ship from one of the windowed corridors in Argos, Marston was reminded of the first time he had glimpsed the *Pericles* more than seven months ago. Today was just like that day in February; space around the planetoid was filled with patrolling Navy ships, mineral-laden mining vessels and transport ships traveling to and from the base. The most notable difference was the relief convoy, a collection of twenty Navy and civilian ships, departing the station to assist the Vinkere-ravaged worlds in Tier 3 Space.

As the convoy disappeared into the asteroid field surrounding Argos, Marston turned his attention back to the *Pericles*. Parts of the damaged exterior had to be removed and replaced before the ship could safely sustain an atmosphere again. Teams of engineers were beginning to remove damaged hull panels while drones carefully maneuvered gleaming new replacements into position.

Marston spotted Winston in the cockpit of a one-man utility vehicle and smiled. The small craft was hovering over the bow of the ship while Winston used its grappler arms to collect damaged panels discarded by the repair teams. The damaged plates would be melted down and remade into useful parts, and then re-incorporated into the *Pericles*, a fact Marston found strangely pleasing. After several minutes observing the repair efforts, he turned away from the window and strode down the corridor toward the nearest monorail station. He had a meeting to attend.

Balzano met Marston outside Navy Command in Argos City and they walked in together. The Operations Center was as busy as ever; the officers were coordinating relief efforts across several nearby sectors of the Commonwealth. Nobody paid them any attention as they crossed the room toward Admiral Garcia's office. Marston pressed the door chime, and after a few moments the doors slid open. They entered, stopping in front of the Admiral's desk and saluting smartly.

"At ease," Garcia said, gesturing for them to sit in the chairs facing his desk. Marston recalled the mixture of excitement and anxiety he had experienced the last time he had sat across from the Admiral.

"Welcome back. You've certainly had an eventful few months," Garcia said.

"We all have," Marston said.

"That's true, and we still have a lot to do in the aftermath of the Vinkere Invasion. Rebuild our worlds and fleets. Find and apprehend those Vinkere who were stranded in the Commonwealth. The next several months are likely to be just as eventful."

Garcia's comment prompted Marston to ask: "Admiral, can you tell us what happened to our Vinkere prisoner?" He hadn't heard anything about S'Geliss since the *Pericles* had left ISER Station for the Storm Nebula.

Garcia nodded. "As you know, the starship *Callisto* was part of Admiral Haftel's fleet that journeyed to ISER Station, but it was too damaged to partake in the Blue Star Campaign. After transferring S'Geliss from your ship to their brig, they delivered him back to the Commonwealth. At this time, he is being held in a secure facility while we decide whether to try him here or extradite him to Tuulan Vee. In either case, you can be sure he will be brought to justice."

"Good," said Balzano.

"The purpose of this meeting isn't to discuss the Vinkere, although we will want to hear all about your experiences with them and everything that happened while you were out of contact with the Navy. You can expect to be fully debriefed over the next couple of days," Garcia told them. "Today's meeting is about another threat, and I've asked one of the Navy's leading experts on the subject to join us."

On cue, the door opened and an older, heavy-set man in an admiral's uniform entered the office. Marston couldn't help smiling as he rose to his feet and saluted the man. "Admiral Mackenzie!"

The older man nodded his white-haired head in greeting. "At ease, gentlemen."

Marston shook his hand warmly. Mackenzie had promoted him to captain, and then been his staunchest defender when the decision proved contentious. The last time Marston had seen him was on Earth nine months earlier.

"It's good to see you again, Admiral," Marston said. "I didn't realize you were in Argos."

"I'm just passing through," Mackenzie said. He took a seat beside Admiral Garcia so they were both facing Marston and Balzano. Mackenzie gestured to Garcia. "Please continue, Admiral."

"As I was saying, the past few months have been extremely eventful," Garcia said. "Not just for the Commonwealth, but for the whole Locality."

"And you and your crew managed to put yourselves right in the middle of it all," Mackenzie chuckled, clasping his hands together in his lap. Marston and Balzano smiled uneasily.

Garcia looked at Marston. "As you know, there were some admirals who at the beginning of this year did not consider you a viable candidate for captaincy. Suffice it to say, the success of your mission to the Blue Star has won many of them over."

Mackenzie snorted. "It's about time they came around."

"You have both proven that you are more than capable," Garcia continued. "There will be no looking over your shoulders to make sure you do your jobs properly."

"Including from Admiral Bryant," Mackenzie added. Marston wondered if Mackenzie had heard about his run-in with Bryant over selecting Winston as his chief engineer. Several months ago, it would have troubled Marston to know he was the subject of controversy. Now he didn't care as long as they kept it behind the scenes and let him do his job. "That's good to hear," he said.

As though reading his thoughts, Mackenzie said, "It's time we told you the truth about the reason for your promotion and the controversy it created. Let's start with some context. What do you know about the Human-Draxilan Armistice?"

The question was unexpected. "It's the peace treaty between the Commonwealth and the Draxilan Empire," Balzano said, recalling his middle school modern history class on the subject.

"That's right. It ended the War of the White Passage with a forty-year truce," Mackenzie said. "The penalty for breaking the truce was military intervention by the Ankari Assembly against the aggressor."

"Ankari intervention was a safeguard against renewed Draxilan aggression," Garcia explained.

"What most people have lost sight of is that the truce ends in a few months. And from what we can tell, the Draxilans are counting down the days." Mackenzie looked grim. "Long-range surveillance suggests they're preparing for conflict. We think they have been for years."

"The Draxilans want to start another war?" Balzano repeated.

"Our intelligence units have observed a build-up of military infrastructure and an increase in ship-building in the Empire. They're definitely preparing to attack someone. Their Imperator is expected to announce a new age of expansion, the decree could come any day now," Garcia said. "Even if we were only 20% sure we were the target, our job is to assess threats to the Commonwealth and prepare accordingly, *if* our worst fears turn out to be true."

Mackenzie stood up and began pacing, as he often did when frustrated or restless. "Unfortunately, the Kalavat Plague has only strengthened their position in the Locality," he said. "The Draxilans weren't affected by it. We don't know if it's because they're immune or if they just managed to avoid it, but right now they could be the strongest military power in the Locality, possibly even strong enough to challenge the Ankari in their weakened state."

"We, on the other hand, have just fought off an alien invasion," Marston said grimly.

"And it cost us. Badly," Mackenzie said flatly. "Aside from the losses of population and infrastructure in Tier 3 and Tier 4 Space, we estimate the Navy's losses to be up to twenty five percent."

Marston was astonished; it was worse than he had imagined. Equally troubling was the fact that the Draxilans had been preparing for war while humanity had grown complacent about the threat they posed. Most of humanity, anyway; for veterans like Mackenzie and Garcia, the original conflict was still within living memory.

"Our concern before the Vinkere Invasion was that we weren't ready to face a renewed Draxilan offensive. Now…" Mackenzie let his words trail off as they absorbed the full impact of his meaning.

"But we didn't fight off one set of invaders to be conquered by another," Garcia said firmly. "Our tactical preparedness has long been a concern. That's why five years ago, we developed Operation: Marathon. Named after the Battle of Marathon between the ancient Persians and the Greeks. The Greeks, although seemingly outmatched, won the battle."

"Operation: Marathon encompasses all of our preparations for a possible future war with the Draxilans," Garcia said. "New infrastructure on the outer planets, weapon emplacements, developing new shield and engine technologies… Marathon was the reason we were able to halt the Vinkere advance. If we hadn't been implementing Marathon, the Vinkere would have gotten a lot farther and done a lot more damage."

Mackenzie continued. "The *Pericles* was designed and built as part of the Interceptor Project. Our fleet needed a faster, more maneuverable ship to match the new ships the Draxilans are fielding."

"I did wonder how they managed to build the *Pericles* in just two years," Marston admitted.

"We're working to refine the construction process; on a war-time footing the shipyards here at Argos should be able to construct a frigate like the *Pericles* in six months, and a corvette in five," Garcia said.

"Obviously, constructing more ships is only part of the solution," Mackenzie continued. "We also need people to crew them, and the ability to recruit and train officers rapidly, particularly in the advent of a prolonged war in which the Navy suffers high casualties. For this purpose, the Advanced Tactical Training Program was developed. The graduates of our first class, of which you were one, Captain Marston, were to be our proof of concept. To demonstrate that the type of individual we're looking for could be trained quickly and promoted in a crisis to defend the Commonwealth."

"The Vinkere Invasion caught us all off guard, but it was exactly the sort of crisis we needed to be prepared for," Garcia said. He looked at Marston. "The importance of Operation Marathon and our ATTP graduates in the Commonwealth's defense cannot be overstated."

"I wondered if there was more to the advanced tactical training," Marston admitted. "But none of my classmates knew any more than I did, and our instructors were… vague when we asked them about it."

"They were ordered to be," Mackenzie told him. "Operation: Marathon is still classified."

"Why are you telling us now, then?" Marston asked.

"Because you deserved to know. You faced difficult circumstances and overcame them. Even before the Vinkere," Mackenzie said.

Balzano shook his head in amazement. "So, preparations for conflict with the Draxilans inadvertently saved us from the Vinkere."

"Yes. Unfortunately, our losses have set us back significantly," Mackenzie said grimly, "But we're considering other options. We've begun some high-level negotiations with ISER, so we'll see if anything comes from that." He didn't elaborate, so Marston didn't press him for details.

"We are also building alliances," Garcia said. "The Commonwealth Senate is considering mutual defense treaties with the Arretrian Kingdoms and the Republic of Tuulan Vee."

"If we can be of service, just tell us," Marston said. "My crew and I will do what we can to help." Balzano nodded in firm agreement.

"Good. All of us may soon be called upon to defend the Commonwealth again," Garcia said. "We live in uncertain times. The Vinkere have disrupted the balance of power in the Locality. We'll need all the good officers we can get." Mackenzie nodded in agreement. He privately hoped that the new generation of captains and commanders were as intelligent and brave as his protégé. *They would surely need to be*, he thought grimly.

"The Vinkere data core you retrieved may contain information on Vinkere or Ankari technology that could give us an edge. Our specialists are analyzing it now," Garcia said. "We'd also like to know everything about the artificial intelligence Amalthea."

"I'll tell you everything I can," Marston said, "But I regret that we have no idea whether she is still functioning or not. The last time we saw her was just before she uploaded into the *Antruvion*'s computer system."

Mackenzie shook his head in wonderment. "An AI born on a starship. Incredible. We still don't fully understand what led to her creation, but it's prompted some... interesting discussions with the other Commonwealth AIs. President Hasina and Admiral Makeba personally interrogated Earth AI."

That piqued Marston's interest. "Earth AI? What did it say?"

"Well, now that the cat's out of the bag, they've been surprisingly forthcoming. If we can recreate the circumstances of her creation, we may be able to build a new generation of stable AIs. Artificial intelligence is one of the few areas where we have an advantage over the Draxilans. If Amalthea is still out there, retrieving her will be one of our top priorities."

Marston was relieved to hear that. He still felt guilty for abandoning Amalthea. Sirroyo's words echoed through his mind: *If she were human, you wouldn't even hesitate to save her.*

"Lieutenant Sirroyo, will be able to tell you a lot more about her than we can," Balzano told the admirals.

"We'll debrief her as soon as she returns," Garcia said.

Mackenzie raised his eyebrows. "Returns? From where?"

"She's on another mission right now."

"Doing what?" Mackenzie inquired.

Marston smiled mysteriously. "Fulfilling a promise."

*

A Class 1 shuttle emerged from the slipstream in an uninhabited system visited by the *Pericles* a few months earlier. Using sub-light engines, Tahir Hasan guided the small ship toward the asteroid belt orbiting the system's dwarf star. As they approached their target, he turned to Katarina Sirroyo, seated to his right. "Activate the beacon," he instructed.

"Beacon activated... I'm receiving a response," Sirroyo confirmed without looking up from her console. Elzor Drin peered eagerly over her shoulder at the monitor. She frowned, but shifted to allow him a clear view.

Hasan highlighted their target on the viewscreen. "There's your ship, right where we left her," he said, and Drin beamed happily. The *Wealth and Grandeur,* still anchored to its asteroid, had remained hidden and unharmed.

Hasan guided the shuttle carefully through the asteroids until it drew alongside the cargo ship. Drin bid him and Sirroyo farewell and then he and Henry Clarke left the cockpit. There was a spring in his step as they made their way to the airlock.

"What will you do now?" Clarke asked him. "It's a long journey home."

"My home is my ship," Drin said, and Clarke nodded in appreciation. "If referring to the Merchant Republic is what you are doing, then yes, it is far. But had I not left it behind I never would have been positioned to rescue Minister Jadus and Professor Minnen!" He tapped his chest. "I am a man of destiny, and in the Commonwealth is where my immediate future lies. Find a new crew and then help your people rebuild is what I will do!"

"Good luck," Clarke said, offering his hand. Drin, who had spent enough time with humans to understand the gesture, shook it vigorously.

Clarke watched him disappear through the airlock of the *Wealth and Grandeur*. When the hatch closed, he grinned, imagining the Vlind captain appearing in some port and proclaiming himself an agent of destiny.

He returned to the cockpit and took his seat as the *Wealth and Grandeur* was detaching from the asteroid. The Vlind ship accelerated away and the shuttle followed it. When the two ships were clear of the asteroid belt they separated.

"Farewell, my friends!" Drin broadcast. A portal blossomed in front of the bulbous cargo ship and it dove into the slipstream, leaving the Navy shuttle alone.

Hasan grinned. "Mission accomplished."

"Let's get back to our home," Sirroyo said. Clarke looked at her in surprise; expressions of sentimentality were uncharacteristic, but he made no comment. Instead, he instructed Hasan to set a course for Argos and engage the slipstream drive.

*

Justin Caleb

October 1, 2438
Plague Control Initiative Headquarters, Strahnti
Kelzanti Galactic Federation
Ral Hokono loved Strahnti at night. Streetlights and flashing billboards created bright valleys between the towering monoliths of the capital's skyscrapers. Neat lanes of air traffic divided the night sky into squares, and Hokono smiled. Today, like all the days before it since taking his new job, had been frantically busy. But today had been *good* busy. Reports of the success of Minnen the Learned's antivenom were coming in from infected worlds across the Federation. There was still a lot to be done, but it no longer appeared that civilization teetered on the brink of ruin. So, for the next few hours, Hokono could relax. His personal communicator beeped, and he accepted the incoming message from his daughter Sandesha.

"Hi Dad, I'm leaving home now. I'll meet you at the restaurant in fifteen minutes," she said.

"I will see you there shortly," Hokono promised her. The evening was pleasant, and he planned on walking to the restaurant. He lifted his jacket from the back of his chair and left the office, looking forward to a night spent with his daughter. Maybe one day soon his wife could join them again. Behind him the lights turned off automatically and the room fell into darkness, lit only by the glow from the lively city outside.

*

October 4, 2438
In orbit of Telvarn, Telvarn System
Republic of Tuulan Vee
The serene, blue-green world rotating beneath their ship was as familiar as Jadus' own reflection.

"Home," she breathed quietly. She always felt the same sentimental longing upon seeing her home world. Telvarn's oceans glistened in the sunlight, but even from this altitude Jadus could see something was different. Patches of glowing amber and faint trails of smoke could be seen through the clouds above the eastern continent where the Republic's military had been forced to "cleanse" plague-affected regions with fire. The ships responsible formed a protective ring around the planet, and although Jadus was happy to be back, it troubled her to see her home planet under blockade.

It's only for a season, she reminded herself. That was their destination: the eastern continent, to oversee distribution of the Kalavat Plague antivenom.

The transport ship landed on the edge of an overgrown field near a farmhouse. Rows of overripe grain rippled in the breeze. There had been no harvest this season, and the unharvested grain had turned a deep gold.

Antak was in the cockpit, but his voice filtered over the intercom: *"You're clear to disembark."*

"I strongly urge caution, Minister," the Republic's military commander for the eastern continent said gruffly. "This is essentially a war zone."

"Your advice is noted," Jadus said curtly. She had no intention of remaining behind. She turned to the group of soldiers and doctors assembled near the airlock. "Is everyone ready?"

They nodded. "Ready as we'll ever be," Jarren confirmed, hefting a case filled with vials of antivenom.

"We'll go first and make sure the area is secure," Korosa said, gesturing for her fellow security officers to follow. Rifle raised, she leapt out of the ship and onto the ground. Her security team followed her, fanning out in a widening circle.

When Korosa gave them the all-clear, Jadus and the rest of the group disembarked and walked across the field toward the farm complex. They passed an empty stable and farming equipment that looked as though it had been abandoned in a hurry. Twin grain silos rose up behind the main building; this was one of the communal farmhouses favored by the Aforay, a Tuulan For ethnic minority who preferred to live in small agricultural communities.

From the safety of the farmhouse cautious eyes watched them through cracks in the boarded-up windows. As Jadus' group approached the building, the front door opened and a group of people emerged. They wore the clothes of agricultural workers and wielded old rifles or farming implements as weapons. They hastily took up positions behind the makeshift barricade protecting the veranda and their leader, an older male, signaled for the newcomers to halt.

"Identify yourself," he called. Jadus paused several meters from the house. She could see the rifle shaking in his hands, hear his voice wavering. He was a civilian, an old farmer. The ship's sensors had indicated at least two dozen other people inside the farmhouse, probably scared and hungry.

"It's alright," Jadus called out in a calm voice. She gestured to Jarren, who held up the case of antivenom vials for the farmer to see. "We are here to help you, friend."

Epilogue

October 18, 2438
ISER Station, Gandra Sector
Unclaimed

The corridors of the station felt empty to Uxxio, but he supposed the quiet was normal for the scientists who lived here. The battered but victorious remnants of the allied fleet had returned to ISER Station following their successful campaign in the Carina Nebula, and for a brief time, the halls had been filled with celebration. It had been short-lived however, and the scientists had returned to their work, while the ships of the fleet returned to their respective homes, their cargo holds filled with vials of Professor Minnen's antivenom, now produced in batches designed to be more effective for the different species of the Locality.

Uxxio walked into the station's cafeteria. It was empty, except for one table of scientists and another occupied by crewmen from the *Vigilant and Strong*, the Vlind Merchant Navy ship permanently assigned to guarding the station now that its location was no longer a secret. Uxxio approached the kitchen staffer on duty, who smiled knowingly. "The usual?"

Uxxio nodded. "Yes, please."

The kitchen hand passed Uxxio a thermos of coffee, made to Professor Minnen's liking. He thanked the man and left.

He walked back to the lab, humming a tune, and was about to enter when the doors opened and Minnen the Learned emerged, nearly colliding with him.

"Oh, thank you," Minnen said, taking the coffee from Uxxio.

"Sir, where are you going?"

"To speak with Overseer Vashon. Are you coming?"

Uxxio lingered in the doorway. "I could, or I could keep going with—"

"The computer tells me she is currently with Sul."

"I am more than happy to accompany you, sir, if you would like me to," Uxxio said hastily, moving to catch up with the professor. He didn't see the smile that flashed across Minnen's face.

As they walked, Uxxio updated him on the reports coming in from across the Locality. "The antivenom has proven quite successful so far. It seems to work as well for the species of the Locality as it does for the Vinkere."

"Its long-term effects are virtually unknown to us, Uxxio," Minnen said. "I would like to continue to monitor its use."

"Of course, sir."

Minnen drank from his coffee cup, feeling reinvigorated with every sip. He was seriously considering asking one of the human scientists on the station about coffee plants. If he could take some home and cultivate them...

They reached the communications center and entered. They spotted Overseer Vashon in one of the combooths, and beside her was Minnen's daughter, Sul. He was surprised to see they were talking to a human male wearing the dark blue uniform of the Commonwealth Navy.

As they drew closer, he was able to hear the end of their conversation: *"... at your location six weeks from today. Mackenzie out."* The call ended and the Navy officer disappeared from the screen. Vashon and Sul turned to find Minnen regarding them curiously.

"Hello, father," Sul said. She didn't seem concerned at his eavesdropping.

"How can we assist you, Professor?" Vashon asked.

Minnen wanted to speak to Vashon about collaborating with the other ISER stations on a long-term study of the Kalavat Plague antivenom's effects on the host. But that could wait a moment.

"I apologize for intruding. Are you expecting more guests?" he asked.

"Not exactly," Sul said with a sidelong look at Vashon. She stood up and took Minnen's arm. "Father, I'll be leaving the station in a few weeks. An organization is interested in a project my team and I have been working on. They're coming to pick it up, and I've agreed to go with them to test it."

"You're leaving?" Uxxio said, unable to mask his disappointment.

Sul smiled at him. "Only for a short time."

Minnen was equally surprised. "Where are you going, daughter?" he asked.

Sul squeezed his arm excitedly. "The former center of Vinkere power in the Locality. The Storm Nebula!"

About the Author

Justin Caleb grew up in the leafy suburbs of northwest Sydney, Australia. Since 2015 he has worked as a freelance editor. A lifelong reader and science fiction fan, Justin dreamed of writing science fiction the way he thought it should be written; with engaging characters, exotic locations, and adventures that grant the reader hours of escapism. The Blue Star is his first novel. In his free time Justin enjoys tennis, stand-up paddle boarding and quality time with his pets.

Made in the USA
Las Vegas, NV
03 January 2024

83834374R00267